CONTENTS

OXFORD
UNIVERSITY PRESS

Great Clarendon Street, Oxford, OX2 6DP,
United Kingdom

Oxford University Press is a department of the University of Oxford.
It furthers the University's objective of excellence in research, scholarship,
and education by publishing worldwide. Oxford is a registered trade mark of
Oxford University Press in the UK and in certain other countries

Published in the United States of America by Oxford University Press
198 Madison Avenue, New York, NY 10016, United States of America

British Library Cataloguing in Publication Data

Data available

Library of Congress Control Number: 2023933503

ISBN 978-0-19-887152-1

Printed and bound in the UK by
Clays Ltd, Elcograf S.p.A.

OXFORD WORLD'S CLASSICS

MARCEL PROUST

The Swann Way

Translated by
BRIAN NELSON

Edited with an Introduction and Notes by
ADAM WATT

OXFORD WORLD'S CLASSICS

*For over 100 years Oxford World's Classics have brought
readers closer to the world's great literature. Now with over 700
titles—from the 4,000-year-old myths of Mesopotamia to the
twentieth century's greatest novels—the series makes available
lesser-known as well as celebrated writing.*

*The pocket-sized hardbacks of the early years contained
introductions by Virginia Woolf, T. S. Eliot, Graham Greene,
and other literary figures which enriched the experience of reading.
Today the series is recognized for its fine scholarship and
reliability in texts that span world literature, drama and poetry,
religion, philosophy, and politics. Each edition includes perceptive
commentary and essential background information to meet the
changing needs of readers.*

THE SWANN WAY

MARCEL PROUST (1871–1922) is best known as the author of the seven-volume masterpiece *A la recherche du temps perdu* (*In Search of Lost Time*, 1913–27). He was born in Auteuil, to the west of Paris, to well-to-do parents; at the age of 10 he suffered a near-fatal asthma attack and his life from that point onwards was marked by ill health. He began writing reviews, short stories, and society journalism whilst studying at the Lycée Condorcet and published a collection of these pieces, *Les Plaisirs et les jours* (*Pleasures and Days*) in 1896. Family connections and schoolfriends gave him access to the highest Parisian social circles, on which he would later draw for his portrayal of the society life in *In Search of Lost Time*. His first attempt at an extended narrative (posthumously published as *Jean Santeuil*, 1952) was abandoned; subsequent stages in his apprenticeship as a writer include translating works by the English art historian and social critic John Ruskin and producing dazzling pastiches of major French writers. Finally, during 1908–9, whilst working on a critical essay taking to task the great nineteenth-century critic Sainte-Beuve, Proust began to draft fragments of a first-person narrative that coalesced into what would become *In Search of Lost Time*. The first volume appeared in 1913. Unfit for military service, Proust spent the wartime years expanding his novel, the subsequent volumes of which appeared between 1919 and 1927. Proust's devotion to his work, sleeping by day then writing and making additions and revisions through the night, was ruinous for his already fragile health and he died in 1922, while still engaged in the corrections to his final volumes.

BRIAN NELSON is an Emeritus Professor at Monash University, Melbourne, and a Fellow of the Australian Academy of the Humanities. His publications include *Zola: A Very Short Introduction*, *The Cambridge Introduction to French Literature*, *The Cambridge Companion to Zola*, *Zola and the Bourgeoisie*, and translations of Zola's *The Assommoir*, *His Excellency Eugène Rougon*, *Earth* (with Julie Rose), *The Fortune of the Rougons*, *The Belly of Paris*, *The Kill*, *Pot Luck*, and *The Ladies' Paradise*. He has also translated *Swann in Love* by Marcel Proust for the Oxford World's Classics series. He was awarded the New South Wales Premier's Prize for Translation in 2015.

ADAM WATT is Professor of French & Comparative Literature at the University of Exeter, where he is Deputy Pro-Vice-Chancellor of the Faculty of Humanities, Arts and Social Sciences. His books include *Reading in Proust's* A la recherche: *Le Délire de la lecture* (2009); *The Cambridge Introduction to Marcel Proust* (2011); a critical biography of Proust (2013); and, as editor, *Marcel Proust in Context* (2013) and *The Cambridge History of the Novel in French* (2021). He has published comparative work on Proust and a range of writers from Valéry, Rivière, Beckett, and Barthes to Eve Kosofsky-Sedgwick and Anne Carson.

ACKNOWLEDGEMENTS

OUR thanks go to Judith Luna and Chris Mann for reading the translation in its draft form and for making a number of helpful comments; and, for exchanges on Proust and translation matters, to Esther Allen, Andrew Benjamin, Peter Bush, Ilona Chessid, Hélène Jaccomard, Valerie Minogue, Julie Rose, and Robert Savage. We are grateful to Luciana O'Flaherty for her encouragement and wise counsel. Adam Watt is grateful to Stacey Hynd for her support and to Brian Nelson for his patience and goodwill throughout the production of this work.

GENERAL EDITORS' PREFACE

In Search of Lost Time, published between 1913 and 1927, is recognized as the undisputed masterpiece of twentieth-century fiction. Endlessly rich in its themes and idioms, it is a philosophical novel about time, memory, imagination, and art; a psychological novel about human behaviour, love, and jealousy; a social novel about France, especially high society, as it evolved from the end of the nineteenth century to the aftermath of the 1914–18 War; and a comic novel of manners, character, and language. It is also an experimental novel, quite unlike what contemporary readers normally understood to be a work of fiction. Part of Proust's importance historically is that he redefined the boundaries of the genre. Instead of a conventional linear story with a clearly identifiable plot, the *Search* uses a kaleidoscope of memories to create a startlingly new form of narrative. For those who come to the *Search* for the first time, it reads very much like an autobiography. There is an 'I', a first-person narrator who is telling the story of his childhood experiences and the life that follows, adding analytical comments as he goes. But although there are strong autobiographical elements in the novel—the places and characters can be matched with Proust's own experience, and the narrator's name is eventually revealed to be Marcel—these elements have been transformed, and a world created out of them which, though based on real experiences, is an imaginary one, a fictional creation. Moreover, the narrative 'I' is a double 'I', moving fluidly between the present of the narrator and the past of his younger self, building multiple perspectives into a symphonic structure and promoting a dramatic narration as the narrator comes slowly to understand the significance of his past experiences. The novel invites the reader to enter the narrator's mind, to accompany him on his journey of discovery as he explores the workings of his own consciousness and seeks to understand not only the meaning of his own life but also the nature of the human condition.

There is no ideal, ultimate translation of a given original. There cannot be, given that nothing is exactly the same in one language as in another. Moreover, as Kevin Hart has noted, following Jacques Derrida, while any text is always open to translation, 'no version, faithful or free, will ever exhaust its meaning. There will always be a supplement of signification which remains outside even the most successful translation, and that supplement will always entice another translator to begin work.'[1] Classic texts in particular, from Homer onwards, are susceptible of multiple readings and retranslations over time. Gustave Flaubert's *Madame Bovary* has been retranslated into English over twenty times since its publication in 1857. Retranslation of classic works, and the ability to compare different versions of a given text, afford an opportunity to celebrate not only the expressive capacities of the English language, the role of the translator, and the creativity involved in the translator's art, but also 'the rich multiple presence of the translated text'.[2] Our aim with this series of new translations, accompanied by detailed notes and readable introductions by leading scholars, is to contribute to that richness—to widen still further the appeal of a work that offers inexhaustible rewards.

Publication will be in seven volumes. There will be a different translator for each volume (except the first and last). We have chosen to standardize certain terms, recurrent phrases and expressions, modes of address, personal titles, use of elision and so forth across the translations, and, more generally, have attempted to facilitate unity of voice, a stylistic consonance, across the various volumes (while bearing in mind shifts in Proust's voice and tone as his work progressed). The views on translation expressed in the Translator's Note in this volume are, broadly speaking, those of the team. Ultimately, however, the best guarantee that Proust's voice will come through in each volume is the artistry of the translators themselves.

Proust's themes and preoccupations, the threads with which the seven individual volumes of the *Search* are stitched together into a coherent whole, are as relevant and speak as directly to us now as they ever have in the course of the last century. Desire, attraction, betrayal; ageing, memory, and identity; death, loss, and the solace of art: all of these human concerns speak to us from the pages of Proust's novel. But in their interweaving—and this cuts to the core of the

---

[1] Quoted by Paolo Bartoloni, 'The Virtuality of Translation', in Christopher Palmer and Ian Topliss (eds.), *Globalising Australia* (Melbourne: La Trobe University, 2000), 77–83, at 78.

[2] Dominique Jullien, 'The Way by Lydia's: A New Translation of Proust', in Suzanne Jill Levine and Katie Lateef-Jan (eds.), *Untranslatability Goes Global* (New York: Routledge, 2017), 64–76, at 72.

Search's remarkable hybrid status—we encounter a quite extraordinary array of cultural and historical references. From cave paintings to music hall, Renaissance sculpture to advertising hoardings, high culture to lowbrow ephemera, Proust's novel throngs with allusions to centuries' worth of history and cultural production. Though contemporary readers, unlike those of Proust's own time, have the facility of consulting a search engine to learn in a matter of seconds, for example, who painted the Virtues and Vices of Padua, or who Planté and Rubinstein were, we felt nevertheless that incorporating a set of explanatory endnotes in each volume was at once desirable and valuable. Those who choose to ignore them can of course forge ahead in their reading uninterrupted; but those who are curious will find socio-cultural, historical, geographical, and artistic allusions illuminated and contextualized. The notes seek not to offer any sort of critical commentary on Proust's novel, but rather to clarify dates and details that will enrich readers' appreciation of its unique breadth of reference.

The introductory essay to each volume outlines the key concerns and preoccupations of the volume in question, providing a broad frame of reference for readers tackling the novel for the first time and reflecting on the role of that volume in the wider structure of the novel as a whole. These essays will prime readers for the journey that lies ahead but should be read with the awareness that they—inevitably—contain 'spoilers' or anticipations of what is to come.

BRIAN NELSON
ADAM WATT

TRANSLATOR'S NOTE

NEW translations of classic authors are produced to some extent in the shadow of their predecessors, of which they offer, implicitly or not, a kind of critique.[1] In the case of Proust the longest shadow is cast by C. K. Scott Moncrieff. For decades, his translation of *A la recherche du temps perdu* (*A la recherche* for short), published between 1922 and 1931, was the only one available to English-speaking readers unable to read Proust in the original. This translation was monumental in its scale and in many ways admirable in its realization. Moncrieff had a fine ear for the cadences of Proust's prose, and a considerable talent for elegant phrasing. But his language dated over time, especially in dialogue, and from the beginning he was prone to tamper with the text, through embellishment or the heightening of language. His translation also contained various errors and misinterpretations. The reservation most commonly voiced about his translation, however, is that it changed Proust's tone. He tended to make Proust sound precious and flowery, whereas Proust's style is not in the least affected or ornate. His prose is precise, rigorous, exact. Grand rhythm and maxim-like concentration often work together. Proust's sentences, though elaborately constructed, have a beautiful balance, a musicality that becomes particularly apparent when the text is read aloud. As John Sturrock observed, Moncrieff's choice of English title, the 'poetical', Shakespearean *Remembrance of Things Past*, hardly reflects the plainness (or the thematic implications) of *A la recherche du temps perdu*. The contrast is symptomatic, Sturrock noted, of 'the unhappy way in which Scott Moncrieff contrived to play down the stringent intelligence of his author by conveying it in an English prose that is constantly looking to prettify. It's as if the translator had been taken aback by how acrid and how ruthless Proust can be in his exposure of the deep falsities of the inhabitants of the Parisian *beau monde*, and was determined to muffle its cruelty by the gentility of his English.'[2]

[1] Cf. Antoine Berman, *Toward a Translation Criticism: John Donne*, ed. and trans. Françoise Massardier-Kenney (Kent, OH: Kent State University Press, 2009) (French original 1995).

[2] John Sturrock, 'Proust in English', in *The Word from Paris: Essays on Modern French Thinkers and Writers* (London: Verso, 1998), 110–18, at 115.

Since Moncrieff's day, literary translation has become a much more self-conscious practice, while recent years have also seen the rise of the discipline of translation studies. The aim of capturing a writer's style has been equated by some contemporary translators and translation studies scholars with 'foreignization'. This denotes, in its milder form, a determination to stay as close as possible to the original, and, in its most zealous form, a kind of interventionism that heightens one's awareness of the foreign. The latter approach implies the production of a consciously defamiliarized English by the retention of syntactical or grammatical conventions from the source language: to make the translation 'feel French' (or German, etc.) and remind readers that they are reading a translation. Proponents of this approach feel it shows respect for the other and has the merit of alerting readers to the diversity, and the need for diversity, among cultures. There is of course a foreignness inherent in the text, both for linguistic reasons and because different languages reflect different social and cultural worlds. Who would not wish to respect foreignness in the latter sense—for instance, by keeping culturally specific words and phrases in the original? But foreignize stylistically? Proust sounded strange in French, to his French audience, because of the particularity of his voice, a strikingly original new voice given shape in his native language. It is a verbal strangeness—a stylistic otherness— the translator should keep in order to allow the anglophone reader to experience something equivalent to the experience of the native French reader. But this is not the same as trying to make the translation sound French per se. Successful translation of Proust is achieved (unsurprisingly, one might feel) by making him sound like Proust—by giving him an English voice, a voice that conveys his vision, his sensibility, and his unique qualities as a writer. Moreover, Proust in English can be idiosyncratic without ceasing to be idiomatic. Anthea Bell has written: 'translators are in the business of spinning an illusion. The illusion is that the reader is reading not a translation but the real thing'; 'I am not saying, of course, that the illusion should deprive readers of the foreignness of the original text . . . Far from it: I mean only that I hope a translation will read as easily and be as appealing to the reader as if it had been originally written in English.'[3] Surely this

---

[3] Anthea Bell, 'Translation: Walking the Tightrope of Illusion', in Susan Bassnett and Peter Bush (eds.), *The Translator as Writer* (London: Continuum, 2006), 58–67, at 59, 60.

is the highest form of respect a translator can pay a text and its culture, and the readers of the text in the target language.

The task of the translator is to get inside the author's skin. I think of translation as an art of imitation: a quest to find and reproduce a text's 'voice'. It is a kind of performance art, combining close reading and creative (re)writing. A sequence of words in one language is replaced by a sequence of words in another language. Everything is changed so that the text stays the same, that is to say as close as possible to the translator's experience of the original. This involves scrupulous attention to verbal detail—myriad decisions concerning tone, texture, rhythm, register, syntax, sound, connotations: all those things that make up style and reflect the marriage between style and meaning. Proust was the greatest prose stylist of his generation. His style is largely identified with his famous long sentences, with their 'coiling elaboration'.[4] As they uncoil, the sentences express the rhythms of a sensibility, the directions and indirections of desire, the conflicts and convolutions of a mind, the narrator's or Swann's, that forms the framework—indeed the subject matter—of the narrative, as it unfolds, via many detours and with a dynamic backward- and forward-looking movement, from childhood beginnings to mature adulthood. While recognizing the impossibility of exact equivalence, my aim has been to recreate the intricate harmonies of Proust's sentences, and the whole pattern of effects embodied in his prose, in such a way that the translation creates the 'illusion' of which Anthea Bell speaks.

I have tried to maintain the full range of Proust's tones and registers, and the shifts between them. I have also tried to capture as much as possible of his humour. Proust is a deeply serious novelist, but he is also a great comic writer. Comic vision is central to his work, and assumes varied forms. Most obviously, there is the comedy of character: Marcel's invalid Aunt Léonie, who 'never sleeps', lying in bed all day and using her hypochondria as a vantage point from which to satisfy her craving to know everything about the life of the town; his eccentric grandmother; his timid high-minded aunts, unable to thank Swann for a case of wine without expressing their gratitude in such cryptic terms that no one could possibly understand what they mean;

---

[4] Richard Howard, 'Intermittences of the Heart', in André Aciman (ed.), *The Proust Project* (New York: Farrar, Straus and Giroux, 2004), 98.

the buffoon Cottard, with his ludicrous self-consciousness and obsession with puns and figures of speech. There is the social comedy, whether it be the rituals of the narrator's family and the town of Combray or the snobbery of the bourgeois and aristocratic circles of Paris. There is the high comedy of the great set pieces in 'Swann in Love' (the dinner at the Verdurins', the soirée at the Marquise de Saint-Euverte's). There is the irony that suffuses the narrative: the narrator, as he looks back on his younger self, and on Swann's experience of sexual jealousy, chronicles the tantalizing gaps—a tragicomedy of errors—between desire, perception, and reality.

Finally, the title. *The Way by Swann's* I find awkward, while Moncrieff's *Swann's Way* shifts the emphasis somewhat from 'way' (the path along the edge of Swann's estate, one of the two different paths taken by Marcel and his family on their Combray walks) to Swann and sounds oddly ambiguous (as in: what sort of way?). I chose *The Swann Way* because it forms a perfect balance with *The Guermantes Way* (the opposition is an important element in the architecture of the novel) and fits smoothly into the flow of the text (see the first mention of the two 'ways' on pp. 125–6).

B.N.

INTRODUCTION

*Readers new to the novel should note that this Introduction
makes details of the plot explicit.*

A Novel of Time

STALACTITES, reflections, patinas, rays of light, visitors from the past:
early in 1912, these were the notions that Marcel Proust was pondering as he sought out a title for a novel on which he had been working,
with ever-increasing intensity, since 1908.[1] He was fascinated by the
different ways our bodies and brains store up lived experience, intrigued
by the ways in which the past can make itself felt in the present, and
determined to capture these in a narrative form that would communicate a particular subjectivity whilst also exploring the wider world
of which he was part. But finding a title was tricky. Eventually the
stalactites and patinas were rejected and Proust came to focus on the
dimension of human experience that underpins and determines all
experiences of past and present: Time. Minutes that drag lazily on,
hours that skip by unnoticed, years that weather faces and dull what
once was bright: all of this would become the very substance of
Proust's book and, after a number of fits and starts, *A la recherche du
temps perdu* took hold as the overarching title. A literal translation
gives *In Search of Lost Time*, and this indeed is our chosen rendering.
The first published translation took a different, lyrical tack, proffering
Remembrance of Things Past, a borrowing from Shakespeare's rather
maudlin Sonnet 30 ('When to the sessions of sweet silent thought |
I summon up remembrance of things past, | I sigh the lack of many
a thing I sought').[2] What this Shakespearean title puts centre stage is
the importance of memory in Proust's enterprise, but it pushes into

---

[1] Letter to Reynaldo Hahn, first semester of 1912, in *Correspondance de Marcel Proust*,
ed. Philip Kolb, 21 vols. (Paris: Plon, 1970–93), xi. 151.

[2] Proust's first English-language translator was Charles Kenneth Scott Moncrieff
(1889–1930). His *Swann's Way* appeared with Chatto & Windus in 1922, the year of
Proust's death. Scott Moncrieff's labours were not complete at his death in 1930 and the
final volume, *Le Temps retrouvé* (*Time Regained*), was completed by Stephen Hudson (pen
name of Sydney Schiff), appearing in 1931.

the wings any mention of loss, equally important in the French formulation since, as an idiom or standard formulation, 'temps perdu' can be lost or *wasted* time. And *A la recherche du temps perdu* is a massive novel that invites its readers to take a big gamble: read me, it says, page after page, volume after volume, and see what return you might get on your investment. Will it be time well spent or time wasted? Proust's novel, which swelled from its originally planned, relatively modest dimensions of two, perhaps three volumes, to become the seven-volume saga we have today, demands of its readers a very considerable commitment of time. Its sheer length means that if it is read from start to finish, even a speedy reader without undue disruption or delay will be, at the very least, several months older and wiser by the time she finishes her task. The subtle (and the radical) ways in which individuals change over time are at the core of Proust's thinking and are something to which a reading of his novel renders us acutely sensitive. When we live with the cadences of his sentences, the rhythms of his thoughts, the profundity of his insights, and the acuity of his wit, our own being-in-the-world is altered. Our vision is adjusted, our senses delicately recalibrated both to the rich and varied world around us and to our own inner landscape: what we mean and who we are when we say 'I'.

This is in part because *In Search of Lost Time* takes the form of a first-person narrative, a novel built around a narrator-protagonist we meet in the first, enigmatic sentence of the book ('For a long time I went to bed early') and whose company we keep through each of the seven volumes. *The Swann Way*, then, is the doorway to the narrator's world, but what we encounter is not a conventional linear account of his life. Rather, and this is one of the great innovations of Proust's writing and one of the main challenges it poses to readers, we find ourselves plunged into the recollections and reminiscences of the adult narrator, who describes and reflects on moments of his past from positions of varying distance from the events in question. *The Swann Way* is principally concerned with the narrator's childhood (and, in 'Swann in Love', its prehistory) but the narrative perspective repeatedly shifts: at times the voice that speaks is noticeably mature and worldly-wise, at others it has the naïve and unworldly qualities of the youthful protagonist at the time of events portrayed. This shifting focalization creates a dynamism in the narrative that serves to underscore one of Proust's key observations: that our subjectivity, what we mean when we say 'I', is not singular and unchanging. When we consider the duration of a lifetime we realize that 'I' am made up of continuity and change, multiple selves that bloom and recede, traits and proclivities that predominate and subside, characteristics and identities that surge and fade. For Proust, as for Whitman, 'I contain multitudes'. What intrigued Proust was how our past selves, the instantiations of who I was and what I experienced before the present moment, that we may believe to be lost or forgotten, nevertheless linger, latent within us, emerging unexpectedly into the here and now when triggered by the right stimulus. This form of *involuntary* memory (as opposed to our conscious or voluntary efforts that allow us to recall an address or the spelling of a word) is of vital importance in Proust's project. The experience of involuntary memory is staged, most famously, in *The Swann Way* via the narrator's encounter with a madeleine, a small cake to which we will return below. The powerful involuntary experience, when a sensation in the present moment prompts an unbidden memory of a previous encounter with the same sensation, recurs at various points in Proust's narrative, but it is the madeleine scene that has become the defining 'Proustian moment', familiar even to those who have never read a page of *In Search of Lost Time*.

Before we come to a discussion of those pivotal pages and the purpose they serve within *The Swann Way* and the wider novel as a whole, it will be helpful to provide some wider context about the author of this very particular work of fiction that takes subjectivity and individual perspective and knowledge so very seriously. Who was Marcel Proust, and how did he come to write the novel that he did?

Marcel Proust—A Life of Writing

Marcel Proust was the first son born (in 1871) to wealthy, upper-middle-class parents, Adrien Proust, a celebrated physician and public health specialist and his wife Jeanne Proust, née Weil, a highly intelligent woman born into a wealthy Jewish family. While Proust's younger brother Robert, born in 1873, would go on to be a medical man like his father, the young Marcel had no such inclination. His childhood was marked by ill health, in particular acute asthma. Attempts to push him, in time, towards a conventional career came to naught. His desire to write was strong from an early age (already at high school, the Lycée Condorcet in Paris, he established and contributed to a short-lived literary and artistic review with his classmates). He went on to produce a substantial body of journalistic writings, reviews, and essays on literary and artistic topics which illuminate his age and provide a rich sense of how his personal aesthetics developed between his years as a precocious lycée student in Paris in the 1880s and the later period, from 1908 to 1922, in which he devoted (and ultimately sacrificed) his life to the composition and publication of his novel.[3] Early attempts at finding a voice and a vehicle for it can be most profitably read and studied. In 1896 he produced a volume of mannered prose sketches and somewhat derivative poems, mostly previously published in newspapers and journals, entitled *Pleasures and Days* (*Les Plaisirs et les jours*), which insofar as it was critically heeded at all, gave him a reputation as a lightweight society writer, dilettantish and lacking direction. Determined to prove himself, yet uncertain of the best route to take, he subsequently channelled his creative efforts into four partially overlapping projects. First, he produced over fifteen hundred pages of manuscript notes towards a narrative that never quite coalesced into a coherent, structured novel. Begun in 1895, these notes—written in the third person and above all concerned with the thoughts, impressions, and perceptions of a young man by the name of Jean Santeuil—were abandoned by 1899. They were posthumously ordered, edited, and published as *Jean Santeuil* in 1952. Although it contains a good many elements that would be recycled or incorporated in one way or another into *In Search of Lost Time*, the *Jean Santeuil* material is a long way from being an 'early novel'. We might think of it as a set of stepping-stones at best. Secondly, between 1899 and 1906 Proust devoted his time not to the production of fiction (the *Jean Santeuil* notes had left him at something of an impasse) but to the work of translation. In an idiosyncratic yet effective way, Proust worked with his mother and Marie Nordlinger, the English-speaking cousin of his friend Reynaldo Hahn, to produce French versions of two works by the English critic, artist, social thinker, and art historian

[3] This section draws on material previously published as the Introduction to *Swann in Love* (Oxford World's Classics, 2017). For a more detailed account of Proust's life, see my critical biography *Marcel Proust* (London: Reaktion Books, 2013). The 'standard' full biographies in English and French are William C. Carter, *Marcel Proust: A Life* (2000; New Haven: Yale University Press, 2013) and Jean-Yves Tadié, *Marcel Proust: Biographie* (Paris: Gallimard, 1996)—also translated into English by Euan Cameron: *Marcel Proust* (New York: Viking, 2000).

John Ruskin (1819–1900). Proust's heavily annotated translation of *The Bible of Amiens* appeared in 1904, followed by his version of *Sesame and Lilies* in 1906, to which is appended an important prefatory essay, subsequently widely republished as 'Days of Reading'.[4] This essay in particular was a chance for Proust to explore ideas about art, memory, and the nature of subjective experience that would feed into the pages of 'Combray' (and other parts of the *Search*). Ruskin provided lasting lessons in aesthetics, in architectural and art history, and in the less concrete but equally pertinent matter of how as individuals we relate to place and space. Proust is a writer greatly sensitive to the world around him, both its natural and built environments, and Ruskin played a major role in developing that sensitivity. The practice of translation, however, in the end left Proust unfulfilled—it did not feel like 'real' writing, as he put it, but drudgery in the service of others.[5] His father and mother had died in 1903 and 1905 respectively: now he was alone (his brother had married and started a family), his fortieth birthday was on the horizon, and he had precious few accomplishments of which to speak.

The turning point came for Proust during 1908–9 when he embarked on two broadly concurrent undertakings. Following news reports of the extraordinary 'Lemoine Affair'—the tale of a crooked engineer who succeeded, for a time, in swindling the De Beers diamond company out of almost two million francs with the claim that he had mastered a method of manufacturing diamonds—Proust wrote a series of quite brilliant pastiches of well-known writers in the French tradition, based on the outlandish events. He wrote accounts of the affair in the style of (among others) the great nineteenth-century novelists Honoré de Balzac and Gustave Flaubert, as well as the Goncourt brothers, the prolific critic Émile Faguet, and the historian Jules Michelet.[6] The process of identifying and reproducing the salient traits of style of revered authors was a sort of 'literary criticism in action' for Proust

[4] *The Bible of Amiens* (1882) is Ruskin's study of the development of Christianity in France, with a focus on Amiens and its cathedral, originally constructed in the thirteenth century. *Sesame and Lilies* (1865) brings together two lectures Ruskin gave which treat the respective education, duties, and comportment of men and women.

[5] Letter to Antoine Bibesco, 20 December 1902, in *Correspondance de Marcel Proust*, ed. Kolb, iii. 196.

[6] For an incisive and illuminating account of these texts and their relation to Proust's later writing, see Hannah Freed-Thall, '"Prestige of a Momentary Diamond": Economies of Distinction in Proust', *New Literary History* 43/1 (2012), 159–78.

while also, crucially, serving as 'a matter of hygiene...necessary to purge oneself of the most natural vice of idolatry and imitation'.[7] Proust realized that by actively reproducing the writing style of others, he could avoid the risk of unconsciously doing so when creating his own work. He was thus able to arrive at the voice that speaks to us from the pages of *In Search of Lost Time*, but this would only emerge from a final transitional project that was begun at the same time Proust was crafting his pastiches.

In 1908, he started working on a piece of writing we now know as *Against Sainte-Beuve* (*Contre Sainte-Beuve*, posthumously published in 1954), which was ultimately abandoned in favour of the novel that grew out of these notes. *Against Sainte-Beuve* can be read as one might walk around an artist's studio or workshop, examining sketches and maquettes, rough drawings and studies that show the tentative, combinatory steps that precede and foreshadow a masterpiece.[8] Here we can see Proust trying his hand at a variety of approaches to the writerly vocation. Proust started with the idea of a critical essay taking issue with the methods of Charles-Augustin Sainte-Beuve (1804–69), the most influential French literary critic of the nineteenth century. His intention was to write a fictional dialogue between himself and his mother, who would come to his bedside and listen to his account of plans for an article challenging Sainte-Beuve's view that the merits of a given literary work are determined by the moral qualities of the writer who produced it. Proust's view—that a work of art should be judged on its own terms, regardless of the qualities of its creator— prefigures the aesthetic lessons learned in the *Search* by the novel's narrator-protagonist, as well as later twentieth-century literary theoretical writing concerning 'the death of the author' and the autonomy of the work of art. This dialogue-cum-essay, however, grew quickly beyond its anticipated dimensions and in one of Proust's notebooks

---

[7] See *Correspondance de Marcel Proust*, ed. Kolb, viii. 61 and xviii. 380.

[8] A recent discovery of material from this period has added yet further to our understanding of Proust's early steps towards the novel as we have it today. This is the seventy-five pages of draft material begun in late 1907 and elaborated during the first half of 1908 that came to light amongst the papers of Proust scholar Bernard de Fallois at his death in 2018. They show some of the earliest versions of scenes that take their final form in *The Swann Way*, but also in three of the novel's later volumes, showing how adept Proust was at saving, adapting, and redeploying draft material long before word-processing made such things possible at the touch of a button. See Marcel Proust, *Les Soixante-quinze feuillets*, ed. Nathalie Mauriac Dyer (Paris: Gallimard, 2021).

from this time, known as the *Carnet de 1908*, it is possible to trace the fervent, dynamic, multidirectional movements of his thinking: here we find, intermingled with notes relating to potential developments of the essay on Sainte-Beuve, fictional fragments—sketches of scenarios and characters—as well as reading notes and scribbled lists of topics for exploration, and possible structural forms for his narrative.[9] Gradually, in this and a succession of other *carnets* (notebooks) and *cahiers* (school jotters that Proust bought cheaply in large quantities), between 1908 and 1912 a first-person voice and a guiding structure emerged that would, in time, become *A la recherche du temps perdu*, a wholly new sort of text that retains and incorporates traits of the critical or philosophical essay within its hybrid form.

It is commonplace to associate Proust with the image of the ivory-tower artist, a reclusive figure in a cork-lined room, dedicated only to matters of the mind and the production of his novel, swathed in blankets and burning medicated powders to ease the rattling of his asthmatic chest. Such an image has its roots in reality: in 1910 he did have the walls of his Boulevard Haussmann bedroom lined with cork in an attempt to muffle the sound of the busy thoroughfare and the lively neighbourhood beyond his apartment windows, and his poor health, nocturnal regime, peculiar diet, and proclivity for self-medication did lead to the rhythms of his life being idiosyncratic and its duration relatively short, but he was by no means a lifetime recluse or anchorite of art. His relationships were intense (especially with the loves of his adult life—Reynaldo Hahn, Bertrand de Fénelon, and Alfred Agostinelli) and his network of contacts and correspondents varied and extensive. He could not have written the novel he did without a finely calibrated and highly trusted social compass, an awareness of the extraordinary riches that can be gleaned by an attentive observer in a given social setting.[10] Until the last years of his life when respiratory and other health problems curtailed his physical activity, he was a passionate participant in the artistic and cultural life of the French

---

[9] See *Cahiers Marcel Proust*, 8. *Le Carnet de 1908*, ed. Philip Kolb (Paris: Gallimard, 1976). Also available online at https://gallica.bnf.fr/ark:/12148/btv1b6000655q. r=NAF%2016637 (accessed August 2022).

[10] For an insightful overview, see Edward J. Hughes, 'Proust and Social Spaces', in Richard Bales (ed.), *The Cambridge Companion to Marcel Proust* (Cambridge: Cambridge University Press, 2001), 151–67. Michael Lucey's *What Proust Heard: Novels and the Ethnography of Talk* (Chicago: Chicago University Press, 2022) is an immensely valuable, extended account of Proust's novel as a study in the production of sociological knowledge.

capital, its theatres and concert halls, its museums and galleries, private salons and balls. (And even at a time when, by his own account, he had been taking aspirin, morphine, adrenalin, and other substances to manage rheumatic pain, asthma, and fevers, he nevertheless left his bedroom sanctuary in May 1921, just eighteen months before his death, to visit an exhibition of Vermeer paintings at the Musée du Jeu de Paume.[11]) Though his travels were largely domestic, and never took him further than Belgium, Holland, Switzerland, and Venice, via tireless reading and astonishing volumes of correspondence, he kept himself apprised of matters ranging from politics and international affairs to share trading, gastronomy, horticulture, and of course literature and the arts. Limitations of space preclude us from expanding further here on the details of Proust's life, though many of them emerge in the following pages: the novel grew and evolved symbiotically with the arc of his life, as we shall see. In a long letter of January 1920, he wrote: 'I sacrifice to this work my pleasures, my health, my life.'[12] Such hyperbole in Proust's correspondence is common, but in this he was accurate. The intensity with which he dedicated himself to his literary enterprise almost certainly curtailed his life, but the quid pro quo was the singular work of literature that we have today.

Composition and Structure of In Search of Lost Time

Proust's novel is the story, told in the first person, of how an individual comes to recognize that he is ready and able to fulfil his vocation as a writer. The narrator-protagonist's life is not especially eventful, but the society in which he moves, the relationships he forms, and the struggles he endures with his health serve nevertheless, for most of his life, to prevent him from getting down to work. The complexity—and astonishing accomplishment—of the novel is in the telling, in the non-linear structure of the narrative, in the variability in perspective of the voice that leads us through the tale and the multiple speeds at which it moves. A brief event or a fleeting impression may be dwelt on for pages, while months, even years, can pass in a brief parenthetical remark. As noted above, at times we hear the voice of the youthful

---

[11] See *Correspondance de Marcel Proust*, ed. Kolb, xx. 163.
[12] *Correspondance de Marcel Proust*, ed. Kolb, xix. 78.

protagonist, close in to the action of which he is part, at others we are in the company of a more worldly, adult narrator looking back on the events of his life. This plurality of perspective and approach is mirrored in the composition history of the work, which rapidly and untidily grew well beyond its original anticipated parameters.

The novel's seven volumes did not materialize, of course, all at once. Proust began with *The Swann Way*, which appeared in 1913, but the second volume published, *In the Shadow of Girls in Blossom* (1919), was not the second to be written. Proust began by writing 'Combray', the opening part of the first volume, more or less as we have it, and then wrote what we now know as the closing part of the final volume, *Time Regained*. These bookends were in place by 1910–11 and the writing of the latter parts of the first volume and what would become the third volume, *The Guermantes Way*, followed in 1911–12. Prior to this Proust had envisaged a novel in two parts, the volumes entitled *Le Temps perdu* and *Le Temps retrouvé* (*Time Lost* and *Time Regained*), but as the first volume grew, for practical reasons a certain amount of material had to be excised and placed at the beginning of a second volume. With the publication of *The Swann Way* in 1913 a three-volume structure was therefore anticipated: the second would be *The Guermantes Way* and the last *Time Regained*. The planned overarching title at this stage was *Les Intermittences du cœur* (*The Intermittencies of the Heart*). Proust's writing, however, never tended towards concentration: proliferation, rather, is the watchword of his creative process and in 1914 the material of that envisaged second volume was in fact separated out, spliced with new drafts and expansions, to form the basis of *In the Shadow of Girls in Blossom* and *The Guermantes Way*.

Two major events of 1914—one personal, one geopolitical—had further and fundamental impact on the development of Proust's novel. The outbreak of war meant the suspension of the publication of Proust's work, though ill health meant he was not engaged for service and was thereby at liberty to continue to develop his novel during the years of the conflict. It is likely that Proust's relationship with a young man seventeen years his junior, Alfred Agostinelli, was a motivating force in his developing the story of the protagonist's relationship with a girl named Albertine, encountered among a group of young friends in the fictional resort town of Balbec. Agostinelli was a 19-year-old taxi driver when Proust first met him during his vacation in the Normandy seaside town of Cabourg in the summer of 1907. They saw each other regularly—Proust spent the summer in Cabourg every year from 1907 to 1914—and eventually, in the spring of 1913, Proust installed Agostinelli in his Paris apartment, ostensibly to serve as a secretary. When, unannounced, Agostinelli fled the capital in December 1913 for Monte Carlo, Proust was distraught and went to great lengths (in vain) to secure his return. Using money Proust had given him, Agostinelli registered at a flying school under the assumed name of 'Marcel Swan'.[13] When news reached him that Agostinelli had drowned after crashing his plane into the sea off Antibes in May 1914, Proust was devastated. These events contributed to the drafting of two volumes of *In Search of Lost Time* that took shape during the war years: *The Captive*, which tells of the narrator's fraught existence with Albertine in Paris, and *The Fugitive*, which deals with her flight and death in a horse-riding accident. The story of the narrator's relationship with Albertine begins in *In the Shadow of Girls in Blossom*, which became the *Search*'s second volume, published to significant acclaim—and the award of the Prix Goncourt—in 1919. *The Guermantes Way*, which offers an anatomy of Parisian high society life during the Belle Époque period, followed in two instalments in 1920 and 1921, with the *Search*'s fourth volume, *Sodom and Gomorrah*, the heart of its radical exploration of the various shadings of human sexuality and also largely the product of the war years, appearing in two instalments in 1921 and 1922, the year of Proust's death. *The Captive* and *The Fugitive*, sometimes known as the 'Albertine cycle', were published posthumously, in 1923 and 1925 respectively, their editing (and that of *Time Regained*) completed by Proust's brother Robert and his editor Gaston Gallimard. Finally, having been repeatedly revised, expanded, and adjusted by Proust up to the end of his life, so as to take into account the developments of the intervening volumes unforeseen when it was first drafted in 1910–11, and dealing in

---

[13] Biographers and scholars had until recently reproduced Proust's own belief, mentioned in a note to an essay in the *Pastiches et mélanges* volume published in 1919, that the pseudonym was Marcel Swann. (See *Pastiches et mélanges* in *Contre Sainte-Beuve précédé de Pastiches et mélanges et suivi de Essais et articles*, ed. Pierre Clarac and Yves Sandre, Bibliothèque de la Pléiade Paris: Gallimard, 1971), 66. Recent archival research has shown otherwise: see Jean-Marc Quaranta, 'Marcel Swan', in *Un amour de Proust: Alfred Agostinelli (1888–1914)* (Paris: Bouquins, 2021), 251–4.

significant measure with the effects of the war on life in Paris, *Time Regained* eventually appeared in 1927.[14]

Overture

Many readers find their initial encounter with Proust's writing to be a destabilizing, even a daunting, experience. This is not because the themes are especially challenging; rather, it is because of the uncertainties that underpin the writing itself: we are plunged straight into the thoughts of a narrator who seems to be lacking all bearings, unsure where and, perhaps even more troublingly, *who* he is. He is existentially unmoored and readers have to embrace the heave and sway of his thoughts and preoccupations as he reflects on questions of memory and identity, the experience of waking from sleep and the hinterland between the unconscious and conscious realms of existence that we usually traverse quite unthinkingly. This is a novel that does not eschew the conventional narrative props of time, location, and character, but rather tweaks or modifies them in unexpected ways, creating friction or turbulence in our reading. The comfortingly unequivocal narrative openings of much nineteenth-century realist fiction give way to a swirl of memory, dream, speculation, and uncertainty. We know that a first-person voice speaks to us, but is he young or old? He recalls a number of bedrooms and sleeping arrangements, but where is he now, as he recalls his memories and early versions of his self? There is a good deal of interplay of light and dark in these opening pages (the real candles and curtains, windows and shadows of the rooms in which the protagonist slept, the darkness of unknowing and the figurative illumination or enlightenment of understanding that comes by and by to the narrator and his reader). As the narrator searches for his bearings, conversationally weaving through reminiscences that expand and bloom from within, growing with layers of metaphor, analogy, and association, we realize that as readers we are sharing in this enterprise: our reading of Proust's opening pages is

[14] For a concise and authoritative account of these matters, see Nathalie Mauriac Dyer, 'Composition and Publication of *A la recherche du temps perdu*', in Adam Watt (ed.), *Marcel Proust in Context* (Cambridge: Cambridge University Press, 2013), 34–40. Those interested in the timeline of events that can be construed from a reading of the novel will learn much from Gareth H. Steel's *Chronology and Time in* A la recherche du temps perdu (Geneva: Droz, 1979).

supposed to be uneasy and uncertain—if it weren't, we wouldn't be immersing ourselves in the mental space of the first-person guide who will be our companion over the course of the volumes to come.

The opening pages, then, take a gamble—they invite us to share an experience of instability and lost or unknown identity in order, gradually, page by page, to find our way again with the narrator as he settles into the account of his life, seeing, hearing, and encountering the world as he does. And this is what, ultimately, *In Search of Lost Time* is—the story of a life—but to think of it as no more than a fictional autobiography strips it of its riches, its extraordinary breadth and scope. We might think we know the shape of a life, the possible trajectories an individual might take from childhood through adolescent discoveries, adult accomplishments or disappointments, to late life fulfilment (or otherwise). These more or less familiar paths are the heart of the tradition known in German as the *Bildungsroman*—the novel of formation or becoming—the classic example being *Wilhelm Meister's Apprenticeship* (1795–6) by Goethe (1749–1832). While we do find these elements in Proust, they represent only the most rudimentary outline of what is in fact an astonishingly complex and multifaceted structure, as if we were comparing a photograph of a massive hedge-maze taken from ground level with one taken from above. *In Search of Lost Time* invites us repeatedly to rethink and reassess what we thought we knew and its author delights in the revelations that come from a change in perspective. It is a novel about love and relationships, the many forms they take and the ways in which they are doomed to fail; it is about the sparkling allure and ultimate emptiness of social life; the contemplation of beauty in nature; the enrichment provided by our interactions with art; the ways through which we seek to understand who we are and come to an understanding of the wider world and our place in it; how we are affected by loss; and how our minds struggle to cope with the things we can't control and tend to shut down (or go into overdrive) as means of self-protection. Proust's novel explores all of this and much, much more besides, and intimations of these vast vistas of human experience, via explicit references, subtle foreshadowings, or what nowadays some readers might know as 'Easter eggs', are there to be had in the course of the opening volume. *The Swann Way*, to use a musical term employed by Proust himself, is a sort of overture to the work as a whole, an introduction to the key themes, people, and places of the

Proustian world, such as one finds in the opening musical sequence of an opera. Across the opening ten or so pages, in particular, Proust makes us privy to the main locations of the novel, mentions many of the key dramatis personae, and starts to draw us into the themes of time, memory, identity, and belonging that will be sustained throughout each of the successive volumes.

Structure

The Swann Way has a peculiar and somewhat uneven structure. In what follows I will consider key aspects of each part in turn, beginning with a brief overview of the volume as a whole.

The opening part of the volume is 'Combray', which takes its title from the name of the provincial town where during the narrator's childhood his family would spend time away from Paris, at the house of his great-aunt. This part is subdivided into two sections that are qualitatively very different: 'Combray I' recounts the limited aspects of his childhood that the narrator could voluntarily recall of his early life prior to the 'madeleine moment' mentioned above, the period when his only consolation during the trauma of going to bed was his mother's kiss, often denied him when his parents had guests. Many years later, tasting a madeleine dipped in lime-blossom tea, the memory of the rest of his childhood existence in Combray is suddenly restored to him. 'Combray II' narrates the far more expansive, richly detailed account of this period that comes flooding back to him as a result of that experience. We learn about the narrator's family; their servant Françoise; their friend Charles Swann; we witness the caste-like divisions and cyclical minor dramas of small-town life in Combray; we glimpse the aristocratic Guermantes family and the narrator's first indications of wanting to become an artist. The second part of the volume then steps abruptly some way backwards in time: 'Swann in Love' is a discrete narrative in its own right, the interpolated story, told in the third person, of the troubled love affair between the family friend Charles Swann and the woman who would become his wife, Odette de Crécy. She is a woman of relatively low social standing and one of the little clan of 'faithfuls' at the home of the Verdurins, a socially ambitious bourgeois couple. Swann moves in the highest social circles and we encounter some of the prominent figures at a soirée he attends, held by the Marquise de Saint-Euverte. This part of the novel chronologically long predates the narrator's own story and may be seen as a sort of blueprint for it. It can be read as a stand-alone novella, a bite-sized Proust for those without the time or volition to launch into the *Search* as a whole, but it also serves a key function as part of the 'overture' to the wider work, staging the great risks we face (betrayal, jealousy, self-deception, ridicule) when we fall in love, risks the narrator will in turn run as his own amorous life develops. The relation of 'Swann in Love' to *The Swann Way* and the wider novel as a whole is most instructive: it gives us a model, a set of worked examples, as it were, from which we can extrapolate laws or generalizations about love, society, human behaviour, and relationships. Proust is fascinated by the relation of part to whole, microcosm to macrocosm, and 'Swann in Love' is the first substantive manifestation of this in the novel. We see how Swann behaves, we see how he is treated by those around him, and we may recall the patterns and pitfalls of his experience when in later volumes the narrator in turn goes out into society and seeks comfort and pleasure from the company of others. Before then, however, the volume closes with a brief final part entitled 'Place Names: The Name', which begins with a discussion of the evocative power of place names, before switching to the time when the narrator would play in the Champs-Élysées with Swann's daughter Gilberte (first met in Combray). The narrator loves Gilberte but soon she disappears, leaving him bereft. The volume closes with a passage, narrated from a much later point in time, reflecting on the irrevocable changes that have occurred in the Bois de Boulogne since that distant period of the narrator's childhood. He sombrely acknowledges the unrelenting advance of time and the impossibility of holding on to, or voluntarily recreating, the past.

The Swann Way: *Key Moments*

More than the work of any other author, it seems, Proust's vast literary edifice is with great regularity reduced to a single scene that is taken as representative of the writer's achievements. That scene, spanning little more than three pages, is—of course—the madeleine scene, mentioned above. A number of factors determine why it should have become emblematic of Proust's writing even for those who have never read the novel. The scene is brief (in contrast to the novel that runs so counter to our modern taste for instantaneity, and Proust's many much more extended set-pieces that unfold, quite unhurriedly, at very great length); it is memorable (by dint of its intensity, striking imagery, and rich, sensory nature); and the scene has a universality to it, what some might nowadays call a 'relatable' quality (in this novel where, as I have been arguing, so much about the narrator is idiosyncratic, rarefied, one-off, the madeleine scene recounts an experience each of us can and will have). The madeleine moment, then, is brief, memorable, and universal: a surging, soaring instance of exultant happiness when—albeit fleetingly and without warning—the narrator suddenly relives a moment from his past in the actuality, the very presentness, of the here and now. The intensity of the experience, by Proust's account, comes from the *sensory* nature of the stimulus. The narrator does not actively seek to recall his childhood through a voluntary act of intellectual engagement. His mind is elsewhere, he acts 'mechanically', and abruptly it is the taste sensation that triggers something within him:

It had instantly made the vicissitudes of life unimportant to me, its disasters innocuous, its brevity illusory, acting in the same way that love acts, by filling me with a precious essence: or rather, this essence was not in me, it was me. I no longer felt mediocre, contingent, mortal. Where could it have come from, this powerful feeling of joy? (p. 45)

The prose here is rich, but its structures are simple, a rapid flow of thoughts divided only by the gentlest of pauses imposed by Proust's commas. After a slew of questions and ponderings, active mental endeavours, and renewed, inquisitive mouthfuls of tea and cake that yield no answers, once his mind is left idling, the realization comes to him: 'The taste was the taste of the little piece of madeleine that my aunt Léonie would dip in her infusion of tea or lime blossom and give me when I went into her bedroom to kiss her good morning on Sundays' (p. 46). And all that he had thought to be forgotten, condemned to oblivion (the French 'oubli' covers both of these bases) is revitalized through the catalyst of the narrator's cup of tea. '[W]hen nothing subsists of one's distant past,' he observes, 'smell and taste live on for a long time, alone':

more fragile but more enduring, more immaterial but more persistent, more faithful; they are like souls, remembering, waiting, hoping, amid the ruins of all the rest, bearing unfalteringly on their almost impalpable little drop, the vast edifice of memory. (pp. 46–7)

And this radical juxtaposition of the impalpable little drop and the vast edifice is highly characteristic of the insights of Proust's writing, writing that draws us into the finest of details, the most fleeting of moments, to allow us better to understand the role they play in our existence and better to appreciate the magnitude of the lessons we can derive from them. Proust's madeleine reminds readers that our past is never fully out of reach, that we contain depths well beyond what is voluntarily accessible via intellectual means. And it reminds us of the wonders that are to be found in the humblest of things: like his contemporaries, the cubists, incorporating everyday objects, newsprint, rope, wallcoverings, into their revolutionary collages and *papiers collés*, Proust finds revelation and euphoria in what Samuel Beckett called 'the shallow well of a [tea]cup's inscrutable banality'.[15]

Structurally the madeleine moment is crucial—it brings 'Combray I' to a close and permits access to the rich and varied textures of 'Combray II': the narrator's account of provincial life, local gossip, and family events and traditions, the forces and structures that shaped his childhood. Many vignettes stand out: the depiction of Aunt Léonie, the elderly hypochondriac who shares a range of traits with the young protagonist and his older self; his youthful infatuation with the beauty of nature, the hawthorn blossom, the vistas that meet his eyes on country walks after long afternoons spent reading; and the vision of Gilberte, his first love, emerging from amongst the blooms in Swann's park at Tansonville. On one level these and many other scenes are so many disparate episodes of a comfortable, cosseted middle-class childhood. But examined again, with a closer attention to structuring and themes, we realize that every scene that makes up the narrative of 'Combray II' is a lesson of one sort or another for the young protagonist and a lesson from which readers also profit in turn. The jolt of an unexpected ethical dilemma when the saintly Françoise is witnessed brutally killing a chicken in the kitchen yard; confusion when encountering adult attitudes and conventions, with the alluring lady in pink or the snobbish Legrandin; fascination and mystery prompted by same-sex desire as witnessed between Mademoiselle Vinteuil and her friend at Montjouvain; and so on. Repeatedly the world and the people in it prove to be more complex, more given to

---

[15] Samuel Beckett, *Proust* (1931), in *Proust and Three Dialogues with Georges Duthuit* (London: John Calder, 1987), 35.

mutability and variance than to stability and stasis. They are, in the words of the poet Louis MacNeice, 'incorrigibly plural'. Coming to terms with this plurality, the condition that MacNeice memorably qualifies as 'the drunkenness of things being various', is a major dimension of Proust's novel.[16] As the mature narrator looks back on his youthful experiences—the conclusions he jumped to, the comments he misconstrued, and the situations he misread—he realizes with increasing certainty how important perspective, vision, and point of view are when it comes to understanding the world and our place in it. This is a theme that is introduced in 'Combray' and sustained, with varying intensities, across the full extent of the *Search*. The local priest is among the first to draw attention to the benefits of changing perspective: climb the tower of the Combray church, for instance, and, as he puts it, 'the great thing is you can see at the same time things you can normally only see separately' (p. 100). The narrative sets up a world of divisions and distinctions: the family and the servants; the peasant class, middle classes, and the aristocracy; the Swann way and the Guermantes way; the differently experienced spaces of home, town, church, and countryside; childhood and adulthood; weekdays and weekends. But learn a person's back story (as we do in 'Swann in Love') or look back with the wisdom of hindsight and adult understanding on what was bewildering to a child (as the narrator does repeatedly), and things take on a different colouring. This process of temporal reappraisal and review is a gradual and repeatedly iterated one that shapes the novel and our relationship with the narrator.

Another formative lesson takes place in these pages that introduces us to the experience of perspective and point of view in relation to space. Following a family walk, the young protagonist gains a new vision of his environment when he rides next to the coachman in Dr Percepied's carriage:

At a bend in the road, all of a sudden, I experienced that special pleasure, unlike any other, when I caught sight, first, of the twin steeples of Martinville, which were lit up by the setting sun and seemed to keep changing position with the movement of the carriage and the twists and turns of the road, and then the steeple of Vieuxvicq, which, though separated from

---

[16] Louis MacNeice, 'Snow', in *The Collected Poems of Louis MacNeice* (Oxford: Oxford University Press, 1967), 30.

the others by a hill and a valley, and situated on higher ground in the distance, seemed to be right next to them. (p. 167)

The experience of shifting perspective from a moving point of observation fills the protagonist with a joy he cannot fully comprehend. Instead of being remote, fragmented, and able to be witnessed only separately, familiar elements of the landscape appear to interact, to dance before his eyes. As in the madeleine scene, the experience yields a notion of revelation or disclosure, a deeper access to the world, combined with an almost overpowering giddiness, akin to MacNeice's 'drunkenness' quoted above. The protagonist beholds the dance of the steeples and has his first impulse to write, to translate his feelings into language:

Soon their lines and their sunlit surfaces split apart, as if they were a kind of bark, a little of what was hidden inside them appeared, a thought that had not existed a moment before occurred to me, taking shape in words inside my head, and the pleasure I'd felt at the sight of them was so increased by this that, overcome by a sort of drunkenness, I could think of nothing else. (p. 168)

Following this, we then are privy to the words he jots down in the moment, inlaid in the narrative of 'Combray'. A narrative is born of shifting perspectives and the young protagonist's trajectory towards his vocation as a writer is begun.

The volume shifts tack significantly in its second part, 'Swann in Love', which is not only narrated in the third person, but also takes place at a temporal moment some time before the narrator's childhood that is recounted in 'Combray'.[17] Here we have what is at once a stand-alone narrative—the tale of a courtship, a fraught love affair across social boundaries—and a crucial part of the novel's overall architecture. I suggested above ways in which 'Combray' provides a sort of overture to *In Search of Lost Time*. With 'Swann in Love' we get a new relation of part to whole, in that this portion of the novel provides us (albeit highly condensed, in fewer than two hundred pages) with a sort of miniature of the protagonist's later adult experiences that we encounter in subsequent volumes. The thematic preoccupations of 'Swann in Love' are cut from very much the same

[17] What follows draws in part on my Introduction to *Swann in Love*, trans. Brian Nelson (Oxford: Oxford World's Classics, 2017), pp. vii–xvii.

cloth as the rest of the *Search*: we find the exploration of how social context colours the way individuals interact, how they relate to works of art, how infatuation leads to what we call love, and how this can spill over into jealousy. It is a study in desire, an examination of how the pursuit of pleasure inevitably brings with it some measure of suffering. It also returns repeatedly to the question of truth in human relations and how capable we are of telling lies (even, or especially, to ourselves) when it suits us, yet we cower and crumble when we discover (or merely suspect) that our beloved might have lied to us. In all of this 'Swann in Love' anticipates the larger movements of Proust's novel, outlined above.

Just a very few pages into *The Swann Way*, the narrator indicates that Monsieur Swann's visits 'became less frequent after his unfortunate marriage, as my parents had no desire to receive his wife' (p. 16). At the time, no explanation or further detail is provided for these enigmatic comments; 'Swann in Love' provides the basis for his parents' damning judgement. Swann, a highly cultured and well-connected man-about-town, frequents the most distinguished salons and socializes with those whose well-shod feet tread the corridors of power. 'Swann in Love' opens, however, in a resolutely bourgeois context, in the salon of Madame Verdurin who, as the narrator puts it, 'came from a respectable, extremely wealthy, and utterly undistinguished family' (p. 177), poles apart from the storied lineage of the Guermantes, for instance, with whom Swann is intimately connected. Swann, however, is a special case, a sort of amphibious creature, welcomed and comfortable amongst those with crowned heads and ancient titles and also able to make small talk in the much less rarefied circle of Madame Verdurin's 'little clan'. He is a man of means and has no qualms in pursuing sexual pleasure outside the circle of the upper crust or *gratin* of Belle Époque society. He does not consider social standing as a barrier to possible sexual gratification. Thus he becomes acquainted with Odette de Crécy, whose background is neatly (and discreetly) summed up by the narrator as being 'almost of the demi-monde' (p. 177) and who invites him to join her *chez* Verdurin.

We noted above the important role of the madeleine scene in 'Combray'. 'Swann in Love' also includes a similar experience of involuntary memory, though rather than being associated with joy and exhilaration as it is for the protagonist in 'Combray', for Swann it is an experience that teaches him lessons about love that are far harder to palate than a spoonful of cake crumbs dissolved in tea. The seeds of Swann's love for Odette are sown when he unexpectedly hears in her presence a piece of music he had listened to once before. The unanticipated pleasure and contentment derived from re-hearing the Sonata for Piano and Violin by the fictional composer Vinteuil (the sometime piano teacher in Combray) are projected on to the relationship that subsequently develops between Swann and Odette: they come to think of the sonata as the 'national anthem of their love'. In the latter stages of 'Swann in Love', having all but separated from Odette and purposefully avoided the sonata, Swann hears it once more and finds himself involuntarily confronting his feelings for the woman he cannot but associate with a particular 'little phrase' from that sonata. The little phrase, fleeting and condensed as it may be, contains by turns the tenderness of Klimt's *Kiss* and the aching turmoil of Munch's *Scream*.[18]

While the opening part of *The Swann Way* presents the provincial, slow-paced, often quaint, familial setting of Combray, 'Swann in Love' announces the more dynamic societal world of Paris that will be the setting for much of the remainder of the *Search*. Love is undoubtedly an important theme in 'Combray' but the focus there is principally on the protagonist's childhood love for his mother, whose attention and embrace at bedtime he was on occasion forced to forgo as a result of the presence of a dinner guest who kept his mother from him. That guest, 'the unwitting author of my sufferings' (p. 43), as the narrator puts it, was Charles Swann. In 'Swann in Love' we find that he was already the author of a good deal of suffering of his own. But the pattern of suffering in love that we encounter there, which takes a series of forms—from infatuation, blinkeredness, and possessiveness to creeping suspicion and crushing jealousy—recurs not only in the protagonist's later relationship with Albertine but also in the relations of characters whose roles develop in later volumes such

---

[18] Gustav Klimt (1862–1918) and Edvard Munch (1863–1944) were both contemporaries of Proust, though it seems he did not encounter their work. Munch's *The Scream* was painted in 1893, during approximately the period dealt with in 'Swann in Love'; Klimt's *The Kiss* dates from 1907–8, the year that *In Search of Lost Time* began to take shape in Proust's notebooks. The Chilean filmmaker Raoul Ruiz directed films relating to both artists: his fascinating, surrealistic *Le Temps retrouvé* (*Time Regained*) appeared in 1999, whilst his biopic *Klimt* appeared in 2006. John Malkovich, who plays the Baron de Charlus in *Time Regained*, also plays the title role in *Klimt*.

as Robert de Saint-Loup and his mistress Rachel or the Baron de Charlus and the violinist Charlie Morel. Human desire, by Proust's account, whether directed towards the same or the opposite sex, tends sooner or later to lead individuals to behave in ways that are damaging to themselves and hurtful to those they love.

Works of art—and not just Vinteuil's sonata—punctuate Swann's trajectory in 'Swann in Love'. Two main periods stand out as the most frequently occurring: the first is the nineteenth century, which is to say the period contemporary to the narrative. 'Swann in Love' can be read as a commentary on the fascinating coexistence of various cultures—high-, middle- and low-brow—in the Paris of the Belle Époque. A marked conflict of taste exists between Swann, who attended the École du Louvre (the establishment that produces museum conservators trained in subjects such as art history and archaeology), and the bourgeois denizens of the Verdurin circle, especially Odette, whose tastes are, in the main, diametrically opposed to his own. The second period spans the fifteenth to the seventeenth century: time and again in these pages we find allusions to artists of the Renaissance, to Botticelli and to Michelangelo, to Mantegna, and to others that followed, in particular Rembrandt, and Vermeer. The eyes through which Swann sees the world are those of a connoisseur (perhaps a dilettante) but not the eyes of an artist—for these we must look to Proust's fictional figures who all, as the *Search* progresses, serve in a variety of ways as tutors or models for the protagonist: the composer Vinteuil, the painter Elstir, and the writer Bergotte.

Swann's points of reference are the old masters; Odette's are twee, popular numbers from the theatre and vaudeville, even the mention of which would normally cause Swann to recoil in discomfort. Curiously, though, it is his learning and culture that lead him, in part, to fall for Odette. The enchantment of the little phrase from Vinteuil plays its role, but so does Swann's tendency to find in visual art substitutes or replacements for the figures he encounters in real life. In the footmen on the stairs of Madame de Saint-Euverte's residence, for example, Swann sees figures from Mantegna and Dürer, and in the kitchen maid at Combray he sees an embodiment of Giotto's *Charity* from the Arena (Scrovegni) Chapel in Padua. However, his most enduring artistic substitution comes with Odette. What captures his imagination is the resemblance she bears to the figure of Jethro's daughter, Zipporah, as depicted, famously, in Botticelli's fresco of *Scenes from the Life of Moses* (1481–2). Swann is quickly in thrall to the notion that Odette is an embodiment of an ideal of beauty and grace otherwise only accessible via a reproduction in a book or, at best, by craning one's neck and squinting up at the ceiling in the Sistine Chapel itself. His admiration for art blinkers him to the actual failings of the flesh-and-blood Odette and clouds his awareness of their incompatibilities. And so it is that their 'love', as Proust presents it, gathers strength and its hold over Swann: since his imagination is captured by the emotive power of Vinteuil's music and the entrancing quality of Botticelli's Zipporah, his rational judgement is suppressed or ignored. Love, in Proust's vision of things, is a contrary force and as 'Swann in Love' unfolds it becomes more and more clear that rather than being soulmates somehow cosmically destined to share a life together, as a conventionally romantic love story might have it, Swann and Odette are in fact bonded by his idolatrous relation to art.[19]

To read 'Swann in Love' as a love story, as we have seen, involves coming up against Proust's gloomy, not to say pessimistic, view of human relations. It should be noted, however, that Proust's presenta-tion of sexual identity and preference as qualities that shift and vary throughout a person's life and according to circumstance was radical in its time. Both Odette and Albertine have affairs with lovers of both sexes and Swann's fears about Odette's lesbian affairs adumbrate those that preoccupy the protagonist to the point of obsession in his relations with Albertine. In *In the Shadow of Girls in Blossom*, Proust's protagonist, even while their relationship is in its earliest stages, expresses suspicions about Albertine's intimacy with the other girls at Balbec. He pries, he questions, he insinuates, just as Swann had before him. Later in the novel it is the belief that he has 'proof' of her lesbian past in a remark she makes about a close friendship with the composer Vinteuil's daughter, known to be a lesbian, that prompts the protagonist to move Albertine into his Paris apartment where he hopes he can prevent her from further indulging such proclivities. In *The Captive*, we find that the narrator's mind, even more inquisitive than Swann's, proves to be a yet richer source of hypothetical situations

---

[19] Swann's tendency towards mediated forms of desire or, to put it another way, his habit of investing in interposed, substitute objects is memorably epitomized in his allu-sion to their lovemaking as 'doing a cattleya', in reference to the flowers Odette wore in her corsage when they consummated their relationship.

in which his beloved may or may not have deceived him or betrayed him with other young women, or with men. And the fear of otherness—in this case, the straight man's fear of lesbian betrayal—is interestingly illustrative of the socio-cultural climate at the time of which Proust writes.

On the basis of 'Swann in Love', one might not initially consider Swann himself to be an individual with whom one would associate alterity or outsider status: he is an associate of the Prince of Wales, a close friend of the President of the Republic, a member of the exclusive Jockey Club. Yet for all these seemingly unequivocal marks of being an elite 'insider' (the status, indeed, that keeps the Verdurins, as aspiring bourgeois, from ever fully accepting him) in late nineteenth-century France, one detail of Swann's identity indelibly marks him out from those with whom he associates: his Jewishness. Swann's origins as the son of a Jewish stockbroker, about which readers learn in 'Combray', differentiate him from his blue-blooded friends and associates. The shifting attitudes towards him and his family (and towards other Jewish characters) as the Dreyfus Affair unfolds are explored by Proust in particular in *The Guermantes Way* and in *Sodom and Gomorrah*, where the plight of Jews in contemporary society is compared at length with that of another persecuted minority group: homosexuals.[20] Social acceptance—being 'in' or 'out', fashionable or behind the times, up-to-date or out-of-touch—is a major theme of 'Swann in Love', which is, after all, more than a 'mere' love story. It offers a snapshot of various strata of French society at the *fin de siècle*; the contemporary artistic allusions that underpin the novella

[20] The Dreyfus Affair grew out of the case of Alfred Dreyfus, a Jewish captain in the French army who in 1894 was convicted of treason for allegedly selling secrets to the Germans. Dreyfus was publicly degraded then deported and held in solitary confinement in dreadful conditions on Devil's Island (off the coast of French Guiana). The case stirred powerful and widespread anti-Semitism in France throughout the 1890s. Public pressure, including the campaigning of the novelist Émile Zola (1840–1902), his emphatic public letter 'J'accuse' and the 'Manifesto of the Intellectuals', a petition on which Proust's signature appears (both were published in 1898), led to Dreyfus's retrial. Despite the weight of the case against the army, for their framing of Dreyfus and the various cover-ups that had ensued, Dreyfus, farcically, was found guilty a second time. He was eventually pardoned in 1899 and reinstated in the army, but the divisions the affair had caused ran deep. For an incisive overview, see Edward J. Hughes, 'The Dreyfus Affair', in Watt (ed.), *Marcel Proust in Context*, 167–73; for an accessible, authoritative historical account, see Ruth Harris, *The Man on Devil's Island: Alfred Dreyfus and the Affair that Divided France* (London: Allen Lane, 2010).

point towards this, as suggested above, but a range of other elements in the narrative are also revealing of the societal backdrop of 1880s Paris.[21]

Proust's novel is structured throughout with parallelisms, mirrorings, and echoes, and within 'Swann in Love' we find an illuminating structural parallel between the bourgeois salon of the Verdurins and the aristocratic Saint-Euverte salon at which Swann suffers his final realizations about the state of his relationship with Odette towards the end of this part of the novel. What Proust presents here are two worlds that exist in parallel. While each social class outwardly condemns the other as variously vulgar, tawdry, lacking in taste, dull, and unthinkably boring, we glimpse how the attraction of the unknown creates an allure around the aristocratic milieux in the eyes of the bourgeois and how the aristocrats themselves seem desperate to hold on to a world that is increasingly under threat of extinction. Proust uses the two salons to hold up a range of characters to satirical scrutiny, and neither side, bourgeois or aristocratic, is portrayed in a particularly endearing light. A notable contrast is that a good number of the guests at the Verdurin salon have professions: Cottard is a doctor, Monsieur 'Biche' a painter, Brichot an academic at the Sorbonne, and Saniette an archivist. As such they have a degree of anchorage in the world beyond the drawing room and dining table that is rather more substantive than that of the aristocrats that mingle *chez* Saint-Euverte. Swann, although loosely engaged in writing a study of the Dutch artist Vermeer (1632–75), is essentially a man of leisure. Proust sensitizes us to the class divides in French society while at the same time alerting us to the foibles and insecurities that are common to all human subjects, regardless of heredity or income. *Chez* Verdurin, Dr Cottard is perpetually fearful of having misunderstood a coded reference or blundered over a question of etiquette and so constantly churns out puns, clichés, and non sequiturs in the hope of keeping face, while the painter revels in vulgarity, knowing that his status as an

---

[21] It is unusual, in discussion of Proust's novel, to be able to identify with certainty the period of a given episode, for reasons outlined above in relation to the novel's shifting narrative perspectives. The autonomy of 'Swann in Love' as a retrospective account of a single set of events makes it a case apart. Indeed, there are more explicit references to concrete dates and events in these pages than anywhere else in the *Search*. Swann, for example, is said to be a regular diner with Président Grévy: Jules Grévy's presidential term ran from 1879 to 1887.

artist in such surroundings grants him immunity from criticism. Meanwhile, in the Saint-Euverte salon we find minor aristocrats eager to ensure that others are aware of their more distinguished connections and, just as Madame Verdurin perpetually overemphasizes how moved she is by the works of art she encounters, we find a competitive edge to the way Madame de Saint-Euverte's guests record their appreciation of the music being played. In short, we see variations on effectively the same anxieties and the same compensatory, defensive responses to them. The two salons are arenas for the observation of human interaction—it is not by chance that the novelist encountered at Madame de Saint-Euverte's indicates that he is there 'as an observer' (p. 303)—and Proust's astonishing ear for argot and sociolects, as well as his eye for the physical tics and twitches that mark us out individually and as groups within groups, provide much of the liveliness and energy of these scenes.

Swann is unique in his participation in both salons, but another element is also common to both and for Swann this spells disaster: it is the piece of music that is played, Vinteuil's Sonata for Piano and Violin. When Swann and the Princesse des Laumes meet at Madame de Saint-Euverte's salon their conversation is a joy to behold: it is easy-going and understated, much is unsaid, insinuated. The wit, humour, and mutual understanding of two old friends, meeting in territory familiar to them both, are captured wonderfully, and strike a marked contrast to Swann's more reserved interactions with the Verdurin set. His spark and verve are quickly extinguished, however, once the strains of Vinteuil's sonata reach his discerning ears. Hearing the sonata once again brings about the involuntary memory of happier times with Odette but also brings with it the realization that the relationship has left him 'a wretched figure' he struggles even to recognize (p. 321).

With the short closing part of *The Swann Way*, 'Place Names: The Name', Proust loops us back to the considerations of sleeping and waking with which the volume began, pulling us out of Swann's doldrums and right back into the sensory, hyper-alert register of the narrator we came to know in Combray:

Of all the bedrooms I pictured to myself as I lay awake at night, none was less like the rooms at Combray, powdery with a grainy, pollenated, almost edible atmosphere, redolent of piety, than the room at the Grand-Hôtel de la Plage at Balbec, whose enamel-painted walls contained, like the polished sides of a swimming pool that tint the water blue, a pure, azure air, smelling slightly of sea salt. (p. 357)

The evocative power of place names (all the more evocative for those, like the protagonist, who are so often unable to travel due to ill health) is introduced as a topic for reflection. The seaside town of Balbec is evoked, along with more distant sites—Florence, Venice, Parma, Pisa. Since the narrator is unable to visit these places in person, their names take on a powerful, heady allure, his imagination and powers of association filling in the gap between the word and the thing itself, in this case the Italian cities so redolent of art, architecture, and beauty in all its forms. This contemplative mood continues and soon we are shifted into a passage of recollection of another place, this time in Paris—the Champs-Élysées—where the protagonist would play with Gilberte, now a fixture in his childhood and the object of his intense affections, some time after that first glimpse of her through the hedge in her father's park at Tansonville. In this context we meet Swann once more, not the lovestruck man-about-town of 'Swann in Love' but now the husband of Odette, father to Gilberte, and a source of great fascination for the young protagonist. Equally fascinating is Madame Swann, of whom, when she takes her daily walk in the Bois de Boulogne, he tries to catch a glimpse, as do many of the older male denizens of Paris, familiar with her reputation prior to her marriage.

Separated from the preceding section by just a small textual break—a white space on the page—and concerning the same physical space (the Bois de Boulogne), the closing pages of the volume are in fact separated from what comes before by a considerable temporal distance. Tone and perspective have radically shifted: no longer focused on the child accompanied on his walks by the ever-present Françoise, the narrative tells now of the experience of a much older narrator, who leaves his 'closed room' (reminiscent of the enclosed, cork-lined environment in which much of Proust's novel was written) to walk across the Bois to Trianon. In so doing he reflects on different scales of temporal change, on the cyclical, seasonal alterations to the wood's natural environment, and the starker shifts in fashion and technology he perceives around him: motor cars have replaced carriages, the women he sees seem less elegant, the fashions and behaviours seem vulgar in comparison with the treasured impressions of this enchanted place that he had for so long stored up in his mind. And so it is that the volume that opened in the dark with an exploration of spaces mental and physical comes to its conclusion with a somewhat gloomy realization about space and place and identity. We risk great and inevitable disappointment, the narrator notes, if we seek out in reality confirmation of the images we carry around in our heads. Realities change and our memories, source of comfort though they may be, are always only partial, contingent, fugitive.

Critical Reception

There is a vast volume of criticism on Proust's novel, as well as accounts of his life and times and what one might term 'Proustiana', the extensive fringe of writing, both creative and critical, prompted by or in homage to the author and his novel. For a century critics and scholars have tackled the major themes of time, art, and memory, love, desire, and sexuality, singly and in combination and with reference to many of Proust's myriad sub-themes and preoccupations. (A representative choice of the best such studies is included in the Select Bibliography.) His immense correspondence is an invaluable source of evidence, information, and gossip. It exists in a serviceable twenty-one-volume scholarly edition in French and a generous selected edition in English translation. A digitization project is now underway.[22]

The initial reception of Proust's work was complicated by the extended period over which it was published (1913–27) and the great socio-cultural changes that took place during that period.[23] Early critics tended to consider Proust's novel as thinly veiled autobiography, treating author and narrator-protagonist as one and the same. They

---

[22] 'Corr-Proust', a project to start the digitization of Proust's letters, is a collaboration between the Proust–Kolb Archive at the University of Illinois, the Université Grenoble-Alpes, and the Institut des textes et des manuscrits modernes (ITEM), Paris. It represents a first stage in providing a digital, open-access edition of Proust's letters, including diplomatic transcriptions and high-resolution images of original documents. See http://proust.elan-numerique.fr/ (consulted August 2022).

[23] On the early reception of Proust's work, see Anna Magdalena Elsner, 'Critical Reception during Proust's Lifetime' and Vincent Ferré, 'Early Critical Responses, 1922–1950s', in Watt (ed.), *Marcel Proust in Context*, 183–90 and 191–8 respectively. For a selection of contemporary responses, from reviews of *Pleasures and Days* in the 1890s to the 'Hommage' published after Proust's death by the *Nouvelle revue française* (*NRF*) and the earliest critical essays of the 1930s, see Leighton Hodson (ed.), *Marcel Proust: The Critical Heritage* (London: Routledge, 1989).

struggled with the style and syntax that made them work hard for their readerly gratification and enlightenment. Even some of the biggest names of twentieth-century literature in French, such as Jean-Paul Sartre, criticized Proust for snobbishness and elitism and to an extent wrote off his work for reasons similar to those that had caused André Gide initially to reject *Du côté de chez Swann* on behalf of the *NRF* imprint (though he would later repent and the novel, with the publication of its second, Goncourt Prize-winning volume, *A l'ombre des jeunes filles en fleurs*, transferred to the publisher directed by Gaston Gallimard).[24] It is with the development of phenomenological criticism in the 1950s, associated with figures such as Georges Poulet and Jean-Pierre Richard, and structuralist and post-structuralist thought and theory in France in the 1960s and 1970s, in particular the work of critics and thinkers such as Gérard Genette, Roland Barthes, and Gilles Deleuze, that the vast spectrum of interest—philosophical, philological, sociological, aesthetic—to be found in Proust's novel, came properly to be acknowledged, picked apart, and accounted for.

The first reviews of *The Swann Way* were largely lukewarm: Proust's elaborate syntactical structures and shifting perspectives left many early readers somewhat perplexed. The initial breakthrough for Proust and the *Search* came with the renewed impetus and publicity the work received in 1919 with the change of publisher from Grasset to the imprint of the *NRF*, the publication of *In the Shadow of Girls in Blossom*, and the award of the Goncourt Prize to this volume. After an opening part set in Paris, Proust's second volume then transports its readers to the seaside and immerses us in a bright and enchanting world of sea-spray and sunrises, of adolescent infatuation and the protagonist's various, continuing initiations into the domains of society, of love, and of art, away from the confines of family life in Combray and Paris. The idea that, in Proust's novel, the protagonist's journey

---

[24] Early exceptions to this rule (the dismissal of Proust as indulgent and difficult) include the work by Samuel Beckett already mentioned, as well as the following immensely insightful studies: Ernst Robert Curtius, *Marcel Proust* (1928; Frankfurt am Main: Schöffling & Co., 2021); Walter Benjamin, 'The Image of Proust' (1929), in *Illuminations*, trans. Harry Zohn, ed. Hannah Arendt (London: Jonathan Cape, 1970; Pimlico, 1999), 197–210; Eric Auerbach, *Mimesis: The Representation of Reality in Western Literature*, trans. Willard Trask (Princeton: Princeton University Press, 1953); J. M. Cocking, *Proust* (London: Bowes & Bowes, 1956); and Leo Spitzer, 'Le Style de Marcel Proust' (1961), in *Études de style*, trans. Alain Coulon (Paris: Gallimard, 1970), 397–473.

towards fulfilling his vocation as a writer takes the form of a series of apprenticeships, or processes of learning how to interpret the world around him in all its multifariousness, has been an influential one in Proust criticism and stems principally from a critical study titled *Proust et les signes* (*Proust and Signs*), first published by Gilles Deleuze in 1964 and reissued, with revisions and additions, in its final form in 1970.[25] Society, love, and art all involve us in emitting or interpreting signs of various sorts: by Deleuze's reading, this situation is complicated by the fact that in society and in love people are in the habit of projecting images or emitting messages that are not wholly or consistently truthful. And art, Deleuze argues, is made up of signs that do not correlate to material referents in the world, and as such are a purer, higher order of 'sign' (take, for example, the little phrase in Vinteuil's sonata, which Swann loads with significance yet which has no objective existence or referent beyond the fleeting sound signature emitted by the instruments that produce it).

The first scholarly edition of *A la recherche* was published, in three volumes, in the prestigious 'Bibliothèque de la Pléiade' series in 1954, giving readers and scholars a standard point of reference. Shortly after, in 1962, the main body of the 'fonds Proust'—the material, archival substance of Proust's novel, in the form of jotters and notebooks, loose leaves and extraordinary paper confections (*paperasses*) held together by glue, pins, and good fortune—was acquired by the Bibliothèque nationale in Paris and since then, in parallel (and at times in concert with) the developments outlined above, scholars of 'genetic criticism' have worked tirelessly to elucidate Proust's working practices, his modes and means of composing, editing, revising, and reshaping his work through time. This editorial activity and associated scholarly publications have provided remarkable insights into how Proust's ideas evolved; how his sentences grew (and shrank); how certain notions, themes, or preoccupations were amplified or refined, adjusted or reframed; how certain units of text were moved around, spliced, or filleted. They have also brought to light a staggering amount of cultural-historical data about Proust's Paris and contemporary French society, as well as information relating to what and how Proust read, whom he interacted with, and how all this

[25] On the criticism of this period, see Thomas Baldwin, 'Mid-Twentieth-Century Views, 1960s to 1980s', in Watt (ed.), *Marcel Proust in Context*, 199–205.

came to nourish the novel that would be published between 1913 and 1927.

The 1971 centenary of Proust's birth prompted a new wave of scholarly editions as well as critical studies and reappraisals. Two more weighty volumes were added to the Pléiade collection—*Contre Sainte-Beuve*, published together with Proust's pastiches, essays, and articles, and *Jean Santeuil*, published alongside *Les Plaisirs et les jours*. Jean-Yves Tadié published his landmark study *Proust et le roman* (Proust and the Novel) in 1971 and would go on to direct the 'new Pléiade' edition of *A la recherche*, bringing together a broad team of genetic scholars to create a modern edition with a vast critical apparatus and selections of *esquisses* (early draft sketches of given passages) that appeared in four volumes between 1987 and 1989.[26] Tadié's doorstop biography of 1996, mentioned above, is an outstanding achievement (published in English translation by Euan Cameron in 2000) and numerous illuminating studies have subsequently followed from his pen.

As I (and others) have argued elsewhere, Proust is very much a pivot point between two eras in European literature, the grand realist tradition of the nineteenth century and the modernist innovations of the early to middle years of the twentieth century. On one hand scholars have sought to shed light on Proust's debts to his predecessors (key figures include Balzac and Flaubert, Baudelaire and Nerval, but also more temporally distant figures such as Saint-Simon or La Fontaine, and writers of other languages that Proust encountered in translation such as Hardy, Tolstoy, and Dostoevsky). On the other hand, Proust has often been read, quite rightly, as a modernist, and so he is compared and contrasted with writers of his time as diverse as James Joyce, Virginia Woolf, and Robert Musil, whose publishing trajectories and writerly preoccupations overlapped with those of Proust to varying degrees. He is 'the first contemporary writer of the twentieth century', as Edmund White has it, 'for he was the first to describe the permanent instability of our times'.[27] Proust's experimentation with the possibilities of first-person narrative lead back to Augustine

---

[26] The most recent, and hugely substantive, addition, to the scholarly editing of Proust's work comes in the shape of a new Pléiade volume (re)collecting Proust's nonfictional writings: see *Essais*, ed. Antoine Compagnon, Christophe Pradeau, and Matthieu Vernet, Bibliothèque de la Pléiade (Paris: Gallimard, 2022).

[27] Edmund White, *Proust* (London: Weidenfeld & Nicolson, 1999), 140.

and Montaigne while concurrently stretching forward to anticipate the writings of Samuel Beckett and announce what will come to be known in the later twentieth century as autofiction. This plurality, a sort of self-renewing plasticity in the literary qualities we find in the novel from one reading to the next, would suggest that *In Search of Lost Time* will remain a vitally important touchstone for critics and general readers alike for a long time to come.

Later twentieth-century scholarship has provided some scintillating studies that avoid the trap of claiming Proust for any one school and embrace the destabilizing, at times frustrating, plurality of his writing.[28] High points include Malcolm Bowie's peerless *Proust Among the Stars* (1998), Christopher Prendergast's *Mirages and Mad Beliefs: Proust the Skeptic* (2013), and Michael Lucey's *What Proust Heard: Novels and the Ethnography of Talk* (2022). Rewarding critical appreciations of Proust's writing, his place in Belle Époque culture, and his relation to his contemporaries, the novel's structure, themes, and legacies can be found in the essays collected in *The Cambridge Companion to Proust*, edited by Richard Bales (2001); *Marcel Proust in Context*, edited by Adam Watt (2013); and two introductory works that offer helpful volume-by-volume analysis and discussion: David Ellison's *A Reader's Guide to Proust's 'In Search of Lost Time'* (2010) and my *Cambridge Introduction to Marcel Proust* (2011). Readers seeking brief and accessible overviews in essay format are well served from recent companions and histories.

---

[28] For an overview of scholarship, focusing on the period from 2013 to 2018, but with a range of references further back into the late twentieth and early twenty-first century, see my 'État présent: Marcel Proust', *French Studies* 72/3 (2018), 412–24. Here I discern six main areas of critical interest in Proust: correspondence, biography, and genetic criticism; philosophy; the arts; intertextual, contextual, and thematic studies; modernism; creative responses.

NOTE ON THE TEXT

OUR translation is based on the 'new Pléiade' edition of Proust's novel in French: *A la recherche du temps perdu*, ed. Jean-Yves Tadié et al., 4 vols., 'Bibliothèque de la Pléiade' (Paris: Gallimard, 1987–9). This edition provides the text for the single-volume French edition of the novel, *A la recherche du temps perdu*, 'Quarto' (Paris: Gallimard, 1999), which is an economical means of obtaining a hard-copy version of all seven volumes. The Pléiade text is also reproduced in individual volumes in the readily available paperback series 'Collection Folio' (published 1988–90, Gallimard) and 'Collection Blanche' (published 1992, Gallimard).

SELECT BIBLIOGRAPHY

We have indicated the standard editions of key works by Proust in French. For practical reasons, we have included only secondary sources written in English or those readily available in English translation.

Works by Proust

A la recherche du temps perdu, ed. Jean-Yves Tadié et al., Bibliothèque de la Pléiade, 4 vols. (Paris: Gallimard, 1987–9).

Contre Sainte-Beuve précédé de Pastiches et mélanges et suivi de Essais et articles, ed. Pierre Clarac and Yves Sandre, Bibliothèque de la Pléiade (Paris: Gallimard, 1971).

Against Sainte-Beuve and Other Essays, trans. John Sturrock (Harmondsworth: Penguin, 1988).

Essais, ed. Antoine Compagnon, Christophe Pradeau, and Matthieu Vernet, Bibliothèque de la Pléiade (Paris: Gallimard, 2022).

Jean Santeuil précédé de Les Plaisirs et les jours, ed. Pierre Clarac and Yves Sandre (Paris: Gallimard, 1971).

Jean Santeuil, trans. Gerard Hopkins (1955; Harmondsworth: Penguin, 1985).

Pleasures and Days, trans. Andrew Brown (London: Hesperus, 2004).

Correspondence

'Corr-Proust' Digitization Project: http://proust.elan-numerique.fr/

Correspondance de Marcel Proust, ed. Philip Kolb, 21 vols. (Paris: Plon, 1970–93).

Marcel Proust: Selected Letters, 4 vols., ed. Philip Kolb et al., trans. Ralph Manheim (vol. i), Terence Kilmartin (vols. ii and iii), and Joanna Kilmartin (vol. iv) (New York: Doubleday; London: Doubleday/Collins/HarperCollins, 1983–2000).

Marcel Proust: Lettres 1879–1922, ed. Françoise Leriche (Paris: Plon, 2004).

Biography

Carter, William, *Marcel Proust: A Life* (2000; New Haven: Yale University Press, 2013).

Picon, Jérôme, *Marcel Proust: Une vie à s'écrire* (Paris: Flammarion, 2015).

Tadié, Jean-Yves, *Marcel Proust* (1996), trans. Euan Cameron (New York: Viking, 2000).

Watt, Adam, *Marcel Proust*, Critical Lives (London: Reaktion Books, 2013).

White, Edmund, *Proust* (London: Weidenfeld & Nicolson, 1999).

Critical Studies

Bales, Richard (ed.), *The Cambridge Companion to Proust* (Cambridge: Cambridge University Press, 2001).

Beckett, Samuel, *Proust* (1931), in *Proust and Three Dialogues with Georges Duthuit* (London: John Calder, 1987).

Benjamin, Walter, 'The Image of Proust' (1929), in *Illuminations*, trans. Harry Zohn, ed. Hannah Arendt (London: Jonathan Cape, 1970; Pimlico, 1999), 197–210.

Bowie, Malcolm, *Proust Among the Stars* (London: HarperCollins, 1998).

Compagnon, Antoine, *Proust Between Two Centuries*, trans. Richard Goodkin (New York: Columbia University Press, 1992).

Deleuze, Gilles, *Proust and Signs*, trans. Richard Howard (London: The Athlone Press, 2000).

Ellison, David, *A Reader's Guide to Proust's 'In Search of Lost Time'* (Cambridge: Cambridge University Press, 2010).

Elsner, Ann, and Stern, Thomas (eds.), *The Proustian Mind* (London: Routledge, 2022).

Hughes, Edward J., 'The Renewal of Narrative in the Wake of Proust', in John D. Lyons (ed.), *The Cambridge Companion to French Literature* (Cambridge: Cambridge University Press, 2016), 187–203.

Karpeles, Eric, *Paintings in Proust: A Visual Companion to 'In Search of Lost Time'* (London: Thames & Hudson, 2008).

Landy, Joshua, 'Proust, His Narrator, and the Importance of the Distinction', *Poetics Today* 25/1 (2004), 91–135.

Lucey, Michael, 'Becoming Proust in Time', in Christopher Prendergast (ed.), *A History of Modern French Literature: From the Sixteenth Century to the Twentieth Century* (Princeton: Princeton University Press, 2017), 514–33.

Lucey, Michael, *What Proust Heard: Novels and the Ethnography of Talk* (Chicago: Chicago University Press, 2022).

McDonald, Christie, and Proulx, François (eds.), *Proust and the Arts* (Cambridge: Cambridge University Press, 2015).

Prendergast, Christopher, *Mirages and Mad Beliefs: Proust the Skeptic* (Princeton: Princeton University Press, 2013).

Schmid, Marion, 'Marcel Proust (1871–1922): A Modernist Novel of Time', in Michael Bell (ed.), *The Cambridge Companion to European Novelists* (Cambridge: Cambridge University Press, 2012), 327–42.

Watt, Adam, *The Cambridge Introduction to Marcel Proust* (Cambridge: Cambridge University Press, 2011).

Watt, Adam, 'État présent: Marcel Proust', *French Studies* 72/3 (2018), 412–24.

Watt, Adam, 'Marcel Proust's *A la recherche du temps perdu*', in Adam Watt (ed.), *The Cambridge History of the Novel in French* (Cambridge: Cambridge University Press, 2021), 456–72.

Watt, Adam (ed.), *Marcel Proust in Context* (Cambridge: Cambridge University Press, 2013).

Further Reading in Oxford World's Classics

Flaubert, G., *Sentimental Education*, trans. Helen Constantine, ed. Patrick Coleman.

Joyce, J., *Ulysses*, ed. Jeri Johnson.

Kafka, F., *The Metamorphosis and Other Stories*, trans. Joyce Crick, ed. Ritchie Robertson.

Proust, M., *Swann in Love*, trans. Brian Nelson, ed. Adam Watt.

Woolf, V., *Jacob's Room*, ed. Urmila Seshagiri.

A CHRONOLOGY OF MARCEL PROUST

1871 (10 July) Marcel Proust is born to Jeanne Proust née Weil and Dr Adrien Proust in the village of Auteuil, to the west of Paris. He is very weak in infancy.

1872 The Proust family moves to an apartment on the Boulevard Malesherbes in the 8th *arrondissement* of Paris.

1873 (24 May) Robert Proust, Marcel's brother, is born.

1878–86 Family holidays at Illiers (renamed Illiers-Combray in 1971) in the Eure-et-Loir.

1881 Proust's first, and near fatal, asthma attack. Respiratory and other health problems will henceforth be a permanent part of his life.

1882–9 Proust attends the Lycée Condorcet (named Lycée Fontanes until 1883); attendance poor due to ill health, but various friendships formed.

1889 Proust turns 18. *Classe de philosophie*; (Nov.) signs up for one year's voluntary military service.
Inauguration of the Eiffel Tower as the entrance arch to the World's Fair.

1890 (3 Jan.) Death of Proust's maternal grandmother, Adèle Weil. Enrols at the Faculty of Law and the School of Political Science.

1891 Journalism appears in *Le Mensuel*.
Thomas Hardy, *Tess of the D'Urbervilles*.

1892 Proust and friends from Condorcet found a review, *Le Banquet*. Increased socializing.

1893 Publications in the important journal *La Revue blanche*. Completes *Licence en droit*.

1894 (June) President Carnot assassinated in Lyons by an anarchist. (December) Court martial judges Captain Albert Dreyfus guilty.

1895 Completes *License ès lettres*. Unpaid position at the Bibliothèque Mazarine; scarcely attends due to 'ill health'. Stay in Brittany with Reynaldo Hahn. Begins notes towards *Jean Santeuil*.
Trial of Oscar Wilde.

1896 (Mar.) Publication of *Les Plaisirs et les jours*.

1897 Duels with journalist Jean Lorrain over Lorrain's public insinuations of Proust's homosexual relation with Lucien Daudet.
Henry James, *What Maisie Knew*.

1898 (13 Jan.) Zola's 'J'accuse' in *L'Aurore*. Later in the year Proust attends Zola's trial.

1899 *Jean Santeuil* abandoned; Proust starts work on a translation of Ruskin's *The Bible of Amiens*.
Freud, *Die Traudeutung* (*The Interpretation of Dreams*); Conrad, *Heart of Darkness*.

1900 Proust publishes a series of articles on Ruskin. (Apr.) Travels to Venice with his mother and friends; (Oct.) returns to Venice alone.
Deaths of Ruskin and Nietzsche.

1901 Thomas Mann, four years Proust's junior, publishes *Buddenbrooks*.

1902 Travels to Belgium and Holland with Hahn, visits Bruges and Amsterdam amongst other places. Sees Vermeer's *View of Delft* and numerous old Dutch masters.

1903 (Feb.) Marriage of Robert Proust. Society journalism published in *Le Figaro*. (Nov.) sudden death of Proust's father.
Gertrude Stein moves to Paris from the United States.

1904 *La Bible d'Amiens* published; translation of Ruskin's *Sesame and Lilies* begun; society journalism continues.

1905 (June) Proust's important essay on reading, the preface to *Sésame et les lys*, is published. (July) Madame Proust is taken ill in Évian and rushed back to Paris by Robert; (26 Sept.) Death of Madame Proust. (Dec.) Proust checks in to the clinic of Dr Sollier, fulfilling a promise to his mother.
French government passes a law separating Church and State.

1906 (Aug.–Dec.) Sollier's treatment having made little difference to his health, he stays in the Hôtel des Réservoirs in Versailles, unwilling to be alone in the family home. *Sésame et les lys* is published. He resolves to move into what was his great-uncle Georges Weil's Paris residence, 102 Boulevard Haussmann.
Dreyfus reinstated in the Army.

1907 Various articles and stories published. Summer in Cabourg on the Normandy coast. Meets Alfred Agostinelli, a young taxi-driver. Proust will return to Cabourg every year between 1907 and 1914.
Picasso's *Demoiselles d'Avignon* completed in Paris.

1908 Plans a project 'Against Sainte-Beuve', part critical essay, part dialogue. Features of what will become *A la recherche du temps perdu* take shape. Succession of brilliant pastiches, around the Lemoine Affair, appear in *Le Figaro*.

1909 *Contre Sainte-Beuve* amounts to around 400 pages; publishers show no interest.

Marinetti's first *Manifesto of Futurism* in Paris; Gustav Mahler's Symphony No. 9.

1910–11 Develops the core sequences of his novel that will become *Du côté de chez Swann*, *Le Temps retrouvé*, part of *Le Côté de Guermantes* and, latterly, parts of *A l'ombre des jeunes filles en fleurs*.

1912–13 Successive rejections from publishers.

1913 (Spring) Agostinelli moves into Proust's apartment as secretary. *Du côté de chez Swann* is accepted for publication at the author's expense by Grasset and (14 Nov.) is published.

Stravinsky's *Rite of Spring*; Lawrence's *Sons and Lovers*; Duchamp's *Bicycle Wheel*.

1914 (May) Agostinelli dies, drowned in the Mediterranean as a result of a flying accident. Céleste Albaret officially enters Proust's service.

(Aug.) French forces mobilized; printing presses cease activity during the war. James Joyce, *Dubliners*.

1915 Proust develops *Sodome et Gomorrhe* and the 'Albertine cycle', *La Prisonnière* and *Albertine disparue*.

1916 Negotiations with the *Nouvelle revue française* (*NRF*) who wish to take over publication of *A la recherche* from Grasset. (May) Proust reports suffering a seventy-hour period of insomnia.

(July) First Dada manifesto proclaimed in Zurich.

1917 (18 May) In Paris, Proust attends the premiere of *Parade*, performed by the Ballets Russes, with a scenario by Cocteau, score by Satie, set and costumes by Picasso, and programme notes by Apollinaire. (Feb. and Oct.) Revolution in Russia.

1918 Proust's health, always fragile, becomes a near-constant preoccupation as he devotes more and more time to correcting his novel.

1919 (June) NRF reissues *Du côté de chez Swann*, publishes *Pastiches et mélanges* and *A l'ombre des jeunes filles en fleurs*. The relative who owned 102 Boulevard Haussmann decides to sell and Proust has to move twice; eventually settling (Oct.) at 44 Rue Hamelin. (Dec.) *A l'ombre* awarded the Prix Goncourt.

1920 André Breton employed by Gallimard as proofreader for *Le Côté de Guermantes*. (Oct.) *Le Côté de Guermantes I* published.

(May) Breton and Soupault's *Les Champs magnétiques*, the first work of surrealist (or proto-surrealist) 'automatic writing'.

THE SWANN WAY

*For Monsieur Gaston Calmette**
As a token of profound
and affectionate gratitude.

PART ONE
COMBRAY

I

FOR a long time, I went to bed early. Sometimes, my candle barely out, my eyes would close so quickly that I didn't even have time to think: 'I'm falling asleep.' And half an hour later the thought that it was time to try to sleep would wake me; I'd try to put aside the book I imagined I still had in my hands, and blow out the light; while I was asleep, I'd gone on thinking about what I'd just been reading, but these thoughts had taken a rather curious turn—it seemed to me that I myself was the subject of the book, whether it was a church, a quartet, or the rivalry between François I and Charles V.* This impression would stay with me for a few seconds after I woke; it didn't offend my reason, but it lay like scales on my eyes and prevented me from realizing that the candle was no longer burning. Then it would begin to seem unintelligible, as the thoughts of a former existence must do after reincarnation; the subject of the book would detach itself from me, leaving me free to see myself in it or not; and all at once I would regain my sight and realize in amazement that I was surrounded by darkness, which my eyes found pleasant and restful, but my mind perhaps even more so, finding it incomprehensible, without cause, something truly dark. I'd wonder what time it might be; I could hear the whistling of trains, sometimes close by, sometimes far away, plotting distances like bird calls in a forest, evoking for me the stretch of deserted countryside through which a traveller is hurrying towards a nearby station; and the path he's taking will be engraved on his memory by the excitement of new places, unaccustomed activities, recent conversations beneath an unfamiliar lamp, words of farewell that continue to echo in his ears in the silence of the night, and the happy prospect of returning home.

I'd lay my cheeks gently on the soft cheeks of the pillow, as plump and cool as the cheeks of childhood. I'd strike a match to look at my watch. Nearly midnight. The hour when a sick man, obliged to go on a journey and to sleep in a strange hotel, might wake up feeling unwell and is pleased to see a strip of light under his door. What a relief, it's already morning! In a moment the servants will be up, he'll be able to ring for someone to come and care for him. This expectation gives him the strength to bear his discomfort. In fact he thinks he can hear footsteps; they come closer, then go away again. And the strip of light under the door has disappeared. It's midnight; someone has just turned off the gas; the last servant has gone to bed, and he has no choice but to lie there all night and suffer.

I'd go back to sleep, and sometimes for the rest of the night I'd wake only for a few moments, just long enough to hear the regular creaking of the woodwork, to open my eyes and stare at the kaleidoscopic darkness, and savour in a momentary glimmer of consciousness the deep slumber of the furniture and the room, that whole of which I was but a small part and to whose state of insensibility I would soon return. Or else while sleeping I'd drifted back to one of the earliest stages of my life, for ever gone, and was gripped anew by one of my childish terrors, such as the fear that my great-uncle would pull at my curls, a terror which was not dispelled until the day—the dawn for me of a new era—when they were cut off. I'd forgotten that event while I slept, but as soon as I succeeded in making myself wake up to escape my great-uncle's clutches, I remembered it again, and as a precautionary measure I'd wrap the pillow right round my head before returning to the world of dreams.

At other times during my sleep, just as Eve was created from one of Adam's ribs,* a woman would come into being as a result of an unusual position of my thigh. Formed from the pleasure I was on the point of enjoying, it was she, I imagined, who was offering it to me. My body, feeling its own warmth in her body, would strive to become one with it, and I'd wake up. No other member of humanity was remotely interesting to me compared with the woman whose company I'd left scarcely a few moments before; my cheek was still warm from her kiss, my body ached from the weight of hers. If, as sometimes happened, she had the features of a woman I'd known in real life, I would resolve to devote myself entirely to the goal of finding her again, like people who set out on a journey to see with their own eyes a city they have always longed to visit, and imagine they can enjoy in reality the charm of a dream. Little by little my memory of her would fade, and the girl in my dream would be forgotten.

When a man is asleep, he has in a circle round him the sequence of the hours, the order of the years, and the worlds he has known. He checks with them instinctively as he wakes and in a second reads in them the spot he occupies on the earth, the time that has elapsed up to his waking; but their order can become jumbled and broken. If,

towards morning, after a sleepless night, he drops off while he's reading, in a position too different from the one in which he usually sleeps,
it's enough for his raised arm to halt the sun and make it retreat, and,
for a few moments after he wakes, he will no longer know what time it
is, he'll think he has only just gone to bed. If he dozes off in a position
even more displaced and divergent, for instance sitting in an armchair after dinner, then the chaos of his worlds will be complete, the
magic armchair will transport him at top speed through time and
space,* and on opening his eyes he'll imagine that he went to bed
several months earlier, in another country. But for me it was enough
if, in my own bed, I slept soundly and my mind relaxed entirely; then
I'd lose all sense of the place where I'd fallen asleep, and when I woke
in the middle of the night, since I didn't know where I was, I didn't
even know for a moment who I was; all I had, in its primal simplicity,
was the dim sense of existence as it may quiver in the consciousness
of an animal; I was more bereft than a caveman; but then the
memory—not yet of the place where I was, but of several other places
where I'd lived and where I might now be—would come to me like
help from on high to pull me out of the void from which I couldn't
have got out on my own; I'd pass over centuries of civilization in
a single second, and the image confusedly glimpsed of oil lamps, then
of wing-collar shirts, would gradually recompose the original features
of my self.

Perhaps the immobility of the things around us is imposed on
them by our certainty that they are themselves and not anything else,
by the immobility of our mental conceptions of them. It was certainly
the case that when I awoke like this, and my mind struggled vainly to
establish where I was, everything revolved around me in the darkness:
things, places, years. My body, too heavy with sleep to move, would
try to determine, according to the form of its fatigue and the position
of its limbs, where the wall and furniture were, and thus to reconstruct and put a name to the house in which it lay. Its memory, the
memory in its ribs, its knees, its shoulder blades, offered it in succession several of the bedrooms in which it had slept, while around it the
unseen walls, changing place according to the shape of each imagined
bedroom, whirled giddily in the dark. And even before my mind, trying
to sort out these different shapes and times in my life, had identified
the house by piecing together the relevant circumstances, it—my
body—would remember for each dwelling the particular type of bed,

the position of the doors, the angle at which the light came in through the windows, the presence of a passage, and also my thoughts as I fell asleep and that I rediscovered when I awoke. My numb side, for example, trying to get its bearings, would imagine it lay facing the wall in a big canopy bed, and I would immediately think: 'Goodness, I must have dropped off even though Maman didn't come up to say goodnight.' I was in the country at my grandfather's, who'd died years before; and my body, the side on which I was lying, faithful guardian of a past which my mind should never have forgotten, summoned up the flame of the night light in its urn-shaped bowl of Bohemian glass that hung by chains from the ceiling, and the mantelpiece of Siena marble,* in my bedroom in Combray, at my grandparents' house, in those far-off days which at this moment I imagined to be in the present without picturing them exactly and which I'd see more clearly in a little while when I was fully awake.

Then the memory of a fresh position would rise up in my mind, and the wall would slide away in another direction: I was in my room at Madame de Saint-Loup's house in the country; good Lord, it must be at least ten o'clock, they'll have finished dinner! I must have overslept when I took the nap I take every evening after coming in from a walk with Madame de Saint-Loup and before dressing for dinner. For many years have passed since those Combray days, when, even after our longest walks, I'd still be able to see the reflections of the red sunset in the panes of my bedroom window. Nowadays it's a very different kind of life we lead at Tansonville, at Madame de Saint-Loup's, and a different kind of pleasure I take in going out only in the evenings, walking by moonlight along the lanes where I used to play in the sunshine; and as for the room in which I must have fallen asleep instead of dressing for dinner, I can see it in the distance as we come back from our walk, its lamp shining through the window like a lone beacon in the night.

These shifting and confused flashes of memory never lasted for more than a few seconds; and often, in these fleeting moments of uncertainty as to where I was, I was unable to distinguish the various suppositions of which that uncertainty was composed any better than, when we see a horse running, we can separate the successive positions of its body as shown by a kinetoscope.* But, each time, I'd seen one or other of the bedrooms in which I'd slept during my life, and in the end I'd remember every one of them in the course of my long reveries on waking: winter bedrooms in which, as soon as you lie down, you bury your head in a nest woven out of the most disparate things— a corner of the pillow, the edge of the blankets, the fringe of a shawl, the side of the bed, and an issue of the *Débats roses**—which in the end, with infinite birdlike patience, you mould together into a whole; where, in freezing weather, you enjoy the feeling of being shut off from the outside world (like the tern which makes its nest deep in a tunnel in the warmth of the earth) and where, as the fire is kept going all night, you sleep in a great cloak of warm, smoky air, lit up intermittently by flaring embers, a sort of alcove without walls, a cave of warmth dug out of the room itself, a heated zone whose boundaries are constantly shifting and altering in temperature as gusts of cool air blow on your face from the corners of the room, away from the fire-place, or from near the window;—summer bedrooms, where you love being part of the balmy night, where the moonlight pushes its way through the half-open shutters and throws its enchanted ladder across the floor to the foot of the bed, where you sleep as if in the open air, like a titmouse rocked by the breeze at the end of a moon-beam;—sometimes the Louis XVI bedroom,* so bright and cheerful that even on my first night there I hadn't been too unhappy, the room where the slender columns that effortlessly supported the ceiling drew aside with such grace to reveal the place reserved for the bed; sometimes, on the other hand, the little bedroom with the very high ceiling, hollowed out in the form of a pyramid, two storeys high and partly panelled in mahogany, where, the moment I set foot in it, I felt as if drugged by the unfamiliar smell of vetiver* and became convinced of the hostility of the violet curtains and the indifference of an insolent clock, which kept chattering loudly to itself as though I were not there; where a strange and pitiless rectangular cheval glass,* cutting off obliquely one corner of the room, removed from my usual wide field of vision a little area I hadn't expected to be taken from me; where my mind, struggling for hours to contort itself, to stretch upwards so as to take on the exact shape of the room and man-age to fill its enormous funnel right up to the top, had endured many a long night as I lay there, my eyes wide open, my ears anxiously cocked, my nostrils flaring, my heart beating, until habit changed the colour of the curtains, silenced the clock, taught pity to the cruel cheval glass, disguised or even drove away the smell of vetiver, and appreciably reduced the apparent height of the ceiling. Habit!—that slow but skilful worker who begins by letting our minds suffer for weeks in temporary quarters, but whom we are nonetheless happy to discover at last, for without the help of habit, left to our own devices, we would be powerless to make any abode habitable.

By this time I'd be wide awake, my body had veered round one last time, and the good angel of certainty had brought everything around me to a standstill, had set me down under my bedclothes, in my bedroom, and put back in their approximate positions in the dark my chest of drawers, my desk, my fireplace, the window overlooking the street, and both doors. But even though I knew I wasn't in any of the houses of which the uncertainty of my first waking moment had instantly, if not presented me with a distinct picture, at least made me believe in their possible presence, my memory had been set in motion; usually I didn't try to go back to sleep at once, but would spend most of the night recalling our life in the old days, in Combray in my great-aunt's house, in Balbec, Paris, Doncières, Venice,* and elsewhere, remembering the places, the people I'd known there, what I'd seen of them, what I'd been told about them.

In Combray, every day towards the end of the afternoon, long before I had to go up to bed and lie there unable to sleep, separated from my mother and grandmother, my bedroom became the focus of all my melancholy thoughts. In an attempt to keep me amused on evenings when I looked especially miserable, someone had had the bright idea of giving me a magic lantern, which would be set on top of my lamp while we waited for dinner time to arrive; and, after the manner of the first architects and master glaziers of the Gothic age,* it replaced my opaque walls with impalpable iridescences, multi-coloured supernatural apparitions, where legends were depicted as on a flickering and transitory stained-glass window. But this only increased my unhappiness, because the mere change in lighting destroyed the familiarity of my bedroom, thanks to which, except for the torment of going to bed, it had become tolerable. Now I no longer recognized it, and felt uneasy in it, as if I were in a room in some hotel or 'chalet' in a place where I had just arrived by train and was visiting for the first time.

Golo,* riding at a jerky trot, and thinking of nothing but his monstrous plan, would emerge from the little triangular forest that covered with a velvety dark green the slope of a hill, and go lurching across towards the castle of poor Geneviève de Brabant.* One side of this castle was curved, for it was in fact the edge of one of the oval glass slides arranged in the frame that had to be fitted into the grooves of the lantern. It was only the wing of a castle, and in front of it stretched a moor where Geneviève stood dreaming, wearing a blue belt. The castle and the moor were yellow, but I didn't have to wait to see them to know their colour, for before the slides came round, the old-gold sonority of the name Brabant had given me an obvious clue. Golo would pause for a moment to listen sadly to the patter read out by my great-aunt, which he seemed to understand perfectly, for he would modify his bearing, with a docility not devoid of a certain majesty, so as to match the words of the text; then he'd ride on at the same jerky trot. And nothing could stop his slow progress. If the lamp was moved I could still see his horse making its way across the curtains, swelling out with their folds and slipping down the ravines between them. Golo's own body, being of the same supernatural essence as his steed, accommodated itself to every material obstacle, every object that might impede his progress, by taking it as his skeleton and absorbing it into himself—even the doorknob, which he immediately adapted to and floated invincibly over with his red cloak or his pale face, as noble and melancholy as ever, and betraying not the least concern at this transvertebration.

These brilliant projections were not without their attraction, of course, seeming as they did to come straight out of the Merovingian past* and to spread around me reflections of ancient history. But I can't express the unease I felt at this intrusion of mystery and beauty into a room I'd succeeded in filling with my own personality to the point of seeing it as an extension of myself. The anaesthetizing effect of habit having been destroyed, I'd begin to think, and to feel, and this always brings unhappiness. The doorknob of my room, which for me was different from all the other doorknobs in the world in that it seemed to open of its own accord, without my having to turn it, so unconscious had my handling of it become, was now serving as an astral body for Golo. And as soon as the dinner bell rang I would run down to the dining room, where the big hanging lamp, which knew nothing of Golo and Bluebeard* but was well acquainted with my family and beef casserole, shed the same light as on every other evening; and I would fall into the arms of my mother, whom the misfortunes of Geneviève de Brabant had made all the dearer to me, while Golo's villainy had forced me to examine my conscience more carefully.

Soon after dinner, alas, I had to leave Maman, who stayed talking with the others, in the garden if the weather was fine, in the little drawing room to which everyone retired if the weather was bad. Everyone, that is, except my grandmother, who felt it was 'a pity to stay shut up indoors in the country' and on the wettest days would have endless little arguments with my father, because on those days he'd send me to my room with a book rather than let me stay outside. 'That's not the way to make him strong and healthy,' she'd say sadly, 'especially not that boy—he needs building up and to get a bit of character!' My father would just shrug and study the barometer, for he took an interest in meteorology, while my mother, keeping very quiet so as not to disturb him, would watch him with loving respect, but not too intently, so as not to risk penetrating the mysteries of his superior mind. But as for my grandmother, she went out in all weathers, even when it was pouring and Françoise had to dash out to rescue the precious wicker chairs; there she would be, all by herself in the deserted rain-lashed garden, pushing back her dishevelled grey hair so that her forehead could have the full health-giving benefit of the wind and water. She'd say: 'Some fresh air at last!' and would trot up and down the sodden paths—too symmetrically arranged for her liking by the new gardener who lacked any feeling for nature and whom my father had been asking since morning if the weather was likely to clear up. Her eager, jerky little step was regulated by the various emotions inspired in her by the excitement of the storm, the power of healthy exercise, the misguidedness of my upbringing, and the symmetry of the gardens, rather than by the desire (quite unknown to her) to protect her plum-coloured skirt from the mud-stains that would soon cover it to a height that was the constant despair of her maid.

When these garden walks of my grandmother's took place after dinner, only one thing could make her come back in. This was when she heard my great-aunt calling to her at one of the times when her circular itinerary periodically brought her back, like an insect, into the light from the little drawing room where the liqueurs were set out on the card table: 'Bathilde! Come and stop your husband from drinking cognac!' Simply to tease my grandmother (who had brought into the family a mentality so different that everyone made endless fun of her), my great-aunt would induce my grandfather to drink a few drops of alcohol, though he was under doctor's orders not to touch it. My poor grandmother would come in and implore her husband not to drink the cognac; he would get angry and gulp it down despite her, and she would go out again saddened and discouraged, but smiling, for she was so humble of spirit and so sweet that her love for others and her lack of concern for herself and her own torments came together in a smile which, unlike those seen on the faces of so many people, was ironic only towards herself, while for the rest of us kisses seemed to issue from her eyes, for she could never look upon those who were dear to her without wanting to caress them with her gaze. The torment my great-aunt inflicted on her, the sight of my grandmother's vain entreaties, and of her feeble attempts, doomed in advance, to take the glass away from my grandfather—these were the sorts of things you get so used to in later life that you laugh at them, and take the persecutor's side unhesitatingly and cheerfully enough to persuade yourself that no persecution is involved at all; at the time, however, they filled me with such horror that I felt like hitting my great-aunt. But as soon as I heard: 'Bathilde! Come and stop your husband from drinking cognac!', showing myself to be already a man by my cowardice, I did what we all do when we're grown up and witness suffering and injustice: I chose not to see them; I'd go upstairs to the very top floor next to the schoolroom, right under the roof, and sob by myself in a little room that smelled of orris root and was filled also by the fragrance of a wild blackcurrant bush that had climbed up between the stones of the outside wall and thrust a flowering branch through the half-open window. This room, from which, in the daytime, you could see as far as Roussainville-le-Pin, was intended for more specialized and vulgar use, and for a long time served as a place of refuge for me, no doubt because it was the only room I was allowed to lock, whenever I engaged in any of the four occupations for which I required absolutely privacy: reading, daydreaming, tears, and sensual pleasure. Alas, I didn't know that, far more than her husband's little deviation from his regimen, it was my weak will, my delicate health, and the uncertainty they cast on my future, that preyed on my grandmother's mind in the course of her incessant perambulations, afternoon and evening, when we'd see her lovely face passing hither and thither, tilted towards the sky, showing her brown furrowed cheeks that advancing age had turned almost mauve, like ploughed fields in autumn, and which were concealed, if she was going out, by a half-raised veil, while upon them either the cold or some sad thought invariably left traces of an involuntary tear.

My sole consolation, when I went upstairs for the night, was that Maman would come and kiss me goodnight once I was in bed. But this goodnight was so brief, she went down again so soon, that the moment when I heard her coming up, and then rustling along the corridor with its double doors in her garden dress of blue muslin, hung with little tassels of plaited straw, was for me a painful moment. For it heralded the moment that would follow it, when she'd left me and gone back downstsirs. So I reached the stage of hoping that this goodnight I loved so much would take place as late as possible, so as to prolong the period of respite during which Maman had not yet come. Sometimes, when after kissing me she opened the door to go, I wanted to call her back and say 'Give me another kiss', but I knew that would immediately make her put on her cross face, because the concession she made to my sadness and anxiety by coming up to give me this soothing kiss always annoyed my father, who found such rituals absurd, and she would have liked to make me lose the need for it, the habit of it, rather than let me acquire the new habit of asking for an extra kiss just as she was opening the door to leave. And to see her displeasure destroyed all the calm she'd brought me a moment before, when she'd bent her loving face over my bed and held it out like the host at Communion, so that my lips could draw from it her real presence* and the power to go to sleep. But those evenings when Maman stayed such a short time in my room were bliss compared to the ones when people came to dinner and, for that reason, she didn't come up to say goodnight. These people were usually limited to Monsieur Swann, who, apart from the odd person who happened to be passing through, was almost the only person who came to our house in Combray, sometimes for a neighbourly dinner (though this became less frequent after his unfortunate marriage, as my parents had no desire to receive his wife), sometimes after dinner, unexpectedly. On those evenings when, as we sat round the iron table under the big chestnut tree at the front of the house, we heard, at the far end of the garden, not the shrill, aggressive little bell that spattered and deafened with its ferruginous, icy, interminable sound any person in the household who set it off by coming in 'without ringing', but the double tinkle, timid, oval, golden, of the visitors' bell, everyone would murmur at once: 'A visitor! Who can that be?' but we knew perfectly well it could only be Monsieur Swann; my great-aunt, trying to set an example by speaking quite loudly, in a tone she strained to make natural, would tell us not to whisper like that; that nothing is more off-putting for a visitor on arriving at your house, because it makes them think you're saying things you don't want them to hear; and my grandmother, always glad of an excuse to walk once more round the garden, would be sent out to reconnoitre, and would surreptitiously take advantage of it to pull up, as she passed, the stakes of a rose bush or two, so as to make the roses look a little more natural, as a mother might run her fingers through her son's hair to ruffle it up after the barber has smoothed it down too much.

We'd all sit there in suspense, waiting for my grandmother's report from enemy lines, as if there was a whole range of possible assailants to choose from, until, after a short while, my grandfather would say: 'I recognize Swann's voice.' And indeed he could be recognized only by his voice; it was difficult to make out his face with its Roman nose and green eyes, and his high forehead framed by fair, almost auburn hair, cut in the Bressant style,* because in the garden we used as little light as possible, so as not to attract mosquitoes. I would slip away unobtrusively to say that the cordials should be brought out, as my grandmother felt it was important, altogether nicer, that they should not seem anything out of the ordinary, served only when we had visitors. Though a much younger man, Monsieur Swann was very attached to my grandfather, who had been one of the closest friends of his father, an excellent but rather strange person the ardour of whose feelings and the course of whose thoughts could be disturbed or diverted by the most trivial thing. Several times a year, as we sat at table, I'd hear my grandfather telling the same unvarying stories about the behaviour of old Monsieur Swann on the death of his wife, by whose bedside he'd sat day and night. My grandfather, who hadn't seen him for a long time, had rushed down to be with him at the Swanns' property near Combray and, so that he wouldn't be present when the body was laid in the coffin, managed to entice him for a few moments, weeping copious tears, out of the death chamber. They took a few steps in the park, where there was a little sun. Suddenly Monsieur Swann seized my grandfather by the arm and exclaimed: 'I say, old friend, how wonderful it is to be walking here together in such nice weather! Don't you think it's pretty, with all these trees, my hawthorns, and my new pond, on which you've never congratulated me? Why are you looking so down in the dumps! Just feel this breeze! You can say what you like, Amédée old man, it's good to be alive!' All of a sudden the memory of his dead wife came back to him and, no doubt thinking it would be too complicated to try to understand why, at such a time, he could have felt an upsurge of joy, he confined himself to a gesture he often made whenever a difficult question came into his mind: he passed his hand across his forehead, rubbed his eyes, and wiped the lenses of his lorgnon. Yet he never got over the loss of his wife, but during the two years by which he survived her he'd say to my grandfather: 'It's funny, I think of my poor wife very often, but I can't think of her for long at a time.' 'Often, but just a little at a time, like poor old Swann,' became one of my grandfather's catchphrases, which he would apply to all manner of things. I would have formed the view that this father of Swann's was a monster, if my grandfather, whom I considered a much better judge of people than myself, and whose pronouncements were Holy Scripture to me and often helped me later on to forgive offences I might have been inclined to condemn, hadn't cried: 'What do you mean? He had a heart of gold!'

For many years my great-aunt and my grandparents had no inkling that this same Monsieur Swann the younger, who often came to see them in Combray (especially before his marriage), had entirely ceased to move in the kind of society frequented by his parents and that, under the sort of incognito which the name Swann gave him among us, they were harbouring—with all the innocence of law-abiding inn-keepers giving unwitting shelter to a notorious highwayman—one of the leading members of the Jockey Club,* a special friend of the Comte de Paris* and the Prince of Wales,* and one of the men most sought after by the high society of the Faubourg Saint-Germain.*

Our ignorance of the brilliant social life Swann led was obviously due in part to his natural reserve and discretion, but also to the fact that bourgeois people in those days had a somewhat Hindu conception of society, and saw it as being made up of a number of closed castes, in which everyone, from birth, found himself placed in the station occupied by his parents and from which nothing, except a particularly illustrious career or an unusually brilliant marriage, could remove you and elevate you to a superior caste. Monsieur Swann the elder had been a stockbroker, and so 'young Swann' was destined his entire life to belong to a caste in which fortunes were defined, as in a tax bracket, by such and such limits of income. It was known with whom his father had associated, and therefore with whom he would associate, the people he would be 'in a position' to know. If he knew others, they could only be acquaintances from his bachelor days to whom old friends of his family, such as my relatives, could easily turn a blind eye, given that Swann himself, after the death of his parents, still came most faithfully to see us; but we'd have been ready to wager that any of his acquaintances who were unknown to us were of the sort he'd have preferred to ignore if he'd met them in our company. If it had been absolutely necessary to assign a social coefficient peculiar to him, as distinct from all the other sons of stockbrokers in the same position as his father, this coefficient would have been a little lower than theirs because, being very simple in his ways and having always had a 'craze' for antiques and paintings, he now lived in an old house that was full of his collections and that my grandmother longed to visit, but which was situated on the Quai d'Orléans,* a neighbourhood where my great-aunt would have been ashamed to live. 'But are you really a connoisseur?' she'd say to him; 'I'm only asking for your sake, because I'm sure you let those dealers palm off on you all sorts of dreadful daubs.' She was convinced he lacked all competence and, even in terms of intelligence, had no high opinion of a man who in conversation avoided serious subjects and simply recited prosaic factual details, not only when he gave us cooking recipes down to the last ingredient but even when my grandfather's sisters talked to him about art. When they urged him to give his opinion about a painting or to explain why he admired it, he would remain so reticent that he seemed almost rude, and he would then try to make up for it by providing (if he could) some fact or other about the gallery in which the painting was hung or the date when it was painted. But usually he'd content himself with trying to amuse us with some new story involving people we knew, such as the Combray pharmacist, our cook, or our coachman. These stories certainly made my great-aunt laugh, but she was never sure whether this was because Swann always played in them the role of a fool or because he was such a witty raconteur: 'You really are a card, Monsieur Swann!' Being the only member of our family who was at all common, she never failed to remark to strangers, when Swann was mentioned, that he could easily have lived in the Boulevard Haussmann or the Avenue de l'Opéra,* and was the son of old Monsieur Swann who must have left four or five million francs, but that he was eccentric enough not to do so. An eccentricity which, moreover, she thought bound to amuse other people so much that, in Paris, when Monsieur Swann called on New Year's Day to give her her bag of marrons glacés,* she always made a point of saying, as she peeped over her lorgnon at the other visitors: 'Ah, it's Monsieur Swann! Do you still live next door to the wine depot,* to be sure not to miss your train when you go to Lyons?'

But if anyone had told my great-aunt that this Swann, who, as the son of old Monsieur Swann, was fully 'qualified' to be received by all the 'best' upper-bourgeois families, by the most respected notaries and solicitors in Paris (a privilege he seemed inclined to let lapse), had a different, almost secret life; that when he left our house in Paris saying he must go home to bed, he would no sooner have turned the corner than he would stop, retrace his steps, and go straight to some salon that no stockbroker or associate of his had ever set foot in, this would have seemed to my great-aunt as extraordinary as, to a better-educated lady, would the thought of being on close terms with Aristaeus and learning that, after having had a chat with her, he'd plunge into the realm of Thetis, into an empire hidden from the eyes of mortals and in which Virgil shows him being welcomed with open arms;* or—to confine oneself to an image that was more likely to occur to her, for she had seen it painted on the dessert plates in Combray—as the thought of having had to dinner Ali Baba, who, as soon as he's alone, will go off to his glittering cave full of secret treasure.*

Once in Paris he dropped in on us after dinner, apologizing for being in evening clothes. After he'd left, Françoise said his coachman had told her he'd been dining 'with a princess'. 'Yes, a princess of the demi-monde!'* my aunt had responded serenely, shrugging her shoulders and not even bothering to look up from her knitting.

And so my great-aunt treated him in quite an offhand manner. Since she was of the view that he should be flattered by our invitations, she found it quite natural that he never came to see us in summer without bringing a basket of peaches or raspberries from his garden, and that from each of his trips to Italy he'd bring back for me photographs of old masters.

They didn't think twice about sending for him when they needed a recipe for *gribiche* sauce* or pineapple salad for a big dinner party to which he hadn't been invited, being deemed insufficiently distinguished to be served up to people who might be coming to the house for the first time. If the conversation turned to the princes of the House of France, 'people you and I will never know, will we, and can manage without, can't we?' my great-aunt would say to Swann, who might well have had a letter from Twickenham* in his pocket; and on evenings when my grandfather's sister sang for us, my great-aunt made Swann move the piano and turn the pages of the music, treating him, so sought-after elsewhere, with the unthinking roughness of a child playing with a valuable collector's piece as if it were a cheap toy. Clearly, the Swann who was a familiar presence in all the clubs at that period was very different from the one created by my great-aunt when, in the evening, in the little garden in Combray, after the two timid tinkles of the bell, she would inject and invigorate with everything she knew about the Swann family the dim, indeterminate figure who emerged, followed by my grandmother, from a background of shadows, and whom we recognized only by his voice. But then, even in the most insignificant details of our lives, none of us constitutes a material whole, identical for everyone, which people have only to go and look up like a list of specifications or the text of a will; our social personality is a creation of the minds of others. Even the simple act we describe as 'seeing someone we know' is in part an intellectual activity. We fill the physical appearance of the individual we see with all the notions we have about him, and in the total picture of him that we compose in our minds those notions certainly play the greatest role. In the end they fill out his cheeks so perfectly, follow so exactly the line of his nose, and are so adept at giving his voice its special intonation that each time we see his face and hear his voice, it's as though he's wearing a transparent disguise and what we really see and hear are the notions we've already formed. And so, no doubt, in the Swann they had constructed for themselves, my family had failed, in their ignorance, to include a host of details from his life in the fashionable world, details that made other people, when they met him, see elegance written all over his face, stopping at his aquiline nose as at a natural frontier; but they had also been able to inject into the empty spaces of this face, divested of all glamour, and into the depths of his undervalued eyes, their vague, half-forgotten memories of the pleasant hours they'd idled away with him after our weekly dinners, round the card table or in the garden, during our neighbourly country life. Our friend's corporeal envelope had been so well stuffed with these memories, as well as with various recollections of his parents, that my family's version of Swann had become a complete and living being; nowadays, indeed, I have the impression that I'm moving between two completely different people when, casting my mind back, I recall first the Swann I came to know intimately in later life and then the earlier Swann—that early Swann in whom I rediscover the charming mistakes of my youth, and who in fact is less like the later Swann than he's like the other people I knew at the time, as though one's life were a picture gallery in which all the portraits of a particular period have a family likeness, the same distinctive tonality—that early Swann abounding in leisure, fragrant with the scent of the big chestnut tree, the baskets of raspberries, and a sprig of tarragon.

And yet one day, when my grandmother had gone to ask a favour of a lady she'd known at the Sacré-Cœur* (and with whom, because of our family's notions of caste, she'd almost lost touch, despite their liking for each other), this lady, the Marquise de Villeparisis of the famous Bouillon family,* had said to her: 'I believe you know Monsieur Swann very well? He's a great friend of my nephews, the des Laumes.'* My grandmother had returned from her visit full of enthusiasm about the house, which overlooked some gardens and in which Madame de Villeparisis had encouraged her to rent an apartment, and also about a tailor and his daughter, who had a little shop in the courtyard and whom my grandmother had asked to mend her skirt, which she'd torn coming down the stairs. She couldn't speak too highly of these people: the girl, she said, was an absolute gem and the tailor was one of the finest gentlemen she'd ever met. Because for her, distinction had nothing whatever to do with social class. She was ecstatic about something the tailor had said to her, declaring to Maman: 'Sévigné couldn't have put it better!';* whereas, in contrast, her comment on a nephew of Madame de Villeparisis to whom she'd been introduced was: 'Oh, my dear, you can't imagine! He's so common!'

As for the remark about Swann, its effect had been, not to raise him in my great-aunt's estimation, but to lower Madame de Villeparisis. It was as though the respect which, on my grandmother's authority, we accorded Madame de Villeparisis created an obligation on her part to do nothing that would render her less worthy of our regard, and that she'd failed in this duty by becoming aware of Swann's existence and allowing members of her family to associate with him. 'What! She knows Swann? A person you told us was related to Marshal MacMahon!'* This low opinion of Swann's social connections was

confirmed later by his marriage to a woman of the worst type, virtually a prostitute—not that he ever tried to introduce her to my family,
for he continued to come to our house alone, though less and less; but
they felt, in their ignorance of his private life, that she enabled them
to judge the social circle in which he moved—assuming it was there
that he'd found her.

But on one occasion my grandfather read in a newspaper that
Monsieur Swann was one of the most regular guests at the Sunday
lunches given by the Duc de X . . ., whose father and uncle had been
the most prominent statesmen during the reign of Louis-Philippe.*
My grandfather, it should be noted, was interested in any snippet of
information that might help him to picture the private lives of men
like Molé, the Duc Pasquier, and the Duc de Broglie,* and he was
delighted to learn that Swann associated with people who'd known
them. My great-aunt, on the other hand, interpreted this piece of
news in a way that was unfavourable to Swann: anyone who chose to
consort with people outside the caste into which he'd been born, outside his 'station' in life, went sharply down in her estimation. It
seemed to her that to become déclassé was to abdicate any claim to the
benefits of the many excellent connections with well-placed people
which prudent parents cultivate and store up for their children (and
she had even stopped seeing the son of a lawyer we knew because he'd
married a woman of noble birth and therefore demoted himself from
the respectable position of a lawyer's son to that of one of those
adventurers, former footmen or stable-boys mostly, on whom, they
say, queens have sometimes bestowed their favours). She was opposed,
therefore, to my grandfather's plan to question Swann, when next he
came to dinner, about these friends of his. At the same time my grandmother's two sisters, old maids who shared her nobility of character
but lacked her intelligence, declared they couldn't understand what
pleasure their brother-in-law could find in talking about such trifling
matters. These ladies had such elevated aspirations that they were
incapable of taking any interest in what is known as tittle-tattle, even
if it had some historical interest, or, more generally, in anything that
was not directly associated with some aesthetic object or uplifting
subject. They were so utterly uninterested in anything remotely connected with worldly matters that their sense of hearing—realizing its
temporary uselessness as soon as the tone of the conversation at the
dinner table became frivolous or concerned merely with the mundane,

despite their best efforts to guide it back to the subjects dear to them—would switch off its receiving apparatus to the point of incipient atrophy. If, at such times, my grandfather wanted to attract their attention, he had to resort to the kind of physical stimuli doctors adopt in dealing with patients suffering from distraction: tapping a glass several times with a knife while calling their names and staring at them—violent methods often used by psychiatrists even in their everyday dealings with people who are quite normal, either from professional habit or because they think everybody is slightly mad.

They became interested, however, when, the day before Swann was to come to dinner, and had sent over a case of Asti wine as a personal gift, my great-aunt, as she was reading that morning's *Figaro*, saw, next to the name of a painting in a Corot* exhibition, the words: 'From the collection of Monsieur Charles Swann.' 'Have you seen this?' she exclaimed. 'Swann is being noticed in *Le Figaro* now.'*

'But I've always told you he has excellent taste,' said my grandmother.

'You would, of course! You'd say anything just to be different from us,' retorted my great-aunt. Knowing that my grandmother never agreed with her, and not being quite sure it was her own opinion that we shared, she wanted to extort from us a wholesale condemnation of my grandmother's opinions, against which she was trying to force us into solidarity with her own. But we remained silent. When my grandmother's sisters expressed their intention of mentioning to Swann the reference to him in *Le Figaro*, my great-aunt advised them against it. Whenever she saw others enjoying some advantage, however small, that she didn't have, she would persuade herself that it wasn't an advantage but a disadvantage, and would pity them so as not to envy them. 'I don't think he'd like that; I know I wouldn't like to see my name splashed over the pages of the newspaper like that, and I wouldn't be at all pleased if people mentioned it to me.' But there was no need for her to press the point, for my grandmother's sisters had such a horror of vulgarity that they'd made so fine an art of concealing any personal allusion beneath ingenious circumlocutions that it often went unnoticed even by the person to whom it was addressed. As for my mother, her only thought was of trying to induce my father to talk to Swann, not about his wife but about his daughter whom he adored and, it was said, was the reason why he'd finally decided to marry. 'You need only ask how she is. It must be so hard for him.' But my father would become annoyed: 'Absolutely not! You make the silliest suggestions. It would be ridiculous.'

But the only one of us in whom the prospect of Swann's visit caused particular anxiety was myself. This was because on the evenings when there were visitors, or just Monsieur Swann, Maman didn't come up to my room. I'd eat before the others and afterwards sit at the table until eight o'clock, when it was understood I had to go upstairs; the precious, fragile kiss Maman normally bestowed on me when I was in bed and about to fall asleep had to be transported from the dining room to my bedroom and kept intact during the whole time it took me to undress, without my letting its sweet charm be broken, without letting its volatile essence escape and evaporate; and it was precisely on those evenings when I needed to receive it with special care that I had to take it, snatch it brusquely and publicly, without having the time or the absence of distractions to bring to what I was doing the obsessive attention of those in the grip of some mania who, while closing a door, strive not to think of anything else, so that when their neurotic uncertainty comes back, they can confront it triumphantly with the memory of the precise moment when they did close the door. We were all in the garden when the two timid little tinkles of the bell sounded. We knew it was Swann, but we all looked at each other questioningly and my grandmother was sent on reconnaissance. 'Make sure you make yourselves understood when you thank him for the wine,' my grandfather said to his two sisters-in-law. 'You know how good it is, and it's such a big case.'

'Don't start that whispering,' said my great-aunt. 'It's not very nice to come into a house where everybody is speaking in an undertone!'

'Ah, here's Monsieur Swann! Let's ask him if he thinks it'll be fine tomorrow,' said my father.

My mother thought a word from her would wipe out all the distress my family might have caused Swann since his marriage, and she found an opportunity to take him aside. But I followed her, unable to let her out of my sight, thinking that in a few minutes I'd have to leave her in the dining room and go up to bed without the usual consolation of her coming up to kiss me goodnight. 'Now, Monsieur Swann,' she said, 'do tell me about your daughter. I'm sure she already has a taste for beautiful things, like her father.'

'Come and sit with us on the verandah,' said my grandfather, walking over. This prevented my mother from continuing, but she managed to turn this constraint to good effect and to express a further delicate thought, like good poets whom the tyranny of rhyme forces into the discovery of their best lines: 'We can talk about her when we're by ourselves,' she murmured to Swann. 'Only a mother can really understand these things. I'm sure her mother would agree.'

We all sat down round the iron table. I would have preferred not to think about the painful hours I'd have to spend that evening alone in my room, unable to go to sleep; I kept telling myself that my distress was of little consequence, since I'd have forgotten about it by the morning, and I tried to think only about the future, as though this would carry me, as if on a bridge, across the terrifying abyss that was about to open up at my feet. But my mind, tense with foreboding and as focused as the looks I kept shooting at my mother, was impervious to any extraneous impressions. Thoughts still entered my mind, but only after they had left outside any element of beauty, or even playfulness, that might have moved me or made me laugh. Just as a patient, thanks to a local anaesthetic, can look on, fully conscious but not feeling anything, while an operation is being performed on him, I could recite to myself some of my favourite lines of poetry, or observe my grandfather's attempts to engage Swann in conversation about the Duc d'Audiffret-Pasquier,* without the former making me feel any emotion, or the latter any amusement. My grandfather's efforts were quite fruitless. He'd barely had time to ask Swann about the orator when one of my grandmother's sisters, in whose ears the question resounded like a profound and untimely silence that should be broken for the sake of politeness, said to her sister:

'I must tell you, Céline—the other day I met a young Swedish governess who told me all about the cooperative movement in Scandinavia. She was most interesting. We must have her to dinner one evening.'

'By all means!' replied her sister Flora,* 'but I haven't been wasting my time either. I was at Monsieur Vinteuil's house the other day and met a very clever old gentleman who knows Maubant* very well, and Maubant has been telling him all about the way he works up the roles he plays. He was quite fascinating. He's a neighbour of Monsieur Vinteuil's, which I never knew. He's very nice.'

'Monsieur Vinteuil isn't the only one who has nice neighbours,' exclaimed my aunt Céline in a voice that was too loud (because of her shyness) and sounded artificial (because her remark was premeditated);

and as she spoke, she gave Swann a glance she was wont to call 'meaningful'. At the same time my aunt Flora, who'd realized that this utterance of Céline's was her way of thanking Swann for the Asti, was also gazing at Swann with an expression that combined congratulation and irony, either because she simply wanted to reinforce her sister's little quip, or because she envied Swann for having inspired it, or because she imagined he was embarrassed, and couldn't resist making fun of him since she thought he was being put on the spot.

'I think we can get the gentleman to come to dinner,' continued Flora. 'You know, once he starts on Maubant or Madame Materna,* he goes on for hours.'

'That sounds marvellous,' sighed my grandfather, in whose mind Nature had unfortunately failed to include any capacity whatever for becoming passionately interested in the Swedish cooperative move-ment* or the way Maubant prepares for his roles, just as it had forgot-ten to make sure my grandmother's two sisters had the little grain of salt one must add oneself, in order to find any savour in it, to a story about the private life of Molé or the Comte de Paris.

'Let me tell you something,' said Swann to my grandfather, 'and this has more to do than you might think with what you were just asking me, because in some ways things have changed very little. This morning I was reading Saint-Simon,* and I came across a passage you would have enjoyed. It's in the volume that deals with his mission to Spain. I wouldn't say it's one of the best volumes, it's just a diary, really, an account of the day's events, but at least it's wonderfully well written, which is far more than we can say for those boring news sheets we think we have to read every morning and evening.'

'Oh, I don't agree. There are some days when I find reading the papers very pleasant indeed,' interjected Aunt Flora, this being her way of showing Swann that she'd seen the note about his Corot in *Le Figaro*.

'Yes, especially when they mention things and people we're inter-ested in!' added Aunt Céline, to make sure the point wouldn't be lost.

'You may be right,' replied Swann, looking rather surprised. 'But what I find wrong with the newspapers is that every day they do noth-ing but draw our attention to absolute trivia, whereas only three or four times in our lives do we read books that tell us something truly important. The way people tear the wrapper off their paper every morning makes you want to change everything and publish in the newspaper something like, say . . . Pascal's *Pensées*!'* (He pronounced the title with an ironic emphasis so as not to appear pedantic.) 'And then, in the leather-bound tome we open once every ten years,' he added, showing the disdain for worldly things some men of the world like to affect, 'you could put that the Queen of the Hellenes has gone to Cannes or that the Princesse de Léon has given a fancy dress ball.* That would restore a proper sense of proportion.' Then, sorry he'd allowed himself to speak even light-heartedly about serious matters, he added ironically: 'What a lofty conversation we're having! How did we reach such heights?' and turning to my grandfather: 'Well, Saint-Simon tells how Maulévrier* had the audacity to offer his hand to his sons. You remember, it's Maulévrier of whom he says: "Never did I see in that coarse bottle anything but ill humour, boorishness, and stupidity." '*

'Coarse or not, I know some bottles in which there's something quite different!' interjected Flora, anxious to add her thanks to those of her sister, since the Asti was meant for both of them. Céline laughed.

Swann, disconcerted, went on: 'Saint-Simon puts it this way: "I can't say whether it was out of ignorance or as a trap that he wanted to shake hands with my sons. I noticed in time to prevent him." '*

My grandfather was already in ecstasies over 'through ignorance or as a trap' when Mademoiselle Céline, in whom the name of Saint-Simon—a man of letters—had arrested the complete atrophy of her auditory faculties, burst out indignantly:

'What! You admire that? Well, that's a fine thing, I must say! Think what it means; isn't one man as good as the next? What difference does it make whether he's a duke or a coachman, as long as he's intelligent and a good person? He had a funny way of bringing up his children, your Saint-Simon, if he didn't teach them to shake hands with all decent people. It's abominable, it really is. And you dare to quote him on the subject!' My grandfather, bitterly disappointed and realizing how impossible it would be, in the face of this obstruction, to get Swann to tell the stories that would have amused him, murmured to my mother: 'What was that line you quoted to me that comforts me so much at times like this? Oh, yes: "How many, Lord, are the virtues you make us abhor!"* What a marvellous line it is.'

I couldn't take my eyes off my mother. I knew that when we were at table I wouldn't be allowed to stay until the end of the meal and that Maman, so as not to annoy my father, would not let me kiss her several times in front of everybody, as she would have done in my room. And so I promised myself that in the dining room, as they began the meal and I felt bedtime approaching, I'd prepare myself as best I could for my kiss, which would be so brief and furtive: I'd choose the precise spot on Maman's cheek that I'd kiss, and would so prepare my thoughts that I would be able, thanks to this mental rehearsal, to devote the entire minute she'd grant me to the sensation of her cheek against my lips, just as a painter who can have only short sittings with his model prepares his palette and does as much as he can in advance from memory and from his notes. But all of a sudden, before the dinner bell had sounded, my grandfather said with unwitting cruelty: 'The boy looks tired, he ought to go up to bed. Besides, we're having dinner late tonight.'

Whereupon my father, who wasn't as scrupulous as my grandmother and my mother about honouring treaties, said: 'Yes, off you go, up to bed with you.'

I made as if to go and kiss Maman, but at that very moment the bell was rung for dinner, and my father said:

'No, leave your mother in peace. You've already said goodnight to each other quite enough. These performances are ridiculous. Go on upstairs!'

And so I had to leave without my viaticum;* I had to climb each step of the staircase 'with a heavy heart', as the phrase goes, for my heart wanted to go back down to my mother who, by not kissing me, hadn't given my heart permission to go with me. Those hateful stairs, which I always climbed with such sadness, gave out a smell of varnish that had absorbed and crystallized, so to speak, the special kind of sorrow I felt every evening, and made it perhaps even more unbearable because, when it assumed that olfactory form, my intellect could no longer engage with it. When we're asleep and we're aware of a raging toothache only as of a drowning girl whom we try, over and over again, to pull out of the water, or a line by Molière* we repeat incessantly to ourselves, it's a great relief to wake up, so that our intellect can divest the idea of toothache of its disguise of heroism or rhythmic cadence. It was the opposite of this relief that I felt when my distress at having to go up to my room invaded my consciousness in a manner infinitely swifter, almost instantaneous, at once insidious and abrupt, through the inhalation—more deadly than intellectual penetration—of the smell of varnish peculiar to that staircase. Once in my room, I had to seal myself in, close the shutters, dig my own grave by turning down the bed-covers, and put on the shroud of my nightshirt. But before burying myself in the iron bed they'd moved into the room because I was too hot in the summer behind the rep curtains of the four-poster, I felt a surge of rebellion and attempted a final, desperate, life-or-death stratagem. I wrote a note to my mother begging her to come upstairs because of something important I couldn't commit to paper. I was afraid that Françoise, my aunt's cook who was charged with looking after me when I was in Combray, would refuse to take my note. I suspected that, for her, to deliver a message to my mother when there was a guest would be as inconceivable as for the doorman at a theatre to hand a letter to an actor onstage. When it came to things that could or could not be done, she held to a code at once imperious, far-reaching, subtle, and uncompromising on pointless or imperceptible distinctions (which made it rather like the legal codes of ancient times that, while prescribing such savage practices as the slaughter of babes-in-arms, had the excessive sensitivity to forbid boiling a kid in its mother's milk or eating the sinew from an animal's thigh*). This code, judging from her sudden obstinacy when she didn't want to carry out certain of our instructions, seemed to have been conceived for social complexities and refinements of etiquette which nothing in her previous associations or in her life as a servant in a little town could have put into her head; and we were obliged to conclude that she carried within her something of France's ancient past, noble and little understood, as in those manufacturing towns where grand old houses remain to remind us of courtly days, and where the employees of a chemical factory work amid delicate sculptures depicting the miracle of Saint Theophilus* or the legend of the four sons of Aymon.* In this particular case, the article of Françoise's code which made it unlikely that, except in the event of a fire, she would go and disturb Maman in the presence of Monsieur Swann for so insignificant a person as myself was the one that embodied the respect she professed not only for the family—as for the dead, for priests, and for kings—but also for the stranger within our gates; a respect I might have found touching in a book, but always irritated me on her lips, because of the solemn, maudlin tone she used when invoking it, and especially so this evening, when the sacred character she accorded to dinner parties might have the effect of making her decline to disturb its ceremonial. But to give myself a better chance, I had no hesitation in lying, telling her that the idea of writing to Maman was not my idea at all, but that it was Maman who, as she said goodnight to me, had told me not to forget to let her know about something she'd asked me to look for; and she'd certainly be very angry if my note wasn't taken to her. I think Françoise didn't believe me, for, like primitive man whose senses were so much keener than ours, she was able to detect, from signs imperceptible to the rest of us, any trickery we might want to hide from her; she studied the envelope for five minutes as though an examination of the paper and the look of my handwriting would tell her what was inside, or which article of her code she should apply. Then she went out with an air of resignation that seemed to say: 'To be sure it's terrible for parents to have a child like that!' She came back a moment later to tell me they were still only at the ice cream stage and it was impossible for the butler to deliver the note at once, in front of everybody, but when the finger bowls were put round he'd find a way of passing it to Maman. My anxiety instantly subsided; it was now no longer, as it had been a moment before, until the next morning that I'd be cut off from my mother, since my note, though it would no doubt annoy her (and doubly so because my little trick would make me look ridiculous in Swann's eyes), would at least admit me, invisible and delighted, into the same room as her, and would whisper about me in her ear; now that Maman was about to read what I'd written, that forbidden, hostile dining room, where just a moment before even the ice cream—the *granita*—and the finger bowls seemed to me to speak of pleasures that hurt and saddened me profoundly because Maman was enjoying them while I was far away, had opened its doors and, like a ripe fruit bursting through its skin, was about to pour, to project, into my ecstatic heart all the sweetness of Maman's attention. Now I was no longer separated from her; the barriers were down, an exquisite thread united us. And that was not all: Maman would surely come!

I thought that if Swann had read my note and guessed its purpose he would have laughed at the anguish I'd just experienced; whereas, on the contrary, as I was to learn later, a similar anguish had tormented him for many a long year, and no one, perhaps, could have understood me as well as he; in his case, the anguish that comes from the feeling that the person you adore is in a place of enjoyment where you are not, where you cannot follow, was the result of love, to which it is in a sense predestined, by which it will be taken over and possessed;

but when, as in my case, it takes hold before love has made its appearance in our life, it drifts as it awaits it, free and indeterminate, without a clear focus, attaching itself to different feelings on different days, at times to our love for a parent, at others to our fondness for a friend. And the joy with which I served my first apprenticeship when Françoise came back to tell me the note would be delivered, Swann too had known—that deceptive joy which a friend or relative of the woman we love can give us when, on arriving at the house or theatre where she is, for some ball or party or first night at which he's going to meet her, he sees us wandering about outside, waiting desperately for an opportunity to communicate with her.

He recognizes us, gives us a friendly greeting, and asks what we're doing there. And when we invent some story about having an urgent message to give to his relative or friend, he assures us that nothing could be simpler, takes us in at the door, and promises to send her down straight away. How we love him, as at that moment I loved Françoise—the well-meaning go-between who with a single word has transformed into something tolerable, human, almost reassuring the unspeakable, infernal scene of pleasure into the midst of which we'd been imagining that hostile, perverse, alluring forces were carrying away from us the woman we love, and even making her laugh at us! If we are to judge by him, this relative who has greeted us and is himself one of the initiates in these cruel mysteries, then the other guests cannot have anything very demonic about them. Those inaccessible, excruciating hours during which she was about to taste unimaginable pleasures—now, through an unexpected breach, we are breaking into them; now we can imagine clearly, we begin to control, we take part in, we have almost created, one of the moments which, in succession, would have composed those hours, a moment as real as the others, perhaps even more important to us because she is more directly involved: the moment when she's about to be told that we are waiting downstairs. And no doubt the other moments that evening wouldn't have been very different in essence from this one, would have been no more delectable and hurtful to us, since this well-intentioned friend has assured us: 'Of course, she'll be delighted to come down! She'd much rather chat with you than be bored up there.' Alas! Swann had learned from experience that the good intentions of a third party are powerless to influence a woman who is annoyed to find herself pursued even into a party by a man she doesn't love. Often the friend comes down again alone.

My mother didn't come, and without consideration for my pride (which depended on her maintaining the fiction that she was supposed to have asked me to tell her if I'd found what she'd asked me to look for) told Françoise to reply, flatly: 'There's no answer'—a phrase I have so often heard since then being said by the doormen of swanky hotels or liveried flunkeys in gambling dens to some poor girl who exclaims in surprise: 'What! He didn't say anything? That's not possible. You gave him my note, didn't you? All right, then, I'll just wait a bit longer.' And, just as she invariably assures him that she doesn't need the extra gas jet which the doorman offers to light for her, and carries on sitting there, hearing nothing further except an occasional remark about the weather the doorman exchanges with a pageboy whom he sends off suddenly, when he notices the time, to put a customer's drink on ice, so, having declined Françoise's offer to stay with me or to make me some tea, I let her go back to her pantry, got into bed, and shut my eyes, trying not to hear the voices of my family who were having coffee in the garden. But after a few seconds I began to feel that, by writing that note to Maman, by risking her anger by approaching so close to her that I could almost reach out and seize the moment when I could see her again, I'd closed off the possibility that I might fall asleep without seeing her again, and my heart began to beat more painfully with each passing minute because I was making myself more agitated by telling myself to keep calm and to accept my misfortune. Then, suddenly, my agitation subsided and a kind of rapture swept over me, as when some powerful medication begins to take effect and our pain vanishes: I'd resolved to stop trying to go to sleep without seeing Maman again when she came up to bed, to kiss her whatever the cost, even though I knew full well she'd be cross with me for a long time afterwards. The calm that came with the end of my distress combined with my sense of anticipation, and my thirst for and fear of danger, to give me an extraordinary feeling of exhilaration. I opened the window without a sound and sat down on the foot of my bed; I hardly moved so as not to be heard from below. Outside, too, things seemed to be standing silent and still, as if struck dumb and trying not to disturb the moonlight which, duplicating and distancing everything by extending its shadow before it, denser and more concrete than itself, had at once shrunk and enlarged the landscape like a map that had been folded and was now spread out. What needed to move, like the foliage on the chestnut trees, moved. But its minute quivering, total and self-contained, executed with all its subtleties and soft tremors, didn't blend with the rest of the scene, it remained circumscribed. Exposed against this silence, which absorbed nothing of them, the most distant sounds, those that must have come from gardens at the far end of the town, could be heard distinguished one from the other with such 'finish' that the impression they gave of coming from a distance seemed due to their pianissimo execution, like those muted motifs* performed so well by the Conservatoire orchestra that, even though you don't miss a single note, you think they are being played somewhere outside, a long way from the concert hall, and that all the elderly subscribers—and my grandmother's sisters too, when Swann gave them his seats—strained their ears as if they were listening to the distant approach of an army on the march that hadn't yet turned the corner of the Rue de Trévise.*

I knew that the position in which I was placing myself couldn't have graver consequences in terms of my parents' reaction, far graver in truth than a stranger would have imagined, the sort he would have believed could be produced only by misdeeds of the most shameful kind. But in the upbringing my parents gave me, the order of misdeeds was not the same as for other children, and I'd been taught to place at the top of the list (no doubt because they were the ones from which I needed to be more carefully protected) those whose common characteristic, as I can now see clearly, is that one commits them by giving in to a nervous impulse. But at the time this was never said in my hearing, no one had ever mentioned the cause of my temptations, for to do so might have made me believe I was excusable for giving in to them or even that I was incapable of resisting them. I could recognize them clearly enough, however, from the anguish that preceded them as well as from the rigour of the punishment that followed; and I knew that the one I'd just committed was in the same category as others for which I'd been severely punished, but infinitely more serious. When I went to surprise my mother on her way to bed, and she saw I'd stayed up to say goodnight again in the passage, I'd be banished from the house and sent off to boarding school the very next day, that much was certain. But no matter! Even if I'd have to throw myself out of the window straight afterwards, I'd have preferred that. What I wanted now was Maman, to say goodnight to her, I'd gone too far along the road that led to the satisfaction of that desire to turn back.

I heard my parents' footsteps as they accompanied Swann to the gate; and when the sound of the bell told me he'd left, I went to the window. Maman was asking my father if he'd enjoyed the lobster, and whether Monsieur Swann had had a second helping of the coffee-and-pistachio ice cream. 'I thought it was very ordinary,' she said. 'We should try a different flavour next time.'

'I must say,' said my great-aunt, 'I can't get over how much Swann has changed. He looks so old!' My great-aunt was so used to seeing Swann as an eternal adolescent that she was forever surprised to find him suddenly less young than the age she continued to give him. And my parents too were beginning to notice in him the abnormal, excessive, shameful, culpable senescence of the unmarried, of all those for whom it seems that the great day that has no tomorrow is longer than for others, because for them it's empty and time, throughout the day, is merely an accumulation of moments rather than being divided among children.

'I think that wretched wife of his gives him no end of trouble. The whole of Combray knows she's living with a certain Monsieur de Charlus. It's the talk of the town.'

My mother remarked that, in spite of this, he'd been looking much less unhappy of late. 'And he doesn't make that gesture as often, so like his father, rubbing his eyes and passing his hand across his forehead. I think he doesn't love that woman any more, when all's said and done.'

'Of course he doesn't love her any more,' answered my grandfather. 'He wrote me a letter about it ages ago, which I made a point of ignoring but which left me in no doubt about his feelings towards his wife, at least as far as love is concerned.' And he added, turning to his sisters-in-law: 'Well, what did I tell you, you didn't thank him for the Asti.'

'What do you mean, "didn't thank him"?' replied Aunt Flora. 'I must say, I think I put it very neatly.'

'Yes,' said Aunt Céline, 'you did it extremely well. I was very impressed.'

'And you were very good too.'

'Yes, I was quite proud of what I said about nice neighbours.'

'What! You call that thanking him?' exclaimed my grandfather. 'I heard what you said, but not for the life of me did I think it was meant for Swann. You can be sure he had no idea.'

'Oh, come, come, he's not a fool! I'm sure he understood. I could hardly refer to the number of bottles and how much the wine cost!'

My father and mother were left alone and sat down for a moment; then my father said: 'Well, shall we go to bed?'

'If you like, my dear. I don't feel at all sleepy, though. It can't be that bland coffee ice cream which has made me so wakeful. But I can see a light in the pantry: poor Françoise has been waiting up for me, so I'll go and ask her to unhook me while you get undressed.'

My mother opened the latticed door that led from the hall to the stairs. Soon afterwards, I heard her coming upstairs to close her window. I slipped quietly into the passage; my heart was beating so hard I was hardly able to stand upright, but at least it was no longer pounding from anxiety, but from terror and joy. I saw the light from Maman's candle in the stairwell. Then I saw Maman herself and ran up to her. For a moment she looked at me in amazement, not understanding what was happening. Then an expression of anger came over her face, she said not a word to me, and indeed for much less than this they would sometimes not speak to me for several days. If Maman had said something, it would have been an admission that speaking to me was still a possibility, which in any case might have seemed even more terrible to me, as a sign that, in comparison with the punishment that would be visited upon me, silence and black looks would be as nothing. A word from her at this moment would have been like the calm way you address a servant you've just decided to dismiss; or the kiss you give a son you're sending off to enlist, whereas you would have withheld it if it had simply been a matter of being annoyed with him for a few days. But she now heard my father coming up from the dressing room where he had gone to get ready for bed, and, to avoid the scene he'd make if he saw me, she said in a voice choking with anger: 'Quick—go back to your room! Don't let your father see you standing here as if you've lost your senses!' But I kept saying: 'Come and kiss me goodnight,' terror-struck as I saw the light from my father's candle already coming up the wall, but also using his approach as a means of blackmail, hoping that Maman, to avoid his finding me there if she didn't agree, would say: 'Go back to your room, I'll come.' But it was too late, my father was there in front of us. I mumbled instinctively, though neither of them heard: 'I'm done for!'

It was not so, however. My father would constantly refuse me things that had been granted by my mother and grandmother, because he didn't care about 'principles' and because for him there was no 'law of nations'.* For some totally arbitrary reason, or even for no reason at all, he would at the last minute deny me a certain walk, one so customary, so hallowed, that to deprive me of it was a clear breach of faith; or, as he'd done this evening, long before the ritual hour, he'd say: 'Off to bed with you now, and no arguments!' But by the same token, because he had no principles (in my grandmother's sense), he wasn't strictly speaking intransigent. He looked at me for a moment with an expression of surprise and annoyance, and then when Maman had told him, not without a certain embarrassment, what had happened, he said: 'Go with him, then. You were just saying you don't feel sleepy, stay in his room for a little while. I don't need anything.'

'But, my dear,' replied my mother timidly, 'whether I feel sleepy or not isn't the point, we can't let the boy get into the habit . . .'

'But it isn't a question of habit,' said my father, shrugging his shoulders, 'you can see he's upset. He looks very sad. We're not brutes, are we? You'll end up making him ill, and we don't want that! There are two beds in his room, so just tell Françoise to make up the big one for you and sleep there tonight. I'm going to bed now. I'm not as neurotic as you two. Goodnight.'

It wasn't possible to thank my father; he would have been irritated by what he called 'sentimentalism'. I stood there, not daring to move; he was still in front of us, a tall figure in his white nightshirt and with the pink and violet Indian cashmere he'd taken to wrapping round his head since his first attacks of neuralgia,* looking like Abraham in the engraving after Benozzo Gozzoli* that Monsieur Swann had given me, telling Sarah she must abandon Isaac. This all happened a long time ago. The wall on which I saw the glimmer of his candle as he came upstairs was pulled down long since. In me, too, many things that I thought would last for ever have been destroyed, and new ones have arisen, producing new sorrows and new joys which I couldn't have foreseen then, just as now the old ones have become difficult to understand. It's a long time, too, since my father stopped being able to say to Maman: 'Go with the boy.' Such moments will never again be possible for me. But recently I've begun to hear again very clearly, if I take care to listen, the sound of the sobs I was strong enough to contain in front of my father and that didn't burst out until I was alone with Maman. In truth, they've never stopped; and it's only now, when the sounds of life are dying out around me, that I can hear them again, like convent bells so fully drowned out by the noises of the town during the day that you think they've stopped altogether, until you hear them pealing out once more in the silence of the evening.

Maman spent that night in my room; I'd just committed an offence I thought would entail my banishment from the house, and yet my parents were granting me more than I could ever have won from them as a reward for a good deed. Even at the moment when it manifested itself through his act of clemency, my father's behaviour towards me still had the arbitrary and unwarranted quality that was so characteristic of him and was due to the fact that generally he acted in response to chance circumstances rather than a conscious plan. It may even be that what I called his severity, when he sent me to bed, deserved that name less than my mother's or my grandmother's way of thinking, because in certain respects his nature was less like mine than theirs, and this had probably prevented him from realizing until then how unhappy I was every evening, whereas my mother and grandmother knew perfectly well; but they loved me enough not to spare me my suffering, so as to teach me to master it, to reduce my nervous sensitivity and strengthen my will. My father's affection for me was of a different sort, and I don't know if he would have had that kind of courage: the one time he realized I was upset, he'd said to my mother: 'Go and comfort him.' So Maman spent the night in my room; and, as if not to allow any hint of remorse to spoil those hours that were so different from what I had any right to expect, when Françoise, realizing that something extraordinary was happening when she saw Maman sitting next to me, holding my hand and letting me cry without scolding me, asked: 'Dear me, Madame, what's makin' the young master cry like this?' Maman replied: 'He doesn't even know himself, Françoise. It's his nerves. Make up the big bed for me quickly and then go up to bed yourself.' In this way, for the first time, my sadness was regarded no longer as a punishable offence but as an involuntary ailment that had just been officially recognized, a nervous condition for which I was not responsible; I thus felt relieved at no longer having to mingle qualms of conscience with the bitterness of my tears— I could cry without sin. I was also more than a little proud that Françoise should be present at this turnaround in human affairs which, an hour after Maman had refused to come up to my room and had sent the disdainful message that I should go to sleep, raised me to the exalted status of a grown-up and brought me all of a sudden to a sort of puberty of sorrow, an emancipation through tears. I ought to have been happy; I was not. I felt that my mother had just had the painful experience of giving in to me for the first time, that this was a first step on her part towards abdication from the ideal she'd conceived for me, and that, for all her courage, this was her first admission of defeat. I felt that, if I'd just won a victory, it was over her, that I'd succeeded, as sickness or sorrow or old age might have done, in weakening her resolve, in undermining her faith in her judgement—that this evening marked the beginning of a new era, and would remain a sad day. If I'd dared, I would have said: 'No, Maman, please don't sleep here, I don't want you to.' But I was aware of the practical wisdom, the realism as it would be called now, that tempered the ardent idealism she'd inherited from my grandmother, and I knew that, now the damage was done, she would prefer to let me enjoy the soothing pleasure of her presence, and not disturb my father. To be sure, my mother's beautiful face still shone with youth that evening, as she gently held my hands and tried to stop my tears; but it was precisely this that I felt should not have happened; her anger would have saddened me less than this new gentleness, so unfamiliar in my childhood; I felt that with an impious and secret hand I'd just traced upon her soul a first wrinkle and caused a first white hair to appear. The thought made me sob even more, and then I saw that Maman, who never let herself get emotional with me, was suddenly overcome by my tears and struggled to hold back her own. When she saw I had noticed, she said with a laugh: 'Come on, you silly little ninny, you'll make your Maman as silly as you are if this goes on much longer! Look, if you're not sleepy and Maman isn't either, let's stop upsetting each other and do something, let's read one of your books.' But I had none in my room. 'Well, would it spoil things for you if I got the books your grandmother will be giving you for your saint's day?* Think carefully: you won't be disappointed if there are no surprises the day after tomorrow?' On the contrary, I was delighted, and Maman went to fetch a parcel of books, of which I could only make out, through the wrapping paper, their short wide shape, but which, even at this first glimpse, fleeting and unclear as it was, already eclipsed the paintbox I'd been given on New Year's Day and the silkworms of the year before. The books were *La Mare au Diable*, *François le Champi*, *La Petite Fadette*, and *Les Maîtres sonneurs*.* My grandmother, as I learned afterwards, had at first chosen the poems of

Musset, a volume of Rousseau, and *Indiana*;* for though she deemed frivolous reading to be as unwholesome as sweets and cakes, she didn't think that the powerful breath of genius could have a more dangerous and less invigorating influence on the mind of a child than would fresh air and sea breezes on his body. But when my father on learning which books she wanted to give me came close to calling her mad, she'd gone back to the bookshop in Jouy-le-Vicomte herself, to make sure I'd not go without my present (it was a boiling-hot day and she'd come home feeling so unwell that the doctor had warned my mother not to let her tire herself out like that again), and she'd fallen back on the four pastoral novels of George Sand. 'My dear,' she said to Maman, 'I couldn't bring myself to give the child something that was not well written.'

In fact, she could never reconcile herself to buying anything from which no intellectual benefit was to be derived, especially the benefit beautiful things afford us by teaching us to seek our pleasure elsewhere than in the satisfactions of material comfort and vanity. Even when she had to give presents of the kind called 'useful', when she had to give an armchair or a cutlery set or a walking stick, she looked for 'old' things, as though their desuetude had erased their usefulness and made them better suited to educate us about the lives people led in the past than to serve the needs of our own lives. She would have liked me to have in my room photographs of the most beautiful buildings and landscapes. But at the moment of buying them, and even though the subjects themselves had aesthetic value, she found that vulgarity and utility played too great a part in them, through the mechanical process of their reproduction by photography. In an attempt to reduce this element of commercial banality, if not to abolish it entirely, she tried the stratagem of replacing it as far as possible with further forms of art, thus including several levels of art in the one picture: instead of photographs of Chartres Cathedral, the fountains at Saint-Cloud, or Mount Vesuvius, she would ascertain from Swann whether some great painter had not depicted them, and preferred to give me photographs of *Chartres Cathedral* by Corot, *The Fountains at Saint-Cloud* by Hubert Robert, and *Vesuvius* by Turner, thus adding another layer of art to the picture.* But although the photographer had been excluded from representation of the masterwork or the scene from nature, and replaced by a great artist, he could still come back into his own when it came to reproducing the artist's interpretation. Having reduced the risk of vulgarity to this extent, my grandmother would try to reduce it even further. She would ask Swann if the work had not been engraved, preferring, whenever possible, old engravings that also had an interest beyond themselves, for example those that show us a masterpiece in a state in which we can no longer see it today (like Morghen's engraving of Leonardo's *Last Supper** before it began to deteriorate). It must be said that my grandmother's approach to the art of giving presents didn't always produce brilliant results. The idea I formed of Venice from a drawing by Titian* that is supposed to have the lagoon in the background was certainly far less accurate than the one I would have derived from simple photographs. We could no longer keep count, at home, when my great-aunt wanted to arraign her sister before the family, of all the armchairs she'd given to couples as wedding or anniversary presents which, at the first attempt by the recipients to sit in them, had promptly collapsed. But my grandmother would have thought it petty to concern herself overmuch with the solidity of a piece of furniture if it was still possible to make out on it a small flower, a smile, sometimes some creative invention from the past. And even if there were features of the furniture that answered a need, the fact that they did so in a manner to which we are no longer accustomed enchanted her, like old forms of speech in which we find metaphoric expressions that have disappeared from modern usage, worn down by habit. In fact, the pastoral novels by George Sand she was giving me for my saint's day were like old pieces of furniture in that they were full of expressions that have fallen out of use and become quaint and picturesque, of the sort you only hear nowadays in the speech of country folk. And my grandmother had bought them in preference to other books, just as she would have preferred to rent a house with a Gothic dovecote or some other such 'old' thing as would exercise a beneficial influence on the mind by provoking in it a longing for impossible journeys back through time.

Maman sat down by my bed; she had picked up *François le Champi*, whose reddish cover and incomprehensible title gave it, for me, a distinct personality and a mysterious attraction. I hadn't yet read any real novels. I'd heard people say that George Sand was a classic example of a novelist. This predisposed me to imagine that *François le Champi* contained something inexpressibly delightful. Narrative devices designed to move the reader or arouse his curiosity, certain

modes of expression that unsettle or sadden him, and that a reader
with any education will recognize as common to many novels, seemed
to me—for whom a new book wasn't just one example among many
similar ones, but was as unique as a human being, with no reason for
existing except in itself—simply a disturbing emanation of *François
le Champi*'s peculiar essence. Beneath the everyday events it described,
the ordinary objects and common words it contained, I sensed
a strange, individual voice and intonation. The plot got under way; it
seemed to me all the more obscure because in those days, when I read,
I spent whole pages daydreaming about something completely different. And further gaps were left in the story by the fact that, when
Maman read aloud to me, she skipped over all the love scenes. This
meant that all the odd changes that take place in the attitudes of the
miller's wife and the boy towards each other, which can only be
explained by the gradual growth of love, seemed to me marked by
a profound mystery whose source, I imagined, must lie in the strange
and pleasant name 'Champi',* which cast upon the boy, who bore it
I had no idea why, its lovely, bright, reddish glow. If my mother was
not always a faithful reader, she was, in the case of books in which she
found a note of true feeling, an admirable one because of the respectful simplicity of her performance and the gentle beauty of her voice.
Even in real life, when it was people and not works of art that aroused
her sympathy or admiration, it was touching to observe how thought-
fully she removed from her voice, from her gestures, from what she
said, any note of gaiety that might distress some mother who had once
lost a child, any mention of a saint's day or a birthday that might
remind some old gentleman of his advanced age, any talk about
housekeeping matters that might appear tedious to some young
scholar. In the same way, when she read the prose of George Sand,
which is suffused with the generosity, the moral distinction which
Maman had learned from my grandmother to value above all else in
life, and which I was to teach her only much later not to consider
superior to all else in books, she took care to keep out of her voice any
hint of pettiness or affectation that might have prevented it from
expressing that powerful flow of language, and she imparted all the
natural tenderness, all the deep feeling they demanded to sentences
that seemed written for her voice and accorded perfectly, so to speak,
with the natural registers of her sensibility. To tackle them in the
appropriate tone, she found the warm inflection that pre-existed and

dictated them, but is not to be found in the words themselves; in this way she smoothed away any discordance in the tenses of the verbs, gave the imperfect and the past historic the gentleness implicit in kindness and the melancholy in love, guiding the sentence about to end towards the one that was about to begin, sometimes hurrying the syllables along, sometimes slowing them down, so as to bring them, despite their unequal numbers, into a uniform rhythm, and breathing into this plain prose a continuous current of emotion.

My feelings of guilt had subsided; I let myself be borne along by this gentle night on which I had my mother by my side. I knew that such a night couldn't be repeated; that my greatest desire in the world, to keep my mother in my room during the sad hours of darkness, was too much at variance with the general scheme of things and the wishes of others for its fulfilment, granted that evening, to be anything other than an artificial exception. Tomorrow my anguish would return and Maman wouldn't stay with me. But when my anguish was allayed, I no longer understood it; and in any case, tomorrow night was still a long way off; I told myself I would have time to think of something, although the intervening time wouldn't give me any extra resources, since these things had nothing to do with the exercise of my will and seemed avoidable now only because of the interval that still separated them from me.

So it was that, for a long time, when I lay awake at night and remembered Combray again, all I ever saw of it was a single luminous panel, standing out against a shadowy background, like the panels which a Bengal light* or a searchlight will cut out and illuminate in a building whose other parts remain plunged in darkness: the rather broad base contained the little sitting room, the dining room, the top of the dark path trodden by Monsieur Swann, the unwitting author of my sufferings, the hall through which I would make my way to the foot of the stairs, so painful to climb, that formed the very narrow trunk of this irregular pyramid; and, at the top, my bedroom with the little passage through whose glass-paned door Maman would enter; in a word, always seen at the same time of day, separate from everything that might surround it, standing out on its own in the darkness, the bare minimum of scenery necessary (like the props prescribed on the title page of old plays for performances in the provinces) for the drama of my undressing; as if the whole of Combray consisted only of two floors connected by a slender staircase and as if it had always been seven o'clock in the evening there. To tell the truth, if anyone had asked, I would have been able to say that Combray included other things and did exist at other times of the day. But since what I would then have remembered would have been supplied only by my conscious memory, the memory of the intellect, and since the information this type of memory provides about the past preserves nothing of it, I would never have had any desire to think about the rest of Combray. It was all quite dead for me.

Dead for ever? Quite possibly.

There is a great deal of chance involved in all this, and a second kind of chance, that of our death, often prevents us from waiting very long for the favours of the first.

I find very reasonable the Celtic belief that the souls of those we have lost are held captive in some lower form of life, in an animal or a plant or some inanimate thing, and are lost to us until the day (which for many never comes) when we happen to pass close to the tree or gain possession of the object that is their prison.* Then they quiver and call out to us, and as soon as we recognize them the spell is broken. They are set free, they have overcome death, and they return to share our lives.

It is the same with our past. If we try to recall it, we strive in vain: all the efforts of our intellect are to no avail. The past is hidden somewhere beyond its realm, beyond its reach, in some material object (or rather, in the sensation that object would give us) of which we have no inkling. And it's a question of chance whether or not we come upon this object before we die.

Many years had passed, and everything about Combray that was not part of the theatre and drama of my bedtime had ceased to exist for me, when one winter's day, when I came home, my mother, seeing I was cold, suggested that I have a cup of tea, something I didn't normally do. I declined at first, but then, I don't know why, changed my mind. She sent for one of those small, plump sponge cakes called 'petites madeleines', which look as though they've been moulded in the corrugated valve of a scallop shell.* And soon, mechanically, oppressed by the gloomy day and the prospect of a similar day to follow, I raised to my lips a spoonful of the tea in which I'd softened a piece of the cake. But at the very moment when the mouthful of tea and cake-crumbs touched my palate, a thrill ran through me and

I immediately focused my attention on the extraordinary thing that was happening inside me. A delicious feeling of pleasure had invaded me, isolating me, without my having any inkling as to its cause. It had instantly made the vicissitudes of life unimportant to me, its disasters innocuous, its brevity illusory, acting in the same way that love acts, by filling me with a precious essence: or rather, this essence was not in me, it was me. I no longer felt mediocre, contingent, mortal. Where could it have come from, this powerful feeling of joy? I sensed that it was connected to the taste of the tea and the cake, but that it went far beyond it, couldn't be of the same nature. Where did it come from? What did it mean? How could I grasp it? I drink a second mouthful, in which I find nothing more than in the first, then a third that tells me rather less than the second. It's time for me to stop, the potion seems to be losing its effect. It's clear that the truth I'm seeking is not in the drink but in me. The drink has awoken it within me, but doesn't know what it is, and can only repeat indefinitely, with less and less force, the same testimony, which I, too, don't know how to interpret, though I hope at least to be able to call upon the tea again and to find the truth there, intact and at my disposal, for definitive clarification. I put down the cup and turn to my mind. It's up to my mind to find the truth. But how? What grave uncertainty, whenever the mind feels overtaken by itself; when it, the seeker, is also the dark region where it must seek and where all its attributes will be of no avail. Seek? Not only that: create. My mind is faced with something that does not yet exist and that only it can bring into being and into the light.

And I ask myself once more what it could have been, this unfamiliar state which brought with it no logical proof, but the manifest reality, of bliss, a feeling so real that it made other states of consciousness fade away. I want to try to make it reappear. I go back over my thoughts to the moment when I drank the first spoonful of tea. This produces the same feeling but still no clarity. I ask my mind to make a fresh effort, to bring the fleeting sensation back once more. And, so that nothing will impede the leap of my mind as it tries to recapture that sensation, I shut out every obstacle, every extraneous idea, I stop my ears and my perception from the noises in the next room. But, feeling my mind growing tired without achieving anything, I now make it accept the distraction I've just denied it, to think of other things, to gather its strength before making a last, supreme effort. Then for a second time I create an empty space before it, I confront it once more with the still recent taste of that first mouthful and I feel a faint tremor inside me; something is moving and trying to rise up, something that had been anchored at a great depth; I don't know what it is, but it's coming up slowly; I can feel the resistance and I can hear the murmur of the spaces traversed.

What is throbbing like this deep inside me must surely be the image, the visual memory linked to that taste, trying to reach me. But its struggles are too far away, too blurred and confused; I can only just make out the neutral reflection in which is blended the indistinguishable vortex of swirling colours; but I can't make out its shape, I can't ask it, as the one possible interpreter, to translate for me the evidence of its contemporary, its inseparable companion, the taste, or ask it to tell me what particular circumstance is being evoked, and from what period of my past life.

Will it emerge into the light of my consciousness, this memory, this old moment which the attraction of an identical moment has travelled so far to summon, to move, to raise up from the depths of my being? I don't know. Now I no longer feel anything, it has stopped, gone back down perhaps; who knows if it will ever climb out of the darkness? Ten times I have to start again, lean down towards it. And each time, the faint-heartedness that deters us from every difficult task, from every important undertaking, has counselled me to leave it, to drink my tea and think only about my present concerns and my desires for the future, which can be mulled over painlessly.

And suddenly the memory came to me. The taste was the taste of the little piece of madeleine that my aunt Léonie would dip in her infusion of tea or lime blossom and give me when I went into her bedroom to kiss her good morning on Sundays (because on Sundays in Combray I never went out before it was time for Mass). The sight of the little madeleine hadn't reminded me of anything before I tasted it; perhaps because I'd often seen them since, without eating them, on pastry-cooks' trays, and their image had become detached from those Combray days and associated with more recent times; perhaps because my recollections of those times had been so long out of mind that nothing survived, everything had crumbled away; the shapes of things—including the shape of the little scallop-like cake, so richly sensual under its severe, religious folds—had either disappeared altogether or had lain dormant and lost the power of expansion that would have allowed them to come back into my consciousness. But when nothing subsists of one's distant past, when the people one knew are dead, when things have been obliterated, smell and taste live on for a long time, alone, more fragile but more enduring, more immaterial but more persistent, more faithful; they are like souls, remembering, waiting, hoping, amid the ruins of all the rest, bearing unfalteringly on their almost impalpable little drop, the vast edifice of memory.

And no sooner had I recognized the taste of the piece of madeleine dipped in lime-blossom tea that my aunt used to give me (though I didn't yet know and had to put off until much later discovering why this memory made me so happy) than the old grey house on the street, where her bedroom was, appeared before me like a stage-set and attached itself to the little cottage, opening on to the garden, that had been built behind it for my parents (the truncated section which until that moment had been all I could see); and with the house the town, at all hours of the day and in all weathers, the Square where they used to send me before lunch, the streets where I went on shopping errands, the country lanes we walked along if it was fine. And just as in the magic trick where the Japanese have fun filling a porcelain bowl with water and steeping in it little pieces of paper which, the moment they become wet, begin to stretch and open, assuming different colours and shapes, turning into flowers, houses, human figures, solid and recognizable, so now all the flowers in our garden and in the grounds of Monsieur Swann's country house, and the water lilies on the Vivonne, and the good folk of the town and their little houses and the church and the whole of Combray and its surroundings, all of this took on shape and substance, and emerged, town and countryside alike, from my cup of tea.

COMBRAY at a distance, for forty kilometres around, seen from the train when we arrived there the last week before Easter, was no more than a church symbolizing the town, representing it, speaking of it and for it as far as the eye could see, and then, as you drew near, appearing like a shepherdess sheltering her sheep from the wind in an open field, gathering close round its long dark cloak the grey fleecy backs of its flock of houses, which the remnants of its medieval ramparts enclosed here and there within a line as perfectly circular as a little town in a primitive painting. To live in, Combray was somewhat dreary, like its streets, whose houses, built of the blackish stone of the locality, fronted by outside steps and capped with gables that cast long shadows in front of them, were so dark that as soon as the daylight began to fade it was necessary to draw back the curtains in the front rooms; streets with the solemn names of saints (several of whom were connected with the early lords of Combray): the Rue Saint-Hilaire, the Rue Saint-Jacques in which my aunt's house stood, the Rue Sainte-Hildegarde which ran past her railings, and the Rue du Saint-Esprit on to which opened the little side gate in the garden; and these streets exist in such a remote part of my memory, painted in colours so different from those in which I now see the world, that all of them, together with the church towering above them in the Square, actually seem even more unreal to me than the images projected by my magic lantern; and at times I feel that to be able to walk across the Rue Saint-Hilaire again, to be able to take a room in the Rue de l'Oiseau—in the old Oiseau Flesché inn, from whose basement windows rose a smell of cooking that, now and then, still rises up within me in the same warm, intermittent bursts—would be to enter into contact with the Beyond in a way more marvellously supernatural than getting to know Golo or chatting with Geneviève de Brabant.

My grandfather's cousin—my great-aunt—in whose house we stayed, was the mother of that same Aunt Léonie who, after the death of her husband, my uncle Octave, was no longer disposed to leave, first Combray, then her house, then her bedroom, then her bed, and now never 'came down', but lay in a perpetual, ill-defined state of grief, physical debility, illness, obsession, and piety. Her own room

looked out on the Rue Saint-Jacques, a long street that led eventually
to the Grand-Pré (as opposed to the Petit-Pré, a green in the middle
of the town where three streets met) and which, in its uniform grey
and with three high sandstone steps in front of nearly every door,
seemed like a narrow passage hewn by a sculptor of Gothic images
out of the very stone he would have used to carve a calvary or a crib.*
My aunt effectively confined her life to two adjoining bedrooms,
spending her afternoons in one of them while the other was being
aired. They were the sort of rooms you find in country houses and
which—just as in some parts of the world whole zones of the air or
sea are illuminated or scented by myriads of protozoa* we can't
see—delight us with the thousand smells emanating from their particular virtues, wisdom, habits, a whole secret, invisible, superabundant, and moral life which the atmosphere holds in suspense; smells
still natural, to be sure, and reflecting the weather like the smells of
the surrounding countryside, but already indoor smells, human and
musty, an exquisite, ingenious, limpid jelly of all the fruits of the year
that have left the orchard for the cupboard; smells changing with the
season, but domestic and homely, offsetting the sharpness of hoar-
frost with the sweetness of warm bread, smells as lazy and punctual as
a town clock, vagrant and settled, carefree and prudent, linen smells,
morning smells, pious smells, happy in a peace that brings an increase
of anxiety, and with a prosaicness that serves as a great reservoir of
poetry to a passing stranger who doesn't live among them. The air
was saturated with a perfect silence, so nourishing, so succulent, that
I could never move through it without a sort of sensual appreciation,
especially on those chilly mornings just before Easter, when I enjoyed
it all the more because I'd only just arrived in Combray: before I went
in to say good morning to my aunt, I had to wait for a little while in
the outer room, where the sun, still wintry, had come to warm itself
before the fire, which was already burning between its two bricks and
was filling the whole room with a sooty smell, turning it into one of
those big frontages you find on farmhouse ovens or one of those
overmantels framing an open hearth in a château, which you sit under
hoping that outside there will be rain or snow or even some catastrophic
deluge, adding the charm of hibernation to the feeling of snug seclusion; I would take a few steps from the prayer stool to the embossed
velvet armchairs always protected by crocheted antimacassars,* while
the fire baked like dough the appetizing smells that clotted the air of the

room and which the sunny, damp coolness of the morning had already leavened, flaking them, browning them, fluting them, and swelling them into an invisible but palpable country cake, an enormous *chausson** to which, barely having tasted the crisper, more delicate, more highly esteemed but drier aromas of the cupboard, the chest of drawers, the floral wallpaper, I always came back, with unacknowledged gluttony, to wallow in the ordinary, sticky, stale, indigestible, and fruity smell of the flowered bedspread.

In the next room I could hear my aunt talking quietly to herself. She always spoke softly because she thought something in her head had broken and become loose and that she would have displaced it if she spoke too loudly, but she never remained for long without saying something, even when alone, believing it was good for her throat and that by keeping the blood circulating there she would reduce the frequency of her bouts of breathlessness and anxiety; besides, in the state of total inertia in which she lived, she attached extraordinary importance to her slightest sensations, endowing them with a motility that made it difficult for her to keep them to herself, and since she had no confidant with whom to share them, she announced them to herself in a never-ending monologue that was her sole form of activity. Unfortunately, having formed the habit of thinking out loud, she didn't always make sure there was no one in the next room, and I would often hear her say to herself: 'I mustn't forget I didn't sleep last night' (for never sleeping was her great claim, a claim recognized and respected in the language of the entire household: in the morning Françoise didn't come to 'wake' her, but simply 'went in'; when my aunt felt like having a nap during the day, we said she wanted to 'think about things' or 'have a rest'; and when she happened to forget herself while chatting, and went so far as to say: 'what woke me up' or 'I dreamt that', she would blush and correct herself at once).

After a moment I would go in and kiss her; Françoise would be brewing her tea; or, if my aunt felt agitated, she would ask instead for her tisane, and it would be my job to take the chemist's little bag and tip on to a plate the right amount of dried lime blossom for infusion in the boiling water. The drying of the stems had twisted them into a fantastic trellis in whose interlacings the pale flowers opened as if they'd been arranged by a painter for the most decorative effect. The leaves, whose original appearance had been lost or altered, looked like the most disparate objects, a fly's transparent wing, the blank side of a label, a rose petal, but they'd all been heaped together, crushed or interwoven as in the construction of a nest. The charming extravagance of the pharmacist had produced all sorts of small details that would have been eliminated in an artificial preparation, but, like a book in which you're amazed to find the name of a person you know, this gave me the pleasure of realizing that these stems were actually the stems of real lime flowers, like the ones I saw in the Avenue de la Gare, only different, precisely because they were not imitations but the same flowers that had grown old. And since each new feature among them was only the metamorphosis of an old feature, in some little grey balls I could see green buds plucked before they could open; but it was especially the pink glow, lunar and soft, that made the flowers stand out amid the fragile forest of stems where they hung like little golden roses—a sign, like the bright patch on a wall that marks the place of a vanished fresco, of the difference between where the flower had blossomed and where it hadn't—that showed me that these petals were in fact the same ones that, before filling the chemist's bag with their fragrance, had scented the spring evenings. That rosy candle-glow was still their colour, but it was dulled and deadened in the diminished life that was theirs now, and which could be called the twilight of the flowers. Shortly my aunt would be able to dip into the boiling infusion, whose taste of dead leaves or withered blossom she so relished, a little madeleine, and then, when it was sufficiently soft, hand me a piece.

On one side of her bed was a large yellow chest of drawers made of lemonwood and a table that served as a kind of dispensary-cum-high-altar, on which, beneath a statuette of the Virgin Mary and a bottle of Vichy-Célestins, could be found her missals and her medical prescriptions, everything she needed for the observance, in bed, of both religion and regimen, for not missing the correct times for pepsin and Vespers.* On the other side of the bed was the window: she had the street there before her, and from morning to night, to break the tedium of her life, like a Persian prince,* she would read in it the daily but immemorial chronicles of Combray, upon which she and Françoise would comment afterwards.

I wouldn't have been with my aunt five minutes before she sent me away for fear I might tire her. She would present to my lips her sad, pale, lifeless forehead, on which, at this early hour, she would not yet have arranged her false hair where the vertebral shapes could be made out like a crown of thorns or the beads of a rosary, and she would say: 'Well, off you go, my dear; get ready for Mass; and if you see Françoise downstairs, tell her not to spend too long with you all down there, she should come up soon to see if I need anything.'

Françoise, who had been in her service for years and at that time did not suspect that one day she would enter exclusively into ours, did in fact neglect my aunt a little during the months when we were there. There had been a time in my childhood, before we went to Combray, when Aunt Léonie still spent the winter in Paris with her mother, and when I knew Françoise so little that, on New Year's Day, as we arrived at my great-aunt's house, my mother would put a five-franc coin in my hand and say: 'Be sure you don't give it to the wrong person. Wait until you hear me say, "Good morning, Françoise"; at the same time, I'll give you a little nudge.' No sooner had we set foot in my aunt's dim hall than we saw in the shadows, beneath the flutes of a dazzling white bonnet as stiff and fragile as if it had been made of spun sugar, the concentric creases of an anticipatory smile of gratitude. This was Françoise, standing motionless, framed in the little doorway of the corridor like the statue of a saint in its niche. When our eyes had become accustomed to the church-like darkness, we could discern on her face the disinterested love of humanity, the fond respect for the upper classes, that the hope of a New Year's present inspired in the nobler regions of her heart. Maman pinched my arm hard and said in a loud voice: 'Good morning, Françoise.' At this signal my fingers opened and I released the coin, which dropped into an embarrassed but welcoming hand. But from the time we started to pay regular visits to Combray, there was no one I knew better than Françoise. We were her favourites, and in the early years at least she not only treated us with the same consideration as my aunt, but also showed a keener appreciation of our company, since, in addition to our prestige as members of the family (she had the respect of a Greek tragedian for the invisible bonds that a common bloodline forms in a family*), we had the attraction of not being her usual employers. And so with what joy she would welcome us, commiserating with us that we didn't have better weather, the day of our arrival, just before Easter, when there was often an icy wind; and Maman would ask after her daughter and her nephews, whether her grandson was a good boy, what future they planned for him, whether he was going to take after his granny.

And when there was no one else there, Maman, who knew that Françoise still mourned her parents who'd been dead for years, would speak about them kindly, asking all sorts of questions about the lives they'd led.

She had guessed that Françoise didn't like her son-in-law and that he spoiled her pleasure in being with her daughter, with whom she couldn't chat freely when he was there. So, when Françoise was setting off for their house, a few kilometres from Combray, Maman would say with a smile: 'I'm sure, Françoise, that if Julien has been called away and you have Marguerite all to yourself for the whole day, you'll be sorry, but you'll make the best of it, won't you?' And Françoise would say, laughing: 'Oh, Madame knows everything; Madame is worse than those X-rays they brought for Madame Octave that see the things you've got in your heart' (she pronounced the 'X' with an affectation of difficulty and a self-deprecatory smile for daring—she, an uneducated woman—to use that clever term*); and she would disappear, embarrassed that anyone should take an interest in her, perhaps so that we wouldn't see her cry: Maman was the first person to give her the heartwarming feeling that her life as a country-woman, with its simple pleasures and sorrows, could be of interest, a reason for joy or sadness, to someone other than herself. My aunt would resign herself to managing without her to some extent during our visits, knowing how much my mother appreciated the services of this hard-working and intelligent maid, who looked as nice at five o'clock in the morning in her kitchen, in her cap whose brilliant, tightly crimped pleats seemed made of porcelain, as she was when dressed for High Mass; who did everything well and worked like a horse, whether she was feeling well or not, and without fuss, as though it were nothing; the only one of my aunt's maids who, when Maman asked for hot water or black coffee, brought it boiling hot; she was one of those servants who, in a household, impress strangers the least, perhaps because they don't bother to ingratiate themselves with them, knowing perfectly well they have no real need of them, that these guests are at greater risk of no longer being invited than they are of being dismissed; but who, on the other hand, are those most valued by employers who have tested them and recognized their qualities, and don't care about the superficial pleasantness, the servile chit-chat that might make a good impression on visitors but often conceals irredeemable incompetence.

When Françoise, having made sure that my parents had everything they needed, went back upstairs for the first time to give my aunt her pepsin and ask what she'd like for lunch, she'd rarely escape being called upon to give her opinion or provide an explanation about some momentous event:

'D'you know, Françoise, Madame Goupil went past more than a quarter of an hour late to fetch her sister; if she hangs about on the way, I wouldn't be at all surprised if she arrives after the Elevation.'*

'No, that wouldn't be surprising,' Françoise would answer.

'Françoise, if you'd come five minutes earlier you'd have seen Madame Imbert go past with some asparagus twice the size of what old Madame Callot sells; try to find out from her maid where she got it. You've been serving up asparagus dishes all the time this year; you could have got some like that for our visitors.'

'I wouldn't be surprised if they came from Monsieur le Curé's* garden,' Françoise would say.

'What an idea, my poor Françoise!' my aunt would reply with a shrug. 'From Monsieur le Curé's garden! You know full well the asparagus he grows is very stringy, no good at all. I tell you, the asparagus I saw was as thick as a person's arm. Not your arm, of course, but my poor arm, which has got thinner than ever this year . . . Françoise, didn't you hear the bell just now? It nearly split my head open!'

'No, Madame Octave.'

'You must have a thick skull, then, my poor girl; you can thank God for that. It was Maguelone coming to get Doctor Piperaud. He came straight back out with her and they turned into the Rue de l'Oiseau. Some child must be ill.'

'Oh dear, dear,' Françoise would sigh, unable to hear of a misfortune befalling a stranger, even in some remote part of the world, without beginning to bewail it.

'Françoise, now who were they ringing the passing bell for? Oh, dear God, it must have been for Madame Rousseau. Fancy me forgetting she passed away the other night. It's really time the good Lord called me home too, I've had a head like a sieve since I lost my poor Octave. But I'm wasting your time, my girl.'

'Not at all, Madame Octave, my time's not as precious as all that; the One who made it gave it to us for nothing. I'm just going to make sure my fire hasn't gone out.'

In this way, in these morning sessions, Françoise and my aunt appraised the first events of the day. Sometimes, however, these events assumed a character so mysterious and so alarming that my aunt felt she couldn't wait until it was time for Françoise to come up, and then four tremendous peals of her bell would resound through the house.

'But Madame Octave, it isn't time for your pepsin yet,' Françoise would say. 'Are you feeling faint?'

'Not at all, Françoise,' my aunt would say. 'I mean, yes: you know, of course, that these days there's very seldom a time when I don't feel faint; one day I'll pass away like Madame Rousseau before I know what's happening; but that's not why I rang. You won't believe it, but I've just seen, with my own eyes, Madame Goupil with a little girl I didn't know at all. Run over to Camus's and get two sous' worth of salt.* It's not often that Théodore can't tell you who a person is.'

'But that'll be Monsieur Pupin's daughter,' Françoise would say, preferring to settle on an immediate explanation, since she'd already been down to Camus's shop twice that morning.

'Monsieur Pupin's daughter! What an idea, Françoise! Don't you think I'd have recognized her?'

'But I don't mean the tall one, Madame Octave; I mean the little one who goes to school in Jouy. I think I seen her once already this morning.'

'Ah! That must be it,' said my aunt. 'She must have come back for the holidays. That's it! There's no need to ask, she'll be here for the holidays. But in that case we'll soon see Madame Sazerat come and ring at her sister's, for lunch. Yes, that'll be it! I saw Galopin's delivery boy go past with a tart. You'll see, that tart was for Madame Goupil.'

'Once Madame Goupil has a guest, it won't be long before you see all her folk going in to have lunch, because the time's getting on,' said Françoise, who was anxious to get back downstairs to see to our own lunch and wasn't sorry to leave my aunt with the prospect of such a distraction.

'Yes, but not before twelve!' my aunt would reply in a tone of resignation, casting an uneasy glance at the clock, but furtively, so as not to let it be seen that she, who had renounced all earthly joys, could still find great pleasure in learning whom Madame Goupil was having to lunch, a pleasure for which she'd have to wait, unfortunately, at least another hour. 'And it'll happen right in the middle of my lunch!'

she'd murmur to herself. Her lunch was sufficient distraction in itself
that she didn't want any other at the same time. 'You won't forget to
give me my creamed eggs on a flat plate, will you?' These were the
only plates with pictures on them, and my aunt amused herself at
every meal by reading the caption on whichever one she happened to
be given that day. She would put on her glasses and read out: Ali Baba
and the Forty Thieves, Aladdin and the Magic Lamp, and say with
a smile: 'Very good, very good indeed.'*

'I'd have gone down to Camus's . . .', Françoise would say, seeing
that now my aunt was not going to send her.

'No, no, there's no point now, it's bound to be the Pupin girl. My
poor Françoise, I'm sorry I made you come up for nothing.'

But, as my aunt knew perfectly well, it was not for nothing that
she'd rung for Françoise, since, in Combray, to see a person 'nobody
knew' was as inconceivable as to encounter a character from Greek
mythology, and indeed no one could remember when, each time one
of these amazing apparitions had materialized in the Rue du Saint-
Esprit or in the Square, careful research hadn't succeeded in reducing the fabulous character to the proportions of a person who 'was
known', either personally or by proxy, in his or her civil status, to be
more or less closely related to some family in Combray. It would be
Madame Sauton's son who was just back from military service, Abbé
Perdreau's niece who had just finished convent school, or the curé's
brother, a tax-collector at Châteaudun, who'd just retired or had
come back for the holidays. On first seeing them, people were amazed
to think there might be in Combray certain individuals they didn't
know at all, but that was simply because they hadn't been recognized
and identified at once. And yet long beforehand Madame Santon and
the curé had made it known they were expecting their 'travellers'. In
the evening, when we came back from our walk and I went upstairs to
tell my aunt about it, and was rash enough to mention that near the
Pont-Vieux we'd passed a man my grandfather didn't know, she
would exclaim: 'A man Grandpa didn't know! What an idea!'
Nevertheless, she'd be a little disturbed by this news and would want
to have the matter cleared up, and so my grandfather would be summoned: 'Who was it, now, that you passed near the Pont-Vieux,
Uncle? A man you didn't know?'

'Of course I knew him,' my grandfather would reply. 'It was
Prosper, Madame Bouillebœuf's gardener's brother.'

'Ah! Good!', my aunt would say, reassured but slightly flushed; then, with a shrug and an ironic smile, she'd add: 'And he told me you passed a man you didn't know!' After which they'd tell me to be more careful about what I said next time and not to upset my aunt with thoughtless remarks. In Combray everybody knew each other so well, animals as well as people, that if my aunt had happened to see a dog go by that she 'didn't know at all', she wouldn't be able to stop thinking about it and would devote to this incomprehensible event all her leisure hours and all her powers of induction.

'That'll be Madame Sazerat's dog,' Françoise would suggest, without any great conviction but in an attempt to pacify my aunt and stop her from getting 'all worked up' about it.

'As if I don't know Madame Sazerat's dog when I see it!' would reply my aunt, whose critical mind would not so readily accept such an assertion.

'Then it'll be the new dog Monsieur Galopin brought back from Lisieux.'

'Ah! That could be it.'

'I hear it's a very friendly creature,' would add Françoise, who'd been told about the dog by Théodore, 'very clever, even-tempered, always friendly and obedient. It's not often such a young dog is so well behaved. But Madame Octave, I'll have to leave you now, I haven't got time to stay here enjoying myself, it's nearly ten o'clock, I haven't even started lighting up my stove yet, and I've still got to trim my asparagus.'

'What, Françoise, more asparagus! You've got a real mania for asparagus this year. You'll make our Parisians go off it completely!'

'No, no, Madame Octave, they really like it. They'll come home hungry from church and you'll see, they won't be picking at their food.'

'Church! They must be there already; you've got no time to lose. Off you go and see to your lunch.'

While my aunt was gossiping with Françoise, I went to Mass with my parents. How I loved our church, how clearly I can see it still! The old porch by which we entered, black and pockmarked, was worn out of shape and deeply furrowed at the edges (like the stoup just inside), as if, over the centuries, the gentle brushing of the countrywomen's cloaks as they entered the church, and of their timid fingers taking holy water, could acquire a destructive force, warp the stone, and carve ruts in it like those made by cartwheels bumping into a boundary-stone every day. Its tombstones, under which the noble dust of the abbés of Combray, who were buried there, formed for the choir a sort of spiritual pavement, were themselves no longer hard and inert matter, for time had softened them and made them flow like honey beyond their own square-shaped confines, so that in one place a flowered Gothic capital* had run like a golden wave on to the violets of the white marble floor; and elsewhere they had shrunk, cramping still further their elliptical Latin inscriptions, adding another touch of fantasy to the arrangement of the compressed characters, closing together two letters of a word of which the other letters had become stretched out of all proportion. Its windows never shone so brightly as on the days when the sun hardly appeared, so that if it was dull outside the church you could be sure it would be fine inside. One window was completely filled by a single figure like a king on a playing card, who lived up there between heaven and earth, under his canopy of stone (and in whose slanting blue light, on weekdays sometimes, at noon, when there's no service—at one of those rare moments when the empty, airy church, with sunlight on its rich furnishings, seemed a more human and luxurious place, almost as habitable as the hall of some medieval-style mansion, all sculpted stone and painted glass—you might see Madame Sazerat kneel for a moment, placing on the next prayer stool a neatly tied packet of petits fours she'd just collected from the baker's opposite the church and was going to take home for lunch); in another, a mountain of pink snow, at whose foot a battle was being fought, seemed to have frosted the glass itself, which it swelled with its cloudy sleet like a windowpane to which a few flakes still clung, but flakes lit up by the glow of dawn (the same, no doubt, that tinged the altarpiece with tints so fresh they seemed thrown on it fleetingly by the gleaming light outside, which would vanish at any moment, rather than by the colours adhering for ever to the stone); and all were so old that here and there you could see their silvery age sparkling with the dust of centuries and showing, in their now threadbare brilliance, the weft of their soft tapestry of glass. One of them, a tall panel, consisted of a hundred little rectangular panes in which blue predominated, like a great pack of cards of the kind devised to amuse King Charles VI;* but a moment later, either because a sunbeam was coming through or because my shifting gaze had extinguished and then rekindled an extraordinary flickering fire in

the coloured panes, it had taken on the shimmering radiance of a peacock's tail, then quivered and rippled in a flaming, fantastic shower of
rain that streamed down from the top of the dark, rocky vault, along
the damp walls, as if I was walking through the nave of some dazzling
grotto full of sinuous stalactites, following my parents with their
prayer books; a moment later the little lozenge-shaped panes had
assumed the profound transparency and unbreakable hardness of
sapphires clustered together on the front of a priest's enormous ornamented vestment, behind which could be sensed, more precious than
all these riches, a fleeting smile from the sun; it was as recognizable in
the soft blue stream with which it bathed the jewelled windows as on
the cobbles in the Square or the straw in the marketplace; and even on
our first Sundays, when we arrived before Easter, this sunshine consoled me for the black, bare earth outside, by bringing into bloom, as
in some historical springtime dating from the age of Saint Louis's
successors,* this dazzling, gilded carpet of glass forget-me-nots.

Two tapestries of high warp represented the coronation of Esther*
(tradition had it that Ahasuerus had been given the features of a king
of France and Esther those of a lady of Guermantes* with whom he'd
fallen in love), to which the colours, by running into each other,
had added expression, relief, and light: a touch of pink had strayed
beyond the outline of Esther's lips; the yellow of her dress was so
creamy and rich that it had acquired a kind of solidity and stood out
boldly against the muted background; and the green of the trees, still
bright in the silk and wool of the lower parts of the panel but faded at
the top, set off in a paler tone, above the dark trunks, the yellowing
upper branches, gilded and half obliterated by the sharp, slanting
rays of an invisible sun. All this, and even more so the treasures that
had come into the church from figures who for me were almost
legendary (the gold cross worked, it was said, by Saint Éloi and presented by Dagobert, the tomb of the sons of Louis the Germanic,
made of porphyry and enamelled copper*), because of which I walked
forward into the church, as we made our way to our seats, as into
a valley visited by fairies, in which a country person is amazed to see
in a boulder or a tree or a pond the palpable traces of their supernatural passage—all this made the church, for me, something entirely
different from the rest of the town: a building occupying, so to speak,
a four-dimensional space—the fourth being Time—extending over
the centuries its nave which, from bay to bay, from chapel to chapel,

seemed to straddle and conquer not only a few metres of ground but successive eras of history from which it had emerged victorious; hiding the brutal, barbaric eleventh century in the thickness of its walls, through which nothing could be seen of the heavy arches, plugged and blinded by crude blocks of quarry stone, except where, near the porch, a deep cleft had been hollowed out by the tower staircase, and even there the barbarity was concealed by the graceful Gothic arcades that crowded coquettishly in front of it like smiling older sisters trying to prevent strangers from seeing their ill-mannered, ill-dressed bumpkin of a younger brother; raising into the sky above the Square its tower, which had looked down on Saint Louis and seemed to see him still; and thrusting down with its crypt into a Merovingian darkness, in which, guiding us as we groped our way under the shadowy vault, powerfully ribbed like the wing of an immense stone bat, Théodore and his sister would show us by candlelight the tomb of Sigebert's little daughter,* on which a deep, valve-shaped cavity—like the bed of a fossil—had been dug, it was said, 'by a crystal lamp which, on the night when the Frankish princess was murdered, had detached itself, of its own accord, from the golden chains by which it hung on the site of the present apse and, without its glass being broken or its flame going out, had sunk into the stone, which had given way beneath it'.*

And the apse of the Combray church: what can be said about it? It was so crude, so devoid of artistic beauty, and even of religious feeling. From the outside, since the intersection of streets it overlooked was on a lower level, its blank wall rose up from a sub-foundation of unfaced rock studded with pebbles, and it had nothing particularly ecclesiastical about it, its windows seemed to have been set far too high, and the whole thing looked more like a prison wall than the wall of a church. And certainly, years later, when I thought back on all the glorious apses I'd seen, it would never have occurred to me to compare the apse of Combray with any of them. But one day, when I turned a corner in a little country town, I came upon three alleys that converged, and opposite them I saw a rough-hewn and unusually high wall, with windows set near the top and the same lopsided appearance as the apse in Combray. At that moment I didn't ask myself, as I would have in Chartres or Rheims,* how powerfully it expressed religious feeling, but instinctively exclaimed: 'The Church!'

The church! A familiar friend, flanked in the Rue Saint-Hilaire, where its north door was situated, by its two neighbours, Monsieur Rapin's pharmacy and Madame Loiseau's house, whose walls it abutted without the slightest gap; a simple citizen of Combray that could have had its own street number if the streets of Combray had had numbers, and at whose door you felt the postman should stop on his morning rounds, before going into Madame Loiseau's and after leaving Monsieur Rapin's; there existed, however, between it and everything in Combray that was not it a line of demarcation which my mind has never been able to cross. Even though Madame Loiseau had a window box full of fuschias that developed the bad habit of forever letting their stems run wild with their heads down, and whose flowers had no more important business, when they were big enough, than to go and cool their flushed, violet cheeks against the dark front of the church, to me this didn't make the fuschias in any way holy; although to my eye there was no gap between the flowers and the blackened stone against which they leaned, in my mind they were worlds apart.

The steeple of Saint-Hilaire could be seen from a long way off, inscribing its unforgettable shape on a horizon where Combray hadn't yet appeared; when my father caught sight of it from the train bringing us down from Paris in Easter week, he'd say, as it slid this way and that over all the furrows of the sky and sent its little iron weathercock spinning in all directions: 'Come on, fold the rugs up, we're here.' And on one of the longest walks we used to take from Combray, there was a spot where the lane suddenly opened out on to a great plateau closed off at the horizon by a jagged ridge of forest above which the only thing that could be seen was the delicate tip of the steeple of Saint-Hilaire, but so slender, so pink, that it seemed scratched on the sky by a fingernail that wanted to give the landscape, a pure tableau of nature, this little artistic touch, this single indication of human existence. When you drew near and could see the remains of the square, half-ruined tower, still standing next to the steeple but not as high, what struck you most was the dark, reddish tone of the stones; and on a misty morning in autumn you might have thought, to see it rising above the stormy violet of the vineyards, that it was a ruin of crimson, almost the colour of Virginia creeper.

Often, when we were on the way home after a walk, my grand-mother would make me stop in the Square to look up at it. From the windows of the tower, placed two by two one above the other, with that perfect and original proportion in their spacing that gives beauty and dignity not just to human faces, it released, it let fall at regular intervals flocks of crows which for a little while would wheel about cawing, as if the old stones, which usually let them hop and flutter about without seeming to notice, had become inhospitable and were discharging some kind of extreme agitation that had suddenly struck them and driven them out. Then, after criss-crossing in all directions the violet velvet of the evening air, they would return, suddenly calm, to become part of the tower, baneful no longer but once more benign, several of them perched here and there, seeming not to move but occasionally snapping up some insect on the top of a turret, like a seagull, motionless with the stillness of an angler, on the crest of a wave. Without really knowing why, my grandmother found in the steeple of Saint-Hilaire the same absence of vulgarity, pretension, and meanness of spirit that made her love and deem rich in beneficent influence not only nature (when the hand of man had not, unlike my great-aunt's gardener, diminished it) but also works of artistic genius. And indeed, every part of the church we could see was distinguished from any other building by a kind of inherent thoughtfulness, but it was in its steeple that it seemed to display full self-awareness, to affirm its individual and responsible existence. It was the steeple that spoke for the church. I think, really, that in her confused way my grandmother found in the steeple of Combray what she prized above anything else in the world: an air of naturalness and an air of distinction. Knowing nothing about architecture, she would say: 'My dears, you can laugh at me if you like, it's not what most people would call beautiful, but there's something about its funny old face that I like. If it could play the piano, I'm sure it wouldn't play without feeling.' And when she looked up at it, following the gentle tension, the fervent inclination of its slopes of stone, which came together as they rose, like hands joined in prayer, she became so absorbed in the expressive power of the spire that her gaze seemed to yearn upwards with it; and at the same time she would smile amiably at the worn old stones, of which the setting sun now illuminated only the topmost parts and which, the moment they entered that sunlit zone and were softened by it, seemed suddenly to have risen much higher, like distant-sounding falsettos singing an octave above the rest of the choir.

It was the steeple of Saint-Hilaire that gave every occupation, every hour of the day, every point of view in the town their shape, their crown, their consecration. From my bedroom I could see only its base, which had been freshly covered with slates; but when, on warm Sunday mornings in summer, I saw them blazing like a black sun, I'd say to myself: 'Good heavens! Nine o'clock! I must get ready for Mass if I want to have time to go and give Aunt Léonie a kiss first,' and I'd already know the exact colour of the sun in the Square, feel the heat and dust of the market, and see the shadow cast by the awning of the shop Maman might drop into on her way to Mass, breathing in its smell of unbleached linen, to buy a handkerchief or something which the draper would have her shown, puffing out his chest; he would have been getting ready to close, having just gone into the back shop to slip on his Sunday jacket and wash his hands, which he was in the habit, every few minutes and even on the saddest occasions, of rubbing together in a businesslike, self-satisfied manner.

When, after Mass, we went in to ask Théodore to bring a larger brioche than usual because our cousins had taken advantage of the fine weather to come over from Thiberzy to have lunch with us, we had the steeple there in front of us, itself baked golden-brown like a much larger holy brioche, flaky and sticky because of the sun, pointing its sharp tip into the blue sky. And in the evening, when I was coming in from a walk and thinking about the impending moment when I'd have to say goodnight to my mother and see her no more, the steeple was by contrast so soft in the fading light that it looked as if it had been set down and pushed like a brown velvet cushion against the pale sky which had yielded under its pressure, had given way a little to make room for it, and had consequently risen on either side; while the cries of the birds that wheeled around it seemed to intensify its silence, make its spire stretch even higher, and invest it with a quality no words could express.

Even when we had to do some shopping in the streets behind the church, where it couldn't be seen, everything seemed arranged in relation to the steeple, which would rise up here and there between the houses, and was perhaps even more affecting when it was seen thus, without the church. And indeed, there are many steeples that look best when seen that way; I can call to mind vignettes of rooftops surmounted by steeples that are far more aesthetically pleasing than those composed by the dreary streets of Combray. I will never forget, in a quaint Normandy town near Balbec, two venerable, charming eighteenth-century houses, dear to me for many reasons, between

which, when you look up at them from the lovely garden that slopes
down from the front steps to the river, the Gothic spire of a church
hidden behind them soars up, seeming to crown and complete their
façades, but in a material so unusual, so lovely, so ribbed, so pink, so
polished, that you can see at once that it is no more a part of them than
the crimson crinkled spire of some seashell, tapered like a turret and
glazed with enamel, is a part of the pretty pair of pebbles between
which it has been caught on the beach. Even in Paris, in one of the
ugliest parts of the city, I know a window from which you can see,
beyond a foreground, a middle ground, and even a third ground made
up of the serried roofs of several streets, a violet bell-like shape, at
times reddish, at other times, in the best 'proofs' produced by the
atmosphere, an ashy black; it turns out to be the dome of Saint-
Augustin, and it gives this view of Paris the feel of certain views of
Rome by Piranesi.* But however adept my memory was at conjuring
up these little engravings, it was incapable of putting into any of them
what I had long lost—the feeling that makes us see a thing not as
a spectacle, but believe in it as a unique being; and so, none of them has
such a powerful hold over a whole submerged part of my life as does
the memory of those views of the Combray steeple from the streets
behind the church. Whether we saw it at five o'clock, when we went to
collect letters from the post office, a few doors away from us on the
left, suddenly punctuating the ridge of rooftops with its isolated peak;
whether, on the other hand, we wanted to call on Madame Sazerat, our
eyes would follow the same roofline, lower again after the descent of its
other slope, knowing we would have to take the second turning on the
left after the steeple; whether, if we went further, to the station, we saw
it obliquely, showing in profile fresh angles and surfaces, like a solid
body surprised at some unknown point in its revolution; or whether,
seen from the banks of the Vivonne, the apse, gathering itself muscu-
larly and heightened by the perspective, seemed to spring upwards
with the effort the steeple was making to thrust its spire far into the
sky: it was always to the steeple that we had to return, always the
steeple that dominated everything, summoning the houses with its
unexpected pinnacle, raised before me like the finger of God, whose
body might be hidden in the crowd of mortals but without any danger
of my not being able to distinguish it from them. And even today, if
I lose my way in a large provincial town or an unfamiliar part of Paris,
and a helpful passer-by shows me in the distance, as a reference point,

some hospital belfry, or a convent steeple lifting the peak of its ecclesi-astical cap at the corner of a street I should take, my memory has only to find in it a faint resemblance to that dear, long-vanished outline; the passer-by, should he turn to make sure I'm going the right way, would be amazed to find me still standing there, motionless, gazing at the steeple for hours, forgetting my walk or the place where I was supposed to be going, trying to remember, feeling deep within me lands reclaimed from oblivion beginning to dry out and buildings rising up on them again; and at that moment I'm no doubt again trying to find my way, but more anxiously than just now when I asked the passer-by for directions—I'm turning a corner . . . but . . . my path is in my heart.

As we walked home from Mass we'd often meet Monsieur Legrandin, who was detained in Paris by his professional duties as an engineer and, except during the summer holidays, could come down to his property in Combray only from Saturday evening until Monday morning. He was one of those men who, quite apart from a brilliantly successful scientific career, have acquired an entirely different kind of culture, in literature and the arts, which plays no part in their profes-sional specialization but enriches their conversation. Better read than many men of letters (we didn't know at the time that Monsieur Legrandin had a certain reputation as a writer and we were very sur-prised to learn that a well-known composer had set some verses of his to music) and possessing a greater talent than many painters, they imagine the life they are leading is not the one for which they are best suited, and they carry out their regular occupations either with a nonchalance tinged with whimsy, or an application that is unrelent-ing and supercilious, scornful, bitter, and conscientious. Tall, with a handsome bearing, a delicate, thoughtful face, a long blond mous-tache, and melancholy blue eyes, beautifully courteous, a conversa-tionalist the like of whom we'd never known, he was in the eyes of the family, who always held him up as an example, the epitome of a gentle-man, approaching life in the noblest, most sensitive way. My grand-mother's only criticism was that he spoke a little too well, a little too much like a book, that in the way he used language there was none of the naturalness of his loosely knotted Lavallière cravats* or his short, straight, almost schoolboyish coat. She was also surprised by the ferocious tirades he'd often unleash against the aristocracy, fashion-able society, and snobbery ('certainly the sin Saint Paul has in mind when he talks about the sin for which there is no forgiveness'*).

Worldly ambition was something my grandmother was so incapable of experiencing, or even understanding, that she couldn't see the point of attacking it with such passion. Besides, she didn't think it in very good taste that Monsieur Legrandin, whose sister near Balbec was married to a titled gentleman from Lower Normandy, should indulge in such violent invective against the nobility, going so far as to say he was sorry the Revolution had failed to have them all guillotined.

'Greetings, friends!' he'd say when we met. 'You're lucky to be able to spend so much time here; tomorrow I'll have to go back to Paris, to my little kennel. Of course, I admit,' he'd add, with his particular smile—slightly ironic, disillusioned, distracted—'I've got every useless thing in the world in my house. The only thing I don't have is the one essential thing, a great patch of blue sky like this one here. Always try to keep a patch of blue sky over your life, my boy,' he added, turning to me. 'You've got a fine soul, of rare quality, an artist's nature; you must never let it go without what it needs.'

When we got home my aunt wanted to know if Madame Goupil had arrived late for Mass, but we were unable to enlighten her. Instead, we increased her unease by telling her there was a painter at work in the church copying the window of Gilbert the Bad.* Françoise was despatched at once to the grocer's, but came back none the wiser owing to the absence of Théodore, whose two occupations, as cantor with a role in the maintenance of the church and grocer's assistant, gave him connections with all sections of Combray society and therefore encyclopedic knowledge of all things pertaining to them.

'Oh dear!' sighed my aunt. 'I wish it was time for Eulalie to come. She's really the only one who can tell me.'

Eulalie was a deaf and energetic spinster with a limp who had 'retired' after the death of Madame de la Bretonnerie, with whom she'd been in service ever since she was a child, and had then taken a room next to the church, from which she was constantly emerging either for the services or, if there was no service, to say a little prayer or to give Théodore a hand; the rest of the time she would visit the sick, such as Aunt Léonie, to whom she would relate everything that had happened at Mass and Vespers. She was not averse to adding some occasional pocket money to the little pension she received from her former employers by going now and again to see to the curé's linen or that of some other notable personage in the clerical world of Combray. Above her cloak of black cloth she wore a little white coif, almost like a nun's, while a skin disease gave her crooked nose and parts of her cheeks the bright pink colour of an impatiens flower.* Her visits were the one great source of entertainment left to Aunt Léonie, who hardly received anyone else now, apart from Monsieur le Curé. My aunt had gradually got rid of all the other visitors because in her eyes they were all guilty of belonging to one or the other of the two categories of people she detested. One group, the worse of the two, whom she'd got rid of first, consisted of those who'd advised her not to 'mollycoddle' herself, and were adherents (if only negatively, through the occasional disapproving silence or sceptical smile) of the subversive doctrine that a little walk in the sun and a good rare steak would do her more good (when just two miserable sips of Vichy water stayed undigested in her stomach for fourteen hours!) than her bed and her medicines. The other group was made up of the people who appeared to believe she was more seriously ill than she thought, that she was as seriously ill as she said she was. And so, those she had allowed, after some hesitation and only as a result of Françoise's polite insistence, to come upstairs, and who in the course of their visit had shown how unworthy they were of the favour being granted by venturing a timid 'Don't you think that if you got out a bit when the weather's fine . . .?' or who, on the other hand, when she said: 'I'm in a bad state, very bad, I can't have much time left . . .', had replied: 'Oh, you poor thing, it's awful when your health goes! Still, you may last a while yet', all alike could be sure that her door would never be opened to them again. And if Françoise was amused by my aunt's look of horror when she peered down from her bed and saw one of these people in the Rue du Saint-Esprit apparently on their way to pay her a visit, or when she heard the doorbell, she laughed even more, as at a clever trick, by the unfailing stratagems used by my aunt to have them turned away, and by their discomfited expressions as they walked off without having seen her; and she would be filled with secret admiration for her mistress, whom she felt to be superior to all these people since she didn't want to see them. In short, my aunt demanded that anyone allowed to see her should, at one and the same time, approve of her regimen, sympathize with her for her sufferings, and reassure her as to her eventual recovery.

This was where Eulalie excelled. My aunt might say twenty times in a minute: 'The end is near, my poor Eulalie,' each time Eulalie would reply: 'Knowing your illness as you do, Madame Octave, you'll live to be a hundred, as Madame Sazerin was saying to me only yesterday.' (One of Eulalie's most deeply rooted beliefs, which the huge number of corrections she'd received over the years had failed to dislodge, was that Madame Sazerat's name was Madame Sazerin.)

'I'm not asking to live to a hundred,' my aunt would say, preferring not to have assigned too precise a term to her life.

And since, along with this, Eulalie knew better than anyone how to entertain my aunt without tiring her, her visits, which took place regularly every Sunday unless something unforeseen prevented them, were for my aunt a pleasure the prospect of which kept her on those days in a state that was at first pleasant, but soon became painful, like mounting hunger, if Eulalie was a moment late. If unduly prolonged, the rapture of expectation turned to torture, and my aunt would look constantly at the clock, yawning and feeling faint. The sound of Eulalie ringing the bell, if it came at the very end of the day, when she was no longer expecting it, would make her feel almost ill. The fact was that on Sundays she thought of nothing else but this visit, and as soon as lunch was over Françoise would be keen for us to leave the dining room so she could go upstairs to keep my aunt 'occupied'. But (especially after the fine weather was set fair in Combray) the proud hour of noon, descending from the belfry of Saint-Hilaire which it emblazoned with the twelve brief fleurons of its sonorous crown, would long since have sounded in our ears as we sat at table, with our *Arabian Nights* plates and the consecrated bread which, in its familiar way, had also come in with us from the church; and we'd carry on sitting there, weighed down by the heat and especially by the meal. For, to the permanent foundation of eggs, cutlets, potatoes, preserves, and cakes, which she no longer even announced she was serving, Françoise would add—according to the labours in the fields and orchards, the harvest of the tides, bargains in the market, the kindness of neighbours, or what her own inventiveness might provide, so that our menu, like the quatrefoils* carved on the portals of cathedrals in the thirteenth century, reflected somewhat the changing seasons as well as the chance events of daily life—a brill because the fishmonger had guaranteed it was fresh; a turkey because she'd seen a beauty at the market in Roussainville-le-Pin; cardoons with marrow because she'd never done them that way for us before; a leg of mutton because fresh air gives you an appetite and there'd be plenty of time for it to be digested before dinner at seven; spinach, just for a change;

apricots because they were still hard to get; redcurrants because in two weeks there would be none left; raspberries that Monsieur Swann had brought specially; cherries because the tree in the garden had borne fruit for the first time in two years; cream cheese, which I really liked in those days; an almond cake because she'd ordered it the day before; a brioche because it was our turn to provide one for Easter Mass. And when all this had been consumed, there would be placed before us a creation expressly made for us but more particularly for my father, who was extremely fond of it: *crème au chocolat*, a special invention of Françoise's, as ephemeral and light as an 'occasional' piece of music into which she had poured the whole of her talent. Anyone who declined it, saying: 'No, thank you, I've had enough, I couldn't eat any more,' would have been relegated immediately to the rank of those barbarians who, even when an artist makes them a gift of one of his works, consider only its weight and material, whereas the sole thing of value is the artist's intention and signature. To have left a single drop in the dish would have been to show as much discourtesy as to walk out of a concert during a performance under the nose of the composer.

Eventually my mother would say: 'Come on now, don't sit here all day, go up to your room if you're too hot outside, but get some fresh air first so you don't start reading the moment you leave the table.' I'd go and sit by the pump and its trough, which was often ornamented, like a Gothic font, with a salamander whose allegorical tapering body looked like a sculpted mobile relief on the rough stone; I'd stay there a while, on the backless bench shaded by a lilac tree, in the little untended corner of the garden that opened via a service gate on to the Rue du Saint-Esprit, and where, up two steps, the scullery was to be found, jutting out from the house, almost like a separate building. With its red-tiled floor gleaming like porphyry, it looked not so much like Françoise's lair as a little temple dedicated to Venus. It overflowed with the offerings of the dairyman, the fruiterer, and the greengrocer, who came sometimes from quite distant villages to dedicate to the goddess the first fruits of their fields. And its roof was always crowned with a cooing dove.

In earlier years I never lingered in the sacred grove that surrounded the scullery, for, before going upstairs to read, I'd go into the little sitting room that my uncle Adolphe, a brother of my grandfather's and an old soldier who'd retired as a major, occupied on the ground floor, a room that, even when its windows were open and it let in the heat, if not the rays of the sun, which seldom reached that far, gave off perpetually that strange, cool smell, redolent of both wooded estates and Old France, that sends your nostrils into a daydream when you venture into certain abandoned hunting lodges. But for a number of years now I hadn't been into Uncle Adolphe's little room, since he'd stopped coming to Combray because of a quarrel that had arisen between him and my parents, through my fault. It had happened as follows:

Once or twice a month, in Paris, I'd be sent to visit him, as he was finishing lunch, wearing a loose informal coat, waited on by his manservant in a work jacket of violet and white striped twill. He'd complain that I hadn't come to see him in ages, that we were forgetting him; he'd offer me a piece of marzipan or a tangerine, and we'd go through a drawing room in which no one ever sat, where no fire was ever lit, whose walls had gilded mouldings, its ceiling painted blue to look like the sky and its furniture upholstered in satin, as at my grandparents', only yellow; and we'd arrive in what he called his 'study', hung with those prints depicting, against a dark background, a plump pink goddess riding a chariot, bestriding a globe, or wearing a star on her forehead, that were popular during the Second Empire* because it was felt there was something Pompeian about them, which were later hated, and are now coming back into favour for one simple reason (despite the other reasons given), namely, that they are reminiscent of the Second Empire. I'd stay with my uncle until his servant came up to say the coachman was asking when he should bring the carriage round. My uncle would then become lost in thought, while his bemused servant, not daring to make the least movement lest he disturb him, stood there waiting for an answer, which never varied. At last, but most hesitantly, he would unfailingly utter the words: 'A quarter past two', which the servant would repeat with an air of surprise, but without disputing them: 'A quarter past two? Very good . . . I'll go and tell him.'

In those days I was in love with the theatre (but platonically, because my parents had not yet allowed me to set foot inside a theatre), and the way I imagined the pleasures to be enjoyed there was so inaccurate that I almost believed each member of the audience looked as though through a stereoscope at a scene on the stage that existed for him alone, but was similar to the hundreds of others being looked at, quite separately, by the other spectators.

Every morning I'd run to the Morris column* to see what plays were being advertised. Nothing was ever more pleasant or disinterested than the daydreams inspired in my imagination by these posters, daydreams created by the images inscribed in the words that made up the plays' titles and also by the damp, paste-blistered bills on which the titles stood out. Except for strange works such as *Le Testament de César Girodot* or *Œdipe-Roi*, which were printed not on the green posters of the Opéra-Comique but the claret-coloured posters of the Comédie-Française, nothing seemed to me more different from the sparkling white plume of *Les Diamants de la Couronne* than the smooth, mysterious satin of *Le Domino Noir*,* and since my parents had told me that, for my first visit to the theatre, I would have to choose between these two plays, which I knew only by their titles, I would ponder the mystery of each title in turn, to grasp in each a foretaste of the pleasure it held in store and to compare it to the pleasure that lay concealed within the other title, until in the end I managed to picture to myself so vividly, on the one hand a play that was dazzling and dramatic, on the other a play that was soft and velvety, that I was as incapable of deciding which one I'd prefer to see as if, for dessert, I had to choose between rice pudding *à l'Impératrice*** and *crème au chocolat*.

All my conversations with friends were about actors, and acting, though as yet I knew nothing about it, was, of all the art forms, the one that gave me a presentiment of what Art was. Between one actor's way of inflecting his voice in a major speech and another's, the minutest differences seemed to me of the utmost importance. I would rank them, according to what I'd been told about them, in order of talent, making lists that I'd recite to myself all day long, and in the end these lists became hardened in my brain, obstructing it with their immovability.

Later, when I was at high school, each time the teacher's back was turned and I wrote a note to a new friend, my first question was always whether he'd been to the theatre and whether he thought Got really was the greatest actor, Delaunay second-best, etc. And if, in his opinion, Febvre came below Thiron, or Delaunay below Coquelin, the sudden mobility that the name of Coquelin, losing its stony rigidity, would acquire in my mind, enabling it to move into second place, and the miraculous agility and vitality that made it possible for Delaunay to drop down to fourth, would stimulate and fertilize my brain, returning it to an invigorating sense of flexibility.*

But if these actors preoccupied me so, if the sight of Maubant*
coming out of the Théâtre-Français one afternoon had filled me with
the joy and suffering of love, how much more did the name of a leading lady emblazoned outside the doors of a theatre, how much more,
at the window of a brougham* passing by in the street with its horses'
headbands decked with roses, did the face of a woman I thought
might be an actress leave me in a prolonged state of agitation, as
I made a painful, futile attempt to imagine the kind of life she must
lead! I'd rank the most illustrious in order of talent: Sarah Bernhardt,
La Berma, Bartet, Madeleine Brohan, Jeanne Samary; but I was
interested in them all.* It happened that my uncle knew many of
them and also some courtesans whom I was unable to distinguish
clearly from the actresses. He used to entertain them at his house. If
we went to see him only on certain days, that was because on the other
days he was at home to women whom his family could not very well
have met—that, at least, was what they thought, whereas my uncle,
on the contrary, was only too ready to show his politeness by introducing to my grandmother pretty widows who had perhaps never
been married and countesses with impressive-sounding titles which
were no doubt assumed, or even of making these ladies a present of
some of our family jewels. This had got him into hot water with my
grandfather more than once. Often, when some actress's name was
mentioned in conversation, I'd hear my father say to my mother with
a smile: 'One of your uncle's friends'; and I'd think that the fruitless
novitiate which men of high standing might have to endure, perhaps
for years on end, waiting at the door of some woman who would
ignore their letters and ask her doorman to turn them away, could
have been spared a boy like me by my uncle, who could introduce me
in his own home to the actress who, though inaccessible to so many
others, was his close friend.

And so—using the excuse that a lesson had been moved and had
prevented me several times and would continue to prevent me from
seeing my uncle—one day which was not one of the days set apart for
our visits, I took advantage of the fact that my parents had had lunch
early, slipped out of the house, and instead of going to look at the
theatre posters on the Morris column, which I was allowed to do on
my own, ran to his house. Outside his door I saw a carriage and pair,
with red carnations on the horses' blinkers and in the coachman's
buttonhole. As I was climbing the stairs I heard a laugh and a woman's

voice, and then, as soon as I rang, a silence followed by the sound of doors being closed. The valet came to the door, and on seeing me he seemed embarrassed and said my uncle was very busy and probably couldn't see me; however, he went to tell him of my arrival, and the same voice I'd heard before said: 'Oh, do let him come in, just for a minute, I'd love that. In that photograph you've got on your desk, he looks exactly like his mother, your niece; that's her photograph next to his, isn't it? I'd so like to see the kid, if only for a second.'

I heard my uncle grumble and sound cross; finally the valet showed me in.

The usual plate of marzipan stood on the table and my uncle was wearing his customary tunic; but opposite him, in a pink silk dress with a long string of pearls round her neck, sat a young woman who was just finishing a tangerine. My uncertainty as to whether I should address her as Madame or Mademoiselle made me blush and, not daring to look too much in her direction in case I'd have to speak to her, I went over to give my uncle a kiss. She looked at me and smiled; my uncle said: 'My nephew', without telling her my name, or me hers, probably because, since his difficulties with my grandfather, he'd been trying as far as possible to prevent members of his family from having any kind of contact with acquaintances of this sort.

'He looks so much like his mother,' she said.

'But you've only ever seen my niece in photographs,' my uncle said gruffly.

'I beg your pardon, my dear, I passed her on the stairs last year when you were so ill. It's true I only saw her for a second or two and your stairs are very dark, but it was enough for me to see how beautiful she is. This young man has her lovely eyes, and also *this*,' she said, drawing a finger across her forehead. 'Does your lady niece have the same name as you, my dear?'

'He looks mainly like his father,' growled my uncle, who was no keener to effect an introduction by proxy, by mentioning Maman's name, than to do so in person. 'He's just like his father and also my poor mother.'

'I don't know his father,' said the lady in pink, tilting her head slightly to one side, 'and I never knew your poor mother, my dear. You remember, it was soon after your sad loss that we met.'

I felt a certain disappointment, for this young lady was no different from the other pretty women I'd seen from time to time in our family circle, especially the daughter of a cousin of ours whose parents we visited every New Year's Day. My uncle's friend was better dressed, but she had the same lively, good-natured look, the same open, affectionate manner. I could find no trace in her of the theatrical appearance I admired in photographs of actresses, nor of the diabolical expression that would have been in keeping with the life she must lead. I found it hard to believe she was a courtesan, and I would certainly never have believed she was one of the high-class courtesans had I not seen the carriage and pair, the pink dress and the pearl necklace, and had I not known that my uncle associated only with the most exclusive sort. I kept wondering how the millionaire who paid for her carriage, her town house, and her jewellery could enjoy throwing his money away on someone who, in appearance, was so simple and proper. And yet, when I thought about what her life must be like, the immorality of it disturbed me more, perhaps, than if it had been displayed before me in some clear, concrete form—it was so invisible, like the code in some romantic novel, some scandal that had driven her out of the home of her bourgeois parents, given her to everyone, brought her beauty to full bloom, and propelled her into the demimonde and notoriety; and yet I couldn't help seeing in the play of her features and the intonations of her voice, which were similar to those of other young women I knew already, a girl from a good family, who now belonged to no family at all.

We'd gone into the 'study', and my uncle, seeming somewhat ill at ease because of my presence, offered her the cigarette box.

'No thank you, my dear,' she said. 'You know I can only smoke the ones the Grand Duke sends me. I told him they make you jealous.' And she produced from a case some cigarettes covered in gold lettering in a foreign script. 'Of course!' she exclaimed, 'I must have met this young man's father here, in your house. Isn't he your nephew? How could I have forgotten? He was very nice, most charming.' She said this softly and with some feeling, but, knowing as I did how stiff and cold my father was, I thought that his 'charming' behaviour was in all likelihood quite ungracious, and I felt embarrassed, as though he'd committed some indiscretion, by the disparity between her fulsome appreciation and his lack of amiability. Since then it has struck me that one of the touching aspects of the part played in life by these idle but assiduous women is that they devote their generosity, their talents, a disposable dream of sentimental beauty (for, like artists, they never

seek to realize their dream, or carry it into the realm of a shared existence), and a type of gold that costs them little, to providing a precious
and refined setting for the rough, unpolished lives of men. And just as
this one sat with my uncle in his plain tunic, filling the smoking room
with her lovely person, her dress of pink silk, her pearls, and the distinction that derived from her friendship with a Grand Duke, so in the
same way she had taken some simple remark of my father's, fashioned
it most delicately, bezelled it, given it a proper finish and an impressive
name, set in it the gem of one of her glances, a gem of the first water,
tinged with humility and gratitude, and handed it back transformed
into a jewel, a work of art, something 'most charming'.

'Come on, it's time you were off,' said my uncle.

I stood up, gripped by a desire to kiss the hand of the lady in pink,
but feeling that to do so would be as bold as attempting to abduct her.
My heart pounded as I wondered: 'Should I or shouldn't I?', and
then I stopped asking myself what I ought to do in order actually to
do something. Blindly, madly, not thinking of any of the reasons in its
favour I'd thought of a moment before, I raised to my lips the hand
she was holding out.

'Oh, he's so sweet! Quite a little ladies' man! Just like his uncle!'
she said. And clenching her teeth to give her words a slightly British
accent, she added: 'He'll be a perfect *gentleman*. Couldn't he come
and see me some time for *a cup of tea*, as our neighbours the English
say? He'd just need to send me a "blue" in the morning.'*

I had no idea what a 'blue' was. I didn't understand half of what the
lady was saying, but my fear that her words might conceal some question which it would have been impolite of me not to answer stopped
me from not listening carefully, and I began to feel very tired.

'No, that wouldn't be possible,' said my uncle with a shrug. 'He's
kept very busy, he works very hard.' Then, lowering his voice so that
I wouldn't hear the falsehood he uttered, and contradict him, he
added: 'He wins all the school prizes. Who knows? He may turn out
to be a little Victor Hugo—you know, someone like Vaulabelle.'*

'I adore artists,' replied the lady in pink, 'they're the only ones who
understand women . . . Apart from a few very special men like you.
Forgive my ignorance, my dear, but who is Vaulabelle? Are you talking
about those gilt-edged volumes in the little glass bookcase in your
sitting room? You remember you promised to lend them to me; I'll
take care of them.'

My uncle, who hated lending his books, said nothing and took me out into the hall. Madly in love with the lady in pink, I covered my old uncle's tobacco-stained cheeks with wild kisses, and while, with some embarrassment, he gave me to understand without daring to tell me openly that he'd rather I didn't talk about this visit to my parents, I told him, with tears in my eyes, that I'd never forget his kindness and that one day I'd certainly find a way to show my gratitude. My desire to show my gratitude was so great, in fact, that two hours later, after a few cryptic remarks that didn't seem to me to give my parents a clear enough idea of the new importance with which I'd been invested, I thought it better to describe to them in plain terms, and in every last detail, the visit I'd just paid my uncle. I didn't think that in doing so I was creating trouble for him. How could I have thought that, since I didn't wish it? And I had no way of knowing that my parents would see any harm in a visit in which I saw none. How frequently it happens that a friend asks us to be sure to apologize for him to some woman to whom he has been prevented from writing, and we neglect to do so, feeling that this woman can't attach any importance to a lack of communication that has no importance for ourselves? I imagined, like everyone else, that the brains of other people were inert, passive receptacles without the power to react specifically to whatever was introduced into them; and I was in no doubt that when I deposited in my parents' minds the news of the acquaintance I'd made through my uncle, I was transmitting to them at the same time, as I wished to, my own favourable view of that introduction. Unfortunately, my parents judged my uncle's conduct by a set of principles that were entirely different from those I was implying they should adopt. I heard indirectly that my father and grandfather both spoke to him in the strongest terms. A few days later, I saw my uncle passing in an open carriage, and I felt at once all the distress, gratitude, and remorse I would have liked to convey to him. But it seemed to me that, compared to the immensity of these emotions, merely to raise my cap would appear quite paltry and might make him think I didn't feel I owed him more than the most elementary form of courtesy. I decided to refrain from such an inadequate gesture and turned my head away. My uncle thought that in doing so I was following my parents' orders, he never forgave them, and he died many years later without any of us seeing him again.

And so I no longer went into Uncle Adolphe's sitting room, now kept shut, and would hang around near the scullery until Françoise emerged from her temple and said: 'I'm going to let the scullery maid serve the coffee and take up the hot water, I've got to run up and see to Madame Octave,' whereupon I would decide to go back in and go straight to my room to read. The scullery maid was an abstract personality, a permanent institution whose unvarying set of attributes gave a sort of continuity and identity to the succession of temporary forms in which she was incarnated, for we never had the same girl two years running. The year we ate so much asparagus, the scullery maid whose job was to 'pluck' them was a poor, sickly creature, in a state of advanced pregnancy when we arrived at Easter; we were surprised that Françoise let her do so much work and run so many errands, for she was beginning to have difficulty carrying before her the mysterious basket that grew fuller and larger every day, and whose impressive shape could be discerned beneath the folds of her ample smocks. These smocks were reminiscent of the cloaks worn by some of Giotto's allegorical figures in his frescoes, of which Monsieur Swann had given me photographs.* In fact it was he who had pointed out the similarity, and whenever he asked after the scullery maid he'd say: 'And how is Giotto's Charity?' And indeed the poor girl, whose pregnancy had fattened her, even in her face, so that her cheeks had a straight, square-cut shape, distinctly resembled those strong, mannish virgins (matrons, rather) in whom the seven Virtues are personified on the walls of the Arena Chapel. I realize now that those Virtues and Vices of Padua resembled her in another way, too. Just as the image of this girl was extended by the added symbol she carried before her without appearing to understand its meaning, without showing in her facial expression any appreciation of its beauty and spiritual significance, but bore it as if it were no more than a heavy burden, similarly the strapping housewife portrayed in the Arena Chapel beneath the caption 'Caritas', a reproduction of whose portrait hung on the wall of my schoolroom in Combray, embodies that virtue without seeming to suspect it, without the slightest suggestion of a charitable thought ever having flitted across her strong, vulgar features. The painter has managed beautifully to show her trampling on the treasures of the earth, but for all the world as if she were treading grapes, or rather, as if she had climbed on a pile of sacks to get higher; and she's holding out to God her impassioned heart, or, to be more precise, she's handing it to Him, as a cook might hand a corkscrew through the skylight of her basement kitchen to someone who's asking for it at the ground-floor window. Envy, too, might have had more of an envious expression. But in this fresco the symbol again occupies such a large place and is represented with such realism; the hissing serpent issuing from Envy's lips is so thick, it fills her wide-open mouth so completely, that in order to contain it the muscles of her face are distended, like those of a child blowing up a balloon, and since Envy's attention (and ours as well) is entirely focused on the action of her lips, she hardly has time for envious thoughts.

In spite of the great admiration Monsieur Swann professed for these frescoes of Giotto, it was a long time before I could take any pleasure in contemplating in our schoolroom (where the reproductions he'd brought back for me were hung) that Charity without charity; that Envy who looked more like a plate in a medical textbook illustrating compression of the glottis or the uvula by a tumour on the tongue or by the introduction of a surgical instrument; or that Justice who had the same mean and colourless regularity of features as certain pretty, pious, desiccated bourgeois ladies of Combray I saw at Mass, some of whom had long since enlisted in the reserve militia of Injustice. But in later years I came to understand that the arresting strangeness and special beauty of these frescoes lay in the special role played in them by symbolism, and that, since this symbolism was represented, not in figurative terms (the ideas symbolized being left unexpressed) but as something real, something actually experienced or materially handled, this added something more literal and precise to their meaning, something more concrete and striking to the lesson they were intended to convey. In the case of the poor scullery maid, similarly, our attention was constantly drawn to her belly by the weight it was carrying; and in the same way, again, the thoughts of the dying often turn towards the actual, painful, dark, visceral aspect of death, its underside, which is precisely the side it presents to them and forces them so cruelly to feel, resembling much more closely a crushing burden, a difficulty breathing, a need to drink, than what we call the idea of death.

Those Virtues and Vices of Padua must have had a strong element of the real in them, for they seemed to me as alive as the pregnant servant girl, while she herself appeared scarcely less allegorical than they. And it may be that this lack (or apparent lack) of participation of a person's soul in the virtue of which he or she is the agent, is not simply of aesthetic value but also embodies a reality that, if not psychological, is at least, as they say, physiognomic.* Since then, whenever I've had occasion to meet, in convents for example, truly saintly embodiments of practical charity, they have generally had the brisk, purposeful, unemotional, somewhat abrupt manner of a busy surgeon, the sort of face that shows no sign of commiseration or compassion at the sight of human suffering, and no fear of offending people—the impassive, antipathetic, sublime face of true goodness.

While the scullery maid—unwittingly setting off the superior qualities of Françoise, just as Error, by contrast, makes the triumph of Truth appear even more dazzling—served coffee which, according to Maman, was nothing more than hot water, and then took up to our rooms hot water that was barely tepid, I had lain down on my bed, a book in my hand; my room trembled with the effort to protect its frail transparent coolness from the afternoon sun behind almost closed shutters, through which a gleam of reflected light had nonetheless contrived to slip in on its golden wings, and remained motionless between the wood and the windowpane, in a corner, like a butterfly in repose. There was barely enough light to read, and my sense of the day's splendour was given to me only by Camus (whom Françoise had told that, since my aunt was not 'resting', he could make a noise) as he hammered away in the Rue de la Cure at some dusty packing cases, creating reverberations in the sonorous atmosphere peculiar to hot weather, and seeming to send bright red stars flying up into the air; and also by the flies, performing before me their little concert—the chamber music of summer, so to speak, which does not evoke summer in the same way as human music which you may hear by chance during the hot weather and will remind you of it later, for the music of the flies is connected to the summer in a more compelling way: born of sunny days, reborn only with them, containing something of their essence, it not only awakens their image in our memory, it guarantees their return, their actual, ambient, tangible presence.

The cool gloom of my room was to the broad daylight of the street what a shadow is to a sunbeam, that is to say, it was equally luminous and offered my imagination the entire spectacle of summer, which my senses, if I'd been out walking, could have enjoyed only in fragments; and so it was quite in harmony with my state of repose, which (because of the stirring adventures related in my books) sustained, like a hand held motionless in a stream of running water, the shock and animation of a torrent of activity.

But my grandmother, even if the hot weather had turned bad and a thunderstorm or just a squall had broken, would come up and beg me to go outside. And since I didn't want to stop reading, I'd take my book down into the garden and install myself under the chestnut tree, in a little hooded chair of wicker and canvas in which I'd sit and think I was hidden from the eyes of anyone who might call to see my parents.

And wasn't my mind also a kind of crib in which I remained ensconced even as I observed what was happening in the outside world? When I saw an external object, my awareness that I was seeing it would remain between me and it, surrounding it with a thin spiritual border that prevented me from ever directly touching its material substance; it would dissolve somehow before I could make contact with it, just as an incandescent body moved close to something wet never actually touches the moisture because it's always preceded by a zone of evaporation. On the sort of screen dappled with different states of mind which my consciousness would unfold as I read, and which ranged from my most deep-seated longings to the wholly external picture of the horizon spread out before my eyes at the bottom of the garden, what was the primary, most intimate part of me, the vital mechanism whose workings controlled everything else, was my belief in the beauty and philosophic richness of the book I was reading, and my desire, whatever the book might be, to appropriate them for myself. For even if I'd bought it in Combray, having seen it outside Borange's (whose grocery shop was too far away from the house for Françoise to go there as often as she went to Camus's, but was better for stationery and books) held in place by string in the mosaic of brochures and monthly serials that covered both leaves of the door, a door more mysterious, more replete with ideas than that of a cathedral, it was because I'd recognized it as a book highly recommended by whichever teacher or classmate seemed to me at the time to be privy to the secret of truth and beauty, things I only half apprehended, half understood, and were the vague but perennial object of my thoughts.

After this central belief, which as I read produced constant movement from my inner self towards the outside world in my search for truth, came the emotions aroused in me by the action in which I was taking part, for those afternoons were filled with more drama than occurs, often, in a whole lifetime. This drama consisted of the events happening in the book I was reading. It's true that the characters involved in these events were not 'real people', as Françoise would say. But all the feelings aroused in us by the joys or misfortunes of a real person are produced only through a mental image of those joys or misfortunes; and the ingeniousness of the first novelist lay in his understanding that, since that image is the one essential element in the complicated structure of our emotions, the simplification that would follow from the abolition of real people would be a definite step forward. A real person, however profoundly we sympathize with him, is perceived by us in large measure via our senses, that is to say, he remains opaque, he presents a dead weight that our sensibility cannot lift. If some misfortune befalls him, it's only in one small part of our total idea of him that we can feel emotional sympathy; indeed, it's only in one part of his own total idea of himself that he can feel emotion. The novelist's inspired idea was to replace the parts impenetrable by the heart with an equal quantity of immaterial parts—that is, of the sort the spirit can assimilate. After this it matters little that the actions and feelings of this new order of creatures appear to us to be true, since we've made them our own, since it is within ourselves that they come into being, and that, as we feverishly turn the pages of the book, they control the rapidity of our breathing and the intensity of our gaze. And once the novelist has put us in that state, in which, as in all purely mental states, every emotion is heightened and his book can disturb us in the manner of a dream, but a dream that will be clearer than those we have while asleep and will leave a more lasting memory, then, for the space of an hour, he sets off in us all possible states of happiness and unhappiness, only a few of which we might experience in real life over a period of years and the most intense of which would never be revealed to us because the slowness with which they develop prevents us from being aware of them (that is how the human heart changes in life, and it is the greatest anguish; but we know it only through reading, through our imagination; in reality it changes so gradually, like certain natural phenomena, that even if we are able to observe successively each of its different states, we are still spared the actual experience of feeling it change).

Next in my experience of reading, less internalized than the lives of the characters, was the landscape in which the action took place; half projected before me, it made a much stronger impression on my mind than the actual landscape that met my eyes when I looked up from my book. In this way, for two consecutive summers, as I sat in the heat of our Combray garden, the book I was reading filled me with longing to be in a land of mountains and streams, where I'd see countless saw-mills, and where, deep in the clear water, pieces of wood would lie rotting in beds of watercress; and close by, climbing along low walls, would be clusters of red and violet flowers. And since the dream of a woman who would love me was always present in my mind, during those two summers the dream was suffused with the fresh coolness of running water; and whatever kind of woman I pictured, clusters of red and violet flowers immediately sprang up on either side of her like complementary colours.

This was not only because any mental image produced in our rev-eries is for ever stamped, and its beauty enhanced, by the random colours that happen to surround it as we daydream; for the landscapes in the books I read were for me not merely landscapes more vividly depicted in my imagination than those Combray set before my eyes, but remained very similar to them. By virtue of the author having chosen them, by virtue of the faith with which my mind anticipated his printed word, as if it were a revelation, these landscapes gave me the impression—one I hardly ever gained from the place where I happened to be, and never from our garden, the undistinguished product of the conventional imagination of the gardener so despised by my grandmother—of actually being part of Nature, and worthy of being studied and explored.

If my parents had allowed me, when I was reading a book, to go and visit the region it described, I would have believed I was taking an invaluable step forward in the conquest of truth. For although we have the sensation of being for ever enclosed by our own self, it doesn't feel like a static form of imprisonment: rather, we are as if borne along with it in a perpetual struggle to transcend it, to become part of the world outside ourselves, and we feel a certain discouragement when we hear around us always the same sound, which is not an echo from outside but the resonance of a vibration from within. We try to discover in things the reflection our self has projected on to them, making them precious to us; and we are disappointed when we find that in reality they seem to lack the charm they owed, in our minds, to their associ-ation with certain ideas; sometimes we convert all our inner resources into cleverness, into brilliance, so as to have an effect on people of whose separate existence we are well aware and whom we know are beyond our reach. And so, if I always imagined the woman I loved in the context of the places I most longed at that time to visit, if I wanted her to be the one to show me those places, to open doors to unknown worlds, it wasn't because of a simple chance association of ideas; no, it was because my dreams of travel and love were just moments—which I'm artificially separating today as if cutting sections at different heights in an iridescent, apparently motionless jet of water—in a single irresistible upsurge of all the energy of my life.

Finally, as I continue to trace from the inside outwards these simultaneously juxtaposed states of my consciousness, and before I come to the real horizon that bounds them, I discover pleasures of another kind, the pleasure of being comfortably seated, of breathing in the clean-scented air, of not being disturbed by visitors; and, when an hour rang out from the bell-tower of Saint-Hilaire, of noting what was already spent of the afternoon fall piece by piece until I heard the last chime, which enabled me to add up the total, after which the long silence that followed seemed to mark the beginning, in the blue sky above, of the long stretch of the day I still had left for reading, until the good dinner Françoise was preparing and which would help me to recover from my efforts, during the reading of the book, to keep up with the hero and his adventures. And as each hour rang out it seemed to me that no more than a few seconds had elapsed since the previous hour had struck; the most recent would inscribe itself, close to its predecessor, in the sky, and I could hardly believe that sixty minutes could fit into the little blue arc between their two golden points. Sometimes an hour would even ring prematurely, tolling two strokes more than the last; there must therefore have been an hour I hadn't heard being struck, something that had happened hadn't happened for me; the fascination of my book, as magical as a deep sleep, had tricked my enchanted ears and erased the golden bell from the azure surface of the silence. Those lovely Sunday afternoons under the chestnut tree in the garden in Combray, from which I carefully eliminated all the ordinary events of my own existence and which I replaced with a life of extraordinary adventures and quests in the far reaches of a land washed by running waters—they bring that life back to me when I think of them, for it is for ever contained in those afternoons which, as I went on reading and the heat of the day subsided, slowly encircled and enclosed it in the crystalline succession, slowly changing and dappled with foliage, of their silent, sonorous, fragrant, limpid hours.

Sometimes, in the middle of the afternoon, I'd be torn away from my book by the gardener's daughter, who'd run past like a mad thing, knocking over an orange tree in a tub as she went, cutting a finger, breaking a tooth, and shouting: 'They're coming! They're coming!' so that Françoise and I should run out too and not miss any of the show. This was on the days when the cavalry garrisoned in Combray went out on manoeuvres, usually passing along the Rue Sainte-Hildegarde. The servants had been sitting on a row of chairs outside the garden fence, looking at the people of Combray taking their Sunday walk and being looked at in turn, and the gardener's daughter, through a gap between two distant houses in the Avenue de la Gare, had caught sight of helmets glinting in the sun. The servants would hurry to bring in their chairs, for when the cuirassiers* paraded down the Rue Sainte-Hildegarde they filled the whole width of the street, and the cantering horses brushed against the walls of the houses, occupying both pavements, which were like banks unable to contain a river in flood.

'Those poor boys!' said Françoise, already in tears before she'd even reached the fence; 'those poor youngsters, going off to be cut down like grass in a field!' And she added: 'Just thinking of it shocks me,' putting her hand on her heart, as if to indicate where she had felt the shock.

'It's a wonderful sight, isn't it, Madame Françoise, all those young lads not caring if they lose their lives?' said the gardener, just to pull her leg.

His gambit worked admirably:

'Not caring if they lose their lives? What should we care about if it's not for our lives? It's the only gift the Lord never gives twice. But alas, it's true, they don't care! I saw them in '70;* when they get involved in those wretched wars they lose all fear of death; they turn into madmen; and then they're not worth the rope to hang 'em with; they're not men any more, they're lions.' (For Françoise, the comparison of a man to a lion, which she pronounced lie-on, was anything but a compliment.)

The Rue Sainte-Hildegarde turned too sharply for us to be able to see people coming from far off, and it was only through the gap between the two houses in the Avenue de la Gare that we could still make out more helmets speeding towards us, shining in the sun. The gardener wanted to know if there were many more still to come, because the sun was hot and he was thirsty. So, suddenly, his daughter sallied forth, as if from a besieged city, made a sortie as far as the corner of the street, and after braving death a hundred times, came back with a carafe of liquorice water and the news that there were at least a thousand of them coming in a continuous stream from the direction of Thiberzy and Méséglise. Françoise and the gardener, their earlier disagreement forgotten, discussed how people should behave in time of war.

'As I see it, Françoise,' said the gardener, 'revolution's better, because when a revolution's declared the only ones that take part are those that want to.'

'Oh, yes, well I can see your point there. It's fairer.'

The gardener was also of the view that, as soon as a war was declared, they would stop all the trains.

'Of course!' responded Françoise. 'So as nobody can run away.'

'Aye. They're very crafty!' said the gardener, who would never accept that war was anything other than a nasty trick the State tried to play on the people, or that there wasn't a man in the world who wouldn't run away if he had half a chance.

But Françoise would hurry back to my aunt, I would return to my book, and the servants would resume their positions outside the gate to watch as the dust settled and the excitement caused by the soldiers subsided. Long after calm had descended, the streets of Combray would still be unusually crowded with people out walking. And in front of each house, even those where it wasn't the custom, the servants, and sometimes even the masters, would sit and stare, festooning their doorsteps with a dark, irregular border, like the border of seaweed and shells that a high tide leaves on a beach, like embroidered crêpe, after the water has receded.

Except on days like these, however, I could usually read in peace. But on one occasion I was interrupted by the arrival of Swann, whose comments on the book I was reading—by an author quite new to me, Bergotte*—had the consequence that for a long time afterwards it wasn't against a wall graced with tall clusters of violet flowers, but against a quite different background, the porch of a Gothic cathedral, that I pictured one of the women of whom I dreamed.

I'd heard Bergotte mentioned for the first time by a friend who was older than me and whom I greatly admired, Bloch. When he heard me admit how much I liked *La Nuit d'Octobre*, he burst his sides laughing and said: 'You must get over your dreadful infatuation with Master de Musset.* He's quite odious, an absolutely malign creature. I must admit, though, that he and even that Racine fellow did manage, once in their life, to turn out one quite rhythmical line of verse that also has the great merit, for me, of meaning absolutely nothing. They are: "La blanche Oloossone et la blanche Camyre" and "La fille de Minos et de Pasiphaé".* They were pointed out in defence of those two rogues by my very dear master, the venerable Leconte,* beloved of the immortal gods. Speaking of whom, here's a book I don't have time to read just now, a book recommended, it would seem, by the aforementioned splendid fellow. I've been told he regards the author, a certain Master Bergotte, as a bloke of the highest water; and although at times his judgements are unaccountably generous, for me his word is as sound as the Delphic Oracle.* So do read this lyrical prose, and if the stupendous rhymester responsible for "Bhagavat" and "Le Lévrier de Magnus" has spoken true, then, by Apollo, you will taste, dear master, the ambrosial joys of Olympus.'* It was in a sarcastic tone that he'd asked me to call him, and he'd called me, 'dear master'. But, truth to tell, we took a certain pleasure in this game, for we were still at the age when we believe we make something exist by simply giving it a name.

Unfortunately I was unable to have any further conversations with Bloch and ask him to clarify what he'd said, so that I might assuage the confusion he'd sown in my mind by telling me that beautiful lines of poetry (from which I expected nothing less than a revelation of truth) were all the more beautiful if they had no meaning at all. For Bloch wasn't invited to the house again. At first he'd been made welcome. It was true that my grandfather made out that each time I formed a close attachment to one of my friends and brought him home, he was always a Jew, which wouldn't have bothered him in principle—even his own friend Swann was of Jewish extraction—had he not felt that those I chose as friends were not usually of the best sort. And so when I brought home a new friend, he seldom failed to hum: 'O God of our fathers' from *La Juive* or 'Israel, break thy chain', singing only the tune (tra-la-la . . .), of course, but I'd be afraid my friend might know it and would supply the words.*

Before even seeing them, simply on hearing their names, which often had nothing especially Jewish about them, he'd guess not only the Jewish background of those of my friends who did happen to be

Jewish, but even any skeletons their family might have in their cupboard.

'And what's the name of this friend of yours who's coming this evening?'

'Dumont, Grandpa.'

'Dumont! Oh, I'll be on high alert!'

And he would sing:

> *Archers, faites bonne garde!*
> *Veillez sans trêve et sans bruit;**

Then, after asking a few adroit questions, he would cry out: 'On guard! On guard!' or, if the victim himself had already arrived and had been forced unwittingly, by my grandfather's subtle interrogation, to reveal his origins, then my grandfather, to show us he no longer had any doubts, would simply gaze at us and hum almost inaudibly:

> *De ce timide Israélite*
> *Quoi, vous guidez ici les pas!**

or:

> *Champs paternels, Hébron, douce vallée.**

or occasionally:

> *Oui je suis de la race élue.**

These little eccentricities of my grandfather implied no ill will on his part towards my friends. But Bloch fell out of favour with my family for other reasons. He'd begun by irritating my father, who, noticing his clothes were wet, had asked with keen interest:

'What's the weather like, Monsieur Bloch? Has it been raining? That's odd: the barometer told us it would be perfectly dry.'

To this Bloch had merely replied:

'Monsieur, I'm quite unable to tell you whether it has rained or not. I live so resolutely beyond physical contingencies that my senses don't bother to inform me of them.'

'Well, my dear boy, that friend of yours is an idiot,' my father said when Bloch had left. 'He can't even tell me what the weather's like! As if there's anything more interesting! He's a total halfwit.'

Bloch had also managed to irritate my grandmother because, after lunch, when she said she wasn't feeling well, he'd stifled a sob and wiped away a tear.

'How can he possibly be sincere?' she said. 'It's not as if he knows me. He could be mad, of course.'

And finally, he'd annoyed everybody by turning up an hour and a half late for lunch, covered in mud, and then, instead of apologizing, saying:

'I never let myself be influenced by atmospheric disturbances or conventional ways of measuring time. I'd be very happy to see the reintroduction of the opium pipe and the Malay kris,* but I'm totally ignorant when it comes to the use of those other two implements, which are infinitely more pernicious as well as being dismally bourgeois: the watch and the umbrella.'

In spite of all this he would still have been able to come back to Combray, though he was not, of course, the sort of friend my parents would have chosen for me. In the end they'd decided that his tears over my grandmother's indisposition were genuine; but they knew, either instinctively or from their own experience, that our emotional impulses have little to do with our subsequent actions or the conduct of our lives, and that respect for moral obligations, loyalty to friends, tenacity in completing a task, adherence to a regimen, have a more secure foundation in blind habit than in the fervent and sterile transports of the moment. They would have preferred me to have, instead of Bloch, friends who would have given me no more than it is proper, according to the rules of bourgeois morality, for boys to give one another; who wouldn't unexpectedly send me a basket of fruit because, on that particular day, they'd been thinking of me with affection, but who, being incapable of tipping in my favour, by a simple impulse of their imagination and sensibility, the fine balance of friendship's duties and demands, would be equally incapable of tipping it against me. Even our faults will not easily divert from their duty towards us those natures of which the model was my great-aunt, who, though estranged for years from a niece to whom she never spoke, made no change to the will in which she left that niece her entire fortune, because she was her next of kin and it was the 'done thing'.

But I liked Bloch, my parents wanted me to be happy, and the insoluble problems I posed for myself concerning the meaningless beauty of the daughter of Minos and Pasiphaë left me more exhausted and feeling more unwell than further conversations with him would have done, even though my mother thought they would do me more harm than good. And he would still have been welcome in Combray had it not been for the fact that, after that dinner, having just informed me—a piece of information that was to have a great influence on my life, first by making it happier, then unhappier—that the only thing women thought about was love and that no woman was immune to seduction, he went on to assure me that he'd heard from a very reliable source that my great-aunt had led a scandalous life in her youth and had been known as a kept woman. I could not prevent myself from telling my parents what Bloch had said; the next time he called he was not invited in, and when I met him in the street one day, he gave me a very chilly greeting.

But what he'd said about Bergotte was true.

For the first few days, like a tune you'll come to love but is not yet imprinted on your mind, it wasn't clear to me what I liked so much about his style. I couldn't put down the novel of his that I was reading, but what fascinated me, I thought, was only the subject, as in the early phase of love when you go to some party or entertainment so that you can see a particular woman, though you think what attracts you is only the prospect of enjoying those gatherings themselves. Then I noticed the rare, almost archaic expressions he liked to use at certain points, when a hidden wave of harmony, an inner prelude, would heighten his style; and it was at these points, too, that he would speak of the 'vanities of life', of 'beautiful insubstantial shapes', the 'sterile, delicious torment of understanding and loving', or the 'moving effigies that for ever ennoble the charming and venerable façades of our cathedrals';* that he would express a whole philosophy, new to me, through images so marvellous that it seemed it was they that had awakened the harp-song which then arose and to which they provided a sublime accompaniment. One of these passages from Bergotte, the third or the fourth I'd marked out from the rest of the book, gave me a feeling of joy incomparably greater than that I'd had on reading the first one, a feeling I experienced at a deeper, vaster, more unified level of my being, from which all obstacles and partitions seemed to have been removed. What had happened was that, recognizing the same taste for unusual expressions, the same bursts of musicality, the same idealist philosophy that, without my realizing it, had been the source of my pleasure in the earlier passages, I no longer had the impression I had before me a particular passage in a certain book by Bergotte, tracing on my mind a purely linear figure, but rather the 'ideal passage' from Bergotte, common to all his books, to which all the similar passages that merged into it had added a kind of density and volume by which my mind seemed enlarged.

I wasn't quite Bergotte's sole admirer; he was also the favourite writer of a friend of my mother's, a very well-read lady, while Doctor du Boulbon would keep patients waiting in order to carry on reading his latest book; in fact it was from his consulting room and from a park near Combray that some of the first seeds of a general liking for Bergotte were spread abroad, a very rare species of plant in those days, but now so widespread that throughout Europe and America, even in the tiniest villages, you'll find that its perfect blooms are loved by all. What my mother's friend and, it seems, Doctor du Boulbon liked above all in Bergotte's books was what I liked too: the melodic flow, the old-fashioned expressions, and certain others, simple and familiar, but which, from the way he highlighted them in the text, suggested a particular kind of taste on his part; and also, in the sad passages, a kind of brusqueness, a tone that was almost harsh. And he himself, no doubt, must have felt that these were his greatest charms. For in his later books, if he came upon some great truth or the name of a famous cathedral, he would interrupt his narrative and, in an invocation, an apostrophe, an extended prayer, would give free rein to the lyricism that in his early works had remained internal to his prose, discernible only in ripples on its surface, and was perhaps even more delightful and harmonious because it was veiled and the reader was unable to tell with any precision where it began and where it died away. These passages in which he took such delight were our favourites. I knew them by heart. I was disappointed when he took up his narrative again. Each time he spoke of something whose beauty had until then been hidden from me, of pine forests or hailstorms, of Notre-Dame cathedral, of *Athalie* or *Phèdre*,* with a single image he would make that beauty burst around me. And so, being aware that so many aspects of the world would remain beyond my limited apprehension unless he made them accessible to me, I wanted to have his opinion, or a metaphor of his, in relation to everything, especially those things I might have an opportunity of seeing for myself, particularly some of the historic buildings of France and certain seascapes, because the emphasis with which he referred to them in his books proved how rich in meaning and beauty they were for him. Unfortunately, on almost everything his opinion was unknown to me. I had no doubt that his opinions would be utterly different from mine, since they came down from an unknown world towards which I was striving to rise; convinced that my thoughts would have seemed pure ineptitude to that perfect mind, I'd so thoroughly got rid of them all that if I happened to find in one of his books an idea that had already occurred to me, my heart would swell with pride and gratitude as if some benevolent deity had given it back to me, had pronounced it to be beautiful and true. Now and then I would come upon a page of his that said the same things I often wrote to my grandmother and my mother when I was unable to sleep, so that the page by Bergotte read like a collection of epigraphs that could stand at the top of my letters. And even, years later, when I began writing a book, and the quality of some of my sentences discouraged me from carrying on, I would find their equivalent in Bergotte. But it was only then, when I read them in his work, that I could find any pleasure in them; when I was the one composing them, I was too preoccupied with making them reflect exactly what I perceived in my mind, and too afraid that they would not be 'true to life', to have time to ask myself whether what I was writing would read well! But in reality there was no kind of sentence, no kind of ideas that I loved, except these. My fraught and fretful efforts were themselves a token of my love, a love without pleasure but profound. And so, when I suddenly came upon similar phrases in a book by someone else, that is, without having to endure my usual qualms and strictures and self-torment, I indulged to the full my taste for them, like a cook who, for once, doesn't have to do the cooking and has the time to appreciate what he's eating. One day, when I discovered in a book by Bergotte a joke about an old family servant which the writer's majestic style had made even more ironical, but which was the same joke I'd often told my grandmother about Françoise, and another time, when I noticed that he didn't think it unworthy to include in those mirrors of truth that were his writings a remark similar to one I'd had occasion to make about our friend Monsieur Legrandin (remarks about Françoise and Legrandin that were certainly among those I would have sacrificed most willingly for Bergotte, in the belief that he would find them uninteresting), it seemed to me all at once that the gulf between my humble existence and the realms of truth was not as great as I'd thought, that they actually coincided at certain points, and in my new feeling of confidence and joy I wept over the pages of this writer, as though in the arms of a long-lost father.

From his books, I imagined Bergotte to be a frail, disappointed old man who'd lost several children and never got over it. This was why, as I read him, I sang his prose in my mind, more *dolce*, more *lento* perhaps than he'd intended,* and the intonation of the simplest sentence sounded to me as if it was full of feeling. Above all I loved his philosophy, and had pledged myself to it for life. It made me impatient to reach the age when I'd be able to take the class at secondary school called 'Philosophy'. But I didn't want to do anything else in that class but live exclusively by the tenets of Bergotte, and if I'd been told that the metaphysicians to whom I'd be attracted there wouldn't be like him at all, I'd have felt the despair of a young lover who wants his love to last his whole life and meets someone who tells him about the other women he will love in times to come.

One Sunday, as I was reading in the garden, I was disturbed by Swann, who had come to see my parents.

'What are you reading? Can I have a look? Ah, Bergotte! Who told you about him?'

I said it was Bloch.

'Oh, yes, that boy I saw here once, the one who looks so much like Mohammed II in the portrait by Bellini.* The resemblance is quite striking! He's got the same circumflex eyebrows, the same hooked nose, the same high cheekbones. When he has a goatee beard, they'll look exactly alike. In any case, he has good taste, Bergotte has a charming mind.' And seeing how much I seemed to admire Bergotte, he was kind enough to break his usual rule of never talking about people he knew: 'I know him very well. If you'd like him to write a few words on the title page of your book, I could ask him for you.'

I didn't dare accept his offer, but I did ask him a number of questions about Bergotte: 'Can you tell me who is his favourite actor?'

'Actor? I don't know. But I do know he doesn't think there's any male actor to match La Berma; he thinks she's in a class of her own. Have you ever seen her?'

'No, Monsieur, my parents don't let me go to the theatre.'

'That's a pity. You should insist. La Berma in *Phèdre* or *Le Cid** is only an actress, of course, but, you know, I'm not much of a believer in the "hierarchy" of the arts.' (As he said this I noticed something that had often struck me in his conversations with my grandmother's sisters: whenever he spoke of serious matters, and used an expression that seemed to imply an opinion about an important subject, he took care to mark it off by using a particular tone, mechanical and ironic, as if he'd put the expression in quotation marks, seeming to distance himself from it and say in effect: '*hierarchy*, you know, as silly people say'. But then, if it was so silly, why did he use the word at all?) A moment later he added: 'Her acting will move you as deeply as any artistic masterpiece, as—oh, I don't know . . .'—(and he began to laugh) 'as the Queens of Chartres!'* Until then I'd taken his horror of ever expressing a serious opinion to be a mark of Parisian sophistication, as opposed to the provincial dogmatism of my grandmother's sisters; and I also suspected it was a form of wit in the circles in which Swann moved, where, in reaction to the lyricism of previous generations, excessive importance was attached to small points of fact, formerly regarded as vulgar, and anything that smacked of 'phrase-making' was banned. He seemed afraid to have an opinion about anything, and not to be at his ease unless he had some scrupulously precise details of fact to offer. But in so doing he didn't realize that to postulate that the accuracy of these details was important was in itself an expression of opinion. I thought again of the dinner when I'd been so miserable because Maman wouldn't be coming up to my room and when he'd said that the balls given by the Princesse de Léon were of no importance whatsoever. And yet it was precisely to that kind of pursuit that he devoted his life. I found all this contradictory. Was he waiting for the next life to say seriously what he thought about things, to formulate opinions he didn't have to put in quotation marks, and no longer indulge with punctilious politeness in occupations which, at the same time, he pronounced absurd? I noticed, too, in the way he talked about Bergotte something that was by no means peculiar to him, but was shared at the time by all the writer's admirers, including my mother's literary friend and Doctor du Boulbon. Like Swann, they would say of Bergotte: 'He has a charming mind, so original, he has a way of saying things that's absolutely his own—a little overdone but very charming. You don't have to look for his name on the cover, you can tell it's by him straight away.' But none of them would have gone so far as to say: 'He's a great writer, he's got great talent.' They didn't even say he had talent. They didn't say so because they weren't aware of it. We are very slow to recognize in the particular features of a new writer the model that is labelled 'great talent' in our museum of general concepts. Precisely because these features are new, we don't think they fully resemble what we call talent. Instead, we talk about originality,

charm, subtlety, power; and then one day we realize that these qualities are the very things that constitute talent.

'Are there any books by Bergotte in which he talks about La Berma?'
I asked Monsieur Swann.

'I think so, in his little volume on Racine. But it must be out of
print now. But there may have been a reprint. I'll find out. Anyhow,
I can ask Bergotte anything you want to know; he comes to dinner at
our house once a week, without fail. He and my daughter are great
friends. They go off on little trips together, to look at old towns and
cathedrals and castles.'

Since I had no notion of gradations of social status, the fact that my
father found it impossible for us to see anything of Madame Swann
and her daughter had long since had the perverse effect, by making
me imagine there was a huge gulf between us, of giving them great
prestige in my eyes. I was sorry that my mother didn't dye her hair
and wear lipstick, as I'd heard our neighbour Madame Sazerat say
Madame Swann did, to please, not her husband, but Monsieur de
Charlus; and I thought that, to her, we must be an object of scorn,
which distressed me especially because of Mademoiselle Swann;
from what I'd gathered, she was a very pretty little girl, and I often
dreamed about her, imagining her each time with the same arbitrary
charming face. But when I learned that day that Mademoiselle Swann
was a creature living in such rare circumstances, bathing as though in
her natural element in a world of such privilege that when she asked
her parents if anyone was coming to dinner, she would be answered by
those two radiant syllables, by the name of the golden guest who, for
her, was simply an old friend of the family: Bergotte; that the dinner
table talk she heard, the equivalent of what my great-aunt's conversation was for me, would be Bergotte's pronouncements on all the subjects he hadn't been able to treat in his books, and on which I would
have liked to hear him deliver his oracles; and that, when she went to
visit other towns, he would be walking beside her, in glorious ano-
nymity, like the ancient gods who would come down to dwell among
mortals: from that moment I became aware of the worth of a person
like Mademoiselle Swann and, at the same time, how coarse and
ignorant I would appear to her, and I felt so keenly how delightful and
yet how impossible it would be for me to become her friend that I was
filled at once with longing and despair. From then on, whenever
I thought of her, I would see her most often standing in front of

a cathedral porch, explaining to me what the various statues meant, and, with a smile that said she liked me, introducing me as her friend to Bergotte. And invariably the charm of all the associations of cathedrals that sprang up in my mind, the charm of the hills of the Île-de-France and the plains of Normandy, were reflected on to the picture I had formed of Mademoiselle Swann: I was now more than ready to fall in love with her. Of all the preconditions of love, the one that is most essential and makes us set little store by the rest is our belief that the other person partakes of some unknown mode of existence which his or her love will enable us to share. Even women who claim to judge a man by his physical appearance alone see that appearance as the outward form of a special kind of life. This is why they love soldiers and firemen—the uniform makes them less particular about the face; they think that, under his breastplate, the man they are kissing has a heart that is different, more adventurous, softer; and a young monarch or a crown prince may make the most gratifying conquests in the foreign countries he visits, while having none of the classic good looks that, say, a man who trades in stocks behind the scenes would possibly find indispensable.

While I sat reading in the garden, something my great-aunt would not have understood my doing except on a Sunday, a day when it's forbidden to engage in any serious activity and when she didn't sew (on a weekday she would have said: 'What's this? Are you *amusing* yourself again with a book? It isn't Sunday, you know,' making the word 'amusing' imply childishness and waste of time), Aunt Léonie would gossip with Françoise until it was time for Eulalie to arrive. She would announce that she'd just seen Madame Goupil go by 'without an umbrella, in that silk dress she had made specially in Châteaudun. If she's got far to go before Vespers, she could easily get it soaked through.'

'Maybe, maybe,' said Françoise, meaning maybe not, so as not to rule out the possibility of a happier alternative.

'Bless me!' said my aunt, clapping a hand to her forehead. 'That reminds me—I never found out if she got to church too late for the Elevation. I must remember to ask Eulalie . . . Françoise, just look at that black cloud behind the steeple, and the nasty-looking light on the slates. We're bound to have rain before the day's out. It couldn't possibly stay like this, it's been too hot. The sooner it breaks the better, because my Vichy water won't go down properly until then,' added my aunt, since, in her mind, the desire to accelerate the digestion of her Vichy water was infinitely greater than her fear that Madame Goupil's dress might be ruined.

'Maybe, maybe.'

'And the thing is, when it rains in the Square there isn't much shelter.' Then my aunt suddenly turned pale and exclaimed: 'What, three o'clock already! Vespers have begun and I've forgotten to take my pepsin! Now I know why my Vichy water has been lying on my stomach.'

Grabbing a missal bound in violet velvet, with gilt clasps, out of which, in her haste, she let fall a shower of holy pictures, each with a lacy fringe of yellowing paper, which she used to mark the pages of the feast days, my aunt, while swallowing her drops, began to gabble the words of the sacred text, her understanding of them slightly impaired by her anxiety as to whether her pepsin, taken so late, would be able to catch up with her Vichy water and help it go down. 'Three o'clock! It's incredible how time flies!'

There was a little tap on the windowpane, as if something had struck it, followed by a sustained, light sprinkling sound as though grains of sand were being dropped from an upper window; then the sound increased, taking on a regular rhythm, becoming liquid, loud, musical, immeasurable, universal: it was the rain.

'There, Françoise, what was I just saying? Look at it coming down! But I think I heard the bell at the garden gate: go and see who can be outside in this weather.'

Françoise came back, and said:

'It was Madame Amédée' (my grandmother). 'She said she was going for a walk. It's raining hard, though.'

'Yes, I'm not a bit surprised,' said my aunt, glancing up at the sky. 'I've always said her way of thinking isn't like anybody else's. I'm glad it's her and not me who's outside just now.'

'Madame Amédée is the exact opposite of other folk,' said Françoise, sounding quite benign, refraining until she was alone with the other servants from saying she thought my grandmother was a bit 'dotty'.

'Oh, the Benediction's over!* Eulalie won't be coming now,' sighed my aunt. 'The weather must have put her off.'

'But it's not five o'clock yet, Madame Octave, it's only half past four.'

'Only half past four? And here's me having to draw back the net curtains just to let some light in. At half past four! A week before the Rogations!* Ah, my dear Françoise, the Lord must be angry with us. I mean, what's happening to the world? As my poor Octave used to say, we've been neglecting the Lord and He's getting his own back.'

A bright flush rose to my aunt's cheeks: Eulalie had arrived. Unfortunately, no sooner had she been shown in than Françoise reappeared and, with a smile that was meant to reflect the joy she was sure my aunt would feel on hearing her words, which she enunciated very carefully to show that, despite her use of the indirect form, she was reporting, good servant that she was, the very words the visitor himself had deigned to use, she said:

'Monsieur le Curé would be pleased, indeed delighted, if Madame Octave was not resting and could see him. Monsieur le Curé does not wish to disturb Madame Octave. Monsieur le Curé is downstairs; I said to him to go into the front room.'

To tell the truth, the curé's visits didn't give my aunt as much pleasure as Françoise supposed, and the air of jubilation with which Françoise saw fit to light up her face each time she had to announce his arrival didn't entirely correspond to the feelings of the invalid. The curé (an excellent man, with whom I'm sorry I didn't speak more often, for though he had no feeling for the arts, he was well versed in etymologies), accustomed as he was to telling distinguished visitors all about his church (he even planned to write a book about the parish in Combray), would weary her with his interminable expatiations, which, moreover, never varied. But when his visit coincided exactly with Eulalie's, it became a real annoyance for my aunt. She would have preferred to make the most of Eulalie and not have everyone at the same time. But she didn't dare send the curé away and had to content herself with making a sign to Eulalie not to leave when he did, so that she could have her to herself for a while after he'd gone.

'Well, Monsieur le Curé, what's this I've been hearing? An artist has set up his easel in your church to copy one of the windows? I must say in all my long days I've never heard of such a thing! What is the world coming to! And it's the ugliest thing in the church, too!'

'I wouldn't go so far as to say it's the ugliest, because if there are some things in Saint-Hilaire that are well worth a visit, there are other things in my poor basilica that are very old; it's the only one in the whole diocese that has never been restored. Lord knows the porch is dirty and ancient, but it's not without a certain majesty; and the same can be said of the Esther tapestries—personally I wouldn't give two sous for them, but the experts rank them second only to the ones in Sens.* I can quite see, too, that apart from some details that are rather crude, they are others that show a real gift for observation. But don't talk to me about the stained-glass windows. What sense is there in preserving windows that don't let in any daylight and actually confuse your sight with those flashes of colour I can't even describe, in a church where there aren't even two flagstones on the same level that they won't have replaced because, they say, they're the tombstones of the abbés of Combray and the lords of Guermantes, the old Comtes de Brabant:* the direct ancestors of the present Duc de Guermantes, and of the Duchesse too because she's a Guermantes who married her cousin?' (My grandmother, whose steadfast refusal to take any interest in the private lives of these people had made her get all their names mixed up, would claim, each time the Duchesse de Guermantes was mentioned, that she must be related to Madame de Villeparisis. The whole family would then burst out laughing, and she would try to defend herself by invoking some notification she'd received of a christening or a funeral: 'I seem to remember there was mention of a Guermantes in it somewhere.' And for once I would side with the others, refusing to admit that there could be any connection between her friend from boarding school and the descendant of Geneviève de Brabant.) 'Look at Roussainville,' the curé went on. 'Today it's just a parish of farmers, although in ancient times the place enjoyed a booming trade in felt hats and clocks. (I'm not sure about the derivation of Roussainville. I rather think the original name was Rouville (from *Radulfi villa*), just as Châteauroux comes from *Castrum Radulfi*—but I won't go into that now.) Anyway, the church there has superb windows, nearly all modern, including the very impressive *Entry of Louis-Philippe into Combray*, which it would be more appropriate to have here, in Combray, and which is just as good, they say, as the famous windows at Chartres. Only yesterday I bumped into Doctor Percepied's brother, who knows about these things, and he told me he regards it as a finer piece of work. But, as I said to the artist fellow (who seems very civil, by the way, and is apparently a real virtuoso with his brush): "What's so special about this window, which is even darker than the others?"'

'I'm sure if you asked the Bishop he wouldn't refuse you a new window,' said my aunt in a feeble voice, beginning to think she would soon feel 'tired'.

'You can depend on it, Madame Octave,' replied the curé. 'But, you know, it was His Excellency himself who started all the fuss about the wretched window by proving it represented Gilbert the Bad (a knight of Guermantes and a direct descendant of Geneviève de Brabant, who was a daughter in the Guermantes family) receiving absolution from Saint Hilaire.'

'I don't remember seeing Saint Hilaire in the window.'

'But she's there—have you never noticed a lady in a yellow dress in one corner of the window? Well, that's Saint Hilaire, who is also known in certain provinces, you remember, as Saint Illiers, or Saint Hélier, and even, in the Jura, Saint Ylie.* And these various corruptions of *sanctus Hilarius* are not, by the way, the most curious that have occurred in the names of the blessed. Take, for example, your own patron saint, my dear Eulalie: *sancta Eulalia*. Do you know what she's turned into in Burgundy? *Saint Éloi*, would you believe! She's become a male saint! You see, Eulalie? After you die they'll turn you into a man.'

'Monsieur le Curé will have his little joke.'

'Gilbert's brother, Charles the Stammerer, was a devoutly religious prince, but he lost his father when he was very young; that was Pépin the Mad,* who died as a result of mental illness; Charles wielded power with all the arrogance of a man who'd never known discipline in his youth, to such an extent that if he visited a town and saw a man he didn't like the look of, he'd have the entire population massacred. Gilbert, wanting to take revenge on Charles, had the church in Combray burned down, the original church I mean, which Théodebert,* when he and his court set off from the country house he had near here, at Thiberzy (*Theodeberciacus*, that is), to do battle with the Burgundians, had promised to build over the tomb of Saint Hilaire if the saint brought him victory. All that's left of the original church, because Gilbert burned the rest, is the crypt, which I dare say Théodore has shown you. In the end, Gilbert defeated the unfortunate Charles with the help of William the Conqueror'* (the curé pronounced the name Will'am), 'which is why we have so many English visitors. But it would seem he wasn't able to win over the people of Combray, for they fell upon him as he was coming out of Mass and chopped his head off. Théodore has got a little book he lends to people, which tells the whole story.

'But without a doubt the most extraordinary thing about our church is the view from the belfry, which is superb. In your case, though, since you're not in the best of health, I'd certainly not recommend that you climb our ninety-seven steps, which happens by the way to be exactly half the number they have in the famous cathedral in Milan.* It's quite a job even for a healthy person, especially since you have to go up bent double if you don't want to split your head open, and you get covered in all the cobwebs on the stairs. In any case you'd need to be well wrapped up,' he went on (failing to notice my aunt's indignation at the suggestion that she might be able to climb up to the belfry), 'because there's quite a breeze, once you get to the top! Some people have told me they've felt the chill of death up there. Even so, on Sundays there are always groups that come, sometimes from quite far off, to admire the beautiful panorama, and they go away delighted. Next Sunday, for example, if the weather holds, there'll definitely be lots of people, since it's Rogation Sunday. There's no doubt, though, that the view from up there is magical, with sudden vistas over the plain that are quite special. On a clear day you can see as far as Verneuil. But the great thing is you can see at the same time things you can normally only see separately, like the course of the Vivonne and the ditches at Saint-Assise-lès-Combray, which are separated by a screen of tall trees, or the different canals at Jouy-le-Vicomte (*Gaudicus vice comitis*, as I'm sure you know). Each time I've been to Jouy I've seen part of a canal, easily enough, and then I've turned a corner and seen another part, by which time I couldn't see the previous part. I tried to imagine them all together, but that didn't give the proper picture. From the top of Saint-Hilaire, though, it's a different matter, you can see how the network of canals covers the whole area. Only you can't see any water; it looks as if deep cuts have been made through the town, dividing it into sections, like a brioche sliced into pieces but still holding together. To get a perfect sense of it all you'd have to be in two places at once—at the top of Saint-Hilaire and down at Jouy-le-Vicomte.'

The curé left my aunt so exhausted that no sooner had he gone than she had to send Eulalie away too.

'Here, my dear Eulalie,' she said in a faint voice, taking a coin from a little purse she kept within reach, 'this is so you won't forget me in your prayers.'

'Oh, Madame Octave! I don't know if I should; you know that's not why I come!' Eulalie would say each time, as awkward and embarrassed as if it were the first, and with a look of displeasure that amused my aunt and gave her a certain satisfaction, because if it happened that Eulalie looked a little less displeased than usual as she took the money, my aunt would say afterwards:

'I don't know what's got into Eulalie; I gave her the same as usual, but she didn't seem very happy.'

'I don't think she's got anything to complain about,' Françoise would sigh, for she was inclined to regard as small change anything my aunt gave her for herself or her children, and as treasure squandered on an ingrate the little coins dropped into Eulalie's hand every Sunday, but so discreetly that Françoise never managed to see them. It wasn't that she wanted for herself the money my aunt gave Eulalie. She derived enough pleasure from my aunt's affluence, knowing that the wealth of the employer elevates the servant, giving her prestige in the eyes of the world, and that she, Françoise, was distinguished and renowned in Combray, Jouy-le-Vicomte, and further afield, on account of my aunt's many farms, the curé's frequent and lengthy visits, and the extraordinary quantity of Vichy water she consumed. Françoise was avaricious only on my aunt's behalf; if she'd been in charge of her fortune, which would have been her dream, she would have guarded it against the designs of others with a maternal ferocity. She wouldn't have objected, however, if my aunt, whom she knew to be incorrigibly generous, had gone on giving her money away, as long as it went to rich people. Perhaps she felt that the rich, having no need of gifts from my aunt, couldn't be suspected of liking her on that account. Besides, gifts made to people of wealth and position, like Madame Sazerat, Monsieur Swann, Monsieur Legrandin, or Madame Goupil, all of them people 'of the same rank' as my aunt, and who 'went well with each other', appeared to Françoise to be a natural feature of the strange and brilliant life led by the rich— a life of hunting and shooting, invitations to balls, and visits to each other's houses, the sort of life she approved of and admired. But it wasn't the same if the beneficiaries of my aunt's generosity were what Françoise referred to as 'people like me' or 'people no better than me', the sort she most looked down on unless they called her 'Madame Françoise' and considered themselves her inferiors. And when she saw that, despite her counsel, my aunt continued to do as she pleased and threw her money away—as Françoise saw it, at least—on creatures who were unworthy of her, she began to think that the gifts she received from my aunt were very modest compared to the sums she imagined were being lavished on Eulalie. There was not one farm in the neighbourhood so substantial that Françoise didn't assume Eulalie could easily have bought it with the money derived from her visits (though it should be noted that Eulalie had formed the same estimate of the vast and secret riches of Françoise). Every time, after Eulalie had gone, Françoise made baleful prophecies about her likely fate. She detested her, but was also afraid of her and felt that when she was there she had to put on a 'good face'. She made up for it after Eulalie's departure, without ever mentioning her by name, but uttering sibylline oracles, or pronouncements of a general nature like those in Ecclesiastes,* whose particular application could not escape my aunt. After peering out from behind the curtain to see whether Eulalie had shut the gate properly, she'd say: 'Flatterers know how to wheedle their way into people's good books and feather their own nests, but be patient and the Good Lord will punish them one day,' with the sidelong, insinuating glance of Joas thinking only of Athalie when he says:

Le Bonheur des méchants comme un torrent s'écoule. *

But when the curé came to call as well and stayed so long, leaving my aunt completely exhausted, Françoise would follow Eulalie from the room, saying:

'I'll let you rest, Madame Octave, you look right peeky.'

And my aunt wouldn't even answer, breathing a sigh so faint it seemed it might be her last, and lying there with her eyes closed, as though already dead. But Françoise would scarcely have arrived downstairs when four peels of a handbell, rung with the utmost violence, would resound through the house and my aunt, sitting bolt upright on her bed, would call out:

'Has Eulalie left yet? Can you believe it? I forgot to ask her if Madame Goupil did get to Mass in time for the Elevation! Quick, run after her!'

But Françoise would come back without having been able to catch up with Eulalie.

'That's most annoying,' said my aunt, shaking her head. 'It was the only important thing I had to ask her!'

In this way life went on for Aunt Léonie, always the same, in the gentle uniformity of what she called, with affected disparagement but real feeling, her 'little routine'. This 'routine'—protected by everyone, not only in the house, where we had all experienced the futility of urging her to adopt a healthier way of life, and so had gradually become resigned to respecting the routine she'd adopted, but also in the town, where the packer who worked three streets away from our house always sent someone to ask Françoise, before driving home his nails, if my aunt wasn't 'resting'—was deeply disturbed on one occasion that year. Like a hidden fruit that had ripened without anyone noticing, and had dropped spontaneously to the ground, one night the scullery maid went into labour. But her pains were unbearable, and since there was no midwife in Combray, Françoise had to set off before dawn to fetch one from Thiberzy. The scullery maid's cries made it impossible for my aunt to 'rest', and since Françoise was gone from the house for a long time, despite the short distance, her services were greatly missed. And so, in the course of the morning, my mother asked me to run upstairs to see if my aunt needed anything. I went into the first room, and through the open door of the other room saw my aunt lying on her side, asleep; I could hear her snoring lightly. I was about to slip away when something, probably the noise I'd made on entering, disturbed her sleep and made it 'change down a gear', as they say about motor cars, for the music of her snoring broke off for a second and began again on a lower note; then she woke up and half turned her face, which I could now see clearly—it bore an expression akin to terror; she had obviously just had a horrible dream. She couldn't see me from where she was lying, and I stayed where I was, unsure whether to go in to her or leave; but already she seemed to have gathered her wits and recognized the falsity of the visions that had terrified her; a smile of joy, of pious gratitude to God for making life less cruel than our dreams, feebly illuminated her face, and with the habit she'd formed of talking to herself half aloud when she thought she was alone, she murmured: 'Praise the Lord! It's only the scullery maid in labour! There I was dreaming, wasn't I, that my poor Octave was raised from the dead and was trying to make me go out for a walk every day!' She stretched a hand out towards her rosary, which was lying on the little bedside table, but as she was dozing off again her arm fell back before she could reach it; and so, her mind at rest, she fell asleep, and I crept out of the room without her or anyone else ever knowing what I'd seen and heard.

When I say that, apart from very rare events, such as the birth of the scullery maid's baby, my aunt's routine never underwent any variation, I don't include those variations which, always the same and repeated at regular intervals, introduced into the heart of that uniformity a kind of secondary uniformity. For instance, every Saturday, since Françoise always went to the market at Roussainville-le-Pin in the afternoon, we had lunch an hour earlier. And my aunt had so thoroughly acquired the habit of this weekly departure from her routine that she was as attached to this habit as to all the rest. She was so 'stuck in the routine', as Françoise would say, that if, one Saturday, she'd had to wait to have lunch at the normal time, this would have 'upset' her as much as if, on another day, she'd had to move her lunch forward to its Saturday time. We all felt, moreover, that this early lunch gave Saturdays a special character, indulgent and congenial. At the time when, normally, there was still an hour to negotiate before the relaxation of mealtime, we knew that in a few seconds we'd see the early appearance of some endives, followed by a gratuitous omelette, and an undeserved steak. The regularity of this asymmetrical Saturday was one of those little events, intramural, local, almost civic, which, in uneventful lives and stable societies, create a kind of national bond and become the favourite theme of conversations, jokes, and stories that can always be embroidered upon in the telling; if any one of us had had an epic turn of mind, it would have provided ready-made material for a cycle of legends. From early in the morning, even before we were dressed, for no reason, except to express our pleasure in our common purpose, we'd say to each other good-humouredly, cordially, patriotically: 'Come on, there's no time to lose—don't forget it's Saturday!' while my aunt, conferring with Françoise, and remembering that the day would be longer than usual, would say: 'You could cook them a nice piece of veal, seeing it's Saturday.' If, at ten-thirty, someone absent-mindedly pulled out his watch and said: 'Oh, still an hour and a half to lunch,' everybody would be delighted to be able to say: 'What are you talking about? You're forgetting it's Saturday!'; and a quarter of an hour later we'd still be laughing and saying we should go upstairs and tell Aunt Léonie about this memory lapse. Even the appearance of the sky seemed changed. After lunch, the sun, knowing it was Saturday, would linger an hour longer high in the firmament, and when someone, thinking we were late for our walk, said: 'What! Is it only two o'clock?' on noting the two peals from the belfry at Saint-Hilaire (which as a rule assail no one out walking in the lanes round about, still deserted because of the midday meal or the ensuing nap, or alongside the clear, swiftly flowing stream that even the angler had abandoned, and pass alone across the vacant sky where only a few lazy clouds floated), we would all chorus: 'Yes, but you're forgetting we had lunch an hour earlier today! Remember—it's Saturday!' The surprise of a 'barbarian' (our name for anyone who didn't know what was special about Saturdays)* who called at eleven o'clock to speak to my father and found us all sitting at table, was an event that caused Françoise as much merriment as anything that had ever happened in her life. But if she found it funny that the dumbfounded visitor had no idea that we had lunch early on Saturdays, she found it even funnier that my father (deeply as Françoise sympathized with his automatic chauvinism) had never imagined that the barbarian might not know this and had responded to his surprise at seeing us already eating with no other explanation than: 'Well, it's Saturday, of course!' At this point in her story, Françoise would pause to wipe the tears of laughter from her eyes, and then, to add to her enjoyment, would embroider the dialogue, inventing a response from the visitor, to whom the mention of Saturday meant nothing. And far from objecting to her embellishment, we would encourage her to add more, and say: 'Yes, but didn't he say something else as well? There was more to the story than that, the first time you told it.' Even my great-aunt would put down her needlework, look up, and peer over her lorgnon.

What was also special about Saturday was that it was the day, during the month of May, that we would go out after dinner to attend the 'Month of Mary'.*

Since we sometimes met there Monsieur Vinteuil, who held very strong views on 'the deplorable slovenliness of young people these days, which actually seems to be encouraged', my mother would make sure there was nothing wrong with my appearance before we left for church. It was in the Month of Mary, I remember, that my fondness for hawthorns was born. Not only were they inside the church (after all, we too were allowed within its holy walls) but they were placed on the altar itself, inseparable from the mysteries they helped to celebrate, the branches mingled with the candles and holy vessels, attached to one another horizontally like festive decorations and made even lovelier by the festoons of their leaves, on which were scattered, as on a bridal train, little clusters of dazzling white buds. Though I dared do no more than steal occasional glances at them, I felt that these showy decorations were somehow alive and that it was Nature herself that, by arranging the leaves into patterns and adding the crowning touch of the white buds, had made the display worthy of what was both a popular festival and a mystical celebration. Here and there on some of the higher branches, a flower was opening with easy grace, retaining so casually like a final and scented attire the bouquet of stamens, delicate as gossamer threads, that enveloped them entirely, that in imagining it, in trying to mimic their flowering in my mind, I imagined it as a quick, insouciant toss of the head, accompanied by a coquettish glance with pupils contracted, of a girl in white, vivacious and care-free. Monsieur Vinteuil had come in with his daughter and had sat down beside us. He was from a good family and had once been piano teacher to my grandmother's sisters, and when, after losing his wife and inheriting some property, he had retired to Combray, we often used to invite him to our house. But he was extremely prudish and stopped coming so as not to see Swann, who had made what he called 'an unsuitable marriage, which seems the fashion these days'. My mother, on hearing that he composed, told him by way of a compliment that, when she came to see him, he would have to play her one of his pieces. Nothing would have given Monsieur Vinteuil more pleasure, but he was so scrupulously polite and considerate that he always tried to see things from the other person's point of view, and was afraid he'd seem a bore or egotistical if he followed or even let them infer his own desires. On the day when my parents had gone to pay him a visit, I'd gone with them, but they allowed me to stay outside and, since Monsieur Vinteuil's house, Montjouvain, stood at the foot of a hillock covered with bushes, among which I went to hide, I found myself on a level with the second-floor drawing room, only a few feet from the window. When a servant came in to announce my parents, I saw Monsieur Vinteuil quickly place a sheet of music in a conspicuous position on the piano. But as soon as my parents entered the room, he took it away again and put it to one side. He was afraid, no doubt, of letting them think he was pleased to see them only because he could play them some of his compositions. Each time my mother returned to the subject in the course of the visit, he said the same thing: 'I don't know who put that on the piano, it doesn't belong there,' and turned the conversation to other topics, precisely because they interested him less. His only passion was for his daughter, and she, with her boyish appearance, looked so strong and healthy that it was impossible not to smile at all the precautions her father took on her account, always having a spare shawl to throw over her shoulders. My grandmother used to remark on the gentle, delicate, almost timid expression that often flitted across the freckled face of this sturdy child. Whenever she said something, she heard her words as they must sound to her listeners, would become worried at the possibility of a misunderstanding, and then, beneath her boyish 'devil-may-care' face, we would see in clear outline, as through a transparency, the finer features of a distressed young girl.

When, before leaving the church, I genuflected before the altar, I suddenly caught, as I stood up, a bitter-sweet smell of almonds coming from the hawthorns, and then I noticed on the white buds little yellowish spots under which I imagined the smell must lie hidden, as the almond taste of a frangipane tart lay beneath the golden-brown crust, or the taste of Mademoiselle Vinteuil's cheeks beneath their freckles. Despite the stillness and silence of the hawthorns, this intermittent fragrance was like the murmuring of their intense life, as if the altar was quivering like a hedgerow swarming with living antennae, of which I was reminded by the sight of certain reddish stamens that seemed to have kept the springtime virulence, the irritant power of insects now metamorphosed into flowers.

On leaving the church we'd chat for a moment with Monsieur Vinteuil in front of the porch. Children would be squabbling in the Square, and he'd intervene, taking the side of the little ones and lecturing the bigger ones. If his daughter said, in her loud voice, how glad she'd been to see us, it would immediately seem as if a more sensitive sister within her was blushing at this unthinking, tomboyish remark, which might easily have made us think she was angling for an invitation to our house. Her father would throw a cloak over her shoulders, they would clamber into a little buggy, which she'd drive herself, and off they'd go to Montjouvain. As for us, since the next day was Sunday and there was no need to get up until it was time for High Mass, if it was warm and there was a clear moonlit sky, instead of taking us straight home, my father, indulging his desire to show off, would take us on a long walk by way of the roadside cross, which my mother, who had no sense of direction and often had no idea even what road she was walking along, would regard as a triumph of strategic genius. Sometimes we'd go as far as the viaduct, whose spans led away from the station like huge stone legs and embodied for me the exile and desolation that lay beyond the civilized world, because every year, when we travelled down from Paris, we were warned to be very careful, as we reached Combray, not to miss the station, to be ready before the train stopped because it would set off again after two minutes and proceed across the viaduct, out of the lands of Christendom, of which Combray represented for me the furthest limit. We'd return along the avenue from the station, which contained the most attractive houses in the municipality. In each garden the moonlight, as in the paintings of Hubert Robert, had scattered its broken staircases of white marble, its fountains, its half-open gates. Its beams had destroyed the Telegraph Office. All that remained of it was a broken pillar, but it retained the beauty of a timeless ruin. I'd be dragging my feet, dropping with tiredness; the lovely smell of the linden trees* seemed to me a reward to be won only at the cost of exhaustion and not worth the effort. From gates far apart, dogs awakened by our solitary steps would begin a series of alternating barks such as I still hear sometimes in the evening and in which the avenue from the station (when the public gardens of Combray were created on its site) must have taken refuge, because, wherever I happen to be, as soon as dogs begin their resounding call and response, I see it once more, with its linden trees and its moonlit pavement.

Suddenly my father would stop us and ask my mother: 'Where are we?' Tired out by the walk but proud of him, she'd confess in her loving way that she had absolutely no idea. He'd shrug his shoulders and laugh. Then, as if he'd produced it with his key out of his jacket pocket, he'd point out, right in front of us, the little back gate of our own garden, which, together with the corner of the Rue du Saint-Esprit, had turned up here, waiting for us at the end of our travels along paths unknown. My mother would gasp admiringly: 'You really are amazing!' And from that moment I didn't have to take another step, the ground moved for me through the garden where for so long my actions had ceased to be accompanied by any conscious attention on my part: Habit had taken me in its arms, and carried me to bed like a little child.

Although Saturdays, by beginning an hour earlier and depriving her of Françoise, passed more slowly for my aunt, she nonetheless looked forward to them throughout the week, because they contained all the novelty and entertainment that her frail and disordered body was still able to endure. This wasn't to say, however, that she didn't hanker from time to time after some greater change, that she didn't experience those unwonted moments when we crave something other than what we have, when those who lack the energy or imagination to find within themselves a source of renewal look to the passing moment or the postman's knock for something new, even if it's something worse, some emotion, some sorrow; when our heartstrings, which contentment has silenced like an idle harp, long to be played upon, even by a rough hand and even if they might suffer damage; when the will, which has with such difficulty won the right to abandon itself freely to its own desires and sufferings, would gladly throw the reins into the hands of imperious circumstance, however cruel. Of course, since my aunt's strength, drained dry by the slightest exertion, returned only drop by drop during her hours of rest, the reservoir was very slow in filling, and months would go by before she reached the slight overflow level which others divert into various forms of activity, but which she was incapable of knowing or deciding how to employ. I have no doubt that then—just as the desire to have her potatoes in béchamel sauce for a change would develop, eventually, out of the pleasure she took in the daily reappearance of the mashed potatoes of which she never 'got tired'—she would derive from the accumulation of those monotonous days she treasured so much the keen expectation of some domestic cataclysm which, though it might last only a moment, would force her to make one of those decisive changes which she knew would be of benefit to her but which she could never make of her own accord. She truly loved us, she would have taken pleasure in mourning us; she must often have dreamed that one day, when she felt well and was not worked up about something, she would be told that the house was on fire, that the rest of us had already perished, and soon not a stone would be left standing, but that she herself, provided she got out of bed at once, would have ample time to make her escape—a dream that offered not only the two secondary advantages of allowing her to savour her affection for us in a long period of mourning and to dumbfound the whole town by leading the funeral procession, courageous but stricken, dying on her feet, but also the much more precious benefit of forcing her, opportunely, without time-wasting or the possibility of tiresome indecision, to go and spend the summer at

Mirougrain, a pretty farm she owned, where there was a waterfall. As no such event had ever occurred, whose successful consequences she would certainly dwell on during her endless, solitary games of patience (and though, if it did happen, she would have been thrown into despair the moment it began, from its first small signs, the first words announcing bad news, the sound of which would prove unforgettable, by anything that bore the imprint of actual death, so different from its logical, abstract possibility), she would occasionally resort to making her life more interesting by introducing into it imaginary dramas, which she would play out in a very spirited manner. She enjoyed suddenly pretending that Françoise was stealing from her, that she had set a trap to make sure, and had caught her red-handed; and just as she was in the habit, when she played cards with herself, of playing both her own hand and her opponent's, so she would speak out loud Françoise's clumsy apologies and then reply with such fiery indignation that if one of us happened to come into the room at that moment, we'd find her covered in perspiration, her eyes blazing, her false hair askew, and her bald pate showing. Françoise might sometimes hear from the next room bitingly sarcastic remarks being addressed to her, for my aunt wouldn't have been satisfied merely to invent these remarks and leave them in a state of unvoiced immateriality—she had to make them more real by muttering them to herself. Sometimes, however, even this 'theatre in bed'* was not enough for my aunt, she wanted to have her plays performed. And so, on a Sunday, with all the doors mysteriously closed, she'd confide to Eulalie her doubts about Françoise's honesty and her intention of getting rid of her, and on another day she'd share with Françoise her suspicions about the trustworthiness of Eulalie, to whom she'd never open her door again; and then, a few days later, she would have lost all faith in her confidante of the day before and patched things up with the villain of the piece, though by the time of the next performance the two of them would once more have swapped roles. But the suspicions Eulalie might occasionally arouse in her were necessarily short-lived, flaring up and burning themselves out quickly for lack of fuel, since Eulalie didn't live in the house. It was very different in the case of Françoise, of whose presence under the same roof my aunt was perpetually conscious, though, for fear of catching a chill if she left her bed, she'd never dare go down to the kitchen to see whether her suspicions were well founded. Gradually her mind became entirely occupied with trying to guess what, at any moment of the day, Françoise might be doing behind her back. She'd note any furtive look on Françoise's face, any inconsistency in what she said, any desire she seemed to be concealing. And she'd show her that she'd found her out, with a single word that made the poor woman turn pale and that my aunt seemed to find cruel amusement in driving into her heart. And the following Sunday, a revelation of Eulalie's—like one of those discoveries that suddenly open up an entirely new field of inquiry in a branch of science that has hitherto trudged along familiar paths—would prove to my aunt that even her worst suspicions fell far short of the truth.

'But Françoise ought to know that,' said Eulalie, 'now that you've given 'er a carriage.'

'Given her a carriage!' gasped my aunt.

'Well, what do I know? I thought so—I saw her go by just now in a calash,* looking as proud as a peacock, on her way to the market in Roussainville. I thought it must be Madame Octave who'd given it to her.'

So, by degrees, Françoise and my aunt, like quarry and hunter, were perpetually trying to anticipate each other's ruses. My mother was afraid Françoise would develop a real hatred for my aunt, who would be as offensive to her as she could. Certainly Françoise came more and more to pay extremely close attention to my aunt's every word and gesture. When she had to ask her for anything, she'd hesitate for a long time, pondering how best to go about it. Then, when she'd ventured to make her request, she'd watch my aunt out of the corner of her eye, trying to guess what she was thinking and what her response would be. And so it was that—unlike some artist who has read seventeenth-century memoirs and, wanting to feel closer to the Sun King,* thinks he's making progress in that direction by fabricating a genealogy that traces his ancestry back to one of the great families of France, or by entering into correspondence with one of the crowned heads of Europe, but is actually turning his back on what he's misguidedly seeking in forms that are mere copies and are therefore dead—an old lady from the provinces, who'd never given a thought to Louis XIV but was simply yielding to her own irresistible eccentricities and to malicious impulses born of idleness, saw the most insignificant of her daily occupations, like her morning toilette, her lunch, her afternoon nap, acquire, by virtue of their despotic singularity, something of the interest of what Saint-Simon called the 'machinery' of life at Versailles,* and could also believe that her silences, or a hint of good humour or disdain in her features, were for Françoise a source of speculation as intense, as fearful, as that engendered by the silence, good humour, or haughtiness of the King when a courtier, or even his greatest nobles, had presented him with a petition in one of the avenues at Versailles.

One Sunday, when my aunt had received simultaneous visits from the curé and Eulalie and had then rested for a while, we all went up to say good evening to her, and Maman commiserated with her on the bad luck that always brought her visitors to her door at the same time:

'I hear things didn't work out well again this afternoon, Léonie,' she said gently. 'You had all your visitors here at once.'

My great-aunt interrupted with: 'Riches piled on riches' because, ever since her daughter had become ill, she believed it was her duty to lift her spirits by always noting the bright side of everything. At this point my father chipped in:

'I'd like to take advantage', he said,' of the whole family being here together to tell you something, so I don't have to say it again to everybody separately. I'm afraid we seem to be in Legrandin's bad books: when I saw him this morning he barely said hello.'

I didn't stay to hear what my father had to say, because I'd been with him after Mass when we met Monsieur Legrandin, and I went down to the kitchen to ask about the menu for dinner, which I always found as interesting as the daily newspaper and as exciting as the programme for some festival. When Monsieur Legrandin had passed us as he was leaving the church, walking with a grand lady from a neighbouring château whom we knew only by sight, my father had greeted him in a friendly but discreet way, without stopping for a chat; Monsieur Legrandin had barely responded, and seemed surprised, as if he didn't recognize us, with that distant look of people who have no desire to be friendly and seem to see you at the end of a very long road and such a long way off that they accord you a barely perceptible nod, in keeping with your puppet-like dimensions.

Now, it should be noted that the lady with Legrandin was virtuous and highly regarded; it was out of the question that he was engaged in an amorous adventure and was embarrassed at being caught, and so my father was left wondering what he could have done to upset him. 'I'd be especially sorry if he's cross about something,' said my father, 'because among all those people got up in their Sunday best there's something about him, with his casual little jacket and his loose cravat, that's so unaffected, so very natural—a kind of innocence that's very appealing.' But the family council was unanimously of the view that my father was imagining things, or that, at the moment in question, Legrandin must have been lost in thought. In any case, my father's fears were dispelled the very next evening. As we were returning from a long walk, we saw Legrandin near the Pont-Vieux (he was spending a few more days in Combray because of the holidays). He came up to us with his hand outstretched. 'My dear young man who is fond of reading,' he said to me, 'do you know this line by Paul Desjardins:

*Les bois sont déjà noirs, le ciel est encor bleu.**

Isn't that a very fine evocation of this time of the day? Perhaps you don't know Paul Desjardins? You should read him, my boy; I'm told that nowadays he's turning into a preacher, but for years he composed the most limpid watercolours in words:

Les bois sont déjà noirs, le ciel est encor bleu.

I hope the sky will always be blue for you, my young friend; and then, even when the time comes, as it is for me now, when the woods are dark, when night is falling fast, you'll find consolation, as I do, by looking up at the sky.' He lit a cigarette and for a long time stood gazing at the horizon. 'Farewell, my friends!' he said suddenly, and walked away.

By the time I usually went downstairs to find out what we were having for dinner, the meal was already being prepared. Françoise, commanding all the forces of nature, which had become her assistants, like the giants in fairy tales who hire themselves out as cooks,* would be poking the coals, putting the potatoes to steam, and using fire to put the finishing touches to culinary masterpieces that had already been prepared in potters' vessels that ranged from big vats, casseroles, cauldrons, and fish kettles to terrines for game, moulds for pastry, and little jugs for cream, and included a whole battery of pots of every shape and size. I'd stand by the table and gaze at the peas, freshly shelled by the scullery maid and drawn up in equal numbers like sets of marbles ready for a game; but what delighted me most would be the asparagus, steeped in ultramarine and pink, whose tips, delicately stippled in mauve and azure, shaded off imperceptibly down to their feet—still smeared with a little soil from their garden bed—with an iridescence that was not of this world. It seemed to me that these celestial hues reflected the enchanting creatures who had happily transformed themselves into vegetables and, through the disguise of their firm, edible flesh, made it possible for me to see in these early tints of dawn, these semi-rainbows, these fading blue evenings, the precious essence I recognized again when, all night long after a dinner at which I'd eaten them, they played their joke, as poetic and coarse as in a Shakespearean comedy, of transforming my chamber pot into a vase of perfume.

Giotto's poor Charity, as Swann called her, charged by Françoise with the task of trimming the asparagus, would have them beside her in a basket, as she sat there looking as doleful as if she was suffering all the woes in the world; and the light crowns of blue that capped the asparagus stalks above their pink tunics were as delicately drawn, star by star, as, in Giotto's fresco, are the flowers tied round the forehead or tucked into the basket of Virtue at Padua. Meanwhile, Françoise would be turning on the spit one of those chickens such as she alone knew how to roast, which had carried far abroad in Combray the sweet aroma of her merits, and which, while she was serving them to us at table, would make the quality of kindliness predominate in my personal conception of her character, the aroma of that cooked flesh that she knew how to make so creamily tender being for me only the specific fragrance of one of her many virtues.

But the day when my father consulted the family council about his encounter with Legrandin and I went down to the kitchen was one of the days when Giotto's Charity, still weak and suffering from her recent confinement, couldn't get out of bed; and Françoise, having no one to help her, was falling behind in her preparations. When I arrived downstairs she was in the back kitchen, which opened on to the poultry yard, in the process of killing a chicken which, by virtue of its desperate and quite natural resistance (accompanied by Françoise's frantic cries of 'Filthy creature! Filthy creature!' as she tried to slit its throat under the ear), made the saintly gentleness and kindness of our servant appear somewhat less in evidence than it would the next day at dinner, when the bird was presented with its skin embroidered with gold like a chasuble and its precious juice drained as from a ciborium.* When it was dead, Françoise drew off its blood, which flowed without dousing her resentment; she had another fit of anger, gazed

down at her enemy's corpse, and said one last time: 'Filthy creature!'
I went back upstairs, all a-tremble; I wanted Françoise to be dismissed
on the spot. But who would there have been to make me such
lovely hot-water bottles and such fragrant coffee, and even . . . those
chickens? . . . And the fact was, everybody else had had to make the same
craven calculation. For Aunt Léonie knew, as I didn't yet know, that
Françoise would gladly have laid down her life for her own daughter
or her nephews, but was as hard-hearted as can be when it came to
other people. In spite of this, my aunt had kept her on, for though
aware of her cruel streak she appreciated her qualities as a servant.
I gradually became aware that Françoise's kindliness, her compunc-
tion, her virtues concealed backstairs tragedies, just as history reveals
that the reigns of the kings and queens portrayed kneeling in prayer
in church windows were stained by violence and bloodshed. I came to
realize that, apart from her own relatives, human beings moved her to
compassion for their misfortunes the further away from her they
lived. The floods of tears she shed while reading in the newspaper
about the disasters that had happened to complete strangers would
dry up quickly if she could picture to herself at all precisely the person
concerned. One night, not long after her confinement, the scullery
maid was seized with the most appalling stomach cramps; Maman got
out of bed and woke Françoise, who, quite unmoved, declared that the
girl's howling was a sham, that she just 'wanted attention'. The
doctor, who'd been afraid of such an attack, had put a bookmark in
a medical dictionary we had, at the page where the symptoms were
described, and told us to refer to this page to find out what sort of first
aid to give. My mother sent Françoise to fetch the book, telling her
not to let the bookmark fall out. An hour went by, and Françoise had
still not returned; my mother became quite annoyed, thinking she'd
gone back to bed, and told me to go to the library to see. There I found
Françoise, who, curious to know what the bookmark indicated, was
reading the clinical description of the attack and, now that she was
dealing with a hypothetical patient with whom she wasn't personally
acquainted, was sobbing quite violently. At each painful symptom
mentioned in the article, she exclaimed: 'Oh Mary, Mother of God!
How can the good Lord make a poor human creature suffer so? Oh,
the poor thing!'

But as soon as I called her and she came back to the bedside of
Giotto's Charity, her tears ceased; she could recognize neither the

pleasant sensation of tenderness and pity which she knew so well and had so often derived from reading the newspapers, nor any other pleasure of the same kind, in the irritation and bother of being dragged out of bed for the scullery maid; and at the sight of the sufferings whose description in printed form had made her cry, her only response was to grumble sullenly and even to make some nasty, sarcastic remarks when she thought we'd gone and were out of earshot: 'Well, she's only got herself to blame! She shouldn't have done what you do to get this way! She got pleasure out of it, so she needn't make a fuss now! And honestly, a lad must be desperate to go with the likes of her. It reminds me of one of my old mum's sayings:

> *Qui du cul d'un chien s'amourose,*
> *Il lui paraît une rose.'**

Although, when her grandson had a slight head cold, she'd go off at night, even if she wasn't well herself and should have stayed in bed, to see if he needed anything, walking the twelve kilometres before daybreak, so as to be back in time to start her housework, this same devotion to her family and her desire to ensure the future greatness of her house was reflected, in her policy with regard to the other servants, in a fundamental precept, which was to make certain that none of them stayed too long in my aunt's service; indeed, she took a sort of pride in not allowing any of them to go near my aunt, preferring, even when she was ill, to get out of bed to administer the Vichy water herself, rather than let the scullery maid enter her mistress's bedroom. She was like the species of hymenoptera described by Fabre,* the burrowing wasp, which, to provide fresh meat for her young after her death, summons anatomy to assist her cruelty and, after capturing a few weevils and spiders, proceeds with marvellous skill and ingenuity to sting them in the nerve centre that controls their use of their legs but none of their other vital functions, so that the paralysed insect, next to which the wasp lays her eggs, will provide the larvae, when they hatch, with prey that is docile, harmless, incapable of flight or resistance, but perfectly fresh and edible; similarly, Françoise, to serve her permanent resolve to make the house uninhabitable to any other servant, found ruses so crafty and merciless that it was not until many years later that we learned that if we'd eaten asparagus nearly every day last summer, it was because their smell had given the poor scullery maid, whose job it was to clean them, such violent attacks of asthma that she was obliged in the end to leave.

Alas, we had to change our minds definitively about Legrandin. On a Sunday several weeks after our encounter with him on the Pont-Vieux, when my father had had to admit his mistake, as Mass was drawing to a close and as the sunlight and noise outside was filling the church with such an unecclesiastical atmosphere that Madame Goupil and Madame Percepied (all those, in fact, who a short while earlier, when I arrived a little late, had been so deep in prayer, with their eyes half closed, that I would have thought they hadn't seen me come in if, at the same time, their feet hadn't gently pushed away the kneeler that was preventing me from getting to my seat) began to chat with us quite loudly about totally secular things as though we were already in the Square, we saw Legrandin standing in the blazing sun just outside the porch, with all the colour and bustle of the market below him, being introduced to the wife of another wealthy local landowner by the husband of the lady with whom we'd recently seen him. His face bore an expression of extraordinary eagerness and animation; he made a deep bow with a secondary recoil that brought his back sharply up to a position behind its starting point, a movement he must have been taught by the husband of his sister, Madame de Cambremer. This sudden straightening caused a sort of intense muscular wave to ripple through Legrandin's bottom, which I hadn't imagined to be so ample; and for some reason that undulation of pure matter, that wholly carnal billow, devoid of any spiritual suggestion and whipped into a fury by a thoroughly contemptible zeal, awoke my mind all at once to the possibility of a Legrandin quite different from the one we knew. The lady asked him to tell her coachman something, and as he walked over to her carriage, his face still bore the expression of shy, joyous devotion stamped upon it by the introduction. He was smiling, as in a kind of rapturous dream; then he hurried back to the lady, but since he was walking more quickly than was his wont, his shoulders swung left and right in a ridiculous manner, and so carried away was he that he looked like a crude, mechanical puppet, the plaything of his own excitement. Meanwhile, we came out through the porch and were about to pass close by him; he was too well mannered to turn his head away, but he suddenly appeared to become lost in thought and fixed his gaze on such a distant point on the horizon that he couldn't see us and so didn't have to greet us. His face retained an air of innocence above his casual little jacket that looked as if it was well aware of being out of place in such detestably luxurious surroundings. And a polka-dotted Lavallière bow tie stirred by the breeze in the Square continued to flutter in front of Legrandin like an emblem of his proud isolation and noble independence. Just as we reached the house, Maman realized we'd forgotten the Saint-Honoré cake* and asked my father to go back with me to the baker's and tell them to deliver one straight away. Near the church we met Legrandin coming towards us with the same lady, whom he was escorting to her carriage. As he brushed past us he carried on talking to his companion, but out of the corner of his blue eye he gave us a little sign that seemed somehow to remain within his eyelid and which, since it didn't involve any movement of his facial muscles, was able to go quite unnoticed by the lady; but, to compensate by intensity of feeling for the somewhat restricted nature of its expression, he made the blue chink assigned to us sparkle with a geniality that was more than merely playful and bordered on the mischievous; he subtilized the refinements of amiability into winks of connivance, insinuations, innuendoes, all the mysteries of complicity; and finally elevated his assurances of friendship into protestations of affection, into a declaration of love, lighting up for us alone, with a secret languor invisible to the lady, a love-smitten eye in a countenance of stone.

It so happened that he'd asked my parents the day before to let me dine with him that evening: 'Come and keep your old friend company,' he'd said. 'Like the bunch of flowers a traveller sends us from a country we will never visit again, come and let me breathe from the distant land of your adolescence the scent of those spring flowers I once enjoyed, so long ago. Come with the primrose, the monk's beard, the buttercup, come with the stonecrop that makes the favourite posies in Balzac's flora,* come with the flower of Resurrection Day, the Easter daisy, and the snowballs of the guelder rose which are sweetening the air in your great-aunt's garden even though the last little snowfalls from Easter have not yet melted. Come with the glorious silk raiment of the lily, worthy of Solomon himself,* and with the multicoloured pansies, but come especially with the breeze, still cool from the last frosts, that will open the first Jerusalem rose* for the two butterflies that have been waiting at its door since morning.'

The family was unsure now whether I should still be allowed to dine with Monsieur Legrandin. But my grandmother refused to believe he'd been rude. 'Even you admit', she said to my father, 'that he comes to church quite simply dressed; you can hardly say he's a man of fashion.' She added that in any case, and at the very worst, if he'd been intentionally rude, it was better to pretend we hadn't noticed. And indeed, though my father was the one most put out by Legrandin's behaviour, he may still have been unsure what it really meant. It was like any attitude or action that reveals a person's true hidden character: it has no connection with anything he has said previously, and we can draw no conclusions from the culprit's testimony, for he will admit nothing; we must fall back on the evidence of our senses, and we are made to wonder, in the face of this isolated and incoherent memory, if our senses have not been the victims of an illusion; with the result that such behaviour, the only sort that has any real importance, often leaves us in a state of puzzlement.

I had dinner with Legrandin on his terrace; the moon was shining: 'There's a lovely quality, is there not,' he said, 'in this silence; a novelist you'll read when you're older says the only solace for wounded hearts like mine is shadow and silence.* And you know, my boy, there comes a time in our lives—a time which for you is still far off—when our weary eyes can tolerate only one sort of light, the light that a lovely evening like this prepares and distils out of the darkness, when the only music our ears can bear is the music played by moonlight on the flute of silence.' I listened to Monsieur Legrandin's words, in which I always took great pleasure; but I was troubled by the recollection of a woman I'd seen recently for the first time, and thinking, now that I knew Legrandin was on friendly terms with several of the local aristocracy, that perhaps he knew this one, I plucked up my courage and asked: 'Monsieur, do you know the lady, I mean, the ladies of the Guermantes family?' And I felt happy that, in pronouncing this name, I'd assumed a sort of power over it, by the mere fact of bringing it out of my daydreams and giving it an objective existence in the world of sound.

But at the mention of the name Guermantes, I saw a little dark notch appear in the middle of each of our friend's blue eyes, as though scratched by an invisible pin, while the rest of the pupil reacted by secreting floods of azure. The rim of his eyelids darkened and drooped. His mouth, which had set in a bitter grimace, was the first to recover, and smiled, while his eyes continued to express his pain, like the eyes of a handsome martyr whose body is bristling with arrows. 'No, I don't know them,' he said, but instead of giving so simple a piece of information, so unsurprising an answer, in the natural conversational tone you'd expect, he uttered it with a stress on each word, leaning forward and nodding, with the assertiveness of someone who wants to give credence to an improbable statement (as though the fact that he didn't know the Guermantes could be due only to a strange quirk of fate) and also with the emphasis of a person who, unable to keep silent about a situation that is painful to him, proclaims it openly so as to give the impression that the confession he's making causes him no embarrassment, is easy, pleasant, spontaneous, that the situation itself (being unacquainted with the Guermantes) might well have been the consequence not of unavoidable circumstance but of his own choice, the result of some family tradition, moral principle, or mystical vow expressly forbidding him from having any association with the Guermantes. 'No,' he went on, his words now explaining his tone, 'no, I don't know them, I've never wanted to, I've always made a great point of keeping my independence; at heart, you know, I'm a Jacobin in the way I see the world,* you know. Lots of people came running, to tell me I was wrong not to go to Guermantes, that I was making myself seem a very uncivilized person, a terrible boor. But that kind of reputation doesn't bother me, it's how I am! In my heart of hearts I care for nothing in the world now except a few churches, two or three books, perhaps a few more paintings, and the light of the moon when the breeze of your youth lets me breathe in the sweet smells of the flower beds that my old eyes can't see any more.' I didn't understand very well how, by not going to the houses of people you didn't know, you were clinging to your independence, or how this made you seem boorish and uncivilized. But what I did understand was that Legrandin was not altogether truthful when he said that he cared only for churches, moonlight, and youth; he cared a great deal for the people who lived in châteaux, and in their presence was so fearful of incurring their displeasure that he dared not let them see that some of his friends were bourgeois people, sons of notaries and stockbrokers, preferring, if this truth had to come out, that it should come out in his absence, far away from him, and 'by default': he was a snob. Of course, he never said any of this in the type of language my family and I enjoyed so much. And if I asked him: 'Do you know the Guermantes?', Legrandin the fine talker would reply: 'No, I've never wanted to get to know them.' But unfortunately the fine talker was the second Legrandin to reply, since a different Legrandin (one he kept carefully hidden inside himself and whom he would never allow to be seen because that Legrandin knew some compromising stories about our Legrandin and his snobbery) had already given his reply in the hurt look, the pained semi-smile, the undue gravity of his tone, the thousand arrows by which our Legrandin had been struck in an instant, bringing him to his knees like a Saint Sebastian of snobbery;* all of which meant: 'Oh, how hurtful that question is! No, I don't know the Guermantes. Please don't remind me of the great sorrow in my life.' And since this troublesome Legrandin, this blackmailer Legrandin, though lacking the other's smooth tongue, had a far quicker way of expressing himself, composed of what are called 'reflexes', when Legrandin the fine talker wanted to silence him, he'd already spoken, and however much our friend might regret the bad impression his alter ego's revelations must have produced, all he could do was try to play it down.

This certainly doesn't mean that Monsieur Legrandin wasn't sincere when he railed against snobs. He couldn't know, in his own mind at least, that he was one, since we are aware only of the passions of others, and what we come to know about our own we learn only from others. Upon ourselves our passions act only indirectly, through our imagination, which substitutes for our primary motives others that are more seemly. It was never Legrandin's snobbishness that impelled him to pay frequent visits to a duchess. Instead, it instructed his imagination to make the duchess appear to him as being endowed with all the graces. He could then begin to cultivate the duchess, his self-esteem enhanced by his belief that he was yielding to the qualities of her mind, and other virtues, which the vile snobs of this world could never appreciate. Only other people were aware that Legrandin was a snob himself; for, because they were incapable of following the intermediary processes of his imagination, they could see, closely juxtaposed, his social activities and their primary cause.

Now, at home, we no longer had any illusions about Monsieur Legrandin, and we began to see much less of him. Maman was highly amused each time she caught him in flagrante delicto, committing the sin he would never admit and which he went on calling the sin for which there was no forgiveness, snobbery. As for my father, he found it hard to take Legrandin's disdainful behaviour in so light and detached a manner; and when, one year, they thought of sending me

to Balbec to spend my summer holidays with my grandmother, he
said: 'I absolutely must tell Legrandin you'll be going to Balbec, to see
if he offers to put you in touch with his sister. He probably doesn't
remember telling us she lives two kilometres from there.' My grandmother, who believed that when you're at the seaside you should be at
the beach from morning to night breathing in the salt breezes, and it
was best not to know anyone in the area because time spent on visits
and excursions was time lost from being in the sea air, said she much
preferred that no mention of our plans should be made to Legrandin,
for she could already see his sister, Madame de Cambremer, arriving
at the hotel just when we were about to go fishing and obliging us to
remain indoors to entertain her. But Maman laughed at her fears,
thinking privately that the danger was not so great, that Legrandin
would be in no hurry to put us in touch with his sister. In the event,
however, there was no need for any of us to mention Balbec, for it was
Legrandin himself who, without the least suspicion that we had ever
thought of visiting the place, walked into the trap unwittingly one
evening when we met him on the banks of the Vivonne.

'There are some lovely shades of violet and blue in the clouds this
evening, don't you think, my friend?' he said to my father. 'A blue,
especially, that's more a flower-blue than a sky-blue—a cineraria blue,
which is surprising in the sky. And that little pink cloud, don't you
think it has the colour of a flower, a carnation or hydrangea? Nowhere,
perhaps, except on the Channel coast, on the border between Normandy
and Brittany, have I come across so many examples of this sort of
plant kingdom in the sky. There, not far from Balbec, in that wild
landscape, there's a charming, quiet little bay, where the sunsets of
the Auge Valley, those red and gold sunsets (which I wouldn't dream
of sneering at, by the way) seem quite ordinary and unremarkable;
but in that moist and mild atmosphere these celestial bouquets, pink
and blue, will blossom all at once, incomparably lovely, and will often
last for hours before they fade. Others lose their blossoms immediately, and then it's even lovelier to see the sky strewn with countless
pink and sulphur-yellow petals.

'In this bay, which they call Opal Bay, the golden sands seem all the
more pleasant because they are bound like blonde Andromedas* to
the frightful rocks of the surrounding coast, to that fatal shore,
notorious for its shipwrecks, where every winter many a vessel is
lost to the perils of the sea. Balbec! The most ancient bone in the

geological skeleton of our land, the true Ar-mor, the Sea, the land's end, the accursed region that Anatole France—a magician our young friend here should read—has described so well, shrouded in its eternal fog, like the veritable land of the Cimmerians in the *Odyssey*.* And the marvellous thing about Balbec especially, where they're already building hotels, superimposing them on the ancient and charming soil which they can't change, is the delight of being able to step out at once into regions so primitive and lovely!'

'I see,' said my father. 'Do you know someone in Balbec? As it happens, this young man will be going there for a couple of months with his grandmother, and my wife too, perhaps.'

Legrandin, caught off guard by this question at a moment when he was looking directly at my father, was unable to avert his eyes, but went on staring more and more intently with each passing second at my father, smiling sadly as he did so, with an expression of frankness and friendliness and of not being afraid to look him straight in the eye, and seemed to look right through my father's face as if it had become transparent, and could now see, a long way beyond and behind it, a brightly coloured cloud that created a mental alibi for him and would allow him to prove that, just when he was being asked whether he knew anyone in Balbec, he'd been thinking of something else and hadn't heard the question. Usually this kind of gaze makes the other person say: 'What are you thinking about?' But my father, becoming annoyed, was determined to have an answer, and asked again:

'You seem to know Balbec very well. Have you got friends there?'

In a last desperate effort, Legrandin's smiling gaze reached its extreme limit of fondness, vagueness, candour, and distraction, but, no doubt realizing there was nothing else he could do but answer, he said:

'I have friends wherever clusters of trees, struggling but not defeated, have come together to supplicate with touching obstinacy an inclement and pitiless sky.'

'That's not what I meant,' interrupted my father, as obstinate as the trees and as pitiless as the sky. 'I'm asking if you know anyone there, in that out-of-the-way place, in case something happens to my mother-in-law and she needs somebody to turn to.'

'There as everywhere, I know everyone and I know no one,' replied Legrandin, who was not going to give in easily. 'I know a lot about things, but very little about people. But the things in that place seem just like people, exceptional people, of a very delicate quality, disappointed

by life. It may be an old fortress you encounter on a cliff, by the side
of a road, where it has stopped to contemplate its sorrows in the still
pink evening while a golden moon rises and homebound boats, cleav-
ing the shimmering water, hoist the flame of evening on their masts
and carry its colours; or it may be a simple house that stands alone,
with a shy but romantic air, hiding from all eyes some eternal secret
of happiness and disenchantment. The place is untruthful,' he added
with Machiavellian subtlety,* 'it's a fictitious place and would make
unwholesome reading for a child; it's certainly not a place I'd choose
or recommend for my young friend here, who is so sensitive and
already so inclined to melancholy. A climate of amorous confession
and vain regret may suit a disillusioned old man like me, but it's
always unhealthy for a temperament that's still unformed. Believe
me,' he went on insistently, 'the waters of that bay, which are already
half Breton, may act as a sedative (though that's debatable) for a heart
like mine that is no longer undamaged, a heart whose wounds can no
longer be healed. But at your age, my boy, those waters are not to be
recommended. Farewell, my friends!' he added, walking away with
the evasive abruptness to which we'd become accustomed; and then,
turning towards us with a doctor's raised finger, he summed up the
consultation: 'No Balbec before you're fifty!' he called out, 'and even
then it will depend on the state of your heart.'

My father raised the subject again each time we met him subsequently, tormenting him with questions, but it was a waste of energy:
like that erudite crook who devoted to the fabrication of false palimpsests* a degree of labour and scholarship a tiny fraction of which
would have been enough to secure him a more lucrative but honest
occupation, Monsieur Legrandin, had we insisted further, would in
the end have constructed a whole system of landscape ethics and
a celestial geography of Lower Normandy, rather than admit that his
own sister lived two kilometres from Balbec and be obliged to offer us
a letter of introduction which would never have been such a terrifying
prospect for him had he been absolutely certain—as indeed he should
have been, given his knowledge of my grandmother's character—that
we wouldn't have taken advantage of it.

We always returned from our walks in good time to see Aunt Léonie
before dinner. At the beginning of the season, when the days were still
short, as we reached the Rue du Saint-Esprit we'd still be able to see

a reflection of the setting sun on the windows of our house and a band of crimson deep in the woods near the roadside cross, which was reflected further on in the pond, a red glow which, often accompanied by a sharp nip in the air, was associated in my mind with the glow of the fire roasting the chicken that would soon allow the poetic pleasure I'd taken in the walk to be succeeded by the pleasures of good food, warmth, and rest. But in summer, when we arrived back at the house, the sun would still not have set; and as we sat with Aunt Léonie, its rays, sinking down until they touched the windowsill, would be caught between the long curtains looped by their ties, split, ramified, filtered, and, encrusting the lemonwood of the chest of drawers with flecks of gold, would fill the room with a soft, slanting, woodland glow. But on some days, though very rarely, the chest of drawers would long since have lost its momentary encrustations, and when we turned into the Rue du Saint-Esprit there would no longer be any reflection of the sunset on the windowpanes, and the pond beneath the roadside cross would have lost its red glow, sometimes it was already opalescent and a long beam of moonlight, its path growing ever wider and broken into pieces by all the ripples of the water, would be lying across it from end to end. Then, as we drew near the house, we'd see a figure standing on the doorstep and Maman would say: 'Oh dear! There's Françoise looking out for us. Your aunt must be worried; it's a fact we're too late back.'

Without wasting time to take off our things, we'd hurry upstairs to Aunt Léonie's room to reassure her that, contrary to what she was already imagining, nothing had happened to us, but that we'd gone 'the Guermantes way', and when we went on that walk, well, as my aunt knew very well, we could never be sure what time we'd be back.

'You see, Françoise, didn't I say they must have gone the Guermantes way? Good heavens, they must be ravenous! And your lovely leg of lamb will be all dried up, after being kept so long. What a time to be coming home! So, you went the Guermantes way!'

'But I thought you knew, Léonie,' said Maman. 'I thought Françoise must have seen us go out by the little gate, through the vegetable garden.'

There are indeed, in the area around Combray, two 'ways' we could take for our walks, and they went in such opposite directions that we'd actually leave the house by a different door, according to the way we wanted to go: the way towards Méséglise-la-Vineuse, which

we also called 'the Swann way' because we walked along the edge of
Swann's estate if we went in that direction, and the Guermantes
way. In truth, I never knew anything about Méséglise-la-Vineuse
except the 'way' and various strangers who used to come and stroll
around Combray on Sundays, people whom, this time, even my
aunt, along with the rest of us, 'didn't know at all' and whom we
would therefore assume to be 'people who must have come over
from Méséglise'. As for Guermantes, I was to know more about it
one day, but only much later; and throughout the whole of my adolescence, if Méséglise was to me something as inaccessible as the
horizon, hidden from view, however far we went, by the folds of
a landscape that looked quite different from the landscape around
Combray, Guermantes, on the other hand, seemed no more than
the end point, more ideal than real, of its own 'way', a sort of
abstract geographical term like the equator, the North Pole, or the
Orient. So, to 'take the Guermantes way' in order to go to Méséglise,
or vice versa, would have seemed to me as nonsensical a notion as to
set off towards the east in order to go west. Since my father always
talked about the Méséglise way as affording the finest view of the
plain that he knew and about the Guermantes way as typical of river
scenery, I came to conceive of them as two distinct entities and
invested each with the cohesion and unity that belong only to the
creations of our mind; the smallest detail of either seemed to me
quite precious and to reveal the particular excellence of the whole,
while in comparison, before we reached the sacred site of one or the
other, the purely physical lanes, in the midst of which they were set
down as the ideal view of the plain or the ideal river landscape, were
no more worth the trouble of looking at than, for a keen playgoer,
are the little streets next to a theatre. But, above all, I set between
them, far more than the simple distance in kilometres that separated them, the distance that lay between the two parts of my brain
in which I thought about them, one of those distances of the mind
which not only keeps things apart but cuts them off completely
from each other and puts them on different planes. And that demarcation was made even more absolute because our habit of never
going both ways on the same day, in a single walk, but the Méséglise
way one day and the Guermantes way another day, shut them off
from one another, made them unknowable to each other, in the
sealed and uncommunicating vessels of different afternoons.

When we decided to walk along the Méséglise way, we'd leave (not too early and even if the sky was overcast, because the walk was not very long and didn't take us too far out of our way), as though we were going nowhere in particular, by the front door of my aunt's house, which opened onto the Rue du Saint-Esprit. We'd be greeted by the gunsmith, we'd drop our letters in the box, we'd tell Théodore from Françoise, as we passed, that she'd run out of oil or coffee, and we'd leave the town by the lane that ran along the white fence of Monsieur Swann's grounds. Before reaching it we'd be met by the scent of his lilacs, coming out to welcome strangers. From among the fresh green little hearts of their leaves, the flowers raised inquisitively over the fence their plumes of white or mauve blossoms, still glossy, even in the shade, from the sunlight in which they had bathed. Some, half hidden by the little tiled lodge called the Archers' House, where the caretaker lived, overtopped its Gothic gable with their pink minaret. The Nymphs of Spring would have seemed vulgar compared with these young houris,* which retained in this French garden the pure and vivid colours of Persian miniatures.* Despite my desire to throw my arms round their supple waists and hold their fragrant heads to my face, we'd walk straight past, for my parents had stopped visiting Tansonville after Swann's marriage, and, so as not to appear to be looking into the grounds, instead of taking the path that ran along the fence and climbed directly into the fields, we'd take another path that also led to the fields, but in a more roundabout way, and brought us out a little too high up. One day my grandfather said to my father:

'You remember Swann said yesterday that his wife and daughter were going off to Rheims and he'd take the opportunity to spend a day in Paris? We could go along by the fence, since the ladies aren't there, and save ourselves the trouble of going the long way round.'

We paused for a moment by the fence. Lilac time was nearly over; some of the trees still thrust into the air, like tall mauve chandeliers, their delicate balls of blossom, but in many places where only a week before they'd still been breaking in waves of fragrant foam, they were now withering into a hollow scum, shrivelled and black, dry and without perfume. My grandfather pointed out to my father in what ways the grounds were still the same, and the ways in which they'd changed, since he'd walked there with old Monsieur Swann, on the day of his wife's death; and he took the opportunity to tell the story of that walk one more time.

In front of us a path bordered with nasturtiums rose in full sun towards the house, while to the right was a stretch of level ground. Here Swann's parents had dug an ornamental pond, which was shaded by a circle of tall trees. Even in his most artificial creations, man must work with the raw materials of nature; certain places will always impose their own particular hegemony on their surroundings, and will flaunt their immemorial insignia in the middle of the grounds of a country house just as they would have done far from any human agency, in a wilderness that for ever returns to surround them, created by the exigencies of the position they occupy and superimposed on the creations of men. So it was that at the foot of the path that led down to the ornamental pond there could be seen, in its double row of forget-me-nots and periwinkles, a natural garland, delicate and blue, encircling the water's shaded brow; and the gladiolus, its sword-shaped leaves drooping down with regal nonchalance, stretched out across the agrimony and the wet-footed frogbit the tattered fleurs-de-lis, violet and yellow, of its lacustrine sceptre.

The absence of Mademoiselle Swann, by sparing me the terrible risk of seeing her appear on one of the paths, and of being recognized and scorned by that privileged little girl who had Bergotte for a friend and used to go with him to visit cathedrals, made Tansonville a place of little interest to me on this first occasion that I was allowed to see it; for my father and grandfather, on the other hand, it seemed to give it added attraction, transitory charm, and, like a cloudless sky on a mountaineering trip, to make the day exceptionally propitious for a walk round; I would have liked their plan to be thwarted, to see Mademoiselle Swann appear by some miracle with her father, so close to us that we'd not have time to avoid her and would be obliged to make her acquaintance. And so, when I suddenly noticed on the grass, like a sign of her possible presence, a straw basket lying forgotten next to a fishing line whose cork was floating in the water, I immediately made my father and grandfather look the other way. But in any case, since Swann had told us it was bad of him to go away at this time, because he had some relatives staying at the house, it was possible the line belonged to one of his guests. There was no sound of footsteps along any of the paths. Somewhere in the top branches of one of the trees an invisible bird was doing its best to make the day seem short, exploring the surrounding solitude with a single continuous note; but it received so unanimous a retort, so powerful a repercussion of silence and stillness, that it seemed as though it had arrested for ever the moment it had been trying to make pass more quickly. The sunlight fell so implacably from a motionless sky that it made you want to escape its attentions, and even the dormant water, its repose perpetually disturbed by insects as it dreamed, no doubt, of some imaginary Maelstrom,* increased the unease I'd felt at the sight of the cork by appearing to draw it at full speed across the silent reaches of the reflected sky; almost vertical, it seemed on the point of plunging down, and I'd already begun to wonder whether, leaving aside my desire to know her and my fear of knowing her, I was not duty-bound to warn Mademoiselle Swann that the fish was biting—when I had to run after my father and grandfather, who were calling me, surprised that I hadn't followed them into the little lane that leads up to the fields. I found the whole lane buzzing with the smell of hawthorn blossom. The hedge resembled a series of chapels that were barely visible under the profusion of flowers heaped up like wayside altars; underneath, the sun cast a latticework pattern of light on the ground, as if shining through a stained-glass window; the perfume that enveloped me was as rich and clearly defined in its range as if I were standing before the altar of the Virgin, and each flower, just as ornamental, held out with a distracted air its glittering bunch of stamens, delicate radiating ribs in the same flamboyant style as those which, in the church, decorated the balustrade of the rood screen or the mullions of the window* and blossomed out into the flesh-like whiteness of strawberry plants in bloom. How simple and rustic, in comparison, the wild roses would seem when, in a few weeks, they'd be climbing the same sunny country lane, in the smooth silk of their blushing pink bodices undone by the slightest breath of wind.

But though I stood for a long time before the hawthorns, breathing in their invisible, unchanging smell, trying to imprint it on my mind which didn't know what to make of it, losing it and then recapturing it, becoming absorbed in the rhythm that tossed their blossoms from side to side with youthful high spirits and at intervals as unexpected as certain intervals in music, they went on offering me the same intense delight, endless and inexhaustible, but without letting me delve more deeply into it, like those tunes you can play a hundred times without coming any closer to the secret of their mystery. Several times I turned away from them for a moment so as to be able to return to them afresh. My gaze travelled beyond the hedge, up the bank that rose steeply to the fields, focusing on a stray poppy or a few straggling cornflowers that decorated the ground here and there like the border of a tapestry on which can be seen hints of the rustic motif that dominates the panel itself; these solitary flowers, spaced out like the lone houses that tell us we're approaching a village, announced the vast expanse of wheat breaking in waves beneath the fleecy clouds, and the sight of a single poppy hoisting its red ensign to the top of its flimsy rigging, where it flapped in the wind above its greasy black buoy, made my heart pound like the heart of a traveller who glimpses an upturned boat being caulked on some low-lying stretch of land, and, before even catching sight of it, cries out: 'The Sea!'

Then I'd go back to my hawthorns as you go back to a work of art which, you think, you'll be able to see more clearly when you've stopped looking at it for a moment, but although I formed a frame with my hands so that I'd have only the blossom before my eyes, the feeling they aroused in me remained vague and obscure, struggling in vain to free itself and to become one with the flowers. The flowers themselves didn't help me to understand their effect on me, and I couldn't turn to other flowers for enlightenment. Then, filling me with the joy we feel when we see a work by our favourite painter that is quite different from those we already know, or when someone takes us to view a painting we've known hitherto only in the form of a pencil sketch, or when a piece of music we've heard played only on the piano is presented to us in all the colours of the orchestra, my grandfather called me over and, pointing at the Tansonville hedge, said: 'You love hawthorns—just look at this pink one! Isn't it lovely?' It was indeed a hawthorn bush, but a pink one, even more beautiful than the white. It, too, was dressed for a festival—for the only true holidays, the holy days of religion, because unlike secular holidays they are not ordained by some arbitrary whim to take place on a quite ordinary day that is not set apart for them and has no festive character— but its attire was especially resplendent, for the blossom that clung to the branches, one on top of another, so thickly as to leave no spot undecorated, like tassels wound round a rococo crook fit for a shepherdess, were 'in colour', and consequently of a superior quality according to the aesthetic standards of Combray, if one were to judge by the scale of prices in 'the store' in the Square, or at Camus's, where the more expensive biscuits were the pink ones. I myself preferred cream cheese when it was pink, when I'd been allowed to mix it with crushed strawberries. And these flowers had chosen precisely the colour of something edible, or of some lovingly chosen embellishment of an outfit for a special occasion, one of those colours which, because they make plain the reason for their superiority over other colours, seem most obviously beautiful to the eyes of children, and for that reason will always seem more vivid and more natural to them than those colours, even after they've realized they don't hold out the promise of delicious food and haven't been specially chosen by the dressmaker. And indeed, I'd felt at once, as I'd felt with the white blossom but with more wonder, that it was in no artificial manner, by no device of human fabrication, that the festive intention of the flowers was expressed, but that it was Nature herself that had spontaneously expressed it with the naïve touch of a village shopkeeper decking out her altar for a church procession, smothering the little bush in rosettes like these, which were too delicate in colour and provincially rococo in style.* At the top of the branches, like those tiny rosebushes in pots wrapped in lace paper, whose spots of colour would enliven the altar on great feast days, a thousand buds were swelling and opening, paler in colour, and each revealing as it opened, as though at the bottom of a little bowl of pink marble, tints of blood-red, expressing even more clearly than the flowers themselves the special and irresistible quality of the bush, which, wherever it budded, wherever it blossomed, could do so in pink alone. Set in the hedge, but as different from it as a young girl in a party dress in a crowd of people in everyday clothes who are staying at home, the shrub was ready for the Month of Mary, and seemed already part of it, smiling and sparkling in its fresh pink outfit, utterly delightful and Catholic.

Through the hedge, in the grounds of Tansonville, we could see a path bordered with jasmine, pansies, and verbenas, among which wallflowers were holding open their bright new purses, in the fragrant faded pink of a piece of fine old cordovan leather, while a long green hosepipe coiled across the gravel path and, at each of the points where it was punctured, spread over the flowers and their fragrances a vertical prismatic fan of multicoloured spray. Suddenly I stopped short, unable to move, as happens when something we see requires not only the attention of our eyes, but involves a deeper kind of perception and takes possession of our entire being. A little girl with auburn hair, who looked as if she'd just been out for a walk, and held a gardening spade in her hand, was looking at us, lifting towards us a face covered in pink freckles. Her black eyes were gleaming, and since I didn't know then, nor have I learned since, how to reduce a strong impression to its objective elements, since I didn't have enough 'power of observation', as they say, to isolate the notion of their colour, for a long time afterwards, whenever I thought of her, I immediately remembered those bright eyes as being a vivid blue, since she was fair-haired; and so it's possible that if her eyes had not been so black—which was what struck one most forcibly on first meeting her—I wouldn't have fallen so much in love, as I did, with her eyes of blue.

I looked at her, at first with that gaze that isn't merely the messenger of the eyes, but a window at which all the senses lean out, anxious and petrified, the sort of gaze that would like to touch the body it is contemplating, capture it and make off with it, and the soul too; then, so afraid was I that my grandfather and father, on seeing the girl, would tear me away from her by telling me to run on ahead, with a different kind of gaze, an unconsciously imploring gaze that was intended to make her pay attention to me, to want to know me! She cast a glance forwards and sideways in order to take stock of my grandfather and father, and no doubt the impression she formed of them was that we were ridiculous, for she turned away and with an air of indifference and disdain, stood at an oblique angle so as to spare her face from being within their field of vision; and while they walked on without noticing her, overtaking and passing me, she carried on looking in my direction, without any particular expression, without appearing to see me, but with a half-smile and such an unwavering gaze that I could only interpret it, according to all the principles of good manners instilled in me, as a sign of utter contempt; and at the same time her hand sketched an indecent gesture for which, when it was directed in public at a person one didn't know, the little dictionary of manners I carried within me supplied only one meaning: a desire to be offensive.

'Come here, Gilberte! What are you doing?' The sharp, imperious voice belonged to a lady in white whom I hadn't noticed, while, standing a short distance from her, a gentleman in a linen suit, whom I didn't know, stared at me with eyes that seemed to be popping out of his head; the little girl's smile disappeared abruptly and, taking her spade, she went off without looking back in my direction, with an air that was docile, inscrutable, and sly.

So it was that the name Gilberte passed close to me, given to me like a talisman that might one day enable me to find her again, this girl whom it had just turned into a person and who, a moment before, had been nothing more than a blurred image. So it passed, uttered over the jasmines and the wallflowers, as sharp and cool as the spray from the green hosepipe; impregnating, iridizing the zone of pure air through which it passed—and which it set apart—with the mystery of the life of the girl it designated for the happy creatures who lived and went about with her; displaying under the pink hawthorn, at the level of my shoulder, the quintessence of their familiarity—for me so painful—with her and with the unknown world of her existence which I'd never be able to enter.

For a moment (as we moved away and my grandfather murmured: 'Poor old Swann! What a merry dance they're leading him: they send him off to Paris so she can be with her Charlus—because that was him, I recognized him! And to think that little girl is mixed up in such scandalous behaviour!') the impression left on me by the despotic tone in which Gilberte's mother had spoken to her without her answering back, by demonstrating that she was obliged to obey another person, that she was not superior to the whole world, relieved my suffering a little, gave me a glimmer of hope, and cooled the ardour of my love. But very soon that love surged up again like a reaction by which my humiliated heart was trying to put itself on the same level as Gilberte or bring her down to its own. I loved her and was sorry I hadn't had the time or the presence of mind to insult her, hurt her, and make her remember me. I thought she was so lovely that I wished I could retrace my steps and shout at her, with a shrug: 'You're so ugly! You're horrible! I hate you!' But I walked away, carrying with me for ever my first glimpse of a type of happiness inaccessible to children like me because of certain laws of nature impossible to transgress, the image of a little girl with auburn hair and pink freckles, holding a spade and smiling as she cast in my direction a series of sly, inscrutable glances. And already the charm with which the incense of her name had imbued the spot under the pink hawthorns where she and I had heard it together, was beginning to touch and impregnate with its perfume everything connected with it: her grandparents, whom my own grandparents had had the ineffable pleasure of knowing, the sublime profession of stockbroker, the dismal neighbourhood of the Champs-Élysées where she lived in Paris.

'Léonie,' said my grandfather when we got home, 'I wish you'd been with us this afternoon. You wouldn't recognize Tansonville. If I'd dared, I would have cut you a branch of that pink hawthorn you used to like so much.' And so my grandfather told Aunt Léonie all about our walk, either to entertain her or because the household hadn't yet lost all hope of getting her to venture out of the house. For at one time she'd been very fond of Tansonville, and Swann had been one of the last visitors she went on receiving after she'd closed her door to everybody else. And just as, when he now called to enquire after her (she was the only person in our family he still asked to see), she would have him informed that she was tired, but that she would let him come in the next time he called, so, this evening, she said to my grandfather: 'Yes, one day when the weather's good, I'll take the carriage and go as far as the main gate of the property.' And in saying this she was quite sincere. She would have liked to see Swann and Tansonville again; but she had only enough strength to express this desire: its fulfilment would have taxed her beyond her limits. Sometimes a spell of good weather restored a little of her energy, and she would get up and dress; but before she'd gone into the other room she'd be tired again and would want to go back to bed. What had begun for her—but earlier than for most people—was the great renunciation that comes with old age as it prepares for death, wraps itself in its chrysalis, and may be observed in people who are very long-lived, even in old lovers who have meant the world to each other, and in friends bound by the closest ties of mutual sympathy, who, one year, stop making the necessary journey or outing to see one another, stop writing, and know they will not communicate again in this world. My aunt must have known perfectly well that she would never see Swann again or set foot out of doors, but this definitive seclusion must have been much easier for her for the very reason that, in our eyes, ought to have made it more difficult: for it was imposed upon her by the gradual diminution in her strength, which she was able to measure each day and which, by making every action, every move-ment a cause of fatigue, if not pain, gave to inaction, isolation, and silence the sweet, restorative blessings of repose.

My aunt didn't go to see the hedge of pink hawthorns, but I never stopped asking my parents if she would go, and if at one time she'd often gone to Tansonville, trying to make them talk about Mademoiselle Swann's parents and grandparents, who seemed to me like gods. The name 'Swann' had taken on an almost mythological aura for me, and when I talked with my family I would yearn for them to say it; I didn't dare pronounce it myself, but I'd draw them on to subjects that were close to Gilberte and her family, that involved her in some way, and in speaking of which I would feel I hadn't been exiled too far from her; and so I would suddenly compel my father, by pretending, for instance, to believe that the public appointment held by my grandfather had already been in our family before his time, or that the hedge with the pink hawthorns that Aunt Léonie wanted to see was on common land, to correct my statements and say, as if I had nothing to do with it and of his own accord: 'No, it was *Swann*'s father who had the appointment,' or 'The hedge is part of *Swann*'s grounds.' Then I'd have to catch my breath, so powerful an effect did that name have on me, coming to rest as it did on that part of me where it was forever inscribed, weighing upon me to the point of suffocation—that name which, the moment I heard it, seemed fuller and richer than any other because it was pregnant with all the times I'd uttered it beforehand in my mind. It gave me a thrill of pleasure I was embarrassed at having dared to demand from my parents, for the pleasure was so great that it must have been very difficult for them to give it to me, and with no reward, since it was not a pleasure for them. So then, out of discretion, I would change the subject. Out of a certain moral scruple, too. All the special allurements I invested in the name Swann I would hear again as soon as it was uttered. And then I suddenly became aware that my parents must also experience these allurements, that they must share my point of view and my longings, condoned them, and espoused them, and I felt saddened, as if I had vanquished and corrupted them.

That year my family decided to return to Paris a little sooner than usual. On the morning of our departure, after they'd had my hair curled for a photograph, carefully placed on my head a hat I'd never worn before, and dressed me in a padded velvet jacket, my mother, after looking for me everywhere, found me in tears on the steep little path next to Tansonville, saying goodbye to the hawthorns, putting my arms round the prickly branches and, like a princess in a tragedy, oppressed by her jewels and veils, in a fit of ingratitude at the meddling fingers that had taken such care to twist up my hair in knots and arrange it on my brow, trampling underfoot the curl-papers I'd torn from my head along with my new hat. My mother was unmoved by my tears, but she couldn't suppress a cry at the sight of my crushed hat and ruined coat. But I didn't hear. 'Oh, my poor little hawthorns,' I said, sobbing, 'you're not the ones who want to make me unhappy, forcing me to leave. You've never done anything to hurt me! I'll always love you!' And, drying my tears, I promised them that when I grew up I would not do the pointless things most men do and that, each spring, even in Paris, instead of paying visits and listening to silly talk, I'd go out into the country to see the first hawthorn blossom.

On the walk towards Méséglise, when we reached the fields we were in open country for the whole of the rest of the walk. The wind that traversed these fields, like an invisible vagrant, was for me the presiding spirit of Combray. Every year, the day we arrived, in order to feel I really was in Combray, I'd climb up the hill to greet it as it raced along the furrows and made me run after it. The wind went everywhere with us on the Méséglise way, across the swelling plain where for long stretches it's unchecked by any unevenness of the ground. I knew that Mademoiselle Swann would often go and spend a few days in Laon, and although it was a fair number of kilometres away, the distance would seem less because of the flatness of the terrain; when, on hot afternoons, I saw a gust of wind coming from the furthest horizon, bending the heads of the wheat in the far-off fields, then rolling like a wave over the whole vast expanse before lying down, warm and rustling, among the sainfoin and clover at my feet, the plain which I shared with her at such moments seemed to draw us together, to unite us, and I imagined that the same gust of wind had passed close to her also, that it was whispering some message from her that I was unable to understand, and I'd kiss it as it went by. On the left was a village called Champieu (*Campus pagani*, according to the curé). On the right, beyond the wheat fields, you could see the two carved rustic spires of Saint-André-des-Champs, themselves as spiky, crinkly, honeycombed, chequered, yellowed, and granular as two ears of corn.

Symmetrically spaced out, among the inimitable ornamentation of their leaves, which are unmistakable for the leaves of any other fruit tree, the apple trees opened their broad petals of white satin or dangled in timid bunches their reddening buds. It was on the Méséglise way that I first noticed the round shadow apple trees cast on the sunlit ground, and also the delicate threads of golden silk that the setting sun weaves obliquely under the leaves, and that I'd see my father cut through with his stick without ever deflecting them.

Sometimes in the afternoon sky the moon would appear, white as a cloud, furtive, without show, like an actress who doesn't have to perform yet, and sits for a moment in the auditorium in her street clothes, quietly watching the other actors, not wanting to attract attention to herself. I liked coming upon its image in paintings and books, but these works of art were very different—at least during my early years, before Bloch had attuned my eyes and mind to subtler harmonies—from those in which the moon would seem beautiful to me today and in which I wouldn't have recognized it then. It might be, for instance, some novel by Saintine,* some landscape by Gleyre,* in which it stands out sharply against the sky like a silver sickle, in some work that was naïvely incomplete, like my own impressions, and which it annoyed my grandfather's sisters to see me enjoy. They believed one ought to present to children, and children showed their innate good taste in admiring, those works of art they will continue to admire in adulthood. No doubt they regarded aesthetic merits as material objects which an open mind cannot fail to appreciate, without needing to slowly nurture their equivalents in one's own heart.

It was along the Méséglise way, at Montjouvain, a house standing by the side of a large pond and backed up against a steep, shrub-covered hill, that Monsieur Vinteuil lived. And so we often met his daughter driving her buggy along the road at top speed. One year, we stopped seeing her on her own, but always with an older friend, a young woman who had a bad reputation in the area and who one day took up permanent residence at Montjouvain. People said: 'That poor Monsieur Vinteuil must be blinded by fatherly love not to see what everybody's talking about. A man like that, shocked if he hears a single unseemly remark, letting a woman of that sort come and live under his roof. He says she's a fine person, with a heart of gold, and that she would have been a brilliant musician if she'd worked on her talents. He can be sure she's not there to make music with his daughter.' Monsieur Vinteuil did say this; and indeed it's remarkable how a person will always inspire admiration for their moral qualities in the family of anyone with whom they are having sexual relations. Physical love, so unjustly decried, compels people to manifest every last particle of generosity and selflessness they possess, so much so that these glowing particles are even visible to the eyes of their closest friends. Doctor Percepied, whose deep voice and bushy eyebrows enabled him to play at will the part of a villain, even though his physique was not suited to the role, without in the least compromising his unshakeable and undeserved reputation as being a kind-hearted but grumpy old man, could make the curé and everyone else laugh until they cried by saying gruffly: 'Well, it seems Mademoiselle Vinteuil is making music with her friend. You seem surprised. I can't really comment. But her father told me yesterday. And she's got a perfect right to enjoy music, that girl. I'd never dream of standing in the way of a child's artistic vocation. Nor would Vinteuil, it seems. He makes music with his daughter's friend too, you know. By Jove, there's endless music-making in that damn place. But why are you all laughing? I'm telling you, they go in for too much of it. The other day I bumped into old Vinteuil near the cemetery. He could hardly stand.'

Anyone who, like us, saw Monsieur Vinteuil at that time, avoiding people he knew, turning away the moment he caught sight of them, growing old in a few months, sunk in his sorrows, incapable of any exertion that didn't contribute directly to his daughter's happiness, spending whole days at his wife's graveside, couldn't have failed to realize he was dying of a broken heart, or to imagine he wasn't aware of the rumours going about. He knew, he may even have believed, what people were saying. There is probably no one, however virtuous, who may not be led one day, by the complexity of circumstance, to live cheek by jowl with the vice he has always categorically condemned—without his fully recognizing it, moreover, beneath the mask of particular details it must wear in order to come into contact with him and make him suffer: strange remarks and unaccountable behaviour, one evening, on the part of someone to whom in other respects he has many strong attachments. But a man like Monsieur Vinteuil must have found it especially painful to resign himself to the sort of situation which it is wrongly believed is exclusive to the bohemian life: it occurs whenever a vice which Nature herself has planted in a child, sometimes merely by blending the virtues of its father with those of its mother, like the colour of its eyes, needs to establish for itself the space and security it requires. But the fact that Monsieur Vinteuil may have been aware of his daughter's behaviour didn't mean he worshipped her any the less. Facts are unable to find a place in the world of our beliefs; they didn't produce our beliefs, they don't destroy them; they may inflict on them repeated refutations without weakening them, and a family may be afflicted by an avalanche of misfortunes and maladies without ever doubting the clemency of its God or the competence of its doctor. But when Monsieur Vinteuil thought about his daughter and himself from the point of view of society, from the point of view of their reputation, when he tried to place himself by her side in the rank they occupied in the general esteem of their neighbours, then he made this social judgement exactly as it would have been made by the most hostile inhabitant of Combray: he saw himself and his daughter as the lowest of the low, and this was why his manner had recently been marked by humility and respect for those he saw as above him and to whom he must now look up (even if they'd been far below him until then), and a tendency to look for ways of climbing back to their level, which is an almost automatic result of any downfall. One day as we were walking with Swann along a street in Combray, Monsieur Vinteuil came round a corner and found himself so suddenly face to face with us that he had no time to avoid us; and Swann, with the arrogant charity of a man who, amid the dissolution of all his own moral prejudices, finds in another's disgrace merely a reason for treating him with the kind of benevolence that is all the more gratifying to his own self-regard because he feels it is so precious to its recipient, stood talking for a long time with Monsieur Vinteuil, though he'd never spoken a word to him until that moment, and before taking his leave invited him to send his daughter over some day to play at Tansonville. This was an invitation which, two years before, would have appalled Monsieur Vinteuil, but now it filled him with such feelings of gratitude that he felt obliged not to be so tactless as to accept it. Swann's friendly attitude towards his daughter seemed in itself such an honourable and delightful a gesture of support that he thought it would perhaps be better not to make use of it, so as to have the wholly platonic pleasure of preserving it.

'What a delightful man!' he said, after Swann had gone, with the same gushing enthusiasm and veneration that make intelligent and attractive middle-class women feel awed by a duchess, even if she's stupid and ugly. 'What a charming man! What a shame he made such an unfortunate marriage!'

And then, since even the most sincere people have in them a streak of hypocrisy which makes them put aside their opinion of a person while they're talking to them, and express it as soon as they're no longer present, my parents joined Monsieur Vinteuil in deploring Swann's marriage, in the name of principles and conventions that (by the very fact that they were at one with him in invoking, like decent folk of the same stamp) they seemed to imply were not being infringed at Montjouvain. Monsieur Vinteuil never sent his daughter to Swann's house, and Swann was the one who regretted it most. For each time after he'd said goodbye to Monsieur Vinteuil, he'd remember afterwards that he'd been meaning to ask him about a person who bore the same name, a relative of his, he assumed. And this time he promised himself that he wouldn't forget to raise the matter when Monsieur Vinteuil brought his daughter to Tansonville.

Since the walk along the Méséglise way was the shorter of the two walks we used to take around Combray, and for that reason was reserved for days when the weather was uncertain, the climate along the Méséglise way was quite rainy and we would take care never to lose sight of the edge of the Roussainville woods, so that, if need be, we could take shelter under the trees.

Often the sun would hide behind a cloud, yellowing its edges and distorting its own round shape. The brightness, but not the light of day, would fade from the landscape, where all life seemed suspended, while the little village of Roussainville sculpted its white rooftops in relief against the sky, with a sharpness of detail that was quite breathtaking. A gust of wind would make a solitary crow flap away and then drop down again in the distance, while against the whitening sky the distant woods assumed a deeper shade of blue, as if they were painted in one of those monochromes used to decorate the overmantels of old houses.

But at other times the rain with which we'd been threatened by the little hooded monk in the optician's window would begin to fall; the drops of water, like migrating birds all taking flight at the same time, would descend from the sky in serried ranks. During their rapid flight, they don't separate at all, or deviate from their course, but each one keeps to its place, drawing along the one that comes after it, so that the sky is darker than when the swallows leave. We'd take refuge under the trees. When it seemed that their flight was over, a few stragglers, weaker and slower, would still come down. But we'd leave our shelter, because raindrops enjoy foliage, and even when the ground was nearly dry, more than one still lingered to play on the ribs of a leaf and, hanging motionless from the tip and glistening in the sun, would suddenly slip off and drop from the entire height of the branch on to our faces.

Often, too, we'd go and take shelter, huddled together with the stone saints and patriarchs, in the porch of Saint-André-des-Champs.

How French that church was! Above the door, the saints, the chevalier kings with fleurs-de-lis in their hands, and scenes of weddings and funerals, were carved as they might have been in Françoise's mind. The sculptor had also recorded certain anecdotes relating to Aristotle and Virgil just as Françoise in her kitchen would casually refer to Saint Louis as if she'd known him personally, usually to put my grandparents to shame by comparison, since they were less 'righteous'.* One felt that the notions the medieval artist and the medieval peasant (surviving into the nineteenth century) had of the ancient world or the history of Christianity, and which were marked as much by inaccuracy as by their naïve simplicity, were derived not from books, but from a tradition that was at once very old and very direct, unbroken, oral, distorted, barely recognizable, but alive. Another character whom I also recognized, potential and prophesied, in the Gothic sculpture of Saint-André-des-Champs, was young Théodore, the delivery boy from Camus's grocery shop. In fact, Françoise had such a strong sense of him as someone from the same part of the world, and a contemporary, that when Aunt Léonie was too sick for Françoise, on her own, to turn her over in bed or carry her to her armchair, rather than let the scullery maid come upstairs and get into my aunt's 'good books', she'd send for Théodore. Now this lad, who was generally regarded, quite rightly, as a bad lot, was so filled with the spirit that had decorated Saint-André-des-Champs, and especially with the feelings of respect that Françoise believed were due to 'poor sick folk' and her 'poor mistress', that as he raised my aunt's head from her pillow he had the same naïve and ardent expression as the little angels thronging round the swooning Virgin with tapers in their hands, as if those faces of sculpted stone, stark and grey like trees in winter, were, like them, asleep only, gathering their strength, ready to come back to life in countless common faces, reverent and sly like Théodore's, glowing and ruddy like ripe apples. Against the wall, not set into it like the little angels but standing on a pedestal as though on a stool to keep her feet off the wet ground, a saint of more than human stature showed the full cheeks, the firm breasts swelling out her gown like a cluster of ripe grapes in a horsehair sack, the narrow forehead, the pert little nose, the deep-set eyes, and the hardy, steady, fearless look of the peasant women of those parts. This resemblance, which invested the statue with a sweetness I hadn't expected to find in it, was often authenticated by some girl from the fields, who, like us, had come to seek shelter, and whose presence, like the leaves of a climbing plant that has grown up next to leaves carved in stone, seemed intended to allow us, by comparing it with nature, to appreciate the authenticity of the work of art. In front of us, in the distance, like a promised or an accursed land, stood Roussainville, whose walls I'd never penetrated; it was now, when the rain had already stopped for us, continuing to be punished, like a village in the Bible, by all the spears of the storm beating down obliquely on the dwellings of its inhabitants, or else had been forgiven by the Lord, who had restored to it the frayed golden shafts of his sun, which fell on it in rays of uneven length, like the rays of a monstrance* on an altar.

Sometimes the weather was so bad that we had to go home and stay shut up indoors. Dotted here and there, far off in the countryside, which because of the wet and the gloom looked like the sea, a few isolated houses clinging to a hillside buried in watery darkness shone out like little boats that had folded their sails and would ride at anchor through the night. But what did the rain matter, what did the storm matter! In summer, bad weather is just a passing, superficial mood of the underlying good weather, which is quite different from the fluid, fickle good weather of winter, and having settled over the land and taken solid form in dense masses of foliage on which the rain may drip without compromising the resistance of their permanent joy, has hoisted for the whole season, even in the streets, on the walls of the houses and their gardens, its banners of white or violet silk. In the little drawing room, where I would sit reading until dinner time, I could hear the water dripping from our chestnut trees, but I knew the rain was only polishing the leaves, which had promised to stay there all through the rainy night, like pledges of summer, to ensure that the good weather would continue; the rain could do its worst, but tomorrow at Tansonville there would be just as many little heart-shaped leaves waving over the white gate; and I was unconcerned as I watched the poplar trees in the Rue des Perchamps praying for mercy, bowing in desperation before the storm, and as I heard, at the bottom of the garden, the last, muffled rolls of thunder among the lilacs.

If the weather was bad all morning, my parents would give up the idea of a walk and I'd stay at home. But later on I took to going out on my own on such days, and would walk along the road to Méséglise-la-Vineuse. This was during the autumn when we had to come down to

Combray to see to Aunt Léonie's estate, for she had died at last, vindicating both those who'd always said that her debilitating way of life would end up killing her, and not less those who maintained that she suffered from an illness that wasn't imaginary but organic, which the sceptics would be forced to accept when she succumbed; in any case, her death was not greatly mourned, except by one person, but the grief of that person was intense. During the two weeks of my aunt's final illness, Françoise never left her for a second, never undressed, let no one else do anything for her, and didn't leave her side until she was in her grave. It was then that we understood that the kind of dread in which Françoise had lived of my aunt's sharp words, her suspicions and bad temper, had developed in her a feeling we'd taken for hatred but was actually veneration and love. Her true mistress, whose decisions were impossible to foresee, whose ruses were difficult to foil, whose kind heart was easy to touch, her absolute ruler, her enigmatic and all-powerful monarch, was no more. Compared with her we counted for very little. The time had long passed when, on our first coming to spend our holidays in Combray, we ranked as highly in Françoise's estimation as my aunt. That autumn, completely taken up as they were by legal formalities and discussions with solicitors and farmers, my parents had little time for walks, which the weather made difficult in any case, and they fell into the habit of letting me go off on my own along the Méséglise way, wrapped up in a big tartan cloak that protected me from the rain and that I was especially pleased to throw over my shoulders because I sensed that its Scottish patterning outraged Françoise, who couldn't comprehend that the colour of one's clothes has nothing to do with mourning and to whom, moreover, the degree of grief we'd shown over my aunt's death was not satisfactory, because we hadn't held a large funeral dinner for the neighbours, we didn't affect a special tone of voice when speaking of my aunt, and I was even heard to hum a tune now and then. I'm sure that in a book—and in this respect I was quite like Françoise—such a conception of mourning, in the manner of the *Chanson de Roland** and the porch of Saint-André-des-Champs, would have appealed to me. But whenever Françoise came near me, some evil spirit would urge me to try to make her angry, and I'd take the slightest opportunity to tell her I missed my aunt because she was a good woman in spite of her ridiculous ways, and not in the least because she was my aunt; that she might easily have been my aunt and still seem odious to me, in which case her death wouldn't have caused me a moment's sorrow—remarks which, in a book, would have struck me as inept.

If Françoise, filled like a poet with a flood of confused thoughts about bereavement, grief, and family memories, protested her inability to answer my theories, saying: 'I don't know how to *espress* myself,' I would exult over this admission with an ironic bluntness worthy of Doctor Percepied; and if she went on: 'After all, she was part of the family geology, and you've always got to respect your geology,' I'd shrug my shoulders and say to myself: 'What am I doing, trying to argue with an illiterate woman who speaks in malapropisms?', dismissing Françoise with the petty-minded attitude you're likely to despise in others when considering them calmly and impartially, but which you're quite capable of adopting yourself when acting out one of life's more vulgar little scenes.*

My walks that autumn were all the more enjoyable because I took them after long hours spent with a book. When I was tired from having spent the whole morning reading in the drawing room, I'd throw my cloak over my shoulders and set out; my body, having been forced to sit still for so long, had built up considerable reserves of energy and speed, and now needed, like a top that had been released, to expend them in all directions. The walls of the houses, the Tansonville hedge, the trees in the Roussainville woods, the thickets at the back of Montjouvain, all received the blows of my walking stick and heard my cries of delight, these blows and cries being no more than expressions of my excitement at certain confused ideas which, because they preferred the pleasure of an easy, immediate outlet, hadn't developed to a point where, after a slow and difficult process of elucidation, they would become clear. Most of our attempts to translate our feelings merely relieve us of them by drawing them out of us in an ill-defined form that does not help us to understand them. When I try to sum up what I owe to the Méséglise way, the humble discoveries for which it was the fortuitous setting or the essential inspiration, I remember it was during that autumn, on one of those walks, near the bushy slope that protects Montjouvain, that I was struck for the first time by this disparity between our impressions and the ways in which we usually express them. After an hour of rain and wind against which I'd fought cheerfully, as I came to the Montjouvain pond, and stood in front of a little shed with a tiled roof in which Monsieur Vinteuil's gardener kept his tools, the sun came out again, and its golden rays, washed clean by the downpour, glistened once more in the sky, on the trees, on the wall of the shed, and on the wet tiles of the roof, along the ridge of which a hen was walking. The wind tugged at the wild grass growing out of the wall and at the hen's downy feathers, both letting themselves be blown out to their full extent with the passivity of inert, weightless things. In the pond, which was making reflections again in the sunlight, the tiled roof looked like a slab of pink marble, which had never struck me before. And seeing on the water, and on the surface of the wall, a pale smile responding to the smiling sky, I cried out in my enthusiasm, brandishing my furled umbrella: 'Zut! Zut! Zut! Zut!' But at the same time I felt I ought not to have been contented with these opaque words, but to try to elucidate my feeling of delight more clearly.

And it was at that moment, too—thanks to a peasant who was passing by and seemed in bad humour, made worse by the fact that my umbrella nearly poked him in the eye, and who replied coolly to my 'Lovely day, isn't it, perfect for a walk'—that I learned that the same emotions are not produced simultaneously in all men, in some preordained order. Later on, every time a rather long session of reading had put me in a mood to chat, the friend I was dying to talk to would himself have just been enjoying a good conversation and now wanted to be left alone with his book. And if I'd been thinking fondly about my parents and making resolutions that would be bound to please them, they would have heard, at precisely the same time, of some peccadillo I'd already forgotten and would take me to task for it just as I was about to fling myself at them for a hug.

Sometimes the exhilaration I felt at being alone was accompanied by another kind that I could never distinguish clearly from the first, and which was caused by my desire to see a peasant girl appear before me and to throw my arms round her. Arising suddenly, and without giving me time to identify exactly what had caused it, from among very different thoughts, the pleasure that accompanied it seemed only slightly greater than the pleasure I derived from those other thoughts. Everything that was in my mind at that moment—the pink reflection of the tiled roof, the wild grass, the village of Roussainville which I'd wanted to visit for so long, the trees in the nearby woods, the steeple of its church—acquired an even greater value as a result of this new emotion that made them appear more desirable only because I thought it was they that had provoked it, and that seemed only to wish to bear me more swiftly towards them when it filled my sails with a powerful, mysterious, and propitious wind. But if this desire that a woman should appear added an element of exhilaration to the charms of nature, these very charms, in their turn, enlarged what I might otherwise have found too limited in the woman's charms. It seemed to me that the beauty of the trees was also hers and that the very soul of the landscape, of the village of Roussainville and the books I was reading that year, would be revealed to me by her kiss; and as my imagination drew strength from my sensuality and my sensuality suffused all areas of my imagination, my desire grew boundless. And at the same time—as in those moments of reverie in the midst of nature when, because the effect of habit is suspended and our abstract notions of things are set aside, we're utterly convinced of the originality, of the uniqueness of the place where we happen to be—the peasant girl of my desire seemed to be not just an unremarkable example of the general category Woman, but a necessary and natural product of this particular soil. For at that time everything that was not me, the earth, and other people, seemed more precious, more important, endowed with a more real existence than they can ever appear to a grown man. Between the earth and people I made no distinction. I desired a peasant girl from Méséglise or Roussainville, a fisher girl from Balbec, just as I desired Méséglise and Balbec. The pleasure they might give me would have seemed less genuine, I'd have had less faith in it, if I'd modified its conditions as I pleased. To meet in Paris a fisher girl from Balbec or a peasant girl from Méséglise would have been like receiving a shell I hadn't come across myself on the beach, or a fern I hadn't found myself in the woods. It would have subtracted from the pleasure she would give me all the other pleasures my imagination had vested in her. But to wander in the woods of Roussainville without a peasant girl to kiss was to see these woods and yet know nothing of their hidden treasure, their profound beauty. For me that girl, whom I always pictured dappled with leaves, was herself like a local plant, but of a higher species than the rest and with a structure that would enable me to come closer than through them to the essential flavour of that part of the country. I could believe this all the more readily (and also that the caresses with which she would reveal that flavour would themselves be of a special kind, offering a kind of pleasure that no other girl's could offer) because I was at an age, and would thus remain for a long time, when we have not yet abstracted this pleasure from the various women with whom we have tasted it, when we have not reduced it to a general idea that makes us regard them from then on as the interchangeable instruments of a type of pleasure that is always the same. This pleasure doesn't even exist, isolated, distinct, and formulated in the mind, as the aim we have in wanting to be with a woman, or as the cause of the anticipatory turmoil we feel. We scarcely think of it as a pleasure to be possessed; rather, we call it her particular charm; for we don't think of ourselves, we think only of stepping out of ourselves. Dimly awaited, immanent and hidden, at the moment when it finally arrives it rouses to such a paroxysm the other pleasures we find in the tender glances, and kisses, of the woman by our side, that it seems, more than anything else, like a spasm of gratitude for her kindness and for her touching predilection for us, which we measure by the blessings and happiness she showers upon us.

Alas, it was in vain that I used to implore the old keep at Roussainville to send me one of the village girls, appealing to it as the only confidant I'd had of my earliest desires, when, at the top of our house in Combray in the little room that smelled of orris root, all I could see through the middle pane of the half-open window was that tower, while, faint with emotion, with the wary heroism of an explorer venturing into the unknown or some desperate wretch on the verge of suicide, I opened up within myself an untrodden path which I feared might prove deadly, until the moment when a natural trail, like that left by a snail, coated the leaves of the wild blackcurrant that leaned through the window towards me. In vain did I appeal to it now. In vain did I hold the whole expanse of the countryside in my field of vision, trying to extract a woman from it with the power of my gaze. I'd go as far as the porch of Saint-André-des-Champs, but I never found there the peasant girl I would certainly have met had I been with my grandfather and thus unable to engage her in conversation. I'd stare endlessly at the trunk of a distant tree, from behind which I thought she might appear and come to me; but however much I scrutinized the horizon, it would remain deserted, night would fall, and I would already have lost all hope as I concentrated my attention, as if to summon from it whatever creatures might be hidden there, on that sterile soil, that barren earth; and it was no longer in high spirits but in rage that I struck at the trees in the Roussainville woods, from among which no more living creatures emerged than if they'd been painted cut-outs in a stage set, when, unable to resign myself to going back home without having held in my arms the woman for whom I yearned, I was nonetheless obliged to turn back towards Combray admitting to myself that the chances of my encountering her along the way were dwindling with each passing moment. And if she had appeared, would I have dared to speak to her? I felt she would have taken me for a madman; and I stopped believing that the desires I formed on my walks, and were never realized, were shared by other people, that they had any reality outside myself. They now seemed no more than the purely subjective, impotent, illusory creations of my temperament. They no longer had any connection with nature or reality, which from then on lost all charm and significance and served merely as a conventional framework for my existence, just as the plot of a novel is framed by the railway carriage in which a traveller sits reading in order to kill time.

It may have been from an impression I received at Montjouvain, a few years later, an impression that remained unclear to me at the time, that emerged long afterwards, my conception of sadism. We'll see in due course that, for quite different reasons, the memory of this impression was to play an important part in my life. It was during a spell of very hot weather; my parents had gone somewhere for the whole day and had told me I could stay out as long as I wanted; and having gone as far as the pond at Montjouvain, where I liked to look at the reflections of the tiled roof, I had lain down in the shade and fallen asleep among the bushes on the slope behind the house, in the same spot where I'd once waited for my father one day when he'd gone to see Monsieur Vinteuil. It was almost dark when I awoke. I began to stand up, but then I recognized Mademoiselle Vinteuil (insofar as I was able to recognize her, because I hadn't seen her very often in Combray, and only when she was still a child, whereas now she was growing into a young woman), who had probably just come home, standing right in front of me, a few centimetres away, in the room where her father had received mine and which she'd turned into a little sitting room for herself. The window was ajar, the lamp was lit, I could watch her every movement without her seeing me, but if I'd taken myself off I would have made a rustling sound in the bushes, she would have heard me, and might have thought I'd been hiding there to spy on her. She was in deep mourning, for her father had recently died. We hadn't gone to see her; my mother hadn't wanted to because of a virtue in her that alone set limits to her kindness: modesty;

but she felt deep sympathy for her. She hadn't forgotten the sad end of Monsieur Vinteuil's life, completely given over first to his playing both mother and nursery maid to his daughter, then filled with the suffering she'd caused him; she could still see the tormented expression on the old man's face during that final period; she knew he'd completely abandoned the task of transcribing in clean copies his work of the last few years, the few poor pieces of an old piano teacher and village organist, which, though we assumed they were of little value in themselves, we didn't disdain, because they'd been of such great value to him, having been his sole reason for living before he'd sacrificed them to his daughter, and most of which would be lost for ever, as they'd not even been written down but had been preserved only in his memory, while a few had been jotted illegibly on loose sheets of paper; my mother recalled, also, the other, crueller renunciation that had been forced upon Monsieur Vinteuil, his dream of a happy, decent, respectable life for his daughter; when she called to mind all the heartache that had been visited on my aunts' old piano teacher, she felt deeply moved and shuddered to think how Mademoiselle Vinteuil must be feeling, for the young woman's grief would be tinged with remorse at having virtually killed her father. 'Poor Monsieur Vinteuil,' my mother would say, 'he lived and died for his daughter, without getting any reward for it. Will he get any now he's dead, and in what form? She's the only one who can provide it.'

At the far end of Mademoiselle Vinteuil's sitting room, on the mantelpiece, stood a little photograph of her father. At the sound of a carriage turning in from the road, she quickly went to fetch it, then threw herself down on a sofa, pulled up a little table, and set the photograph on it, just as Monsieur Vinteuil had once placed beside him the piece of music he wanted to play for my parents. Presently her friend entered the room. Mademoiselle Vinteuil greeted her without standing up, her hands behind her head, and moved to the end of the sofa as though to make room for her. But immediately she felt that by doing this she might seem to be manoeuvring her friend into a position she might find awkward. She thought her friend might prefer to sit at some distance from her, on a chair; she felt she'd been indiscreet, her sensitive heart was uneasy; shifting position again to take up all the room on the sofa, she closed her eyes and began yawning to suggest she'd stretched out as she had only because she was feeling sleepy. Despite the rough and bossy familiarity with which she treated her friend, I recognized her father's obsequious and reticent gestures, his sudden scruples. After a few moments she stood up and pretended to be having difficulty closing the shutters.

'Leave them open, I'm hot,' said her friend.

'But that's annoying! Somebody might see us,' replied Mademoiselle Vinteuil.

But then she must have guessed her friend would think she'd said these words simply to provoke her into responding with certain others that she in fact wanted to hear, but that out of discretion she wanted to let her friend be the first to utter. And so her face, which I couldn't see, must have assumed the expression my grandmother liked so much, as she quickly added:

'When I say see us, I mean see us reading. It's so annoying to think that with every little thing you do, somebody might be watching.'

With instinctive generosity and natural courtesy, she left unspoken the words she'd been thinking of as essential for the full realization of her desire. Again and again, deep inside her, a timid, suppliant virgin pleaded with and pushed back a rough, swaggering bully.

'Yes, people are bound to be watching us at this time of night in such a densely populated part of the countryside!' her friend said sarcastically. 'And what if they are?' she went on (feeling she had to accompany these words with an affectionate, mischievous wink, reciting them good-naturedly like a text she knew Mademoiselle Vinteuil liked, but in a tone to which she tried to give a cynical edge). 'If people are watching us, so much the better.'

Mademoiselle Vinteuil shuddered and stood up. Her scrupulous and sensitive heart didn't know what words ought to issue spontaneously from her lips to suit the scene for which her senses clamoured. She searched as far away from her true moral character as she could to find the right language for the depraved person she wanted to be, but the words she thought would have come naturally to such a person sounded false on her lips. And the little she allowed herself to say was said in a very awkward tone, in which her ingrained shyness paralysed her impulse towards boldness and was interlarded with: 'Are you sure you're not cold? You aren't too hot, are you? Would you rather sit and read by yourself?'

'Mademoiselle seems to be having rather lubricious thoughts this evening,' she managed to say at last, probably repeating a phrase she'd heard her friend use on some previous occasion.

Suddenly Mademoiselle Vinteuil felt her friend plant a kiss in the opening of her crêpe blouse; she gave a little cry, jumped up, and they began to chase each other round the room, leaping about, squawking and chirping like a pair of amorous birds, their wide sleeves flapping like wings. Eventually Mademoiselle Vinteuil collapsed on the sofa, with her friend on top of her. The friend had her back turned to the little table on which the photograph of the old piano teacher had been placed. Mademoiselle Vinteuil realized that her friend wouldn't see it unless her attention was drawn to it, and so she said, as if she'd only just noticed it:

'Oh dear, that picture of my father is looking at us! I don't know who could have put it there. I've told them so often that's not where it belongs.'

I remembered this was what Monsieur Vinteuil had said to my father about the sheet of music. The picture must have been a standard prop in their ritual profanations, for the friend's answer sounded like a familiar liturgical response:

'Oh, leave him where he is! He's not here to bother us any more. Just think how he'd start whining and want to cover you up if he could see you here with the window open, the nasty old ape!'

'Come, come,' replied Mademoiselle Vinteuil, her gentle reproach showing the goodness of her nature—not that her words were prompted by indignation at hearing her father spoken of in this way (for that was clearly a reaction she'd grown used to suppressing at such moments, with the help of who knows what sophistries*), but because they were a sort of curb she wanted to apply, so as not to seem selfish, to the pleasure her friend was trying to give her. Also, it may well have been that the smiling restraint with which she responded to these blasphemies, this mild and hypocritical reproach, appeared to her frank and generous nature as a particularly vile and subtle form of the wickedness she was trying to emulate. But she couldn't resist the temptation of being treated with affection by a woman so implacable towards a defenceless dead man; she jumped on to her friend's lap and chastely presented her forehead for a kiss, as a daughter might have done, feeling a thrill of delight at the thought that the two of them, together, were going to the very limit of cruelty by robbing Monsieur Vinteuil, even in his grave, of his fatherhood. Her friend took her head between her hands and placed a kiss on her forehead with a docility that came easily to her because of her great affection for her, and her desire to bring what distraction she could into the sad life of the orphaned girl.

'Do you know what I'd like to do to this horrid old man?' she said, picking up the photograph.

And she whispered something in Mademoiselle Vinteuil's ear that I couldn't catch.

'Oh! You wouldn't dare!'

'I wouldn't dare spit on him? On *that thing*?' said the friend with calculated savagery.

I heard no more, for Mademoiselle Vinteuil, with an air that was at once weary, awkward, fussy, prim, and sad, walked over and closed the shutters and the window, but by now I knew what Monsieur Vinteuil, after his death, had received from his daughter as his reward for all the pain she'd caused him during his lifetime.

And yet, since then, I've thought that if Monsieur Vinteuil had been able to witness this scene, he might still have continued to believe in his daughter's goodness of heart, and in so doing he might not have been entirely wrong. It was true that in Mademoiselle Vinteuil's behaviour the appearance of evil was so absolute that it would have been hard to find it so perfectly embodied in anyone other than a sadist; it's behind the footlights of a Paris boulevard theatre* rather than in the lamplight of a country house that you might see a girl encouraging her friend to spit on the photograph of a father who lived only for her; and sadism is almost the only thing in real life that provides a basis for the aesthetics of melodrama. It might be possible to find a girl who, though not a sadist, has failings as cruel as Mademoiselle Vinteuil's in regard to the memory and wishes of her dead father, but she wouldn't deliberately express them in an act so crude and unsubtle in its symbolism; the wicked aspect of her behaviour would be less evident to other people, and even to herself, as she would be the one who was doing evil without admitting it. But, leaving aside the question of appearances, the evil in Mademoiselle Vinteuil's heart, at least in the early stages, was probably not undiluted. A sadist of her sort is an artist in evil, which a wholly wicked person couldn't be, for then the evil would not be external to her, it would seem quite natural to her, wouldn't even be distinguishable from herself; and as for virtue, respect for the dead, and filial affection, since she would never have had any conception of these things she would take no sacrilegious pleasure in profaning them. Sadists of

Mademoiselle Vinteuil's sort are creatures so purely sentimental, so naturally virtuous that even sensual pleasure appears to them as something bad, the privilege of the wicked. And when they allow themselves to yield to it for a moment, they are trying to climb into the skin of the wicked, and to make their accomplices do likewise, so as to have the illusion, for a moment, of escaping from their own tender-hearted and virtuous natures into the inhuman world of pleasure. And I understood how much she longed for such an escape when I saw how impossible it was for her to achieve it. At the very moment when she wanted to be so different from her father, what she reminded me of were the old piano teacher's ways of thinking and expressing himself. Far more than his photograph, what she really desecrated, what she was using for her pleasures, though it stood between her and them and prevented her from enjoying them directly, was the likeness between her face and his, his mother's blue eyes which he'd handed down to her like a family heirloom, and those kind, good-hearted gestures that interposed between Mademoiselle Vinteuil's vice and herself a way of talking and a mentality that were not designed for vice and that prevented her from recognizing it as something very different from the numerous little social duties and courtesies that occupied her every day. It was not evil that gave her the idea of pleasure, that seemed attractive to her; it was pleasure itself that she saw as evil. And since, each time she indulged in it, it was accompanied by perverse thoughts that at other times had no place in her virtuous nature, she came to see pleasure as something diabolical, to identify it with Evil. Perhaps Mademoiselle Vinteuil felt that at heart her friend was not altogether bad and was not really sincere when she spoke in such blasphemous terms. At least she had the pleasure of kissing her friend's face with its smiles and glances that, even if they were feigned, were similar in their depraved and base expression to those that would have been apparent on the face not of a kind, suffering person, but one with a taste for cruelty and pleasure. She could imagine for a moment that she was indeed playing the games that, with so perverted an accomplice, might be played by a girl who really did harbour such barbaric feelings towards her father's memory. Perhaps she wouldn't have thought of evil as a state so rare, so extraordinary, so disorienting, and so restful to inhabit now and then, if she'd been able to notice in herself, as in everyone else, that indifference to the pain one inflicts on others, which, whatever other names one gives it, shows the terrible, unchanging shape of cruelty.

If the Méséglise way was fairly easy, it was quite a different matter when we took the Guermantes way, because it was a long walk and we wanted to be sure of the weather. When it looked as if we were going to have a spell of fine weather; when Françoise, in desperation because there wasn't a single drop of rain for the 'poor crops', and seeing only a few white clouds floating on the calm blue surface of the sky, would say with a groan: 'Just look up there! They look like a shoal of porpoises frolicking about and sticking their snouts up in the air! It doesn't occur to them to send down some rain for the poor farmers! But as soon as the wheat is tall and ripe, then the rain'll come down pitter-patter, without stopping, with no idea where it's falling, no more than if it was over the sea'; and when my father had been given the same favourable answer several times by the gardener and the barometer, we'd say at dinner: 'If the weather's the same tomorrow, we'll go the Guermantes way.' We'd leave straight after lunch by the little garden gate that dropped us into the Rue des Perchamps, a narrow little street with a sharp bend in it, filled with patches of grass in which two or three wasps would spend the day botanizing; it was a street as quaint as its name, from which I felt it derived its oddity and its cantankerous personality, but it has long since disappeared, for the town's primary school now stands where it used to be. But in my daydreams (like those architects, pupils of Viollet-le-Duc,* who, thinking they've discovered under a Renaissance rood screen or a seventeenth-century altar the traces of a Romanesque chancel, restore the whole church to the state it must have been in in the twelfth century) I leave not a single stone of the modern school building standing, I break through it and 'restore' the Rue des Perchamps. And for this reconstruction I have at my disposal more precise data than restorers normally have: certain pictures stored in my memory, perhaps the only ones still in existence, and themselves doomed to oblivion, of what Combray looked like when I was a child; and, because it was Combray itself, as it was then, that imprinted them in me before it disappeared, they are as moving—if one may compare an obscure portrait with those glorious works of which my grandmother loved to give me reproductions—as those old engravings of the Last Supper or that painting by Gentile Bellini, in which it's possible to see, in a state in which they no longer exist, da Vinci's masterpiece and the portico of Saint Mark's.*

In the Rue de l'Oiseau we'd walk past the old hostelry of the Oiseau Flesché, in whose courtyard would sometimes appear in the seventeenth century the coaches of the Duchesses de Montpensier, de Guermantes, and de Montmorency* when they had to come down to Combray to deal with some dispute with their tenant farmers, or to receive their homage. We'd come to the avenue, among whose trees the steeple of Saint-Hilaire would appear. And I'd have liked to be able to sit down there and read for the rest of the day to the sound of the bells, for it was so lovely there and so quiet that, when an hour struck, you'd have said not that it broke the calm of the day, but that it relieved the day of what it contained, and that the steeple, with the languid, painstaking precision of a person who has nothing else to do, had simply pressed at the right moment the fullness of the silence in order to squeeze out and let fall the few golden drops that had slowly and naturally accumulated in the heat of the day.

The most attractive thing about the Guermantes way was that we had alongside us, almost all the time, the Vivonne river. We crossed it first, ten minutes after leaving the house, by a footbridge known as the Pont-Vieux. The day after we arrived in Combray, after the sermon on Easter Sunday, if the weather was fine, I'd run to this bridge to see the river (in the disorder that prevails on the morning of a great festival, when the grand preparations make the household utensils that are still lying about appear messier than usual) as it sauntered along, sky-blue already between banks still black and bare, accompanied only by a gaggle of cowslips that had arrived too early, and a few precocious primroses, while here and there a violet with a blue spur drooped down under the weight of the drop of perfume stored in its trumpet. The Pont-Vieux led to a towpath which at this spot would be overhung, in the summer, with the bluish foliage of a hazel tree, beneath which an angler in a straw hat had taken root. In Combray, where I could always identify the blacksmith or the grocer's boy concealed beneath the verger's robes or the choirboy's surplice, this angler was the only person whose identity I was never able to discover. He must have known my parents, because he'd raise his hat when we passed by; whereupon I'd try to ask his name, but they'd signal to me to keep quiet so as not to disturb the fish. We'd follow the towpath, which ran along a bank, several feet above the water; on the other side the bank was lower, and stretched away in broad meadows to the town and to the distant railway station. These meadows were strewn with the remains, half buried in the grass, of the château of the old Comtes de Combray, who, during the Middle Ages, had had the Vivonne on this side as a defence against attacks by the lords of Guermantes and the abbés of Martinville.

All that was left of the château were a few barely visible stumps of turrets, sticking up like hummocks, and a few battlements from which crossbowmen had once hurled down stones and watchmen had kept an eye on Novepont, Clairfontaine, Martinville-le-Sec, and Bailleau-l'Exempt, all of them fiefs of Guermantes forming a circle round Combray, and today as low as the grass and not even as high as the boys from the Christian Brothers' school, who came here to learn their lessons or to play during their breaks—a past that had almost disappeared into the ground, lying at the water's edge like a stroller cooling off, but giving me much to ponder, causing me to enlarge my vision of Combray by adding to it a medieval stronghold, a very different place from the town of today, and teasing my imagination with the mysterious shapes of long ago, which it kept half hidden under the buttercups. The buttercups grew in great numbers in this spot which they'd chosen for their games in the grass, standing singly, in pairs, or in large groups, yellow as the yolk of eggs, and shining all the more, I felt, because, unable to divert into the sensation of taste the pleasure I derived from looking at them, I'd let it accumulate in their golden petals until it became potent enough to produce in my mind an effect of pure, purposeless beauty; and so it had been since my early childhood, when I'd stretch my arms out towards them from the towpath, though I could still not spell correctly their pretty name, which might have been the name of a prince from a French fairy tale, who might have come here from Asia centuries ago but had now become naturalized for ever in our town, content with the modest horizon, fond of the sunlight and the riverbank, loyal to the little glimpse of the station, but still retaining, like some of our old paintings in their folksy simplicity, the poetic lustre of the Orient.

I liked to watch the boys putting jugs in the Vivonne to catch minnows, and to see how they became filled by the water, so that they became at once 'containers' with transparent sides like solidified water and the 'contents' of a larger container of flowing liquid crystal, suggesting a more delicious and tantalizing image of coolness than they would have standing on a table laid for dinner, because they showed that coolness as perpetually in flight between the impalpable water, which my hands could never retain, and the unliquified glass, which could offer no pleasure to my palate. I promised myself I'd go back there later with some fishing lines; I asked if I could have a little bread from the snack we'd brought; I threw a few pellets into the Vivonne, and this seemed all that was required to produce a phenomenon of supersaturation, for the water around them solidified immediately into egg-shaped clusters of hungry tadpoles which until then the river had no doubt been holding in solution, invisible, ready to begin to crystallize.

Soon the course of the Vivonne became obstructed by water plants. At first they appeared singly—a pond lily, for instance, which had grown awkwardly across the path of the current, which allowed it so little rest that, like a self-propelling ferry boat, it had no sooner reached one bank than it returned to the other, thus making a never-ending double journey. Pushed towards the bank, its stem unfurled, lengthened, gathered pace, and stretched almost to breaking point until the current caught it again on the other side, whereupon the green tether would fold up on itself and bring the poor plant back to what could rightly be called its starting point, for it would not stay there more than a second before setting off again to repeat the same manoeuvre. There it would be, every time we walked that way, always in the same predicament, reminding me of certain neurasthenics,* among whose number my grandfather counted Aunt Léonie, who present year after year the unchanging spectacle of their bizarre habits, which they always imagine they're on the point of shaking off, but never do; caught in the machinery of their maladies and manias, their futile attempts to escape simply ensure that they remain trapped and that the mechanisms of their strange, inexorable, deadly regimen remain forever in motion. This pond lily was the same, and it was also like one of those damned souls whose singular torment, repeated indefinitely throughout eternity, aroused the curiosity of Dante, who would have asked the poor creature himself to recount in detail the particular circumstances and reasons for his punishment, had Virgil, striding on ahead, not forced him to run after him to catch up,* as my parents did me.

Further on, however, the current slowed down and the river ran through a private property opened to the public by its owner, who had a taste for aquatic gardening and had turned the little ponds formed by the Vivonne at this point into veritable flower-beds of water lilies. The banks along this stretch were thickly wooded, and the long shadows cast by the trees usually made the water look dark green, though sometimes, when we came home on an evening that was calm again after a stormy afternoon, I saw in its depths a sharp, vivid blue, almost violet, suggesting a cloisonné floor in the Japanese style.* Here and there on the surface, blushing like a strawberry, floated a water lily with a scarlet heart, white on its edges. Further along, the flowers were more numerous, but were paler, less glossy, coarser in texture, creased, and arranged by chance in coils so graceful that you imagined you might be seeing, adrift on the water as after the dismantling of some fête galante,* loosened garlands of moss roses. Another spot seemed reserved for the common species of water lilies, nattily pink or white like sweet rocket, like little china ornaments washed sparkling clean with loving care, while, further on still, others, pressed close together in a true floating flower-bed, were like pansies that had flitted like butterflies out of a garden and settled with their icy blue wings on the oblique transparency of this watery garden—this celestial garden, too, for it gave the flowers a soil of a colour more precious, more affecting than their own, and, whether sparkling beneath the lilies in the afternoon in a kaleidoscope of silent, watchful, mobile contentment, or glowing, towards evening, like some distant harbour, with the rosy dreaminess of the setting sun, forever changing so as to remain always in harmony, around the more constant colours of the flowers themselves, with all that is most profound, most evanescent, most mysterious—all that is infinite—in the passing hour, it seemed to have made them blossom in the sky itself.

On emerging from this park, the Vivonne began to flow more freely again. How often have I seen, and wanted to imitate as soon as I was free to live as I chose, a rower who had shipped his oars and was lying flat on his back in the bottom of his boat, letting it drift with the current, seeing only the sky gliding by above him, and showing on his face a foretaste of happiness and peace.

We'd sit down among the irises at the water's edge. In the holiday sky a leisurely cloud would dawdle past. From time to time, suffocated with boredom, a carp would rise up out of the water with an anxious gasp. It was time for tea. Before setting off again, we'd sit for a long time on the grass eating fruit, bread, and chocolate, and we'd hear the distant peals of the Saint-Hilaire bell, horizontal, faint, but still densely metallic; they hadn't blended at all into the air they had spent so long passing through, and, bunched together by their pulsating waves of sound, they sent out vibrations as they brushed over the flowers at our feet.

Sometimes, at the water's edge and surrounded by trees, we'd come upon a villa of the sort that used to be known as a pleasure house, standing by itself in this secluded spot and seeing nothing of the world except the river lapping at its feet. A young woman whose pensive face and elegant veils suggested she was not from these parts, and who had probably come here to 'bury herself', as the saying goes, to taste the bitter sweetness of knowing that her name, and even more so the name of the man whose heart she'd lost, were unknown here, stood framed in a window that allowed her to see no further than the boat moored by the front door. She would look up distractedly when she heard the voices of passers-by behind the trees along the riverbank, but she could be sure without even glimpsing their faces that they'd never known her faithless lover, nor ever would know him, that nothing in their past lives bore his imprint, and nothing in their future would have occasion to receive it. One sensed that in her withdrawal from the world she'd chosen to avoid the places where she might at least have seen the man she loved, in favour of this place where he'd never set foot. And I'd observe her as she returned from a walk along a lane where she knew he'd never appear, and removed from her resigned hands her long, uselessly elegant gloves.

Never, in our walks along the Guermantes way, were we able to go as far as the source of the Vivonne, of which I'd often thought and which had in my mind an existence so abstract, so ideal, that I was as surprised when I was told it was located within the *département*,* a precise number of kilometres from Combray, as I'd been the day I learned there was a particular place on the earth's surface that in ancient times had been the entrance to the Underworld.* Nor were we ever able to go as far as the other great goal I longed to reach: Guermantes itself. I knew this was where the owners of the château, the Duc and Duchesse de Guermantes, lived, and I knew they were real people of flesh and blood, but whenever I thought about them I pictured them to myself sometimes as figures in a tapestry, like the Comtesse de Guermantes in *The Coronation of Esther* in our church, sometimes in changing colours, like Gilbert the Bad in the stained-glass window where he turned from cabbage green, when I was dipping my fingers in the holy water, to plum blue when I'd reached our row of chairs, sometimes completely impalpable, like the image of Geneviève de Brabant, ancestor of the Guermantes family, which my magic lantern showed walking across the bedroom curtain or climbing up to the ceiling—and always wrapped in the mystery of Merovingian times and bathed, as though in a sunset, in the amber light that emanated from the syllable in their name: 'antes'. However, although I could still see them, as duke and duchess, as real people, even if rather strange ones, their ducal character became inordinately distended, immaterialized, so as to contain within it the Guermantes of which they were duke and duchess, comprising the whole sunlit 'Guermantes way', the course of the Vivonne, its water lilies and its tall trees, and so many lovely afternoons. And I knew that the title of Duc and Duchesse de Guermantes wasn't the only one they bore, that since the fourteenth century, when, after vain attempts to defeat its earlier lords in battle, they'd formed an alliance with them through marriage, they were also Comtes de Combray, and thus the foremost citizens of Combray, and yet the only ones who didn't live there. Comtes de Combray, possessing Combray through their name, embodying it in their persons, and carrying within them, no doubt, the strange and pious melancholy that was peculiar to Combray; proprietors of the town, but not of any particular house there, probably dwelling outdoors, in the street, between heaven and earth, like Gilbert de Guermantes, of whom all I could see, in the windows of the apse of Saint-Hilaire, was the reverse side in black lacquer, if I looked up as I went to buy salt at Camus's grocery.

Along the Guermantes way I'd sometimes walk past damp little fences covered in clusters of dark flowers. I'd stop to look at them, thinking I was about to make some important discovery, for I seemed to have before me a fragment of that land of streams and rivers I'd been longing to know ever since I'd read a description of it by one of my favourite authors. And it was with this imaginary land, traversed by bubbling streams, that Guermantes, changing its appearance in my mind, became identified when I heard Doctor Percepied talk about the flowers and the lovely running waters that could be found in the grounds of the château. I dreamed that Madame de Guermantes, taking a sudden fancy to me, had invited me there, and that she'd spend all day with me, fishing for trout. In the evening, holding me by the hand as we walked past the little gardens of her vassals, she'd show me the flowers that leaned their red and violet spikes against the low walls, and would teach me their names. She'd get me to tell her the subjects of the poems I was going to write. And these dreams made me think that, since I wanted to be a writer one day, it was high time to decide what sort of books I'd write. But as soon as I asked myself this question, and began to cast around for a subject I could invest with deep philosophical meaning, my mind would go blank, I'd see before me nothing but a void, I'd feel I had no talent or that, perhaps, a disease of the brain was preventing me from using it. Sometimes I'd rely on my father to sort that out. He was so powerful, in such favour with people in authority, that he made it possible for us to transgress the laws Françoise had taught me to consider more inexorable than the laws of life and death, as when we were allowed to postpone for a year the cleaning of the walls of our house, the only house so exempted in the whole of our part of Paris, or when he obtained permission from the minister for Madame Sazerat's son, who wanted to spend some time at a spa, to take his *baccalauréat** two months in advance, with the candidates whose names began with an 'A', instead of having to wait his turn with the 'S' contingent. If I'd fallen seriously ill, if I'd been kidnapped by bandits, in my unshakable conviction that my father was on intimate terms with the powers that be, had such compelling letters of recommendation to the Almighty that my illness or captivity couldn't be anything other than pure illusions, and that I could come to no harm, I'd have waited with complete equanimity for my inevitable return to the comfort of reality, and my deliverance from sickness or captivity; and perhaps my lack of talent, the black hole that opened in my mind when I strove to find a focus for my future writings, was itself a mere illusion, and would be brought to an end by the intervention of my father, who would surely have come to an agreement with the government and Providence that I'd be the most celebrated writer of the day. But at other times, as my parents grew impatient at seeing me dawdling along behind them, my present existence, instead of seeming to me an artificial creation of my father's that he could modify at will, appeared, on the contrary, to be part of a larger reality that hadn't been designed for me, against which I had no recourse, within which I had no ally, and beyond which no further possibilities lay concealed. At those times it seemed to me that I existed the same way other men did, that I'd grow old and die like them, and that my only distinguishing characteristic was that I was one of those people who have no aptitude for writing. And so, utterly demoralized, I'd give up for ever my ambition to write, despite the encouragement I'd received from Bloch. No amount of praise that might be heaped on me could dispel the intimate, immediate sense I had of the nullity of my intellect, just as a wicked man whose good deeds are praised by all cannot escape the pangs of his conscience.

One day my mother said: 'You know how you're always talking about Madame de Guermantes. Well, because Doctor Percepied took such good care of her when she was ill four years ago, she's coming to Combray for his daughter's wedding. You'll be able to see her at the church.' It was from Doctor Percepied, in fact, that I'd heard most about Madame de Guermantes. He'd even shown us a copy of an illustrated magazine in which she was depicted in the costume she'd worn at a fancy dress ball given by the Princesse de Léon.*

During the wedding service the verger, by suddenly changing his position, afforded me a glimpse of a fair-haired lady sitting in one of the chapels; she had a large nose, piercing blue eyes, a bright, billowy scarf of shiny, mauve silk, and a little pimple at the corner of her nose. Because, on the surface of her face, which was red, as though she was very warm, I could see elements of similarity, diluted and barely perceptible, with the illustration I'd been shown, and especially because the particular features I noticed in her, when I tried to name them, produced exactly the same terms—a large nose, blue eyes—I'd heard Doctor Percepied use when describing Madame de Guermantes, I said to myself: 'That lady looks like Madame de Guermantes.' The chapel from which she was following the service was that of Gilbert the Bad, where, under the flat tombstones, golden and distended like cells of honeycomb, lay the old Comtes de Brabant, and I remembered hearing that it was reserved for the Guermantes family when any of its members came to Combray for a ceremony; and it was hardly likely that there could be more than one woman who looked like the picture of Madame de Guermantes, and who was sitting in that chapel on the very day when she was expected to be there: it was she! I was most disappointed. My disappointment came from the fact that I'd failed to note, when I thought of Madame de Guermantes, that I was picturing her to myself in the colours of a tapestry or a stained-glass window, as living in another century, and as being of a different substance from the rest of the human race. It had never occurred to me that she might have a red face, or a mauve scarf like Madame Sazerat's; and the oval curve of her cheeks reminded me so much of people I'd seen at our house that the suspicion crossed my mind, though only for a moment, that this lady, in her generative principle, in her entire molecular composition, was perhaps not the substantive Madame de Guermantes, and instead, her body, in ignorance of the name by which it was known, actually belonged to a category of women that included the wives of doctors and shop-keepers. 'So that's Madame de Guermantes! That's all she amounts to!' was the exclamation written on my face as I gazed in astonish-ment at this figure which, naturally enough, bore no resemblance to those other figures that had so often appeared in my dreams under the name of Madame de Guermantes, because, unlike them, she was no arbitrary creation of my own, but had sprung up before me for the first time only a moment ago, in the church: an image which wasn't of the same nature, was not colourable at will like those others that so readily absorbed the amber tint of a syllable, but was so real that everything, even the little red pimple on her nose, attested to her subjection to the laws of life, just as, in a transformation scene in a play, a crease in the fairy's dress, a trembling of her little finger, betray the physical presence of a living actress, whereas, until then, we'd almost been convinced that we were simply looking at a projec-tion from a coloured slide.

At the same time, I was trying to apply another idea (the idea: 'It's Madame de Guermantes') on to this fresh and unalterable image that the prominent nose and piercing eyes had fixed in my mind (perhaps because it was they that had first struck me, had made the first impact on me, before I'd had time to wonder whether the woman before me could actually be Madame de Guermantes); but all I managed to do was place the idea facing the image, like two discs separated by a space. But this Madame de Guermantes of whom I'd so often dreamed, now that I could see she had a real existence independent of me, acquired an even greater hold over my imagination, which, paralysed for a moment on encountering a reality so different from what it had expected, began to react, and said to me: 'The glory of the Guermantes goes back even further than Charlemagne. They had the power of life and death over their vassals. The Duchesse de Guermantes is a descendant of Geneviève de Brabant. She doesn't know, nor would she want to know, any of the people here today.'

And then—oh, how marvellous is the independence of the human gaze, tied to the face by a cord so loose, so long, so extensible that it can wander off alone over great distances—while Madame de Guermantes sat in the chapel above the tombs of her dead ancestors, her gaze strayed here and there, climbed up the pillars, and even settled for a moment on me, like a ray of sunshine making its way along the nave, but a ray of sunshine which, at the moment when I felt its caress, seemed quite conscious of what it was doing. As for Madame de Guermantes herself, since she remained quite still, sitting there like a mother apparently oblivious to all the impudent tricks and pranks of her children, who play about and shout out to people she doesn't know, it was impossible for me to tell whether, in the idleness of her mind, she approved or disapproved of what was presented to her wandering gaze.

I felt it was important that she should not leave the church before I'd looked at her long enough, reminding myself that for years I'd dreamed of having the opportunity to see her; and I didn't take my eyes off her, as if by gazing at her I'd be able to carry away and store up inside me the memory of that prominent nose, those red cheeks, all the particular features that seemed to me so many precious, authentic, singular pieces of information about her face. Now that I was moved to consider this face beautiful because of all the thoughts I'd brought to bear on it—and especially perhaps because of a form of the instinct of self-preservation that makes us want to preserve everything that is best in ourselves, in order to avoid feeling disappointed—and since she was one and the same person as the Duchesse de Guermantes who'd lived until then in my imagination, I set her once again apart from the common run of humanity in which the actual sight of her in the flesh had made me include her, and was irritated to hear people around me say: 'She's better looking than Madame Sazerat' (or Mademoiselle Vinteuil), as if she were comparable to them. Restricting my gaze to her fair hair, her blue eyes, and the shape of her neck, and ignoring the features that might have reminded me of the faces of other women, I exclaimed to myself in admiration before this deliberately unfinished sketch: 'How lovely she is! What true nobility! She is indeed a proud Guermantes and a descendant of Geneviève de Brabant!' And the attention I gave to her face made it stand out so vividly that today, if I think back on that wedding, I find it impossible to visualize a single one of the people present except her and the verger who answered in the affirmative when I asked if the lady really was Madame de Guermantes. But I can still see her, especially at the moment when the procession filed into the vestry, which was lit by the warm, fitful sun of that windy, stormy day, and where Madame de Guermantes found herself surrounded by all those Combray people whose names she didn't even know, whose inferiority proclaimed her supremacy too loudly for her to feel towards them anything but sincere benevolence, and whom, moreover, she hoped to impress even more by her graciousness and simplicity. And so, not being able to deploy those deliberate gazes charged with specific meaning which we direct at people we know, but only to allow her distracted thoughts to flow from her eyes in a stream of blue light which she was powerless to control, she was anxious not to embarrass or to appear to disdain the ordinary mortals around her on whom it kept falling as she walked along. I can still see, above her silky, swelling mauve scarf, the mild surprise in her eyes, to which she'd added, without daring to address it to anyone in particular, so that it might be shared by everyone, the slightly shy smile of a sovereign among her vassals, looking apologetically and fondly upon them. This smile fell on me as I stood there, unable to take my eyes off her. Whereupon, remembering the look she'd given me during the Mass, as blue as a ray of sunlight passing through Gilbert the Bad's window, I thought to myself: 'She has definitely noticed me.' I was now sure she liked me, would go on thinking about me after leaving the church, and would perhaps feel sad that evening, at Guermantes, because of me. And immediately I fell in love with her, for if at times we may fall in love with a woman simply because she looks at us with disdain, as I thought Mademoiselle Swann had done, and because we think she will remain for ever unattainable, at other times it may be enough for her to look on us kindly, as Madame Guermantes was doing, and we think she may one day be ours. Her eyes turned as blue as a periwinkle that was impossible to pick, but which she had dedicated to me; and the sun, emerging from behind a dark cloud and beating down again with its full force on the Square and into the vestry, added a geranium blush to the red carpets that had been rolled out for the occasion and over which Madame de Guermantes advanced with a smile, and covered their woollen surface with a pinkish glow, an

epidermis of light, giving it the sort of tenderness, of solemn sweetness and joy that characterize certain passages of *Lohengrin*,* or certain paintings by Carpaccio,* and help to explain why Baudelaire was
able to apply to the sound of the trumpet the adjective 'delicious'.*

How much more distressing, after that day, in the course of my
walks along the Guermantes way, did it seem to me to have no literary
talent, and to have to give up all hope of ever becoming a famous
writer! The sadness I felt over this, as I lingered behind the others,
lost in my dreams, was so great that in order not to feel it any more, to
overcome my pain, my mind, by a kind of spontaneous act of self-
defence, stopped thinking altogether about verse or novels or any kind
of poetic future to which my lack of talent forbade me to aspire. Then,
independently of all these literary preoccupations and in no way connected with them, a roof, a gleam of sunlight on a stone, or the smell
of a lane would suddenly pull me up short because of a special kind of
pleasure they gave me, and also because they seemed to be concealing, beyond what my eyes could see, something they were inviting me
to come and take from them, but which, despite all my efforts, I could
never manage to discover. Since I felt that this something was to be
found somewhere within them, I'd stand there motionless, looking,
sniffing, trying to use my mind to go beyond what I saw or smelt. And
if I had to proceed on my way and catch up with my grandfather, I'd
try to rediscover them by closing my eyes; I'd concentrate on recalling the precise line of the roof, the exact shade of the stone, which,
without my being able to understand why, had seemed to be bursting
with something, ready to open, to yield up what it was they contained,
and for which they were merely an outer covering. Of course it was
not impressions of this kind that could restore the hope I'd lost of
succeeding one day in becoming a writer and poet, because they were
always related to a particular object with no intellectual value, and
suggesting no abstract truth. But at least they gave me an irrational
pleasure, the illusion of a sort of fecundity, and thereby distracted me
from the tedium and the sense of impotence I'd felt each time I'd
tried to identify a philosophical theme for a great literary work. But
the moral duty imposed on me by these impressions of shapes, scents,
and colours—to try to perceive what lay hidden behind them—was
so arduous that I'd soon be looking for excuses that would relieve me
of such efforts and spare me all the trouble involved. Fortunately, my
parents would call me; I'd feel that, for the moment, I didn't enjoy the

calmness of mind I needed for the successful pursuit of my quest, and that it would be better to stop thinking about it until I was back home, and not to exhaust myself to no purpose in the meantime. So I'd concern myself no longer with the mystery that lay hidden in a shape or a perfume, relaxed in the knowledge that I was taking it home with me, protected by the layer of impressions under which I'd find it still alive, like the fish that, on days when I was allowed to go out with my rod, I'd carry back in my basket covered by a layer of grass to keep them fresh. Once I was back at the house I'd begin to think about other things, and in this way my mind would become filled (as my room was with the flowers I'd picked on my walks, or the objects people had given me) with the play of light on a stone, the sound of a bell, the smell of leaves, a roofline—a welter of perceptions beneath which the reality I sensed, but didn't have the will to bring into full view, had long since died. Once, however—when our walk had taken up much more time than usual, and we had been very glad to be overtaken halfway home, as the afternoon was drawing to a close, by Doctor Percepied, who, speeding along in his carriage, recognized us and gave us a lift—I had an impression of this sort and didn't let it go until I'd explored it a little. I'd been made to climb up next to the coachman and we were going along like the wind because the doctor, on the way back to Combray, had to stop at Martinville-le-Sec to see a patient at whose door he'd asked us to wait. At a bend in the road, all of a sudden, I experienced that special pleasure, unlike any other, when I caught sight, first, of the twin steeples of Martinville, which were lit up by the setting sun and seemed to keep changing position with the movement of the carriage and the twists and turns of the road, and then the steeple of Vieuxvicq, which, though separated from the others by a hill and a valley, and situated on higher ground in the distance, seemed to be right next to them.

As I observed and noted the shape of their spires, the shifting of their lines, the sunlight on their surfaces, I felt I wasn't penetrating to the core of my impression of them, that there was something else behind their mobility and brightness, something they seemed to contain and conceal at the same time.

The steeples appeared so far away, and we seemed to be approaching them so slowly, that I was surprised when, a few moments later, we stopped in front of the Martinville church. I didn't know why the sight of them on the horizon had given me so much pleasure, and the obligation I felt to try and discover the reason for it seemed to me quite irksome; I wanted to store in my head those shapes moving in the sun and not think about them any more now. And it's very likely that, had I done so, the two steeples would have gone for ever to join the many trees, rooftops, fragrances, and sounds I'd distinguished from others because of the obscure pleasure they'd given me and which I've never fully explored. I got down to chat with my parents while we waited for the doctor. Then we were off again, and I was back on the box seat, turning my head to look once more at the steeples, and not long afterwards I glimpsed them one last time as we went round a bend. The coachman didn't seem inclined to talk, and barely acknowledged anything I said, and so, for lack of other company, I was obliged to fall back on my own and try to recall my steeples. Soon their lines and their sunlit surfaces split apart, as if they were a kind of bark, a little of what was hidden inside them appeared, a thought that had not existed a moment before occurred to me, taking shape in words inside my head, and the pleasure I'd felt at the sight of them was so increased by this that, overcome by a sort of drunkenness, I could think of nothing else. At this point, though we were already quite a distance from Martinville, when I turned my head I caught sight of them again, quite black this time, for the sun had now set. From time to time a bend in the road would hide them from me; then they appeared one last time, before disappearing for good.

Although not thinking that what lay hidden behind the steeples of Martinville must be something analogous to a beautiful turn of phrase, since it had appeared to me in the form of words that gave me pleasure, I asked the doctor for a pencil and some paper and to ease my conscience and satisfy my enthusiasm, composed, despite the jolting of the carriage, the following little text which I have since rediscovered and reproduce here virtually unchanged:

'Alone, rising from the level plain, and looking lost in the open country, the twin steeples of Martinville ascended towards the sky. Soon we saw three: the laggard steeple of Vieuxvicq, boldly leaping forward and appearing in front of them, had come to join them. Minutes passed, we were moving along quite fast, and yet the three steeples were still a long way ahead of us, like three birds perched on the plain, motionless and standing out in the sunlight. Then the steeple at Vieuxvicq moved away, receding into the distance, and the steeples of Martinville remained alone, lit up by the setting sun, which even at that distance I could see playing on their sloping sides and smiling. We'd taken such a long time to get close to them that I was wondering how long it would still take to reach them when, all of a sudden, the carriage turned a corner and set us down right next to them; they'd thrown themselves so abruptly in our path that we only just had time to stop to avoid bumping into the porch. We set off again, and left Martinville, which accompanied us for a few seconds before disappearing; but we could still see the church steeples and that of Vieuxvicq, lingering alone on the horizon to watch us go, waving farewell with their sunlit spires. Every little while one of them would draw aside so that the other two could see us clearly for a moment longer; then the road changed direction, they swung round in the evening light like three golden pivots and vanished from sight. But a little later, when we'd nearly arrived in Combray, and the sun had set, I caught sight of them one last time, in the far distance, look-ing now like three flowers painted on the low skyline of the fields. They made me think, too, of the three young maids in a legend, aban-doned in some deserted spot where night had begun to fall; as we moved off at a gallop, I could see them timidly seeking their way and, after a few awkward stumbles from their noble silhouettes, they pressed close together, slipped one behind the other so as to form against the still pink sky a single black shape, charming and resigned, and faded into the night.'

I never thought of this page again, but when I'd finished writing it, perched on the edge of the seat where the doctor's coachman usu-ally placed a basket full of chickens he'd bought at the market in Martinville, I was so happy, I felt it had so freed me from those steeples and the mystery behind them, that, as if I myself was a hen and had just laid an egg, I began to sing at the top of my voice.

All day long, on those walks, I'd been able to dream about the pleasure of being a friend of the Duchesse de Guermantes, of fishing for trout, of going out on the Vivonne in a boat, and, greedy for hap-piness, I asked no more from life at such moments than that it should consist of an endless series of blissful afternoons. But when, on our way home, I saw on the left a farm at some distance from two others that were very close together, from which point, in order to enter Combray, we had only to go down an avenue of oaks bordered on one side by small enclosed fields planted at regular intervals with apple

trees which, when lit by the setting sun, cast across the grass a Japanese
pattern of shadows, my heart would suddenly beat faster, for I knew
that within half an hour we'd be home and that, as was the rule on
days when we'd taken the Guermantes way and dinner would be
served later than usual, I'd be sent to bed as soon as I'd had my soup,
and my mother, kept at table as though there was company for dinner,
wouldn't come up to my room to say goodnight. The world of sadness
I then entered was as distinct from the world in which I'd just been
dancing with joy as, in certain skies, a band of pink is separated as
though by a ruled line from a band of green or black. You may see
a bird flying against a background of pink; it draws near its extremity,
almost touching the band of black, then disappears into it. The desires
that had enveloped me a moment before—to go to Guermantes, to
travel, to be happy—now seemed so remote that their fulfilment
would have given me no pleasure. I'd have foregone them all just to
be able to spend the night sobbing in Maman's arms! Shivering,
I could not take my pleading eyes off my mother's face, which wouldn't
appear that evening in my bedroom, where I could already see myself
in my imagination; I wished I could have died. I'd remain in that state
until the following morning, when the first rays of sunshine, like the
gardener with his ladder, would lean their bars against the wall
covered in nasturtiums that climbed up to my window, and I'd jump
out of bed and run down to the garden, without giving a thought to
the fact that evening must return and, with it, the hour when I'd have
to leave my mother. And so it was from the Guermantes way that
I learned to distinguish those states of mind that, during certain
periods, alternate within me, even dividing each day between them,
the one returning to displace the other, with the regularity of a fever;
contiguous, yet so foreign to each other, so lacking in any means of
communication, that when I'm in one of these states I can no longer
comprehend, or even imagine, what I've desired or feared or accomplished in the other.

So, for me, the Méséglise way and the Guermantes way remain
linked to many of the little episodes in the life which, of all the different parallel lives we lead, is the richest in incident and sudden rever-
sals of fortune: I mean, the life of the mind. No doubt its development
within us is imperceptible, and the discovery of the truths that have
changed its meaning and outlook for us, and opened new perspectives
on it, must have been maturing in us for a long time; but this must

have been largely unconscious; and for us those truths date only from the day and minute when they become apparent. The flowers that danced on the grass, the water that flowed past in the sunlight, the whole landscape in which these things appeared still accompanies the memory of them with its unconscious or heedless face; and, certainly, when they were studied at length by that humble passer-by, that dreaming child—as a king is studied by a chronicler lost in the crowd—that piece of nature, that bit of garden could never have imagined it would be thanks to him that they would be elected to survive in all their most ephemeral details; and yet the scent of hawthorn floating along the hedge where the wild roses will soon replace it, the crunch of feet on a gravel path, a bubble formed against a water plant by the current of the river and immediately bursting—all these things my excitement has borne along with it and kept alive over the years, while around them the paths have vanished and those who trod them, and the memory of those who trod them, have died. Sometimes the fragment of landscape thus transported into the present will detach itself in such isolation from everything else that it floats indistinctly in my mind like a Delos* in full bloom, and I'm unable to say from what place, from what time—perhaps, simply, from what dream—it comes. But it is above all as the foundations of my mental identity, as the solid ground on which I still stand, that I must regard the Méséglise way and the Guermantes way. It was because I believed in things and people when I walked along those two ways that the things and people they revealed to me are the only ones I can still take seriously and that still bring me joy. Whether it's because the spark of creative faith has dried up in me, or because reality takes shape only in memory, the new kinds of flowers I'm shown nowadays never seem to me to be real flowers. The Méséglise way with its lilacs, its hawthorns, its cornflowers, its poppies, its apple trees, and the Guermantes way with its river full of tadpoles, its water lilies and buttercups, provided me with an indelible image of the countryside in which I'd like to live, in which my essential requirements are that I can go fishing, drift about in a boat, see the ruins of Gothic fortifications, and find among the wheat fields a church, like Saint-André-des-Champs, monumental, rustic, and golden as a haystack; and the cornflowers, the hawthorns, the apple trees that I still happen, when travelling, to come upon in the fields, because they exist at the same depth, at the same level as my past, speak immediately to my heart. And yet,

because places have their own unique character, when I have a sudden
desire to see the Guermantes way again, it would not be satisfied by
taking me to the banks of a river where the water lilies were just as
beautiful, or even more beautiful, than in the Vivonne, any more than
in my return home in the evening—at that hour when I felt the stir-
rings of the feeling of anguish that later in life is transferred to love,
and may become forever inseparable from it—I would have wished
for some other mother, more beautiful and more intelligent than my
own, to come and kiss me goodnight. No: just as the one thing necessary to send me to sleep contented—in the complete peace of mind
that no mistress has ever been able to give me since that time, because
we have doubts about them at the very moment when we believe in
them, and can never possess their hearts as I received in a kiss my
mother's heart, whole and complete, without reservation or after-
thought, without the residue of an intention that concerned anyone
but me—was that it should be her that appeared before me, that it
should be her face that leaned over me, the face on which there was
something below the eye that was apparently a blemish but which
I loved as much as the rest, so what I want to see again is the
Guermantes way as I knew it, with the farm that stood a little apart
from the two so close together, at the entrance to the avenue of oaks;
those meadows which, when the sun makes them reflective like
a pond, are etched with the leaves of the apple trees; that whole landscape whose individuality sometimes grips me at night, in my dreams,
with an almost uncanny intensity, and which I can never recapture
after I wake up. No doubt, by virtue of having forever and indissol-
ubly united different impressions in my mind, simply because they
made me experience them at the same time, the Méséglise way and
the Guermantes way made me vulnerable, in later life, to much disappointment and even to many mistakes. For I've often wanted to see
a person again without realizing that it was simply because that person reminded me of a hawthorn hedge, and I've been led to believe,
and to make someone else believe in a renewal of affection, by what
was simply a desire to go on a journey. But it is also true that those two
'ways', by enduring in those of my present-day impressions with
which they can connect, give those impressions a foundation, a depth,
a dimension that other impressions lack. They also invest them with
a charm and a meaning that are for me alone. When, on summer
evenings, the melodious sky growls like a wild animal and everyone is

complaining about the storm, it's because of the Méséglise way that I'm the only one to stand in ecstasy, inhaling through the noise of the falling rain the scent of invisible and enduring lilacs.

In this way I'd often lie awake until morning, thinking back to the time in Combray, to my sad sleepless evenings there, to many other days as well, the memory of which had been restored to me more recently by the taste—what they would have called in Combray the 'fragrance'—of a cup of tea, and, by an association of memories, to what, many years after I'd left the town, I'd been told about a love affair Swann had had before I was born, with a precision of detail it's sometimes easier to obtain for the lives of people who've been dead for centuries than for the lives of our best friends, and which seems as impossible as it used to seem impossible to speak with a person in a different town from one's own—before we knew about the device that enables us to circumvent that impossibility. All these memories, successively added to each other, were no more than a single mass, but it was still possible to distinguish, running between them—between the oldest and those that were more recent, generated by a certain 'fragrance', and then those that actually belonged to somebody else, from whom I'd acquired them—if not real fissures or faults, at least that veining, that variegation in colouring, which in certain rocks and marbles marks differences in origin, age, and 'formation'.

Of course, by the time it was nearly morning, the fleeting uncertainty of my first waking moments would long since have faded; I would know in which room I was lying, I would have reconstructed it around me in the darkness, and (getting my bearings by memory alone, or with the help of a faint glimmer of light, under which I placed the window curtains) would have reconstructed it entirely and furnished it, like an architect and decorator, keeping the original plan of the windows and doors; I would have put the mirrors back where they belonged and pushed the chest of drawers into its usual position. But scarcely had the daylight—and no longer the reflection of a last, dying ember on a brass curtain rod which I'd mistaken for the daylight—traced on the darkness, as though in chalk, its first white, correcting ray, than the window, with its curtains, would leave the door-frame where I'd wrongly placed it, while, to make room for it, the desk which my memory had clumsily installed there would shoot off at top speed, pushing the fireplace before it and sweeping aside the wall of the passage; a little courtyard would take over the spot where just a moment before the dressing room had extended to, and the home I'd reconstructed in the darkness would have gone to join all the other homes I'd glimpsed in the swirling confusion of waking, put to flight by the pale sign traced above the curtains by the raised finger of dawn.

PART TWO
SWANN IN LOVE

To belong to the 'little set', the 'little group', the 'little clan' of the Verdurins, one condition was sufficient but necessary: tacit adherence to a Credo one of whose articles was that the young pianist who was Madame Verdurin's protégé that year and of whom she'd say 'It shouldn't be allowed to play Wagner as well as that!' was 'streets ahead' of both Planté and Rubinstein and that Doctor Cottard was a better diagnostician than Potain.* Any 'new recruit' who couldn't be persuaded by the Verdurins that the evenings people spent in houses other than theirs were as dull as ditchwater was immediately banished. Since the women were in this respect more rebellious than the men, more reluctant to give up their interest in society and their desire to find out for themselves how entertaining the other salons might be, and since the Verdurins felt that this spirit of enquiry and this demon of frivolity might become contagious, and fatal to the orthodoxy of their little church, they had been led to expel, one after another, all those of the 'faithful' who were of the female sex.

Apart from the doctor's young wife, they were reduced almost exclusively that year (even though Madame Verdurin herself was a virtuous woman and came from a respectable, extremely wealthy, and utterly undistinguished family, with whom she'd gradually and deliberately lost contact) to a person almost of the demi-monde, Madame de Crécy,* whom Madame Verdurin affectionately called by her first name, Odette, and declared to be 'a darling', and to the pianist's aunt, who must once have worked as a concierge; both of them were unworldly people who, in their naïvety, had been so easily deluded into believing that the Princesse de Sagan and the Duchesse de Guermantes were obliged to pay certain poor souls in order to have anyone at all at their dinner parties, that if someone had offered to get them invited to the homes of either of these great ladies, the former concierge and the *cocotte** would disdainfully have declined.

The Verdurins never invited one to dinner; one always had one's 'place laid'. There was no fixed programme for the evening's entertainment. The young pianist would play, but only if he 'felt like it', because they never forced anyone to do anything, and, as Monsieur Verdurin would say: 'We're all friends here, long live friendship!' If the pianist wanted to play the 'Ride of the Valkyries' or the Prelude to *Tristan*,* Madame Verdurin would object, not because she disliked those pieces but, on the contrary, because they affected her too much: 'So you want me to have one of my migraines? You know perfectly well the same thing happens every time he plays that! I know what I'm in for! Tomorrow, when I want to get up—Goodbye to that! Out of the question!' If he didn't play, they would chat, and one of their friends, usually their favourite painter that year, would 'launch', as Monsieur Verdurin put it, 'into one of his silly stories that would make them all split their sides', especially Madame Verdurin, who was so apt to take literally the figurative expressions for the emotions she felt that on one occasion Doctor Cottard (a junior doctor at the time) had had to reset her jaw after she dislocated it by laughing too much.

Black tie was forbidden because one was 'among friends' and also because one didn't want to be like the 'bores' whom they avoided like the plague and invited only to the grander soirées, which were held as rarely as possible and only if it might amuse the painter or make the musician better known. The rest of the time they were happy to play charades and have supper in fancy dress, but only among themselves, not allowing any outsiders to mingle with the 'little clan'.

But as the 'special friends' began to occupy an increasingly prominent place in Madame Verdurin's life, the bores, the outcasts, became anything and anybody that kept her friends away from her, anything that occasionally prevented them from being free—the mother of one, the professional occupations of another, the country house or ill health of a third. If Doctor Cottard felt he should leave straight after dinner to make another visit to a patient who was seriously ill, Madame Verdurin would say: 'Who knows, it might be better for him if you don't go and disturb him this evening; if you don't, he'll have a good night's rest; you'll go round early tomorrow morning and find him as right as rain.' By the beginning of December it would make her quite ill to think that the 'faithful' would 'let her down' on Christmas Day and the first of January. The pianist's aunt insisted that on New Year's Day he come to dinner with the family at her mother's house:

'It's not as if your mother might die,' cried Madame Verdurin bitterly, 'if you don't go and have dinner with her on New Year's Day, the way they do *in the provinces*!'

Her anxieties would return during Holy Week: 'Doctor, you're a man of science and a free-thinker, I assume you'll be coming on

Good Friday just like any other day?' she said confidently to Cottard
the first year, as if there could be no doubt as to his answer. But she
trembled as she waited for it, for if he didn't come, she might find
herself alone.

'I'll come on Good Friday . . . to say goodbye, because we're going
to spend the Easter holiday in Auvergne.'

'In Auvergne! You'll be eaten alive by fleas and vermin! It'll serve
you right!' And she added, after a pause: 'If only you'd told us, we
would have tried to organize a party; we could all have gone together
in comfort.'

Similarly, if one of the 'faithful' had a friend or if one of the lady
members had a beau who occasionally might make them 'otherwise
engaged', the Verdurins, who were not upset by a woman having
a lover provided that she had him at their house, loved him in their
midst, and didn't prefer his company to theirs, would say: 'Well,
bring your friend along.' And they would take him on for a trial
period, to see if he was capable of keeping no secrets from Madame
Verdurin, if he was worthy of being enrolled in the 'little clan'. If he
wasn't, the member of the 'faithful' who had introduced him would
be taken aside and very kindly advised to break with his friend or his
mistress. But if everything proved satisfactory, the newcomer would
in his turn become one of the 'faithful'. So when, that year, the demi-
mondaine told Monsieur Verdurin that she'd made the acquaintance
of a charming man, Monsieur Swann, and intimated that he would
very much like to be invited to their house, Monsieur Verdurin trans-
mitted the request to his wife there and then. (He never formed an
opinion about anything until she had formed hers, his particular role
being to carry out her wishes, as well as the wishes of the 'faithful' in
general, with great skill and ingenuity.)

'Madame de Crécy has a request. She'd like to introduce one of her
friends to you, a Monsieur Swann. What do you think?'

'Well, how could anyone refuse anything to such an angel of perfection? You be quiet, nobody asked for your opinion. I'm telling you
you're an angel of perfection.'

'If you say so,' replied Odette in a bantering tone, and then added:
'You know I'm not *fishing for compliments*.'*

'All right, then! Bring your friend along, if he's nice.'

The 'little clan' had absolutely nothing in common with the circles
in which Swann moved, and true socialites would have felt there was

little point in his enjoying his exceptional position in society merely to end up with an introduction to the Verdurins. But Swann was so fond of women that once he'd got to know more or less every lady of the aristocracy and they had nothing more to teach him, he'd come to see the naturalization papers,* almost a patent of nobility, bestowed upon him by the Faubourg Saint-Germain as no more than a sort of negotiable bond, a letter of credit with no value in itself but which enabled him to create an immediate position of prestige in some provincial backwater or some obscure Parisian circle where the daughter of the local squire or town clerk had taken his fancy. For at such times desire or love would revive in him a feeling of vanity which, though he was now entirely free of it in his everyday life, was no doubt what had originally inclined him towards the career as a man of fashion in which he'd wasted his intellectual gifts on frivolous pleasures and used his erudition in matters of art merely to advise society ladies on the paintings they should buy and how they should decorate their houses; and it was this vanity that made him want to shine, in the eyes of any new lady friend with whom he was infatuated, with an elegance which the name Swann didn't in itself confer. This desire was especially strong if the new lady friend was of humble background. Just as it's not to other intelligent men that a man of intelligence will be afraid of appearing stupid, so it's not by a great lord but by a country bumpkin that a man of fashion will fear that his distinction will go unrecognized. From time immemorial, three-quarters of all the mental ingenuity and lies told out of vanity by people who merely demean themselves thereby, have been aimed at inferiors. And so Swann, who could be natural and casual with a duchess, would tremble for fear of being scorned, and immediately put on airs in the presence of a chambermaid.

He wasn't like so many people who, from laziness or a resigned sense of the obligation entailed by their exalted social position to remain moored forever in the same place, abstain from the pleasures life offers them outside the worldly situation in which they remain confined until the day they die, and are content, in the end, to describe as pleasures, once they've become used to them, and for want of anything better, the mediocre distractions, the just bearable tedium, it offers. Swann didn't try to convince himself that the women with whom he spent his time were attractive, but tried instead to spend his time with women he'd already found attractive. And these were often women whose beauty was of a somewhat vulgar kind, since the physical qualities he looked for without realizing it were the exact opposite of those he admired in the women sculpted or painted by his favourite artists. Soulfulness and melancholy froze his senses, but he was instantly aroused at the sight of flesh that was pink, healthy, and abundant.

If on his travels he met a family with whom it would have been more elegant for a gentleman not to wish to seek acquaintance, but which counted among its members a woman who seemed graced with a kind of charm he had not previously encountered, to remain aloof and seek to deny the desire she'd inspired, to substitute a different pleasure for the pleasure he might have known with her by writing to one of his former mistresses to invite her to join him, would have seemed to him as cowardly an abdication in the face of life, as stupid a renunciation of a new form of happiness as if, instead of exploring the country round about, he'd shut himself up in his hotel room and looked at postcards of Paris. He didn't lock himself away in the edifice of his relationships, but had converted it, in order to be able to erect it again on a new spot wherever he encountered a woman he found attractive, into one of those collapsible tents of the kind explorers carry with them. As for what wasn't portable or exchangeable for some new pleasure, he would have given it away, however enviable it might appear to other people. How many times had his credit with a duchess who for years had been wanting to please him in some way, without finding any opportunity to do so, been squandered in one fell swoop by an ill-advised telegram asking to put him in touch immediately, by return cable, with one of her stewards whose daughter had caught his eye in the country, just as a starving man might swap a diamond for a crust of bread. Indeed, he'd even laughed at his behaviour afterwards, for there was in him, albeit redeemed by many rare refinements, a certain boorishness. Moreover, he was one of those men of intelligence who, having led a life of idleness, seek consolation and perhaps an excuse in the idea that their idleness offers their intelligence objects just as worthy of interest as those offered by art or scholarship, that 'Life' contains situations that are more interesting, more novelistic than any novel. This, at least, was what he maintained; and he had no difficulty in convincing even the most refined of his society friends, in particular the Baron de Charlus, whom he liked to amuse with accounts of the racy adventures he'd had, such as his

encounter with a woman on a train whom he'd taken back to his house
and discovered to be the sister of a reigning monarch who at that time
held in his hands all the tangled threads of European politics, with
which Swann was thus kept well informed in the most delightful
manner, or when, through a complex set of circumstances, the choice
about to be made by the conclave determined whether or not he'd be
able to sleep with a scullery maid.

And it wasn't only the brilliant phalanx of virtuous dowagers, gen-
erals, and academicians to whom he was particularly close that Swann
forced with such cynicism to act as his go-betweens. All his friends
were used to receiving periodic letters in which a word of recommendation or introduction was asked of them with a diplomatic skill
which, persisting as it did through his successive love affairs and
varying pretexts, revealed, more clearly than any bungling would have
done, a permanent characteristic and an identical quest. Many years
later, when I began to take an interest in his character* because of the
ways it resembled my own, but in completely different respects,
I often asked to hear how, whenever he wrote to my grandfather (who
wasn't my grandfather yet, for it was at about the time of my birth
that Swann's great love affair began, and for a long time these practices of his were interrupted), the latter, recognizing his friend's
handwriting on the envelope, would exclaim: 'Here's Swann again,
asking for something. On guard!' And, either from distrust or from
the unconscious spirit of devilry that makes us offer something only
to those who have no desire for it, my grandparents would flatly refuse
even his most easily satisfied requests, such as an introduction to
a girl who dined with them every Sunday, which meant that whenever
Swann broached the subject they had to pretend they'd stopped seeing her, although they would be wondering throughout the whole
week who on earth they could invite to dinner with her, and often
ended up with no one, because they didn't want to ask the one person
who would have been delighted to come.

Sometimes a particular couple, friends of my grandparents
who'd been complaining that they never saw anything of Swann,
would announce to them with satisfaction and possibly a desire to
make them envious, that he'd become utterly charming towards
them and was constantly at their house. My grandfather didn't
want to spoil their pleasure but would look at my grandmother and
hum the tune of:

Quel est donc ce mystère?
*Je n'y puis rien comprendre.**

Or:

*Vision fugitive . . .**

Or:

Dans ces affaires
*Le mieux est de ne rien voir.**

A few months later, if my grandfather asked Swann's new friend: 'And Swann? Do you still see a lot of him?', the other person's face would fall: 'Never mention that man's name to me again!'

'But I thought you were such good friends . . .'

For several months, Swann had been on similarly close terms with some cousins of my grandmother, dining at their house nearly every day. Suddenly, without warning, he stopped coming. They thought he was ill, and my grandmother's cousin was about to send someone round to ask after him when she found in the pantry a letter in his hand, which the cook had left by accident in the accounts book. In it he told the woman that he was leaving Paris and wouldn't be able to see her again. She'd been his mistress and when he broke off with her she was the only person he thought he needed to tell.

If, however, his mistress of the moment was a woman of rank or at least one whose background was not too humble nor her reputation too dubious to prevent him from taking her into the world of polite society, then for her sake he'd return to it, but only to the particular sphere in which she moved or into which he'd drawn her. 'No use expecting Swann to drop by this evening,' people would say. 'Remember—it's his American's night at the Opéra.' He would make sure she was invited to the most exclusive salons, where he was always welcome, where he dined weekly or played poker; every evening, when a slight frizz had been added to the brush of his red hair, tempering with a certain softness the sparkle of his green eyes, he'd choose a flower for his buttonhole and go off to join his mistress for dinner at the house of one or other of the women of his circle; then, thinking of the admiration and affection soon to be lavished upon him, in the presence of the woman he loved, by all these fashionable people for whom he could do no wrong and whom he'd meet again there, he rediscovered the charm of that worldly life to which he'd grown indifferent but whose very substance, penetrated and coloured by the warmth of a newly inserted flame which now played on it, seemed to him precious and beautiful, since he'd incorporated into it a new love.

But, in contrast to each of these love affairs, or each of these flirtations, which had been the more or less complete fulfilment of a dream inspired by the sight of a face or a body which Swann had spontaneously, without any kind of effort, found attractive, when he was introduced to Odette de Crécy one evening at the theatre by an old friend of his who'd spoken of her as a ravishing creature with whom he might perhaps come to a pleasant arrangement, but had made her out to be a more difficult proposition than she actually was in order to appear to have done him a bigger favour by introducing her to him, she'd struck Swann as being not without beauty, certainly, but as having a kind of beauty that left him indifferent, that aroused in him no feeling of desire, even gave him a sort of physical repulsion, one of those women such as everyone has known, different for each of us, who are the opposite of the type our senses crave. She had too sharp a profile for his taste, her skin was too delicate, her cheekbones too prominent, her features too drawn. Her eyes were lovely, but so large that they drooped under their own weight, straining the rest of her face and making her always look as if she were ill or in a bad mood. Some time after this introduction at the theatre, she'd written to ask if she could see his art collections, which interested her very much because although she was 'an ignoramus', she 'liked pretty things'; it seemed to her, she said, that she'd understand him better once she had seen him in 'his *home*', where she imagined him 'so relaxed and comfortable with his tea and his books', though she hadn't hidden her surprise that he lived in a part of town that must be so depressing and 'was so un-*smart* for a man who was so very *smart** himself'. And when he'd allowed her to come, she'd told him as she left how sorry she was to have spent such a short time in a house she'd been so glad to visit, speaking of him as though he meant more to her than the other people she knew, and seeming to establish between their two selves a sort of romantic bond that had made him smile. But Swann was already approaching the age of disillusion when one knows how to content oneself with being in love for the sake of being in love without requiring too much reciprocity, when that meeting of hearts, though it's no longer as in early youth the goal towards which love inevitably tends, nevertheless remains a part of it by an association of ideas so strong that it may become the cause of love if it manifests itself first. In his younger days, a man dreams of winning the heart of the woman he loves; later, the feeling that he possesses a woman's heart may be enough to make him fall in love with her. And so, at an age when it would seem—since what one seeks above all in love is subjective pleasure—that one's appreciation of the beauty of a woman should play the largest part in it, love may come into being, love of the most physical kind, without there having been any initial desire. At this stage of life, one has already been a victim of love several times; it no longer evolves by itself in accordance with its own mysterious and immutable laws, to the astonishment of our passive hearts. We come to its aid, we distort it with memory or suggestion; recognizing one of its symptoms, we remember and recreate the rest. Since we know its melody, engraved on our hearts in its entirety, we don't need a woman to remind us how it begins—filled with the admiration which beauty inspires—in order to recall how it goes on. And if she starts in the middle—where the two hearts come together, where it sings of living only for each other—we're familiar enough with the music to be able to join our partner straightaway in the passage where she awaits us.

Odette de Crécy went to see Swann again, then visited him more and more often; and no doubt each visit revived his feeling of disappointment at seeing that face whose details he'd half forgotten in the meantime and which he'd not recalled as being either so expressive or, despite her youth, so faded; as she chatted with him, he regretted that her considerable beauty was not of the sort he would instinctively have preferred. It must be said that Odette's face seemed thinner and sharper than it was because her forehead and the upper parts of her cheeks, those smooth and flatter surfaces, were covered by the masses of hair which women favoured at the time—drawn forward in a fringe, crimped up, or falling in loose ringlets over the ears; and as for her figure, which was most shapely, it was difficult to see it as a coherent whole (because of the fashions of the period, and despite the fact that she was one of the best-dressed women in Paris), the bodice jutting out as if over an imaginary stomach and ending in a sharp point, and the double skirts and bustles swelling like a balloon underneath, making a woman look as if she were composed of different parts that had been badly fitted together; so variously, according to the vagaries of their design or the consistency of their material, did the flounces, the pleats, and the bodice follow the line that led to the bows, the puffs of lace, the fringes of dangling jet beads, or guided them along the corset, but never related in any way to the living body, which, depending on whether the architecture of all these frills and furbelows corresponded to her own shape, or was too thoroughly different, found itself either fiercely gripped or completely lost from sight.

But when Odette had left, Swann would smile as he thought of how she'd said that time would hang heavily until he allowed her to come back again; he'd recall the anxious, shy way in which she'd once begged him that it should not be too long, and the look in her eyes at that moment, fastened on him in fearful entreaty, which made her appear so touching under the bunch of artificial pansies pinned to the front of her round white straw hat with its black velvet ribbons. 'And what about you?' she'd said. 'Couldn't you come and have tea at my house one day?' He'd pleaded pressure of work, an unfinished essay—which, in reality, he'd abandoned years earlier—on Vermeer of Delft.* 'I know I'm useless, a pathetic little creature like me, compared with all you great scholars,' she'd replied. 'I'd be like the frog before the Areopagus.* But I really would love to learn, to know things, be initiated. What fun it must be to study all those books and bury your head in old papers!' She'd added this last comment with the self-satisfied air an elegant lady has when she declares that she likes nothing better than getting her hands dirty doing some messy job, like 'lending a hand in the kitchen'. 'You'll laugh at me, but that painter who keeps you from seeing me' (she meant Vermeer)—'I've never heard of him. Is he still alive? Can I see any of his work in Paris, so I can have an idea of what it is you like and try to work out what's going on inside that great head of yours that works so hard, in that mind I always feel is so busy with its thoughts, so I can say: "Yes, that's what he's thinking about"? How wonderful it would be to share in your work!' He'd regretfully refused, citing his fear of new friendships, for what he'd called, out of gallantry, his fear of being hurt. 'You're afraid of affection? How strange; that's all I ever look for, I'd give my life to find it,' she'd said, in a tone of such unfeigned conviction that he'd been quite moved. 'You must have been hurt by some woman. And you think all other women are like her. She can't have understood you; you're such an exceptional person. That's what I liked about you straightaway, I felt you weren't like anyone else.'

'And you too,' he'd said to her, 'I know very well what women are like, you must be busy with all sorts of things, you can't have much time for yourself.'

'But I never have anything to do! I'm always free, I'll always be free for you. At whatever time of the day or night that might be convenient for you to see me, send for me and I'll be only too happy to come. Will you do that? Do you know what would be nice? If I arranged an introduction to Madame Verdurin, whose house I go to every evening. Imagine if we met there and I thought it was partly for my sake that you'd come!'

As he remembered these conversations and thought about her when he was alone, he was no doubt combining her image with those of many other women in his romantic daydreams; but if, due to some circumstance or other (or even not, since a circumstance that presents itself at the moment when a state of mind, hitherto latent, makes itself felt, may have had no influence on it at all), the image of Odette de Crécy came to absorb all these daydreams, if they were no longer separable from the memory of her, then the imperfections of her body would no longer have any importance, nor would the question of her body being more or less to his taste than any other body, since, now that it had become the body of the woman he loved, it would henceforth be the only one capable of filling him with joy or misery.

It so happened that my grandfather had known the family of these Verdurins (which was more than could be said of any of their current friends). But he'd lost touch completely with 'young Verdurin', as he called him, whom he regarded, more or less, as having fallen—though without losing his grip on his millions—among bohemians and riffraff. One day he received a letter from Swann asking if he could put him in touch with the Verdurins: 'On guard! On guard!' my grandfather had exclaimed. 'I'm not a bit surprised, it's just where Swann was bound to end up. A nice lot! I can't do what he asks because, for one thing, I no longer know the gentleman in question. And for another, there must be some woman involved, and I never get mixed up in that sort of thing. Well, well! It'll be interesting to see what happens if Swann falls in with those young Verdurins.'

And so, my grandfather having declined Swann's request, it was Odette herself who'd taken him to the Verdurins'.

On the day when Swann made his first appearance, the Verdurins had had to dinner Doctor and Madame Cottard, the young pianist and his aunt, and the painter then in favour, and these were joined later in the evening by several other members of the 'faithful'.

Doctor Cottard was never quite sure of the tone he should adopt in response to anyone who addressed him, whether his interlocutor wanted to make a joke or was serious. So, as a precautionary measure, he would add to each of his facial expressions the offer of a conditional and tentative smile whose anticipatory subtlety would exculpate him from the charge of simple-mindedness, if the remark made to him turned out to have been facetious. But since he also had to take the opposite possibility into account, and could not dare to allow this smile to settle clearly on his face, one saw floating over his features a perpetual uncertainty in which could be read the question he never dared to ask: 'Are you serious?' He was no more confident of how to behave in the street, or even in life generally, than in a drawing room, and he might be seen greeting passers-by, carriages, or events with a cunning smile that precluded any attribution of impropriety to his attitude, since it demonstrated that if the attitude turned out to be unsuitable, he was well aware of it, and that if he'd adopted it, it was simply as a joke.

On all points, however, on which a direct question seemed to him permissible, the doctor did not fail to attempt to reduce the field of his doubts and complete his education.

And so, acting on the advice given him by a wise mother on his leaving the provinces for Paris, he never let pass an unfamiliar figure of speech or proper name without trying to secure the fullest information about them.

As regards figures of speech, his thirst for knowledge was insatiable, because, sometimes supposing them to have a more precise meaning than they actually have, he wanted to know exactly what people meant when they used those he heard most often: the bloom of youth, blue blood, a fast life, the moment of truth, elegance personified, to give carte blanche, to be struck dumb, etc., and in what particular circumstances he himself could introduce them into his conversation. Failing these, he'd fall back on a number of puns he'd memorized. As for new names of people mentioned in his presence, he contented himself merely with repeating them in an interrogative tone, which he thought sufficient to elicit explanations without his appearing to ask for them.

Since he completely lacked the critical faculty which he thought he exercised in all things, the refinement of manners that consists in telling a person for whom you're doing a favour that you're greatly obliged to them, without expecting them to believe you, was wasted on the doctor, who took everything literally. Blind though Madame Verdurin was to his faults, and though she continued to find him most clever, she had in the end become irritated to see that, when she invited him to share a stage-box for a performance by Sarah Bernhardt, saying to him, to be especially gracious: 'It was so kind of you to come, Doctor, since I'm sure you've already heard Sarah Bernhardt many times before, and we may also be too close to the stage,' Doctor Cottard, who had entered the box with a half-smile hovering between appearance and disappearance until someone authoritative informed him of the quality of the performance, replied: 'It's true that we're much too close and one *is* beginning to get a little tired of Sarah Bernhardt. But you said you'd like me to come. And your wish is my command. I'm only too happy to do you this little favour. There's nothing I wouldn't do for you, you're so kind!' And he added (in vain hope of comment): 'Sarah Bernhardt—she's what they call "the Golden Voice",* isn't she? And the reviewers often write that she "sets the stage on fire". That's an odd expression, isn't it?'

'You know,' Madame Verdurin had said to her husband, 'I think we're on the wrong track when, out of modesty, we make light of the presents we give the Doctor. He's a man of science, he has no truck with practical matters, he has no idea of the value of things, he relies completely on what we tell him.'

'I hadn't dared to say anything, but I had noticed,' replied Monsieur Verdurin. And the following New Year's Day, instead of sending Doctor Cottard a three-thousand-franc ruby and saying it was just a trifle, Monsieur Verdurin bought an artificial stone for three hundred, while giving the impression that it would be hard to find one as beautiful.

When Madame Verdurin had announced that Monsieur Swann would be joining them that evening, the doctor had exclaimed in a tone coarsened by surprise, 'Swann?'—for the most trivial piece of news always took especially by surprise this man who thought himself always prepared for everything. And seeing that no one answered him, he roared: 'Swann? Who's this Swann?', his attack of anxiety suddenly subsiding when Madame Verdurin said: 'Oh, he's the friend Odette told us about.'

'Ah, I see. That's all right then,' replied the doctor, relieved. As for the painter, he was delighted by Swann's appearance at Madame

Verdurin's, because he assumed he was in love with Odette and he liked to see himself as a matchmaker. 'I absolutely love arranging marriages,' he confided in Doctor Cottard's ear. 'I've already arranged quite a few—even between women!'

By telling the Verdurins that Swann was very '*smart*',* Odette had made them fear he might be a 'bore'. However, he made an excellent impression, of which one of the indirect causes, though they didn't know it, was his belonging to fashionable society. In fact, he enjoyed over men who have never mixed in high society, even men of intelligence, one of the advantages of those who've had some experience of it, which is that they no longer see it transfigured by the desire or the horror it inspires in their imagination, but consider it of no importance. Their amiability, unconnected with snobbery or any fear of seeming too amiable, reflects their independence, showing the ease and grace of movement of gymnasts whose supple limbs perform exactly the movements they want, without any indiscreet or awkward assistance from the rest of the body. The simple, elementary gymnastics of a man of the world extending a gracious hand to the unknown young man being introduced to him, or bowing discreetly to the ambassador to whom he himself is being introduced, had eventually been absorbed, without his being aware of it, into Swann's whole social manner, so that towards people socially inferior to him, like the Verdurins and their friends, he displayed an instinctive warm attentiveness, and made friendly overtures, which, they felt, a 'bore' would never have done. He had a moment of coldness only with Cottard: seeing the doctor wink at him and smile ambiguously before they'd spoken to each other (a particular performance that Cottard called 'Wait and see'), Swann thought the doctor probably remembered him from a chance encounter in some house of ill repute, though he frequented such places very rarely and had never indulged in that form of dissipation. Finding the allusion in bad taste, especially in front of Odette, who might form a bad impression of him because of it, he assumed an icy manner. But on learning that the lady standing near him was Madame Cottard, he thought that so young a husband would not have tried to allude to entertainments of that sort in the presence of his wife; and he stopped reading into the doctor's knowing look the meaning he'd suspected. The painter straightaway invited Swann to visit his studio with Odette; Swann thought how pleasant he was. 'Perhaps you'll be more highly favoured than me,' Madame Verdurin said in a tone of mock resentment. 'Perhaps he'll show you his portrait of Cottard' (which she'd commissioned from the painter). 'Don't forget, Monsieur Biche,' she reminded the painter, for whom it was a time-honoured joke to address him as 'Monsieur', 'to capture that lovely, attractive, shrewd, and amusing look of his eyes. You know what I want most is his smile; that's what I asked you for—a portrait of his smile.' And since this phrase struck her as especially noteworthy, she repeated it very loudly to make sure it would be heard by a large number of guests, some of whom, on a vague pretext, she had induced to come closer before she uttered it again. Swann asked to be introduced to everyone, even to an old friend of the Verdurins, Saniette, whose shyness, simplicity, and good nature had lost him all the esteem he had enjoyed because of his skill as a palaeographer, his large fortune, and the distinguished family he came from. When he talked, he made a kind of burbling sound—an effect people found delightful because they felt it betrayed not so much an impediment of speech as a quality of soul, a vestige as it were of the childhood innocence he had never lost. Each consonant he could not pronounce seemed a further expression of the hardness of which he was incapable. In asking to be introduced to Monsieur Saniette, Swann appeared to Madame Verdurin to be reversing roles (to the extent that, in response, she insisted on the difference: 'Monsieur Swann, would you be so kind as to allow me to introduce our friend Saniette?'), whereas in Saniette it aroused warm feelings towards Swann, which the Verdurins, however, never revealed to him, as they found Saniette rather irritating and had no desire to provide him with new friends. But, on the other hand, they were very touched by Swann's immediate request to be introduced to the pianist's aunt. She was wearing a black dress, as always, because she thought women always looked well in black and nothing could be more distinguished, but her face was extremely red, as it always was after she'd eaten. She bowed respectfully to Swann, but straightened up majestically. Since she was entirely uneducated and was afraid of making mistakes of grammar, she deliberately pronounced words in an indistinct manner, thinking that if she made a blunder it would be so blurred by imprecision that no one could be certain whether she'd made it or not; the result was that her conversation was reduced to a series of vague croakings from which emerged now and then the few words and phrases of which she was fully confident. Swann felt he could poke a little fun at her as he talked with Monsieur Verdurin, but the latter was quite offended.

'She's a splendid woman,' he replied. 'I grant you she's not brilliant; but I assure you she's very pleasant company when you talk to her on your own.'

'I don't doubt it,' Swann hastened to concede, and added: 'I just meant she doesn't strike one as "distinguished"' (giving special stress to the adjective) 'and actually that's a compliment!'

'Well,' said Monsieur Verdurin, 'this will surprise you: she writes delightfully. You've never heard her nephew play? He's marvellous, isn't he, Doctor? Would you like me to ask him to play something, Monsieur Swann?'

'Oh, it would be a joy . . .', Swann started to say, when he was interrupted in a facetious manner by the doctor. Having once heard it said that over-emphasis in conversation and the use of formal expressions were out of date, the doctor thought, whenever he heard a solemn word used seriously (as Swann had just used the word 'joy'), that the speaker was guilty of pomposity. And if, in addition, the word happened to occur in what he called an old cliché, however much it might be in common usage, he would assume that the sentence of which he'd heard the opening words was ridiculous and would complete it ironically with the platitude he seemed to be accusing the speaker of intending to use, though it had never entered the latter's head.

'A joy for ever!' he cried mischievously, throwing up his arms for effect.

Monsieur Verdurin couldn't help laughing.

'What are those good folk laughing about over there?' called Madame Verdurin. 'You seem to be having a jolly time in your little corner.' Then she added, in a tone of mock-childish chagrin: 'Don't imagine I'm enjoying myself over here, sitting in disgrace all by myself!'

Madame Verdurin was sitting on a high Swedish chair of waxed pine, which she'd been given by a violinist from that country and which she kept in her drawing room, though in shape it was rather like a kitchen stool and was quite out of keeping with her beautiful antique furniture; but she made a point of displaying the gifts which the 'faithful' would give her from time to time, so that the givers would have the pleasure of recognizing them when they came to the house. She tried to persuade them to give her only flowers and sweets, which are at least perishable; but she wasn't successful, and the house therefore contained a whole collection of foot-warmers, cushions, clocks, screens, barometers, and vases, in a constant accumulation of the useless and ill-assorted.

From her lofty perch she was able to play a full part in the conversation of the 'faithful', and would delight in their banter, but ever since the accident to her jaw, she had stopped making the effort to explode with laughter and contented herself instead with a kind of dumb show that signified, without tiring her or exposing her to danger, that she was laughing to the point of tears. At the slightest hint of a joke being cracked by one of the 'faithful' at the expense of a 'bore' or a former member of her circle who had been relegated to the camp of the 'bores'—and to the absolute despair of Monsieur Verdurin, who for so long had made himself out to be as affable as his wife, but who now, since his laughter was real, would quickly get out of breath and had thus been outdistanced and defeated by her trick of feigned, incessant hilarity—she would utter a little cry, screw up her birdlike eyes, already slightly clouded by leucoma, and suddenly, as if she had only just had time to block out some indecent sight or parry a fatal blow, burying her face in her hands, which covered it completely and hid it from view, would seem to be doing her utmost to suppress, to annihilate, a fit of laughter which, had she given in to it, would have made her faint. So there she sat, dizzy with the gaiety of the 'faithful', drunk with good fellowship, gossip, and sychophancy, clinging to her perch like a bird whose biscuit has been soaked in mulled wine, sobbing with affability.

Meanwhile, Monsieur Verdurin, after asking Swann's permission to light his pipe ('We don't stand on ceremony here, we're among friends'), went over to ask the young musician to sit at the piano.

'I say, leave him alone! He didn't come here to be pestered like that!' exclaimed Madame Verdurin. 'Don't torment him!'

'But why do you think it might bother him?' said Monsieur Verdurin. 'I dare say Monsieur Swann doesn't know the Sonata in F sharp we've discovered. He'll play the piano arrangement for us.'

'Oh, no! Not my sonata!' cried Madame Verdurin. 'I don't want to cry and get a head cold and neuralgia, like last time. No thank you, I don't want to go through that again! It's all right for the rest of you, it's obvious that you're not the ones who will have to stay in bed for a week!'

This little scene, which was re-enacted each time the pianist sat down to play, never failed to delight her friends as much as if they were seeing it for the first time, for they took it as proof of the enchanting originality of the 'Patronne' and of her sensitivity to music. Those standing near her would gesture to those further away, smoking or playing cards, to come closer, since something was happening, saying 'Listen! Listen!' as they do in the Reichstag* at interesting moments. And the following day they'd commiserate with those unable to attend, reporting that the performance had been even more entertaining than usual.

'Well, all right then,' said Monsieur Verdurin. 'He can just play the Andante.'

'Just the Andante! You can't be serious!' exclaimed Madame Verdurin. 'It's precisely the Andante that breaks me up. Just listen to the Patron! He's priceless! It's as if he said: "It's the Ninth, we'll just listen to the finale", or "It's the *Meistersingers*,* we'll leave after the Overture."'

The doctor, however, urged Madame Verdurin to let the pianist play, not because he thought the distressing effect the music had on her was feigned—he recognized in it certain neurasthenic symptoms—but because he shared the habit, common to many doctors, of immediately reducing the severity of their prescriptions as soon as it strikes them that something more important is involved, such as some fashionable gathering they are attending, and at which the presence of the person they are advising for once to forget their dyspepsia or flu is essential.

'You won't be ill this time, you'll see,' he said, trying to hypnotize her with his gaze. 'And if you are ill, we'll look after you.'

'Really?' replied Madame Verdurin, as if the prospect of such a favour left her no choice but to capitulate. Perhaps, too, by repeatedly saying she'd be ill, there were moments when she forgot it was only a lie, and she actually assumed the disposition of an invalid. And invalids, tired of always having to make the infrequency of their attacks dependent on their prudence, like to believe they can do with impunity whatever gives them pleasure but is usually bad for them, as long as they put themselves in the hands of a person of authority who, without obliging them to make the slightest effort, by uttering a word or dispensing a pill, will get them back on their feet.

Odette had gone to sit on a tapestry-covered couch near the piano. 'You see, I've got my own little spot,' she said to Madame Verdurin.

The latter, seeing Swann sitting by himself on a chair, made him get up: 'You don't look comfortable there. Go and sit next to Odette. You can make room for Monsieur Swann, can't you, Odette?'

'What lovely Beauvais,'* said Swann before he sat down, trying to be pleasant.

'Ah! I'm glad you appreciate my couch,' replied Madame Verdurin. 'But I must tell you, if you think you'll ever see another one as beautiful, you're mistaken. They've never made anything quite like it. And these little chairs are marvellous too. You can have a look at them in a moment. The emblem on each bronze moulding corresponds to the subject on the upholstery; there's a lot to enjoy, you know, if you want to study them. Even the little friezes round the edges—look at them, look at the little vine on the red background in the Bear and the Grapes. It's so well drawn. Don't you think so? They really knew about drawing! Don't the grapes make your mouth water? My husband claims I don't like fruit because I eat less than he does. But the fact is I'm greedier than any of you, but I don't need to put them in my mouth because I can feed on them with my eyes. What are you all laughing at? Ask the doctor, he'll tell you those grapes act on me like a real purgative. Some people go to Fontainebleau for their cure; I stay here for my own little Beauvais cure. Now, Monsieur Swann, you mustn't leave without feeling the little bronze mouldings on the backs. The patina is so soft, isn't it? No, no, with your whole hand—feel them properly.'

'Ah, if Madame Verdurin is going to start fondling her bronzes, we won't have any music tonight,' said the painter.

'You be quiet, you're being naughty! Anyway,' she said, turning to Swann, 'we women are forbidden pleasures far less voluptuous than this. But nothing fleshly can compare with it! When Monsieur Verdurin paid me the compliment of being jealous—come on, at least be polite about it, don't say you were never jealous . . .'

'But I didn't say a word! Doctor, you're my witness: did I say anything?'

Swann carried on feeling the bronzes to be polite, not daring to stop right away.

'Come along, you can stroke them later; now you're the one who's going to be stroked. Your ears are, at least; I think you'll like it; here's the young man who'll be doing it for you.'

When the pianist had finished playing, Swann was even more affable towards him than anyone else in the room. This is why:

The year before, at a soirée, he'd heard a piece of music played on
piano and violin. At first, he'd enjoyed only the physical quality of the
sounds produced by the instruments. And then he'd felt a great pleasure when, beneath the delicate line of the violin, slender but persistent, compact and commanding, he'd suddenly seen, struggling to rise
in a sort of liquid swell, the solid mass of the piano part, multiform
but indivisible, smooth yet tumultuous, like the mauve restlessness of
the waves when charmed and softened by moonlight. But at a certain
moment, though unable to distinguish any clear outline of what he
found so pleasing, or even find words to describe it, suddenly
entranced, he had tried to hold on to the fleeting phrase or
harmony—he didn't know which—that had just been played and had
expanded his soul, as the fragrance of certain roses floating in the
moist evening air has the power to dilate our nostrils. Perhaps it was
his ignorance of music that had given him so confused an impression,
the kind of impression that may, however, be the only one that is
purely musical, immaterial, entirely original, irreducible to any other
order of impressions. An impression of this kind, that vanishes in an
instant, is, so to speak, *sine materia*.* No doubt the notes we hear at
such moments tend already, according to their pitch and frequency, to
spread out before our eyes over surfaces of varying dimensions, to
trace arabesques, to give us sensations of breadth or tenuousness, stability or caprice. But the notes vanish before these sensations have
developed sufficiently to avoid submersion by those already evoked
by the succeeding or even the simultaneous notes. And this impression would continue to envelop with its liquidity and softness the
motifs that momentarily emerge, scarcely discernible, then immediately fall away and disappear, leaving only the particular pleasure they
give, impossible to describe or recall or name, ineffable—were it not
for memory, which, like a labourer trying to build firm foundations
amid the waves, constructs facsimiles of these fleeting phrases, enabling us to compare them to those that follow and to appreciate the
difference between them. Thus, scarcely had Swann's feeling of
delight faded away than his memory provided him with an immediate
transcription, sketchy and provisional, admittedly, but at which he
could glance while the music continued, so that when the same
impression suddenly recurred, it was no longer impossible to grasp.
He could picture to himself its extent, the symmetries of its arrangement, its notation, its expressive value; he had before him something

that was no longer pure music, but a design, an architecture or thought that makes it possible to recall the actual music. This time he had distinguished quite clearly one phrase as it rose above the waves of sound. It had suggested at once sensual pleasures he had never imagined before hearing it, which he felt he could never experience except through that phrase; and it had filled him with a new and strange kind of love.

With its slow rhythm, it led him first in one direction, then another, then yet another, towards a state of happiness that was noble, unintelligible, and precise. Then all at once, having reached a certain point from which he was preparing to follow it, after a momentary pause it abruptly changed direction, and with a new, more rapid movement, subtle, melancholy, persistent, and gentle, it carried him along with it towards new vistas. Then it disappeared. He passionately wanted to see it again a third time. And it did reappear, but didn't speak to him any more clearly, and the sensual pleasure it produced even seemed less profound. But when he'd returned home he felt a need for it, he was like a man into whose life a woman, glimpsed for a moment passing by, has introduced the image of a new kind of beauty that enriches his own sensibility, though he doesn't know whether he will ever be able to see again this woman he already loves, without even knowing her name.

Indeed, it seemed for a moment that this love for a phrase of music would open up for Swann the possibility of a kind of rejuvenation. He had long since abandoned any attempt to devote his life to an ideal goal, limiting it to the pursuit of everyday satisfactions, and he'd come to believe, without ever admitting it to himself in so many words, that this would not change for as long as he lived; worse still, since his mind was empty of lofty ideas, he no longer believed in their existence, though he couldn't deny it entirely. Thus he'd developed the habit of taking refuge in trivial thoughts, which enabled him to ignore the really important things in life. Just as he didn't ask himself if he would have done better not to go into society, but on the other hand had no doubt that if he'd accepted an invitation he ought to turn up and that if he didn't pay a call afterwards he must at least leave his card, so in his conversation he took care never to express his own heartfelt opinion about anything, but simply to offer factual information which had a certain value in itself and enabled him to reveal nothing of his own capacities. He was extremely precise when it came to a recipe, the date of a painter's birth or death, and the titles of his works. Occasionally he'd forget himself and express an opinion about a work or someone's outlook on life, but then he'd give his remarks an ironic tone, as if he wasn't entirely serious in what he was saying. But now, like certain valetudinarians in whom, suddenly, a change of surroundings, or diet, or sometimes a spontaneous and mysterious organic development, seems to bring about such a sudden improvement in their health that they begin to envisage the unhoped-for possibility of belatedly starting a completely new life, Swann found in himself, in the memory of the phrase he'd heard, in certain other sonatas he'd asked people to play for him to see if he might discover his phrase in them, the presence of one of those invisible realities in which he no longer believed and to which, as if the music had had a sort of compelling influence on the inner emptiness from which he suffered, he felt once more the desire, and almost the strength, to devote his life. But, since he hadn't managed to find out who had written the work he'd heard, he hadn't been able to acquire a copy and had eventually forgotten it. During the week after the soirée, he'd bumped into several people who had also been there and he had asked them about the recital; but some had arrived after the music or left before; some had indeed been there while it was performed but had gone into another room to talk, and those who had stayed to listen could tell him no more than the others. As for the hosts, they knew it was a recent work which the musicians they'd hired had asked to play; but since the performers had gone on tour, Swann was unable to discover anything further. Many of his friends were musicians, but though he could recall the special, indescribable pleasure the little phrase had given him, and could actually see the shape of it in his mind's eye, he was incapable of singing it for them. So he stopped thinking about it.

But that evening, at Madame Verdurin's, the young pianist had hardly been playing for more than a few minutes when suddenly, after a high note held through two whole bars, he sensed it approaching, escaping from underneath that sonority, sustained and extended like a curtain of sound veiling the mystery of its incubation, and he recognized the secret and various murmurings of the airy fragrance of the phrase he loved. It was so distinctive, its charm was so unique, so inimitable, that Swann felt as though he'd met in a friend's drawing room a woman he'd admired in the street and despaired of ever seeing again. Finally, it receded, still diligent and purposeful, through all the ramifications of its fragrance, leaving on Swann's face the reflection of its smile. But now he could ask the name of this stranger (they told him it was the Andante from the Sonata for Piano and Violin by Vinteuil); now he possessed it, could have it in his house as often as he liked, could try to learn its language and its secret.

And so, when the pianist had finished, Swann went over and thanked him with a warmth that Madame Verdurin found most gratifying.

'He's a charmer, isn't he?' she said to Swann. 'He's really got the hang of that sonata, the little devil. You didn't know the piano could do all that, did you? My word, it's everything—except a piano! I'm amazed every time; I think I'm hearing an orchestra. Though it's better than an orchestra, more complete.'

The young pianist bowed, and with a smile, emphasizing his words as if he were uttering a witticism, said: 'You're very kind.'

And while Madame Verdurin was saying to her husband: 'Go and get him some orangeade, he deserves it,' Swann was describing to Odette how he'd fallen in love with that little phrase. When Madame Verdurin called over, 'Well now, Odette, it looks as if someone is saying nice things to you,' Odette replied: 'Yes, very nice,' and Swann found her ingenuousness delightful. Meanwhile, he'd been asking people about Vinteuil and his work, the period of his life when he'd composed the sonata, and, the thing he wanted to know most of all, the meaning the little phrase could have had for him.

But all these people who professed to admire the composer (when Swann said that his sonata was truly beautiful, Madame Verdurin exclaimed: 'It most certainly is! No one dares admit they don't know Vinteuil's sonata, not to know it is simply not allowed,' and the painter added: 'Oh, yes! It's a really great piece of work, isn't it? It may not be what you'd call "conventional" or "popular", but it makes a huge impression on us artists')—these people seemed never to have wondered about these questions, for they were incapable of answering them.

In fact, one or two particular comments Swann made about his favourite phrase prompted Madame Verdurin to say: 'Well, that's funny! I never paid much attention; you know, I've never been one for splitting hairs or discussing fine points; we don't waste time nit-picking in this house, it's not our style.' Doctor Cottard gazed at her in speechless admiration, with the zeal of a student, as she revelled in an endless flow of clichés. Both he and his wife, however, with a kind

of common sense that is characteristic of people of humble background, were careful never to offer an opinion or to pretend to admire
a piece of music which, once they were back in the privacy of their
own home, they admitted to each other they didn't understand any
more than they understood the painting of Monsieur Biche. Since
the public's notions of the charm and beauty and forms of the natural
world are derived only from the stereotypes of an art gradually
assimilated, and since original artists start by rejecting those stereotypes, Monsieur and Madame Cottard, typical in this respect of the
public, found neither in Vinteuil's sonata nor in the painter's portraits
what for them constituted harmony in music or beauty in painting. It
seemed to them, when the pianist played the sonata, that he was hitting on the keyboard random notes that bore no relation to the forms
of music they were used to, and that the painter was simply throwing
colour at random on to his canvases. When they were able to recognize a human form in one of the paintings, they found it clumsy and
vulgarized (that is to say, lacking the elegance of the school of painting through which they viewed all living creatures, even those they
saw passing by in the street), and devoid of truth, as if Monsieur
Biche didn't know that shoulders have a particular shape or that
women don't have mauve hair.

However, when the 'faithful' had dispersed, the doctor thought he
had a good opportunity, and while Madame Verdurin was saying
a further word about Vinteuil's sonata, he, like a novice swimmer
throwing himself into the water when there aren't too many onlook-
ers, exclaimed with sudden resolution: 'Yes, he's what you call a musician *di primo cartello*!'*

Swann learned only that the recent appearance of Vinteuil's sonata
had greatly impressed a certain avant-garde school of musicians, but
that it was still completely unknown to the general public.

'Actually, I know someone called Vinteuil,' said Swann, thinking of
the piano teacher who had taught my grandmother's sisters.

'Perhaps it's him,' exclaimed Madame Verdurin.

'Oh, no!' replied Swann, laughing. 'If you'd ever set eyes on him,
you wouldn't think that for a second.'

'Then to ask the question is to answer it?' said the doctor.

'But he could be a relative,' Swann went on. 'That would be rather
sad, but of course a genius can have a silly old fool as a cousin. If that
were the case, I confess I'd accept any torture to get the old fool to

introduce me to the composer of that sonata: starting with the torture of the old fool's company, which would be awful.'

The painter knew that Vinteuil was very ill at the moment and that Doctor Potain was afraid he'd not be able to save him.

'What!' cried Madame Verdurin. 'Do people still consult Potain?'

'Now, now, Madame Verdurin!', said Cottard, in a bantering tone, 'you forget that you're talking about one of my colleagues, in fact one of my mentors.'

The painter had heard a rumour that Vinteuil was on the brink of insanity. And he declared that there were signs of it in certain passages of the sonata. This comment didn't strike Swann as being in any way absurd; but it disturbed him, for, since a work of pure music contains none of the logical connections whose dislocation in language is an indication of insanity, to read insanity in a sonata seemed to him as mysterious as the idea of insanity in a dog or a horse, though such cases have been known.

'Don't talk to me about your mentors, you know ten times as much as he does,' Madame Verdurin said to Doctor Cottard, in the tone of a woman who has the courage of her convictions and stands up to anyone who doesn't agree with her. 'At least you don't kill your patients!'

'But, Madame, he's a member of the Academy,'* replied the doctor ironically. 'If a patient prefers to die at the hand of one of the princes of science . . . It's far more stylish to be able to say: "I'm being treated by Potain." '

'Oh, it's more stylish, is it?' said Madame Verdurin. 'So illness can be a question of style now, can it? I didn't know that . . .' Then, suddenly burying her face in her hands, she exclaimed: 'You're so funny! Silly me, there I was taking you seriously when all the time you were pulling my leg.'

As for Monsieur Verdurin, finding it rather tedious to force a smile over such a trifle, he contented himself with drawing on his pipe and reflecting sadly that, when it came to amiability, he'd never be able to compete with his wife.

'You know, we like your friend very much,' said Madame Verdurin to Odette when the latter was bidding her goodnight. 'He's so unaffected, and very charming; if they're all like that, the friends you'd like to introduce to us, you're very welcome to bring them along.'

Monsieur Verdurin pointed out that Swann had clearly not appreciated the pianist's aunt.

'But the poor man felt a bit out of his element,' answered Madame Verdurin. 'You can't expect him to have caught the tone of the house on his very first visit, like Cottard, who has been one of our little clan for years. The first time doesn't count, but it was useful for getting to know us. Odette, it's agreed that he'll join us tomorrow at the Châtelet. Will you pick him up?'

'No, he doesn't want me to.'

'Very well, as you wish. As long as he doesn't let us down at the last minute!'

To Madame Verdurin's great surprise, he never let them down. He'd join them wherever they happened to be, sometimes in restaurants on the outskirts of Paris which were relatively unfrequented because the season hadn't yet started, but more often at the theatre, which Madame Verdurin liked very much. One day at her house, hearing her say how useful it would be to have a special pass for first nights and gala performances, that it had been a great nuisance not to have one on the day of Gambetta's funeral,* Swann, who never talked about his brilliant connections but only about those who were not well regarded, whom he felt it would be insensitive to conceal, and among whom, in the Faubourg Saint-Germain, he'd taken to including all his contacts in the world of officialdom, responded: 'Don't worry, leave it to me, you'll have one in time for the new production of *Les Danicheff*.* As it happens, I'm having lunch with the Prefect of Police tomorrow at the Élysée.'

'What? At the Élysée?' cried Doctor Cottard, at the top of his voice.

'Yes, where Monsieur Grévy lives,'* replied Swann, a little embarrassed by the effect of his remark.

And the painter said to the doctor by way of a joke: 'Do you have attacks like that very often?'

Usually, once an explanation had been given, Cottard would say: 'Oh, I see! Of course,' and would make no further display of emotion. But this time, Swann's words, instead of having the usual calming effect, raised to fever pitch his astonishment that a man with whom he was actually dining, who had no official position, nor any particular claim to distinction, was on visiting terms with the Head of State.

'What? Monsieur Grévy? You know Monsieur Grévy?' he said to Swann with the stupid, incredulous look of a sentry outside the Palace being asked by a stranger to be allowed to see the President of the Republic, and who, realizing from these words 'the sort of man he's dealing with', as the newspapers say, assures the poor lunatic that he will be granted an immediate audience and directs him to the special infirmary of the Barracks.

'I know him slightly,' replied Swann, trying to erase what had seemed too dazzling, in the doctor's eyes, about his relations with the President of the Republic. 'We have some friends in common.' (He didn't dare say the friend was the Prince of Wales.) 'He invites so many people, you know, and I can assure you his lunches are actually rather tedious; and they're very simple, never more than eight at table.'

Cottard, taking Swann at his word, immediately adopted the view that there was nothing special about an invitation to lunch with the President and that such invitations were freely available to anyone. From then on, he no longer found it surprising that Swann, like so many others, should visit the Élysée, and he even felt a little sorry for him for having to attend lunches which Swann himself admitted were a bore.

'Oh, I see! Of course,' he said, sounding like a suspicious customs officer who, after hearing your explanations, stamps your passport and lets you go through without opening your luggage.

'Yes, I can well believe that those lunches are awfully dull, it's very noble of you to go to them,' said Madame Verdurin, for whom the President of the Republic was a bore to be especially dreaded, in that he had at his disposal means of seduction, and compulsion, which, if employed upon the 'faithful', would be capable of making them desert her. 'They say he's as deaf as a post and eats with his fingers.'

'In that case, it definitely can't be much fun for you to go there,' said the doctor with a note of commiseration in his voice; and then, recalling Swann's mention of eight guests at a time, he asked quickly, less out of idle curiosity than with a linguist's zeal: 'Are they what you'd call "private" luncheon-parties?'

But the prestige of the President in the eyes of the doctor ultimately prevailed over both the modesty of Swann and the malevolence of Madame Verdurin, and every time he sat down to dinner with the Verdurins Cottard would ask anxiously: 'Will we be seeing Monsieur Swann this evening? He's a personal friend of Monsieur Grévy. Does that mean he's what they call a *gentleman*?' He even went so far as to offer Swann an invitation-card to the Dental Exhibition.

'This will let you in, and anyone you might like to take with you, but dogs are not allowed. I'm just mentioning that because some friends of mine didn't know and they could have kicked themselves afterwards.'

As for Monsieur Verdurin, he noted the distressing effect on his wife of the discovery that Swann had friends in high places but had never mentioned it.

If no arrangement had been made to go out somewhere, it was at the Verdurins' that Swann would join the little clan, but he came only in the evenings and hardly ever agreed to have dinner, in spite of Odette's entreaties.

'We could have dinner on our own, if you'd prefer,' she would say.

'And what about Madame Verdurin?'

'Oh, that wouldn't be a problem. I'd just tell her my dress wasn't ready, or my cab was late. One can always think of some excuse.'

'You're very sweet.'

But Swann thought that, if he showed Odette (by agreeing to meet her only after dinner) that there were pleasures he preferred to that of her company, it would be a long time before her interest in him waned. And, in any case, since he much preferred to Odette's type of beauty that of a young working-class girl, as fresh and plump as a rose, with whom he'd become smitten, he liked to spend the early part of the evening with her, knowing that he'd see Odette later on. It was for these reasons that he never agreed to have Odette pick him up on her way to the Verdurins'. The young girl would wait for him near his house at a street corner his coachman Rémi knew; she'd get in beside Swann and remain there in his arms until the carriage drew up outside the Verdurins'. When he walked in, Madame Verdurin would point to the roses he'd sent that morning and say: 'You deserve a good scolding', then send him to his place next to Odette, and the pianist would play, just for the two of them, the little phrase by Vinteuil that had become, so to speak, the national anthem of their love.* He'd begin with the sustained violin tremolos which for several bars were without accompaniment, occupying the whole foreground, then all of a sudden they seemed to move aside and, as in those paintings by Pieter De Hooch* that acquire depth from the narrow frame of a half-open door, in the distance, quite different in colour, in the velvety softness of an intervening light, the little phrase would appear, dancing, pastoral, interpolated, episodic, belonging to another world. It rippled past, simple and immortal, distributing on all sides the gifts of its grace, with the same ineffable smile; but Swann thought he could detect in it now a certain disenchantment. It seemed to realize how vain was the happiness to which it showed the way. In its airy grace there was a suggestion of something over and done with, like the mood of detachment that follows regret. But this hardly mattered to him, he considered the phrase less for what it was in itself—in terms of what it might express for a composer totally unaware of his existence or that of Odette when he wrote it, and for all those who would hear it in the centuries to come—than as a token, a memento, of his love, which even for the Verdurins, even for the young pianist, would remind them of Odette and himself at the same time, and bind them together; so much so that he'd given in to Odette's capricious insistence that he abandon his plan to have some other pianist play the whole sonata for him, and so this passage remained the only one he knew. 'Why do you need the rest?' she'd said. 'This is *our* piece.' Indeed, he even found it painful to think, as the little phrase floated past, so very near and yet so infinitely far away, that although it was addressed to them it did not know them, and he was almost sorry that it had a meaning of its own, its own intrinsic and unalterable beauty, independent of them, just as a gift of jewellery or even letters written by a woman we love may make us resent the water of the gems or the words chosen, because they are not created exclusively from the essence of a passing love affair and a particular person.

It often happened that he stayed so long with the young girl before going to the Verdurins' that, as soon as the little phrase had been played by the pianist, Swann would realize it was almost time for Odette to go home. He'd drive her back as far as the door of her little house in the Rue La Pérouse, behind the Arc de Triomphe. It was perhaps because of this, and so as not to monopolize her favours, that he sacrificed the less necessary pleasure of seeing her earlier in the evening, of arriving with her at the Verdurins', to the exercise of this right to leave together, which she recognized as his and to which he attached greater importance, since it made him feel that no one else would see her, come between them, or prevent her staying with him in thought, after he'd left her.

And so she'd go home in Swann's carriage; one night, when she'd just stepped down and he was saying he'd see her the following day, she ran to pick one of the last remaining chrysanthemums from the little garden in front of the house and gave it to him before he left. He held it pressed to his lips during the drive home, and when after a few days the flower withered, he locked it away with great care in his desk.

But he never went into the house. In fact, he'd only set foot in it on two occasions, in the afternoon, in order to participate in that practice which was of such vital importance for her: 'taking tea'. The loneliness and emptiness of the little streets (nearly all of them lined with small adjoining townhouses, their monotony suddenly broken by some sinister-looking single-storey building, the historical testimony and sordid remains of the time when this part of Paris was still in bad repute), the snow still lying in the garden and on the trees, the unkemptness of the season, and the proximity of nature all added an element of mystery to the warmth and the flowers he'd found inside.

From the ground floor, raised slightly above street level, leaving on the left Odette's bedroom, which looked out at the back onto a little parallel street, a straight staircase led up between dark painted walls hung with Oriental draperies, strings of Turkish beads, and a large Japanese lantern suspended from a silken cord (but illuminated with a gas jet, so as not to deprive visitors of the latest comforts of Western civilization) and brought him to her drawing room and morning room. These were entered via a narrow hallway whose wall was chequered by a wooden trellis of the kind you see on garden walls, but gilded, and lined along its entire length by a rectangular box in which bloomed, as in a greenhouse, a row of those large chrysanthemums which were still rare at the time, yet nothing to compare with the ones horticulturalists have since succeeded in producing. Swann was irritated by the fashion for these flowers, which had begun the previous year, but on this occasion he'd been pleased to see the gloomy hallway streaked with pink, orange, and white rays by these fragrant but short-lived stars which light up on grey days. Odette had received him in a pink silk dressing-gown, her neck and arms bare. She'd made him sit next to her in one of the many mysterious alcoves arranged in the recesses of the room, sheltered by immense palms in china flower-pot holders, or by screens to which she'd attached photographs, fans, and ribbons tied in bows. She'd said: 'You can't be comfortable like that, wait a minute, I'll fix you up,' and with a rather smug little laugh that implied some unique invention of her own, she'd installed behind his head and under his feet cushions of Japanese silk which she kneaded and shaped as if she were prodigal of these riches, regardless of their value. But when the valet brought in, one after the other, the many lamps which, nearly all contained in large Chinese vases, burned singly or in pairs, all on different pieces of furniture as though on altars, and which had turned the already almost nocturnal gloom of that late winter afternoon into a more lasting, more rosy, more human sunset—perhaps making some passing lover stop in the street outside and fall into a reverie at the mystery that was revealed and yet concealed by the glowing panes—she'd kept a sharp eye on the servant to see whether he'd placed each of them in their designated places. She thought that if even one were put where it ought not to be, the overall effect of her sitting room would be destroyed, and her portrait, which rested on a sloping easel draped in plush, would be ill-lit. So she paid fervent attention to the man's every clumsy movement and gave him a stern reprimand for having passed too close to a pair of flower stands which she made a point of cleaning herself for fear that they might get damaged and which she now went over to examine, to make sure he hadn't chipped them. She thought there was something 'quaint' about the shapes of all her Chinese knick-knacks, and also about the orchids, the cattleyas especially, which, along with chrysanthemums, were her favourite flowers, because they had the great merit of not looking like flowers, but of seeming to be made of silk or satin. 'This one looks as if it was cut out of the lining of my coat,' she said to Swann, pointing at an orchid, with a suggestion of respect in her voice for this very 'chic' flower, this elegant, unexpected sister which Nature had given her, so far removed from her on the scale of existence and yet so refined, more deserving than many women of being granted admission to her salon. Drawing his attention, first, to flame-tongued dragons painted on a vase or embroidered on a screen, then to the petals of a bunch of orchids, then to a dromedary of silver inlaid with niello* with its eyes encrusted with rubies, standing on the mantelpiece next to a toad carved in jade, she pretended first to be frightened of the dangerous monsters, then to laugh at their comic appearance, blushing at the impropriety of the flowers, and then feeling an irresistible desire to go and kiss the dromedary and the toad—whom she called her 'little darlings'. And these affectations were in sharp contrast to the sincerity of certain of her religious devotions, for instance to Notre-Dame de Laghet,* who, when she was living in Nice, had cured her of a mortal illness, and whose gold medallion she always wore, attributing to it infinite powers. Odette made Swann her special tea, asked him:

'Lemon or cream?' and when he answered 'cream', said with a laugh: 'A soupçon!' And when he declared it to be very good, she added: 'You see, I know what you like.' The tea had, in fact, seemed as precious a thing to Swann as it did to her, and love has such a need to find a form of justification, a guarantee that it will last, in pleasures which would never have become pleasures without it and cease to be pleasures when love itself ceases, that when he left her at seven o'clock to go and dress for the evening, during the whole journey home in his carriage, unable to contain the great pleasure the afternoon had given him, he kept repeating to himself: 'How nice it would be to have a little woman like that in whose house one could always be sure to find that rare thing—a good cup of tea.' An hour later, he received a note from Odette and immediately recognized the large handwriting, in which an affectation of British stiffness imposed an appearance of discipline on ill-formed characters that might have suggested to eyes less biased than his own an untidiness of mind, a deficient education, a lack of frankness and resolution. Swann had left his cigarette case at her house. 'If you'd left your heart here too, I wouldn't have let you have it back.'

His second visit to her may have been more significant. On his way to the house that day, as always when he was to see her, he pictured her to himself beforehand; and the need he felt, in order to find her face at all pretty, to focus on her fresh, pink cheekbones rather than on the rest of her cheeks, which were so often sallow and drawn, and sometimes marked with little red spots, troubled him insofar as it proved that the ideal is unattainable and happiness limited. He'd brought an engraving she wanted to see. She was a little off-colour, and received him in a dressing gown of mauve crêpe de Chine, pulling the richly embroidered material over her chest like a cloak. As she stood beside him, letting her long hair flow loose down her cheeks, bending one leg rather like a dancer so that she could lean more easily over the engraving, at which she gazed, her head tilted to one side, with those great eyes of hers which seemed so tired and sullen when she was not in good spirits, Swann was struck by her resemblance to the figure of Zipporah, Jethro's daughter,* in a fresco at the Sistine Chapel. This idiosyncrasy of loving to discover in the paintings of the Old Masters not just the general characteristics of the real world around us, but what seems on the contrary the least susceptible of generalization, the individual features of people we know: for example, in a bust of the Doge Loredano by Antonio Rizzo,* he saw the prominent cheekbones, the slanting eyebrows, in fact the spitting image of his coachman Rémi; in the colouring of a Ghirlandaio,* the nose of Monsieur de Palancy; in a portrait by Tintoretto,* the invasion of the fleshy part of the cheek by the side-whiskers, the broken nose, the piercing gaze, the swollen eyelids of Doctor du Boulbon. Perhaps because he'd always felt a certain regret at having limited his life to the social world and to conversation, he believed he'd been granted a kind of indulgent forgiveness by the great artists in the fact that they too had contemplated with pleasure, and incorporated into their work, faces like these, which gave it a special stamp of reality and truth to life, a modern flavour; perhaps, also, he'd let himself become so involved in the frivolous ways of society people that he felt a need to find in an old masterpiece these anticipatory and rejuvenating allusions to personalities of the present day. Perhaps, on the other hand, he still had enough of the artist in him to derive pleasure from the ways in which these individual characteristics took on more general significance as soon as he saw them, uprooted and set free, in the resemblance between an older portrait and a modern original which it was not intended to represent. Whatever the reason, and perhaps because the richness of impressions he'd been experiencing for some time, though deriving from his love of music, had actually enhanced his enjoyment of painting, he now experienced a greater pleasure— and this was to have a lasting effect on him—at that moment, when he noticed the resemblance between Odette and the Zipporah of Sandro di Mariano, who is better known now by his popular nickname of Botticelli, for that name evokes, not the actual work of the Master but the banal and false idea of it adopted in popular culture. He no longer appraised Odette's face according to the finer or poorer quality of her cheeks and the fleshy softness he assumed he'd feel with his lips if he ever dared to kiss her, but as a skein of beautiful, delicate lines that his eyes unravelled, following their curves and windings, connecting the rhythm of her neck to the flow of her hair and the curvature of her eyelids, as if contemplating a portrait of her in which her type became clear and intelligible.

He stood gazing at her; a fragment of the fresco appeared in her face and in her body, and from then on he'd always try to rediscover it in her, whether he was with her or was only thinking about her, and although no doubt he valued the Florentine masterpiece not only because he could rediscover it in Odette, her resemblance to it conferred a certain beauty on her too, and made her more precious. Swann was annoyed with himself for having misjudged the value of a creature whom the great Sandro would have found adorable, and was gratified by the fact that his pleasure in seeing Odette had found some justification in his own aesthetic culture. He reflected that by associating the thought of Odette with his dreams of happiness he had not resigned himself to a second-best as imperfect as he'd hitherto believed, for she satisfied his most refined artistic tastes. He forgot that this did not make Odette any more the sort of woman he found desirable, since his desires had always run counter to his aesthetic tastes. The phrase 'Florentine work of art' was immensely useful to Swann. It enabled him, like a title, to insert Odette's image into a world of dreams from which, until then, she'd been excluded and where she was now invested with a kind of nobility. And while the purely physical view he'd had of this woman, by perpetually renewing his doubts about the quality of her face, her body, the whole nature of her beauty, had weakened his love, these doubts were swept aside and his love confirmed now that he could stand on the firm ground of his aesthetic values; while, in addition, the kiss, the physical possession, which would seem natural and unremarkable if granted by a person of flawed beauty, now coming to crown his adoration of a work of art in a gallery, seemed to hold out the promise of supernatural delights.

And whenever he was tempted to regret the fact that for months he'd done nothing but see Odette, he told himself it was not unreasonable to devote a good deal of his time to a priceless work of art, cast for once in a different and especially delightful material, in an exceedingly rare exemplar which he'd contemplate at some moments with the humility, spirituality, and disinterestedness of an artist, at others with the pride, egotism, and sensuality of a collector.

He placed on his study table, as if it were a photograph of Odette, a reproduction of Jethro's daughter. He'd gaze in admiration at the large eyes, the delicate features with their suggestion of an imperfect complexion, the wonderful locks of hair that fell over the tired cheeks, and, adapting to the idea of a living woman what he'd until then found beautiful in aesthetic terms, he translated it into various physical attractions which he was delighted to see combined in a person he might come to possess. Now that he'd become acquainted, in the flesh, with the original of Jethro's daughter, the vague feeling of sympathy that draws us to a masterpiece as we look at it became a desire that henceforth stood in for the desire that Odette's body had not at first inspired in him. After he'd gazed for a long time at the reproduction of Botticelli, his thoughts would turn to his own Botticelli, even more beautiful in his eyes, and, moving the photograph of Zipporah closer to him, he'd imagine it was Odette he was clasping to his breast.

And yet he strove to think up ways not only of preventing Odette from growing tired of him, but also, sometimes, of preventing himself from becoming tired of her; feeling that Odette, since she'd been able to see him frequently, no longer seemed to have much to say to him, made him fear that the rather uninteresting, monotonous, and seemingly immutable behaviour she now adopted when they were together would eventually destroy his romantic hope that one day she'd declare her passion, a hope which alone had made him fall in love and remain in love. And so, in an attempt to change Odette's too fixed attitude towards him, which he was afraid would make him grow tired of her, he'd suddenly write her a letter full of feigned disappointment and simulated anger, which he'd have delivered to her before dinner. He knew she'd be alarmed, and would answer him, and he hoped that, when the fear of losing him tugged at her heart, words would spring forth that she'd never yet uttered to him; and indeed, it was in this way that he'd obtained the most affectionate letters she'd so far written to him, including one, which she'd sent round at midday from La Maison Dorée* (it was the day of the Paris–Murcia Fête,* held in aid of the victims of the Murcia floods), that began with the words: 'My dear Charles, my hand is shaking so much that I can hardly write,' and that he'd kept in the same drawer as the withered chrysanthemum. Or, if she hadn't had time to write to him, when he arrived at the Verdurins' she'd run up to him, saying: 'I must talk to you,' and he'd gaze curiously at the revelation on her face and in her words of what until then she'd kept hidden in her heart.

Even as he drew close to the Verdurins' house, when he caught sight of the great lamp-lit windows whose shutters were never closed, he felt quite touched at the thought of the charming creature he'd soon see in her full splendour, bathed in the golden light. From time to time the silhouettes of the guests would stand out, slender and black, against the light from the lamps, as if on a screen, like the little pictures fitted at intervals around a translucent lampshade and separated from each other by panels of pure light. He'd try to distinguish

Odette's silhouette. Then, as soon as he arrived, without his being aware of it, his eyes would shine with such joy that Monsieur Verdurin would say to the painter: 'I think things are warming up.' And for Swann, Odette's presence did indeed give the house something that was lacking in the other houses he frequented: a kind of sensory apparatus, a nervous system that extended throughout every room and produced constant tremors of excitement in his heart.

And so, through its simple, regular functioning as a social organism, the 'little clan' automatically arranged Swann's daily meetings with Odette and enabled him to feign indifference as to whether he saw her or not, and even a desire not to see her, a desire that carried no great risk of being fulfilled, since, whatever he wrote to her during the day, he was bound to see her in the evening and take her home.

Once, however, depressed by the thought of the inevitable ride home together, he'd taken his young girl all the way to the Bois so as to delay his appearance at the Verdurins', and he arrived at their house so late that Odette, thinking he wasn't coming, had already left. When he saw she was no longer in the drawing room, Swann felt a pang in his heart; he trembled at the thought of being deprived of a pleasure he was now fully appreciating for the first time, since until then he'd always had the certainty of its being available whenever he wished, which, as with all pleasures, reduces them and may even prevent us from completely realizing their full extent.

'Did you see his face when he realized she wasn't here?' Monsieur Verdurin said to his wife. 'I think we can say he's hooked.'

'Whose face?' asked Doctor Cottard, who had left the house earlier to make a brief visit to a patient, had just come back to fetch his wife, and didn't know whom they were talking about.

'What, didn't you bump into the most handsome of Swanns at the front door . . .?'

'No. Monsieur Swann was here?'

'Oh, just for a moment. We had a very agitated, very anxious Swann. Odette had already left, you see.'

'You mean there's "hanky panky", she's allowed him to "enter the castle"?' asked the doctor, cautiously testing the meaning of these expressions.

'No, no,' replied Madame Verdurin. 'There's certainly nothing going on, and just between ourselves, I think she's making a big mistake and behaving like an absolute ninny—which is what she is, in fact.'

'Now, now, now,' said Monsieur Verdurin, 'how can you be so sure? We haven't exactly been in a position to see for ourselves, have we?'

'She would have told me,' replied Madame Verdurin haughtily. 'She tells me everything! I've told her, since she's not with anyone else at present, she should sleep with him. She makes out she can't, that she was really attracted to him at first but he's shy with her, which makes her shy with him, and anyway she doesn't love him in that way, for her he's a kind of ideal, she's afraid of spoiling her feelings for him, but how would I know? And yet it would be just what she needs.'

'I beg to differ,' said her husband. 'The gentleman isn't quite my cup of tea. I find him rather pretentious.'

Madame Verdurin froze, assumed a blank expression as if she'd turned into a statue, a device that enabled her to appear not to have heard that intolerable word 'pretentious', which seemed to imply that a person could be pretentious in relation to them, and therefore 'superior' to them.

'Anyhow, if there's nothing going on, I don't think it's because the fellow believes she's *virtuous*,' Monsieur Verdurin went on ironically. 'Still, you never know, he does seem to think she's intelligent. I don't know if you heard him holding forth to her the other evening about Vinteuil's sonata; I'm terribly fond of Odette, but to give her lectures on aesthetic theory—really, you'd have to be a complete nincompoop.'

'Come on now, stop saying nasty things about Odette,' said Madame Verdurin, in a 'little girl' voice. 'She's delightful.'

'But she can still be delightful. Nobody's saying nasty things about her, just that she's no genius and no saint. In fact,' he said to the painter, 'are you that keen for her to be virtuous? If she was, we might not find her so delightful.'

On the landing Swann had been stopped by the butler, who hadn't been there when he arrived and had been asked by Odette—but this was already an hour earlier—to tell him, in case he should still come, that she'd probably go and have a cup of chocolate at Prévost's on her way home. Swann set off for Prévost's, but his carriage was forever being held up by other carriages or by people crossing the street, loathsome obstacles he'd gladly have knocked out of the way, were it not for the fact that a policeman's report would have delayed him even more than the passing pedestrians. He counted the minutes as they ticked by, adding a few seconds to each to be sure he was not making them too short and allowing himself to think he had a greater chance than he actually had of arriving early and finding Odette still there. And at one point, like a man in a fever who emerges from sleep and becomes aware of the absurdity of the dreams that had been swirling in his mind without his clearly distinguishing himself from them, Swann suddenly realized the strangeness of the thoughts he'd been turning over since the moment he was told at the Verdurins' that Odette had already left, the unfamiliar aching of his heart, which he noticed now as if he'd just woken up. What! All this agitation because he wouldn't see Odette until tomorrow, precisely what he'd wanted, an hour before, as he was being driven to Madame Verdurin's! He was obliged to acknowledge that in this same carriage which was taking him to Prévost's, he was no longer the same man and was no longer alone, that a new person was there with him, attached to him, a part of him, from whom he might not be able to free himself, whom he was going to have to treat with circumspection, as one behaves towards a superior or copes with an illness. And yet from the moment he'd begun to feel that a new person had been added to him in this way, his life seemed more interesting. It hardly occurred to him that, even if it took place, this possible meeting at Prévost's (the anticipation of which so devastated, so denuded the moments preceding it that he couldn't find a single idea or memory with which to offer his mind some rest) would probably, like the others, not amount to much. As on every other evening, once he was with Odette, casting at her change-able face a furtive glance which he would immediately turn away for fear that she'd see in his eyes his mounting desire and stop believing in his lack of interest, he'd no longer be able to think about her, so busy would he be finding excuses that would enable him not to leave her immediately and yet ensure, without his seeming at all concerned, that he'd see her again the next day at the Verdurins': excuses, in other words, that would enable him to prolong for the time being, and to renew for one more day, the disappointment and torment he was suf-fering because of the pointless presence of this woman to whom he'd made approaches but never dared to take in his arms.

She was not at Prévost's; and so he resolved to look in every res-taurant along the boulevards. To save time, while he looked in some, he sent to the others his coachman Rémi (Rizzo's Doge Loredano), for whom he then waited—not having found Odette anywhere—at a prearranged spot. The carriage didn't reappear, and Swann imagined the coming moment as one when Rémi would say: 'The lady is there,' or when he'd say: 'The lady wasn't in any of the cafés.' And so he saw the remainder of the evening before him, single and yet alternative, preceded either by a meeting with Odette which would put an end to his agony, or by the forced abandonment of his search and acceptance of the need to return home without having seen her.

The coachman returned, but as he pulled up in front of Swann, Swann didn't say: 'Did you find the lady?' but: 'Remind me tomorrow to order some more firewood; I think our stocks are running low.' Perhaps he felt that if Rémi had found Odette in one of the cafés, waiting for him, the end of the ill-fated evening would already be cancelled out by the realization, already forming in his mind, of the happy one, and there was no need for him to rush to seize a happiness that had already been captured, was now held in a safe place, and would never be able to escape. But it was also from the force of inertia; his mind lacked the suppleness some people lack in their bodies, and who, at the moment when they need to avoid a collision, snatch a flame away from their clothing, or perform a sudden movement, take their time, pause for a moment in their present position as if to steady themselves and find their momentum. And no doubt, if the coachman had interrupted him by saying: 'The lady's there,' he might well have replied: 'Oh yes, of course! That errand I sent you on! Well, well! Is that so?' and then continued with what he was saying about the firewood in order to hide the state of his emotions and give himself time to get over his anxiety and devote himself to happiness.

But what the coachman came back to tell him was that he hadn't found her anywhere, and, as a trusted old servant, offered his advice: 'I think all Monsieur can do now is go home.'

But the indifference Swann affected easily enough as long as Rémi could do nothing to change the answer he'd brought back fell away when he saw Rémi attempt to make him give up hope and abandon his search.

'Certainly not!' he cried. 'We must find the lady. It's extremely important. If she doesn't see me, she'll be most annoyed, and offended too. It's about a business matter.'

'I don't see how the lady could be offended,' replied Rémi, 'if she was the one who left without waiting for Monsieur, and said she was going to Prévost's, and then wasn't there.'

By now the restaurants were closing. Under the trees along the boulevards, fewer people were wandering along, barely distinguishable in the gathering darkness. Every now and then the shadowy figure of a woman coming up to him, murmuring in his ear, asking him to take her home, would make Swann start. He brushed nervously against all these dim forms as if, among the shades of the dead, in the kingdom of darkness, he were searching for Eurydice.*

Of all the modes by which love comes into being, of all the disseminating agents of this holy evil, one of the most efficacious is this great breath of agitation that sweeps over us from time to time. For then the die is cast, and the person whose company we enjoy at the time is the one we will love. It isn't even necessary, until then, that we should have been attracted to that person more than to others, or even to the same extent. All that is required is that our predilection becomes exclusive. And that condition is fulfilled when, at a moment when we're deprived of that person's company, the quest for the pleasures their company gave us is suddenly replaced by an anxious need whose object is that very person, an absurd need which the laws of this world make impossible to satisfy and difficult to cure: the senseless and painful need to possess the person entirely.

Swann asked Rémi to drive him to the few restaurants that were still open. The hypothesis of a happy ending to his search was the only one he'd been able to envisage at all calmly; and now he no longer hid his agitation nor the importance he attached to finding Odette; he promised Rémi a reward if they were successful, as though, by inspiring in his coachman a desire to succeed that would reinforce his own, he could make Odette, if she'd already gone home to bed, nevertheless appear in one of the boulevard restaurants. He continued as far as the Maison Dorée, looked in twice at Tortoni's, and, still not seeing her, had just come out of the Café Anglais again, looking quite distraught as he strode back to the carriage, which was waiting for him on the corner of the Boulevard des Italiens, when he bumped into someone coming from the opposite direction: it was Odette. She explained later that there'd been no room at Prévost's and so had gone to have supper at the Maison Dorée in an alcove where he mustn't have noticed her, and was just walking back to her carriage.

His appearance was so unexpected that she stepped back in alarm. Swann, for his part, had been rushing all over Paris not because he thought it was possible to find her, but because he couldn't bear the thought of giving up the attempt. But the happiness which his reason had never stopped telling him would be unattainable, that evening at least, now seemed to him all the more real: for, since he'd played no part in its preparation by foreseeing the likely circumstances in which it might be realized, it remained external to him; he didn't need to draw upon his mind to give it the quality of truth, it contained its own truth, projecting that truth towards him, a truth whose radiance dispelled like a dream the loneliness he'd been dreading, a truth which had now become the basis, the support, for his blissful, unthinking reverie. He was like a traveller arriving at the Mediterranean seaboard on a day of glorious weather, and, no longer certain that the lands he has left behind really exist, lets his eyes be dazzled by the bright reflections from the deep luminous blue of the water, rather than looking at them directly.

He climbed up with her into the carriage that had been waiting for her and told Rémi to follow.

In her hand she was holding a bunch of cattleyas, and Swann could see that, under her lace scarf, she had flowers of the same orchid in her hair, fastened to a plume of swan feathers. Beneath the scarf, she was dressed in flowing black velvet caught up on one side to reveal a broad triangle of undergown in white ribbed silk, and showing a yoke, also of white silk, at the opening of the low-cut bodice adorned with more cattleyas. She'd hardly recovered from the shock of bumping into Swann when some obstacle in the street made the horse shy. They were thrown forward in their seats, she cried out, then sat trembling and breathless.

'It's all right,' he said. 'Don't be frightened.' And he put his arm round her shoulder, supporting her body against his. Then he went on: 'Don't speak, just nod or shake your head until you've got your breath back. You won't mind if I straighten the flowers on your bodice? That jolt has knocked them out of place. I wouldn't want you to lose them, so I'll push them back in a little.'

Odette, who was not used to a man making such a fuss over her, said with a smile: 'Oh, I don't mind at all.'

But he, intimidated by her answer, and perhaps also to make his excuse seem sincere, or even beginning to believe that he'd meant what he said, exclaimed: 'No, don't talk! You'll get out of breath again, you can just make signs, I'll understand perfectly well. You really don't mind? Look, there's a drop of . . . I think some pollen has got sprinkled over you; can I brush it off with my hand? I'm not pressing too hard, I'm not being too rough? I'm tickling you, perhaps? The thing is, I don't want to touch the velvet, it might get crumpled. But you can see they really had to be fastened, or they would have fallen out; I'll push them back in a little further, like this . . . You're sure you don't mind? And if I sniffed them to see if they really have no scent, would that bother you? I've never smelt one, would you believe? You don't mind? Honestly?'

Smiling, she gave a little shrug, as if to say 'You're quite mad; you can see I like it.'

He ran his other hand up Odette's cheek; she gazed at him without blinking, with the grave and languid look of the women of the Florentine master in whose faces he'd found a resemblance with hers; her shining eyes, wide and slender like theirs, seemed to brim at the edge of her lids and to be on the point of welling out like two tears. She tilted her head to one side, as Botticelli's women all do, in the pagan scenes as well as in the religious paintings. And in an attitude that was no doubt habitual, which she knew was appropriate to moments like this and which she made sure she would not forget to adopt, she seemed to need all her strength to hold her face back, as if some invisible force was drawing it to Swann's. And it was Swann who, for a moment, held her face away from his in his hands, before she let it fall, as though in spite of herself, onto his lips. He'd wanted to give his mind time to catch up with him, to recognize the dream it had cherished for so long and to be present at its realization, like a relative invited to share in the success of a child of whom she has always been very fond. Perhaps, too, Swann was also gazing at Odette's face with the eyes of a man who looks intensely at a land-scape he's about to leave forever, as if to carry it away with him, for it was a face he was seeing for the last time: Odette as she was before he slept with her, or even kissed her.

But he was so timid with her that, after ending the evening in her bed, having begun by rearranging her cattleyas, whether from fear of offending her or of appearing in retrospect to have lied, or because he lacked the boldness to formulate a more pressing requirement than the flower-arranging (which he could always resort to again, since it hadn't annoyed Odette the first time), in the days that followed he used the same stratagem. If she was wearing cattleyas on her bodice, he'd say: 'What a shame, the cattleyas don't need to be straightened this evening, they haven't been disarranged as they were the other evening; this one, though, doesn't look very straight. May I see if they have a stronger scent than the others?' Or, if she had none: 'Oh! No cattleyas this evening! That means I won't be able to do any flower-arranging.' So that for some time there was no change to the sequence he'd followed that first evening, starting with his touching Odette's bosom with his fingers and lips, and their love-play still began this way each time; and long afterwards, when the flower-arranging (or the ritual pretence of flower-arranging) had long since fallen into disuse, the metaphor 'do a cattleya', having become a term they used without thinking to refer to the act of physical possession—in which, in fact, one possesses nothing—lived on in their language, commemorating the forgotten custom from which it sprang. And perhaps this particular way of saying 'to make love' did not mean exactly the same thing as its synonyms. Even if we feel blasé about women, seeing in the sexual enjoyment of many different ones the same predictable experience, we can still discover a new kind of pleasure if the women involved are (or are thought to be) difficult enough to oblige us to make it spring from some unexpected incident in our relations with them, as had been for Swann the original arranging of the cattleyas. He tremblingly hoped, that evening (but Odette, he thought, if she was taken in by his stratagem, couldn't guess his intention), that it was possession of this woman that would emerge from the large mauve petals; and the pleasure he felt already and that Odette was tolerating, he thought, only because she had not recognized it, seemed to him, because of that—as it might have seemed to the first man when he tasted it among the flowers of the earthly paradise—a pleasure which had not existed until then, which he was now seeking to create, a pleasure—as indicated by the special name he gave it—entirely new and individual.

Now, every evening, when he took her home, he had to go in, and often she'd come back out in a dressing gown and walk with him to his carriage, and kiss him in full view of the coachman, saying: 'Why should I care what people think?' On evenings when he didn't go to the Verdurins' (which happened occasionally now that he had other ways of seeing her), or on the increasingly rare evenings he spent in fashionable company, she'd ask him to drop in on his way home, whatever the hour. It was spring, a crisp and frosty spring. On leaving a party, he'd climb into his victoria,* spread a rug over his knees, tell the friends who were leaving at the same time and had asked him to join them, that he couldn't, that he was not going their way, and the coachman would set off at a fast trot, knowing exactly where to go. They were surprised at Swann's behaviour, and indeed he was a changed man. No one ever received a letter from him now asking for an introduction to some woman. He no longer paid any attention to women and avoided places where one might normally meet them. In a restaurant, or in the country, his attitude was the opposite of the one by which, only recently, people would have recognized him, and which had seemed that it would always and inevitably be his. Once a passion takes hold of us, it manifests itself as a temporary, different personality that takes the place of our normal personality and obliterates the signs, invariable until then, by which it expressed itself! What never changed now, however, was that wherever Swann might be, he never failed to go and see Odette afterwards. The distance that separated him from her he inevitably covered as though it were the rapid and irresistible slope of his very life. In truth, when he'd stayed out late at some social gathering, he would often have preferred to go straight home without making that long trip, and not see her until the next day; but the very fact of taking the trouble to call in to see her at an unusual hour, of imagining, after he took leave of his friends, that they'd be saying to one another: 'He's very devoted, there must be some woman who makes him go and see her at any time of day or night,' made him feel that he was leading the kind of life led by men who conduct love affairs, and in whom the sacrifice they make of their comfort and other interests to a dream of sensual pleasure generates a sort of inner charm. Then, without his realizing it, the certainty that she was waiting for him, that she wasn't somewhere else with other people, that he wouldn't return home without seeing her, cancelled out the anguish, now forgotten but always ready to be reawakened, that he'd felt on the evening when Odette had left the Verdurins' before his arrival, an anguish of which the present assuagement was so pleasant that it could be called happiness. Perhaps it was to that anguish that he owed the importance Odette had assumed for him. Other people usually mean so little to us that when we invest one of them with such potential for causing us suffering or happiness, that person seems to belong to another world, takes on an aura of poetry, transforms our life into a sort of emotional field in which he or she will be closer or less close to us. Swann found it impossible to think calmly about what Odette might mean to him in the years to come. Sometimes, as he sat in his victoria on those lovely cold nights, he'd see the brilliant moon spreading its light between his eyes and the deserted streets, and would think of that other face, bright and tinged with pink like the moon's, which, one day, had risen in his mind and, since then, had shed upon the world the mysterious light in which he saw it bathed. If he reached Odette's house after the time when she sent her servants to bed, rather than ring the bell at the gate of her little front garden, he'd go round into the other street, over which, on the ground floor, among the identical but unlit windows of the adjoining houses, shone the solitary lighted window of her bedroom. He would tap on the pane, and she, thus alerted, would respond and go and wait for him on the other side, at the front door. He'd find several of her favourite pieces open on the piano: the *Valse des Roses* or *Pauvre Fou* by Tagliafico* (which, she'd written in her will, was to be played at her funeral); he'd ask her to play instead the little phrase from Vinteuil's sonata, even though she played very badly, but the most lasting impression we have of a piece of music is often one that rises above a series of wrong notes struck by clumsy fingers on an out-of-tune piano. For Swann the little phrase continued to be associated with his love for Odette. He was well aware that this love was something that did not correspond to anything beyond itself, observable by others; and he realized that Odette's qualities were not such as to justify the value he placed on the time he spent in her company. And often, when his mind was governed by intelligence alone, he would feel a desire to stop sacrificing so many of his intellectual or social interests to this imaginary pleasure. But the little phrase, as soon as he heard it, was able to open up within him the space it needed, rearranging the shape of his inner self; a margin was left for a pleasure which, similarly, did not correspond to any external object, and yet, instead of being purely individual, like his enjoyment of his love for Odette, assumed for Swann a reality superior to that of concrete things. The little phrase aroused in him a yearning for an unknown delight, but gave him nothing precise with which to assuage it. The result was that those parts of Swann's inner self from which the little phrase had erased all concern for material interests, those human considerations that affect all men, had been left vacant and blank, and in them he was free to inscribe the name of Odette. Also, insofar as Odette's affection appeared somewhat weak and disappointing, the little phrase supplemented it, strengthened it with its own mysterious essence. To see Swann's face as he listened to the phrase, one would have thought he was inhaling an anaesthetic that would enable him to breathe more freely. And the pleasure the music gave him, which was soon to become a form of addiction, did indeed resemble at such moments the pleasure he would have derived from trying out various perfumes, or entering into contact with a world for which we men are not made, which seems formless to us because our eyes cannot see it, meaningless because it eludes our understanding, which we can only grasp through one sense alone. What deep repose, what mysterious renewal for Swann—whose eyes, for all their subtle appreciation of painting, and whose mind, for all its shrewd observation of manners, were indelibly marked by the barrenness of his life—to feel himself transformed into a creature alien to humanity, blind and deprived of any intellectual faculty, almost a fantastic unicorn, a chimerical creature conscious of the world only through its sense of hearing. And since he nevertheless persisted in trying to find in the little phrase a meaning which his intellect could not plumb, what strange intoxication he felt as he divested his innermost self of all the help reason might provide and made it feel its way unaided through the conduit, the dark filter, of sound! He was beginning to become aware of how much suffering, perhaps even some secret and unappeased sorrow, lay hidden in that sweet phrase, but he couldn't feel that suffering. What did it matter that it told him love is fragile, for his own love was so strong! He played with the sadness of it as he felt it pass over him, but he experienced it as a caress that only deepened and sweetened his sense of his own happiness. He'd make Odette play it ten times, even twenty times, insisting that as she played she should not stop kissing him. Each kiss calls forth another. Ah, in those first days of love, kisses come so naturally! So closely, in their profusion, do they crowd together that it would be as hard for lovers to count the kisses they exchange in an hour as to count the flowers in a meadow in the month of May. Then she'd make as if to stop, saying: 'How do you expect me to play if you keep holding me? I can't do everything at once. Decide what you want—am I to play the phrase or am I to play at kissing you?' He'd get annoyed, but she'd burst out laughing, laughter that was then transformed into a shower of kisses. Or she'd look at him sulkily, and once again he would see a face worthy of figuring in Botticelli's *Life of Moses*; he'd place her in it, positioning her head at the required angle; then, once he'd painted her in fifteenth-century tempera, on the walls of the Sistine Chapel, the idea that she was actually still there, by the piano, in the present moment, willing to be embraced and possessed, the idea of her physical existence and life would so intoxicate him that, his eyes wild and his jaws tensed as if ready to devour her, he'd fall upon his Botticelli virgin and start pinching her cheeks. Then, when he'd left, but not before going back in to kiss her once more because he'd forgotten to fix in his memory some detail of her fragrance or her features, as he returned home in his victoria he'd bless Odette for granting him these daily visits, which he felt couldn't give her any great pleasure, but which, by protecting him from jealousy—by removing any possibility of his suffering again from the malady that had taken hold of him the evening when he'd failed to find her at the Verdurins'—would help him to arrive, without having any more of those crises of which the first had been so painful that it must be the last, at the end of this strange period of his life, of these hours that were almost enchanted, like those in which he drove through Paris by moonlight. And noticing during his homeward journey that the moon had changed its position in relation to him and was now almost touching the horizon, he'd think that his love, too, was subject to immutable natural laws, and wonder whether this period he'd entered would last much longer, whether, quite soon, in his mind's eye, he'd no longer see that beloved face except as occupying a distant and diminished position, and on the point of ceasing to shed on him the radiance of its charm. For Swann, now that he was in love, was again finding in the things around him a certain charm, as at the time when, in his adolescence, he'd seen himself as an artist; but it was no longer the same charm, for now their charm was conferred by Odette alone. He felt the inspirations of his youth, which had been dissipated by a life of frivolity, reawakening within him, but they all bore the mark, the reflection, of a particular person; and during the long hours which he now found a delicate pleasure in spending at home, alone with his convalescent soul, slowly he became himself again, but owned by another.

He went to her house only in the evenings, and he was as ignorant of how she spent her time during the day as he was about her past life, so much so that he lacked even that small, initial clue which, by enabling us to imagine what we don't know, makes us want to know it. So he never wondered what she might be doing, nor what sort of life she'd led. He merely smiled to himself at the thought that, a few years earlier, when he didn't know her, someone had mentioned to him a woman who, if he remembered correctly, could only have been Odette, as being a courtesan, a kept woman, one of those women to whom he still attributed, since he'd spent very little time in their company, the wilful, fundamentally perverse character with which they'd for so long been endowed by the imagination of certain novelists. He told himself that as often as not one has only to take the opposite view of the reputation the world has formed of someone in order to judge that person accurately, and when he compared the character of such a woman with that of Odette, so kind, so artless, so idealistic, and so nearly incapable of not telling the truth that, after he begged her one day, so that he could dine with her alone, to send the Verdurins a note saying she was unwell, the next day he'd seen her blushing and stammering as she stood face to face with Madame Verdurin, who was asking her if she felt better, showing on her face, despite herself, how upsetting, how painful it was for her to tell a lie, and, as in her answer she multiplied the fictitious details of her alleged indisposition of the day before, seeming to be asking forgiveness, by her supplicating looks and distressed voice, for the falseness of her words.

However, there were some days, though they were rare, when she came to see him in the afternoon, interrupting his musings or the essay on Vermeer to which he'd recently returned. His servant would come to tell him that Madame de Crécy was in the morning room. He'd go and join her, and when he opened the door, as soon as she saw him, a smile would spread across her rosy face, changing the shape of her mouth, the look in her eyes, the moulding of her cheeks. When he was alone again, he'd see that smile, and also the smile of the day before, and another with which she'd greeted him on a previous occasion, and the one with which she'd responded, in the carriage, when he asked her if she minded his rearranging her cattleyas; and Odette's life at all other times, since he knew nothing about it, appeared to him, with its neutral and colourless background, like those sheets of sketches by Watteau* upon which one sees, here, there, in every corner, from every angle, drawn in three colours on the buff paper, an infinite number of smiles. But sometimes, in a corner of that life which Swann saw as completely blank, even if his mind told him it wasn't, because he couldn't imagine it, some friend who, suspecting they were in love, wouldn't have dared to tell him anything about her that was of the slightest importance, would describe how he'd glimpsed Odette that very morning walking up the Rue Abbatucci, wearing a little cape trimmed with skunk, a Rembrandt* hat, and a bunch of violets in her bodice. This simple sketch was very disturbing to Swann because it suddenly made him realize that Odette had a life that didn't entirely belong to him; he wanted to know whom she'd wanted to please with that outfit, which he'd never seen her wear; and he promised himself that he'd ask her where she'd been going at that moment, as if the whole colourless life of his mistress—almost non-existent, since it was invisible to him—now consisted of just one thing apart from all those smiles she gave him: her walking along a street wearing a Rembrandt hat, with a bunch of violets in her bodice.

Except when he asked her for Vinteuil's little phrase instead of *La Valse des Roses*, Swann didn't try to make her play things that were to his taste alone, or, any more in music than in literature, to correct her bad taste. He was well aware that she wasn't intelligent. When she said she'd love him to tell her about the great poets, she'd imagined she'd immediately get to know heroic and romantic verse in the style of the Vicomte de Borelli, but even more touching.* As for Vermeer of Delft, she asked Swann if the painter had suffered over a woman, if it was a woman who'd inspired him, and when he told her that nobody knew, she lost interest in the man. She often said: 'Poetry, of course—there would be nothing nicer if it was all true, if poets really believed everything they say. But very often those people are even more calculating than anyone else. I know what I'm talking about, because I had a friend who was in love with a poet of sorts. In his poetry all he talked about was love, the sky, and the stars. And she was really taken in! He did her out of more than three hundred thousand francs.' If Swann then tried to make her understand something about beauty in art, or how to appreciate poetry and painting, after a short while she'd stop listening and say: 'Oh! I never imagined it was like that.' And he felt that her disappointment was so great that he preferred to lie and tell her that what he'd said was nothing, that he'd just scratched the surface, that he didn't have time to go into things properly, that there was much more to it. 'More?' she'd say sharply. 'What, exactly? Tell me!' But he wouldn't continue, knowing it would all sound very uninteresting to her, different from what she was hoping for, less sensational and less touching, and fearing that, disillusioned with art, she might at the same time be disillusioned with love.

And in fact she now found Swann less impressive, intellectually, than she'd believed. 'You're always so reserved, I can't make you out.'

She was much more impressed by his indifference to money, his kindness to everyone, his tact. And it often happens, in fact, to greater men than Swann, to a scientist or an artist, when he's not misunderstood by those around him, that the feeling on their part that proves they've been convinced of the superiority of his intellect is not their admiration for his ideas, which are beyond them, but their respect for his kindness. What also inspired her with respect was Swann's position in society, though she had no desire that he should try to secure invitations for herself. Perhaps she felt that any such attempt was bound to fail, or was even afraid that the mere mention of her name would prompt dreadful revelations about her. In any case, she'd made him promise never to speak of her to others. The reason why she didn't want to go into society, she'd told him, was a quarrel she'd once had with a friend who'd avenged herself by speaking ill of her. 'But surely', Swann objected, 'your friend didn't know everybody in society.' 'Well, yes,' she replied, 'but these things get around; you know how cruel people can be.' Swann could make no sense of this story, but he knew very well that sayings such as 'People can be so cruel' and 'There's no smoke without fire' are generally accepted as true; there must be cases to which they were applicable. Was Odette's one of them? He wondered about it, but not for long, because he was subject to the same mental torpor that had afflicted his father whenever he was faced with a difficult problem. In any event, that social world that so frightened Odette didn't, perhaps, inspire her with any great longings, since it was too far removed from the world she knew for her to have any clear picture of it. However, while she'd retained in some respects a genuine simplicity (one of the friendships she kept up, for example, was with a little dressmaker, now retired, whose steep, dark, foul-smelling staircase she climbed almost every day), she had a craving to be 'chic', but did not conceive of it in the same way as society people. For them, being 'chic' is something that emanates from a small number of individuals who project it quite far—but more and more faintly the further one is from their most intimate associates—through the circle of their friends or friends of their friends, whose names form a sort of directory. Society people know this directory by heart, they have in these matters an erudition from which they've extracted a type of taste, or tact, so that if Swann, for example, read in a newspaper the names of the people who were present at a dinner party, he could immediately tell, without having to draw on his knowledge of society, precisely how 'chic' the dinner party was, just as a literary person, by reading a single sentence, can judge exactly the merit of its author. But Odette was one of those people (extremely numerous, whatever society people may think, and to be found in all classes of society) who don't share these notions, but imagine a quite different kind of 'chic', that assumes different guises according to the circle to which they themselves belong, but has the special characteristic— whether it was the version Odette dreamed of or the one revered by Madame Cottard—of being directly accessible to everyone. The other, the 'chic' of society people, is indeed accessible too, but only after a certain lapse of time. Odette would say of someone: 'He only goes to smart places.'

And if Swann asked her what she meant by that, she'd answer almost with contempt: 'I mean smart places! For heaven's sake, if you need to be told, at your age, what the smart places are, you can't be helped! For example, the Avenue de l'Impératrice on Sunday mornings, around the lake at five o'clock, the Éden Théâtre on Thursdays, the Hippodrome* on Fridays, the balls . . .'

'But which balls?'

'The balls people give in Paris! The smart ones, I mean. Herbinger, for instance, you know the one I mean, the one who works for a stock-jobber. You must know who I mean, he's one of the best-known men in Paris, that tall fair-haired young man who's such a snob, always has a flower in his buttonhole, a parting at the back, and a light-coloured overcoat; he's always with that old frump he takes to all the first nights. Well, he gave a ball the other night, and all the smart people in Paris were there. I'd have loved to go! But you had to show your invitation at the door, and I couldn't get one. But actually, I'm just as glad I didn't go, I'd have been trampled underfoot, and I wouldn't have seen a thing. It's all about being able to say you were at Herbinger's ball. And you know how I like to show off! But in any case, you can bet that out of a hundred girls who say they were there, at least half of them are lying . . . But I'm surprised you weren't there, a real "swell" like you.'

Swann made no attempt to induce her to modify her conception of what was 'chic'; thinking that his own was no more authentic, that it was just as foolish and frivolous, he saw no point in educating his mistress about it, with the result that after a few months she took no interest in the people whose houses he frequented, except insofar as they were able to provide enclosure passes for race meetings or tickets for first nights.

She wanted him to cultivate useful connections of that kind, but otherwise she was inclined to think there was nothing very smart about
them, having seen the Marquise de Villeparisis go past in the street
wearing a black woollen dress and a bonnet tied under her chin.

'But, *darling*, she looks like an usherette or an old concierge! And
she's a marquise! I'm no marquise, but you'd have to pay me a lot of
money to be seen in a get-up like that!'

And she couldn't understand why Swann lived in the house on the
Quai d'Orléans, which, though she didn't dare to tell him, she considered unworthy of him.

It was true she liked to think of herself as a lover of 'antiques' and
would assume a rapturous and knowing air when she described how
she adored to spend a whole day looking for 'knick-knacks', hunting
for 'bric-à-brac' and 'period things'. Although it was a sort of point of
honour she insisted on maintaining, as if in deference to some old
family precept, that she should never answer questions or 'account
for' how she spent her days, she once mentioned to Swann a friend
who'd invited her to her house, where she found everything in 'period
style'. But Swann couldn't get her to say what the period was. After
a little reflection, however, she replied that it was 'medieval'. By this
she meant that the rooms had wood panelling. Some time after that,
she mentioned her friend again, and added, in the hesitant tone and
with the knowing air one adopts when referring to a person one has
met at dinner the evening before and of whom one has never heard
until then, but whom one's hosts seem to consider so celebrated that
one hopes the person one is talking to will know who is meant: 'She's
got a dining room that's . . . eighteenth-century!' Personally, she'd
thought it hideous, very bare, as though the house was unfinished;
women looked hideous in it too, and the style would never catch on.
She mentioned it again, a third time, and showed Swann the address
of the man who'd designed the drawing room, and whom she wanted
to send for, when she had enough money, to see if he could design one
for her too, not the same, of course, but the kind she dreamed of having but which unfortunately her little house was not large enough
to accommodate, with tall dressers, Renaissance furniture, and fire-
places like the ones in the château at Blois. On this occasion, she let
slip what she thought of Swann's abode on the Quai d'Orléans; for
he'd criticized her friend for indulging, not in Louis XVI (which, he
said, even though it was quite out of fashion these days, could be

made to look attractive), but in fake antique: 'You wouldn't want her to live like you, with a lot of broken furniture and threadbare carpets, would you!' she said, her bourgeois respect for appearances getting the better, once more, of her *cocotte*'s dilettantism.

People who liked looking for knick-knacks, who loved poetry, who despised crass calculations involving money, and dreamed of honour and love, she saw as an elite class of humanity, superior to all the rest. There was no need actually to have those tastes, as long as one proclaimed them; when a man had confessed to her at a dinner party that he liked to wander about and get his hands dirty in curiosity shops, that he'd never be appreciated in this commercial age, because he didn't care about its concerns, and that because of this he belonged to another age altogether, she'd say on returning home: 'He's such an adorable creature, so sensitive! I had no idea!' and she'd conceive for him there and then a deep bond of friendship. On the other hand, men who, like Swann, had those tastes, but didn't talk about them, left her cold. She had to admit, of course, that Swann wasn't interested in money, but she'd add sulkily: 'But with him, it's not the same thing'; and, in fact, what appealed to her imagination wasn't the practice of disinterestedness, but its vocabulary.

Feeling that, often, he couldn't give her in real life the pleasures of which she dreamed, he tried at least to ensure that she'd be happy in his company, tried not to question the vulgar ideas, the bad taste which she displayed in all things, and which he loved, moreover, like everything that came from her, which enchanted him even, for they were so many characteristic features by which the essence of this woman revealed itself to him. And so, when she looked happy because she was going to see *La Reine Topaze*,* or when her expression became serious, worried, or petulant because she was afraid of missing the flower-show, or simply of being late for tea, with muffins and toast, at the tearooms in the Rue Royale, where she believed that regular attendance was indispensable for the establishment of a woman's reputation for elegance, Swann, enchanted as we all are by the naturalness of a child or the verisimilitude of a portrait so lifelike that it seems about to speak, felt so strongly his mistress's soul rising to the surface of her face that he couldn't resist going over to touch it with his lips. 'Ah! So little Odette wants to be taken to the flower-show, she wants to show herself off. Well, then, we'll take her, because her wish is our command.' As Swann's eyesight was rather poor, he had to resign himself to wearing spectacles for working at home, and to adopting a monocle, which was less disfiguring, for going out in society. The first time she saw him with one in his eye, she was beside herself with delight: 'I must say that, for a man, it's terribly *chic*! It really suits you! You look like a real *gentleman*.'* And she added, with a hint of regret: 'All you need now is a title!' He was happy that Odette was like this, just as, if he'd been in love with a Breton woman, he'd have enjoyed seeing her in a coif and hearing her say she believed in ghosts. Until then, like many men whose taste for the arts develops independently of their sensuality, an odd discrepancy had existed between the satisfactions he'd accord to each, for he enjoyed the seductions of ever more refined works of art in the company of ever more vulgar women, taking a young servant-girl to a private box for a production of a decadent play he wanted to see, or to an exhibition of Impressionist painting, convinced, moreover, that a cultivated society woman wouldn't have understood them any better but would not have been able to stay quiet so nicely. Now, however, ever since he'd fallen in love with Odette, to share her feelings, to be at one with her in spirit, was such a pleasant endeavour that he tried to find enjoyment in the things she liked, and the pleasure he felt, not only in imitating her habits but also in adopting her opinions, was all the greater, since they had no roots in his own intelligence, because they reminded him only of his love for her, which was why he'd preferred them to his own. If he went to more than one performance of *Serge Panine*,* if he looked for opportunities to see Olivier Métra* conduct, it was for the pleasure of being initiated into Odette's whole way of seeing things, of feeling that he had an equal share in all her tastes. This charm, which the things and places she liked possessed, of bringing him closer to her, seemed to him more mysterious than the charm intrinsic to things and places that were of greater beauty but did not remind him of her. Furthermore, since he'd allowed the intellectual beliefs of his youth to weaken, and since, without his being aware of it, they'd been eroded by his man-of-the-world scepticism, he thought (or at least he'd thought thus for so long that he went on saying it) that the things we admire have no absolute value in themselves, but depend entirely on the period in which one lives, the social class to which one belongs, and changing fashions, the most vulgar of which are equal to those that are regarded as the most refined. And just as he considered that the importance Odette attached to being invited to the opening of a painting exhibition was not in itself more ridiculous than the pleasure he used to take in lunching at the home of the Prince of Wales, so he didn't think that the admiration she professed for Monte Carlo or the Righi was more unreasonable than his own liking for Holland, which she imagined to be ugly, or for Versailles, which she found dreary. And so he denied himself the pleasure of visiting those places, delighting instead in the thought that it was for her sake, that he wanted to feel things and love things only with her.

Like everything else that formed part of Odette's environment, and was no more, in a sense, than the means whereby he could see and talk to her, he enjoyed the company of the Verdurins. At their house, since at the heart of all the entertainments, meals, music, games, fancy-dress suppers, excursions to the country and the theatre, even the occasional soirées they put on for the 'bores', there was the presence of Odette, the sight of Odette, conversation with Odette, a priceless gift bestowed upon Swann by the Verdurins' invitations, he was happier among the 'little clan' than anywhere else, and tried to find real qualities in it, imagining that by so doing he would, from choice, be part of it for the rest of his life. Not daring to tell himself, lest he should not believe it, that he'd always love Odette, at least in supposing that he'd go on visiting the Verdurins for ever (a proposition that, a priori, raised fewer objections of principle on the part of his intelligence), he could see himself in the future continuing to see Odette every evening; this did not, perhaps, amount to quite the same thing as loving her for ever, but for the moment, while he loved her, to feel that he wouldn't stop seeing her one day was all he asked. 'What charming people,' he'd say to himself, 'That's the kind of life one should lead! How much more intelligent, more artistic, they are than the people one knows! How genuine, despite some silly little excesses, is Madame Verdurin's love of painting and music, what a passion for works of art, what keenness to encourage artists! Her ideas about society people are not quite right; but then, the ideas society people have about artistic circles are even more wrong! Perhaps I'm not very demanding in terms of intelligent conversation, but I'm perfectly happy with Cottard, despite his awful puns. And as for the painter, he can be dreadfully pretentious when he tries to make an impression on people, but on the other hand he has one of the best minds I've ever come across. The main thing, though, is how free one feels there, one can do as one pleases without any kind of constraint or fuss. So much good humour flows every day through that drawing room! Apart from a few rare exceptions, I will most certainly never go anywhere else. It's where I will feel more and more at home and want to live my life.'

And since the qualities he believed to be intrinsic to the Verdurins were merely the reflection of the pleasures he enjoyed in their house because of his love for Odette, those qualities became more serious, more profound, more vital, when those pleasures were too. Because Madame Verdurin sometimes gave Swann the only thing that could constitute happiness for him; because, one evening when he felt anxious on seeing Odette talking rather more to one of the guests than to any of the others, and when, irritated with her, he didn't want to take the initiative of asking her if she'be coming home with him, Madame Verdurin brought him peace and joy by saying, unprompted: 'Odette, you'll see Monsieur Swann home, won't you?'; because, when the summer holidays were approaching, and he'd been wondering whether Odette might go away somewhere without him, whether he'd still be able to see her every day, Madame Verdurin had invited them both to spend the summer at her house in the country—Swann, unconsciously allowing gratitude and self-interest to infiltrate his intelligence and influence his ideas, went so far as to proclaim that Madame Verdurin was the noblest of souls. If one of his old classmates from the École du Louvre* happened to mention a number of delightful or eminent people, he'd reply: 'I prefer the Verdurins a hundred times over.' And then, with a solemnity that was new to him, he'd declare: 'They are magnanimous people, and magnanimity is, in the end, the only thing that is really important, that confers distinction here on earth. You see, there are only two kinds of people: those who are magnanimous, and the rest; and I've reached an age when one has to choose, to decide once and for all whom one is going to like and dislike, to stick with the people one likes, and, to make up for the time wasted with the others, never leave them again for as long as one lives. And so,' he went on, with the little thrill one feels when, even without quite realizing it, one says something not because it's true but because one enjoys saying it and listens to one's own voice as if it's someone else's, 'the die is cast, I've chosen to love only magnanimous souls, and to live henceforth only in the company of magnanimous people. You ask me whether Madame Verdurin is really intelligent. I can assure you she has shown a nobility of spirit, a loftiness of soul which, you know, no one could possibly attain without an equal loftiness of mind. There can be no doubt that she has a highly intelligent understanding of the arts. But that may not be her most admirable quality; every little thing, ingeniously and exquisitely kind, she has performed for me, every thoughtful action, every little gesture, so natural yet so sublime, reveals a more profound understanding of existence than any philosophical treatise.'

He might have reminded himself, however, that there were some old friends of his parents who were just as simple as the Verdurins, or friends of his youth just as fond of art, that he knew other big-hearted people, but whom, since he'd opted for simplicity, the arts, and magnanimity, he'd stopped seeing altogether. But these people didn't know Odette, and, if they had known her, would never have thought of bringing them together every day.

And so, in the whole Verdurin circle, there was probably not a single one of the 'faithful' who was as fond of them, or thought he was as fond of them, as Swann. Yet, when Monsieur Verdurin had said he didn't care much for Swann, he was not only expressing his own sentiments but also guessing those of his wife. Doubtless Swann's affection for Odette was too exclusive and he'd neglected to make Madame Verdurin his regular confidante: doubtless the very discretion with which he'd availed himself of the Verdurins' hospitality, often refraining from coming to dinner for a reason they never suspected and in place of which they saw a desire not to decline an invitation to the house of some 'bores', and doubtless, too, despite all the precautions he'd taken to keep it from them, their gradual discovery of his brilliant position in society—all this contributed to their irritation with him. But the real, deeper reason for it lay elsewhere. It was that they'd quickly sensed in him an impenetrable, private space, where he continued to maintain silently to himself that the Princesse de Sagan was not grotesque and that Cottard's jokes were not amusing; in short, though he never once dropped his affability or rebelled against their dogmas, the impossibility of imposing them upon him and fully converting him to them, an impossibility such as they'd never encountered in anyone else. They would have forgiven him for associating with bores (to whom, in fact, in his heart of hearts, he infinitely preferred the Verdurins and the whole of the little clan) if only he'd been willing to set a good example by renouncing them in the presence of the 'faithful'. But this was an abjuration which they realized they'd never be able to get out of him.

How different he was from a 'newcomer' Odette had asked them to invite, although she'd met him only a few times, and in whom they were already investing great hopes: the Comte de Forcheville! (It turned out that he was Saniette's brother-in-law, which filled the 'faithful' with amazement: the old palaeographer had such a humble manner that they'd always supposed him to be socially inferior to themselves, and didn't expect to discover that he came from a wealthy and relatively aristocratic family.) Of course, Forcheville was a tremendous snob, whereas Swann was not; of course, he'd never dream of placing the Verdurins' circle above all others, as Swann did. But he didn't have the natural refinement that prevented Swann from being party to the more obviously false criticisms Madame Verdurin made of people he knew. As for the vulgar and pretentious tirades the painter launched into on certain days, and the commercial traveller jokes Cottard ventured, for which Swann, who liked both men, could easily find excuses without having the heart or the hypocrisy to applaud them, Forcheville by contrast was of an intellectual calibre that allowed him to be dumbfounded, awestruck by the first (though he failed to understand a word) and to delight in the second. And indeed the first dinner at the Verdurins' at which Forcheville was present threw into sharp relief all these differences, brought out his qualities, and precipitated Swann's fall from grace.

At this dinner there was, apart from the regulars, a professor from the Sorbonne, a certain Brichot, who'd met Monsieur and Madame Verdurin at a spa somewhere and who, if his university duties and scholarly pursuits hadn't left him little free time, would gladly have come to the house more often. For he had the kind of curiosity and superstition about life which, when combined with a certain scepticism towards the object of their studies, gives some intelligent men in any profession, doctors who don't believe in medicine, schoolteachers who don't believe in Latin compositions, a reputation for having broad, brilliant, and even superior minds. He made a point, at Madame Verdurin's, of seeking the most topical examples when he spoke about philosophy or history, mainly because he thought that such subjects were no more than a preparation for life, and imagined that he was seeing practised in the little clan what he'd previously encountered only in books, and perhaps also because, having had instilled into him in his younger days, and having unconsciously preserved, a respect for certain subjects, he believed he was casting aside his scholarly self by taking conversational liberties with them, although, in fact, this seemed daring to him only because he remained a scholar.

At the beginning of the meal, when Monsieur de Forcheville, seated to the right of Madame Verdurin, who for the benefit of the 'newcomer' had taken great pains over her appearance, said to her: 'It's very unusual, that white dress!', the doctor, who couldn't take his eyes off him, so curious was he to know what kind of man a 'de', as he termed it, would be, and was waiting for an opportunity to attract his attention and engage him in conversation, seized on the word *blanche* and, without raising his eyes from his plate, said: 'Blanche? Blanche de Castille?',* then, without moving his head, looked furtively to right and left, smiling uncertainly. Whereas Swann, with his pained and pointless effort to smile, showed how stupid he found this pun, Forcheville had shown not only that he appreciated the subtlety of Cottard's wit but also that he was a man of the world who knew how to moderate his mirth, which had already greatly pleased Madame Verdurin by its spontaneity.

'What do you make of a scientist like that?' she asked Forcheville. 'It's impossible to have a serious conversation with him, even for two minutes.' And she added, turning to the doctor: 'Is that the sort of thing you say to people at your hospital? If so, it must be a very entertaining place! I can see I must get myself admitted as a patient!'

'I believe I heard the doctor talking about that old harridan, Blanche de Castille, if I may be so bold as to put it that way. Isn't that so, Madame?' Brichot asked Madame Verdurin, who, swooning with laughter, her eyes closed, buried her face in her hands, through which muffled squeals could be heard. 'Good heavens, Madame,' continued Brichot, 'I wouldn't like to alarm the respectful souls, if there are any, round this table, *sub rosa* . . . And I realize, of course, that our ineffable republic, Athenian as it most decidedly is, might wish to pay homage to that obscurantist Capetian lady as the first of our police chiefs with a real grip in things. Yes, indeed, my dear host, yes indeed, yes indeed!' he went on in his sonorous voice, articulating each syllable, in response to an objection by Monsieur Verdurin. 'The *Chronique de Saint-Denis*, an impeccably reliable source, leaves us in no doubt about the matter. There could have been no better choice of patron saint by a secularizing proletariat than that mother of a saint (whom, by the way, she led a dog's life, as we know from Suger and other Saint Bernards*); for with her no one failed to get what was coming to him.'

'Who is that gentleman?' Forcheville asked Madame Verdurin. 'He sounds most impressive.'

'What, you don't know the famous Brichot? He's a celebrity throughout the whole of Europe.'

'Ah! So that's Bréchot!' cried Forcheville, who hadn't quite caught the name. 'You must tell me all about him!', he added, staring goggle-eyed at the great celebrity. 'It's always interesting to have dinner with famous men. I must say, you certainly treat your guests to very select dinner-companions. There's never a dull moment in your house.'

'Oh, you know, the main thing', Madame Verdurin said modestly, 'is that they feel at home. They can say whatever they like, and the conversation goes off like fireworks. Brichot, this evening, is quite off form: you know, I've seen him be absolutely dazzling here in my house; you feel you should go down on your knees before him. But at other people's houses he's just not the same, he has no wit at all, you have to drag the words out of him, he's actually boring.'

'How odd!' said Forcheville, surprised.

Brichot's brand of wit would have been considered pure stupidity by the people among whom Swann had spent his youth, even though compatible with genuine intelligence. And the intelligence of the Professor, which was lively and well nourished, would probably have been envied by many of the society people Swann considered witty. But those people had so thoroughly inculcated in him their own likes and dislikes, at least in all matters to do with social life, including even the ancillary part of it which should, strictly speaking, be a matter of intelligence—namely, conversation—that Swann couldn't help but find Brichot's jokes pedantic, vulgar, and nauseatingly crude. Moreover, accustomed as he was to people with good manners, he was shocked by the brusque military tone adopted by the jingoistic aca-demic towards anyone he happened to address. But the main reason for his attitude may have been that, that evening in particular, he'd lost some of his indulgence towards Madame Verdurin on seeing how friendly she was to this man Forcheville whom Odette, unaccountably, had brought along. She'd asked him when she arrived, in a slightly embarrassed way: 'What do you think of my guest?'

And he, realizing for the first time that Forcheville, whom he'd known for years, might be attractive to women and was quite a hand-some man, had replied: 'Revolting!' It certainly didn't occur to him to be jealous of Odette, but he didn't feel quite as happy as usual, and when Brichot, having begun to tell the story of Blanche de Castille's mother, who 'had been with Henry Plantagenet for years before she married him', tried to get Swann to ask him what happened next by saying: 'Isn't that right, Monsieur Swann?' in the sergeant-majorish tone some people adopt to make themselves understood by a peasant or to put heart into a trooper, Swann spoiled Brichot's effect, and thus infuriated the hostess, by asking to be excused for having so little interest in Blanche de Castille, but there was something he wanted to ask the painter. The latter, in fact, had gone that afternoon to an exhibition by an artist, a friend of Madame Verdurin's who'd recently died, and Swann wanted to find out from him (for he respected his judgement) if there was really anything more in these last works than the virtuosity people had found so astonishing in his earlier works.

'In that respect it was extraordinary, but it didn't seem to me to be the kind of art you might call "elevated",' Swann said with a smile.

'Elevated . . . to the level of an institution,' interjected Cottard, raising his arms with mock solemnity. The whole table burst out laughing.

'You see?' said Madame Verdurin to Forcheville. 'You just can't be serious with him. When you least expect it, he comes out with one of his pieces of nonsense.'

But she noticed that Swann was the only one who hadn't laughed. For one thing, he was displeased that Cottard had made fun of him in front of Forcheville. And then the painter, instead of answering him properly, which he probably would have done if he'd been alone with him, preferred to show off to the other guests by treating them to a little speech about the skill of the deceased master.

'I went up very close to one of the paintings to see how it was done. I stuck my nose right into it. Well, it was amazing! I couldn't for the life of me tell whether it was done with glue, or rubies, or soap, or leaven, or sunshine, or poo!'

'And one makes twelve!' cried the doctor, but too late for anyone to understand his interjection.

'It looks as if it was made out of just anything,' continued the painter. 'There's no way you can work out what the trick is, any more than you can with *The Night Watch* or *The Regentesses*, and the brushwork is even better than Rembrandt or Hals.* It's got everything. No, really, everything! I swear.'

And just as singers who've reached the highest note they can produce continue in a falsetto, very softly, he went on in a murmur, laughing, as if the painting had been preposterously beautiful: 'It smells
nice, it goes to your head, it takes your breath away, it makes you feel
you're being tickled, and you haven't got a clue what it's made with,
it's a kind of sorcery, trickery, an absolute miracle!' Then he burst out
laughing: 'It shouldn't be allowed!' Then he paused, looked up with
a very serious expression, and, adopting a deep bass note which he
tried to bring into harmony, he added: 'and it's so *true*!'

Except at the moment when he'd said the painting was better than
The Night Watch, a blasphemy that had provoked a protest from
Madame Verdurin, for whom *The Night Watch* was the greatest masterpiece in the world along with the Ninth and the *Winged Victory*,* and
at the word 'poo', which had made Forcheville glance quickly round
the table to see whether the word was acceptable and had then formed
his mouth into a prudish and conciliatory smile, all the guests, except
for Swann, had been gazing at the painter, transfixed with admiration.

'He's so marvellous when he gets carried away like that,' cried
Madame Verdurin the moment he'd finished, delighted that the table
talk should have turned out so interesting on the very evening that
Monsieur de Forcheville was dining with them for the first time. 'And
you, what are you doing sitting there like that, with your mouth wide
open like a simpleton?' she said to her husband. 'You know how well
he can talk. Anyone would think', she went on, turning to the painter,
'that he'd never heard you speak before. You should have seen him
while you were talking, he was hanging on every word. And tomorrow
he'll repeat everything you said, word for word.'

'But I'm not joking!' said the painter, delighted with his success.
'You look as if you think I was just spinning a yarn, that I was having
you on; well, I'll take you there and you can see for yourself whether
I'm exaggerating. I bet you anything you like, you'll come away even
more impressed than I was!'

'But we don't think you're exaggerating. We just want you to eat
your dinner, and my husband should too; give Monsieur some more
sole, you can see that his has gone cold. You're serving as if the house
was on fire, we're not in any hurry. Wait a little while before you bring
in the salad.'

Madame Cottard, a modest woman who never said much, didn't
lack self-assurance when a moment of inspiration provided her with

a witty remark. She felt it would be well received, and this increased her confidence, but what she did with it was not so much in order to shine herself as to give support to her husband in his career. And so she didn't allow the word 'salad' to leave Madame Verdurin's lips without saying in an undertone, turning to Odette:

'It's not a Japanese salad, is it?'

Then, in her delight and confusion at the aptness and daring of this allusion, so discreet yet unmistakable, to the highly successful new play by Dumas, she broke into a charming, girlish laugh, not at all loud but so compulsive that for a few moments she couldn't control it. 'Who is that lady?' asked Forcheville. 'She's terribly witty.'

'No, it's not, but you can all have one if you come to dinner on Friday.'

'You'll think I'm terribly provincial, Monsieur,' Madame Cottard said to Swann, 'but I haven't yet seen this famous *Francillon** everybody's talking about. The doctor has been (in fact, I remember he said he had the great pleasure of spending the evening with you) and I must confess I didn't think it would be very sensible for him to book two seats to go again with me. Of course, an evening at the Théâtre-Français is never disappointing, the acting is always so good, but we have some very nice friends' (Madame Cottard rarely uttered a proper name, finding it more 'distinguished' to refer simply to 'some friends of ours' or 'one of my friends', speaking of them in an affected tone and with the self-importance of someone who provides names only when she chooses) 'who often have a box and are kind enough to take us to all the new productions worth seeing, so I'm bound to see *Francillon* sooner or later and be able to make my own mind up about it. I must confess, though, that I feel rather stupid, because in every drawing room I find myself in, naturally the only thing they're all talking about is that wretched Japanese salad.' Then, seeing that Swann seemed less interested than she would have thought in such a burning topic, she added: 'It's actually becoming rather tiresome. But I must admit it can sometimes give people some amusing ideas. I've got a friend, for instance, who's quite eccentric, though she's very pretty as well as being very popular and very sought after, who claims she got her cook to make that Japanese salad in her own kitchen, using all the ingredients mentioned by Dumas *fils* in his play. Then she invited some friends to come and try it. Unfortunately, I was not one of the chosen few. But she told us all about it at her next "at home";

apparently it was revolting, she made us laugh until we cried. But of course it's all in the telling,' she said, seeing that Swann was still not amused.

And imagining that it was perhaps because he hadn't enjoyed *Francillon*, she went on: 'Anyway, I think I'll be disappointed. I don't suppose it's as good as *Serge Panine*, which Madame de Crécy absolutely adores. That play at least has real substance, it makes you think. But to give a recipe for a salad on the stage of the Théâtre-Français! Really! *Serge Panine*, on the other hand . . .! But it's like everything by Georges Ohnet, it's always so well written. You may know *Le Maître de Forges*,* which I like even better than *Serge Panine*.'

'You'll have to forgive me,' Swann said ironically, 'but I must confess that my lack of admiration is divided roughly equally between those two masterpieces.'

'Really? What don't you like about them? Are you sure you're not prejudiced against them? Perhaps you think they're a little too sad? Anyway, as I always say, people should never argue about novels or plays. We've all got our own way of looking at things, and what you might hate I might absolutely love.'

She was interrupted by Forcheville, who'd turned to address Swann. In fact, while Madame Cottard was discussing *Francillon*, Forcheville had been telling Madame Verdurin how much he admired what he called the painter's 'little speech'. 'The gentleman has a way with words! And what a memory!' he said to her when the painter had finished. 'I've rarely come across anything like it. By Jove, I wish I could be like that. He'd make an excellent preacher. With him and Bréchot you have two amazing characters, both virtuosos, though when it comes to the gift of the gab, I think the painter might even beat the professor. He sounds more natural, less affected. Although now and then he does use some words that are a little vulgar, but that's the thing nowadays. But I've seldom seen anyone hold the floor so cleverly—"hold the spittoon", as we used to say in the Army; in fact, I had a friend in my Army days the gentleman rather reminds me of. You could give him any subject, anything at all, this wine glass, for example, and he could rattle on about it for hours; well no, not about this glass, that's a silly thing to say, but about the Battle of Waterloo, or something like that, he'd spin such a yarn out of it! In fact, Swann was in the same regiment; he must have known him.'

'Do you see much of Monsieur Swann?' asked Madame Verdurin.

'Oh no,' replied Monsieur de Forcheville, and then, thinking he'd be able to get closer to Odette if he were pleasant to Swann, he decided to take this opportunity to flatter him by mentioning his distinguished friends, but to do so as a man of the world himself, in a tone of friendly criticism and not as if he were congratulating Swann on some unexpected success: 'Isn't that so, Swann? I never see you. In any case, how could anyone manage to see him? The devil spends all his time with the La Trémoïlles, the Laumes,* and all that lot!. . .' This imputation was especially false since, for the past year, Swann had hardly gone anywhere except to the Verdurins'. But the mere name of people the Verdurins did not know was greeted by them with a disapproving silence. Monsieur Verdurin, fearing the painful effect the names of these 'bores' must have had on his wife, especially when flung at her so tactlessly in front of all the faithful, cast a furtive glance at her, full of worry and concern. But he saw that in her resolve to take no notice, to remain unmoved by the news that had just been imparted to her, not merely to remain dumb but to have been deaf as well, as we pretend to be when a friend who has behaved badly towards us tries to slip into the conversation an excuse we'd seem to accept if we listened to it without objection, or when someone utters in our presence the forbidden name of an enemy, Madame Verdurin, so that her silence should not look like approval but like the meaningless silence of inanimate objects, had suddenly emptied her face of all life, all mobility; her domed forehead had become simply a fine piece of sculpture in the round, which the name of those La Trémoïlles with whom Swann spent all his time had been unable to penetrate; her slightly wrinkled nose revealed the curve of a nostril that seemed copied from life. You would have sworn her half-open mouth was about to speak. She was now merely a wax cast, a plaster mask, a maquette for a monument, a bust for the Palais de l'Industrie,* in front of which the public would be bound to stop to admire the way in which the sculptor, by evoking the inalienable dignity of the Verdurins as opposed to that of the La Trémoïlles and the Laumes,* whose equals they certainly were, just as they were the equals of all the 'bores' on the face of the earth, had managed to give an almost papal majesty to the whiteness and rigidity of the stone. Then at last the marble came to life and was heard to say that people must be very easy to please if they went to that house, because the wife was always drunk and the husband such an ignoramus that he said 'collidor' instead of 'corridor'.

'You'd have to pay me a fortune to let that lot into my house,' concluded Madame Verdurin, casting an imperious glance at Swann.

She could hardly have expected him to be so submissive as to echo the saintly simplicity of the pianist's aunt, who'd exclaimed: 'Would you credit that! It amazes me that they can still find anyone willing to speak to them! I think I'd be too afraid: one can't be too careful. How can there still be people common enough to go running after them?' But he might at least have replied, like Forcheville: 'Well, dash it all, she's a duchess! Some people are still impressed by that sort of thing.' This had at least allowed Madame Verdurin to reply: 'And much good may it do them!' But instead, Swann merely laughed in a way that suggested he couldn't even take such an outrageous remark seriously. Monsieur Verdurin, still casting furtive glances at his wife, was saddened to see, but understood all too well, that she was consumed with rage, like a Grand Inquisitor who has failed to stamp out heresy, and in an attempt to induce Swann to recant, since having the courage of one's convictions always seems to be calculated and cowardly in the eyes of those who don't share those convictions, asked him directly: 'Tell us frankly what you think of them. We'll keep it to ourselves, of course.'

To this, Swann replied: 'Oh, I'm not in the least intimidated by the Duchess (if it's the La Trémoïlles you're talking about). I can assure you everyone likes going there. I wouldn't say she's in any way "profound" ' (he pronounced 'profound' as if it was a ridiculous word, for his speech still bore the traces of mental habits which the recent change in his life, a rejuvenation marked by his enthusiasm for music, had temporarily made him lose, so that sometimes he would state his views quite robustly) 'but, in all honesty, she's an intelligent woman, and her husband is genuinely cultured. They're charming people.'

Whereupon Madame Verdurin, feeling that because of this one infidel she'd be prevented from achieving total orthodoxy among the little clan, was unable to restrain herself in her fury at Swann's stubborn refusal to see how much his words were making her suffer, and screamed at him from the depths of her heart: 'You can think that if you want, but at least don't say so to us.'

'It all depends on what you call intelligence,' said Forcheville, thinking it was his turn to shine. 'Come on, Swann, tell us what you mean by intelligence.'

'Exactly!' exclaimed Odette. 'That's the sort of big subject I'm always asking him to talk to me about, but he never does.'

'Yes I do,' protested Swann.

'Fibber!' said Odette.

'Fibber who?' asked the doctor.

'As you see it,' Forcheville went on, 'does intelligence mean having the gift of the gab, knowing how to ingratiate yourself?'

'Finish your dessert, so they can take your plate away,' Madame Verdurin said rather sourly to Saniette, who was lost in thought and had stopped eating. Then, perhaps a little ashamed at her ungracious tone, she added: 'It's all right, you can take your time. I only said that for the others, because it holds up the next course.'

'That gentle anarchist Fénelon',* said Brichot, rapping out the syllables, 'has a very curious definition of intelligence . . .'

'Listen!' said Madame Verdurin to Forcheville and the doctor. 'He's going to give us Fénelon's definition of intelligence. Most interesting. It's not often you get a chance to hear that!'

But Brichot was waiting for Swann to put forward his definition. Swann, however, was not forthcoming, and by this fresh evasion spoiled the brilliant contest Madame Verdurin had been dying to offer Forcheville.

'You see! He's like that with me,' said Odette sulkily. 'I'm glad to see I'm not the only one he thinks is not up to his standard.'

'Those de la Trémouailles,* whom Madame Verdurin has presented as being so undesirable,' said Brichot, articulating his words with special force, 'are they descended from the de la Trémouailles whom that grand old snob Madame de Sévigné said she was so pleased to know because it made a good impression on her peasants? Of course, the marquise had another reason, which must have been more important for her, because she was a woman of letters to the core, and always put good "copy" before everything else. And in the journal she used to send regularly to her daughter, it was Madame de la Trémouailles, always well informed through all her grand connections, who supplied the foreign politics.'

'Yes, but I don't actually think it's the same family,' hazarded Madame Verdurin.

Saniette, having hurriedly given the butler his untouched plate, had fallen back into a state of silent meditation, but now emerged at last to tell them, with a laugh, about a dinner he'd attended with the Duc de la Trémoïlle where it became clear that the duke did not know that George Sand was the pseudonym of a woman. Swann, who was quite fond of Saniette, felt he ought to give him some facts about the duke's culture proving that ignorance of that sort on his part was utterly impossible; but he suddenly stopped, realizing that Saniette didn't need this proof, but knew already that the story was untrue for the simple reason that he'd just invented it. The worthy man suffered acutely from being regarded as so boring by the Verdurins; and, knowing full well that he'd been even duller than usual at this dinner, he hadn't wanted to let it end without saying something amusing. He capitulated so quickly, looked so crestfallen at his failure to achieve the effect he'd intended, and his reply ('My mistake, my mistake! But it's not a crime to be wrong, is it?') was such an abject appeal to Swann not to persist with a refutation that was now superfluous, that Swann wished he'd been able to say that the story was both true and delightfully funny. The doctor, who'd been listening to them, thought this was the right moment to say *Se non è vero*,* but he was not quite sure of the words and was afraid of getting them wrong.

When dinner was over, Forcheville went up to the doctor:

'She can't have been bad-looking at one point, Madame Verdurin; and she's a woman you can talk to, which is the main thing as far as I'm concerned. Of course she's getting on a bit. But Madame de Crécy—now there's a little lady who's got her wits about her. My word, yes, you can see straight away she's knows what's what! We're talking about Madame de Crécy,' he added, as Monsieur Verdurin joined them, his pipe in his mouth. 'I'd say that as a specimen of the female form . . .'

'I'd rather have her in my bed than have a slap in the face with a wet fish,' blurted Cottard, who for some moments had been waiting for Forcheville to pause for breath so that he could interject that old joke for which he feared there would be no opportunity if the conversation changed course, and which he delivered with the excessive spontaneity and confidence that mask the coldness and anxiety inseparable from a prepared recitation. Forcheville was familiar with the joke, understood it, and was amused. As for Monsieur Verdurin, he was unsparing with his mirth, having recently discovered a way of expressing it that was different from his wife's, but just as simple and obvious. Scarcely had he begun the movement of head and shoulders of a man shaking with laughter than he would immediately begin to cough, as if, in laughing too violently, he'd swallowed a mouthful of pipe smoke. And by keeping the pipe in one corner of his mouth, he was able to prolong indefinitely the pantomime of suffocation and hilarity. Thus both he and Madame Verdurin (who, at the opposite end of the room, was listening to one of the painter's stories and closing her eyes and making ready to bury her face in her hands) were like two theatre masks each representing Comedy in a different way.

Monsieur Verdurin had in fact been wise not to take his pipe out of his mouth, for Cottard, who needed to leave the room for a moment, murmured a witticism he'd only recently picked up and which he repeated each time he had to go to the same place: 'I must go and see a man about a dog.' This resulted in a renewed coughing fit on the part of Monsieur Verdurin.

'Do take that pipe out of your mouth,' said Madame Verdurin, handing round liqueurs. 'You'll choke to death if you try so hard not to laugh.'

'What a charming man your husband is,' declared Forcheville to Madame Cottard. 'He's incredibly witty. Oh, thank you, Madame. An old soldier like me never says no to a drink.'

'Monsieur de Forcheville thinks Odette is charming,' said Monsieur Verdurin to his wife.

'Well, as a matter of fact she'd like to come and have lunch with you one day. We can arrange that, but on no account must Swann hear about it. He tends to put a damper on things, you know. And you can still come to dinner, of course; we hope we'll be seeing a lot of you. With summer coming, we'll often be having dinner out of doors. That won't bother you, will it—little dinner parties in the Bois? Good, good, it'll be very nice.' Then: 'I say, aren't you going to go and do your job?' she cried to the young pianist, in order to display, before a newcomer of Forcheville's importance, both her wit and her despotic power over the 'faithful'.

'Monsieur de Forcheville was saying bad things about you,' Madame Cottard said to her husband when he returned to the drawing room. And he, pursuing the idea of Forcheville's noble birth, which had been preoccupying him all through dinner, said to him: 'I'm treating a baroness at the moment, Baronne Putbus. The Putbuses took part in the Crusades, if I'm not mistaken. They have a lake in Pomerania that must be ten times the size of the Place de la Concorde. I'm treating her for rheumatoid arthritis. Charming woman. I believe she knows Madame Verdurin, actually.'

This enabled Forcheville, a moment later, finding himself alone again with Madame Cottard, to complete the favourable judgement he'd passed on her husband: 'And he's so interesting, you can see he knows a lot of people. My word, those medical men know such a lot!'

'I'm going to play the phrase from the sonata for Monsieur Swann,' said the pianist.

'Good heavens! It's not the "Sonata-Snake", is it?' asked Monsieur de Forcheville, trying to show off.

But Doctor Cottard, who had never heard this pun, did not understand, and thought that Monsieur de Forcheville was making a mistake. He hurried over to correct him. 'No, no, it's not *serpent à sonates*, it's *serpent à sonnettes*,'* he said in a tone of eager, impatient self-congratulation.

Forchevile explained the pun to him. The doctor blushed.

'You must admit it's not bad, Doctor!'

'Oh, I've heard it many times,' answered Cottard.

Then they fell silent; beneath the agitated violin tremolos which protected it with their quivering line two octaves above—as in a mountainous landscape, behind the seeming immobility of a vertiginous waterfall, one sees, two hundred feet below, the tiny figure of a woman walking in the valley—the little phrase had just appeared, distant, graceful, protected by the slow, continuous unfurling of its transparent curtain of sound. And Swann, in his heart, appealed to it as to a confidante of his love for Odette, as to a friend of hers who ought to tell her to pay no attention to that man Forcheville.

'Ah, you're late!' said Madame Verdurin to a regular whom she'd invited to drop in for coffee. 'Brichot was in top form! He's gone now, but he was quite superb! Wasn't he, Monsieur Swann? I believe it was the first time you and he had met,' she added, in order to make the point that he had her to thank for the introduction. 'Wasn't our Brichot delightful?'

Swann bowed politely.

'What? Didn't you find him interesting?' Madame Verdurin asked him rather sharply.

'But of course, Madame, he was most interesting. I was enthralled. He's perhaps a little too arrogant, and a little too jolly, for my taste. I'd prefer it if he were rather less sure of himself, less categorical, now and then, but one can see he knows a lot and he seems a very decent sort.'

It was very late by the time everyone had left. Cottard's first words to his wife were: 'I've rarely seen Madame Verdurin in such good form as she was this evening.'

'What kind of person exactly is this Madame Verdurin of yours? Rather difficult to make out, isn't she?', said Forcheville to the painter, to whom he'd offered a lift.

Odette watched with regret as he went off; she dared not decline to ride with Swann, but she was in a bad mood in the carriage, and when he asked if he could come in, she gave an impatient shrug and said: 'I suppose so.'

When all the guests had gone, Madame Verdurin said to her husband: 'Did you notice the stupid way Swann laughed when we mentioned Madame La Trémoïlle?'

She'd noticed, too, that several times Swann and Forcheville had omitted the 'de' in front of La Trémoïlle. Convinced that they only did this to show they were not intimidated by titles, she wanted to follow suit, but hadn't worked out by which grammatical form to express it. And so her corrupt habits of speech won out over her intransigent republicanism, so she carried on saying 'the de la Trémoïlles', or rather, using an abbreviation common in *café-concert* songs and cartoon captions, which elided the *de*, she referred to them as the d'la Trémoïlles, but compensated for it by saying: 'Madame La Trémoïlle,' adding 'The *Duchess*, as Swann calls her,' with an ironic smile that showed she was just quoting and would accept no responsibility for such a naïve and ridiculous appellation.

'I must say I thought him utterly stupid,' she said.

And Monsieur Verdurin replied: 'He's not sincere. He's quite sly, always sitting on the fence, always wanting to run with the hare and hunt with the hounds. How different from Forcheville! There at least is a man who tells you straight out what he thinks. You either agree with him or you don't. He's not like the other one, who's neither fish nor fowl. Odette certainly seems to prefer Forcheville, and I can't say I blame her. In any case, if Swann wants to show us what a great society man he is, the defender of duchesses, at least the other one has got a title—he is, after all, the Comte de Forcheville,' he added delicately, as if, being familiar with the history of that title, he could very accurately judge its particular value.

'Do you know,' said Madame Verdurin, 'he saw fit to make some nasty and quite ludicrous insinuations about Brichot. Naturally, once he saw that Brichot is well liked in this house, it was a way of getting back at us, and spoiling our party. He's the sort of person who pretends to be your friend and stabs you in the back as soon as he's out of the door.'

'That's exactly what I mean,' replied Monsieur Verdurin. 'He's a typical failure, one of those small-minded individuals who are envious of anything that's at all grand.'

In reality there was not one of the 'faithful' who was not more malicious than Swann; but they all took care to season their slander with familiar pleasantries, with little touches of feeling and cordiality; whereas the slightest reservation Swann allowed himself, unadorned by such conventional formulas as 'I don't mean to be unkind', to which he didn't deign to stoop, seemed to them treachery. There are certain original authors in whom the slightest boldness of expression is found offensive because they haven't begun by pandering to public taste by offering the usual commonplaces; it was by the same process that Swann infuriated Monsieur Verdurin. In his case as in theirs, it was the novelty of his language that was thought to betray the sinister nature of his designs.

Swann was still unaware of the disgrace that threatened him at the Verdurins' and continued to regard their absurdities in a rosy light, through the eyes of love.

More often than not, he met Odette only in the evenings; he was afraid he'd make her tire of him if he visited her during the day as well, but he wanted at least to remain in her thoughts and was always looking for opportunities to make her think of him, in a way that would be pleasant for her. If, in the window of a florist or a jeweller, the sight of a shrub or a precious stone took his fancy, he'd think at once of sending them to Odette, imagining the pleasure they'd given him would be felt by her too, and would increase her affection for him, and he'd have them delivered forthwith to her house in the Rue La Pérouse, so as not to delay the moment when, because she was receiving something from him, he'd feel he was in some way close to her. He was especially anxious for her to receive them before she went out, so that her gratitude would win him a more affectionate welcome when she saw him at the Verdurins'; or, one never knows, if the shopkeeper was especially prompt, there was the chance that she'd send a note of thanks before dinner, or even give him the unexpected bonus of arriving in person at his house. Just as he'd once tested Odette's nature for reactions of resentment, so now he sought by reactions of gratitude to extract from her intimate particles of feeling that she hadn't yet revealed to him.

She often had money troubles and would ask him to help her pay urgent debts. He was happy to assist, as he was happy about anything that could impress Odette with his love for her, or simply with how influential he was and how useful he could be to her. No doubt, if someone had said to him in the beginning: 'It's your position that attracts her,' and now: 'What she loves about you is your money,' he wouldn't have believed it, but wouldn't have minded too much if people thought that her attachment to him, and the union between them, were based on something as powerful as snobbery or money. But even if he'd believed it to be true, he might not have been upset to discover that Odette's love for him had a more durable buttress than his charm or the personal qualities she might see in him: namely, self-interest, a self-interest that would prevent the day ever coming when she might be tempted to stop seeing him. For the moment, by heaping gifts upon her, by doing her favours, he could rely on advantages extraneous to his person or his intellect to relieve himself of the arduous task of making himself attractive to her. And the pleasure of being in love, of living by love alone, the reality of which he sometimes doubted, was greatly enhanced for him, as a dilettante of intangible sensations, by the price he was paying for it—as we see how people who are uncertain whether the sight of the sea and the sound of the waves are really enjoyable become convinced that they are, and convinced also of the rare quality and disinterested nature of their own tastes, by paying a hundred francs a day for a hotel room from which that sight and that sound may be enjoyed.

One day, when reflections of this kind recalled once more the memory of the time when people had spoken of Odette as a kept woman, and he was amusing himself yet again by contrasting that strange personification, the kept woman—a shimmering amalgam of unknown and diabolical elements, set, like some vision by Gustave Moreau,* among poisonous flowers interwoven with precious jewels—with the Odette on whose face he'd seen the same feelings of pity for someone in distress, revolt against an injustice, gratitude for a favour, that he'd seen on his own mother's face and on the faces of his friends, the Odette whose conversation so often turned on the things he knew better than anyone, his collections, his bedroom, his

old servant, the banker who looked after his securities, it happened
that the thought of the banker reminded him that he must call on him
soon to draw some cash. In fact, if this month he was helping Odette
less liberally with her material difficulties than he had the previous
month, when he'd given her five thousand francs, and if he didn't buy
her the diamond necklace she wanted, he wouldn't be renewing her
admiration for his generosity, the gratitude that made him so happy,
and he would even risk making her think, as she saw the tokens of his
love grow smaller, that his feelings for her had also waned. Then, suddenly, he wondered whether this was precisely what was meant by
'keeping' her (as if, in fact, the option of keeping could be derived
from elements not at all mysterious and perverse but from the intimate substance of his daily life, like the familiar and domestic thousand-
franc note, torn and glued together again, which his manservant, after
paying the month's accounts and the rent, had locked in the drawer of
the old desk from which Swann had taken it out again to send it with
four others to Odette) and whether one could not after all apply to
Odette, at least since he'd come to know her (because he didn't suspect for a moment that she could ever have received money from anyone before him), the expression he'd believed so irreconcilable with
her: 'kept woman'. He was unable to pursue this idea any further, for
at that moment an attack of the mental laziness which in him was
congenital, intermittent, and providential extinguished all light in his
brain, just as, at a later period, one could suddenly cut off the electricity in a house. His mind groped for a moment in the dark, he took off
his glasses, wiped the lenses, passed his hand over his eyes, and didn't
see any light until he found himself faced with a completely different
idea, namely that he ought to try to send six or seven thousand francs
to Odette the following month instead of five, because it would give
her such a pleasant surprise.

In the evening, when he didn't stay at home until it was time to go
and meet Odette at the Verdurins', or rather at one of the open-air
restaurants in the Bois and especially at Saint-Cloud, he'd dine at one
of the fashionable houses where he'd once been a habitual guest. He
didn't want to lose touch with people who might one day prove useful
to Odette, and thanks to whom, in the meantime, he often succeeded
in pleasing her. Also, his long acquaintance with the world of high
society and luxurious living had given him both a disdain for that
world and an addiction to it, so that by the time he'd come to consider

the most modest abodes as being exactly on a par with the most pala-
tial, his senses were so accustomed to the latter that he'd have felt quite
uncomfortable to find himself in the former. He had the same
regard—to a degree of identity they wouldn't have believed—for
a petit bourgeois family which invited him to a little party on the fifth
floor, Staircase D, left at the landing, as for the Princesse de Parme,
who gave the most lavish parties in Paris; but he didn't feel he was
actually at a dance as he stood with husbands and fathers in the hostess's bedroom, while the sight of the washstands covered with towels
and the beds transformed into cloakrooms, their quilts piled high with
hats and overcoats, gave him the same stifling sensation that, nowadays, people who have been used to electricity for the past twenty
years may experience at the smell of a smoky oil lamp or a guttering
candle. On the days when he dined in town, he'd have the horses har-
nessed for half past seven; as he dressed, his thoughts would dwell on
Odette, and so he wouldn't feel alone, for the constant thought of her
would give the time during which he was separated from her the same
special charm as the time he spent with her. He'd get into the carriage,
but he felt that this thought had jumped in with him and settled on his
lap like a beloved pet which he'd take everywhere and keep with him at
the dinner table, unbeknown to the other guests. He'd stroke it, warm
himself with it, and, experiencing a kind of languor, would yield to
a slight quivering sensation, quite new to him, that made his neck and
his nostrils tense, as he fastened the bunch of columbines in his
buttonhole. Having felt unwell and depressed for some time, especially since Odette had introduced Forcheville to the Verdurins, Swann
would have liked to go to the country to relax. But he would not have
dared to leave Paris for a single day while Odette was there. The air was
warm; spring was now at its most beautiful. And although he would
traverse a city of stone to immure himself in some town house, what he
constantly saw in his mind's eye were the grounds of a house he owned
near Combray, where, by four in the afternoon, thanks to the breeze
from the meadows of Méséglise, if you walked down to the asparagus
bed you could enjoy the cool evening air beneath an arbour in the garden as much as by the edge of the pool fringed with forget-me-nots
and irises, and where, if he dined out of doors, the table was surrounded by redcurrants and roses, intertwined by his gardener.

After dinner, if the meeting that evening was early, and in the Bois
or at Saint-Cloud, he'd leave so quickly after getting up from the

table—especially if it looked like rain and that the 'faithful' would be forced to go home earlier than usual—that on one occasion the Princesse des Laumes (at whose house they'd dined late and from whom Swann had taken his leave before coffee was served in order to join the Verdurins on the island in the Bois) had said: 'I must say, if Swann was thirty years older and had bladder trouble, no one would mind his running off like that. But he doesn't seem to care what people think.'

He told himself that the delights of spring which he couldn't go and enjoy in Combray he could at least savour on the Île des Cygnes* or at Saint-Cloud. But as he could think only of Odette, he didn't even know if he'd smelt the scent of the young leaves, or if the moon had been shining. He'd be greeted by the little phrase from the sonata, played in the garden on the restaurant piano. If there was no piano there, the Verdurins would take great pains to have one brought down from one of the rooms or from a dining room. Not that Swann was now back in favour; far from it. But the idea of organizing an ingenious form of entertainment for someone, even for someone they disliked, stimulated in them, during the time required for its preparation, transient feelings of warmth and cordiality. Now and then he'd reflect that another spring day was slipping past, and would force himself to pay attention to the trees and the sky. But the agitation he felt in the presence of Odette, together with a slightly feverish indisposition that had persisted for some time now, robbed him of the calm and well-being which are the indispensable background to the impressions we derive from nature.

One evening, when Swann had agreed to dine with the Verdurins, and had mentioned during dinner that the following day he'd be attending the annual banquet of an old comrades' association, Odette had replied across the table, in front of Forcheville, who was now one of the 'faithful', in front of the painter, in front of Cottard: 'Yes, I know you've got your banquet to go to, so I won't see you until I get home, but don't be too late.'

Although Swann had never yet taken serious offence at Odette's friendly relations with one or other of the 'faithful', he felt an exquisite pleasure on hearing her confess in front of everyone, with such calm immodesty, to their nightly meetings, his privileged position in her house, and the preference for him that it implied. It was true that Swann had often reflected that Odette was in no way a remarkable woman, and the supremacy he exercised over a woman so inferior to him was not something that ought to appear especially flattering when proclaimed in this way to all the 'faithful', but ever since he'd noticed that many other men found Odette a beautiful and desirable woman, the attraction her body had for them had aroused in him a painful need to assert his complete mastery of even the tiniest parts of her heart. He'd begun to attach immeasurable value to the times he spent at her house in the evening, when he'd sit her on his knee and make her tell him what she thought about one thing or another, and list the only possessions on earth he still valued. And so, when dinner was over, he took her aside and made a point of thanking her effusively, trying to show her by the degree of his gratitude the great range of the pleasures it was in her power to bestow on him, the supreme pleasure being to safeguard him, for as long as his love should last and render him vulnerable, from attacks of jealousy.

When he came away from the banquet the next day, it was pouring with rain, and all he had was his victoria; a friend offered to drive him home in his brougham, and since Odette, by the fact of having invited him to come, had given him to understand that she wasn't expecting anyone else, he could have gone home to bed, his mind at rest and his heart untroubled, rather than set off in the rain like this. But perhaps, if she saw that he didn't seem to want to insist on spending the late evening with her, without exception, she might neglect to keep it free for him just at a time when he particularly wanted to see her.

It was after eleven when he reached her house, and as he apologized for not having been able to come earlier, she complained that it was indeed very late, the storm had made her feel unwell, she had a headache, and warned him he couldn't stay for more than half an hour, that at midnight she'd send him away; soon afterwards she said she felt tired and wanted to sleep.

'So, no cattleya tonight?' he said. 'I was so looking forward to a nice little cattleya.'

Sounding slightly sulky and irritable, she replied:

'No, no, darling, no cattleya tonight. You can see I'm not well.'

'It might have done you good, but I won't insist.'

She asked him to put out the light on his way out; he drew the bed-curtains and left. But when he was back home, it suddenly occurred to him that Odette might have been waiting for someone else that night, had only pretended to be tired, and had asked him to put out the light simply to make him think she was going to sleep, and that as soon as he'd left she'd lit the lamp again and opened the door for the man who was going to spend the night with her. He looked at the time. It was about an hour and a half since he'd left her. He went back out and took a cab to a spot very close to Odette's house, in a little street perpendicular to the one her house overlooked at the back and where he'd sometimes go and tap on her bedroom window so that she'd let him in. He got out of the cab; the whole neighbourhood was dark and deserted. He walked the few steps to the other little street and came out almost opposite her house. Amid the darkness of the row of windows in which the lights had long since been put out, he saw just one from which there spilled out—between the slats of its shutters, closed like a wine press over its mysterious golden pulp—the light that filled the bedroom and whose message, on so many other nights, as soon as he saw it from afar as he turned into the street, gave him a thrill of excitement with its message: 'She's there, waiting for you,' but which now tortured him by saying: 'She's there, with the man she was expecting.' He wanted to know who it was; he crept along the wall as far as the window, but was unable to see anything between the oblique slats of the shutters; all he could hear in the silence of the night was the murmur of a conversation. It was agonizing for him to see that light and to know that in its golden glow, behind the sash, the hateful, invisible pair were moving about, to hear the murmur of voices that revealed the presence of the man who'd arrived after he himself had left, the duplicity of Odette, and the pleasure she was at that moment enjoying with him.

Yet he was glad he'd come back: the torment that had forced him to leave his house had become less acute now that it had become less vague, now that Odette's other life, of which, before leaving, he'd had a sudden helpless suspicion, was there, within his grasp, fully exposed by the light of the lamp unknowingly imprisoned in that room, and all he had to do, when he chose, was to go in and capture it; or rather, he would knock on the shutters as he often did when he came very late; in that way, at least, Odette would learn that he knew, that he'd seen the light and heard the voices, and that, although a moment ago he'd pictured her laughing with the other man at his illusions, now he was the one who saw them, deceivers mistakenly confident but tricked by him, whom they believed to be far away but who was there, poised to knock on the shutters. And perhaps what he felt at that moment, a feeling that was almost pleasurable, was something more than the calming of doubt or relief from distress: it was an intellectual pleasure. If, since he'd fallen in love, things had regained a little of the delightful interest they held for him in the past, but only insofar as they were illuminated by the thought of Odette, now it was another of the faculties of his studious youth that his jealousy reawakened, a passion for truth, but for a truth that was similarly interposed between himself and his mistress, receiving its light only from her, an entirely personal truth whose sole object, of infinite value and almost disinterested in its beauty, was what Odette was doing, the people she saw, her plans for the future, her past life. At all other periods of his life, the details and everyday actions of another person had always seemed devoid of interest to Swann if reported to him as the subject of gossip; he found such talk meaningless, and, although he listened, it was only the most vulgar part of his mind that was engaged; these were moments when he felt at his most ordinary. But in this strange phase of love, when everything about another person assumes such profound importance, the curiosity he felt awakening within him concerning the most trifling activities of this woman was the same curiosity he'd once had about History. And all the things of which previously he'd have been ashamed, such as spying outside a window, and tomorrow perhaps, for all he knew, wheedling information out of casual witnesses, bribing servants, listening behind doors, seemed to him now to be no different from the deciphering of texts, the weighing of evidence, and the interpretation of monuments—just so many methods of scientific investigation with real intellectual value and appropriate to the search for the truth.

On the point of knocking on the shutters, he felt a pang of shame at the thought that Odette would now know he'd been suspicious, that he'd come back, that he'd posted himself in the street. She'd often told him how much she hated jealous men, lovers who spied. What he was about to do was extremely heavy-handed, and from then on she would detest him, whereas now, for the moment, so long as he hadn't knocked, perhaps even as she was deceiving him, she loved him still. How often we sacrifice the prospect of happiness because of our insistence on immediate gratification! But his desire to know the truth was stronger and seemed to him nobler. He knew that the reality of certain circumstances which he would have given his life to reconstruct accurately could be read behind that window, with its slats of light, as beneath the gold-illuminated cover of one of those precious manuscripts by whose artistic richness itself the scholar who consults them cannot remain unmoved. He felt a sensuous pleasure in learning the truth that so excited him in those unique, ephemeral, and precious pages, on that translucent material, so warm and so beautiful. Moreover, the advantage he felt he had over them—that he so needed to feel he had—lay perhaps less in knowing than in being able to show them he knew. He stood on tiptoes. He knocked. They hadn't heard, he knocked again more loudly, the conversation stopped. A man's voice, which he tried to identify from among the voices of the men-friends of Odette whom he knew, asked:

'Who's there?'

He wasn't sure he recognized it. He knocked once more. The window was opened, then the shutters. It was too late now to draw back and, since she was going to realize what he was doing there, in order not to appear too miserable, too jealous and inquisitive, he simply called out in a cheerful, casual tone:

'Sorry to disturb you. I just happened to be passing and saw the light. I wanted to know if you were feeling better.'

He looked up. Facing him, two old gentlemen were standing at the window, one of them holding a lamp, and then he saw the bedroom, a bedroom he'd never seen before. Since, when he came to see Odette late at night, he was in the habit of recognizing her window by the fact that it was the only one with a light among the windows that were otherwise all alike, he'd made a mistake and had knocked at the window beyond hers, which belonged to the neighbouring house. He went away apologizing and returned home, glad that the satisfaction of his curiosity had left their love intact, and that, having simulated for so long a sort of indifference towards Odette, he hadn't given her, by his jealousy, that proof of loving too much, which, between lovers, for ever exempts the other from loving enough. He never spoke to her about this misadventure, and he gave it no further thought himself. But now and then his wandering thoughts would come across the memory they hadn't noticed, and bump into it, driving it in, and Swann would feel a sudden stab of pain. As though it were an actual physical pain, his mind could do nothing to alleviate it; but at least with physical pain, because it's independent of the mind, the mind can focus on it, note that it has diminished or momentarily ceased. But with this type of pain the mind, merely by recalling it, created it afresh. To wish not to think about it was still to think about it, to continue to suffer from it. And when, talking with friends, he forgot about it, all of a sudden one of them would say something that would make him wince, like a wounded man whom some clumsy person has just carelessly touched on his bad arm or leg. When he left Odette, he was happy, he felt calm, he recalled her smiles, gently mocking when she spoke of other people but affectionate towards him; the weight of her head as she tilted it on its axis to let it fall, almost in spite of herself, on his lips, as she had done the first time in the carriage; the languishing looks she'd given him as she lay in his arms, nestling her head against her shoulder as if shrinking from the cold.

But at once his jealousy, as if it were the shadow of his love, provided him with a complementary version of the new smile with which she'd greeted him that very evening—and which, conversely now, mocked Swann, filled as it was with her love for another—with the same inclination of the head, but leaning towards different lips, with all the marks of affection she'd given him, but given to another man. And all the sensuous memories he carried away from her house were like so many sketches, rough plans like those a decorator might submit, enabling him to form an idea of the passionate or swooning attitudes she might adopt with other men. The result was that he came to regret every pleasure he enjoyed with her, every new caress whose sweetness he'd been so imprudent as to point out to her, every fresh charm he found in her, for he knew that a moment later they'd be added to the collection of instruments in his torture-chamber.

Swann's torment became even more acute when he remembered a fleeting expression he'd noticed a few days earlier, and for the first time, in Odette's eyes. It was after dinner at the Verdurins'. Whether it was because Forcheville, sensing that Saniette, his brother-in-law, was no longer in favour, wanted to use him as a whipping-boy in order to shine at his expense, or because he'd been irritated by a clumsy remark Saniette had made to him, though in fact it had gone unnoticed by the others, who were unaware of any unpleasant allusion it might unintentionally have contained, or because, for some time now, he'd been waiting for an opportunity to have banished from the house someone who knew too much about him, and whom he knew to be so sensitive that at times he felt embarrassed merely by his presence, Forcheville responded to Saniette's clumsy remark in such a crudely aggressive manner, hurling abuse at him, emboldened, the more he shouted, by Saniette's distress, alarm, and entreaties, that the poor man, after asking Madame Verdurin whether he should stay or leave, and receiving no answer, had left the house stammering in confusion, with tears in his eyes. Odette had looked on impassively, but when the door had closed on Saniette, she'd lowered by several notches, as it were, her face's normal expression, so as to put herself on the same level of baseness as Forcheville, and her eyes had gleamed with a sly smile of congratulations for his boldness, and mockery for the man who'd been its victim, she'd cast him a glance of complicity in the crime which so clearly implied: 'That was a real execution, if ever there was one! Did you see how pathetic he looked? He was crying,' that Forcheville, when his eyes met hers, suddenly lost all the anger or the pretence of anger with which he was still flushed, and smiled as he replied: 'Well, if he'd been a bit nicer, he'd still be here. A good dressing-down never does a man any harm, at any age.'

One day when Swann had gone out in the middle of the afternoon to pay a call, and had found that the person he wanted to see wasn't at home, he had the idea of going round to Odette's house instead, at an hour when he never called on her, but when he knew she was always at home having her nap or writing letters before teatime, and when he'd enjoy seeing her for a little while without disturbing her. The concierge told him he thought she was in; he rang the bell, thought he heard a noise, and then footsteps, but no one came to the door. Anxious and irritated, he went round to the little street at the back and stood under Odette's bedroom window; the curtains prevented him from seeing anything, he knocked hard on the windowpanes, and called out; no one opened. He saw that some neighbours were watching him. He went away, thinking that after all he might have been mistaken in thinking he'd heard footsteps; but he remained so preoccupied that he couldn't think of anything else. An hour later, he went back. He found her there; she told him she'd been in the house when he rang, but was sleeping; the bell had woken her, she'd guessed it was Swann, she'd run out to look for him, but he'd already gone. She had, of course, heard him knock at the window. Swann immediately recognized in her story one of those fragments of true fact which liars, when caught off guard, console themselves by introducing into the composition of the falsehood they are inventing, thinking they can incorporate it there and give their story a semblance of Truth. Of course, when Odette had done something she didn't want to reveal, she'd hide it deep inside herself. But as soon as she found herself face to face with the man to whom she intended to lie, she became uneasy, all her ideas evaporated, her faculties of invention and reasoning were paralysed, her brain became empty; yet she had to say something, and all she'd find within reach was the very thing she'd wanted to conceal and which, being true, was all that had remained. She would detach a little piece from it, insignificant in itself, telling herself that, after all, it was the best thing to do, since the detail was authentic and less dangerous, therefore, than a fictitious one. 'At least that bit is true,' she'd say to herself, 'and that's all to the good. He can make enquiries, he'll find it's true, so at least it won't be that that gives me away.' She was wrong, it was precisely what gave her away; she didn't realize that her little fragment of truth had corners that could fit only into the contiguous fragments of the truth from which she'd arbitrarily detached it, corners that, no matter into what invented details she placed them, would always reveal, by the bits that stuck out and the gaps they didn't fill, that that was not where they belonged. 'She admits she heard me ring the bell and then knock, thought it was me, and wanted to see me,' Swann said to himself. 'But that hardly accords with the fact that nobody came to the door.'

But he didn't point out this contradiction, because he thought that, left to her own devices, Odette might produce some falsehood that would give him a faint indication of the truth. She went on talking, and he didn't interrupt, but listened, with an avid, painful piety, to her every word, feeling (rightly so, because she was hiding the truth behind them as she spoke) that, like the sacred veil, they retained a vague imprint, a blurred outline, of that reality so infinitely precious and, alas, undiscoverable—what she'd been doing that afternoon at three o'clock, when he'd called—of which he'd never possess anything other than her lies, illegible and divine traces, and which now existed only in the secretive memory of this woman who could contemplate it without appreciating its value but would never reveal it to him. Of course, it had occurred to him more than once that in themselves Odette's daily activities were not passionately interesting, and that the relationships she might have with other men didn't exhale naturally, universally, and for every intelligent soul a morbid sadness capable of infecting one with a feverish desire to commit suicide. He would then realize that this interest, this sadness, existed in him alone, like a disease, and that, once he was cured of this disease,

Odette's actions, the kisses she might have bestowed, would become once again as innocuous as those of so many other women. But his realization that the painful curiosity he now brought to them had its origin only in himself was not enough to make him think it was unreasonable to consider this curiosity as important and to take every possible step to satisfy it. For Swann was reaching an age when one's philosophy—encouraged by the prevailing philosophy of the day, and also by that of the circle in which he'd spent much of his life, the Princesse des Laumes and her set, where the accepted view was that intelligence is in direct ratio to scepticism and that nothing is real and incontestable except the particular tastes of the individual—is no longer that of youth, but a positivistic, almost medical philosophy, the philosophy of men who, instead of exteriorizing the objects of their aspirations, try to extract from the accumulation of the years a stable residue of habits and passions which they can regard as characteristic and permanent, and which they will deliberately make it their primary concern to satisfy by the kind of life they choose to adopt. Swann thought it wise to make allowance in his life for the pain he felt at not knowing what Odette had been doing, just as he made allowance for the fact that his eczema would become worse in inclement weather; to provide in his budget for sizeable sums to be expended on the procurement of information about how Odette spent her days, without which he'd feel unhappy, just as he reserved certain amounts for the gratification of other tastes from which he knew he could expect to derive pleasure, at least before he'd fallen in love, such as his taste for collecting art and for good food.

When he began to say goodbye to Odette to return home, she asked him to stay a while longer and even held him back by the arm as he was opening the door to go. But he paid no special attention to this, because among the multiplicity of gestures, remarks, and little incidents that go to make up a conversation, it's inevitable that we should fail to notice those that hide a truth our suspicions are blindly seeking, and fasten, on the other hand, on those that conceal nothing. She kept saying: 'What a shame—you never come in the afternoon, and the one time you do come, I miss you.' He knew very well she wasn't so in love with him that she'd been very distressed at having missed his visit, but, because she was good-natured, anxious to please him, and often sad when she'd offended him, he found it quite natural that she should be sorry for having deprived him of the pleasure of spending an hour in her company, which was a very great pleasure, if not for her, then certainly for him. Yet it was a matter of such relative unimportance that eventually the doleful expression she continued to wear began to surprise him. She reminded him, even more than usual, of the faces of some of the women portrayed by the painter of the *Primavera*.* She had at this moment their dejected, sorrowful expression, which seems to betoken the unbearable weight of some terrible burden of grief, whereas they are merely letting the Infant Jesus play with a pomegranate or watching Moses pour water into a trough.* He'd seen her wear this expression of profound sorrow once before, but had forgotten when. Then, suddenly, he remembered: it was when she'd lied to Madame Verdurin the day after the dinner to which she hadn't come on the pretext of illness, but in reality so that she could spend time alone with him. Surely, even if she'd been the most scrupulously honest of women, she would hardly have felt remorseful for such an innocent little lie. But the lies Odette normally told were less innocent, and served to prevent discoveries that might involve her in terrible difficulties with one or another of the people she knew. So when she lied, she felt assailed by fear, poorly prepared for her defence, plagued by doubts, and would be close to tears, from sheer exhaustion, like a child who hasn't slept. She knew, moreover, that through her lie she was usually seriously hurting the man to whom she was telling it, and at whose mercy she would perhaps find herself if she lied badly. And so she felt at once humble and guilty in his presence. And when she had to tell a little white lie, the association of sensations and memories would make her feel faint, as if by overexertion, and penitent, as when one does someone a bad turn.

What depressing lie was she now telling Swann that gave her this pained look, this plaintive voice, which seemed to falter under the effort she was forcing herself to make, to beg for forgiveness? It suddenly crossed his mind that it was not merely the truth about what had occurred that afternoon that she was trying to hide from him, but something more immediate, that had perhaps not yet happened and was quite imminent, something that might enlighten him about the earlier event. At that moment, he heard the bell ring. Odette didn't stop talking, but her words had become a single, long lament: her regret at not having seen Swann that afternoon, at not having opened the door to him, had turned into an endless cry of despair.

The front door could be heard closing, then the sound of a carriage, as if someone was going away—presumably the person Swann was not meant to meet—after being told that Odette was not at home. Then, after reflecting that merely by coming at an unusual time of day he'd managed to disturb so many arrangements she didn't want him to know about, he was overcome with a feeling of despondency, almost of anguish. But since he loved Odette, since he was in the habit of turning all his thoughts towards her, instead of feeling sorry for himself, he felt sorry for her instead, and he murmured: 'Poor darling!' When he finally left, she picked up several letters that were lying on her table and asked him if he could post them for her. He took them with him and, once he was home, realized that they were still in his pocket. He walked back to the post office, took the letters out of his pocket, and, before dropping them in the box, glanced at the addresses. They were all for tradesmen, except one which was for Forcheville. He stood holding the envelope in his hand. 'If I knew what's inside,' he thought, 'I'd know what she calls him, the way she talks to him, if there's anything between them. In fact, if I don't look inside, I'd be doing Odette a disservice, because it's the only way to rid myself of a suspicion that may be slanderous, in any case bound to cause her suffering, and that nothing thereafter can remove, once the letter has been posted.'

He returned home after leaving the post office, but he'd kept this last letter in his pocket. He lit a candle and held up close to its flame the envelope he had not dared to open. At first he couldn't read anything, but the envelope was thin, and by pressing it against the stiff card it contained he managed to make out, through the semi-transparent paper, the concluding words. It was a very stiff, formal ending. If Forcheville had been looking at a letter addressed to him, rather than himself reading a letter addressed to Forcheville, then Forcheville would have seen words far more redolent of affection! He took a firm hold of the card which kept moving about in the envelope, which was too large for it, and then, sliding it with his thumb, brought one line after another under the part of the envelope which was not of double thickness, the only part through which it was possible to read.

But he still had great difficulty in deciphering them. Not that it mattered, because he'd seen enough to realize the letter was about some trivial event that had no connection with a love affair; it was something to do with an uncle of Odette's. Swann had been able to read at the beginning of the line: 'It was just as well I . . .', but couldn't understand what Odette had done that was just as well, when a word he'd not at first been able to decipher suddenly became clear and explained the meaning of the whole sentence: 'It was just as well I opened the door, it was my uncle.' Opened the door! So Forcheville had been there when Swann rang the bell, and she'd made him leave, which was the reason for the noise he'd heard.

Then he read the whole letter; at the end she apologized for having treated him so unceremoniously, and told him he'd forgotten his cigarette-case, the same sentence she'd written to Swann after one of his first visits. But to Swann she'd added: 'If you'd left your heart here too, I wouldn't have let you have it back.' To Forcheville, nothing of the sort, nor any allusion that might suggest they were having an affair. In fact, if anyone was being deceived in all this it was Forcheville, for the purpose of Odette's letter was to make him believe the visitor had been her uncle. So that he, Swann, was the one she really cared about, the one for whom she'd sent the other man away. And yet, if there was nothing between Odette and Forcheville, why hadn't she opened the door right away, why had she said: 'It was just as well I opened the door, it was my uncle'? If she wasn't doing anything wrong, what on earth could Forcheville have made of the fact that she hadn't opened the door? Swann sat there, bewildered, forlorn, yet happy, gazing at this envelope which Odette had entrusted to him without the slightest hesitation, so absolute was her confidence in his integrity, but the transparent screen of which had afforded him a glimpse of a tiny part of Odette's life, revealing a secret he'd never have believed it possible to uncover, like a narrow illuminated section cut directly out of the unknown. Then his jealousy rejoiced at this discovery, as though that jealousy had an independent, selfish existence, voracious for anything that would feed it, even at Swann's own expense. Now it had something to feed on, and Swann could begin to worry every day about the visitors Odette had received at about five o'clock, and begin trying to learn where Forcheville had been at that time. For Swann's affection for Odette still retained the form imprinted on it from the beginning by his ignorance of how she spent her days and by the mental laziness that prevented him from supple-menting his ignorance by his imagination. He hadn't been jealous, at first, of the whole life Odette led without him, but only of the moments when some incident, which he may have misinterpreted, had led him to suppose that Odette might have deceived him. His jealousy, like an octopus which throws out a first, then a second, and finally a third tentacle, battened on that particular moment, five o'clock in the afternoon, then on another, then on yet another. But Swann was not capable of inventing his sufferings. They were merely the memory, the perpetuation, of a suffering that had come to him from elsewhere.

But here, everything brought him more suffering. He decided to remove Odette from Forcheville's company altogether by taking her to the Midi for a few days. But he imagined that all the men in the hotel desired her and that she desired them. And so, although in his travels in the past he'd looked out for new people and new groups, he now seemed unsociable, avoiding company as if it was unbearably hurtful to him. And how could he not be misanthropic, when in every man he saw a potential lover of Odette? And in this way his jealousy, even more than the happy, sensual feelings he'd initially had for Odette, altered Swann's character, completely changing, in the eyes of other people, even the outward signs by which that character manifested itself.

A month after the day on which he'd read Odette's letter to Forcheville, Swann went to a dinner the Verdurins were giving in the Bois. Just as people were getting ready to leave, he noticed a number of confabulations between Madame Verdurin and several of the guests, and thought he heard the pianist being reminded to come to a party at Chatou the next day—to which he, Swann, hadn't been invited.

The Verdurins had spoken only in whispers, and in vague terms, but the painter, probably without thinking, exclaimed: 'We must make sure there's no light, and have him play the "Moonlight" Sonata* in the dark so that we can see by it!'

Madame Verdurin, seeing that Swann was within earshot, assumed the expression in which the desire to silence the speaker and the desire to maintain an air of innocence in the eyes of the listener cancel each other out in a gaze of intense vacuity, in which the motionless sign of complicity is concealed beneath an innocent smile, which, as everyone who has ever noticed a social gaffe is aware, reveals it instantly, if not to its author, at least to its victim. Odette seemed suddenly to have the desperate look of someone who has given up the struggle against the crushing difficulties of life, and Swann anxiously counted the minutes he'd have to endure before he could leave the restaurant and, during the drive home, ask her for an explanation, persuade her not to go to Chatou the next day or make sure he was invited, and find solace in her arms for the anguish he was feeling. At last the carriages were brought round. Madame Verdurin said to Swann: 'So, goodbye. See you soon, I hope?', attempting by her friendly manner and fixed smile to prevent him from realizing that she was not saying, as she'd always said until now: 'We'll see you tomorrow, then, at Chatou, and at my house the day after.'

Monsieur and Madame Verdurin invited Forcheville to get in with them. Swann's carriage had pulled up behind theirs, and he was waiting for them to move on so that he could help Odette into his.

'Odette, you can come with us,' said Madame Verdurin, 'we've kept a little place for you here, next to Monsieur de Forcheville.'

'Yes, Madame,' replied Odette.

'But I thought you were coming with me!' exclaimed Swann, not mincing his words, because the carriage door was open, there were just a few seconds left, and, in the state he was in, he could not possibly leave without her.

'But Madame Verdurin has asked me . . .'

'For heaven's sake!' said Madame Verdurin. 'You can surely go home without her for once; we've let you have her to yourself often enough!'

'But there's something important I need to say to Madame de Crécy!'

'Well, you can write her a letter . . .'

'Goodbye,' said Odette, holding out her hand.

He tried to smile but looked utterly dejected.

'Did you see the way Swann thinks he can treat us now?', said Madame Verdurin to her husband when they were back home. 'I thought he was going to bite my head off, just because we offered Odette a lift! It's quite indecent! He might as well say straight out that he thinks we're running a brothel! It's a mystery to me how Odette can put up with such manners! His whole way of behaving seems to say: "You belong to me." I'll tell Odette exactly what I think, I hope she'll understand.'

A moment later she burst out again: 'No, but really! The filthy creature!', using, without realizing it, perhaps responding to the same obscure need to justify herself—like Françoise in Combray, when the chicken refused to die—the same words which the final convulsions of a harmless animal wring from the peasant engaged in slaughtering it.

When Madame Verdurin's carriage had left and Swann's took its place, his coachman looked at him and asked if he was feeling unwell or whether there had been some accident.

Swann sent him away; he wanted to walk, and he returned home on foot through the Bois. He talked to himself as he walked, and in the same artificial tone he'd always adopted when enumerating the charms of the little clan and extolling the magnanimity of the Verdurins. But just as the conversation, the smiles, the kisses of Odette seemed as hateful to him as he'd once found them delightful, if they were addressed to other men, so the Verdurins' salon, which that very evening had still seemed an agreeable place, inspired with a genuine enthusiasm for art and even with a sort of moral nobility, now that Odette was going there to flirt freely with another man, appeared to him in all its absurdity, in all its shameless inanity.

In complete disgust, he pictured to himself the soirée at Chatou. 'The very idea of going to Chatou anyway! Like a pack of grocers taking a day off! How unspeakably bourgeois they are! They can't actually be real, they must all have stepped out of a play by Labiche!'*

The Cottards would be there, and perhaps Brichot too. 'Could anything be more grotesque than the lives of these nonentities, living constantly in each other's pockets. They'd feel completely lost, I'm sure they would, if they didn't all meet up again tomorrow *at Chatou*!' Oh God! The painter would be there too, the painter who was so fond of 'matchmaking', who would invite Forcheville to visit his studio with Odette. He could see Odette, terribly overdressed for a country outing, 'because she's so vulgar, and especially, the poor thing, so stupid!!!'

He could hear the jokes Madame Verdurin would make after dinner, jokes which, whoever the 'bore' might be at whom they were aimed, had always amused him because he saw Odette laughing, laughing with him, her laughter mingling with his. Now he felt that perhaps they would make Odette laugh at him. 'What a fetid sense of humour they have!' he said, twisting his mouth into an expression of disgust so violent that he could feel the muscles in his neck press against his shirt collar. 'How on earth can a creature whose face is made in God's image find anything to laugh at in those nauseating jokes? Anyone with the slightest sense of smell has to turn away in horror to avoid the offensive stench. It's quite incredible to think that a human being can fail to understand that, by smiling at the expense of a fellow human being who has held out a trusting hand, she's allowing herself to sink into a slimy pit from which it will be impossible, with the best will in the world, ever to rescue her. I exist on a level so far above the swamp where those filthy vermin squat gabbing and blabbing, that I can't possibly be spattered by the jokes of a Verdurin!' he cried, tossing his head and proudly throwing back his shoulders. 'God knows I've honestly tried to pull Odette up out of there, and lift her into a nobler and purer atmosphere. But any human being has just so much patience, and mine is exhausted,' he said to himself, as though this mission to tear Odette away from an atmosphere of sarcasms dated from longer ago than the last few minutes, and as though he hadn't embarked upon it only when it had occurred to him that their sarcasms might be aimed at him and were intended to separate Odette from him.

He could see the pianist sitting down to play the 'Moonlight' Sonata, and the faces Madame Verdurin would pull as she grew increasingly alarmed at the disastrous effect Beethoven's music would have on her nerves: 'Idiot! Liar!' he exclaimed. 'And the woman makes out that she loves *Art*!' She'd say to Odette, after cleverly slipping in a few words of praise for Forcheville, as she had so often done for him: 'Make some room next to you for Monsieur de Forcheville.' 'In the dark, too! She's a pimp! A procuress!' 'Procuress' was the name he applied also to the music that would invite them to sit quietly, to dream together, to gaze into each other's eyes, to take each other by the hand. He felt there was something to be said for the austere view of the arts held by Plato and Bossuet, and the old system of education in France.*

In fact, the life one led at the Verdurins', which he'd so often described as 'the kind of life one should lead', seemed to him now the worst type of all, and their little clan the lowest of social circles. 'They really are', he said, 'at the bottom of the social ladder, Dante's last circle.* It's obvious that that venerable text refers to the Verdurins! When you think about it, real society people, whatever you may say about them, are quite other than that uncouth lot, and demonstrate their profound wisdom in refusing to know them, or so much as sully the tips of their fingers with them! What sound intuition there is in that *Noli me tangere** of the Faubourg Saint-Germain!' He had now left far behind the avenues of the Bois and had almost arrived home, but had still not yet got over his pain and the feats of insincerity which the false tones and artificial sonority of his own voice were raising to ever greater heights, and went on perorating aloud in the silence of the night: 'Society people have their faults, as no one knows better than I do, but all the same they are people for whom certain things are simply impossible. I used to know a certain society lady who was far from perfect, but all the same had a basic delicacy and a sense of honour in her dealings with people that would have made her incapable, under any circumstances, of any sort of treachery, and that's enough to show the vast gulf between her and a harridan like that Verdurin woman. Verdurin! What a name! Oh, we can certainly say they're the perfect, the ultimate specimens of their kind! Thank God, I can now stop demeaning myself by mixing with those vile, appalling people!'

But, just as the virtues he was until that very afternoon still attributing to the Verdurins, even if they'd actually possessed them but had done nothing to foster his love for Odette, wouldn't have been enough to rouse Swann into raptures about their magnanimity—raptures which could only have been inspired in him by the influence of Odette working through others—similarly, the immorality he now saw in the Verdurins, even if it had really existed but they had not invited Odette with Forcheville and excluded him, would have been insufficient to unleash his wrath and induce him to denounce their 'infamy'. And no doubt Swann's voice was more perceptive than he was himself, when it refused to pronounce these words of revulsion towards the Verdurin circle and his joy at being free of it, except in an affected tone, and as if they'd been chosen rather to relieve his anger than to express his thoughts. Indeed, while he was giving vent to his invectives, his thoughts, without his noticing it, were probably occupied with a wholly different matter, for when he arrived home, scarcely had he closed the main door behind him than he suddenly clapped his hand to his forehead and, reopening the door, went out again exclaiming in a natural voice this time: 'I think I've found a way of getting myself invited to the dinner at Chatou tomorrow!' But it must not have been a good way, for he wasn't invited: Doctor Cottard, who'd been called away to attend to a patient in the country and had therefore not seen the Verdurins for several days and had been unable to go to Chatou, said, as he sat down at their table the day after the dinner: 'So, aren't we going to see Monsieur Swann this evening? He's surely what one calls a personal friend of the . . .'

'I should certainly hope not!' exclaimed Madame Verdurin. 'God forbid! He's terribly dull, stupid, and ill-mannered.'

At these words Cottard showed his surprise and, simultaneously, his submission, as though confronted with a truth contrary to everything he'd believed until then, but which was incontrovertibly obvious; and looking rather nervous and fearful, buried his nose in his plate and simply replied: 'Ah! Ah! Ah! Ah! Ah!', traversing, on a descending scale, the entire register of his voice in his forced but orderly retreat into the depths of his being. Swann was never mentioned again at the Verdurins'.

So the drawing room that had brought Swann and Odette together became an obstacle to their meetings. She no longer said, as in the early days of their love: 'We'll see each other tomorrow night anyway, there's a supper at the Verdurins',' but: 'We won't be able to see each other tomorrow night, there's a supper at the Verdurins'.' Or else the Verdurins would have arranged to take her to the Opéra-Comique to see *Une nuit de Cléopâtre** and Swann would read in Odette's eyes her fear of his asking her not to go, to which, quite recently, he wouldn't have been able to stop himself responding with a kiss as it flitted across his mistress's face, but which now exasperated him. 'Yet it's not anger I feel,' he said to himself, 'when I see that she wants to go and dip into that excremental music. It's sadness, not for myself of course, but for her; sadness at seeing that after more than six months of living in daily contact with me, she hasn't managed to change enough to reject Victor Massé spontaneously! Especially that she hasn't managed to understand that there are evenings when a person of any sensitivity at all must be able to give up a pleasure when asked to do so. She ought to be able to say "I won't go," if only because it's the intelligent thing to do, because it's by her answer that her innermost qualities will be judged once and for all.' And having persuaded himself that it really was only in order to have a higher opinion of Odette's spiritual worth that he wanted her to stay with him that evening instead of going to the Opéra-Comique, he followed the same line of reasoning with her, with the same degree of insincerity that he'd used with himself, and even with one degree more, for now he was also in the grip of his desire to catch her through her vanity.

'I swear', he said to her a few moments before she left for the theatre, 'that in asking you not to go, I'd really be wishing, if I were thinking only of myself, that you'd refuse, because I've got so many

things to do this evening and I'll feel caught out and quite annoyed if
you tell me now all of a sudden that you're not going. But my own
occupations, my own pleasures, aren't everything, I must think of you.
The day may come when I won't see you any more, and then you'd
have every right to reproach me with having failed to warn you at the
crucial time, when I felt I was about to pass judgement on you, to make
one of those terrible criticisms that do so much damage to feelings of
love. You see, *Une nuit de Cléopâtre* (what a title!) has nothing to do
with what I'm saying. What's important is whether you're really a creature devoid of all spiritual values, and even lacking in charm, the sort
of despicable creature who always puts her own pleasure first. If that's
what you are, how could anyone love you, because you're not even
a person, a clearly defined entity, imperfect but at least perfectible?
You're just a formless stream of water running down any slope it finds,
a fish devoid of memory, incapable of thought, which no matter how
long it spends in its aquarium, will always mistake the glass for water
and bump against it a hundred times a day. Do you realize that your
answer will have the effect—I won't say of making me stop loving you
immediately, of course, but of making you less attractive in my eyes
when I realize that you're not a person, that you're a slave to everything
and don't know how to rise above anything? Obviously I'd have preferred to ask you as a thing of no importance to give up your *Nuit de
Cléopâtre* (since you make me soil my lips with that despicable name)
in the hope that you'd go anyway. But since I've decided to attach this
importance to your answer and draw these inferences from it, I thought
it would only be fair to let you know.'

For a few moments, Odette had been showing signs of being upset
and confused. Although she was unable to grasp the meaning of this
speech, she did understand that it might belong to the general category of 'scoldings' and scenes of reproach and supplication, and her
familiarity with the ways of men enabled her, without paying attention to the details of what they said, to conclude that they wouldn't
make such pronouncements unless they were in love, and that since
they were in love it wasn't necessary to obey them, as they would only
be more in love afterwards. And so she would have listened to Swann
with the utmost calm if she hadn't noticed that the time was getting
on and that if he went on talking much longer, she would, as she told
him with a smile that was loving, obstinate, and abashed, 'end up
missing the Overture!'

On other occasions he told her that the one thing that was more likely than anything to make him stop loving her was her refusal to stop lying. 'Even from the point of view of your attractiveness as a woman,' he said, 'can't you see how unattractive you make yourself when you stoop to lying? Think how many faults you could redeem with a single confession! You're really far less intelligent than I thought!' But it was in vain that Swann thus expounded for her all the good reasons she had for not lying; they might have undermined some general and systematic approach to lying, but Odette had no such system; whenever she didn't want Swann to know about something she'd done, she simply didn't tell him. In other words, lying was for her an expedient of a particular order; and the only thing that could determine whether she should make use of it or tell the truth was a reason also of a particular order: how likely or unlikely it was that Swann would discover that she hadn't told him the truth.

Physically, she was going through a bad phase: she was putting on weight; and the expressive, doleful charm, the wide, dreamy eyes she used to have seemed to have disappeared with her first youth, with the result that she'd become so dear to Swann at the very moment, as it were, when he found her distinctly less pretty. He'd gaze at her for minutes at a time, trying to rediscover the charm he'd once seen in her, and couldn't find it. But knowing that within the new chrysalis, what lived on was still Odette, still the same will, evanescent, elusive, and sly, was enough to make Swann pursue her with as much passion as before. He would also look at photographs of her taken two years before, and remember how exquisite she'd been. And that would console him a little for all the trouble and distress she caused him.

When the Verdurins carried her off to Saint-Germain, or to Chatou, or to Meulan, as often as not, if the weather was fine, they'd suggest on the spot that they should stay the night and not go back until the next day. Madame Verdurin would try to allay the scruples of the pianist, whose aunt had stayed behind in Paris: 'She'll be very pleased to be rid of you for a day. And why should she be worried, she knows you're with us; in any case, I can take the blame.'

But if she didn't succeed, Monsieur Verdurin would be detailed to find a telegraph office or a messenger and enquire as to which of the 'faithful' had someone they needed to notify. But Odette would thank him and say she didn't need to send anyone a telegram, because she'd told Swann once and for all that if she were to send him one in front of everybody, she'd be compromising herself. There were times when she'd be gone for several days, when the Verdurins took her to see the tombs at Dreux, or, on the recommendation of the painter, to Compiègne to admire the sunsets in the forest, from where they'd go as far as the château at Pierrefonds.

'To think she could visit real historic buildings with me, who studied architecture for ten years and am forever being implored to take people of very high standing to Beauvais or Saint-Loup-de-Naud, but would do it only for her, and instead she goes off with those absolute dullards to swoon over the dejecta of Louis-Philippe and Viollet-le-Duc! If you ask me, you don't need to be very artistic to do that, and you don't need to have a particularly sensitive nose to decide not to spend your holidays in the latrines in order to be closer to the smell of excrement.'

But when she'd left for Dreux or Pierrefonds—without, alas, allowing him to go too, and turn up there as if by chance, because 'that would make a terrible impression' she said—he'd plunge into that most intoxicating of romances, the railway timetable, which showed him the various means by which he could join her, in the afternoon, in the evening, or that very morning! Not just the means, but more than that, almost the authorization. Because, after all, the timetable and the trains themselves were not meant for dogs. If the public was informed, by means of the printed word, that at eight o'clock in the morning a train left for Pierrefonds and arrived there at ten, it could only be because going to Pierrefonds was a lawful act, for which permission from Odette was superfluous; an act, moreover, that could have a motive completely different from the desire to see Odette, since people who had never heard of her performed it every day, and in large enough numbers for it to be worth the trouble of stoking the locomotives.

So, all things considered, she could hardly stop him from going to Pierrefonds if he felt like it! In fact, he felt that he did want to, and that, if he hadn't known Odette, he certainly would have gone. For ages he'd wanted to become more familiar with Viollet-le-Duc's restoration work. And since the weather was so good, he felt an overwhelming desire to go for a walk in the forest at Compiègne.

It really was bad luck that she'd forbidden him the only spot that tempted him today. Today! If he ignored her prohibition and went there, he might see her *today*! But whereas, if at Pierrefonds she'd met someone who didn't matter, she would have said joyfully: 'I say! What are you doing here!', and would have invited him to come and see her at the hotel where she was staying with the Verdurins, if it was him, Swann, that she ran into, she'd be offended, she'd think she was being followed, she'd love him less, perhaps she'd turn away in anger when she saw him. 'So, I'm not allowed to travel any more!' she'd say to him on their return, whereas he was the one who was not allowed to travel!

At one point, he'd had the idea, in order to be able to go to Compiègne and Pierrefonds without making it seem that he was doing so to meet Odette, of arranging to be taken there by one of his friends, the Marquis de Forestelle, who had a château in that part of the country. The marquis, to whom he'd mentioned his plan without revealing the reason for it, was beside himself with joy and marvelled at the fact that Swann, for the first time in fifteen years, was finally consenting to come and see his estate, and since he didn't want to stay there, as he'd told him, at least promised to spend a few days going on walks and excursions with him. Swann could already picture himself with Monsieur de Forestelle. Even before seeing Odette there, or even if he didn't manage to see her, how happy he'd be to set foot on that earth where, not knowing the exact location, at any given moment, of her person, he'd feel all around him the thrilling possibility of her suddenly appearing: in the courtyard of the château, which now seemed so beautiful because it was on her account that he'd gone to see it; in every street of the town, which to his eyes took on a fantastical air; on every path of the forest, rosy in the deep, soft sunset;—in an infinity of alternative nooks where, in the uncertain ubiquity of his hopes, his happy, errant, and divided heart would simultaneously take refuge. 'On no account,' he would warn Monsieur de Forestelle, 'must we run into Odette and the Verdurins. As it happens, I've just heard that they're at Pierrefonds today. We've got plenty of time to see each other in Paris, it would hardly be worth the trouble of leaving Paris if neither of us could take a step without the other.' And his friend would be at a loss to understand why, once he was there, he'd change his plans twenty times a day, inspect the dining rooms of all the hotels in Compiègne without making up his mind to sit down in any of them even though they bore no trace of the Verdurins, seeming to be searching for the very thing he'd said he wanted to avoid (and would indeed avoid) as soon as he found it, for if he'd come upon the little group, he would have made a show of avoiding them, happy to have seen Odette and that she'd seen him, especially that she'd seen him apparently not thinking of her at all. But no, she'd certainly guess it was on her account that he was there. And when Monsieur de Forestelle came to pick him up, and it was time to set off, he said: 'Alas, no, I can't go to Pierrefonds today, Odette's there, you see.' And Swann was happy despite everything to feel that if he, alone among mortals, wasn't allowed to go to Pierrefonds that day, it was because for Odette he was in fact someone different from other people, her lover, and that the restriction that was applied in his case alone to the universal right to freedom was merely one of the forms of that servitude, that love which was so dear to him. It was certainly better not to risk quarrelling with her, to be patient, to wait for her to come back to Paris. He spent his days poring over a map of the forest of Compiègne as though it was the *Carte du Tendre*,* and surrounded himself with photographs of the château at Pierrefonds. On the first day when it was just possible that she might be on her way back, he opened the timetable again, calculated which train she must have taken and, in the event of her being delayed, those she could still take. He didn't leave the house for fear of missing a telegram, didn't go to bed in case she'd returned on the last train and wanted to surprise him by coming to see him in the middle of the night. In fact he heard the bell at the street door, and it seemed to him that they were slow to open it, he wanted to wake up the concierge, went to the window to call out to Odette if it was she, for in spite of the instructions he'd gone down more than a dozen times to give the servants himself, they were quite capable of telling her he was not at home. It was a servant coming in. He noticed the incessant stream of carriages passing by, to which he'd never paid attention in the past. He listened to each one coming from far off, drawing near, and passing his door without stopping, and bearing far away a message that wasn't for him. He waited all night, quite pointlessly, for the Verdurins had decided to come back early, and Odette had been in Paris since noon; it hadn't occurred to her to tell him, and not knowing what to do with herself she'd spent the evening alone at a theatre, had long since gone to bed, and was now asleep.

In fact, she hadn't given him so much as a thought. And occasions such as this, when she forgot Swann's very existence, were more useful to Odette, did more to attach Swann to her, than all her coquetry.

Because in this way he was kept in the state of painful agitation that had already been powerful enough to make his love blossom on the night when he failed to find her at the Verdurins' and had looked for her all evening. And unlike myself as a child in Combray, he didn't have happy days in which to forget the sufferings that return at night. He spent his days without Odette; and there were times when he said to himself that to allow such a pretty woman to go out alone in Paris was like leaving a case full of jewels in the middle of the street. Then he'd glare at all the men passing by as if they were so many thieves. But their faces, formless and collective, escaped the grasp of his imagination and didn't feed his jealousy. Swann's mind would become exhausted until, putting his hand over his eyes, he'd cry out: 'Heaven help me!', like people who have worn themselves out grappling with the problem of the reality of the external world or the immortality of the soul,* and relieve their weary minds with an act of faith. But the thought of his absent mistress was inextricably linked with the simplest everyday actions—having lunch, receiving his mail, leaving the house, going to bed—by the very sadness he felt at having to perform them without her, like the initials of Philippe le Beau, which, in the church at Brou, because of the longing she felt for him, Margaret of Austria intertwined everywhere with her own.* On certain days, instead of staying at home, he'd go and have his lunch in a nearby restaurant to which he'd once been attracted by its good cooking and to which he now went only for one of those reasons, at once mystical and absurd, that we call romantic: because the restaurant (which still exists) bore the same name as the street in which Odette lived—*Lapérouse*. Sometimes, when she'd gone away for a short period, it was only after several days that she thought of letting him know she'd returned to Paris. And then she'd say quite simply, no longer taking the precaution as she once had of covering herself, just in case, with a little fragment borrowed from the truth, that she'd only got back just then by the morning train. This statement was untrue; at least for Odette it was untrue, lacking substance, not having what it would have had if true—a basis in her memory of her arrival at the station; indeed, as she uttered these words, she was prevented from forming a picture to herself of what the words purported to be true by the contradictory image of whatever quite different thing she'd been doing when, according to her, she was getting off the train. In Swann's mind, however, there was no such obstacle to her words and they encrusted themselves, assuming the indelibility of a truth so absolute that if a friend told him he'd come by the same train and hadn't seen Odette, Swann would be convinced that it was the friend who was mistaken about the day or the hour, since his account didn't accord with what Odette had said. Her words would have seemed to him false only if he'd suspected beforehand that they were. For him to believe she was lying, a previous suspicion was a necessary condition. In fact it was also a sufficient condition. Then everything Odette said would seem suspect. If he heard her mention a name, it was certainly the name of one of her lovers; once the supposition was forged, he'd spend weeks in a state of torment; on one occasion he even contacted a private investigator to ascertain the address and occupation of his unknown rival, who would give him no peace until he went away, and who, he eventually learned, was an uncle of Odette's who'd been dead for twenty years.

Although as a rule she didn't allow him to meet her in public places, saying people would talk, it happened now and again that he'd attend a soirée to which she'd also been invited—at Forcheville's, at the painter's, or at a charity ball in one of the ministries—and would find himself there at the same time as she. He saw her but didn't dare to stay for fear of irritating her by seeming to be spying on the pleasures she was enjoying with other people, pleasures which—as he drove home alone, and went to bed as troubled as I was to be some years later, on the evenings when he came to dinner in Combray—seemed to him boundless because he hadn't seen the end of them. And once or twice on such evenings he experienced the sort of happiness which, had it not been so violently affected by the recoil from the sudden cessation of anxiety, it might be tempting to call a tranquil happiness, since it consisted of a return to a state of calm: for instance, he'd dropped in on a party at the painter's and was about to depart, leaving behind him Odette transformed into a brilliant stranger, surrounded by men to whom her glances and her gaiety, which were not for him, seemed to speak of some sensual pleasure to be enjoyed there or elsewhere (perhaps at the 'Bal des Incohérents',* where he dreaded she might go afterwards) and which caused Swann more jealousy even than physical intimacy because he found it more difficult to imagine; he was on the point of going through the studio door when he heard himself being called back with these words (which, by removing from the party the possible ending that had filled him with such dread, transformed it retrospectively into something innocent, made Odette's return home something no longer unimaginable and terrible, but sweet and familiar, something that would stay beside him in his carriage like a part of his everyday life, and divested Odette herself of the excessive brilliance and gaiety of her appearance, showing that it was only a disguise she'd assumed for a moment, for its own sake, not with a view to mysterious pleasures, and of which she was already tired)—with these words that Odette tossed to him as he was crossing the threshold: 'Would you mind staying another five minutes? I'm about to leave, we could go together and you could take me home.'

It was true that on one occasion Forcheville had asked to be taken back at the same time, but when they arrived at Odette's door and he asked to be allowed to come in too, Odette had responded by pointing to Swann and saying: 'Ah! That depends on this gentleman here. Ask him. Well, you can come in for a little while if you want, but you mustn't stay too long, because, I warn you, he likes to have a quiet chat with me, and he doesn't much like me to have visitors when he's here. Ah, if you knew that creature as well as I do! Isn't that so, *my love*,* I'm the only one who really knows you?'

And Swann was perhaps even more touched to see her addressing him in this way, in front of Forcheville, not only with these words of affection and special favour, but also with certain criticisms like: 'I'm sure you haven't answered your friends yet about that dinner on Sunday. Don't go if you don't want to, but at least be polite,' or: 'Now, have you left your essay on Vermeer here so you can do a little more of it tomorrow? You're so lazy! I'll make you work—you'll see!', which proved that Odette kept abreast of his social engagements and his writings on art, and that the two of them really did have a life together. And as she said this she gave him a smile that made him feel she was entirely his.

At moments like this, while she was making orangeade for them, suddenly, as when a faulty reflector starts to cast on the wall, around a certain object, big fantastic shadows, which then shrink and disappear into it, all the terrible shifting ideas he'd formed about Odette would vanish, would dissolve into the charming body Swann saw before him. He had the sudden suspicion that this hour spent at Odette's house, in the lamplight, was perhaps not an artificial hour, invented just for him (intended to disguise that alarming and delightful thing that was constantly in his thoughts without his ever being able to form a clear picture of it, an hour in Odette's real life, in Odette's life when he wasn't there), with stage props and imitation fruit, but was perhaps a real hour of Odette's life, and that if he hadn't been there she would have offered the same armchair to Forcheville and poured him not some unknown drink, but that same orangeade, that the world inhabited by Odette was not that other frightful and supernatural world in which he regularly placed her, and which perhaps existed only in his imagination, but the real world, with no special aura of sadness, and including that table at which he was going to be able to write and that drink which he would be allowed to taste, all those objects which he contemplated with as much admiration and curiosity as gratitude, for if by absorbing his dreams they'd delivered him from them, they in return had been enriched by them, they showed him the palpable realization of those dreams, and they intrigued his mind, taking shape before his eyes at the same time that they soothed his heart. Ah, if Fate had but allowed him to share a single home with Odette, so that in her house he'd be at home, if he asked the servant what there was for lunch, it would have been Odette's menu he was given in reply, and if when Odette wanted to take a morning walk in the Avenue du Bois de Boulogne, his duty as a good husband would have obliged him to accompany her, even if he had no desire to go out, and to carry her coat when she was too warm, and if after dinner she wanted to spend a relaxed evening at home, if he'd been forced to stay with her, doing whatever she asked; then all the trivial details of his life which now seemed to him so sad, even the most familiar of them—like the lamp, the orangeade, the armchair, the things that contained so much of his dreams, materialized so much desire—would have taken on, precisely because they would also be part of Odette's life, a sort of superabundant sweetness and mysterious density.

And yet he suspected that what he yearned for was a state of tranquillity, of peace, which would not have provided a propitious atmosphere for his love. When Odette ceased to be for him a creature always absent, longed for, imagined, when the feeling he had for her was no longer the same mysterious disturbance provoked in him by the phrase from the sonata, but affection and gratitude, when normal relations were established between them, putting an end to his madness and melancholy, then no doubt the actions of Odette's daily life would seem of little interest in themselves—as he'd already suspected on several occasions, for instance on the day when he'd read through the envelope the letter addressed to Forcheville. Contemplating his malady with as much analytical detachment as if he'd inoculated himself with it in order to study it, he told himself that once he'd recovered, whatever Odette might do would be a matter of indifference to him. Even so, the truth was that, in his morbid state, he dreaded such a recovery as much as death itself, for it would in fact have meant the death of everything he then was.

After these quiet evenings, Swann's suspicions would subside; he would think kindly of Odette, and the next day, early in the morning, he would order the finest jewellery to be sent round to her house, because her kind attentions of the night before had excited either his gratitude, or a desire to see them repeated, or a paroxysm of love which needed to find expression.

But at other times his anguish would return, he would imagine that Odette was Forcheville's mistress, and that when, the day before the outing to Chatou to which he hadn't been invited, the two of them had sat watching him from the depths of the Verdurins' landau* in the Bois, as he begged her in vain to go back with him, with that look of despair which even his coachman had noticed, and then turned away, alone and defeated, she must have had, as she drew Forcheville's attention to him and said: 'Look how furious he is!', the same gleam in her eyes, the same malicious, base, sly expression as on the day when Forcheville had driven Saniette from the Verdurins' house.

At moments like this, Swann hated her. 'Just look at me, I'm such a fool,' he'd tell himself. 'I'm actually paying for other people's pleasures. All the same, she'd better be careful and not push her luck, because I might well decide to stop giving her anything at all. At any rate, let's put an end, for the time being, to all the extra favours! To think that only yesterday, when she said she wanted to go to Bayreuth for the season,* I was stupid enough to offer to rent, for the two of us, one of those pretty little castles the King of Bavaria has in the neighbourhood! But she didn't seem awfully keen! She hasn't said yes or no yet; let's hope she'll decide against it. My God! The idea of spending two weeks listening to Wagner with a woman like that, who couldn't care less about music—what fun that would be!' And since his hatred, like his love, needed to find an outlet and be acted upon, he took pleasure in pursuing his evil fantasies further and further, since, because of the perfidies he attributed to Odette, he hated her even more, and, if they turned out to be true (something he tried very hard to picture), he'd have an opportunity to punish her and to vent on her his mounting rage. Thus he went so far as to imagine that he'd soon receive a letter in which she'd ask for money to rent the castle near Bayreuth, but with the warning that he shouldn't go there himself, because she'd promised to invite Forcheville and the Verdurins. How he would have liked her to be so bold! How he would have enjoyed refusing, as he wrote the vengeful answer, the terms of which he took satisfaction in choosing, in declaiming out loud, as if he'd actually received the letter!

Yet, this was what happened the very next day. She wrote that the Verdurins and their friends had expressed a desire to attend the performances of Wagner, and that, if he'd be so good as to send her the money, she would at last have the pleasure, after having been invited so often to their house, of inviting them in her turn. As for him, she said not a word, the implication being that their presence excluded his.

And so, the terrible answer, every word of which he'd carefully chosen the day before without daring to hope that they could ever be used, could now, to his delight, be sent round to her. But sadly, he felt certain that, whether with her own money or with money she could easily find elsewhere, she'd still be able to rent something at Bayreuth, since she wanted to do so, she who was incapable of telling the difference between Bach and Clapisson.* However, she'd have to live more modestly. There was no way, as there would have been had he simply sent her a few thousand-franc bills, of organizing every evening, in some castle, one of those exquisite supper parties after which she might indulge the whim—which it was possible she'd never yet had—of falling into Forcheville's arms. At least he, Swann, wouldn't be the one who would foot the bill for this loathsome trip! If only he could do something to prevent it! If she could sprain an ankle before setting out, or if the coachman who was to take her to the station would agree, at no matter what price, to drive her to some place where she could be kept for a while in seclusion—that perfidious woman, her eyes glittering with a smile of complicity with Forcheville, that Odette had become for Swann in the last forty-eight hours!

But she was never that for very long; after a few days, the sly gleam in her eyes would fade, and the picture of a hateful Odette saying to Forcheville: 'Look how furious he is!' would fade and dissolve. Then, gradually, the face of the other Odette would reappear and rise up, gently radiant, the Odette who also offered a smile to Forcheville, but a smile in which there was nothing but affection for Swann, when she said: 'You mustn't stay too long, because this gentleman doesn't much like me to receive visitors when he's here. Ah, if you only knew this creature as well as I do!'—the same smile she wore when thanking Swann for an instance of his courtesy, which she prized so highly, or for some advice for which she'd asked during one of those times of difficulty when he was the only person she felt she could turn to.

Then, thinking of this other Odette, he'd ask himself how he could have written that outrageous letter, of which until now she'd probably thought him incapable, and which must have brought him down from the high, very special place which by his kindness and devotion he'd won in her esteem. He would now become less dear to her, because it was for those qualities, which she didn't find in Forcheville or in any other man, that she loved him. It was because of them that Odette so often showed a warmth towards him that counted for nothing when he was jealous, because it wasn't a sign of desire, and even gave proof of affection rather than love, but whose importance he began once more to feel in proportion as the spontaneous relaxation of his suspicions, a relaxation often accelerated by the distraction he found in reading about art or in conversation with a friend, caused his passion to become less demanding of reciprocities.

Now that, after this oscillation, Odette had naturally returned to the place from which Swann's jealousy had momentarily removed her, to the angle from which he found her charming, he pictured her to himself as full of tenderness, with a look of consent in her eyes, and so pretty thus that he could not help offering her his lips as if she'd been there and he'd been able to kiss her; and he felt as strong a sense of gratitude towards her for that enchanting, kindly glance as if it had been real, as if he'd not simply conjured it up in his imagination to satisfy his desire.

How he must have hurt her! Of course, he could find valid reasons for his resentment, but they wouldn't have been enough to make him feel that resentment if he hadn't loved her so much. Had he not had equally serious grievances against other women, for whom he would nevertheless have been happy to do favours now, feeling no anger towards them because he no longer loved them? If the day ever came when he found himself in the same state of indifference towards Odette, he would understand that it was his jealousy alone that had made him find something repugnant, unforgivable, in her desire (so understandable, after all, springing as it did from an element of childishness in her nature and also from a certain delicacy of spirit), to be able, since the opportunity had arisen, to return some of the Verdurins' hospitality, and to play the lady of the house herself.

He returned to this other point of view—which was the opposite of the one based on his love and jealousy, and which he adopted sometimes through a sort of intellectual equity and in order to allow for the various probabilities—and tried to judge Odette as if he'd never been in love with her, as if she were like any other woman, as if her life, as soon as he was no longer present, hadn't been different, like a plot being hatched against him behind his back.

Why should he think that there she would enjoy, with Forcheville or with other men, intoxicating pleasures which she'd never experienced with him and which his jealousy alone had fabricated out of nothing? In Bayreuth as in Paris, if Forcheville happened to think of him at all, it would only be as of someone who occupied an important place in Odette's life, to whom he was obliged to defer when they met at her house. If Forcheville and she gloated at the idea of being there together in spite of him, it was he who was to blame for it by trying in vain to prevent her from going, whereas if he'd approved of her plan, which was in fact defensible, she would have appeared to be there on his recommendation, she would have felt that she'd been sent there, housed there by him, and she would have had him to thank for the pleasure of entertaining those people who had so often entertained her.

And if—instead of letting her go off on bad terms with him, without having seen him again—he sent her the money, if he encouraged her to make the trip and did all he could to make it pleasant for her, she would come running, happy and grateful, and he would have the joy of seeing her, a joy he hadn't experienced for nearly a week and which nothing could replace. Because as soon as Swann could picture her without a feeling of revulsion, as soon as he saw once again the warmth of her smile, and as soon as the desire to take her away from any other man was not mixed in with his love by jealousy, that love became once again mainly a taste for the sensations that Odette's person gave him, for the pleasure he took in admiring as a spectacle, or exploring as a phenomenon, the dawn of one of her glances, the formation of one of her smiles, the sound of a certain tone of voice. And this pleasure, different from all others, had in the end created in him a need for her that she alone, by her presence or her letters, could satisfy, almost as disinterested, almost as artistic, as perverse, as another need that characterized this new period in Swann's life, in which the aridity, the depression of earlier years had been succeeded by a sort of spiritual overabundance, without his knowing to what he owed this unexpected enrichment of his inner life, any more than a person of poor health knows why, at a certain moment, he begins to grow stronger, put on weight, and seems for a time to be on the road to a complete recovery: that other need, which was also developing independently of the material world, was the need to hear and learn about music.

And so, through the very chemistry of his disease, after he'd created jealousy out of his love, he began again to manufacture affection and pity for Odette. She'd become once more his sweet, enchanting Odette. He was full of remorse at having treated her badly. He wanted her to come to him, and, before she came, wanted to have prepared for her some pleasure, so as to see her gratitude take shape in her face and mould her smile.

And Odette, certain that she would see him come back to her after a few days, as loving and submissive as before, to ask for a reconciliation, lost all fear of displeasing him or even of making him angry, and refused him, whenever it suited her, the favours he valued most.

Perhaps she didn't realize how sincere he'd been with her during their quarrel, when he'd told her he wouldn't send her any money and would try to hurt her. Perhaps she didn't realize, either, how sincere he was, if not with her, at least with himself, on other occasions when, for the sake of the future of their relationship, so as to show Odette that he was capable of living without her, that a break between them was always possible, he decided to let some time pass without going to see her again.

Sometimes it would be after several days during which she'd given him no fresh cause for anxiety; and since he knew that his next few visits to her house wouldn't give him any great joy, but more probably some annoyance that would put an end to his present state of calm, he'd send her a note to say he was very busy and wouldn't be able to see her on any of the days he'd suggested. Then a letter from her, crossing with his, asked him to change one of those very meetings. He wondered why; his suspicions, his anguish, took hold of him again. In the new state of agitation in which he found himself, he could no longer abide by the commitment he'd made to himself in his earlier state of relative calm, and he'd hurry round to her house and demand to see her on every one of the following days. And even if she hadn't written first, if she merely replied that she agreed to his request that they stop seeing each other for a while, this was enough to make him unable to go on without seeing her. For, contrary to Swann's expectations, Odette's agreement to his suggestion had brought about a complete change in his attitude. Like all those who possess some particular thing, in order to know what would happen if he ceased for a moment to possess it, he'd removed it from his mind, leaving everything else in the same state as when it was there. But the absence of a thing isn't merely that, it isn't simply a partial lack, it's a disruption of everything else, it's a new state which cannot be foreseen in the old.

But there were other occasions—Odette's imminent departure on a trip, for instance—when, using some trivial dispute as his excuse, he'd resolve not to write to her and not to see her again until her return, thus giving the appearance, and expecting the benefit, of a serious break, which she'd perhaps imagine to be final, to a separation the greater part of which was the unavoidable consequence of her trip, which he was simply allowing to begin a little earlier than planned. Already he could picture Odette worried and distressed at having received neither a visit nor a letter from him, and this image of her, by soothing his jealousy, made it easier for him to break the habit of seeing her. At times, no doubt, in a remote part of his mind where his resolution had thrust it because of the long intervening period of the three weeks of accepted separation, it was with pleasure that he contemplated the idea that he'd see Odette again on her return; but this feeling was accompanied by so little impatience that he began to wonder whether he wouldn't happily double the duration of an abstinence so easy to bear. It had lasted so far only three days, a much shorter time than he'd often spent without seeing Odette and without having, as now, planned it in advance. And yet at this point a slight irritation or physical discomfort—by inciting him to regard the present moment as an exceptional moment, outside the rules, one in which common sense would allow him to accept the relief afforded by a pleasure and, until there might be some point in resuming the effort, to give his will a rest—suspended the action of the latter, which relaxed its grip; or, less than that, the recollection of something he'd forgotten to ask Odette, such as whether she'd decided on the colour in which she'd have her carriage repainted, or, with regard to an investment, whether it was ordinary or preference shares that she wanted him to buy (it was all very well to show her he could live without seeing her, but if it meant that the carriage had to be painted all over again, or the shares yielded no dividends, a lot of good *that* would have done him), and, like a taut piece of elastic when you let it go or the air in a compressor when you open it slightly, the idea of seeing her again sprang back from the far distance, where it had been kept, into the field of the present and of immediate possibilities.

It sprang back without meeting any further resistance, and was so irresistible, in fact, that Swann found it had been far less difficult to face the approach, one after another, of the fortnight he was to be separated from Odette than to wait the ten minutes his coachman needed to harness the carriage that was going to take him to her, minutes he spent in transports of impatience and joy, his mind returning constantly, in order to lavish upon it all his affection, to the idea of seeing her again, an idea which, by returning so suddenly, just when he thought it so far removed from him, had leapt back to the forefront of his consciousness. For this idea no longer encountered the obstacle of his desire to attempt immediately to resist it, a desire which had ceased to have any place in Swann's mind since, having proved to himself—or so he believed—that he was so easily capable of resisting it, he no longer saw any risk in postponing a plan of separation that he was now certain he could easily put into operation whenever he wished. Furthermore, this idea of seeing her again came back to him adorned with a novelty, a seductiveness, endowed with a virulence, which habit had dulled but which had been retempered in that privation, not of three days but of two weeks (for a period of abstinence must be calculated, by anticipation, as having lasted already until the final date assigned to it), and had converted what had been until then an expected pleasure that could easily be sacrificed into an unhoped-for happiness he was powerless to resist. Finally, the idea came back to him embellished by his ignorance of what Odette might have thought, might perhaps have done, on seeing that he'd given no sign of life, so that what he was now going to find was the thrilling revelation of an Odette almost unknown to him.

She, however, just as she'd assumed that his refusal to send her money was only a sham, took as a mere pretext to see her his coming to ask about the repainting of the carriage and the purchase of shares. For she was unable to reconstruct the various phases of the crises through which he was passing, and in the notion she'd formed of them there was no attempt to understand the way they worked; she considered them only in the light of what she knew beforehand—their necessary, unfailing, and always identical termination. A notion that was incomplete—and therefore all the more profound, perhaps—if it were to be judged from the point of view of Swann, who would no doubt have thought he was misunderstood by Odette, just as a drug addict or a consumptive, persuaded that they have been prevented, one by some outside event just when he was about to free himself from his habit, the other by a chance indisposition just when he was about to be finally cured, feel misunderstood by the doctor who doesn't attach the same importance to these alleged contingencies, which he sees as mere disguises, assumed, so as to make themselves felt again by his patients, by the vice and the morbid condition which, in reality, haven't ceased to weigh heavily and incurably upon them while they were indulging their dreams of reform or recovery. Indeed, Swann's love had reached the stage where the boldest of doctors or (in certain affections) of surgeons ask themselves whether to deprive a patient of his vice or to rid him of his disease is still reasonable or even possible.

Certainly, of the extent of his love Swann had no direct awareness. When he tried to measure it, it sometimes seemed to him diminished, reduced to almost nothing; for example, on certain days he'd recall the lack of pleasure, amounting almost to displeasure, which, before he fell in love with Odette, he'd felt for her expressive features and dull complexion. 'I'm definitely making progress,' he'd say to himself the next day. 'When I really think about it, I hardly enjoyed myself at all yesterday when I was in bed with her: it's odd, I actually found her ugly.' And, of course, he was quite sincere, but his love extended well beyond the domain of physical desire. Odette's person, in fact, now had very little to do with it. When his eyes fell on the photograph of Odette on his study table, or when she dropped in to see him, he found it difficult to identify her face, in the flesh or on pasteboard, with the constant, painful anxiety in his mind. He'd say to himself, almost with surprise: 'It's her!', as though suddenly we were to be shown in a particular, external form one of our illnesses, and found that it bore no resemblance to our suffering. 'It's her'—he would puzzle over what that actually meant; for what love and death have in common, much more than the vague things people are always saying, is that they make us probe deeper, for fear that its reality will elude us, into the mystery of personality. And this malady which Swann's love had become had spread to such an extent, was so intermingled with all his habits, with his every act and thought, with his health, his sleep, his whole existence, even with what he wished for after his death, was now so much part of him, that it couldn't have been torn out of him without destroying him almost entirely: as they say in surgery, his love was no longer operable.

This love of Swann's had so detached him from all other interests that when by chance he reappeared in society, telling himself that his connections in that world, like a beautiful setting (though Odette would probably not have been able to form any clear estimate of its value) might restore a little of his own value in her eyes (as indeed they might have done had these connections not been devalued by his love, which for Odette depreciated everything it touched by seeming to proclaim them less precious), what he felt there, along with his distress at being in places and among people she didn't know, was the same disinterested pleasure as he would have derived from a novel or a painting depicting the amusements of a leisured class, just as, in his own house, he enjoyed contemplating the smooth functioning of his domestic life, the elegance of his wardrobe and of his servants' liveries, the soundness of his investments, in the same way as, when reading Saint-Simon, who was one of his favourite authors, he enjoyed descriptions of the mechanics of daily life, the menus at Madame de Maintenon's dinners, or Lully's shrewd avarice and lavish lifestyle.* And to the small extent that this detachment was not absolute, the reason for the new pleasure Swann was savouring was that he could migrate for a while into the few and distant parts of himself that had remained almost untouched by his love and his sorrow. In this respect the personality which my great-aunt attributed to him as 'young Swann', as distinct from the more individual personality of Charles Swann, was the one in which he was now happiest. One day, wishing to send the Princesse de Parme some fruit for her birthday (and because she could often be useful to Odette indirectly, by enabling her to have seats at galas and jubilees), but not being sure how to order it, he'd entrusted the task to a cousin of his mother's, a lady who, delighted to run an errand for him, had written to him, when sending the account, that she hadn't ordered all the fruit at the same place, but the grapes from Crapote, whose speciality they were, the strawberries from Jauret, the pears from Chevet, who always had the best, and so on, 'each piece of fruit hand-picked and inspected by me'. And indeed, from the way the princess had thanked him, he'd been able to judge the flavour of the strawberries and the ripeness of the pears. But, above all, the words 'each piece of fruit hand-picked and inspected by me' had soothed his suffering by transporting his mind to a region he rarely visited, even though it was his by right as the heir to a rich upper-bourgeois family which had handed down from generation to generation, at his disposal whenever he wanted, a knowledge of the 'right addresses'* and the art of placing an order.

Indeed, he'd forgotten he was 'young Swann' for too long not to feel, when he became that person again for a moment, a keener pleasure than any he might have felt at other times but which had palled; and if the kindness shown towards him by bourgeois people, for whom he had always been 'young Swann', was less marked than that of the aristocracy (but in fact was more flattering, for with them at least it's always inseparable from respect), no letter from a royal personage, whatever princely entertainment it offered, could ever give him as much pleasure as a letter asking him to be a witness, or merely to be present, at a wedding in the family of some old friends of his parents, some of whom had continued to see him from time to time—like my grandfather, who, the year before, had invited him to my mother's wedding—while others barely knew him personally, but felt certain obligations of courtesy towards the son, the worthy successor, of the late Monsieur Swann.

But, because of his close ties, already so well established, with members of high society, they too, in a sense, were part of his house, his household, his family. Contemplation of his distinguished connections made him feel the same external support, the same reassurance, as when he gazed upon the fine properties, the fine silverware, the fine table linen, that had come down to him from his family. And the thought that if he were struck down at home by a sudden illness, his manservant would naturally run for help to the Duc de Chartres, the Prince de Reuss, the Duc de Luxembourg, and the Baron de Charlus, brought him the same consolation as our old Françoise derived from the knowledge that one day she'd be wrapped in a shroud of her own fine sheets, marked with her name, and not darned (or with such care that it gave an even clearer idea of her skill as a seamstress), a shroud which, since she saw it so often in her mind's eye, gave her a certain satisfying sense, if not of well-being, at least of self-esteem. But above all, since every action or thought of Swann's that concerned Odette was shaped and controlled by his unavowed feeling that he was, if not less dear to her, at any rate less pleasant to be with than anyone, even the most boring of the Verdurins' faithful—when he returned to a social world in which he was regarded as the very incarnation of elegance, was constantly sought after, whom people were always sorry not to see, he began once again to believe in the existence of a happier life, almost to feel an appetite for it, like an invalid who, bedridden for months, and on a strict diet, suddenly sees in a newspaper the menu for an official luncheon or an advertisement for a cruise round Sicily.

The excuses he made to these society friends were for not visiting them, while those he made to Odette were for not staying away from her. He even paid for his visits to her (asking himself at the end of each month, imagining he'd tried her patience somewhat by going to see her too often, whether it would be enough if he sent her four thousand francs) and for each one found a pretext, a present to take her, a piece of information she needed, or Monsieur de Charlus who happened to be on his way to see her and had insisted that he come with him. Or, in the absence of an excuse, he'd ask Monsieur de Charlus if he'd run over to her house and mention in the course of conversation, as if spontaneously, that he'd just remembered something he had to tell Swann, and would she be so kind as to ask him to come round right away; but more often than not Swann would wait in vain, and Monsieur de Charlus would tell him in the evening that his ruse hadn't worked. The result was that not only was she frequently away from Paris, even when she was there she saw very little of him, and now, each time he wanted to see her, she who, when she was in love with him, used to say: 'I'm always free' and 'What do I care what people think?', would invoke social conventions or plead some prior engagement. When he mentioned that he might be going to a charity event, or a private viewing, or a first night which she, too, would attend, she'd tell him that he was trying to flaunt their affair, that he was treating her like a prostitute. It reached the point that, in order to avoid being debarred from meeting her anywhere, Swann, knowing that she was acquainted with and was very fond of my great-uncle

Adolphe, and having once been a friend of his himself, went to see him one day in his little apartment in the Rue de Bellechasse to ask him to use his influence with Odette. Since she always adopted a lyrical tone when she spoke to Swann about my uncle, saying: 'Ah, yes, he's not like you, his friendship with me is such a splendid thing, a great and beautiful thing! He'd never have so little regard for me that he'd want to be seen with me everywhere in public!', Swann was perplexed, and did not know quite how lofty his own tone should be in talking about Odette to my uncle. He began by invoking her a priori excellence, her axiomatic and seraphic superhumanity, the revealed truth of her virtues, which could neither be demonstrated nor deduced from experience. 'I must talk to you. You know what an adorable creature Odette is, an absolute angel. And you also know what people are like in Paris. Not everyone sees Odette the way you and I see her. There are some people who think I'm cutting a rather ridiculous figure; she won't even let me be seen with her, at the theatre, for example. She respects your opinion enormously, so couldn't you have a word with her for me, to assure her she's exaggerating the harm I might be doing to her reputation by greeting her in public?'

My uncle advised Swann not to see Odette for a little while, saying that this would make her love him all the more; and he advised Odette to let Swann meet her wherever he liked. A few days later, Odette told Swann she'd just had the disappointing experience of discovering that my uncle was no different from other men: he'd tried to rape her. She calmed Swann down, for his first impulse was to go and challenge my uncle to a duel, but the next time they met he refused to shake his hand. He regretted this falling-out all the more because he'd hoped, had he seen my uncle again a few times and had managed to chat with him in strict confidence, to get him to shed some light on certain rumours regarding the life Odette had led when she lived in Nice. For my uncle was in the habit of spending his winters there, and Swann thought it might even have been there that he'd first met Odette. The few words someone had let slip in Swann's presence about a man who'd purportedly been Odette's lover had greatly disturbed him. But the things which, before knowing them, he would have regarded as terrible to learn and impossible to believe, were incorporated for ever, when he did learn of them, into his general sadness; he accepted them, he would have found it inconceivable that they might never have occurred. But each one of them left an indelible mark on the

picture he was forming of his mistress. He was even given to understand, at one point, that Odette's easy virtue, which he'd never have
suspected, was more or less common knowledge, and that in Baden
and Nice, when she used to go and spend a few months there, she'd
had a sort of amorous notoriety. He sought out certain womanizers, to
question them; but they were aware that he knew Odette; and besides,
he was afraid of reminding them of her, of putting them on her track.
But he, to whom nothing hitherto could have seemed as tedious as
everything relating to the cosmopolitan life of Baden or Nice, having
learned that Odette had perhaps led a rather wild life in those two
pleasure-spots, though he could never find out whether it had been
solely to satisfy financial needs which, thanks to him, she no longer
had, or from some form of capricious desire which might easily
return, now leaned in impotent, blind, dizzy anguish over the bottom-
less abyss that had swallowed up the early years of the Septennate,*
when one spent the winter on the Promenade des Anglais and the
summer beneath the linden trees at Baden, and saw in them a painful
but magnificent profundity, such as a poet might have lent them; and
if the reconstruction of the petty details of life on the Côte d'Azur
in those days could have helped him to understand something of
Odette's smile or the look in her eyes—candid and straightforward
though they were—he would have devoted to it more passion than an
aesthete studying the extant documents of fifteenth-century Florence
to gain greater insight into the soul of Botticelli's Primavera, his fair
Vanna, or his Venus.* He'd often sit gazing at her pensively, not saying
a word, and she'd say: 'You look so sad!' It was not so very long since
he'd switched from the idea that she was a good person, the equal of
the finest women he had ever known, to the idea that she was a kept
woman; conversely, he'd reverted more recently from the Odette de
Crécy who was perhaps too well known among a merry crowd of rakes
and philanderers, to this face whose expression was at times so gentle,
to this nature so human. He would ask himself: 'What does it matter
that in Nice everyone has heard of Odette de Crécy? Reputations
like that, even if true, are based on gossip and rumour.' He'd reflect that
the legend surrounding Odette, even if it was authentic, was something extraneous to her, was not innate, an irreducible and pernicious
aspect of her personality; that the creature who might have been led
into bad ways was a woman with kind eyes, a heart full of pity for the
suffering of others, a docile body which he'd held in his arms and felt

with his hands, a woman whom he might one day come to possess
entirely, if he succeeded in making himself indispensable to her.
She'd sit there, often tired, her face drained for a moment of that
febrile, excited preoccupation with the unknown things that made
Swann suffer; she'd push back her hair with her hands; her forehead,
her whole face, would seem larger; then, suddenly, some ordinary
human thought, some generous feeling such as may be found in all
individuals when, in a moment of relaxation or reclusion, they are
able to be themselves, would spring from her eyes like a beam of
golden sunlight. And immediately her whole face would light up like
a dull landscape covered in clouds that suddenly part, leaving it transfigured by the setting sun. The life he glimpsed in Odette at such
moments, and the future she seemed to be dreaming about, Swann
could have shared with her; no troubling disturbance seemed to have
left its residue there. Rare though they became, these moments were
not without value. In memory, Swann joined the fragments together,
abolished the intervals between them, cast, as if in gold, an Odette of
kindness and calm, for whom in later years (as we shall see in the second part of this story*) he made sacrifices which the other Odette
would never have won from him. But how rare these moments were,
and how seldom he now saw her! Even in the case of their evening
rendezvous, she told him only at the last minute if she'd be able to see
him, for she counted on his always being free and she wanted first to
make sure that no one else would invite her out. She'd claim she had
to wait for an extremely important message, and if, after she'd already
told Swann he could come, some friends asked her, halfway through
the evening, to join them at the theatre or at supper, she'd jump for
joy and run off to dress. As she progressed in her preparations, every
movement she made brought Swann closer to the moment when he'd
have to leave her, when she'd dash off on an irresistible impulse; and
when at last she was ready, shooting a final glance at the mirror, her
eyes sharp and bright with concentration, she applied a little more
lipstick, fixed a stray lock of hair over her forehead, and called for her
sky-blue evening cape with gold tassels, Swann would look so down-
cast that she'd be unable to repress a gesture of impatience, and would
snap: 'So that's the thanks I get for letting you stay here until the last
minute. And I thought I was being nice. I'll know better next time!'
Sometimes, at the risk of annoying her, he resolved to try to find out
where she'd gone, and he even imagined an alliance with Forcheville,

who might perhaps have been able to enlighten him. In any case, when he'd established with whom she was spending the evening, it wasn't difficult for him to discover, among his acquaintances, someone who knew, if only indirectly, the man in question, and could easily obtain this or that piece of information about him. And while he was writing to one of his friends, to ask him for help in clearing up some point or other, he'd feel a sense of relief on ceasing to ask himself his unanswerable questions and on transferring to someone else the tiring task of interrogation. It's true that Swann was hardly better off for the information he did obtain. Knowing something doesn't always enable us to prevent it, but the things we know, we can at least hold on to, if not with our hands, at least in our minds, where we can do with them what we like, which gives us the illusion of having some sort of control over them. He was happy whenever Monsieur de Charlus was with Odette. He knew that nothing would happen between Charlus and her, that when Monsieur de Charlus went out with her, it was out of friendship for him and he'd have no qualms about telling him what she'd done. Sometimes her refusal to see Swann on a particular evening would be so categorical, she'd seem so keen to go out somewhere, that Swann would feel it most important that Charlus should make himself available to go with her. The next day, not daring to question Charlus too closely, he'd pretend to misunderstand his answers, thus obliging him to give further details; and after each further answer he'd feel more relieved, because it would soon become clear that Odette had occupied her evening with the most innocent of pleasures: 'What are you saying, Mémé old chap?* I don't quite follow . . . You didn't go straight to the Musée Grévin from her house? You went somewhere else first? No? How funny! You don't know how entertaining you are, Mémé old boy. What a strange idea of hers to go on to the Chat Noir afterwards. But quite typical . . . No? Oh, it was your idea? How odd. But not such a bad idea, really; she must have seen a lot of people she knew there? No? She didn't speak to anyone? That's extraordinary. So you sat there, the two of you, all by yourselves? I can just picture it. What a good chap you are, my dear Mémé. I'm very fond of you.' Swann felt relieved. It had occasionally happened to him, when chatting casually with people to whom he was barely listening, to hear certain stray remarks (such as: 'I saw Madame de Crécy yesterday with a gentleman I don't know'), remarks which, as soon as they entered his heart, turned into a solid state, grew hard like an encrustation, and cut into him, became irremovable; so that he was greatly soothed, in contrast, by the words: 'She knew no one, she spoke to no one,' which flowed freely through him, fluid, easy, breathable! And yet, a moment later, he was telling himself that Odette must find him very dull if those were the pleasures she preferred to his company. And their triviality, though reassuring, also pained him as if they'd been an act of infidelity.

Even when he was unable to find out where she'd gone, it would have been enough, to alleviate the anguish he felt at such times, and for which Odette's presence, the sweet pleasure of being with her, was the sole remedy (which in the long run aggravated the disease, like many remedies, but at least brought temporary relief), it would have been enough for him, if only Odette had allowed it, to remain in her house while she was out, to wait for her until the time of her return, when other times, which some special quality or magic spell had made him believe to be different from all others, would have merged into it. But she didn't want this; he had to return home; he forced himself, on the way, to form various plans, he stopped thinking about Odette; he even succeeded, as he undressed, in turning over in his mind some quite cheering thoughts; and it was with a heart full of hope of going to see some great painting the next day that he got into bed and put out the light; but as he prepared to go to sleep, no sooner did he cease to exert the self-control of which he was not even aware, because it had become so habitual, than at that very instant an icy shiver would run through him and he'd begin to sob. He didn't even want to know why, he wiped his eyes, and said to himself with a little laugh: 'That's nice! I'm turning into a real neurotic!' After which, he could only think with a feeling of great weariness that the next day he'd have to resume his quest to find out what Odette had been doing, and think of what influences he could bring to bear in order to see her. This compulsion to engage in activity that was relentless, unchanging, and fruitless, was so painful that one day, noticing a swelling in his abdomen, he felt genuinely delighted at the thought that he might have a fatal tumour, that he'd no longer need to bother about anything, that illness would take over, make him its plaything, until his imminent demise. And indeed if, during this period, it often happened that, without admitting it to himself, he longed for death it was in order to escape not so much from the intensity of his suffering as from the monotony of his struggle.

And yet he'd have liked to live until such time as he no longer loved her, when she'd have no reason to lie to him, and he could at last learn from her whether, that afternoon when he'd dropped in to see her, she was or was not in bed with Forcheville. Often, for several days, the suspicion that she was in love with someone else would draw his mind away from that question about Forcheville, would make it almost a matter of indifference to him, in the way that a new stage in an illness can seem to provide momentary relief from the preceding stages. There were even days when he was not tormented by any suspicions. He thought he was cured. But the next morning, when he woke up, he felt the same persistent pain which, the day before, he'd diluted with a stream of different sensations. But the seat of the pain was unchanged. In fact, it was the sharpness of the pain that had woken him.

Since Odette never gave him any information about the very important things that occupied so much of her time every day (although he'd lived long enough to know that these things are never anything other than pleasures), he couldn't try to imagine them for very long at a time; his brain would become quite empty; then he'd pass a finger over his weary eyelids, as if wiping his pince-nez, and stop thinking altogether. But floating up from that great unknown were certain occupations that reappeared from time to time, vaguely connected by Odette to some obligation towards distant relatives or old friends who, since they were the only ones she regularly mentioned as preventing her from seeing him, seemed to Swann to form the necessary, fixed framework of her life. Because of the tone in which she referred from time to time to 'the day I go to the Hippodrome with my woman-friend', if, having felt unwell and thought: 'Perhaps Odette will be prepared to come and see me,' he suddenly remembered it was one of those days, and said to himself: 'Oh, no! There's no point in asking her to come. I should have thought of it before, today's her day for going to the Hippodrome with her woman-friend. Let's confine ourselves to what's possible; there's no point wearing ourselves out suggesting things that are unacceptable and have already been ruled out in advance.' The duty incumbent upon Odette of going to the Hippodrome, to which Swann thus gave way, seemed to him not only inescapable, but the mark of necessity with which it was stamped seemed to make plausible and legitimate everything that was in any way related to it. If a man passing in the street greeted Odette and thus aroused Swann's jealousy, she answered his questions by linking the man to one of the two or three great duties to which she regularly referred; if, for example, she said: 'He was in my friend's box at the Hippodrome,' this explanation would allay Swann's suspicions, since it struck him as inevitable that the friend would have other guests besides Odette in her box, but he had never tried or managed to form any clear picture of them. How he would have loved to make the acquaintance of the friend who went to the Hippodrome, and to be invited along with Odette! How gladly he would have given up all his elegant society friends in exchange for a single person Odette was in the habit of seeing, even a manicurist or a shop assistant! He'd have gone to more trouble for them than for a queen. Wouldn't they have given him, with the knowledge of Odette's life they bore within them, the only effective sedative for his pain? With what joy he would have hastened to spend his days at the home of one or other of those humble people with whom Odette kept up friendly relations, whether out of self-interest or genuine simplicity! How gladly he would have elected to live the rest of his days in the garret of some sordid but enviable apartment house where Odette went but never took him and where, if he'd lived with the little retired dressmaker, whose lover he would willingly have pretended to be, he would have had a visit from Odette nearly every day! In these almost working-class neighbourhoods, what a modest existence, abject but sweet, and filled with calm and happiness, he would gladly have led for ever.

It still happened occasionally that when, after meeting Swann somewhere, Odette saw some man approaching whom he didn't know, he could see on her face the same look of dismay she'd worn on the day he'd come to see her while Forcheville was there. But this was rare; for on the days when, despite everything she had to do, and her fear of what people might think, she managed to see Swann, the main impression she gave now was self-assurance: in striking contrast, whether unconscious compensation or a natural reaction, to the timidity she'd shown in the early days of their relationship, even when she wasn't with him, when she began a letter with the words: 'My dear Charles, my hand is shaking so much that I can hardly write' (at least so she claimed, and a little of that emotion must have been sincere for her to want to feign more). She'd felt attracted to Swann then. We only ever tremble for ourselves, or for those we love. When our happiness is no longer in their hands, what calm, what ease, what boldness we enjoy in their presence! When she spoke to him or wrote him a note, she no longer used any of those words with which she'd once pretended that he belonged to her, creating opportunities for saying 'my' or 'mine' when she referred to him—'You are my possession, it's the sweet scent of our friendship, and I shall keep it'—and for talking to him about the future, about death itself, as if it were something they would share together. In those days, to everything he said she'd answer admiringly: 'You're so unlike other people!'; she'd gaze at his long face and his balding head (which made those who knew of his success with women think: 'He's not conventionally good-looking, it's true, but he has style: that quiff, that monocle, that smile!'), and, perhaps more out of curiosity to know what he was really like than a desire to become his mistress, she'd say: 'If only I knew what goes on in that head of yours!'

Now, however, whatever Swann said, she would respond in a tone that was sometimes irritable, at other times indulgent: 'Can't you ever be like other people!' She would look at his face, which was only a little aged by worry (but about which everyone now thought, with the same aptitude that enables one to discover the meaning of a piece of symphonic music after reading the programme, or to see family resemblances in a child once one knows its parentage: 'He's not exactly ugly, it's true, but he's really quite ridiculous: that monocle, that quiff, that smile!'—creating in their suggestible imaginations the invisible boundary that separates, by a few months, the head of an adored lover from the head of a cuckold), she'd say: 'Oh, if only I could change what goes on in that head of yours and put some sense into it!' Always ready to believe in the truth of what he hoped, if Odette's behaviour towards him left the slightest room for doubt, he'd seize on her words, and say: 'You can if you want.'

And then he'd try to convince her that to comfort him, guide him, make him work, would be a noble task, to which many women would ask nothing better than to devote themselves, though it's only fair to add that in their hands the noble task would have seemed to him a tactless and intolerable usurpation of his freedom: 'If she didn't love me a little,' he would tell himself, 'she wouldn't want to change me. And if she wants to change me, she'll have to see me more often.' Thus he saw her reproaches as proof of her interest, of her love perhaps; and indeed she now gave him so few of those that he was obliged to regard as such the various prohibitions she imposed on him. One day she declared that she didn't like his coachman, who, she felt, was perhaps turning Swann against her, and in any case didn't show the punctiliousness and deference towards him that she would have liked to see. She felt that Swann wanted her to say: 'Don't use him any more when you come to see me,' just as he might have wanted her to kiss him. Since she was in a good mood, she said it; he was touched. That evening, talking to Monsieur de Charlus, with whom he could at least enjoy the relief of being able to talk about her openly (since every word he uttered now, even to people who didn't know her, always related in some way to her), he said: 'I do believe, though, that she loves me; she's so nice to me, and she certainly seems interested in what I do.' And if, when he was setting off to her house, getting into his carriage with a friend to whom he was giving a lift, the friend said: 'I say, that's not Lorédan on the box,' with what melancholy joy Swann would reply:

'Indeed not! I can't use Lorédan, you know, when I go to the Rue La Pérouse. Odette doesn't like me to use Lorédan, she doesn't think he behaves properly towards me. Well, what can one do? You know what women are like! It would really upset her. Oh, yes, if I used Rémi, I'd never hear the end of it!'

This new manner Odette had adopted towards him, indifferent, offhand, irritable, certainly made him suffer; but he wasn't aware of the extent of his suffering; since it was only gradually, day by day, that Odette had cooled towards him, it was only by comparing what she was now with what she'd been in the beginning that he could have measured the magnitude of the change that had taken place. Yet that change was his deep, secret wound, which hurt him day and night, and every time he felt that his thoughts were straying a little too close to it, he'd quickly lead them in another direction for fear of suffering too much. He'd say to himself in an abstract way: 'There was a time when Odette loved me more,' but he didn't have a clear memory of that time. Just as there was a desk in his study that he managed not to look at, which he made a detour to avoid as he came and went, because in one of its drawers he'd locked away the chrysanthemum she'd given him that first evening when he'd driven her home, and the letters in which she'd said: 'If you'd left your heart here too, I wouldn't have let you have it back,' and: 'At whatever time of the day or night that might be convenient for you to see me, send for me and I'll be only too happy to come,' so there was a place inside him that he never allowed his thoughts to approach, forcing them, if necessary, to make the detour of a lengthy argument so that they wouldn't have to pass in front of it: this was the place in which dwelt his memory of happier times.

But his extreme caution was foiled one evening when he'd gone out to a party.

It was at the home of the Marquise de Saint-Euverte, the last, for that year, of the evenings on which she invited people to hear the musicians she'd use, later on, for her charity concerts. Swann, who had intended to go to each of the previous evenings in turn but hadn't been able to make up his mind, was dressing for this one when he received a visit from the Baron de Charlus, who had come to offer to accompany him to the party, if this would help him to be a little less bored there, a little less miserable. But Swann responded:

'You know, of course, how much I'd like to go with you. But the greatest pleasure you can give me is to go and see Odette instead. You know what an excellent influence you have on her. I don't think she'll be going anywhere this evening before she goes to see her old dress-maker, and I'm sure she'd be delighted if you went with her. In any case, you'll find her at home before that. Try to entertain her, and see if you can talk some sense into her. Perhaps you can arrange something she would like for tomorrow, something the three of us could do together . . . And try to make a few suggestions for the summer, see if there's anything she might want to do, a cruise all three of us could go on, something like that. As for tonight, I don't expect to see her; but if she did want to see me, or you thought of something, you'd need only to send me a word at Madame de Saint-Euverte's up until midnight, and afterwards here at home. Thank you for everything you do for me. You know how fond I am of you.'

The Baron promised to pay the visit Swann wanted after depositing him at the door of the Saint-Euverte house, where Swann arrived calmed by the thought that Monsieur de Charlus would be spending the evening in the Rue La Pérouse, but in a state of melancholy indifference to everything that did not concern Odette, and especially to everything connected with fashionable life—a state which gave these things the charm to be found in anything which, when it's no longer an object of our desire, appears to us in itself. As soon as he stepped down from the carriage, in the foreground of that fictitious summary of their domestic life which hostesses like to offer their guests on ceremonial occasions, and in which they strive to observe accuracy of costume and setting, Swann was very pleased to see the descendants of Balzac's 'tigers',* the grooms, who normally followed their mistress on her daily outing, but who were now hatted and booted and posted outside in front of the house on the soil of the avenue, or in front of the stables, like gardeners lined up next to their flower-beds. The tendency he'd always had to look for analogies between living people and portraits in art galleries was still active, but in a more constant and general way; it was fashionable society as a whole, now that he was detached from it, that presented itself to him as a series of pictures. In the entrance hall (which in the old days, when he still attended such functions, he'd have entered wrapped in his overcoat and left in his tails, without knowing what had happened during the few moments he'd spent there, his mind having been either still at the party he'd just left or already at the party into which he was about to be introduced) he noticed for the first time, roused by the unexpected arrival of such a tardy guest, the scattered pack of tall, magnificent, idle footmen who were dozing here and there on benches and chests, and who, raising their noble, sharp, greyhound profiles, now rose to their feet and gathered round him in a circle.

One of them, particularly ferocious-looking, and rather like the executioner in certain Renaissance paintings depicting scenes of torture, stepped forward with a ruthless air to take his things. But the hardness of his steely gaze was compensated for by the softness of his cotton gloves, so that, as he approached Swann, he seemed to exhibit both contempt for his person and regard for his hat. He took it with a care to which his posture imparted something meticulous and a delicacy that was rendered almost touching by his evident strength. Then he passed it to one of his inexperienced and timid assistants, who expressed the terror he was feeling by casting wild glances in all directions, and showing the agitation of a captive animal in its first hours of domestication.

A few feet away, a burly fellow in livery stood musing, motionless, statuesque, useless, like the purely decorative warrior one sees in the most tumultuous paintings by Mantegna, lost in thought, leaning on his shield, while those around him are rushing about slaughtering each other; standing apart from the group of his colleagues as they bustled round Swann, he seemed similarly resolved to take no part in this scene, which he followed vaguely with his cruel sea-green eyes, as if it had been the Massacre of the Innocents or the Martyrdom of Saint James. Indeed, he seemed to belong to that vanished race—if, in fact, it ever existed, except in the altarpiece of San Zeno and the frescoes of the Eremitani,* where Swann had come in contact with it, and where it dreams on still—which issued from the impregnation of an ancient statue by one of the Master's Paduan models or one of Albrecht Dürer's Saxons.* And the locks of his red hair, crinkled by Nature but glued by brilliantine, were treated as they are in the Greek sculptures which the painter from Mantua never stopped studying and which, if out of all creation it represents only man, is at least able to derive from his simple forms such rich variations, as though borrowed from the whole of animate nature, that a head of hair, in the smooth rolls and sharp beaks of its curls, or in the superimposition of the triple diadem of its tresses, can look at once like a bunch of seaweed, a brood of doves, a bed of hyacinths, and a coil of snakes.

Still others, also colossal, stood on the steps of a monumental staircase for which their decorative presence and marmoreal immobility might have inspired the same name as the one in the Doges' Palace—'The Giants' Staircase'*—and which Swann began to climb with the sad thought that Odette had never climbed it. Oh, with what joy, by contrast, he would have gone up the dark, evil-smelling, rickety flights to the little dressmaker's, in whose garret he'd gladly have paid more than the price of a weekly stage-box at the Opéra for the right to spend the evening there when Odette came to visit, and even on other days, so that he could have talked about her, been among the people she was in the habit of seeing when he wasn't there, and who for that reason seemed to possess a part of his mistress's life that was more real, more inaccessible, and more mysterious than anything he knew. In the old dressmaker's foul-smelling but longed-for staircase, since the building had no service stair, one saw in the evening outside every door an empty, unwashed milk-can put out in readiness on the mat; whereas on the magnificent but despised staircase Swann was now climbing, on either side, at different levels, in front of each recess made in the wall by the window of the concierge's lodge or the door to an apartment, representing the domestic service which they controlled and paying homage to the guests, a concierge, a majordomo, a steward (worthy men who for the rest of the week lived semi-independently in their own quarters, dined there by themselves like small shopkeepers, and might before long take up more prosaic service

in the household of a doctor or factory owner), all of them careful to
carry out to the letter the instructions they had been given before
being allowed to put on the dazzling livery they wore only at rare
intervals and in which they didn't feel entirely at ease, stood beneath
the arch of their doorways, their stately splendour tempered by their
plebeian friendliness, like saints in their niches, while an enormous
usher, dressed like a church verger, struck the flagstones with his staff
as each new guest passed by. At the top of the staircase, up which he'd
been followed by a pale-faced servant with his hair tied with a ribbon
in a short pigtail, like one of Goya's sextons* or a notary in an old
play, Swann passed in front of a desk at which valets seated like scriv-
eners before huge registers stood up and inscribed his name. He then
crossed a little hall which—like certain rooms arranged by their
owners to serve as the setting for a single work of art, and are left
deliberately bare except for that work, from which they take their
name—displayed at its entrance, like some priceless statue of a watchman by Benvenuto Cellini,* a young footman, his body bent slightly
forward, his face, even redder than his red gorget, blazing with diffi-
dence and zeal; piercing with his intense, impetuous, vigilant gaze the
Aubusson tapestries* hung before the room where the music was
being performed, he seemed, with his expression of soldierly impas-
siveness or supernatural faith—allegory of alarm, incarnation of
alertness, or commemoration of the call to arms—to be watching,
angel or sentinel, from the tower of a castle or cathedral, for the
approach of the enemy or for the Day of Judgement. Now Swann had
only to enter the concert room, the doors of which were opened for
him by an usher bedecked with chains who bowed low before him as
though handing him the keys of a conquered city. But he thought of
the house in which he might have been at that very moment, if Odette
had allowed it, and the memory of an empty milk can glimpsed on
a doormat wrung his heart.

    Swann quickly recovered his sense of how ugly the male of the
species can be when, beyond the tapestry hanging, the spectacle of the
servants was followed by that of the guests. But even the ugliness of
these faces, though so familiar, seemed new to him now that their
features—instead of being signs of practical utility in the identifica-
tion of this or that person who until then had represented a set of
pleasures to pursue, annoyances to avoid, or courtesies to repay—now
rested on purely aesthetic connections, on the autonomy of their

lines. And in the midst of this press of men, everything, down to the monocles that many of them wore (and which previously would at most have enabled Swann to say they were wearing monocles), released from indicating a habit, the same one for all of them, now appeared to him to be endowed with a sort of individuality. Perhaps because he now saw General de Froberville and the Marquis de Bréauté, who were chatting just inside the door, as no more than two figures in a painting, whereas they were the old, useful friends who'd introduced him to the Jockey Club* and supported him in duels, the general's monocle, stuck between his eyelids like a piece of shrapnel in his vulgar, scarred, triumphant face, standing out in the middle of his forehead like the single eye of the Cyclops, looked to Swann like a monstrous wound that might have been glorious to receive but was indecent to display; whereas the monocle the marquis had added, as a sign of festivity, to his pearl-grey gloves, opera hat, and white tie, substituting it (like Swann himself) for the familiar pince-nez when attending social functions, bore, glued to its other side like a natural history specimen under a microscope, an infinitesimal gaze that swarmed with affability and never ceased to sparkle with delight at the loftiness of the ceilings, the excellence of the entertainment, the interesting programmes, and the quality of the refreshments.

'I say, fancy seeing you! We haven't seen you for ages,' said the general to Swann. Then, noticing how drawn he looked and thinking that a serious illness might have kept him away, he added: 'You're looking very well, old chap!' while Monsieur de Bréauté exclaimed: 'My dear fellow, what on earth are you doing here?' to a society novelist who had just slotted into the corner of his eye a monocle that was his sole instrument of psychological investigation and merciless analysis, and who replied with an air of mystery and self-importance, rolling the 'r's: 'I'm here as an observer!'

The Marquis de Forestelle's's monocle was minute and rimless, and, as it required a constant, painful clenching of the eye in which it was encrusted like a superfluous piece of cartilage whose presence was inexplicable and its composition very rare, gave his face an expression of melancholy refinement, and made women imagine that he was capable of suffering greatly in love. But Monsieur de Saint-Candé's monocle, encircled by a huge ring, like Saturn, was the centre of gravity of a face that continually adjusted itself in relation to it, a face whose quivering red nose and sarcastic thick-lipped mouth attempted by their grimaces to keep up with the endless sparks of wit gleaming in the glass disc, and saw itself preferred to the most handsome eyes in the world by snobbish and depraved young women in whom it inspired dreams of artificial charms and exquisite sensual pleasures; meanwhile, behind him, Monsieur de Palancy, who with his big carp's head and bulging eyes moved slowly through the festivities clenching and unclenching his mandibles as if to orient himself, seemed to be carrying about on his person only an accidental and perhaps purely symbolic fragment of the glass of his aquarium, a part intended to represent the whole, reminding Swann, a great admirer of Giotto's *Vices* and *Virtues* at Padua, of the figure of Injustice, by whose side a leafy bough evokes the forests where his lair lies hidden.

Swann had moved further into the room at Madame de Saint-Euverte's insistence, and in order to listen to an aria from *Orfeo* that was being performed on the flute, had positioned himself in a corner where, unfortunately, his view was blocked by two ladies of mature years seated next to each other, the Marquise de Cambremer and the Vicomtesse de Franquetot, who, because they were cousins, spent all their time at parties wandering about clutching their handbags and followed by their daughters, looking for each other as though at a railway station, and could never relax until they'd reserved two adjacent chairs with a fan or a handkerchief: Madame de Cambremer, since she knew hardly anyone, being all the more glad to have a companion, Madame de Franquetot, who, in contrast, was extremely well connected, thinking there was something elegant and original about showing all her fine friends that she preferred to their company an insignificant lady with whom she shared youthful memories. Full of melancholy irony, Swann watched them as they listened to the piano intermezzo (Liszt's *Saint Francis Preaching to the Birds**) which had come after the flute, and followed the dizzy feats of the virtuoso, Madame de Franquetot appearing anxious, her eyes almost popping out of her head as if the keys over which he ran his fingers so nimbly were a series of trapezes from which he might fall from a height of eighty metres, and at the same time casting at her companion looks of astonishment and disbelief, as if to say: 'This is amazing! I'd never have thought a man could do that!', Madame de Cambremer, as a woman who'd received a sound musical education, beating time with her head, like a metronome pendulum which swung so far and so fast from side to side (and with the sort of wild abandonment in her eyes that suggested a level of pain that had gone beyond what was bearable, can no longer be controlled, and cries out: 'I can't help it!') that her diamond earrings kept getting caught in the straps of her bodice and she was obliged to straighten the black grapes she had in her hair, while continuing to accelerate her wild oscillations. On the other side of Madame de Franquetot, but a little further forward, was the Marquise de Gallardon, absorbed in her favourite subject for reflection, namely her relationship to the Guermantes, which in her eyes and, she believed, the eyes of the world was a source of great glory as well as some shame, for the most brilliant of the Guermantes kept her at a certain distance, perhaps because she was a bore, or because she was unkind, or because she came from an inferior branch of the family, or possibly for no reason at all. When she found herself next to someone she didn't know, as at this moment with Madame de Franquetot, she suffered terribly from the fact that her awareness of her kinship with the Guermantes couldn't be made outwardly manifest in visible characters like those which, in the mosaics in Byzantine churches, placed one beneath another, inscribe in a vertical column next to some holy personage the words he's supposed to be uttering. At this moment she was pondering the fact that, in the six years that her young cousin the Princesse des Laumes had been married, not once had she received an invitation or a visit from her. This thought filled her with anger, but also with pride; for, by dint of saying to people who expressed surprise at not seeing her at Madame des Laumes's house that it was because she risked meeting the Princesse Mathilde there—for which her ultra-Legitimist family would never have forgiven her*—she'd come to believe this was the reason why she never visited her young cousin. Yet she remembered having asked Madame des Laumes several times whether there was some way she could meet her, but remembered this only vaguely and, in any case, more than neutralized this slightly humiliating recollection by muttering to herself: 'After all, it's not up to me to make the first move, I'm twenty years older than she is.' Fortified by these muttered words, she threw her shoulders proudly back so that they seemed detached from her torso, while her head was positioned almost horizontally upon them in a manner reminiscent of the 'restored' head of a roast pheasant that is brought to the table with all its feathers. Nature had endowed her with a squat, plump, mannish figure; but the snubs she'd received had straightened her up like those trees which, having taken root in an unfortunate position on the edge of a cliff, are forced to grow backwards to keep their balance. Obliged, in order to console herself for not being altogether the equal of the other Guermantes, to tell herself incessantly that it was because of her uncompromising principles and her pride that she saw so little of them, this thought had ended up moulding the very shape of her body and giving her a kind of bearing that passed among bourgeois ladies as a sign of breeding, and at times even generated a flicker of desire in the jaded eyes of old clubmen. If Madame de Gallardon's conversation had been subjected to those analyses which, by establishing the frequency of given words and phrases, enable one to discover the key to a coded text, it would have become clear that no expression, even the most common, recurred in it as often as 'at my cousins the Guermantes's', 'at my aunt Guermantes's', 'Ezéar de Guermantes's health', 'my cousin de Guermantes's box'. When anyone spoke to her about a celebrated personage, she'd reply that, although she didn't know him personally, she'd seen him hundreds of times at the home of her aunt de Guermantes, but she'd deliver this reply in such a glacial tone and in a voice so low that it was clear that if she didn't know him personally it was because of all the stubborn and ineradicable principles which her shoulders leaned against, like the ladders on which gymnastic instructors make you stretch in order to develop your chest.

As it happened, the Princesse des Laumes, whom no one would have expected to see at Madame de Saint-Euverte's, had just arrived. To show that she wasn't trying to flaunt her superior rank in a salon to which she'd come only out of condescension, she'd entered with shoulders hunched, her arms pressed close to her sides, even though there was no crowd to squeeze through and no one attempting to get past her, and she stayed deliberately at the back of the room, with the air of being in her proper place, like a king queueing at the door of a theatre for as long as the management are unaware of his presence; and there she stood, confining her gaze to the study of a pattern in the carpet or in her own skirt, so as not to appear to be attracting attention to herself or expecting favoured treatment, occupying the spot that had seemed to her the most unassuming, next to Madame de Cambremer, whom she didn't know (but knowing full well that she'd be drawn from there by a cry of delight from Madame de Saint-Euverte as soon as the latter noticed her). She stood watching her neighbour's pantomime of musical appreciation, but refrained from imitating it. This didn't mean that, having for once agreed to spend a few minutes at the Marquise de Saint-Euverte's, she didn't wish (so that the courtesy she was doing her hostess might count double) to show herself as agreeable as possible. But she had a natural horror of what she called 'overdoing things', and would make it very clear that she 'had no intention' of indulging in displays of emotion that were not in keeping with the 'tone' of her usual circle; but, for all that, she couldn't help but be impressed by such displays by virtue of the spirit of imitation akin to timidity which is developed even in the most self-confident people by the atmosphere of a new social environment, even if it's inferior to their own. She began to wonder whether Madame de Cambremer's gesticulations were not, perhaps, a necessary response to the piece being played, which bore little resemblance to the type of music she was used to hearing, and whether to refrain from such behaviour might not be taken as evidence of incomprehension with respect to the work and rudeness towards the lady of the house: with the result that, by way of a compromise between her contradictory inclinations, at one moment she merely straightened her shoulder-straps or raised a hand to her fair hair to secure the little balls of coral or pink enamel, flecked with diamonds, which formed her simple and charming headdress, and the next moment she studied her impassioned neighbour with cold curiosity, while keeping time to the music for a few moments with her fan, but, so as not to forfeit her independence, on the wrong beat. When the pianist had finished the Liszt intermezzo and begun a prelude by Chopin,* Madame de Cambremer gave Madame de Franquetot a fond smile of knowing satisfaction and allusion to the past. As a girl she had learned how to caress those long sinuous phrases of Chopin, so free, so flexible, so tactile, which begin by seeking out and exploring a place for themselves far outside and away from the direction in which they started, far beyond the point which one might have expected them to reach, and which disport themselves in these byways of fantasy only to return more deliberately—with a more premeditated reprise, with more precision, as upon a crystal bowl that resonates until it makes you want to cry out—to strike you in the heart.

Having been brought up in a provincial household that had little contact with anyone, hardly ever going to a ball, she'd become intoxicated, in the solitude of her old manor house, with the idea of all those dancing couples, imagining their movements, slowing them down, speeding them up, scattering them like flowers, even leaving the ball-room for a moment to listen to the wind blowing in the pine trees at the edge of the lake, and seeing all of a sudden, as he came towards her, more unlike anything one had ever dreamed of than an earthly lover could be, a slender young man in white gloves whose voice had a strange and false lilt to it. But nowadays the old-fashioned beauty of this music seemed stale. Having fallen, during the last few years, in the esteem of the discriminating public, it had lost its place of honour and its charm, and even those with poor taste no longer took more than moderate and unavowed pleasure in it. Madame de Cambremer cast a furtive glance behind her. She knew that her young daughter-in-law (full of respect for her new family, except for the things of the mind, about which, with her knowledge of Harmony and even Greek, she was especially enlightened) despised Chopin, and felt almost ill when she heard him played. But Madame de Cambremer, freed from the vigilant eye of the Valkyrie, who was sitting at a distance with a group of people of her own age, was now able to abandon herself to a few moments of sheer delight. And the Princesse des Laumes shared this delight. Though she didn't have a natural gift for music, she'd had lessons fifteen years earlier from a piano teacher in the Faubourg Saint-Germain, a woman of genius who at the end of her life had fallen on hard times and had turned, at the age of seventy, to giving lessons to the daughters and granddaughters of her old pupils. She was now dead. But her method, her lovely style of playing, came back to life sometimes under the fingers of her pupils, even those who had become in other respects very ordinary people, had given up music, and hardly ever opened a piano. And so Madame des Laumes could nod approvingly, very knowledgeably, with a true appreciation of the way the pianist was playing this prelude, which she knew by heart. The final notes of the phrase he'd just begun came spontaneously to her lips. And she murmured: 'It's always so *ch*arming', with a double *ch* at the beginning of the word which was a mark of refinement and with which she felt her lips crinkling so romantically, like a beautiful flower, that she instinctively brought her eyes into harmony with them by giving them at the very same time an expression of dreamy sentimentality. Meanwhile, Madame de Gallardon was thinking how annoying it was that she had so few opportunities to meet the Princesse des Laumes, for she wanted to teach her a lesson by snubbing her. She didn't know her cousin was actually there. But as Madame de Franquetot moved her head, the princess came into view. Immediately Madame de Gallardon rushed over to her, disturbing everybody; but although she was keen to maintain a distant and glacial manner that would remind everyone that she had no desire to be on friendly terms with a person in whose house one might find oneself coming face to face with the Princesse Mathilde, and to whom it wasn't for her to make the first overture since she belonged to 'a different generation', she decided to make up for this air of haughtiness and reserve by some simple remark that would justify her approach and force the princess to engage in conversation; and so, when she reached her cousin, Madame de Gallardon, with a stern expression and a hand thrust out as if trying to 'force' a card, said 'How's your husband?' in the concerned tone she would have used if the prince had been seriously ill. The princess, bursting into her own unique style of laughter, which was calculated both to show she was making fun of someone and to make herself look prettier by concentrating her features around her animated lips and sparkling eyes, replied: 'Oh, he's never been better!' And she went on laughing.

Whereupon Madame de Gallardon, drawing herself up and putting on an even chillier expression, and still concerned about the Prince's health, said to her cousin:

'Oriane' (and at this point Madame des Laumes looked with an air of surprise and amusement in the direction of an invisible third party, before whom she seemed anxious to testify that she had never authorized Madame de Gallardon to call her by her first name), 'I'd be so pleased if you'd drop in for a moment tomorrow evening to hear a clarinet quintet by Mozart.* I'd love to know what you think of it.'

She seemed not so much to be making an invitation as asking a favour, and to want the princess's appraisal of the Mozart quintet as if it were a dish prepared by a new cook, whose culinary skills she was keen to have assessed by a gourmet.

'But I know that quintet, and I can tell you now . . . that I like it!'

'You know, my husband isn't well; it's his liver . . . He'd be so very pleased to see you,' resumed Madame de Gallardon, thus making it a charitable obligation for the princess to appear at her soirée.

The princess never liked to tell people she didn't want to visit them. Every day she would write notes expressing her regret at having been prevented—by an unexpected visit from her mother-in-law, by an invitation from her brother-in-law, by the Opéra, by an outing to the country—from attending a soirée to which she'd never have dreamed of going. In this way she gave many people the joy of believing that she was one of their friends, that she would have been glad to visit them, and that she'd been unable to do so because of some aristocratic contretemps which they were flattered to see competing with their own soirée. Also, since she belonged to that witty Guermantes set in which there survived something of the quick wit, unburdened by platitudes and conventional sentiments, which goes back to Mérimée and has found its latest expression in the plays of Meilhac and Halévy,* she adapted it to her social relations, transposing it even into her style of politeness, which endeavoured to be positive and precise, to approximate to the plain truth. She would never develop at any length to a hostess the expression of her desire to attend her soirée; she thought it kinder simply to put to her a few little facts on which would depend whether or not it was possible for her to come.

'Well, the fact is,' she said to Madame de Gallardon, 'tomorrow evening I must go and see a friend who's been asking me for ages to fix a day. If she takes us to the theatre, with the best will in the world there'll be no chance I could come to you; but if we stay in the house, since I know there won't be anyone else there, I'll be able to slip away.'

'By the way, did you see your friend Monsieur Swann?'

'What? My darling Charles is here? I had no idea. I must try to catch his eye.'

'It's funny he should come to old Saint-Euverte's,' remarked Madame de Gallardon. 'Of course, I know he's very clever' (by which she meant he was very crafty), 'but all the same—a Jew in the house of the sister and sister-in-law of two archbishops!'

'Well, I'm ashamed to say I'm not at all shocked,' said the Princesse des Laumes.

'I know he's a convert, and even his parents and grandparents before him. But they say it's the converted ones that stay more attached to their religion than the rest, that it's all for show. Is that true, do you think?'

'I have no idea about those things.'

The pianist had by now finished the prelude, the first of the two Chopin pieces he was to play, and went straight into a polonaise. But from the moment Madame de Gallardon told her cousin that Swann was in the room, Chopin himself could have risen from the grave and played his entire repertoire without Madame des Laumes paying the slightest attention. She belonged to that half of the human race in whom the curiosity the other half feels about the people it doesn't know is replaced by an interest in those it does. As with many women of the Faubourg Saint-Germain, the presence, in a place where she was, of another member of her set, even though she had nothing in particular to say to him, monopolized her attention to the exclusion of everything else. From that moment, in the hope that Swann would notice her, the princess, like a tame white mouse when a lump of sugar is offered to it and then taken away, kept turning her face, filled with a thousand signs of complicity, quite unrelated to the mood of Chopin's polonaise, in the direction where Swann was standing and, if he moved, she would make a corresponding adjustment to the direction of her magnetic smile.

'Oriane, please don't be angry,' resumed Madame de Gallardon, who could never prevent herself from sacrificing her highest social ambitions, and her hope of one day dazzling the world, to the imme-diate, obscure, and private pleasure of saying something disagreeable, 'but there are people who claim that your Monsieur Swann is the sort of man one can't have in one's house. Is that true?'

'But surely you of all people know it's true,' replied the Princesse des Laumes, 'since you've invited him scores of times and he hasn't been to your house once.'

Then, leaving her cousin to her mortification, she burst out laugh-ing again, scandalizing the people who were listening to the music, but attracting the attention of Madame de Saint-Eurverte, who had stayed near the piano out of politeness and only now caught sight of the princess. Madame de Saint-Euverte was especially delighted to see Madame des Laumes because she'd thought she was still at Guermantes looking after her sick father-in-law.

'Good heavens, Princesse! I didn't know you were here!'

'Yes, I've been here in my little corner, and I've been hearing such lovely things.'

'What! You've been here for quite a while?'

'Oh, yes, quite a long while, but it has seemed quite short; if it was long, it was only because I couldn't see you.'

Madame de Saint-Euverte offered the princess her armchair, but she declined, saying:

'Oh, please, no! There's no need. I don't mind where I sit.' And deliberately choosing a low seat without a back, the better to show off her lordly simplicity, she said: 'There, this pouffe is good enough for me! It'll make me sit up straight. Oh dear, I'm making too much noise again; if I'm not careful, I'll get myself thrown out!'

The pianist was now forcing the pace, the musical excitement was reaching a climax, a servant was passing round refreshments on a tray and making the spoons rattle, and, as happened every week, Madame de Saint-Euverte signalled to him, without his seeing her, to go away. A newly-wed, who had been told that a young woman should never appear bored, was smiling with pleasure, and was trying to catch the hostess's eye in order to send her a look of gratitude for having 'thought of her' for such a delightful occasion. However, although she remained calmer than Madame de Franquetot, it was not without some uneasiness that she followed the music; the object of her concern, however, was not the pianist, but the piano, on which a candle, jumping at each fortissimo, seemed in danger, if not of setting its shade on fire, at least of dripping wax on to the rosewood. In the end she could bear it no longer and, mounting the two steps of the dais on which the piano was placed, rushed to remove the candle-holder. Her hands were just about to touch it when a final chord rang out, the polonaise came to an end, and the pianist stood up. Nevertheless, the young woman's bold initiative, and the moment of confusion between her and the instrumentalist that resulted from it, produced a generally favourable impression.

'Did you see what that young woman did, Princesse?' said General de Froberville to the Princesse des Laumes, having come over to greet her as Madame de Saint-Euverte moved away for a moment. 'Quite odd, wasn't it? Is she one of the performers?'

'No, she's just some young thing by the name of Cambremer,' replied the princess without thinking, and then hastened to add: 'I'm only repeating what I've heard—I have no idea who she is, someone behind me was saying they're neighbours of Madame de Saint-Euverte in the country, but I don't think anyone knows them. They must be "country cousins"! By the way, I don't know whether you're on familiar terms with all the brilliant people here tonight, but I can't put a name to any of them. What do you think they do when they're not attending one of Madame de Saint-Euverte's soirées? She must have hired them along with the musicians, the chairs, and the refreshments. You must admit these guests from the Belloir agency* are most impressive. How can she have the nerve to hire all these "extras" week after week? I've never seen anything like it!'

'Ah! But Cambremer is a good name, and old too,' said the general.

'It may well be,' snapped the princess, 'but that doesn't mean it's *euphonious*.' She gave a special emphasis to the word, as though putting it in quotation marks, a little affectation of speech that was peculiar to the Guermantes set.

'Really? She's quite gorgeous, though,' said the general, keeping his eyes fixed on Madame de Cambremer. 'Don't you think so, Princesse?'

'She's too forward; I don't think that's very nice in such a young woman. Of course, she's not my generation,' replied Madame des Laumes, using an expression that was common to the Gallardons and the Guermantes. Then, seeing that the general could not take his eyes off Madame de Cambremer, she added, half out of spite towards the young woman, half out of indulgence towards the general: 'Not very nice . . . for her husband! I'm sorry I don't know her, seeing that you're so taken with her; I could have introduced you' (which, if she had known her, she would have made a point of not doing). 'I'll have to say goodnight soon; it's the birthday of a friend of mine today, and I must go and give her my best wishes.' Her tone of matter-of-fact modesty reduced the fashionable gathering to which she was going to the level of a tiresome ceremony which she was obliged, yet touched, to attend. 'And I have to meet Basin there, too. While I've been here, he's been seeing some friends of his; I believe you know them, they're called after a bridge—the Iénas.'

'It was the name of a victory before it was a bridge,* Princesse,' said the general. 'You know,' he went on, removing his monocle and wiping it, as he would have changed the dressing on a wound, while the princess instinctively looked away, 'for an old trooper like me, that Empire nobility, it wasn't the same, of course, but, for what it was, it was very fine in its own way. Those people really fought like heroes.'

'Oh, I have the greatest respect for heroes,' said the princess in a slightly ironic tone. 'If I don't go with Basin to see this Princesse d'Iéna, it's not because of that, not at all, it's simply because I don't know them. Basin knows them, he's very fond of them. And it's not what you might think—there's no flirting involved, there's no reason for me to object. Besides, what good does it do when I object!' she added in a melancholy voice, for everyone knew that the day after the Prince des Laumes married his ravishing cousin, he'd been unfaithful to her, and hadn't stopped being unfaithful ever since. 'It isn't that at all, they're old friends of his, he gets on swimmingly with them and I'm very pleased for him. In any case, what he's told me about their house is enough. Can you imagine, all their furniture is "Empire"!'

'Naturally, Princesse; it was their grandparents' furniture.'

'I'm not saying it wasn't, but that doesn't make it less ugly. I understand very well that people can't always have nice things, but at least the things they have shouldn't be ridiculous. I really can't think of anything more pretentious, more bourgeois, than that horrible style—cabinets with swans' heads, like bathtubs.'

'Nevertheless, I believe they do have some beautiful things; they must have that famous mosaic table that was used for the Treaty of . . .'*

'Oh, I'm not saying they haven't got a few things that are interesting from a historical point of view. But they can't be very nice because . . . they're simply horrible! I've got things like that myself, which Basin inherited from the Montesquious. Only they're in the attics at Guermantes, where nobody can see them. But, in any case, that's not the point, I'd rush round to see them with Basin, I'd even see them among all their sphinxes and brasses if I knew them, but . . . I don't know them! I was always told when I was little that it isn't polite to call on people one doesn't know,' she said, putting on a childish voice. 'So I'm just doing what I was taught. Just imagine how those good people would react if someone they don't know came bursting into their house. They might give me a very hostile reception!'

And she coquettishly enhanced the charm of the smile which this supposition had brought to her lips, by giving her blue eyes, which were fixed on the general, a dreamy, gentle expression.

'Oh, Princesse, you know full well they'd be utterly delighted . . .'

'Not at all. Why would they?' she asked him very sharply, either because she didn't want to give the impression that she knew it would be because she was one of the foremost ladies in France, or to have the pleasure of hearing the general tell her so. 'Why? What makes you say that? It might be most disagreeable for them. I don't know, but speaking for myself, I find it tiresome enough to see the people I know, and I'm quite sure that if I had to see people I don't know, even if they had "fought like heroes", I'd go mad. In any case, except when it's an old friend like you, whom one knows quite apart from that, I'm not sure that heroism gets people very far in society. I often find it boring enough to give a dinner party, but if I had to take the arm of Spartacus . . .* No, really, if I had to make up the numbers, I'd never dream of asking

Vercingetorix . . .* I think I'd keep him for large-scale occasions. And since I don't have any of those . . .'

'Ah, Princesse, you're not a Guermantes for nothing. You've got all the family wit!'

'People always say "the Guermantes' family wit". I've never understood why. Do you know any *others* who have it?' she added, with a burst of joyful, bubbly laughter, all her features concentrated, combining to reinforce her vivacity, her eyes sparkling, blazing with a radiant sunny gaiety that could be kindled only by remarks, even if made by the princess herself, in praise of her wit or her beauty. Then she said: 'Look, there's Swann. He seems to be talking to your young Cambremer; over there, next to old Madame Saint-Euverte, can't you see him? Go and ask him to introduce you. But you'd better hurry, he's getting ready to leave!'

'Did you notice how dreadfully ill he's looking?' said the general.

'My dear Charles! Ah! He's coming over at last. I was beginning to think he didn't want to see me!'

Swann was very fond of the Princesse des Laumes, and the sight of her reminded him of Guermantes, the estate near Combray, and the whole of the surrounding countryside which he loved so much and had ceased to visit so as not to be away from Odette. In conversation with the princess, he used the semi-literary, semi-courtly way of talking which he knew she enjoyed, and which came back to him quite naturally as soon as he immersed himself for a few moments in his old social milieu, and he wanted anyway, for his own satisfaction, to express the longing he felt for the country:

'Ah!' he said to the company at large, in order to be heard both by Madame de Saint-Euverte, to whom he was speaking, and by Madame des Laumes, for whom he was speaking, 'Behold the charming Princesse! See, she's come up from Guermantes for the express purpose of listening to Liszt's *Saint Francis of Assisi*, and has only just had time, like a pretty little titmouse, to steal a little fruit from the plum trees and hawthorns to put in her hair; there are even a few drops of dew on them still, a little of the hoar-frost that must be making the Duchesse shiver. It's very pretty indeed, my dear Princesse.'

'What! The Princesse has come up specially from Guermantes? But that's really too much! I didn't know; I feel quite embarrassed,' exclaimed Madame de Saint-Euverte naïvely, unaccustomed as she was to Swann's wit. Then, examining the princess's headdress, she said: 'Yes, you're right, it's meant to look like . . . I'm not quite sure, not chestnuts, no—oh, it's a lovely idea! But how could the Princesse have known what was going to be on my programme! The musicians didn't even tell me.'

When Swann was in the company of a woman with whom he'd kept up the habit of addressing in gallant language, he usually said things in such a delicately nuanced way that many society people found him incomprehensible, and he didn't condescend to explain to Madame de Saint-Euverte that he'd been speaking metaphorically. As for the princess, she exploded with laughter, because Swann's wit was highly appreciated in her set, and also because she could never hear a compliment addressed to her without finding it exquisitely subtle and irresistibly amusing.

'Oh, I'm so pleased, Charles, that you like my little hips and haws. But what were you doing talking to that Cambremer woman? Is she a neighbour of yours in the country, too?'

Madame de Saint-Euverte, seeing that the princess appeared happy to chat with Swann, had moved away.

'But she's your neighbour as well, Princesse!'

'My neighbour as well? Then they must have country houses everywhere, those people! I wouldn't mind being in their shoes!'

'No, not the Cambremers; her own family. She's the Legrandin girl who used to come to Combray. I don't know whether you realize that you are the Comtesse de Combray, and that the Chapter owes you dues.'

'I don't know what the Chapter might owe me, but I do know that the curé touches me for a hundred francs every year, and I'd be very pleased if he stopped! But I must say, those Cambremers have an extraordinary name! It ends just in time, but it ends badly!' she said with a laugh.

'And it doesn't begin any better,' Swann replied.

'Yes! The double abbreviation . . .'*

'Someone very angry and very proper didn't dare finish the first word.'

'But since he couldn't prevent himself from beginning the second, he should have finished the first—then he'd have had done with it. I must say, we're making some very tasteful jokes today, my dear Charles.' Then she added, in a caressing tone: 'You know, it's such a shame I don't see you any more, I do so enjoy talking to you. That old fool Froberville, for example, would never have understood what I meant about the Cambremers having an extraordinary name. You must admit life can be awful. The only time I don't feel bored is when I'm with you.'

This was probably untrue. But Swann and the princess had the same way of looking at the little things of life, the effect of which—unless it was the cause—was a great similarity in their ways of expressing themselves and even in their pronunciation. This resemblance was not easily noticeable because their voices were so utterly different. But if in one's imagination one managed to divest Swann's remarks of the sonority in which they were wrapped, of the moustache from beneath which they emerged, one realized that these were the same phrases, the same inflections, the whole general style of the Guermantes set. When it came to important matters, Swann and the princess could never agree about anything. But ever since Swann had become so melancholy, always in the tremulous state that precedes tears, he felt the same need to talk about his suffering as a murderer has to talk about his crime. When he heard the princess say that life can be awful, he felt as comforted as if she'd been talking about Odette.

'Yes, indeed, life can be awful. We should see each other soon, my dear Oriane. What's so nice about you is that you're never cheerful. We should spend an evening together.'

'What a good idea! Why don't you come down to Guermantes? My mother-in-law would be delighted. People say it's a very unattractive part of the world, but I must say I don't dislike it at all; I hate "picturesque" places.'

'Yes, absolutely, it's delightful,' replied Swann. 'It's almost too beautiful, too alive for me just now; it's a place to be happy in. Perhaps it's because I've lived there, but there are so many things there that speak to me! As soon as a little breeze gets up, and the cornfields begin to stir, I feel someone is about to appear, that I'm going to receive some news; and those little houses by the water . . . I'd be quite miserable there!'

'Oh, look out! There's that awful Rampillon woman. She's seen me; you must hide me. Remind me what it was that happened to her; I get it all mixed up; she's just married off her daughter, or her lover, I can't remember which; perhaps both . . . to each other! . . . Oh, no, I remember now, she's been dropped by her prince . . . Pretend you're talking to me, so that that old Bérénice* won't come over and invite me to dinner. In any case, I must be off. Listen, my dear Charles, now that I've seen you for once, won't you let me carry you off and take you to the Princesse de Parme's? She'd be so pleased to see you, and so would Basin—he's meeting me there. You know, if we didn't get news of you from Mémé . . . Do you realize I never see you at all now!'

Swann declined; having told Monsieur de Charlus he'd go straight home from Madame de Saint-Euverte's, he didn't want to run the risk, by going to the Princesse de Parme's, of missing a message he'd been hoping all evening to be brought in to him by a servant, and that perhaps he'd now get from his concierge. 'Poor Swann,' said Madame des Laumes that night to her husband, 'he's always so pleasant, but he seems so miserable. You'll see him yourself, because he's promised to come to dinner one of these days. I find it absurd that a man of his intelligence should suffer over a woman like that. She isn't even interesting; I'm told she's quite stupid,' she added, with the wisdom of people, not in love themselves, who think that a clever man should be unhappy only over a person who's worth it; which is rather like being surprised that anyone should condescend to suffer from cholera because of so insignificant a creature as the comma bacillus.

Swann was looking for an opportunity to leave, but just as he was about to make his escape, General de Froberville asked him for an introduction to Madame de Cambremer, and he was obliged to go back into the drawing room to look for her.

'I say, Swann, I'd rather be married to that little lady than slaughtered by savages! What do you say?'

The words 'slaughtered by savages' affected Swann profoundly; and at once he felt the need to continue the conversation:

'Well, you know,' he said, 'some very fine men have died that way For example, there was that navigator whose ashes were brought back by Dumont d'Urville—La Pérouse . . .'* (and Swann was at once happy again, as if he'd been talking about Odette). 'He was a fine character, that La Pérouse, and very interesting,' he added with a melancholy air.

'Oh yes, of course, La Pérouse,' said the general. He's very well known. There's a street named after him.'

'Do you know someone in the Rue La Pérouse?' asked Swann in some agitation.

'Only Madame de Chanlivault, the sister of that fine fellow Chaussepierre. She gave a very good theatre-party the other evening.

Now there's a salon that will be very chic one of these days, mark my words!'

'Ah, so she lives in the Rue La Pérouse. It's pleasant—a pretty street, and so sad-looking.'

'Not at all. You can't have been there for quite a while; there's nothing sad about it these days, there's a lot of building going on throughout that whole neighbourhood.'

When Swann finally introduced Monsieur de Froberville to the young Madame de Cambremer, since it was the first time she'd heard the general's name, she gave him the smile of delight and surprise with which she'd have greeted him if no other name but his had ever been uttered in her presence, for as she didn't know any of the friends of her new family, whenever someone was introduced to her she assumed he must be one of them, and thinking it would be tactful to look as though she'd heard such a lot about him since her marriage, she'd hold out her hand with a hesitant air that was meant as proof both of the inculcated reserve she had to overcome and the spontaneous warmth of personality that enabled her to do so. And so her parents-in-law, whom she still regarded as the most eminent people in France, declared she was an angel; all the more so because, in marrying their son to her, they preferred to appear as if they'd yielded to the attraction of her fine qualities rather than her great wealth.

'You clearly have the soul of a musician, Madame,' said the general, unconsciously alluding to the incident of the candle.

Meanwhile the concert had resumed, and Swann realized he wouldn't be able to leave before the end of the new item. He was unhappy at having to remain imprisoned among all these people whose stupidity and absurd ways were all the more painful because, being unaware of his love and incapable, had they known about it, of taking any interest in it or doing more than smile at it as at some childish nonsense or deplore it as sheer madness, they made it appear to him as a purely subjective state which existed for him alone, whose reality could not be confirmed by any external thing; he suffered above all, to the point where even the sound of the instruments made him want to cry out, from having to prolong his exile in this place to which Odette would never come, where no one and no thing knew of her existence, from which she was totally absent.

But suddenly it was as though she'd entered the room, and this caused him such intense pain that he couldn't help clutching at his heart. What had happened was that the violin had risen to a series of high notes on which it lingered as though waiting for something, holding them in a prolonged state of expectancy, in the exaltation of already seeing the object of its expectation approaching, and with a desperate effort to try to last until its arrival, to welcome it before expiring, to keep the way open for it a moment longer, with its last remaining strength, so that it could come through, as one holds open a door that would otherwise close. And before Swann had time to understand, and say to himself: 'It's the little phrase from Vinteuil's sonata—don't listen!', all his memories of the time when Odette was in love with him, which he'd managed until now to keep hidden in the deepest part of his being, deceived by this sudden beam of light from the time of love which they believed had returned, had taken wing, and risen to sing madly in his ears, with no pity for his present misfortune, the forgotten refrains of happiness.

In place of the abstract expressions 'the time when I was happy', 'the time when I was loved', which he'd often used before now without suffering too much, for his mind had invested them only with spurious extracts of the past that preserved nothing of its reality, what came back to him now was everything that had fixed for ever the specific, volatile essence of that lost happiness; he saw it all again: the curled, snow-white petals of the chrysanthemum she'd tossed to him in his carriage, which he'd kept pressed to his lips—the embossed address of the 'Maison Dorée' on the notepaper on which he'd read: 'my hand is shaking so much that I can hardly write'—the way her eyebrows had drawn together when she said pleadingly: 'You won't leave it too long before getting in touch?'; he could smell the curling-tongs of the barber, who would crimp his hair while Lorédan went to fetch the young girl; he could feel the torrential rain that fell so often that spring, the drive home in his victoria on those icy moonlit nights; the whole network of thought-patterns, seasonal impressions, and physical reactions which had woven over a number of weeks a uniform mesh in which his body was once again held. At that time he'd been satisfying a sensual curiosity by experiencing the pleasures of people for whom love is everything. He'd believed he could stop there, that he wouldn't be obliged to know their sorrows too; but how small a thing Odette's charm was for him now compared with the dreadful terror thrown out from it, like a murky halo, by the immense anguish of not knowing at every moment what she'd been doing, of not possessing her everywhere and always! Alas, he recalled the tone of her voice when she'd exclaimed: 'But I never have anything to do! I'm always free!'—she who was never free now!—and the interest, the curiosity she'd shown in his life, the passionate desire that he should do her the favour—which in fact he'd then dreaded as a tedious and inconvenient waste of his time—of allowing her to be part of it; how she'd had to beg him to let her introduce him to the Verdurins; and, when he'd allowed her to come and see him once a month, how she'd had to tell him over and over again, before he allowed himself to give in, how delightful it would be to make a practice of seeing each other every day, a habit she longed for whereas to him it seemed only a tiresome imposition, of which she'd then grown tired and finally broken off, while for him it had become such an irresistible and painful need. He had no idea how truly he spoke when, the third time he saw her, as she said to him yet again: 'But why don't you let me come more often?', he'd said to her with a laugh, gallantly: 'for fear of being hurt'. Now, alas, she still wrote to him occasionally from a restaurant or hotel on notepaper that bore the establishment's printed name, but printed as if in letters of fire that burned him. 'She wrote this from the Hôtel Vouillemont. What can she have gone there for? With whom? What happened there?' He remembered the gas lamps being extinguished along the Boulevard des Italiens, when he'd bumped into her against all hope among the wandering shades on that night which had seemed to him almost supernatural and which indeed—since it belonged to a period when he didn't even have to ask himself if he would annoy her by looking for her and finding her, so sure was he that her greatest pleasure was to see him and let him take her home—was part of a mysterious world to which one may never return once its doors have closed. And Swann saw, standing motionless before that scene of remembered happiness, a wretched figure who filled him with pity because he didn't recognize him at first, and he had to lower his eyes so that no one would notice they were full of tears. It was himself.

When he realized this, his pity vanished, but he was jealous of that other self she had loved, he was jealous of those men of whom he'd often thought, without too much suffering, 'perhaps she loves them', for now he'd exchanged the vague idea of loving, in which there is no love, for the petals of the chrysanthemum and the letterhead of the Maison d'Or, which were full of it. Then, his distress becoming too intense, he drew his hand across his forehead, let his monocle drop, and wiped it. If he'd seen himself at that moment, he might have added, to the collection of those he'd already observed, the monocle he was now removing like an importunate thought and from whose misted surface he was trying, with a handkerchief, to wipe away his cares.

There are tones in the violin—if we don't see the instrument and therefore can't relate what we hear to its shape, which modifies its sound—so similar to those of certain contralto voices that we have the illusion that a singer has been added to the concert. When we look up we see only the wooden cases of the instruments, as delicate as Chinese boxes, but at times we are still tricked by the deceptive call of the siren; at times, too, we think we can hear a captive genie struggling, like a demented thing, deep inside the erudite, enchanted, quivering box; while at other times it's like a pure and supernatural being that goes by, unrolling its invisible message.

As though the musicians were not so much playing the little phrase as performing the rituals it required in order to make its appearance, and proceeding to the incantations necessary to obtain, and prolong for a few moments, the wonder of its evocation, Swann, who was no more able to see it than if it had belonged to an ultraviolet world, and who was experiencing something like the refreshing sense of a metamorphosis in the momentary blindness with which he was struck as he approached it, felt it to be present, like a protective goddess, a confidante of his love, who, to be able to come to him through the crowd and take him aside to speak to him, had assumed the disguise of this sonorous apparition. And as she passed, light and soothing as a perfume, telling him what she had to say, every word of which he studied closely, sorry to see them fly away so quickly, he involuntarily made with his lips the motion of kissing the harmonious, fleeting form as it went by. He no longer felt exiled and alone, since the little phrase was speaking to him, talking to him quietly about Odette. For he no longer had the impression, as he once had, that he and Odette were unknown to the little phrase. It had so often witnessed their moments of happiness! True, it had just as often warned him how fragile these moments were. And in fact, whereas in those days he'd read suffering in its smile, in its limpid, disillusioned tones, he now found in it the grace of a resignation that was almost happy. Of those sorrows, of which the little phrase used to speak to him and which, without his being affected by them himself, he'd seen it carry past him, smiling, on its rapid and sinuous course, of those sorrows, which had now become his own, without his having any hope of ever being free of them, it seemed to say to him, as it had once said of his happiness: 'What does it all matter? None of it means anything.' And for the first time Swann's thoughts turned with a surge of pity and tenderness to Vinteuil, to that unknown, sublime brother who must also have suffered greatly. What must his life have been like? From the depths of what sorrows had he drawn that godlike strength, that unlimited power to create? When it was the little phrase that spoke to him about the vanity of his sufferings, Swann found solace in that very wisdom which, just moments before, had seemed to him unbearable when he thought he could read it on the faces of indifferent strangers who regarded his love as a minor aberration. For the little phrase, unlike them, whatever its opinion of the brevity of such conditions of the soul, saw in them something not less serious than everyday life, as these people did, but on the contrary, something so superior that it alone was worth expressing. The charms of an inner sadness—they were what it sought to imitate, to recreate, and their very essence, even though it consists in being incommunicable and appearing trivial to everyone but the one who experiences them, had been captured and made visible by the little phrase. So much so that it caused their value to be acknowledged, their divine sweetness savoured, by those same people in the audience—if they were at all musical—who would afterwards fail to recognize these charms in real life, in every individual love that came into being before their eyes. Doubtless the form in which it had codified them could not be resolved into arguments or reasonings. But ever since, more than a year before, the love of music had, for a time at least, been born in him, revealing to him many of the riches of his own soul, Swann had regarded musical motifs as actual ideas, belonging to another world, another order, ideas veiled in shadow, unknown, impenetrable to the human mind, but nonetheless perfectly distinct from one another, unequal among themselves in value and significance. When, after the Verdurin evening, he'd had the little phrase played over for him again, and had sought to solve the puzzle of how it was that, like a perfume, like a caress, it took hold of him, enveloped him, he'd realized that it was to the narrow intervals between the five notes that composed it, and to the constant repetition of two of them, that the impression of a sweetness tremulously offered and withdrawn was due; but in reality he knew that he was drawing this conclusion not from the phrase itself, but from equivalents substituted, for his mind's convenience, for the mysterious entity he'd perceived, before knowing the Verdurins, at that party where he'd heard the sonata for the first time. He knew that the very memory of the piano falsified still further the perspective in which he saw the elements of the music, that the field open to the musician is not a miserable keyboard of seven notes, but an immeasurable keyboard as yet almost entirely unknown on which, just here and there, separated by shadows thick and unexplored, a few of the millions of keys of tenderness, of passion, of courage, of serenity, which compose it, each one as different from the others as one universe differs from another, have been discovered by a few great artists who do us the service, by awakening in us feelings that correspond to the theme they've discovered, of showing us what richness, what variety lies hidden, unbeknownst to us, within that great unfathomed and alarming night of our soul which we take to be vacuity and nothingness. Vinteuil had been one of those musicians. In his little phrase, although it might present to the intelligence an obscure surface, one sensed a content so solid, so precise, to which it gave a force so new, so original, that those who'd heard it preserved it within themselves on the same footing as the ideas of the intellect. Swann referred back to it as to a conception of love and happiness whose distinctive character he recognized at once, as he would that of *La Princesse de Clèves* or of *René*,* if the titles of either of those works occurred to him. Even when he wasn't thinking of the little phrase, it existed latent in his mind on the same level as certain other notions without material equivalents, like the notions of light, of sound, of perspective, of physical pleasure, which are the rich possessions that diversify and adorn our inner life. Perhaps we'll lose them, perhaps they will fade away, if we return to nothingness. But for as long as we are alive, we can no more divest ourselves of our experience of them than we can do so in relation to some material thing, than we can, for instance, doubt the light of the lamp we have lit and which transforms all the objects in our room, from which even the memory of darkness vanishes. In this way Vinteuil's phrase, like some theme, say, in *Tristan*, which may also represent to us a certain emotional accretion, had espoused our mortal condition, had taken on something human that was quite affecting. Its destiny was linked to the future, to the reality of our soul, of which it was one of the most special, the most distinctive ornaments. Perhaps it's the nothingness that is real and our entire inner life is non-existent, but in that case we feel that these phrases of music, and these notions that exist in relation to that life, must be nothing also. We shall perish, but we hold as hostages these divine captives who will follow us and share our fate. And death in their company is somehow less bitter, less inglorious, perhaps less probable.

Swann was, therefore, not wrong to believe that the phrase of the sonata really existed. However, though human in that respect, it belonged nevertheless to a species of supernatural creatures we've never seen, but whom, in spite of that, we recognize with delight when some explorer of the unseen succeeds in capturing one, and brings it back from the divine realm to which he has access, to shine down for a few moments on ours. This was what Vinteuil had done with the little phrase. Swann sensed that the composer had merely unveiled it, made it visible, with his musical instruments, following and respecting its outlines with a hand so loving, so prudent, so deli-cate, and so sure that the sound changed at every moment, fading to indicate a shadow, enlivened when it had to follow the track of a bolder contour. And one proof that Swann was not mistaken in believing in the real existence of this phrase was that any music lover with the least discernment would at once have noticed the imposture if Vinteuil, lacking the power to see its outlines clearly and to render them accur-ately, had added a few touches of his own here and there in order to conceal the deficiencies of his vision or the lapses of his hand.

It had disappeared. Swann knew it would reappear at the end of the last movement, after a long passage that Madame Verdurin's pian-ist always skipped. There were in that passage some marvellous ideas which Swann had not noticed on first hearing the sonata but which he noticed now, as if, in the cloakroom of his memory, they had divested themselves of the uniform disguise of novelty. He listened to all the diverse themes that would enter into the composition of the phrase, like the premises on which an inevitable conclusion is built; he was witnessing its genesis. 'What daring!' he said to himself. 'This Vinteuil is as inspired, perhaps, as Lavoisier or Ampère,* conducting his experiments, discovering the secret laws that govern an unknown force, driving, across a region unexplored, towards the only possible goal, the invisible team in which he has placed his trust and which he'll never see!' How beautiful was the dialogue Swann heard between the piano and the violin at the beginning of the last section! The suppression of human speech, far from letting fantasy reign there, as one might have thought, had eliminated it; never had spoken language been subject to such rigid necessity, never had it known such pertinent questions, such irrefutable answers. At first the piano alone lamented, like a bird abandoned by its mate; the violin heard it and responded, as from a nearby tree. It was as at the beginning of the world, as if there were as yet only the two of them on the earth, or rather in this world removed from everything else, constructed by the logic of its creator so that there would never be more than the two of them: the world of this sonata. Was it a bird, was it the soul of the little phrase, not yet fully formed, was it a fairy—this creature invisibly lamenting, whose plaint the piano tenderly repeated? Its cries were so sudden that the violinist had to snatch at his bow to gather them up. Marvellous bird! The violinist seemed to want to charm it, tame it, capture it. Already it had passed into his soul, already the violinist's body, truly possessed, was shaking like a medium's with the presence of the little phrase. Swann knew it was going to speak one more time. And he'd so completely divided himself in two that the wait for the imminent moment when he'd find himself confronting it again made him shudder with one of those sobs which a beautiful line of poetry or a sad piece of news wrings from us, not when we're alone, but when we repeat them to friends in whom we can see ourselves as another person whose probable emotion affects them too. It reappeared, but this time to remain suspended in the air and play there for a moment only, as though motionless, before dying. And so Swann concentrated intently on this brief extension of its life. It was still there, like an iridescent bubble floating by itself. Like a rainbow, whose brilliance weakens, fades, then returns, and before dying away altogether, glows for a moment more gloriously than ever: to the two colours it had so far allowed to appear, it added others, chords of every hue in the prism, and made them sing. Swann didn't dare to move, and would have liked to make all the other people in the room stay still too, as if the slightest movement might compromise the fragile, exquisite, supernatural magic that was so near to vanishing. No one, in fact, dreamed of speaking. The ineffable word of one man, who was absent, perhaps dead (Swann didn't know if Vinteuil was still alive), breathing out above the rites of these celebrants, was enough to hold the attention of three hundred people, and made of the dais, where a soul had thus been conjured into being, one of the noblest altars on which a supernatural ceremony could be performed. So that, when the phrase had unravelled itself at last, floating in fragments in the motifs that followed and had already taken its place, if at first Swann was irritated to see the Comtesse de Monteriender, famous for her naïvety, lean towards him to confide her impressions even before the sonata had ended, he couldn't help smiling, and perhaps also found a deeper meaning, which she couldn't see, in her words. Marvelling at the virtuosity of the musicians, the countess exclaimed to Swann: 'It's amazing! I've never seen anything like it . . .' But then, with a scrupulous regard for accuracy, she corrected her first assertion, and qualified her remark by adding: 'anything like it . . . since the table-turning!'

From that evening on, Swann knew that the love Odette had once felt for him would never return, that his hopes of happiness would never be fulfilled. And on the days when she again happened to show some kindness and affection towards him, if she showed him particular attention, he'd note these ostensible and deceptive signs of a slight renewal of feeling with the kind of loving, sceptical concern, the desperate joy of people who, caring for a friend in the last days of an incurable illness, report as facts of great significance such things as: 'Yesterday he did his accounts himself, and he managed to spot a mistake we'd made in adding up; today he ate an egg and enjoyed it—if he manages to digest it we'll try a cutlet tomorrow,' although they know these things are meaningless in the face of imminent and inevitable death. No doubt Swann was sure that if he'd now been living far away from Odette, he would eventually have lost interest in her, so that he would have been glad if she'd left Paris for ever; he would have had the courage to remain; but he could not bring himself to leave.

He had often considered leaving. Now that he was once again at work on his study of Vermeer, he needed to return, for a few days at least, to The Hague, Dresden, and Brunswick. He was convinced that a *Diana with Her Companions* which had been bought by the Mauritshuis at the Goldschmidt sale as a Nicolas Maes was in fact a Vermeer.* And he would have liked to be able to examine the painting on the spot, in order to confirm his belief. But to leave Paris while Odette was there, or even when she wasn't there—for in new places where our sensations haven't been dulled by habit, we refresh and reanimate an old pain—was for him so cruel a notion that he was able

to think about it constantly only because he knew he was resolved
never to put it into effect. But sometimes, while he was asleep, the
intention of taking the trip would come back to him—without his
remembering that it was out of the question—and in his sleep he
would take the trip. One night he dreamed that he was going away for
a year; he was leaning out of the train window towards a young man
on the platform who was weeping as he bade him farewell, and was
trying to convince him to come away with him. The train began to
move, he awoke in alarm, and remembered that he wasn't going away,
that he would see Odette that evening, the next day, and almost every
day thereafter. Then, still shaken by his dream, he blessed the special
circumstances that had made him independent, so that he could
remain near Odette, and also succeed in getting her to allow him to
see her occasionally; and, as he recapitulated all these advantages—his
social position; his wealth, from which she was too often in need of
assistance not to shrink from contemplating a serious break with him
(to the extent, some said, of secretly hoping he would marry her); his
friendship with Monsieur de Charlus, which in truth had never been
of any great advantage to him in his dealings with Odette, but gave
him the consolation of feeling that she heard flattering things about
him from this mutual friend whom she admired so much; and even
his intelligence, which he employed entirely in devising every day
a new scheme that would make his presence, if not agreeable, at least
necessary to Odette—he thought about what would have become of
him if he hadn't had all this; he thought that if, like so many men, he'd
been poor, humble, wretched, forced to accept any kind of work, or
tied down by his family or a wife, he might have been obliged to leave
Odette, and that dream, the terror of which was still so fresh in his
mind, might even have come true; and he said to himself: 'You don't
know when you're well off. You're never as unhappy as you think.'*
But he reflected that this way of life had now been going on for years,
that all he could now hope for was that it would last for ever, that he
would sacrifice his work, his pleasures, his friends, in fact his whole
life to the daily expectation of a meeting that could bring him no happiness, and he wondered whether he was not deceiving himself,
whether the circumstances that had favoured his love affair and kept
it from ending had not been detrimental to the whole course of his
life, whether the most desirable outcome would not in fact have been
the one which, to his great delight, had only happened in a dream: his

own departure; and he told himself: 'You don't know when you're badly off. You're never as happy as you think.'

Sometimes he hoped she would die, painlessly, in an accident, for she was out of doors, in the streets, on the roads, from morning to night. As she always returned safe and sound, he would marvel at the human body's suppleness and resilience, at its ability to outwit and keep at bay all the perils that beset it (and which to Swann seemed innumerable now that his secret desire had assessed them), and so allowed people to abandon themselves daily and almost with impunity to their work of mendacity, their pursuit of pleasure. And he felt a bond of sympathy with Mohammed II, whose portrait by Bellini he liked so much,* who, realizing that he'd fallen madly in love with one of his wives, stabbed her to death in order, as his Venetian biographer ingenuously says, to recover his independence of mind. Then he would feel shocked that he should be thinking thus only of himself, and the sufferings he'd endured would seem to him to deserve no pity since he himself had set so low a price on Odette's life.

Incapable as he was of cutting himself off from her altogether, if at least he'd been able to see her when he wanted, without impediment, his suffering would in the end have subsided and perhaps his love would have died. And since she didn't want to leave Paris for ever, he wished she would never leave. As he knew that her only extended absence was the annual one in August and September, at least he had ample opportunity, several months in advance, to dissolve the bitter thought of it in all the Time to come which he carried within him in anticipation, and which, composed of days identical with those of the present, flowed through his mind, transparent and cold, nourishing his sadness but without causing him too much pain. But that inner future, that limpid free-flowing river, was suddenly disturbed by a single remark of Odette's that pierced Swann's heart, immobilized it like a block of ice, hardened its fluidity, froze it completely; and he suddenly felt he was filled with an enormous and infrangible mass that pressed on the inner walls of his being until it nearly burst; Odette had simply said, observing him with a sly smile: 'Forcheville is going on a lovely trip at Whitsun.* He's going to Egypt,' and Swann had immediately taken this to mean: 'I'm going to Egypt at Whitsun with Forcheville.' And in fact, if Swann said to her several days later: 'About that trip you said you were going to take with Forcheville,' she would answer without thinking: 'Yes, my dear, we're leaving on the nineteenth. We'll send you a postcard of the Pyramids.' Then he longed to know if she was Forcheville's mistress, to ask her point-blank. He knew that, superstitious as she was, there were some per-juries she would not commit, and besides, the fear, which had held him back up to now, of annoying her with questions, of making her hate him, had vanished now that he'd lost all hope of ever being loved by her.

One day he received an anonymous letter telling him that Odette had been the mistress of countless men (several of whom it named, among them Forcheville, Monsieur de Bréauté, and the painter), and of women too, and that she frequented houses of ill repute. He was tormented by the thought that among his friends there was a person capable of sending him this letter (because certain details revealed that its author was someone who had an intimate knowledge of Swann's life). He wondered who it could be. But he'd never had any suspicion with regard to the unknown actions of other people, those which had no visible connection with what they said. And when he began to wonder whether it was beneath the apparent character of Monsieur de Charlus, or Monsieur des Laumes, or Monsieur d'Orsan, that he would have to locate the uncharted region in which this ignoble act had been conceived, since he'd never heard any of these men speak in favour of anonymous letters, and since everything they'd ever said to him implied that they condemned them, he saw no reason to connect this infamy with the character of any one of them rather than the others. Monsieur de Charlus was somewhat eccentric, but basically good and kind; Monsieur des Laumes was a little hard, but sound and straightforward. As for Monsieur d'Orsan, Swann had never met anyone who, in even the most depressing circumstances, would approach him with more heartfelt words, in a more tactful and fitting manner. So much so that he couldn't understand the rather indelicate role people ascribed to Monsieur d'Orsan in the love affair he was having with a rich woman, and whenever Swann thought of him he was obliged to disregard the bad reputation which was so irreconcilable with the many clear proofs of his considerate nature. For a moment Swann felt his mind clouding over, and he thought about something else in order to see things more clearly. Only then did he have the strength to return to his reflections. But now, having been unable to suspect anyone, he was forced to suspect everyone. After all, Monsieur de Charlus was fond of him and had a heart of gold. But he was a neurotic—one day he might be upset on hearing that Swann was unwell, and another day, out of jealousy, or anger, or acting on a sudden impulse, he might want to hurt him. Really, that kind of man was the worst of all. Of course, the Prince des Laumes was not nearly as fond of Swann as Monsieur de Charlus. But for that very reason he didn't have the same susceptibilities with regard to him; and also, his was a nature which, though undoubtedly cold, was as incapable of base as of magnanimous actions. Swann regretted that he hadn't formed attachments exclusively to such people. Then he mused that what prevents men from doing harm to their fellow men is goodness of heart, that really he could answer only for men whose natures were similar to his own, as was, so far as the heart was concerned, that of Monsieur de Charlus. The mere thought of causing Swann so much distress would have revolted him. But with an insensitive man, of another order of humanity, like the Prince des Laumes, how could one begin to imagine the actions to which he might be led by motives that sprang from a totally different nature? To have a kind heart is everything, and Monsieur de Charlus had one. Monsieur d'Orsan was not lacking in heart either, and his relationship with Swann—cordial but not close, arising from the pleasure which, since they thought the same way about everything, they found in talking together—was more stable than the high-strung affection of Monsieur de Charlus, who was capable of committing acts of passion, for good or ill. If there was anyone by whom Swann had always felt himself understood and liked in a discriminating way, it was by Monsieur d'Orsan. Yes, but what of the disreputable life he led? Swann regretted that he hadn't been more mindful of it in the past, having often confessed jokingly that he'd never felt such keen feelings of sympathy and respect as in the company of a scoundrel. 'It's not for nothing', he said to himself now, 'that when men pass judgement on their fellows, it's in terms of their actions. They are the only things that mean something, as opposed to what we say or what we think. Charlus and des Laumes may have their faults, but they are still honourable men. Orsan may not have any such faults, but he's not an honourable man. He may have acted dishonourably once again.' Then Swann suspected Rémi, who, it was true, could only have provided inspiration for the letter, but for a moment he felt he was on the right track. In the first place, Lorédan had reasons for bearing a grudge against Odette. And then, how can we not imagine that our

servants, living in a situation inferior to ours, adding to our wealth
and our weaknesses imaginary riches and vices for which they envy
and despise us, will inevitably be led to act quite differently from the
people of our own class? He also suspected my grandfather. Every
time Swann had asked a favour of him, hadn't he always refused?
Besides, with his bourgeois ideas, he might have thought he was acting in Swann's own interest. Swann also suspected Bergotte, the
painter, and the Verdurins, and in passing admired once more the
wisdom of society people in keeping their distance from those artistic
circles in which such things are possible, perhaps even openly
accepted as amusing pranks; but then he recalled some of the honest
traits displayed by those bohemians, and contrasted them with the life
of expediency, almost of fraudulence, to which a lack of money,
a craving for luxury, and the corrupting influence of their pleasures
often drive members of the aristocracy. In short, the anonymous letter
proved that he numbered among his acquaintances a person capable
of villainy, but he could see no more reason why that villainy should
be hidden in the unfathomed depths of the man of sensibility rather
than in the unfeeling man, in the artist rather than the bourgeois, in
the great lord rather than the valet. What criterion should one adopt
to judge one's fellows? In truth, there was not a single person among
those he knew who might not be capable of infamy. Must he then stop
seeing them all? His mind clouded over; he drew his hands two or
three times across his brow, wiped the lenses of his pince-nez with his
handkerchief, and, reflecting that, after all, men as good as himself
associated with Monsieur de Charlus, the Prince des Laumes, and the
rest, he persuaded himself that this meant, if not that they were
incapable of infamy, at least that it was a necessity of life, to which
everyone must submit, to associate with people who were perhaps not
incapable of it. And he continued to shake hands with all the friends
he'd suspected, with the purely formal reservation that each one of
them had possibly sought to drive him to despair. As for the actual
content of the letter, he didn't worry about it, because not one of the
charges levelled against Odette was remotely plausible. Like many
people, Swann had a lazy mind and lacked imagination. He knew very
well as a general truth that people's lives are full of contrasts, but for
each particular individual he imagined the part of his or her life of
which he knew nothing as being identical to the part he knew. He
imagined what he was not told on the basis of what he was told.

During the times when Odette was with him, if their conversation turned to some dishonest act committed or some unworthy sentiment expressed by a third party, she would condemn them by virtue of the same principles that Swann had heard professed by his parents and to which he'd always remained faithful; and then she would arrange her flowers, drink tea with him, or enquire after his work. So Swann extended these habits to the rest of Odette's life, and saw her going through these motions whenever he wanted to picture to himself the times when she was away from him. If anyone had portrayed her to him as she was, or rather as she'd been with him for so long, but with another man, he would have been distressed, because that picture of her would have seemed quite plausible. But the idea that she went to procuresses, took part in orgies with other women, and led the dissolute life of the most abject creatures—what an insane aberration, for the realization of which, thank God, the imagined chrysanthemums, the endless partaking of tea, the virtuous indignation left no room! However, from time to time he'd give Odette to understand that, for some malicious reason, someone had been reporting to him about everything she did; and by making use of an insignificant but true detail which he'd learned by chance, he would imply that he'd accidentally divulged a tiny fragment, among a great many others, of a complete reconstruction of Odette's life which he held in his mind, thus making her suppose that he was well informed about things that in reality he didn't know or even suspect, for if quite often he adjured Odette never to tamper with the truth, it was only, whether he realized it or not, so that she would tell him everything she did. No doubt, as he said to Odette, he loved sincerity, but he loved it as a procuress who could keep him informed about his mistress's life. And so his love of sincerity, not being disinterested, hadn't made him a better person. The truth he cherished was the truth Odette could tell him; but, to obtain that truth, he wasn't afraid to resort to falsehood, the very falsehood which he never stopped portraying to Odette as leading every human being to degradation. In short, he lied as much as Odette because, while unhappier than she, he was no less selfish. And she, hearing Swann tell her the things she'd done, would stare at him with a look of mistrust, and put a touch of annoyance into her expression just in case, so as not to appear to be humiliated and to be blushing for her actions.

One day, during the longest period of calm he'd yet been able to go through without suffering fresh attacks of jealousy, he'd agreed to go to the theatre that evening with the Princesse des Laumes. Having opened his newspaper to find out what was being played, the sight of the title, *Les Filles de Marbre* by Théodore Barrière,* struck him such a painful blow that he recoiled and turned his head away. Illuminated as though by footlights, in the new spot where it now appeared, the word 'marble', which he'd lost the ability to notice, so accustomed was he to seeing it before his eyes, had suddenly become visible again, and had immediately reminded him of the story Odette had told him long ago of a visit she'd paid to the Salon at the Palais de l'Industrie with Madame Verdurin, who'd said to her: 'Be careful, now! I know how to melt you. You're not made of marble, you know.' Odette had sworn it was only a joke, and he'd attached no importance to it at the time. But he'd had more confidence in her then than he had now. And the anonymous letter had indeed alluded to affairs of that kind. Not daring to lift his eyes to the newspaper again, he unfolded it, turned a page in order not to see the words '*Les Filles de Marbre*', and mechanically began to read the news from the provinces. There had been a storm in the Channel, damage was reported in Dieppe, Cabourg, and Beuzeval.* He recoiled again in horror.

The name Beuzeval had reminded him of another place in the same area, Beuzeville, whose name is linked by a hyphen to another, Bréauté, which he'd often seen on maps, but without ever noticing it was the same as that of his friend Monsieur de Bréauté, whom the anonymous letter mentioned as having been Odette's lover. After all, in the case of Monsieur de Bréauté, there was nothing implausible about the charge; but as far as Madame Verdurin was concerned, it was a sheer impossibility. The fact that Odette sometimes lied didn't mean one could assume she never told the truth, and in the remarks she'd exchanged with Madame Verdurin and which she herself had described to Swann, he'd recognized one of those pointless and dangerous little pleasantries which, from inexperience of life and ignorance of vice, are made by women whose very innocence they reveal and who—like Odette for instance—are least likely to feel passionate love for another woman. Whereas on the contrary the indignation with which she'd denied the suspicions she'd unintentionally aroused in him for a moment with her account accorded with everything he knew about his mistress's tastes and temperament. But at this moment, through one of those inspirations typical of jealous men, analogous to the inspiration which reveals to a poet or a scientist, who thus far has nothing but a single rhyme or observation, the idea or law that will give them all the power they need, Swann recalled for the first time a remark Odette had made to him at least two years before: 'All Madame Verdurin thinks about these days is me! I'm her little pet. She kisses me, she wants me to go shopping with her, and to call her *tu*.' Far from seeing, at the time, any connection between this comment and the silly remark reported to him by Odette and meant to suggest some sort of depravity, he'd welcomed it as proof of a warm friendship. But now the memory of Madame Verdurin's expressions of affection had suddenly blended with the memory of her unseemly conversation. He could no longer separate them in his mind, and saw them mingled in reality too, the affection lending a certain serious-ness and importance to the pleasantry which, in turn, made the affec-tion seem somewhat less innocent. He went to see Odette at her house. He sat down at a distance from her. He didn't dare kiss her, not knowing whether it would be affection or anger that a kiss would pro-voke, either in her or in himself. He sat there, saying nothing, watch-ing their love die. Suddenly he made up his mind.

'Odette, my dear,' he said, 'I know I'm being awful, but there are a few things I must ask you. Do you remember the idea I got into my head about you and Madame Verdurin? Tell me, was it true, with her or with anyone else?'

She shook her head, pursing her lips, a sign people often use to indicate that they will not go, because it bores them, if someone asks: 'Are you coming to watch the procession go past? Will you be at the review?' But a shake of the head usually applied to an event in the future, by that very fact, imparts a degree of uncertainty to the denial of an event in the past. Furthermore, it suggests only reasons of per-sonal expediency rather than disapproval or moral impossibility. When he saw Odette signal to him thus that it was untrue, Swann realized it might well be true.

'I've told you. You know very well,' she added, looking irritated and unhappy.

'Yes, I know, but are you sure? Don't say, "You know very well"; say, "I have never done anything of that sort with any woman." '

She repeated his words, as if it were a school lesson, ironically, and as if she wanted to get rid of him: 'I've never done anything of that sort with any woman.'

'Can you swear it on your medal of Our Lady of Laghet?'

Swann knew Odette would never swear a false oath on that medal.

'Oh, stop being so horrible to me!' she exclaimed, swiftly side-stepping his question. 'Can't you stop this? What's the matter with you today? You seem determined to make me hate you, absolutely loathe you. I wanted to have a nice time with you again, the way we used to, and this is how you thank me!'

But Swann, not letting go, like a surgeon waiting for a spasm to subside that has interrupted his operation but will not make him abandon it, continued:

'You'd be quite wrong if you thought I'd hold it against you in any way, Odette,' he said with a persuasive and deceptive gentleness. 'I only talk to you about things I know, and I always know much more than I say. But only you can mitigate by your confession what will go on making me hate you as long as I only have other people's word for it. Any anger I might feel has nothing to do with your actions, I forgive you everything because I love you; it's because of your duplicity, the ridiculous duplicity that makes you persist in denying things I know to be true. How can you expect me to go on loving you when I see you insisting on, swearing to, something I know is untrue? Odette, don't prolong the agony of this moment, it's unbearable for both of us. If you want to, you can end it in a second, you'll be free of it for ever. Tell me on your medal, yes or no, if you ever did things like that.'

'But I've got no idea!' she exclaimed angrily. 'Perhaps a very long time ago, without knowing what I was doing. Perhaps two or three times.'

Swann had considered in advance every possibility. Reality must therefore be something that bears no relation to possibilities, any more than the thrust of a knife into one's body bears any relation to the gradual movement of the clouds overhead, for the words 'two or three times' carved a kind of cross in the tissues of his heart. How strange that the words 'two or three times', mere words, words spoken into the air, at a distance, could so lacerate the heart, as if they'd actually touched it, could make a man ill, as if he'd swallowed poison. Instinctively Swann thought of the remark he'd heard at Madame de Saint-Euverte's: 'I've never seen anything like it since the table-turning.' The pain he now felt was unlike anything he'd thought possible. Not only because, even in his moments of deepest distrust, he'd rarely imagined such an extremity of evil, but because, even when he did imagine it, it remained vague, ambiguous, not clothed in the particular horror that had arisen from the words 'perhaps two or three times', not armed with that specific cruelty, as different from anything he'd ever known as a disease with which one is stricken for the first time. And yet Odette, the source of all his pain, was no less dear to him, was on the contrary more precious, as if, as his suffering increased, so did the value of the sedative, of the antidote which this woman alone possessed. He wanted to devote more care to her, as to a disease one suddenly discovers is more serious. He wanted the terrible thing she'd told him she'd done 'two or three times' not to happen again. To ensure this, he had to watch over Odette. People often say that when we tell a friend about the misdeeds of his mistress, we succeed only in making him more attached to her, because he doesn't believe what he's told; but how much more so if he does! But, Swann wondered, how could he manage to protect her? He could perhaps keep her safe from a particular woman, but there were hundreds of others, and he realized what madness had come over him when, on the evening when he hadn't found Odette at the Verdurins', he'd begun to want something that was always impossible—to possess another person. Happily for Swann, underneath the new sufferings that had entered his soul like an invading horde, there lay a natural foundation, older, gentler, and quietly industrious, like the cells of a damaged organ that at once prepare to mend the affected tissues, or like the muscles of a paralysed limb that strive to recover their normal movements. For a time, these older, more autochthonous inhabitants of his soul employed all Swann's strength in the mysterious labour of reparation that gives one an illusion of relief during convalescence, after an operation. This time it wasn't so much, as it usually was, in Swann's mind that this respite took effect, through exhaustion; it was rather in his heart. But all the things that have ever existed in life tend to recur, and like a dying animal seized anew by a convulsion that had seemed over, on Swann's heart, spared for a moment, the same agony returned of its own accord to retrace the same cross. He remembered those moonlit evenings when, leaning back in the victoria that was taking him to the Rue La Pérouse, he would voluptuously savour the emotions of a man in love, unaware of the poisoned fruit they would inevitably bear. But all these thoughts lasted no more than a second, the time it took to raise his hand to his heart, catch his breath, and manage a smile to hide his torment. Already he was beginning to ask further questions. For his jealousy, which had taken more pains than an enemy would have done to strike this blow, to make him feel the most intense suffering he'd yet known, wasn't satisfied that he'd suffered enough, and sought to expose him to a wound that was deeper still. Thus, like a malevolent deity, Swann's jealousy inspired him, driving him on towards his ruin. It was not his fault, but Odette's alone, if at first his torment didn't grow worse.

'My darling,' he said, 'it's all in the past now. Was it with anyone I know?'

'No, no, I swear it wasn't. Anyway, I think I exaggerated, I don't think I went that far.'

He smiled and went on: 'As you like. It doesn't really matter, but it's a shame you can't tell me the name. If I could picture the person it would keep me from ever thinking about it again. I say this for your sake, because then I wouldn't bother you about it any more. It's such a relief to be able to picture something in your mind! The things that are really horrible are those you can't imagine. But you've already been so nice about it, I don't want to keep on at you. I'm so very grateful to you for being so good to me. I've quite finished now. Just one more thing, though: how long ago was it?'

'Oh, Charles, can't you see you're killing me? It was all so long ago. I never gave it another thought. And now it's as if you're determined to put those ideas in my head again.' And with unconscious stupidity but deliberate spite, she added: 'A lot of good it'll do you!'

'Oh, I only wanted to know if it had happened since I've known you! It would be natural enough. Did it happen here? Can't you tell me which particular evening, so I can picture what I was doing at the time? You must realize it isn't possible you don't remember who it was with, Odette, my love.'

'But I don't, really I don't; I think it was in the Bois one evening when you came to meet us on the island. You'd had dinner with the Princesse des Laumes,' she added, happy to give him a specific detail that would attest to her truthfulness. 'There was a woman at the next table I hadn't seen for ages. She said: "Come round behind that little rock and see how the moonlight looks on the water." At first I just yawned, and said: "No, I'm tired, I'm quite happy where I am." She insisted there had never been moonlight quite like it. "Oh, come on!" I said. I knew very well what she was after.'

Odette was almost laughing as she related this, either because it seemed to her quite natural, or because she thought she would thereby make it seem less important, or so as not to appear humiliated. But, at the sight of Swann's face, she changed her tone:

'You're a beast, you like torturing me, making me tell you lies, so you'll leave me in peace.'

This second blow was even more terrible for Swann than the first. Never had he imagined it to have been so recent, hidden from his unseeing eyes not in a past he hadn't known about, but in evenings he could remember so clearly, evenings he'd spent with Odette, which he'd believed he knew all about but now seemed, in retrospect, horrible and full of deceit; among them, suddenly, there opened up a great chasm, that moment on the island in the Bois. Odette, without being intelligent, had the charm of naturalness. She had described, she had mimed the scene with such simplicity that Swann, gasping, saw everything: Odette's yawn, the little rock. He heard her answer—gaily, alas!—'Oh, come on!' He felt she would tell him nothing more that evening, that no further revelation could be expected for the moment; so he said: 'My poor darling, please forgive me, I can see I've hurt you; but it's all over now, and I won't think about it any more.'

But she saw that his eyes remained fixed on the things he didn't know and on that past time of their love, monotonous and sweet in his memory because it was vague, which was now being torn open like a wound by that moment on the island in the Bois, in the moonlight, after his dinner with the Princesse des Laumes. But he was so accustomed to finding life interesting—to admiring the strange discoveries one can make—that even while suffering to the point of thinking he couldn't endure such pain for long, he said to himself: 'Life is really amazing; it's full of big surprises; immorality is actually more common than one would think. Here's a woman I trusted, who seems so simple, so honest in any case, even though her morals were a little loose, who seemed quite normal and healthy in her tastes; after an implausible denunciation, I question her, and the little she admits reveals far more than I'd ever have suspected.' But he was unable to limit himself to these detached observations. He tried to form a precise estimate of the significance of what she'd told him, in order to know if he ought to conclude that she'd done this sort of thing often and was likely to do so again. He repeated her words: 'I knew very well what she was after', 'two or three times', 'Oh, come on!', but they didn't reappear in his memory unarmed, each of them held a knife and used it to strike further further blows. For a long time, just as a sick man can't stop himself from trying repeatedly to make the motion that causes him pain, he kept saying these words to himself: 'I'm quite happy where I am', 'Oh, come on!', but the pain was so intense that he had to stop. He was amazed that acts he'd always dismissed light-heartedly as being quite trivial had now become as serious as a mortal illness. He knew many women he could have asked to keep an eye on Odette. But how could he expect them to adopt the point of view he now had and not hold on to the point of view he'd had for so long, that had always guided him in love affairs, and not say to him, laughing: 'You awful jealous man, trying to rob other people of their pleasure'? Through what trapdoor, suddenly opened, had he (who in the past had derived only refined pleasures from his love for Odette) been plunged into this new circle of Hell from which he couldn't see how he would ever escape? Poor Odette! He didn't hold it against her. She was only half to blame. Didn't people say it was her own mother who had handed her over to a rich Englishman in Nice when she was still little more than a child? But what painful truth was now contained for him in those lines from Alfred de Vigny's *Journal d'un poète* which in the past had left him quite unmoved: 'When you feel you are falling in love with a woman, you should say to yourself: Who are her friends? What kind of life has she led? All one's future happiness depends on the answers.'* Swann was amazed that simple statements repeated in the mind, like 'Oh, come on!' or 'I could see very well what she was after', could hurt so much. But he realized that what he believed to be simple statements were merely parts of the framework that still contained, and could still bring back to him, the pain he'd felt when Odette was telling her story. For it was indeed the same pain that he was now feeling again. Even though he now knew—and even if, with the passage of time, he'd forgotten a little, and forgiven—the moment he repeated these words to himself all his old suffering turned him once again into the person he'd been before Odette had spoken: ignorant, trustful; his unrelenting jealousy placed him once again, so that he might be hurt all the more by Odette's confession, in the position of a man who doesn't yet know, and after several months he could still be stricken by her story as if he'd only just heard it. He marvelled at the terrible recreative power of his memory. It was only by the weakening of that generative force, whose fecundity diminishes with age, that he could hope for an easing of his torment. But as soon as the power of any one of Odette's remarks to make him suffer seemed nearly exhausted, one of those on which Swann's mind had dwelt less until then, a remark that was almost new, would come to replace the others and strike at him with undiminished vigour. The memory of the evening when he'd dined with the Princesse des Laumes was painful to him, but it was only the core of his sickness, which spread out confusedly all around into the days before and after it. And whatever point in it he tried to touch in his memories, it was the whole of that season, during which the Verdurins had dined so often on the island in the Bois, that hurt him. So badly that the curiosity which his jealousy kept provoking in him was gradually neutralized by his fear of the new torments he would inflict on himself by satisfying it. He realized that the entire period of Odette's life that had elapsed before she met him, a period he'd never tried to imagine, was not the abstract length of time he'd vaguely pictured, but had consisted of specific years, each one filled with concrete incidents. But if he were to learn more about them, he was afraid that that past of hers, colourless, fluid, and tolerable, might assume a hideous, tangible shape, a particular, diabolical form. And he continued to make no effort to imagine it, no longer from laziness of mind, but from fear of suffering. He hoped that, one day, he might at last be able to hear mention of the island in the Bois or the Princesse des Laumes without feeling the old rending of his heart, and thought it would be imprudent to provoke Odette into supplying him with more words spoken, names of places, and different circumstances which, when his suffering had barely abated, might rouse it again in another form.

But often the things he didn't know, that he dreaded now to learn, were revealed spontaneously by Odette herself, and without her realizing it; in fact the gap that depravity put between Odette's real life and the comparatively innocent life which Swann had believed, and often still believed, that his mistress led, was far wider than she realized: a depraved person, always affecting the same virtue in the eyes of the people by whom he doesn't want his vices to be suspected, has no gauge by which to recognize how far those vices, whose continuous growth is imperceptible to himself, are gradually drawing him away from normal ways of living. In the course of their cohabitation, in Odette's mind, along with the memory of the actions she was hiding from Swann, other actions were gradually coloured by them, infected by them, without her being able to see anything strange about them, without their seeming out of place in the particular surroundings where she kept them inside her; but if she described them to Swann, he would be horrified by the revelation of the environment they betrayed. One day he was trying, without hurting Odette, to ask her if she had ever had any dealings with procuresses. He was convinced, in fact, that she hadn't; the anonymous letter had lodged the idea in his mind, but in a mechanical way; it had met with no credence there, but had remained there, and Swann, in order to be rid of the purely material but nonetheless awkward presence of the suspicion, wanted Odette to remove it. 'Oh, no! Not that they don't pester me,' she added with a smile of satisfied vanity, no longer able to realize it couldn't seem acceptable to Swann. 'There was one here yesterday who stayed more than two hours waiting for me, offered me any amount I wanted. Apparently some ambassador had said to her: "I'll kill myself if you don't bring her to me." They told her I'd gone out. In the end I went and spoke to her myself so she would go away. I wish you could have seen the way I treated her; my maid could hear me from the next room and said I was shouting at the top of my voice: "Haven't I told you?" I said, "I don't want to! That's how it is, I just don't feel like it! Really, I should hope I'm still free to do as I please! If I needed the money, I could understand . . ." I've given the concierge strict instructions not to let her in again. He's to say I've gone to the country. Oh, I wish you'd been hiding somewhere. I think you'd have been pleased, my dear. Your little Odette has some good in her, you see, even though some people don't appreciate her at all.'

Moreover, her very admissions, when she made any, of faults that she supposed he'd discovered, served Swann as starting points for new doubts rather than putting an end to the old. For they never exactly matched his suspicions. Though Odette might remove from her confession all the essentials, there remained in the accessories something Swann had never imagined, that crushed him anew, and led him to expand the terms of his jealousy. And these admissions he could never forget. His soul bore them along, cast them aside, cradled them like dead bodies, and was poisoned by them.

On one occasion she mentioned a visit Forcheville had paid her on the day of the Paris–Murcia Fête. 'What? You already knew him then? Oh, yes, of course you did,' he said, correcting himself so as not to show he hadn't known. And suddenly he began to tremble at the thought that, on the day of the Paris–Murcia Fête, when he'd received from her the letter which he'd so carefully preserved, she had perhaps been having lunch with Forcheville at the Maison d'Or. She swore she hadn't. 'But the Maison d'Or does remind me of something or other which I found out later wasn't true,' he said in order to frighten her. 'Yes, that I hadn't been there at all that evening when I told you I'd just come from there, and you'd been looking for me at Prévost's,' she replied (thinking from his manner that he knew this) with a decisiveness in which there was, not cynicism, but timidity, a fear of upsetting Swann, which out of self-respect she wanted to hide, as well as a desire to show him she was capable of being frank. And so she struck with the precision and force of an executioner, though quite without cruelty, for she had no conception of the hurt she was causing Swann; and she even began to laugh, but perhaps this was mainly so as not to appear apologetic or embarrassed. 'It's quite true, I hadn't been to the Maison Dorée; I'd just been at Forcheville's house. I actually had been to Prévost's, I didn't make that up, and he met me there and asked me to come in and look at his engravings. But then someone else called to see him. I told you I was coming from the Maison d'Or because I was afraid you'd be annoyed. You see? That was rather kind of me, wasn't it? Even if it was wrong of me, at least I'm telling you about it now. What would I have to gain by not telling you I had lunch with him the day of the Paris–Murcia Fête, if it was true? Especially since, at the time, we didn't know each other very well, did we, darling?' He smiled at her with the sudden, craven weakness of the broken creature these crushing words had made of him. So, even during the months he'd never dared to think about again because they'd been too happy, during those months when she'd loved him, she was already lying to him! Besides the time (the first evening they had 'done a cattleya') when she'd told him she'd just come from the Maison Dorée, how many others there must have been, each of them also concealing a lie which Swann had never suspected. He remembered that one day she'd said: 'I'd just tell Madame Verdurin my dress wasn't ready, or my cab came late. One can always think of some excuse.' From him too, probably, when she'd murmured the little phrases that explain a delay or justify changing the time of a meeting, they must often have concealed, without his suspecting it then, something she was going to do with another man, a man to whom she'd said: 'I'll just tell Swann my dress wasn't ready, or my cab came late. One can always think of some excuse.' And beneath all of Swann's fondest memories, beneath the simplest words Odette had said to him in those early days, which he'd believed like the words of the Gospel, beneath the daily doings she'd recounted to him, beneath the most ordinary places, her dressmaker's apartment, the Avenue du Bois, the Hippodrome, he could sense, concealed within the superfluity of time which even in the busiest days still leaves some leeway, some room, and can serve as a cover for certain acts, he could sense the intrusion of a possible undercurrent of lies that debased everything that had remained most dear to him (his happiest evenings, the Rue La Pérouse itself, which Odette must always have left at times different from those she'd reported to him), spreading everywhere a little of the murky horror he'd felt on hearing her admission about the Maison Dorée, and, like the loathsome creatures in the Desolation of Nineveh,* dismantling stone by stone the entire edifice of his past. And if, now, he turned away whenever his memory pronounced the cruel name of the Maison Dorée, it was no longer, as still quite recently, at Madame de Saint-Euverte's party, because the name reminded him of the happiness he'd long since lost, but because it evoked the unhappiness he'd only just discovered. Then the same thing happened with the name of the Maison Dorée as with that of the island in the Bois, it gradually lost its power to inflict pain on him. For what we believe to be our love, or our jealousy, is not a single passion, continuous and indivisible. It's composed of an infinity of successive loves, of different jealousies, which are ephemeral but by their uninterrupted multiplicity give the impression of continuity, the illusion of unity. The life of Swann's love, the fidelity of his jealousy, were formed of the death, the infidelity, of innumerable desires, innumerable doubts, all of which had Odette as their object. If he hadn't seen her for a long time, those that died wouldn't have been replaced by others. But the presence of Odette continued to sow in Swann's heart alternate seeds of affection and suspicion.

On certain evenings she'd suddenly be full of affection towards him again, and warn him severely that he ought to take advantage of it right away, under penalty of not seeing it repeated for years to come; they had to go back to her house immediately to 'do a cattleya', and this desire which she claimed to feel for him was so sudden, so inexplicable, so imperious, the caresses she lavished on him so demonstrative and unwonted that this brutal and improbable fondness made Swann as unhappy as any lie or act of spite. One evening when, in obedience to her command, he'd again gone home with her and she was kissing him and whispering to him with a passion quite unlike her usual coldness, he suddenly thought he heard a noise; he got up, looked everywhere, found no one, but was unable to bring himself to lie down again next to her, whereupon she flew into a rage, broke a vase, and said: 'It's impossible to do anything right with you!' And he was left wondering whether she'd hidden some man in the room with the aim of provoking his jealousy or inflaming his senses.

Sometimes he visited brothels in the hope of learning something about her, though without daring to say her name. 'I've got a nice young one I know you'll like,' the Madam would say. And he would stay there for an hour chatting gloomily to some poor girl who was surprised that he went no further. One who was very young and beautiful said one day: 'What I'd like would be to find a man who'd be a real friend to me; then he could be sure I'd never go with another man again.'

'Really? Do you think it's possible for a woman to be touched that a man loves her, and never be unfaithful to him?' Swann asked anxiously.

'Oh yes! It would all depend, though, on what she's like!'

Swann couldn't help saying to these girls the sorts of things the Princesse des Laumes would have enjoyed. To the one who was looking for a friend, he said with a smile: 'How nice, you've put on blue eyes to go with your sash.'

'And you too, you're wearing blue cuffs.'

'What a nice conversation we're having, in a place like this! I'm not boring you, am I? Or stopping you from doing something else?'

'No, I've got plenty of time. If you'd been boring me, I'd have said so. I like listening to you.'

'I'm very flattered . . . Aren't we having a nice little chat?' he said, turning to the Madam, who'd just come in.

'Yes, that's just what I was thinking. How good they're being, I thought! People are coming here now just to talk. The Prince was telling me only the other day that it's much nicer here than at his wife's house. It seems that nowadays all the society women put on such airs. It shouldn't be allowed! But I'll leave you in peace, I know when I'm in the way.' And she left Swann alone with the girl with blue eyes. But soon he stood up and took his leave. She no longer interested him, she didn't know Odette.

The painter had been unwell, and Doctor Cottard recommended that he go on a sea-voyage; several of the faithful said they'd go with him; the Verdurins couldn't face the prospect of being left alone, rented a yacht, then purchased it; thus Odette went on frequent cruises. Each time she'd been gone for a little while, Swann felt he was beginning to detach himself from her, but as if this mental distance were proportional to the physical distance, as soon as he heard she was back, he couldn't rest until he'd seen her. Once, having gone off for only a month, so they thought, either because they were tempted in the course of the journey, or because Monsieur Verdurin had cunningly arranged things beforehand to please his wife and had informed the faithful only bit by bit as they went along, from Algiers they went to Tunis, then to Italy, then to Greece, Constantinople, and Asia Minor. The trip had lasted nearly a year. Swann felt perfectly relaxed, almost happy. Even though Madame Verdurin had tried to persuade the pianist and Doctor Cottard that the aunt of the one and the patients of the other had no need of them, and that in any case it was unwise to let Madame Cottard return to Paris which, Monsieur Verdurin claimed, was in the throes of a revolution, she was obliged to grant them their freedom at Constantinople. And the painter left with them. One day, shortly after the return of the three travellers, Swann, seeing an omnibus go by heading for the Luxembourg, where he had some business, had jumped on and found himself sitting opposite Madame Cottard, who was doing the rounds of the ladies whose 'day' it was; she was in full regalia, an ostrich feather in her hat, a silk dress, a muff, a parasol, a little case of visiting cards, and freshly laundered white gloves. Arrayed with these insignia, in fine weather she would go on foot from one house to the next in the same neighbourhood, but when she had to proceed to a different neighbourhood would use the omnibus system, changing as necessary. For a few minutes, before the woman's native amiability broke through the starched surface of the little bourgeoise, and not being sure whether she ought to talk about the Verdurins to Swann, she produced quite naturally, in her awkward, slow, soft voice, which from time to time was drowned out completely by the rattling of the omnibus, remarks selected from those she'd heard and repeated in the twenty-five houses whose stairs she climbed in the course of a day.

'I don't need to ask you, Monsieur, if a man so in the swim as yourself has been to the Mirlitons to see the portrait by Machard* which the whole of Paris is rushing to see? Do tell me what you think of it. Whose camp are you in, those who approve or those who don't? It's the same in every house now, the only thing they talk about is Machard's portrait; you aren't fashionable, you aren't really cultured, you aren't up-to-date unless you can give your opinion of Machard's portrait.'

Swann replied that he hadn't seen the portrait, and Madame Cottard was afraid she'd offended him by obliging him to confess it.

'Well, that's all right! At least you admit it straightaway, you don't think you're in disgrace because you haven't seen Machard's portrait. I think that's admirable of you. Well, I've seen it. Opinion is divided, you know, some people think it's too polished, rather like whipped cream, but I think it's just perfect. Of course, she's not like the blue-and-yellow women of our friend Biche. But I must tell you frankly (you'll think I'm terribly old-fashioned, but I always say what I think): I don't understand his work. Of course, I can see the good points in his portrait of my husband, it's not as strange as what he usually does, but even so he had to go and give him a blue moustache. Whereas Machard! Just imagine, the husband of the friend I'm just on my way to see now (which has given me the great pleasure of your company) has promised her that, if he's elected to the Academy (he's one of the doctor's colleagues) he'll get Machard to paint her portrait. Now that's a really lovely idea! I've got another friend who says she really prefers Leloir.* I'm just an ignoramus, and for all I know Leloir may be better technically. But I think the most important thing in a portrait, especially when it's going to cost ten thousand francs, is that it should be a good likeness, and nice to look at.'

Having made these pronouncements, to which she had been inspired by the loftiness of her plume, the monogram on her card case, the little number inked inside her gloves by the cleaner, and the embarrassment of speaking to Swann about the Verdurins, Madame Cottard, seeing that the omnibus was still a fair distance from the corner of the Rue Bonaparte, where the driver was to let her off, listened to her heart, which counselled other words.

'Your ears must have been burning, Monsieur,' she said, 'while we were on our voyage with Madame Verdurin. We talked about you all the time.'

This came as a great surprise to Swann, for he assumed his name was never uttered in the presence of the Verdurins.

'Of course,' Madame Cottard went on, 'Madame de Crécy was there, and that says it all. Wherever Odette is, she can never go for long without talking about you. And you can well imagine it's never unfavourably. What! You don't believe me?' she added, seeing that Swann looked sceptical.

Carried away by the sincerity of her conviction, and giving no negative edge to the word, which she used purely in the sense in which one employs it to speak of affection between friends, she continued: 'She *adores* you! Oh, I'm quite sure one could never say a bad word about you in front of her! That would spell trouble! Apropos of anything at all, if we were looking at a painting, for instance, she'd say: "Now, if he was here, he'd be able to tell us whether it's genuine or not. There's nobody like him for that." And she'd be constantly saying: "I wonder what he's doing at this moment? If only he'd do a little work! It's dreadful that a man with such gifts should be so lazy." (You'll forgive me, won't you?) "I can see him now, he's thinking about us, he's wondering where we are." And one thing she said I found quite charming; Monsieur Verdurin said to her: "How on earth can you see what he's doing at this moment, when he's a thousand miles away?" And Odette replied: "To the eye of a friend, nothing is impossible." No, I swear, I'm not saying this just to flatter you; you have a true friend in her, such as you don't often find. I can tell you, too, that if you don't know it, you're the only one who doesn't. Madame Verdurin told me as much herself on our last day with them (you know how it is, one always talks more freely just before saying goodbye): "I'm not saying Odette isn't fond of us, but anything we might say to her doesn't count for much compared to what Monsieur Swann might say." Oh, my goodness! The driver's stopping for me! I've been chatting away so much, I nearly missed the Rue Bonaparte . . . Would you be so kind as to tell me if my feather's straight?'

And Madame Cottard withdrew from her muff, and proffered to Swann a white-gloved hand from which there escaped, along with a transfer ticket, a vision of upper-class life that filled the omnibus, mingled with the smell of newly cleaned kid leather. And Swann felt himself overflowing with affection for her, as much as for Madame Verdurin (and almost as much as for Odette, for the feeling he now had for her, being no longer mingled with pain, was hardly love any more), while from the platform of the omnibus he followed her with loving eyes as she boldly made her way up the Rue Bonaparte, her plume erect, her skirt held up in one hand, while in the other she held her parasol and her card case with its monogram fully displayed, her muff dancing in front of her as she went.

To counteract the morbid feelings Swann had for Odette, Madame Cottard, in this respect a better physician than her husband would have been, had grafted onto them other feelings, normal ones, of gratitude and friendship, feelings which in Swann's mind would make Odette appear more human (more like other women, because other women too could inspire these feelings in him), and would hasten her final transformation into the Odette he'd loved with untroubled affection, who had brought him back one evening after a party at the painter's home to drink a glass of orangeade with Forcheville, the Odette with whom Swann had glimpsed the possibility of living in happiness.

In the past, having often thought with terror that one day he would fall out of love with Odette, he had resolved to be vigilant and, as soon as he felt his love was beginning to leave him, to cling to it and hold it back. But now, to the weakening of his love there corresponded a simultaneous weakening of his desire to remain in love. For a person can't change, that is to say become someone else, while continuing to be governed by the feelings of the person they no longer are. Occasionally a name glimpsed in a newspaper, that of one of the men he thought might have been Odette's lovers, revived his jealousy. But it was very mild, and as it proved to him that he hadn't yet completely emerged from the time when he'd suffered so much—but also known so voluptuous a way of feeling—and that the hazards of the road ahead might still enable him to catch a furtive, distant glimpse of its beauties, this jealousy actually gave him a pleasant thrill, just as to the sad Parisian leaving Venice to return to France a last mosquito proves that Italy and the summer are still not too remote. But more often than not, when he made the effort, if not to remain in that particularly distinctive period of his life from which he was emerging, at least to retain a clear view of it while he still could, he discovered that already it wasn't possible; he would have liked to observe, as if it were a landscape about to disappear, that love which he'd just left behind; but it's so difficult to assume a kind of double vision and create for oneself an accurate representation of a feeling one no longer has that soon, darkness gathering in his brain, he could see nothing at all, gave up looking, took off his pince-nez, wiped its lenses; he told himself that it would be better to rest a little, that there would be time enough later on, and settled back with the incuriosity, the torpor of the drowsy traveller in a railway carriage who pulls his hat down over his eyes in order to sleep as he feels the train carrying him faster and faster away from the country where he has lived for so long and which he'd vowed not to let slip past without giving it a last farewell. Indeed, like the same traveller if he does not wake until he arrives back in France, when Swann chanced upon proof close at hand that Forcheville had been Odette's lover, he realized that it caused him no pain, that his love was now far away, and he was sorry he'd had no warning of the moment when he was about to leave it behind for ever. And just as, before kissing Odette for the first time, he'd tried to imprint on his memory the face which had been familiar to him for so long and was about to be transformed by the memory of that kiss, so he would have wanted, in his thoughts at least, to have been able to make his farewells, while she still existed, to the Odette who'd inspired him with love and jealousy, to the Odette who had made him suffer and whom he would now never see again. He was mistaken. He did see her again, one more time, a few weeks later. It was while he was asleep, in the twilight of a dream. He was walking with Madame Verdurin, Doctor Cottard, a young man in a fez whom he could not identify, the painter, Odette, Napoleon III, and my grandfather, along a path that followed the line of the coast and overhung the sea, at times by a great height, at others by just a few metres, so that they were constantly climbing and descending; those who were descending were already no longer visible to those who were still climbing; what little daylight remained was failing, and it seemed as though they were about to be shrouded in darkest night. At times the waves leapt right up to the edge, and Swann could feel the spray of icy water on his cheek. Odette told him to wipe it off, but he couldn't, and was embarrassed by this in front of her, as he was embarrassed to be in his nightshirt. He hoped that, in the darkness, no one would notice, but Madame Verdurin gave him a long stare of surprise during which he saw her face change shape, her nose grow longer, and she sprouted a large moustache. He turned away to look at Odette, her cheeks were pale, with little red spots, her features drawn, ringed with shadows, but she was looking at him with eyes full of tenderness that were about to fall upon him like teardrops, and he felt he loved her so much that he'd have liked to take her away with him at once. Suddenly Odette turned her wrist, glanced at a tiny watch, and said: 'I must go.' She took leave of everyone, in the same manner, but without taking Swann aside, without telling him where they were to meet that evening, or another day. He didn't dare to ask her; he would have liked to follow her but was obliged, without turning back towards her, to answer with a smile a question from Madame Verdurin, but his heart was pounding horribly, he felt he hated Odette, he would gladly have gouged out those eyes that he'd loved so much just a moment ago, and crushed those pale cheeks. He walked on up the slope with Madame Verdurin, which meant that with each step he moved further away from Odette, who was going back down the way they had come. One second later she'd been gone for hours. The painter remarked to Swann that Napoleon III had disappeared a moment after she had. 'They obviously arranged it in advance,' he added. 'They must have met at the foot of the cliff, but they didn't want to say goodbye at the same time for the sake of appearances. She's his mistress.' The young stranger began to cry. Swann tried to comfort him. 'You know, what she's doing is for the best,' he said, drying his eyes and taking off his fez to make him feel more at ease. 'I told her dozens of times she should do it. So why be upset about it? He's the one who can really understand her.' Thus did Swann reason with himself, for the young man he'd failed to identify at first was also himself; like certain novelists, he'd divided his personality between two characters, the one having the dream, and the other he saw before him wearing a fez.

As for Napoleon III, this was the name he'd given to Forcheville because of a vague association of ideas, then a certain change in the baron's usual features, and lastly the broad ribbon of the Legion of Honour on his chest; but in reality, and in everything that the character in the dream represented and reminded him of, it was indeed Forcheville. For, from incomplete and changing images, Swann in his sleep drew false deductions, having for a moment such creative power that he reproduced himself by simple division, like certain lower organisms; with the warmth he felt in his own palm he modelled the hollow of an imaginary hand which he thought he was holding, and from feelings and impressions of which he was not yet conscious he produced a set of events which, through their sequential logic, would engender at just the right moment in his sleep the person required to receive his love or make him wake up. In an instant utter darkness descended upon him, an alarm sounded, people ran past him, escaping from their blazing houses; Swann heard the sound of the surging waves, and of his own heart, which with equal violence was pounding anxiously in his breast. Suddenly these palpitations quickened, he felt an inexplicable pain and nausea; a peasant, covered in burns, called out as he ran: 'Come and ask Charlus where Odette ended up this evening with her friend. He used to go about with her at one time, and she tells him everything. They're the ones who started the fire.' It was his valet, who had come to wake him and was saying: 'Monsieur, it's eight o'clock and the hairdresser's here. I've told him to come back in an hour.'

But these words, reaching Swann through the waves of sleep in which he was submerged, had reached his consciousness only by undergoing the refraction that causes a ray of light in the depths of water to look like a sun, just as, a moment earlier, the sound of the door-bell, resounding in the depths with the sonority of an alarm, had given birth to the episode of the fire. Meanwhile, the scene before his eyes turned to dust, he opened his eyes, heard one last time the sound of a wave in the sea as it receded. He touched his cheek. It was dry. And yet he could remember the sensation of the cold spray and the taste of the salt. He got out of bed and dressed. He'd asked the hairdresser to come early because he'd written to my grandfather the day before to say he'd be going to Combray in the afternoon, having learned that Madame de Cambremer—Mademoiselle Legrandin—was spending a few days there. The association in his memory of the charm of that young face with the charm of a countryside he hadn't visited for so long offered him a combined attraction that had made him decide to leave Paris for a few days at least. As the different chance events that bring us into contact with certain people don't coincide with the time during which we're in love with them, but, overlapping it, may occur before love has begun and may be repeated after it has ended, the earliest appearances in our lives of a person destined to attract us later on assume retrospectively in our eyes the significance of an omen, a portent. This was how Swann had often looked back at the image of Odette when he met her at the theatre, on that first evening when he hadn't dreamed he would ever see her again—and how he now recalled the party at Madame de Saint-Euverte's at which he'd introduced General de Froberville to Madame de Cambremer. So many are our interests in life that it isn't uncommon, on the self-same occasion, for the foundations of a happiness that doesn't yet exist to be laid alongside the aggravation of a sorrow from which we're still suffering. And undoubtedly this could have happened to Swann elsewhere than at Madame de Saint-Euverte's. Who indeed can say whether, had he found himself elsewhere that evening, he would have known other joys, other sorrows, which later would have come to seem inevitable? But what did seem to him to have been inevitable was what had taken place, and he was not far short of seeing something providential in the fact that he had decided to go to Madame de Saint-Euverte's party, because his mind, anxious to admire life's rich possibilities, and incapable of engaging for long with a difficult question, such as the question of what was most to be wished for, felt that in the sufferings he'd experienced that evening and in the pleasures, as yet unsuspected, that were already germinating— the balance between which was too difficult to establish—there was a sort of necessary connection.

But an hour after he'd woken, while he was giving instructions to the hairdresser to see that his newly cut hair shouldn't become disarranged on the train, he thought about his dream again, and saw once again, as he'd felt them close behind him, Odette's pale complexion, her too thin cheeks, her drawn features, her tired eyes, everything that—in the course of the successive expressions of affection which had made of his abiding love for Odette a long oblivion of the first image he'd formed of her—he'd ceased to notice since the earliest days of their affair, days to which, no doubt, while he slept, his memory had returned to seek their exact sensation. And with the intermittent boorishness that reappeared in him as soon as he was no longer unhappy and his moral standards dropped accordingly, he exclaimed to himself: 'To think I've wasted years of my life, that I wanted to die, that I felt my deepest love, for a woman who didn't really appeal to me, who wasn't my type!'

PART THREE
PLACE NAMES: THE NAME

OF all the bedrooms I pictured to myself as I lay awake at night, none was less like the rooms in Combray, powdery with a grainy, pollenated, almost edible atmosphere, redolent of piety, than the room at the Grand-Hôtel de la Plage at Balbec, whose enamel-painted walls contained, like the polished sides of a swimming pool that tint the water blue, a pure, azure air, smelling slightly of sea salt. The Bavarian decorator charged with fitting out the hotel had used different design schemes for the various rooms, and along three sides of the room I happened to occupy he'd set low bookcases with glass fronts, whose panes, depending on where they stood, and by an effect he hadn't foreseen, reflected this or that section of the ever-changing spectacle of the sea, unfurling a frieze of bright seascapes, interrupted only by the mahogany of the shelves. The result was that the whole room looked like one of those model dormitories featured in 'modern style'* home exhibitions, which are hung with works of art thought likely to appeal to the person who will be sleeping there, and representing subjects in keeping with the kind of site where the dwelling will be built.

Nor was there anything less like the real Balbec than the one I'd often imagined on stormy days when the wind was so strong that Françoise, when she took me to the Champs-Élysées, would warn me not to walk too close to the houses for fear that a flying tile would land on my head, and would recount, groaning the while, the many shipwrecks and natural disasters reported in the newspapers. I would have liked nothing more than to contemplate a storm at sea, not so much because it would be a beautiful spectacle as because it would be a momentary revelation of the real workings of Nature; or rather, the only spectacles I found truly beautiful were the ones which I knew were not artificially contrived for my entertainment, but were necessary and unchangeable—the beauty of a landscape or of a great work of art. I was curious and eager to know only what I believed to be more real than myself, things whose value for me was that they gave me a glimpse into the mind of a great genius, or of the power and grace of Nature as she appeared when left to herself, without human interference. Just as it would be no consolation for the death of our

mother to have nothing but the beautiful sound of her voice on
a gramophone record, so a mechanical imitation of a storm would
have left me as cold as the illuminated fountains at the Exposition.*
And to ensure that the storm would be absolutely real, I also wanted
the shore itself to be a natural shore, not a jetty recently created by
a municipality. In fact, because of all the feelings it aroused in me,
nature struck me as the diametrical opposite of all the mechanical
creations of men. The less it bore their imprint, the more scope it
gave for my heart to expand. And I'd remembered the name Balbec,
mentioned to us by Legrandin, as that of a beach very close to 'those
death-dealing cliffs, famous for their many shipwrecks, wrapped six
months of the year in a shroud of fog and foam from the waves'.

'You can still feel there,' he said, 'far more than at Finistère* (and
even though hotels are being built all over it, but without being able to
change the ancient skeleton of the earth), you can still feel there the real
land's end, of France, of Europe, of the Ancient World. And it's the last
encampment of fishermen, those men who've lived like that since the
world began, facing the eternal kingdom of darkness and sea mists.'

In Combray one day I'd mentioned this beach at Balbec in the
presence of Monsieur Swann in the hope of finding out from him
whether it was the best spot from which to see the most violent storms.
He'd responded: 'Oh yes, I know Balbec very well! The church at
Balbec dates from the twelfth and thirteenth centuries; it's still half
Romanesque, but I'd say it's also one of the most interesting examples
of Norman Gothic, and so unusual that you might almost say it's
Persian in style.'

And that region, which until then I'd regarded as being part of the
immemorial world of nature, contemporaneous with the great phenomena of geology—and as far removed from human history as the
Ocean itself or the Great Bear, with those wild fishermen for whom
there had been no Middle Ages, any more than for the whales—
underwent a delightful transformation in my mind, by suddenly
taking its place in the sequence of the centuries, now that it had
experienced the Romanesque period; and it was a joy to know that the
Gothic trefoil had come at the proper time to leave its pattern on
those wild rocks, like the frail but hardy plants which, when spring
comes, spangle here and there the polar snow. And if the Gothic style
brought to these places and to these men a definition which they previously lacked, they in their turn gave some definition to it in return.

I tried to picture how these fishermen had lived, the timid and unwitting experiment in social relations they had attempted there, in the Middle Ages, clinging together on a promontory somewhere on the shores of Hell, with the cliffs of Death towering above them; and the Gothic style seemed to me more alive now that it was detached from the towns where until then I'd always imagined it, enabling me to see how, in one particular instance, on remote and forbidding rocks, it had taken root and flowered into a delicate spire. I was taken to look at reproductions of the most famous statues in the Balbec church—the shaggy, snub-nosed apostles, the Virgin in the porch—and I could scarcely breathe for joy at the thought that it was within my power to go and see the originals standing out in three-dimensional relief against the eternal briny mist. After that, on mild, stormy evenings in February, the wind blew into my heart, shaking it no less violently than it shook my bedroom chimney, a plan to visit Balbec—combining within me a desire to look at Gothic architecture and my desire to see a storm at sea.

I would have liked to take, the very next day, the gracious, welcoming train at one twenty-two, whose departure time, displayed on the railway company's posters and advertisements for round trips, I could never read without my heart beating faster: it seemed to cut a delectable notch at a precise point in the afternoon, a mysterious mark from which the diverted hours still led, of course, towards evening and the following morning, but an evening and morning I would experience, not in Paris, but in one of the towns the train passed through and where I might choose to get off—for it stopped at Bayeux, at Coutances, at Vitré, at Questambert, at Pontorson, at Balbec, at Lannion, at Lamballe, at Benodet, at Pont-Aven, at Quimperlé, and progressed magnificently overloaded with proffered names among which I was unable to choose, so impossible was it to sacrifice a single one. Or, without even waiting until the next day, if I dressed quickly and left that very evening (if my parents had let me), I could have arrived at Balbec as dawn was breaking over the raging sea, and taken refuge from the drifting spray in the Persian-style church. But at the approach of the Easter holidays, which my parents had promised to let me spend for once in the north of Italy, in place of the dreams of storms that had filled my head with visions of huge waves rolling in from all sides, higher and higher, and crashing onto a wild and lonely shore, close to churches as steep and rugged as cliffs, in whose towers the sea-birds would be shrieking, came another dream; all at once my dreams of storms were erased, deprived of all charm, excluded from my mind by a totally different, incompatible dream, the converse dream of the most glorious of springs, not the Combray spring which still pricked us with all the needle-points of the frost, but the spring which was already covering the fields of Fiesole with lilies and anemones and giving Florence a dazzling golden background like those in the paintings of Fra Angelico.* From then on, nothing seemed to me to have any value except sunlight, colours, and perfumes; for the replacement of one dream world by another had brought about a change of front in my desire, and a complete change of key—as abrupt as any that may occur in music—in my sensibility. Then it came about that a slight change in the weather was enough to provoke this modulation within me, without any need to wait for the return of a particular season. For often in one season we find a day that has strayed from another, that transports us at once into that season, evokes its particular pleasures, makes us desire them, and interrupts the dreams we were having, by detaching that single page from a different chapter and inserting it out of place in the interpolated calendar of Happiness. But soon, just as those natural phenomena from which our comfort or health may derive only scant and accidental benefit until the day when science takes hold of them and, by making it possible to produce this benefit at will, gives us the power to enjoy it free of the control and consent of chance, so the production of these Atlantic and Italian dreams ceased to depend purely on the changes of season or weather. To make them reappear, I needed only to pronounce the names—Balbec, Venice, Florence—within whose syllables had gradually accumulated the longing inspired in me by the places they designated. Even in spring, if I came across the name Balbec in a book, it was enough to awaken my longing for storms at sea and the Norman Gothic; and even on a stormy day the name of Florence or Venice filled me with a desire for the sun, for lilies, for the Doges' Palace, and for Santa Maria del Fiore.*

However, although these names absorbed completely the image I'd formed of the various places, it was only by transforming that image, by making its reproduction in my mind subject to their own laws; as a result, they made it more beautiful, but at the same time more different from anything that the towns of Normandy or Tuscany could be in reality, and, by increasing the arbitrary delights of my imagination, compounded the disappointments I would experience later, on my travels. They magnified my image of certain places on the surface of the globe, making them more special and consequently more real. At that time I didn't represent to myself cities, landscapes, or famous buildings as more or less pleasant pictures, cut out here and there from the same material, but as unknown things, each one different in essence from the others, for which my soul hungered and which it would benefit from knowing. And they assumed even greater individuality from being designated by names, names that were theirs alone, names like the names people have. Words give us clear and familiar little pictures of things, like the pictures hung on the walls of schoolrooms to give children an example of what is meant by a workbench, a bird, or an anthill, things taken to be typical of all others of the same sort. But names give us a confused image of people (and of towns, which they accustom us to regard as individual and unique, like people)—an image that derives from them, from the brightness or darkness of their sound, the colour in which it is uniformly painted, like one of those posters, entirely blue or entirely red, in which, because of the limitations of the process of their reproduction, or a whim on the designer's part, not only the sky and sea are blue or red, but also the boats, the church, the people in the streets. The name of Parma, one of the towns I most wanted to visit ever since reading *La Chartreuse de Parme*,* seemed to me to have a compact, mauve, smooth, soft quality; and if anyone mentioned the possibility of my staying in a house in Parma, this would afford me the pleasure of thinking I'd be living in a house that was compact, mauve, smooth, and soft, that was quite unlike the houses in any other town in Italy, since I'd created it in my imagination out of the heavy first syllable of the name *Parme*, in which no air circulates, and out of the Stendhalian softness and tint of violets with which I'd imbued the name. And when I thought of Florence, I thought of a town miraculously fragrant and like the petals of a flower, because it was known as the City of Lilies and the name of its cathedral was Our Lady of the Flowers. As for Balbec, it was like one of those names in which, as on an old piece of Norman pottery that keeps the colour of the earth from which it was made, you can still see a representation of some outmoded custom, some feudal right, an inventory from long ago, or an obsolete type of pronunciation which had formed its two incongruous syllables and which I was sure I'd find used there even by the innkeeper who would serve me coffee on my arrival and then take me down to look at the raging sea in front of the church, and whom I'd picture as disputatious, solemn, and medieval, like a character out of an old *fabliau*.*

If my health were to improve and my parents allowed me, if not to stay in Balbec, at least to become acquainted with some of the architecture and landscapes of Normandy or Brittany by actually taking that train at one twenty-two which I'd boarded so many times in my imagination, I'd have wanted to get off in the most beautiful towns; but compare them as I might, how could I choose, any more than between individual people who are not interchangeable, between Bayeux, so lofty with its noble russet lacework, its highest point illuminated by the old gold of its second syllable, and Vitré, whose acute accent barred its ancient glass with black wooden lozenges; or gentle Lamballe, whose whiteness ranged from eggshell yellow to pearl grey; or Coutances, a Norman cathedral, whose final diphthong, rich and yellowing, crowned a tower of butter;* or Lannion, with the noise, in the middle of its main street, of the coach pursued by the fly;* or Questambert and Pontorson, naïve and ridiculous, all white feathers and yellow beaks strewn along the road to those poetic riverside spots; or Benodet, a name that has almost slipped its moorings, which the stream seems to want to carry away in its tangled algae; or Pont-Aven, like a pink-white flutter of a winged, lightly poised coif shimmeringly reflected in the greenish water of a canal; or Quimperlé, more firmly moored, ever since the Middle Ages, among babbling streams beading the air with a pearl-grey mist, like the dim glow made through the cobwebs of a stained-glass window by the tarnished silver of hazy sunbeams.

These images were misleading for another reason—namely that they were necessarily very simplified. No doubt whatever it was that my imagination aspired to and that my senses took in only partially and without immediate pleasure, I'd committed to the safe custody of names; no doubt because I'd loaded them with dreams, these names acted on my desires like magnets; but names aren't very capacious and the most I could do was include in them two or three of the towns' 'main attractions', which would lie there side by side, without any connecting element; thus, in the name of Balbec, as in the magnifying glass in the penholders you can buy at seaside resorts, I saw waves surging round a church built in the Persian style. Perhaps indeed the simplification of these images was one of the reasons why they came to have such a hold on me. When my father decided, one year, that we'd spend the Easter holidays in Florence and Venice, finding there wasn't enough room to insert into the name Florence the elements that usually make up a town, I was forced to create a supernatural city out of the impregnation, by certain scents of spring, of what I believed to be, in essence, the spirit of Giotto. At the very most—and because no name can be made to carry with it much more time than space—like some of Giotto's paintings which show us the same figure engaged in two different actions, one when he's lying in bed and another when he's preparing to mount his horse, the name Florence was divided into two compartments. In one, under an architectural canopy, I was gazing at a fresco over which was partly drawn a curtain of morning sunlight, dusty, oblique, and gradually spreading; in the other (for since I didn't think of names as inaccessible ideals but as containing an atmospheric sense of the reality in which I was going to immerse myself, the life not yet lived, the pure and intact life I saw in them, gave to the most material pleasures and the simplest scenes the kind of attraction they have in the works of the Primitives*), I was walking quickly—eager to enjoy the lunch, complete with fruit and a carafe of Chianti, that awaited me—across a Ponte Vecchio strewn with daffodils, narcissi, and anemones. That, even though I was in Paris, was what I saw, and not my actual surroundings. Even from the simplest, most realistic point of view, the places we long for occupy a far larger place in our life, at any given moment, than the place in which we happen to be. No doubt, if I'd paid more attention at the time to what was in my mind when I pronounced the words 'going to Florence, to Parma, to Pisa, to Venice', I'd have realized that what I saw bore not the slightest resemblance to a town, but was as unlike anything I knew, and as delightful, as a marvellous spring morning might be for a race of men whose whole existence had consisted of nothing but gloomy winter afternoons. These images—fixed, unchanging, unreal, filling my nights and my days—differentiated this period of my life from those that had gone before (and which might have been confused with it by an observer who could see things only from the outside, that is to say who saw nothing), just as, in an opera, a particular melodic phrase introduces a change of mood in a way that can't be anticipated by anyone who has only read the libretto, still less by anyone simply standing about outside the theatre, filling in time. And besides, even from the point of view of mere quantity, the days that make up our lives are not all equal. To get through each day, people who are at all highly strung, like myself, are equipped, like motor cars, with different gears. There are arduous, mountainous days that require a painfully long time to climb, and downward-sloping days you can descend at full tilt, singing as you go. During that month—in which I constantly turned over in my mind, like a tune of which you never tire, those images of Florence, Venice, and Pisa of which the desire they provoked in me retained something as profoundly individual as if they were a person with whom I was in love—I never ceased to believe that they corresponded to a reality outside myself, independent of me, and they aroused in me feelings of hope as exalted as those which an Early Christian might have known on the eve of his entry into Paradise. So, without my worrying about the contradiction inherent in my desire to see and feel, to experience with my bodily senses, what I'd created out of my day-dreams and not out of my senses at all—and was all the more tempting to them, since it was so different from anything they knew—it was whatever reminded me of the reality of these images that most inflamed my desire, by seeming to hold out the promise that it would be fulfilled. And although my excitement was fuelled by a desire for aesthetic enjoyment, it was sustained by guidebooks rather than by books about aesthetics, and by railway timetables even more than by guidebooks. What excited me was the thought that the Florence I saw in my imagination, so near and yet so impossibly far, and which wasn't accessible by any inner journey, within myself, could be reached indirectly, if I were to take a detour via the land route. It's true that I felt happy when I repeated to myself, thus giving a special value to what I was going to see, that Venice was 'the School of Giorgione, the home of Titian, the most comprehensive museum of medieval domestic architecture'.* But I felt even happier when, out on an errand and walking briskly because of the weather, which after a few days of precocious spring had relapsed into winter (like the weather that usually awaited us in Combray during Holy Week), I saw the chestnut trees along the boulevards, steeped in the chilly air as liquid as water, but, like punctual guests dressed for the occasion and undaunted by the weather, beginning to shape and chisel the frozen masses of burgeoning greenery whose steady growth was hindered but not halted by the severity of the cold, and I reflected that by now the Ponte Vecchio would be heaped high with hyacinths and anemones, and that the

spring sunshine would already be tinting the water in the Grand Canal
with so deep an azure and such brilliant emeralds that when it came to
lap around the base of Titian's canvasses it would surely rival them in
the richness of its colours. I couldn't contain my joy when my father,
even as he consulted the barometer and bemoaned the cold, began to
look for the best trains, and when I realized that by proceeding one day
after lunch to that sooty laboratory, and stepping into the magic chamber charged with effecting a metamorphosis of everything around it,
I could wake up the following morning in the city of marble and gold,
'bossed with jasper', 'paved with emerald'. This convinced me that
Venice and the City of Lilies were not just a set of artificial images
I could conjure up at will in my imagination, but existed at a precise
distance from Paris that I would absolutely have to cover if I wanted to
see them, at a particular place on the earth's surface and nowhere
else—in a word, I was now convinced that these places were entirely
real. They became even more real for me when my father, by saying:
'Well, it looks as if the two of you could stay in Venice from the twentieth to the twenty-ninth of April and arrive in Florence on Easter
morning', made both towns emerge not simply from abstract Space
but from the imaginary Time in which it's possible for us to undertake
not just one journey at a time but others simultaneously, none of which
need excite us too much since they are only possibilities—the Time
that recreates itself so effectively that we can spend it again in one town
after we've already spent it in another—and assigned to them some of
those specific calendar days that certify the authenticity of the activities on which we spend them, for these unique days are consumed by
being used, they never come back, they can't be relived in one place
after they've been lived in another; I felt that these days would fall
during the week that would begin with the Monday on which the laun-
drywoman was to bring back the white waistcoat which I'd spilt ink all
over, and that the two Queen Cities were now moving towards that
week, to become absorbed in it as they emerged from the ideal Time in
which they didn't yet exist—those two Queen Cities whose domes and
towers I'd soon be able, by the most thrilling kind of geometry, to fit
into the puzzle of my life. But I was still merely on the way to the ultimate
degree of bliss; I reached it finally (for not until then did the revelation
come to me that the following week, on the eve of Easter, walking along
Venice's splashing streets, reddened by the reflections from Giorgione's
frescoes, there would be none of those men, whom I continued to

imagine, despite so much advice to the contrary, as 'majestic and terrible as the sea, bearing armour that gleamed with bronze beneath the folds of their blood-red cloaks',* but that I myself might be the tiny figure, in a large photograph of Saint Mark's that someone had lent me, whom the illustrator had portrayed, in a bowler hat, in front of the portico) when I heard my father say: 'It must still be quite cold on the Grand Canal; you'd do well to pack your overcoat and warm jacket, just in case.' At these words I was lifted into a state akin to ecstasy; I felt I was truly making my way—something I had until then thought impossible—between those 'rocks of amethyst, like a reef in the Indian Ocean';* by a supreme muscular effort, far beyond my normal capacity, I divested myself of the air that surrounded me in my bedroom, as though it were a shell that served no purpose, and replaced it by an equal quantity of Venetian air, that sea air as indescribable and particular as the air one breathes in dreams, which my imagination had implanted in the name of Venice; I felt myself undergoing a miraculous disincarnation, which was immediately accompanied by the vague nausea you feel when you've come down with a bad sore throat, and my parents had to put me to bed with such a persistently high temperature that the doctor declared it was not only out of the question to let me leave now for Florence and Venice, but that, even when I'd fully recovered, they should wait at least another year before letting me make any further travel plans, and spare me anything that might over-excite me.

And also, alas, he strictly forbade my parents from allowing me to go to the theatre to hear La Berma, the sublime artist whom Bergotte had proclaimed a genius, who might have consoled me for not going to Florence and Venice, or Balbec, by introducing me to something that was perhaps as significant and beautiful as those places. They had to be content with sending me every day to the Champs-Élysées in the charge of a person who would make sure I didn't tire myself, namely Françoise, who had entered our service after the death of Aunt Léonie. Going to the Champs-Élysées was unbearable to me. If Bergotte had described it in one of his books, I would no doubt have wanted to get to know it, like all those things of which a 'double' had first been introduced into my imagination. For this breathed warmth and life into them, gave them a personality, and made me want to experience them in reality; but in this public garden there was nothing that had the slightest connection with my dreams.

One day, because I was bored in our usual spot, next to the merry-go-round, Françoise took me on an expedition, venturing across the frontier guarded at regular intervals by the little bastions of the barley-sugar ladies into those neighbouring but foreign regions where the faces are unfamiliar, where there are goat-cart rides; then she went back to collect her things from her chair, which stood with its back to a clump of laurels. As I waited for her, pacing about on the broad expanse of patchy, close-cropped, sun-baked lawn, at the far end of which is an artificial pond with a large statue in the middle, I suddenly heard the sharp tones of a little girl; she was putting on her coat and fastening her racquet, and calling out to another little girl with auburn hair who was playing with a shuttlecock in front of the basin: 'Goodbye, Gilberte, I'm going home now. Don't forget we're coming to your house tonight, after dinner.' That name, Gilberte, passed close by me, evoking all the more forcefully the existence of the girl it designated in that it didn't simply name her in her absence but was directly addressed to her; in other words, as it passed by me, in action so to speak, its force was increased by the curve of its trajectory and the proximity of its target: carrying within it, I felt, all the familiarity with the girl to whom it was addressed, all the impressions of her that belonged not to me but to the friend who was calling to her, everything that, as she uttered it, she could visualize, or at least had stored in her memory, of their daily companionship, of the visits they paid to each other's houses, of that unknown existence which was all the more inaccessible and painful to me because, conversely, it was so familiar, so tractable to this cheerful girl who let it brush past me without my being able to penetrate it, who had tossed it into the air with a simple cry, sending into the atmosphere the delicious emanation it had released with its precise touch from certain invisible parts of Mademoiselle Swann's life, such as the evening to come at her home, after dinner; forming, on its celestial passage through the children and their nannies, a little, exquisitely coloured cloud, like one of those clouds curling above a garden by Poussin,* that reflect minutely, like a cloud in an opera full of horses and chariots, some scene from the life of the gods; casting, finally, on the meagre grass, at the spot where it was not only a patch of withered lawn but also a moment in the afternoon of the fair-haired shuttlecock player (who went on hitting and picking up her shuttlecock until she was called away by a governess with a blue feather in her hat), a marvellous little band of light, the colour of heliotrope, as impalpable as a reflection and spread out over the lawn like a carpet on which I walked up and down with slow, sacrilegious steps, reluctant to leave, until Françoise cried out: 'Come on, button up your coat and let's get going!' and I noted to myself for the first time, with irritation, how common her speech was and that she had, alas, no blue feather in her hat.

Would she ever come back to the Champs-Élysées? The next day she wasn't there; but I did see her on the following days, and I spent so much time hovering about the spot where she played with her friends that one day, when they found they were short of players for a game of prisoner's base,* she sent someone to ask me if I'd make up the numbers on their side, and from that day I played with her every time she came to the Champs-Élysées. But that wasn't every day; there were days when she was kept from coming by her lessons, her catechism class, or a tea party, that whole life separate from mine which on two occasions, condensed into the name Gilberte, I'd felt pass so painfully close to me, once in the steep little lane in Combray and for the second time on the grass of the Champs-Élysées. On those days she'd announce in advance that we wouldn't be seeing her; if it was because of her school work, she'd say: 'What a bore! I can't come tomorrow, you'll all be having fun without me,' with a sorrowful air that consoled me somewhat; if, on the other hand, she'd been invited to a party, and I, not knowing this, asked her if she'd be coming out to play, she'd reply: 'I certainly hope not! I'm hoping Maman will let me go to my friend's party.' At least on days like that I knew I wouldn't see her, whereas there were other days when her mother would unexpectedly take her shopping, and the next day she'd say: 'Oh yes, I went out with Maman,' as though it was perfectly natural and not, for someone else, the worst possible calamity. There were also the days when the weather was bad, and her governess, who particularly disliked the rain, didn't want to take her to the Champs-Élysées.

So if the sky looked unsettled, from early morning I'd study it at regular intervals, and I'd note every omen. If I saw the lady opposite standing at her window and putting on her hat, I'd say to myself: 'That lady's going out, so it's the sort of weather people can go out in: why wouldn't Gilberte do what the lady's doing?' But the weather would cloud over, my mother would say it might brighten up again, a single ray of sunshine would be enough, but it was more likely it would rain; and if it rained, what was the point of going to the

Champs-Élysées? So from lunch onwards my anxious eyes remained fixed on the unsettled, cloudy sky. It remained dark. The balcony in front of the window was grey. Suddenly I saw, on the sullen stone, not a colour less dull, but something that made me sense a sort of striving towards a colour less dull, the pulsation of a hesitant ray struggling to release its light. A moment later, the balcony was as pale and reflective as a pool at dawn, and a thousand reflections of the wrought iron of its balustrade had alighted on it. A breath of wind dispersed them, the stone darkened again, but, as though tamed, they returned; imperceptibly the stone grew lighter once more, and in one of those sustained crescendos which, in music, at the end of an overture, carry a single note to the highest fortissimo, making it pass rapidly through all the intermediate stages, I saw it reach that fixed, unalterable gold of fine days, against which the clear-cut shadow of the iron lacework stood out in black like strange, intricate vegetation, with a delicacy in the delineation of its slightest details that made it appear like the work of a painstaking artistic sensibility, and with such sharp relief, such a velvety effect in the restfulness of its dark, soothing masses that in truth the broad, leafy reflections on that lake of sunshine seemed to know they were pledges of calm and happiness.

Instantaneous ivy, fixed yet fleeting! The least colourful, the saddest, in the opinion of many, of all that creep on walls or decorate windows; for me the dearest plant of all from the day it appeared on our balcony, like the very shadow of the presence of Gilberte, who was perhaps already in the Champs-Élysées, and as soon as I arrived would greet me with: 'Let's start playing prisoner's base straight away, you're on my side'; fragile, swept away by the slightest breath, but also in harmony, not with the season but with the hour; promise of the immediate happiness which the day will bring or deny, and thereby of that immediate happiness par excellence, the happiness of love; softer, warmer on the stone even than moss; and so hardy that it needs the merest glimmer of sunlight, even in the heart of winter, to start budding and burst joyfully into blossom.

And even on those days when all other vegetation had disappeared, when the lovely green leather wrapped round the trunks of the old trees was hidden under snow, and when the snow had stopped falling but the sky was still too overcast to hope that Gilberte would go out, suddenly my mother would exclaim: 'Look, the sun's come out! Perhaps you could go to the Champs-Élysées after all,' and on the mantle of snow covering the balcony the sun that had appeared would be weaving a tracery of gold threads and black shadows. On such days we'd find no one, or a solitary girl about to leave, who would assure me that Gilberte wouldn't be coming. The chairs, deserted by the grand assembly of shivering governesses, stood empty. Alone, by the lawn, sat a lady of a certain age who came in all weathers, always decked out in the same magnificent, dark costume, and to make whose acquaintance I would at that time have sacrificed, if the exchange had been possible, the greatest privileges of my entire future life. For Gilberte went over to greet her every day, and she always asked after Gilberte's 'darling mother', and it seemed to me that, if I'd known this lady, Gilberte would have seen me in a very different light, as someone who knew her parents' friends. While her grandchildren went to play a little distance away, she would read *Les Débats*, which she called 'my good old *Débats*', and when she referred to the police-man on the corner or the woman who hired out the chairs, she'd say, with aristocratic affectation, 'My good friend the policeman', or 'The chair-lady and I, who are old pals'.

Françoise found it too cold to sit down, so we walked to the Pont de la Concorde* to look at the Seine, which was frozen solid; everyone, even children, was coming up to it, quite unafraid, as though it was a huge, beached whale, defenceless and about to be cut up. I went back to the Champs-Élysées with Françoise, dragging myself along disconsolately between the motionless merry-go-round and the white expanse of lawn, caught in the black web of paths from which the snow had been cleared, while the statue that surmounted it held in its hand a long icicle, which seemed to have been added to it to explain its gesture. Even the old lady, after folding her *Débats*, asked a passing nanny what time it was, thanking her with: 'That's awfully kind of you!' Then she begged the street-sweeper to tell her grandchildren to come, because she was feeling the cold, adding: 'That would be ter-ribly nice of you! I don't know how to thank you!' Then, all at once, the earth shifted on its axis: between the puppet theatre and the merry-go-round, against the now bright horizon and the clearing sky, I'd just spotted, like a miraculous sign, Mademoiselle's blue feather. The next moment Gilberte was running at full tilt towards me, her eyes sparkling, her face all rosy under a toque trimmed with fur, in high spirits because of the cold, her late arrival, and her eagerness for a game; just before she reached me, she slid along the ice and, either to help keep her balance, or because she thought it more graceful, or pretending to move like a skater, her arms opened wide as she came forward smiling, as if she wanted to embrace me. 'Bravo! Bravo!' cried the old lady, expressing, on behalf of the silent Champs-Élysées, their thanks to Gilberte for having come without letting herself be put off by the weather. 'That was splendid. If I didn't belong to a different generation, if I wasn't so very old, I'd say, like you young people, that it was "super", "grand". You're like me, faithful to our good old Champs-Élysées. We're brave souls, aren't we? I so love it here, even when it's like this. Don't laugh, but the snow makes me think of ermine!' And the old lady herself began to laugh.

The first of the days to which the snow, a symbol of the forces that might prevent me from seeing Gilberte, imparted the sadness of a day of farewells, even of a day when one leaves home to go on a journey (because it changed the appearance and almost prevented the use of the scene of our only encounters, by transforming it, covering it, as it were, in dust-sheets), marked, none the less, a stage in the development of my love, for it was like a first shared experience of sorrow. There were just the two of us out of our whole little gang, and to be alone there with her was not only like the beginning of a close friendship, but also (as though she'd come out in such weather especially for me) seemed to me as touching a gesture on her part as if, on one of those days when she'd been invited to a party, she'd decided not to go in order to be with me in the Champs-Élysées; I gained more confidence in the vitality and future of our friendship, which had remained so alive amid the stillness, solitude, and ruin of our surroundings; and as she stuffed snowballs down my neck, I smiled with emotion at what seemed to me both a preference she was showing me by tolerating me as her travelling companion in this new and wintry land, and a sort of loyalty she was maintaining for me in these difficult times. Soon, one after another, like timid sparrows, her friends arrived, black against the snow. We got ready to play, and since this day that had begun so sadly was destined to end in joy, when I walked over, before the game started, to the friend with the sharp voice I'd heard that first day calling Gilberte by name, she said: 'No, no, we know you'd much rather be on Gilberte's side. Anyway, look—she's calling you over.' She was indeed summoning me over to join her team on the snow-covered lawn, which the sun, picking out on it the pink gleam and worn metallic sheen of an old brocade, was turning into a Field of the Cloth of Gold.*

So that day, which I had so dreaded, was in fact one of the few on which I was not too unhappy.

For, though I now thought of nothing else but of not letting a single day go by without seeing Gilberte (so much so that once, when my grandmother hadn't come home by dinner time, I couldn't help thinking that if she'd been run over in the street and killed, I wouldn't be able to go to the Champs-Élysées for some time: one love takes all), yet those moments I spent in her company, for which I'd waited so impatiently since the day before, quivering with excitement, and for which I'd have sacrificed everything else in my life, were by no means happy moments, and how well I knew it, for they were the only moments in my life on which I focused meticulous, fierce attention, and yet found in them not one iota of pleasure.

All the time I was away from Gilberte, I felt I needed to see her because, by trying so hard to picture her, in the end I was unable to do so, and had no clear sense of what, precisely, my love represented. And she'd never told me she loved me. In fact, she'd often said there were boys she liked better than me, that I was just a friend she was happy enough to play with, though she found me too distracted, not involved enough in the game; furthermore, she'd often shown signs of apparent coldness towards me that might have shaken my belief that for her I was someone different from the others, had that belief been based on any love Gilberte might have felt for me, and not, as was the case, on the love I felt for her, which made it far more resistant to my doubts, since this made it depend entirely on the manner in which I was obliged, by an inner compulsion, to think of her. Besides, I myself hadn't yet said anything to Gilberte about my feelings for her. True, on every page of my exercise books, I wrote out endlessly her name and address, but when I gazed at those faint lines, which I scribbled without her thinking of me any the more, which made her assume so much importance in my life without being any more involved in it, I felt discouraged, because they spoke to me, not about Gilberte, who would never so much as see them, but about my own desire, which they seemed to show me as something purely personal, unreal, tedious, and ineffectual. The most pressing thing was that we should see each other, Gilberte and I, and that we should have an opportunity to declare our love for each other, for until then our love could hardly be said to have begun. No doubt the various reasons that made me so impatient to see her would not have seemed so pressing to a grown man. When we're older, and more skilled in the cultivation of our pleasures, we're content to enjoy thinking about a woman in the way I thought about Gilberte, without worrying about whether the image corresponds to the reality, and we're also happy to love her without needing to be sure that she loves us; we may even forgo the pleasure of confessing our affection for her, so as to preserve and enhance the affection she has for us, like those Japanese gardeners who obtain a more beautiful flower by sacrificing several others. But at the time when I was in love with Gilberte, I still believed that Love really existed outside ourselves; that, although allowing us at the very most to overcome the obstacles in our way, it offered its blessings in an order we were not free to alter in any way; it seemed to me that if, on my own initiative, I'd substituted for the sweetness of avowal the simulation of indifference, not only would I have deprived myself of one of the joys I'd most longed for, but I'd have fabricated for myself, just as I pleased, a kind of love that was artificial and worthless, that bore no relation to true love, whose mysterious and foreordained paths I would have ceased to follow.

But when I arrived in the Champs-Élysées, and thus was able to bring my love face to face with its living cause in the real world, so as to make any necessary rectifications to it, no sooner did I set eyes on Gilberte Swann, whose presence I'd been counting on to refresh the images of her that had become blurred in my memory, the Gilberte Swann with whom I'd been playing only the day before, and whom I'd just been prompted to recognize and greet by a blind instinct like the one that makes us walk by putting one foot in front of the other, without giving us time to think about it, than it began to seem that she and the little girl who was the object of my dreams were two different people. If, for instance, I'd retained in my memory from the day before two blazing eyes and two full, shining cheeks, Gilberte's face now presented me insistently with the very feature I'd completely forgotten, a certain sharp tapering of the nose which, instantaneously associating itself with other features, assumed the importance of those characteristics which in natural history define a species, and transformed her into a little girl of the kind that have pointed snouts. While I was preparing to take advantage of this longed-for moment and to submit the image of Gilberte I'd prepared before coming, but which had now disappeared from my mind, to the process of adjustment that would allow me, in the long hours I spent alone, to be sure

it was truly she I was recalling, truly my love for her that I was aug-
menting little by little like a book in the process of composition, she
would hold out a ball; and, like the Idealist philosopher whose body
takes account of the external world in the reality of which his intellect
doesn't believe, the same self which had just made me greet her before
I'd recognized her now urged me to take the ball (as if she were simply
a friend with whom I'd come to play, and not the soulmate with whom
I'd come to commune), made me exchange with her, out of decorum,
until the time came when she had to go, a thousand and one polite and
trivial remarks, and so prevented me from remaining silent, which
would have enabled me to recapture the urgent truant image of her,
and from uttering the words that might have brought about the decisive step forward in our love, which I was always obliged to postpone
until the following afternoon.

Our love did, however, make some progress. One day we went with
Gilberte to the stall of the woman who was always especially nice to
us—for it was to her that Monsieur Swann used to send for his *pain
d'épice*,* of which, for health reasons, he consumed a great deal, suffering, as he did, from ethnic eczema and the constipation of the
Prophets;* Gilberte pointed out to me with a smile two little boys
who were like the little artist and the little naturalist in children's
storybooks. One of them didn't want a red stick of barley sugar
because he preferred the violet, and the other, with tears in his eyes,
was refusing the plum his nanny wanted to buy him because, as he
finally said with passion: 'I want the other one! It's got a worm in it!'
I bought two one-sou marbles. I stood gazing admiringly at the agate
marbles, luminous and captive in their special wooden bowl; they
seemed very precious to me because they were as fair and smiling as
young girls and because they cost fifty centimes each. Gilberte, who
was given a great deal more pocket money than I was, asked me which
one I thought the most beautiful. They had the molten transparency
of life itself. I didn't want any of them singled out to the exclusion of
all the others. I would have liked her to buy them, and liberate them,
all. Nevertheless I pointed to one that had the same colour as her eyes.
Gilberte picked it up, turned it over until she found its shining seam
of gold, fondled it, paid its ransom, and handed me the liberated captive, saying: 'Take it, it's a present, it'll remind you of me.'

On another occasion, still obsessed by the desire to hear La Berma
in a classical play, I asked her if she happened to have a copy of a booklet

of Bergotte's about Racine, which was now out of print. She asked me to remind her of the exact title, and that evening I sent her an express letter, writing on the envelope the name, Gilberte Swann, which I'd so often inscribed in my exercise books. The next day she brought me a little parcel tied with mauve ribbon and sealed with white wax; it contained the booklet, which she'd asked someone to find for her. 'You see? It's what you asked for,' she said, taking from her muff the note I'd sent her. But in the address on the blue letter-form—which only the previous day had been nothing, merely an express letter written by me, and which, now that a telegraph boy had delivered it to Gilberte's concierge and a servant had carried it to her room, had become one of those priceless things: one of the express letters she'd received that day—it was hard for me to recognize the futile and forlorn outlines of my handwriting under the circular postmarks and the pencilled inscriptions added by a postman, the signs of its translation into actuality, certificatory stamps administered by the outside world, violet-ringed emblems of real life, which for the first time had managed to match, affirm, enhance, and delight my dreams.

And there was another day when she said: 'You know, you can call me Gilberte. In any case, I'll call you by your first name. It's silly otherwise.' Yet for a while she went on addressing me as *vous*, and when I remarked on this, she smiled, and made up a sentence like those artificial ones used in grammar books of foreign languages whose only object is to teach us how to use a new word, and ended it with my first name. When I recalled later on what I'd felt at that moment, what came back to me was the impression of having been held briefly in her mouth, my innermost self as if stripped bare, without any of the social limits and conventions that applied both to her other playmates and, when she used my surname, to my parents, and of which her lips, in the effort she made, not unlike her father, to articulate the words to which she wanted to give special emphasis, seemed to divest me, as you peel a piece of fruit of which only the pulp can be eaten, while her gaze, adopting the same new degree of intimacy as her words, seemed not only to make more direct contact with me but also showed with a simultaneous smile its awareness of that intimacy, the pleasure it took in it, and even the gratitude it felt.

But at that actual moment I was incapable of appreciating these new pleasures at their true value. They were given not by the little girl I loved to the me who loved her, but by the other, the one with whom

I used to play, to that other me, who possessed neither the memory of the true Gilberte, nor the inalienable heart which alone could have known the value of a happiness which it alone had desired. Even after I returned home, I was unable to find enjoyment in these pleasures, for every day the need that made me hope that the next day I'd enjoy at last a clear, calm, happy contemplation of Gilberte, that she would at last confess her love for me, explaining why she'd had to hide it from me until now, that same daily need forced me to regard the past as of no account, to look forward into the future only, to consider the small attentions she'd shown me not in themselves and as if they were self-sufficient, but as fresh rungs of the ladder on which I might set my feet, which would enable me to advance one step further in my quest for the happiness that had so far eluded me.

Although she gave me these occasional signs of friendship, she also hurt me by seeming not to be pleased to see me, and this often happened on the very days I'd been most counting on for the realization of my hopes. I was sure Gilberte would come to the Champs-Élysées, and I felt a kind of delight that seemed, nevertheless, no more than a vague anticipation of great happiness, when—going into the drawing room in the morning to kiss Maman, who was already dressed to go out, her turret of black hair fully assembled, and her lovely plump white hands still smelling of soap—the sight of a free-standing column of dust above the piano and the sound of a barrel organ playing 'En revenant de la revue'* under the window made it clear that winter had received, until nightfall, the unexpected visit of a radiant spring day. While we were eating lunch, the lady opposite suddenly opened her window, prompting a sunbeam that had settled next to my chair for its afternoon siesta to leap the whole length of our dining room in a single bound, before returning to continue its siesta a moment later. At school, during the one o'clock class, the sun made me sick with impatience and boredom as it let fall a golden stream on the edge of my desk, like an invitation to a party I wouldn't be able to get to before three o'clock, when Françoise would meet me at the school gate and we'd make our way to the Champs-Élysées through streets gilded with sunlight and thronging with people, above which the balconies, detached from the fronts of the houses by the sun and vaporized, seemed to be floating in the air like clouds of gold. But alas! In the Champs-Élysées there was no Gilberte; she hadn't arrived yet. Under an invisible sun which picked out here and there the glowing tip of a blade of grass, standing motionless on the lawn, with pigeons that looked like ancient sculptures dug up by a gardener's pick out of the venerable soil of some classical landscape, I kept my eyes fixed on the horizon, expecting at any moment to see Gilberte, walking in the wake of her governess, passing behind the statue which seemed to be invoking the sun's blessing on the child, drenched with light, it was holding in its arms. The old lady who read *Les Débats* was sitting on her chair, in her usual place, and had just called out 'What a lovely day!' to a park-keeper, giving him a friendly wave as she did so. And when the chair woman came up to collect the money for the chair, she simpered away as she put the ten-centime ticket in the opening of her glove, as if it was a bouquet of flowers she wanted to show off, out of consideration for the giver. When she'd found the best place for the ticket, she made a swivelling movement with her neck, primped her boa, and as she showed the woman the scrap of yellow paper sticking out from her glove, she gave her the sort of smile with which a woman, pointing to her bosom, says to a young man: 'Look, I'm wearing your roses.'

In the hope of meeting Gilberte, I took Françoise as far as the Arc de Triomphe; there was no sign of her, and I was on my way back to the lawn, convinced by now that she wouldn't be coming, when, as I reached the merry-go-round, the girl with the sharp voice ran up to me and said: 'Quick, quick! Gilberte's been here for the last fifteen minutes! She'll be going soon. We're waiting for you to make up a team for prisoner's base.' While I'd been walking up the Avenue des Champs-Élysées, Gilberte had arrived via the Rue Boissy-d'Anglas, her governess having taken advantage of the fine weather to do some shopping for herself; and Monsieur Swann would be coming to pick up his daughter. So it was my fault; I shouldn't have left the lawn, for it was never possible to know for sure from what direction Gilberte would come, nor whether she'd be early or late; and this uncertainty ended up colouring not only the whole of the Champs-Élysées and the entire length of the afternoon, like a vast expanse of space and time on every point and at every moment of which it was possible that Gilberte's image would appear, but also that image itself, because behind it I felt that there lay concealed the reason why it had shot an arrow into my heart at four o'clock instead of half past two, wearing a formal hat rather than a playtime beret, and in front of the Ambassadeurs* instead of between the two puppet theatres. I assumed that these variations corresponded to one or other of the occupations in which I was unable to follow Gilberte: I had encountered the mystery of her unknown life. It was this mystery that troubled me when, as I ran forward at the bidding of the girl with the sharp voice, to begin our game of prisoner's base right away, I saw Gilberte, who could be so brusque and offhand with us, curtseying to the old lady with *Les Débats* (who said: 'What a lovely sun, it seems on fire'), and talking to her with a shy smile and a formality of manner that made me imagine the different little girl Gilberte must be at home with her parents, with the friends of her parents, or when paying calls, in the whole of that other existence of hers that lay beyond my reach. But no one gave me such a powerful impression of that other existence than Monsieur Swann, who arrived soon afterwards to fetch his daughter. That was because he and Madame Swann, inasmuch as their daughter lived with them, and her studies, her games, her friendships depended on them, embodied for me an impenetrable mystery, a painful kind of charm; I felt this in Gilberte, too, but more so in her parents, for as gods all-powerful in relation to her, they must be the source of that mystery. Everything about them was the object of so constant a preoccupation on my part that on the days when, as on this day, Monsieur Swann (whom I'd seen so often in the past without his having aroused my curiosity, when he was on friendly terms with my parents) came to pick Gilberte up in the Champs-Élysées, once the pounding of my heart provoked by the sudden sight of his grey hat and hooded cape had subsided, his appearance continued to excite me as if he were a historical character about whom we'd just been reading a series of books and the smallest details of whose life fascinate us. His acquaintance with the Comte de Paris, which had been a matter of indifference to me when I heard it mentioned in Combray, now became in my eyes something to marvel at, as if no one else had ever known any member of the House of Orléans; it made him stand out vividly against the vulgar background of passers-by of different classes who were cluttering that path in the Champs-Élysées, in the midst of whom I admired that he condescended to appear without demanding any special form of deference, which as it happened none of them dreamed of paying him, so profound was the incognito he'd assumed.

He responded politely to the greetings of Gilberte's friends, even to mine despite the fact that he'd fallen out with my family, though he didn't seem to realize who I was. (This reminded me that, after all, he'd seen me quite often in the country—a memory I'd retained somewhere in my mind but kept in the shadows, because, ever since I'd seen Gilberte again, Swann had become above all else her father, and was no longer the Swann of Combray; the ideas with which I now linked his name were different from the network of associations to which he'd once belonged and which I no longer used when I had occasion to think about him, and he'd thereby become another person; nevertheless, I still attached him by an artificial thread, secondary and transversal, to our guest of earlier times; and since nothing had any value for me any more except to the extent that my love might profit by it, it was with a sudden feeling of shame, and regret at not being able to erase them, that I recalled the years when, in the eyes of this same Swann who at this moment stood before me in the Champs-Élysées and to whom, with luck, Gilberte hadn't mentioned my name, I'd so often, in the evenings, made a fool of myself by sending word asking Maman to come up to my room to say goodnight, while she was having coffee with him, my father, and my grandparents at the table in the garden.) He told Gilberte that he'd let her play one game, that he could wait a quarter of an hour; and, sitting down like any normal person on one of the iron chairs, paid for his ticket with the hand which Philippe VII* had so often held in his, while we began playing on the lawn, scattering the pigeons which, with their beautiful iridescent bodies, heart-shaped and looking like the lilacs of the bird kingdom, took refuge as if in so many sanctuaries, one on the great stone basin which, as the bird's beak was invisible below the rim, seemed to make the gesture and to have been designed for the purpose of offering in abundance the fruit or grain at which its feathered friend appeared to be pecking, another on the head of the statue, which it seemed to crown with one of those enamelled objects whose polychrome relieves the monotony of the stone in certain sculptures of antiquity, and with a quality that, when attributed to the goddess, entitles her to a particular epithet and makes of her, as a different first name makes of a mortal woman, a new divinity.

On one of those sunny days that had failed to fulfil my hopes, I was quite unable to hide my disappointment from Gilberte.

'There were so many things I wanted to ask you,' I said. 'I thought today was going to be an important day in our friendship. But no sooner do you get here than you have to go away again! Try to come early tomorrow, so I can talk to you.'

Her face lit up and she jumped for joy as she answered: 'Tomorrow? Oh, you can be sure, my friend, I won't be coming. I've got a special tea party! And the day after, I'm going to a friend's house to watch the arrival of King Theodosius* from her windows—won't that be marvellous?—and the day after that I'm going to see *Michel Strogoff*,* and soon after that there'll be Christmas and the New Year holidays. Perhaps they'll take me to the Midi. That'd be super! Though it would mean I wouldn't have a Christmas tree; anyway, even if I stay in Paris, I won't be coming here because I'll be out visiting with Maman. Oh, there's Papa calling me—bye-bye.'

I walked back home with Françoise through streets still bedecked with sunshine, as on the evening of some festive day now over. I could hardly drag my legs along.

'I'm not a bit surprised,' said Françoise. 'It's been far too warm today, not normal for this time of year. Dearie me, there's bound to be lots of poor folk feeling sick today. Anyone would think things aren't right up there in heaven, either!'

Stifling my sobs, I kept repeating to myself what Gilberte had said in expressing her joy at the prospect of not coming to the Champs-Élysées for a long time. But already the charm with which, by the mere act of thinking, my mind was filled as soon as I thought about her, and the special, unique position—painful though it was—in which I was inevitably placed in relation to Gilberte by the inner constraint of a mental habit, had begun to add, even to this sign of indifference, something romantic, and in the midst of my tears a smile formed that was simply the timid beginnings of a kiss. And when it was time for the postman to arrive, I said to myself that evening, as on every evening: 'There'll be a letter from Gilberte, she's going to tell me at last that she's always loved me, and she'll explain the mysterious reason why she's been forced to hide her love for me until now, to pretend she can be happy without me, and why she's pretended to be the other Gilberte, simply the girl I play with.'

Every evening I liked to imagine receiving this letter, believing I was reading it, reciting each sentence to myself. But suddenly, I stopped in alarm, realizing that if I were to receive a letter from Gilberte, it couldn't be this one, since it was I who had written it. And from then on I would make every effort not to think of the words I would have liked her to write, for fear that, by using them myself, I would be excluding those very words—the dearest, the most desired—from the field of all possible compositions. Even if, through some unlikely coincidence, I'd received a letter from Gilberte identical to the one I'd invented, I'd have recognized my handiwork and wouldn't have had the impression of receiving something that hadn't come from me, something real and new, a feeling of happiness external to my mind, independent of my will, a true gift of love.

Meanwhile I read and reread a page which, though it hadn't been written to me by Gilberte, had at least come to me from her, that page of Bergotte's on the beauty of the ancient myths from which Racine drew his inspiration, and which, along with the agate marble, I kept near me always. I was touched by her kindness in having had someone seek it out for me; and since everyone needs to find some reason for his passion, so much so that he's happy to recognize in the person he loves qualities that, as he has learned from literature or conversation, are among those worthy of arousing love, he assimilates them by imitation and turns them into new grounds for love, even though these qualities may be diametrically opposed to the ones his love would have sought after as long as it was spontaneous—as Swann had once done, with the aesthetic nature of Odette's beauty—I, who had begun to love Gilberte, in Combray, because of everything that was unknown about her life, into which I would have liked to launch myself, taking root, casting aside my own life as something of no account, I thought of it now as having inestimable value, and that of that familiar, contemptible life of mine Gilberte might one day become the humble servant, the companionable, comforting collaborator who, in the evenings, helping me in my work, would collate for me my collection of pamphlets. As for Bergotte, that infinitely wise, almost divine old man, because of whom I'd first loved Gilberte, before I'd even seen her, now it was above all because of Gilberte that I loved him. I studied the pages he'd written about Racine and, with equal pleasure, the wrapping paper, folded under great seals of white wax and tied with long coils of mauve ribbon, in which she'd brought those pages to me. I kissed the agate marble, which was the better part of my love's heart, the part that was not frivolous but faithful, and which, though adorned with the mysterious charm of Gilberte's life, dwelt close beside me, inhabited my room, slept in my bed. But as for the beauty of that stone, and the beauty also of those pages of Bergotte which I was so pleased to associate with the idea of my love for Gilberte, as if, in the moments when that love seemed to me to amount to nothing, they gave it a kind of consistency, I saw that they were anterior to that love, and bore no resemblance to it, that their elements had been determined by the writer's talent or by the laws of mineralogy before Gilberte knew me, that nothing in the book or in the stone would have been different if Gilberte hadn't loved me, and that nothing, consequently, entitled me to read in them a message of happiness. And while my love, forever expecting that the next day would bring Gilberte's avowal of her love, spent each evening cancelling and unravelling the poorly done work of the day, in an obscure part of me an unknown seamstress refused to abandon the discarded threads, but rearranged them, without any intention of pleasing me or working for my happiness, according to the different pattern she gave to all her work. Without showing any special interest in my love, nor beginning by deciding that I was indeed loved, she gathered up those of Gilberte's actions that had seemed to me inexplicable along with her faults, which I had excused. Then everything took on a meaning. It seemed to tell me, this new pattern, that when I saw Gilberte, instead of coming to the Champs-Élysées, go to a party, go shopping with her governess, or prepare to be away over the New Year holidays, I was wrong to think: 'It's because she's frivolous or submissive.' For she would have ceased to be either if she'd loved me, and if she'd been forced to do what she'd been told, she would have felt the same despair I felt on the days when I didn't see her. It showed me further, this new pattern, that I must after all know what it meant to love, since I loved Gilberte; it drew my attention to my constant anxiety to make a good impression on her, which explained why I kept trying to persuade my mother to buy Françoise a raincoat and a hat with a blue feather, or, better still, to stop sending me to the Champs-Élysées with a servant who embarrassed me (to which my mother replied that I was being unfair to Françoise, that she was a good woman who was devoted to us all), and also my obsessive need to see Gilberte, the result of which was that, months in advance, I thought of nothing else but how to find out exactly when she'd be leaving Paris and where she'd be going, making me feel that the most attractive spot in the world would be a place of exile if she was not going to be there, and wanting to stay for ever in Paris as long as I could see her in the Champs-Élysées; and it had no difficulty making me see that, in Gilberte's behaviour, there was no hint of the same anxiety or need. She, on the contrary, appreciated her governess, and was unconcerned about what I might think of the woman. She found it quite natural not to come to the Champs-Élysées if she was to go shopping with Mademoiselle, and pleasant if she was going out with her mother. And even supposing she'd ever allow me to spend my holidays in the same place as herself, when it came to choosing that place she'd take into account her parents' wishes, and the many attractions she'd been told about, and not at all that it should be the place where my family was planning to send me. When she told me, as she sometimes did, that she liked me less than one of the other boys, less than she'd liked me the day before, because by playing badly I'd made her side lose the game, I'd ask her forgiveness and beg her to tell me what I should do to make her like me again as much as, or more than, the other boys; I wanted her to tell me she'd already forgiven me, I begged her to like me, as if she could change her feelings for me at will, or as I wished, in order to please me, simply by the words she would utter, according to whether my conduct was good or bad. Didn't I know, then, that what I felt for her depended neither on her actions nor on my own will?

It showed me, finally, the new pattern devised by the invisible seamstress, that though we may hope that the actions of a person who has hurt us up until now prove not to have been in character, there is in their consistency a clarity against which our hopes are powerless and it's to that clarity that we must attend, rather than to our hopes, if we want to know what that person's actions will be in the future.

These new words of advice were heard by my love; they persuaded it that the next day would be no different from all the days that had gone before; that Gilberte's feelings for me, too well established now to be able to change, amounted to indifference; that in my friendship with her, I was the only one who was in love. 'It's true,' my love replied, 'there's nothing more to be made of this friendship. It won't change.' And so, the very next day (or from the next public holiday, if there was one coming up soon, or an anniversary, or the New Year perhaps, one of those days that are unlike other days, when time starts afresh, detaching itself from the heritage of the past, rejecting its legacy of sorrows) I would ask Gilberte to give up our former relationship and help to lay the foundations of a new one.

I always had within reach a street map of Paris which, because I could see on it the street where Monsieur and Madame Swann lived, seemed to me like a map of buried treasure. And for pure pleasure, as well as from a sort of chivalrous loyalty, on any kind of pretext I would say the name of that street, until my father, not being aware of my love, unlike my mother and grandmother, asked: 'Why are you always talking about that street? There's nothing special about it. It's a very pleasant street to live in because it's so close to the Bois, but there are a dozen other streets of which one can say the same.'

I contrived at every turn to make my parents say Swann's name; of course I repeated it over and over in my own mind, but I also needed to hear its sweet sound, to have someone else play for me that music whose silent reading was not enough. What's more, the name Swann, which I'd known for such a long time, had now become for me, as happens to some aphasics* with the most everyday words, a new name. It was always present in my mind, yet my mind couldn't get used to it. I studied it and spelled it out to myself, but the sequence of its letters always came as a surprise. And together with its familiarity, it had lost its innocence. The pleasure I felt on hearing it now struck me as so guilty that I had the impression, when talking with other people, that they could read my mind and would change the subject if I tried to lead them towards mentioning Swann. I fell back on subjects that still concerned Gilberte, I repeated over and over again the same words, and although I knew they were only words—words uttered in her absence, which she couldn't hear, words without potency, able merely to invoke a state of affairs but not to influence it—it seemed to me nonetheless that by dint of sifting through and stirring up everything even remotely connected to Gilberte, I might perhaps make something approximating to happiness emerge. I kept telling my parents that Gilberte was very fond of her governess, as though that statement, by being repeated a hundred times, would have the effect of making Gilberte suddenly walk into the room, having decided to come and live with us for ever. I sang the praises of the old lady who read *Les Débats* (having already hinted to my parents that she was an ambassadress or even possibly of royal blood) and I continued to celebrate her beauty, her splendour, her noble bearing, until the day I mentioned that, from what I'd heard Gilberte call her, her name must be Madame Blatin.

'Oh, now I know who you mean,' exclaimed my mother, while I felt myself blushing with shame. 'On guard! On guard! as your poor grandfather would have said. So she's the one you find so beautiful! But she's a dreadful woman and always has been. She used to be married to a bailiff. You probably can't remember, when you were little, the lengths I went to to avoid her at your gym lessons. She kept trying to come and talk to me—though she didn't know me at all—with the excuse of wanting to tell me you were "too nice-looking to be a boy". She always had a mania for getting to know everybody, and if she does know Madame Swann, she can't be right in the head, which is what I always thought. Because, although she comes from a very common family, I've never heard people say anything really bad about her. It's just that she always had that mania for trying to get in with the right people. She's dreadful, terribly vulgar, and a trouble-maker into the bargain.'

As for Swann, in order to try to look like him, I spent all my time at the dinner table pulling my nose and rubbing my eyes. 'The boy's an idiot!' my father would say. 'He'll make himself look hideous.' I would especially have liked to be as bald as Swann. He seemed to me a being so extraordinary that I found it miraculous that people I knew actually knew him too, and might, in the course of an ordinary day, chance to meet him. And one time, my mother, while she was telling us, as she did every evening at dinner, what she'd been doing that afternoon, merely by saying: 'By the way, guess who I saw in the Trois Quartiers,* at the umbrella counter—Swann!' caused her story, which I had been finding so tedious, suddenly to blossom with a mysterious flower. What a melancholy pleasure, to learn that, that very afternoon, allowing his supernatural form to be outlined against the crowd, Swann had gone to buy an umbrella. Among the events of my mother's day, great and small, but all equally insignificant, that one aroused in me those peculiar vibrations by which my love for Gilberte was perpetually stirred. According to my father, I took no interest in anything because I didn't listen when there was talk about the possible political consequences of the visit of King Theodosius, at that moment the guest of France and, it was claimed, the nation's ally. But I did take the keenest interest in knowing whether Swann had been wearing his hooded cape!

'Did you say hello to each other?' I asked.

'Of course,' answered my mother, who always seemed afraid that if she admitted they were not on friendly terms with Swann, people would try to arrange a closer reconciliation than she wished, because of Madame Swann, whom she didn't want anything to do with. 'He was the one who came up and spoke to me. I hadn't seen him.'

'So you haven't fallen out?'

'What? What makes you think we might have fallen out?' she replied rather sharply, as if I'd cast doubt on the fiction of her good relations with Swann and was trying to bring about a 'rapprochement'.

'He might be cross because you don't invite him any more.'

'We don't have to invite everyone, do we? He doesn't invite me, does he? And I don't know his wife.'

'But he used to come and see us in Combray.'

'Yes, that's true, but in Paris he's got other things to do, and so have I. In any case, I can assure you we didn't look a bit like two people who had some kind of falling-out. We stood there together for a little while because he had to wait for his parcel. He asked after you and told me you played with his daughter.' I was stunned by the stupendous revelation that I existed in Swann's mind, and even more, that I existed there in so complete a form that when I stood before him, trembling with love, in the Champs-Élysées, he knew my name, who my mother was, and could even bring together around my capacity as playmate of his daughter certain facts about my grandfather, their family, the place where we lived, and certain details of our past life that perhaps even I didn't know. But my mother didn't seem to have taken any great delight in that counter at the Trois Quartiers where, at the moment when Swann had caught sight of her, she'd represented for him a particular person with whom he shared sufficient memories to impel him to go up to her and greet her.

Nor did she, nor indeed my father, seem to be overcome with delight when they mentioned Swann's grandparents or alluded to the profession of honorary stockbroker. My imagination had singled out and sanctified a particular family in the social world of Paris, just as it had singled out from the Paris of bricks and mortar a particular house whose carriage entrance it had sculpted and whose windows it burnished. But these embellishments were visible to no one but me. In the same way that my parents regarded the house Swann lived in as similar to the other houses built at the same time in the neighbourhood of the Bois, so Swann's family seemed to them to be in the same category as many other stockbroker families. They judged it more favourably or less according to the degree to which it shared in merits common to the rest of the universe, and could see nothing unique in it. Indeed, what they appreciated in it they could find in equal, or greater, measure elsewhere. And so, having agreed that the house was well situated, they went on to talk about some other house that was even better situated (but had nothing to do with Gilberte) or about certain financiers who were a cut above her grandfather; and if they'd seemed for a moment to be of the same opinion as me, that was because of a misunderstanding that was soon dispelled. The fact was that, in order to perceive in everything that touched on Gilberte an unknown quality analogous in the world of emotions to what infra-red may be in the world of colours, my parents would have needed to have that sixth sense with which love had temporarily endowed me.

On the days when Gilberte had told me she wouldn't be coming to the Champs-Élysées, I'd try to arrange walks that would bring me into some kind of contact with her. Sometimes I'd take Françoise on a pilgrimage past the house where the Swanns lived. I'd make her repeat endlessly what she'd learned from the governess about Madame Swann. 'It seems she sets great store by her medals.* You'll never catch her leaving on a journey if she's heard the hooting of an owl, or some noise like a clock ticking in the wall, or she's seen a cat at middlenight,* or a piece of furniture starts creaking. Oh yes! she's a very religious lady, is Madame Swann!' I was so madly in love with Gilberte that if we ran into their old butler out walking a dog, I'd be so overcome that I'd stop in my tracks and gaze piningly at his white whiskers. And Françoise would say: 'What's wrong with you?'

Then we'd continue on our way until we reached their carriage entrance, where a concierge, unlike any other concierge in the world, and saturated, down to the very braid of his livery, with the same melancholy charm I'd sensed in the name Gilberte, looked as though he knew I was one of those people in whom an original unworthiness would for ever prevent them from penetrating into the mysteries of the life he was charged with guarding and which the ground-floor windows seemed equally conscious of protecting, as they stood there, tightly shut, resembling far less other windows, between the stately folds of their muslin curtains, than Gilberte's own glances. At other times we'd go along the boulevards, and I'd take up a position at the corner of the Rue Duphot, where, I'd been told, Swann was often to be seen walking past on his way to the dentist; and my imagination so differentiated Gilberte's father from the rest of humanity, his pres-ence in the midst of the real world introduced into it such magic, that even before we reached the Madeleine* I'd be full of excitement at the thought that I was approaching a street where at any moment I might come face to face with that supernatural being.

But more often than not, on the days when I knew I wouldn't be seeing Gilberte, I'd steer Françoise in the direction of the Bois de Boulogne, as I'd been told that Madame Swann went for a walk nearly every day along the Allée des Acacias, round the Grand Lac, and down the Allée de la Reine-Marguerite.* For me the Bois was like one of those zoological gardens in which you can see in one place a whole variety of flora and oddly assorted landscapes—a hill, a grotto, a meadow, some boulders, a stream, a dry moat, another hill, a marsh—which you know are there only to enable the hippopotamus, zebras, crocodiles, white rabbits, bears, and heron to disport themselves in an appropriate or picturesque setting; bringing together a complex mixture of self-contained little worlds—first a small plantation of red trees and American oaks, like a farm in Virginia, then a group of conifers by the edge of the lake, or a forest grove from which a fleet-footed walker would suddenly emerge, clad in soft furs, with the lovely eyes of an animal—the Bois was the Garden of Woman; and, planted for them with trees of one kind only, like the myrtle grove in the *Aeneid*,* the Allée des Acacias was much frequented by the famous beauties of the day. Just as, from a distance, the sight of the edge of the rock from which the sea lion will plunge into the water thrills the children who know they are about to see the animal, so, well before I arrived in the Allée des Acacias, first their scent, radiating all around, made me feel the proximity and singularity of a powerful, soft, vegetable personality, then, as I drew near, the sight of their topmost branches, light and delicate, with their simple elegance, coquettish outline, and fine tissue, on which hundreds of flowers had alighted like throbbing colonies of precious parasites, and, finally, their feminine names, indolent and sweet—all of this made my heart pound, but with a worldly desire, like those waltz tunes that remind us only of the names of the beautiful women the usher announces as they enter the ballroom. I'd been told that I'd see in the avenue certain elegant women who, though not all of them had ever been married, were regularly mentioned in the same breath as Madame Swann, but most often by their assumed name; their married name, when they had one, was only a sort of incognito which men who wanted to talk about them were careful to lay aside in order to make themselves understood. Believing that Beauty—in the matter of feminine elegance—was governed by secret laws that had been made known to these women, and that they had the power to bring that Beauty into existence, I had already accepted in advance like a revelation the spectacle of their clothes, their carriages and horses, and a thousand other details to whose fleeting, ever-changing pageant my belief imparted a sort of inner soul which gave it the cohesion of a masterpiece. But it was Madame Swann I wanted to see, and I waited for her to go past, as nervous as if she were Gilberte herself, for Gilberte's parents, imbued like everything else in her life with her special charm, inspired in me as much love as she did, indeed a feeling of agitation that was even more painful (because their point of contact with her was the intimate part of her life from which I was excluded) and also (for, as will be seen, I was soon to learn that they didn't like her to play with me) the feeling of veneration we always have for those who have unlimited power to hurt us.

I assigned first place, in terms of aesthetic merit and distinction in fashion, to simplicity, whenever I glimpsed Madame Swann, on foot, wearing a simple cloth polonaise,* a little toque trimmed with a pheasant's wing, a bunch of violets on her bodice, hurrying across the Allée des Acacias as if it were merely the shortest way home, and acknowledging with a wink the greetings of gentlemen in carriages who, recognizing her figure from a distance, raised their hats and said to themselves that she was the smartest of them all. But instead of simplicity, it was luxury that I put in first place if, after I'd forced Françoise, who was exhausted and said she was on her 'last legs', to walk up and down with me for an hour, I managed to see at last, emerging from the avenue that leads to the Porte Dauphine,* a resplendent carriage—an image for me of royal glamour, the passage of a sovereign, making an impression on me such as no real queen has ever made since, because my notion of their power is now less vague, more founded on experience; the carriage was borne along by two flying horses as slender and sleek as in the drawings of Constantin Guys,* carrying on its box an enormous coachman wrapped in furs like a Cossack, beside him a tiny groom who called to mind the 'tiger' of 'the late Baudenord';* what I saw (or rather, felt being engraved on my failing heart with the clean strokes of a knife) was an incomparable victoria, a little high in its design and hinting despite its up-to-the-minute style of opulence at a more traditional carriage, within which was Madame Swann, reclining luxuriously, her hair now blonde with a single grey lock, held in place by a thin band of flowers, mostly violets, from which hung long floating veils, in her hand a mauve parasol, on her lips an ambiguous smile which to my eyes expressed the beneficence of a monarch, though in fact, as she bestowed it sweetly on the men who greeted her, it was the provocative smile of the courtesan. It was a smile that said to some: 'Oh yes, I remember; it was wonderful!'; to others: 'I wish we could have! Fate was against us!'; and to others: 'Yes, if you like! I'll just stay in this line for a minute, and as soon as I can I'll double back.' When strangers passed, a languorous smile still played on her lips, as if she was looking forward to seeing, or was remembering, a friend, which made people comment: 'What a lovely woman!' And for some men, just a few, she had a smile that was sour, stiff, reticent, and cold, and meant: 'Yes, you rat, I know you, and that nasty tongue of yours, that you can't control! But do I attack you?' Coquelin* went past holding forth to a group of friends hanging on his words, and waving theatrically to the people in the carriages. But I thought only of Madame Swann, and even pretended not to have seen her, because I knew that when her carriage drew level with the clay-pigeon shooting range she'd tell her coachman to pull to one side and let her down so that she could walk back the way she'd come. On the days when I plucked up enough courage to pass close by her, I'd drag Françoise in that direction. And, sure enough, before long I'd see Madame Swann walking towards us on the footpath, the long train of her mauve skirts spread out behind her, dressed, as the common people imagine queens to be dressed, in finery no other woman wore, glancing down now and then at the handle of her parasol, and hardly seeming to notice the passers-by, as if her sole concern was to take some exercise, without thinking she was being observed and that all heads were turned towards her. Now and then, however, when she looked back to call her greyhound, she'd cast an imperceptible glance all round.

Even strangers were alerted by something special and extravagant about her—or perhaps by the sort of telepathic suggestion that used to set off bursts of applause by an ignorant audience at moments when La Berma was sublime—that she must be someone well known. They would ask one another: 'Who is she?', or ask a passing stranger, or remember exactly how she was dressed in order to tell some better-informed friend, who might then enlighten them. Others, pausing in their walk, would say:

'Do you know who that is? Madame Swann! That doesn't mean anything to you? Odette de Crécy, then?'

'Odette de Crécy! Of course, I thought it might be. Those sad eyes . . . Well, she can't be as young as she used to be, eh? I remember I slept with her on the day MacMahon resigned.'*

'You'd better not remind her. She's Madame Swann now, the wife of a gentleman in the Jockey Club, a friend of the Prince of Wales. But she still looks superb.'

'Yes, but if you'd known her then! She was so lovely! She lived in a very odd little town house full of Chinese bric-à-brac. I remember we were bothered by the paper boys shouting the news in the street. In the end she made me get up and leave.'

I couldn't hear these comments, but I could feel, all around her, the vague murmur of celebrity. My heart pounded with impatience at the thought that another few moments must go by before all these people (among whom I was dismayed not to see a certain half-caste banker who, I felt, despised me) could witness this woman, whose reputation for beauty, misconduct, and elegance was universal, being greeted by the unknown youth to whom they'd paid not the slightest attention (and who hardly knew her, but thought he had the right to greet her because his parents were acquainted with her husband and he sometimes played with her daughter). But I was already very close to her, and doffed my hat to her with such an extravagant and extended gesture that she couldn't help smiling. People laughed. Madame Swann, it must be said, had never seen me with Gilberte and didn't know my name; for her I was like one of the park-keepers, or the boatman, or the ducks on the lake to which she threw bread—just one of the familiar, nameless, minor figures, as nondescript as an 'extra' onstage, who happened to appear as she took her walks in the Bois. There were other days when, not having seen her in the Allée des Acacias, I'd come upon her in the Allée de la Reine-Marguerite, where women go who want to be alone, or to appear to want to be alone; she was never alone for long, but was soon joined by some gentleman friend, often wearing a grey 'topper', whom I didn't know, and who would chat with her for a long time, while their two carriages followed behind.

The complexity of the Bois de Boulogne, which makes it an artificial place and, in the zoological or mythological sense, a Garden, struck me again this year as I walked through it on my way to Trianon,* on one of those mornings in early November when, in Paris, cooped up indoors, we're so close to the spectacle of autumn, and yet excluded from it, as it draws rapidly to a close without our witnessing it, that we feel a yearning, a veritable craving for falling leaves that can even prevent us from sleeping at night. In my closed room, they had been present for a month now, summoned by my desire to see them, slipping between my thoughts and the object I was trying to concentrate them on, swirling before me like those yellow spots that sometimes, whatever we may be looking at, dance before our eyes. And that morning, no longer hearing the rain falling as on the previous few days, and seeing the smile of fine weather at the corners of my drawn curtains as at the corners of closed lips that betray the secret of their happiness, I'd felt I might be able to go and look at those yellow leaves with the light shining through them, in their supreme beauty; so, no more able to resist my urge to go to see the trees than, in my childhood days, when the wind howled in the chimney, I'd been able to resist my longing to visit Balbec and gaze at the sea, I'd left the house to walk to Trianon by way of the Bois de Boulogne. It was the time and the season when the Bois seems perhaps at its most multiform, not only because it's more subdivided, but also because it's subdivided differently. Even in the open parts, with their sweeping vistas, here and there in front of a dark, distant mass of trees, now leafless or with their summer foliage still intact, a double row of orange-red chestnuts seemed, as in a picture just begun, to be the only thing painted so far by an artist who hadn't yet applied any colour to the rest, and to be offering their avenue, in full daylight, for the group of strollers that would be added to the picture later on.

Further off, where the trees were still all green, one alone, small, squat, lopped, but stubborn in its resistance, was tossing in the wind its unkempt head of red hair. Elsewhere, again, could be seen the first awakening of this May-time of the leaves, and those of a porcelain vine as marvellous and cheering as a winter-fruiting pear had that very morning all come out in blossom. And the Bois had the temporary, artificial look of a nursery garden or a park, where for botanical purposes or in preparation for a festival, they have recently planted, among the trees of a common sort that have not yet been transplanted elsewhere, two or three rare species, with fantastic foliage, that seem to be reserving an empty space around themselves, giving air, creating light. Thus it was the time of year when the Bois de Boulogne displays the greatest number of different species and brings together in a composite whole more distinct elements than in any other season. It was also the time of day. In the places where the trees had not yet lost their leaves, they seemed to be undergoing a change of substance starting from the point where they were touched by the light of the sun, almost horizontal in the morning, as it would be again a few hours later in the gathering dusk, when it flares up like a lamp, projects over a distance on to the foliage a warm and artificial glow, and ignites the topmost leaves of a tree that remains the shadowy and incombustible candelabrum of its burning tip. At one point, it thickened the leaves of the chestnut trees so that they seemed like bricks, cementing them crudely against the sky like a piece of yellow Persian masonry patterned in blue; at another, it detached them from the sky as they clutched at it with their fingers of gold. Halfway up a tree clothed in Virginia creeper, it had grafted and brought into bloom an enormous cluster of what appeared to be red flowers, too dazzling to identify but possibly a variety of carnation. The different parts of the Bois, which in summer blend into each other in a single dense mass of greenery, were now clearly divided. Open spaces made visible the entrance to almost every one of them, or else a superb mass of foliage designated it like a banner. It was possible to distinguish, as on a coloured map, Armenonville, the Pré Catelan, Madrid, the race course, and the shores of the lake.* Here and there some useless construction would appear, a fake grotto, a windmill for which the trees stood aside to make room, or which was borne on the soft green platform of a grassy lawn. One could feel that the Bois wasn't just a wood, that it fulfilled a purpose foreign to the life of its trees; the exhilaration I felt was caused not merely by my admiration of autumn, but by a desire—fount of the joy the soul feels at first without being aware of its cause, without understanding that it comes from no external source. And so I gazed at the trees with an unsatisfied longing that went beyond them and was directed, without my knowing it, towards those masterpieces of feminine beauty, the lovely women for whose walks, a few hours every day, they serve as setting. I walked towards the Allée des Acacias. I passed through groves which the morning light had divided into new sections, pruning the trees, joining some of them together, blending their branches. It drew deftly towards it a pair of trees; making effective use of its great scissors of light and shade, it cut off from each one half of its trunk and branches and, weaving together the two halves that remained, made of them either a single pillar of shade, defined by the surrounding light, or a single luminous phantom whose quivering, artificial contour was ringed by a dark web of shadows. When a ray of sunshine gilded the highest branches, they seemed to sparkle with moisture, to have just emerged from the liquid, emerald-green atmosphere in which the whole grove was plunged as though under the sea. It was evident that the trees continued to live with a vitality all their own, and when they'd lost their leaves, that vitality shone all the more brightly from the sheath of green velvet round their trunks or in the white enamel of the mistletoe berries that spangled the topmost branches of the poplars, as round as the sun and the moon in Michelangelo's *Creation*.* Forced for so many years by a sort of grafting to live alongside women, they reminded me of the dryads, the lovely quick and colourful ladies of the world whom they cover with their branches as they pass beneath them, obliging them to feel, as they do, the power of the season; they reminded me of the happy days of my youth when I believed the world was a thing of beauty, when I would eagerly come to the places where masterpieces of female elegance were created for a few moments among the unconscious, complicitous trees. But the beauty which the pines and acacias of the Bois de Boulogne made me desire (these trees being more disturbing because of this than the chestnuts and lilacs of Trianon that I was on my way to see) was not fixed outside me in the mementoes of some historical period, in works of art, in a little temple to the god of Love whose entrance is piled with gold-webbed leaves. I reached the shores of the lake, and walked on as far as the clay pigeon range. The idea of perfection which at that time I carried within me I'd conferred upon the height of a victoria, upon the slenderness of its horses, as fierce and light as wasps, their eyes bloodshot like the cruel steeds of Diomedes,* and which now, filled as I was with a desire to see again what I had once loved, a desire as ardent as that which had driven me down these same paths many years before, I wanted to behold once more at the moment when Madame Swann's enormous coachman, watched over by the tiny groom as childlike as Saint George,* struggled to control their wings of steel which twitched and quivered. Now, alas, there were only motor cars driven by moustachioed gentlemen with tall footmen by their sides. I wanted to see in the present, so as to know if they were as charming as they appeared in my memory of them, women's little hats worn so low that they seemed to be simple crowns. But all the hats were now immense, covered with fruit and flowers and a variety of birds. Instead of the lovely dresses that had made Madame Swann look like a queen, I now saw Graeco-Saxon tunics with Tanagra folds,* or sometimes in the style of the Directoire,* Liberty chiffons* with floral patterns like wallpaper. The gentlemen who might have strolled with Madame Swann in the Allée de la Reine-Marguerite were no longer wearing the grey top hats of earlier times, nor any other kind. They all went about bareheaded. And I no longer had any belief to infuse into all these new elements of the spectacle, to give them substance, unity, life; they went past in a fitful, random, mean-ingless fashion, containing in themselves no beauty that my eyes might have tried, as they had in earlier times, to form into a compos-ition. They were just ordinary women, in whose elegance I had no faith and whose dress seemed to me unimportant. But when a belief disappears, there survives—more and more tenaciously so as to mask the loss of our ability to give reality to new things—a fetishistic attachment to the old things which our belief once animated, as if it were in them and not in ourselves that the divine resided and as if our present lack of belief had a contingent cause, the death of the gods.

I thought: How awful! How can anyone think these motor cars are as elegant as the old carriages and pairs? I'm probably too old already, but I wasn't made for a world in which women stagger about in dresses that aren't even made of cloth. What's the point of walking among these trees, if there's nothing left of all those gatherings under the delicate reddening leaves, if vulgarity and idiocy have replaced the exquisite things they once framed? How awful! My only consola-tion is to think about the women I once knew, now that that world of elegance has disappeared. But how could anyone looking at these hor-rible creatures, with hats like birdcages or kitchen gardens, begin to appreciate what was so charming about the sight of Madame Swann in a simple mauve bonnet or a little hat crowned with just a single iris on its stem? Could I even have made them understand why I felt excited on winter mornings when I met Madame Swann when she was out walking, wearing her sealskin coat and a simple beret with two blade-like partridge feathers sticking up, and wrapped as well in the artificial warmth of her apartment, which was suggested by nothing more than the bunch of violets pressed to her breast, whose blue flowers in the freezing air looked so bright against the grey sky and bare trees, and had the same charming effect of using the season and the weather merely as a setting, and of living in a human atmosphere, in the atmosphere of this woman, as had, in the vases and flower stands of her drawing room, next to the blazing fire, in front of the silk-covered sofa, the flowers that looked out through the closed window at the falling snow? But in any case it would not have been enough for me for the clothes to be the same as in those earlier times. Because of the interdependence of the different parts of a memory, parts which our memory keeps in a balanced whole, from which we are not allowed to abstract or reject anything, I would have liked to be able to go and spend the rest of the day in the home of one of those women, sipping tea, in an apartment with walls painted in dark colours, as Madame Swann's still was (in the year after the one in which the first part of this story ends) and in which the orange gleam, the red combustion, the pink-and-white flame of the chrysanthemums would glow in the November twilight, in moments similar to those in which (as we'll see later) I'd been unable to discover the pleasures for which I yearned. But now, even though they had led to nothing, those moments seemed to me to have been charming enough in themselves. I wanted to find them again as I remembered them. Alas, there was nothing now but Louis XVI apartments, all white, and dotted with blue hydrangeas. Moreover, people didn't return to Paris, now, until much later. Madame Swann would have written to me from a country house to say she wouldn't be back until February, well after the chrysanthemum season, had I asked her to reconstruct for me the elements of that memory which I felt belonged to a distant year, to a vintage to which I was not allowed to go back, the elements of that longing which had itself become as inaccessible as the pleasure it had once vainly pursued. And I would also have needed them to be the same women, those whose dress interested me because, at the time when I still had faith, my imagination had individualized them and given each of them a legend. Alas, in the Avenue des Acacias—the Allée de Myrtes—I did see some of them again, grown old, now no more than terrible shadows of what they had once been, wandering, desperately searching for who knows what in the Virgilian groves. They fled, but I still stood there long after, vainly questioning the deserted paths. The sun had disappeared. Nature was resuming its reign over the Bois, from which the idea that it was the Elysian Garden of Woman had vanished; above the imitation windmill the real sky was grey; the wind wrinkled the Grand Lac with little wavelets, like a real lake; large birds flew swiftly over the Bois, as over a real wood, and with shrill cries settled, one after another, in the tall oaks which, under their druidical crowns and with a Dodonean majesty,* seemed to proclaim the inhuman emptiness of this deconsecrated forest, and helped me to understand what a contradiction it is to search in reality for the pictures that reside in our memory, for they would never have the charm bestowed on them by memory itself and from not being perceived through the senses. The reality I'd known no longer existed. It was enough that Madame Swann did not arrive at the same time as before, looking exactly as she had done then, for the whole avenue to be altered completely. The places we've known don't belong only to the world of space in which we situate them for our own convenience. They were only ever a thin slice among contiguous impressions that formed our life at that time; the memory of a particular image is only regret for a particular moment; and houses, roads, avenues are as fleeting, alas, as the years.

EXPLANATORY NOTES

COMBRAY

3 *Gaston Calmette*: Proust's dedicatee, Calmette (1858–1914), was the editor of *Le Figaro*, the newspaper in which Proust published numerous articles between 1900 and his death in 1922. Calmette died after being shot, in his office at *Le Figaro*, by the wife of Joseph Caillaux, a politician and former prime minister against whom Calmette's paper had been waging a campaign in its pages.

7 *the rivalry between François I and Charles V*: François I (1494–1547) was king of France from 1515 to 1547; he was defeated by Charles V (1500–58), king of Spain from 1516 to 1556, in the election to the position of Holy Roman Emperor. Proust may be alluding here to a book on this subject, François Mignet's *Histoire de la rivalité de François Ier et de Charles-Quint* (1875).

8 *just as Eve was created from one of Adam's ribs*: Proust boldly undercuts the biblical story of the creation of Eve (Genesis 2:7) by comparing it to the emergence of a fantasized female figure in the protagonist's erotic dream.

9 *at top speed through time and space*: a probable allusion to H. G. Wells's science fiction classic *The Time Machine* (1895).

10 *its urn-shaped bowl of Bohemian glass . . . and the mantelpiece of Siena marble*: glass produced in Bohemia and Silesia (now the Czech Republic) has a centuries-old reputation for quality and beauty, as does the honey-yellow marble quarried around the Tuscan city of Siena. These precisions are characteristic of the narrator's eye for detail.

as shown by a kinetoscope: a precursor to modern moving-picture projectors, the kinetoscope, devised by the American inventor Thomas Edison in the early 1890s, gave an individual the impression of seeing moving pictures via a scroll of photographic stills viewed through a peephole in the top of a cabinet-sized device.

11 *an issue of the Débats roses*: the evening edition of the newspaper the *Journal des débats*, its name deriving from the colour of the paper on which it was printed.

the Louis XVI bedroom: 'Louis Seize' style refers to furniture, architecture, and decoration developed during the reign of Louis XVI, the last king of France before the Revolution of 1789. The style was characterized by classical influences in contrast to the ornate qualities of the baroque period that came before.

the unfamiliar smell of vetiver: vetiver is a fragrant grass; essential oils extracted from the root have a range of medicinal properties, including use as a soporific.

11 *rectangular cheval glass*: a long mirror mounted on a swivel that allows it to be tilted.

12 *Balbec, Paris, Doncières, Venice*: the narrator here lists what are, in addition to the fictional Combray, the primary geographical locations of the novel. Balbec is a fictional seaside town based on Cabourg on the Normandy coast, whilst Doncières is a fictional garrison town where the narrator later visits his friend Robert de Saint-Loup, stationed there in *The Guermantes Way*.

the Gothic age: in architecture, the Gothic period spans from the mid-twelfth to the mid-fifteenth centuries. Proust's interest in cathedral design and construction stems from his study of, amongst others, the art historians John Ruskin (1819–1900) and Émile Mâle (1862–1954).

Golo: in the medieval legend of Geneviève de Brabant, a tale of falsely accused infidelity upon which Jacques Offenbach based an operetta of the same name, Golo is the wicked suitor who accuses Geneviève of adultery when she turns down his amorous advances.

poor Geneviève de Brabant: the heroine of the medieval legend depicted in the protagonist's magic lantern slides. Proust's fictional Guermantes are descendants of the Brabant line.

13 *the Merovingian past*: the Merovingian kings were the first dynasty to rule Frankish Gaul, between the fifth and eighth centuries.

Bluebeard: *Barbe bleue* is a French folk-tale, the best-known version of which was written by Charles Perrault (1628–1703) in 1697. The eponymous Bluebeard is a wealthy nobleman who marries and murders a series of wives.

16 *like the host at Communion . . . her real presence*: in Christianity, bread and wine, respectively representing the body and blood of Christ, are consecrated and shared in the rite of Communion. 'Real presence' is the Christian doctrine that Christ is present in a substantial way, not only symbolically, in the consecrated bread or wafer known as the 'host'.

17 *the Bressant style*: Prosper Bressant (1815–86) was an actor who popularized a hairstyle combining longer, bouffant hair at the back and sides of the head with shorter hair on top.

18 *the Jockey Club*: one of the most exclusive gentlemen's clubs in Paris, founded in 1833–4. Swann's membership (since he was Jewish and neither an aristocrat nor a leader of industry), and the friendships mentioned in these lines, are indicative of his exalted social position.

Comte de Paris: Philippe d'Orléans (1838–94) was the grandson of King Louis-Philippe.

Prince of Wales: the future Edward VII was Prince of Wales from 1841 to 1901.

the Faubourg Saint-Germain: the exclusive district on the left bank of the Seine, around the church of Saint-Germain-des-Prés, site of many of the capital's finest *hôtels particuliers* (private mansions) and historically home to the high nobility.

19 *the Quai d'Orléans*: a street overlooking the Seine, situated on the south side of the Île Saint-Louis; at the time it was not an especially desirable address.

the Boulevard Haussmann or the Avenue de l'Opéra: two of the city's grandest thoroughfares, created in the course of the programme of urban renewal and renovation known as 'Haussmannization' (1853–70), after its architect Baron Georges-Eugène Haussmann (1809–91), prefect of Paris. Proust lived at 102 Boulevard Haussmann from 1906 to 1919 and wrote the majority of *A la recherche du temps perdu* there.

20 *marrons glacés*: candied chestnuts, often given as a New Year's Day gift.

the wine depot: the 'Halle aux vins' was located on the left bank of the Seine, opposite the Quai d'Orléans.

Virgil shows him being welcomed with open arms: Proust's reference here is to the pastoral poems, the *Georgics*, by the Roman poet Virgil (70–19 BC): a shepherd, Aristaeus, visits the world beneath the ocean ('the realm of Thetis', a sea nymph and mother to Achilles) where he is welcomed by his own mother, also a water nymph.

glittering cave full of secret treasure: the story of Ali Baba and the forty thieves is a story of Syrian origin added by Antoine Galland to his French translation (1704–17) of the collection of folk-tales compiled in Arabic between the seventh and fourteenth centuries, known as *Les Mille et une nuits* in French (*The Thousand and One Nights* or *The Arabian Nights* in English).

a princess of the demi-monde!: the 'demi-monde' refers to the hedonistic fringes of respectable society ('le monde' or 'le beau monde') where elite men would indulge their desires with women of lower social standing ('demi-mondaines' or courtesans) whom they supported materially and financially. This world was at its peak during the period known as the Belle Époque, from around 1871 to 1914.

gribiche sauce: a sauce typically eaten with cooked meats, made with an emulsion of oil, mustard, and cooked egg yolks; chopped gherkins and egg whites; capers, chervil, tarragon, and parsley.

21 *a letter from Twickenham*: the Comte de Paris (of the Orléans family, 'princes of the House of France') lived in exile at Twickenham, to the south-west of London, until 1871. The events recounted, however, are clearly subsequent to that date: Proust's handling of precise dates and 'real world' chronology is idiosyncratic.

22 *the Sacré-Cœur*: a Parisian boarding school for girls run by the nuns of the Basilica of the Sacré-Cœur.

Marquise de Villeparisis of the famous Bouillon family: Proust has his fictional characters related to a branch of the (real) aristocratic La Tour d'Auvergne family. The mothers of Basin de Guermantes, Oriane de Guermantes, and Madame de Villeparisis are sisters, born Bouillon.

the des Laumes: before inheriting his father's title, the Duc de Guermantes was Prince, and his wife Oriane Princesse des Laumes. See note to p. 241.

22 '*Sévigné couldn't have put it better!*': Marie de Rabutin-Chantal, Marquise de Sévigné, known as Madame de Sévigné (1626–96) is a major figure in seventeenth-century literature. She is celebrated for her much-read letters to her daughter, which combine wisdom, wit, vivacity, and tenderness.

related to Marshal MacMahon: Patrice MacMahon (1808–93) led the French army in the Franco-Prussian War and was president of the Third Republic of France from 1873 to 1879. His relation to the fictional Madame de Villeparisis is Proust's invention.

23 *during the reign of Louis-Philippe*: Louis-Philippe was king of the French from 1830 until the February Revolution of 1848, which led to his abdication.

men like Molé, the Duc Pasquier, and the Duc de Broglie: all three were ministers under the 'July Monarchy' (the name given to Louis-Philippe's reign): Louis Mathieu, Comte Molé (1781–1855) was prime minister from 1836 to 1839 and elected to the Académie française in 1840. Étienne-Denis Pasquier (1767–1862), president of the Chamber of Peers from 1830 to 1837, was ennobled as Duc de Pasquier by Louis-Philippe in 1842 and, like Molé, an *académicien*, elected in 1842. Victor, Duc de Broglie (1785–1870) was a career statesman, holding various posts including minister for foreign affairs (1832).

24 *Corot*: Jean-Baptiste-Camille Corot (1796–1875) was an influential nineteenth-century painter of landscapes and portraits, much admired by Claude Monet (1840–1926) amongst others.

'*Swann is being noticed in Le Figaro now*': Le Figaro, as noted above, was the daily newspaper that published many of Proust's early writings and was France's leading newspaper when Proust was writing his novel.

26 *the Duc d'Audiffret-Pasquier*: Gaston Audiffret-Pasquier (1823–1905), was grand-nephew and adopted son of the Duc de Pasquier, mentioned above. He too was a centre-right politician and *académicien*.

her sister Flora: Proust mistakenly attributes both comments in this exchange to the same sister.

Maubant: Henri-Polydore Maubant (1821–1902), was an actor at the revered Comédie-Française, specializing in older, patrician characters.

27 *Madame Materna*: Amalie Materna (1844–1918) was a celebrated Austrian operatic soprano who originated some of the greatest roles of Richard Wagner (1813–83).

Swedish cooperative movement: the cooperative movement grew in Britain and France in the late eighteenth and early nineteenth century, developing in Sweden by the 1880s.

Saint-Simon: Louis de Rouvroy, Duc de Saint-Simon (1675–1755) was a diplomat and writer whose voluminous *Mémoires* provide an extraordinary account of Louis XIV's court at Versailles and the Regency period of Louis d'Orléans, between 1694 and 1723. His mission as *ambassadeur-extraordinaire* to Spain was in 1720–3.

Pascal's Pensées: Blaise Pascal (1623–62) was a mathematician, philosopher, and theologian and a contemporary of René Descartes (1596–1650). Pascal's *Pensées*, published posthumously in 1670, is a collection of fragmentary writings that offer a defence of Christianity.

28 *the Queen of the Hellenes has gone to Cannes . . . the Princesse de Léon has given a fancy dress ball*: Olga Constantinovna (1851–1926), niece of Tsar Nicolas I, was married to King George I of Greece (1845–1913) and thus 'Queen of the Hellenes' from 1867 to 1913. Herminie de La Brousse de Verteillac (1853–1926) was an aristocratic poet who bore the title Princesse de Léon from 1872 to 1893, before becoming Duchesse de Rohan.

Maulévrier: Jean-Baptiste-Louis Andrault, Marquis de Maulévrier-Langeron (1677–1754), was the French ambassador to Spain during Saint-Simon's mission there in 1720–3.

"Never did I see . . . stupidity": a direct quotation from Saint-Simon's *Mémoires* for 1721.

"I can't say . . . to prevent him": again, a direct quotation from Saint-Simon's *Mémoires* for 1721.

"How many, Lord, are the virtues you make us abhor!": here the grandfather quotes a line spoken by Pompey's mourning widow in the Roman tragedy *The Death of Pompey* by Pierre Corneille (1606–84), which was first performed in 1643.

29 *viaticum*: the name given, in the Catholic Church, to the Eucharist (the act of Holy Communion) when it is administered to someone thought to be near death. Metaphorically it can refer to provisions given to a traveller about to undertake a journey.

Molière: Jean-Baptiste Poquelin (1622–73), known as Molière, was a comic playwright, actor, and rival of Pierre Corneille (see note to p. 28).

30 *from an animal's thigh*: these references to 'legal codes of ancient times' are biblical allusions: see Exodus 34:26 and Genesis 32:33.

Saint Theophilus: having rashly signed a pact with the Devil, Theophilus, a sixth-century churchman in Cilicia (modern-day Turkey) displayed such repentance that he was saved by an intercession from the Virgin and granted a saintly death. This story is thought to be one of the Virgin's miracles that is most commonly depicted in church art, as a key representation of the Virgin's power. Proust may also have in mind Rutebœuf's mystery play *Le Miracle de Théophile* (?1261).

Aymon: the story of the four sons of Aymon is another popular medieval tale, recounted in the late twelfth-century *Geste de Renaud de Montaubon*, involving four brothers who clash with King Charlemagne and which forms part of the mythic fabric of early French history.

34 *muted motifs*: mutes are mechanical devices used on musical instruments to muffle the tone.

the Conservatoire orchestra . . . Rue de Trévise: the Paris Conservatoire de musique opened in 1795 and was located at the corner of the Rue du

Conservatoire and the Rue Bergère in the 9th *arrondissement* until 1911. Rue de Trévise is a very short walk away.

37 *'law of nations'*: the *Droit des gens* (*Law of Nations*, 1758) was a groundbreaking text written by the Swiss jurist Emer de Vattel (1714–67), which laid the foundations of modern international law and citizens' rights.

neuralgia: the experience of shooting, burning pain deriving from a damaged or irritated nerve.

Benozzo Gozzoli: (?1421–97), celebrated Renaissance painter best known for his fresco *The Procession of the Magi* in the Palazzo Medici Riccardi in Florence. He depicted various scenes from the Old Testament, though there is no record of a painting depicting Abraham's gesture as suggested here.

39 *for your saint's day*: the calendar of saints is the traditional means of organizing the liturgical year, with one or more saints being celebrated each day. Some of these remain widely observed, such as St Andrew's Day and St David's Day in Scotland and Wales respectively.

The books were La Mare au Diable, François le Champi, La Petite Fadette, and Les Maîtres sonneurs: the four titles mentioned here are pastoral novels of country life in the Berry region of France by George Sand (1804–76), published respectively in 1846, 1848, 1849, and 1853.

40 *the poems of Musset, a volume of Rousseau, and Indiana*: Alfred de Musset (1810–57) was a novelist, dramatist, and poet associated with Romanticism. Jean-Jacques Rousseau (1712–78) was a philosopher and writer and one of the architects of the Enlightenment in Europe. *Indiana* (1832) was an early romantic novel by Sand, which treats the themes of female desire, marriage, and adultery. As these brief summaries make clear, the grandmother's views of what might be suitable reading for the child protagonist make no concession for his age and are aligned with what the narrator has just called her 'ardent idealism'.

Chartres Cathedral . . . thus adding another layer of art to the picture: Corot (see note to p. 24), painted a view of Chartres Cathedral in 1830, which is now in the collection of the Louvre in Paris. Hubert Robert (1733–1808) was a painter of Romantic landscapes (of France and Italy, often depicting ruins). He painted *Le Parc de Saint-Cloud* and *Le Jet d'eau*: Proust appears to conflate them here; an extended description of a fountain such as Robert depicts features in *Sodom and Gomorrah*. J. M. W. Turner (1775–1851) was a prolific English Romantic painter and forerunner of impressionism. He visited Naples and climbed Vesuvius in 1819, and subsequently produced various depictions of the volcano, some of which Proust encountered as reproductions in the pages of the works of John Ruskin.

41 *Morghen's engraving of Leonardo's Last Supper*: the best-known engraving by Raphaël Morghen (1758–1833) is his work, completed in 1800, based on the mural *The Last Supper* (*c*.1495–8), painted by Leonardo da Vinci (1452–1519) in the refectory of the Santa Maria delle Grazie convent in Milan.

Titian: Tiziano Vecellio (?1490–1576), known in English as Titian, is one of the best-known European painters of early modern Europe. Based in Venice (a frequent backdrop to his work), Titian painted frescoes, land-scapes, and portraits that were widely sought after. Venice later becomes an important site in Proust's novel (the protagonist finally visits the city in *The Fugitive*).

42 *'Champi'*: a dialect word from the Berry region, where the book is set, *champi* means 'foundling'. In Sand's novel, François is adopted by a miller's wife named Madeleine.

43 *Bengal light*: a sort of flare giving off an intense bluish light; previously used for signalling, now a type of firework.

44 *the object that is their prison*: the narrator's allusion to a 'Celtic belief' about souls becoming entrapped in material objects may refer to certain Breton legends recounted in works with which Proust was familiar: *Histoire de France* (1855) by the historian Jules Michelet (1798–1874), *Souvenirs d'en-fance et de jeunesse* (1883) by the scholar and critic Ernest Renan (1823–92), and the memoir-novel *Pierre Nozière* (1899) by Anatole France (1844–1924).

a scallop shell: madeleines are made in the shape of a scallop shell. Historically, pilgrims travelling the Way of St James (Jacques in French) to his shrine at Santiago de Compostela in northern Spain would wear scallop shells since the shell was traditionally the emblem of St James (hence 'coquilles Saint Jacques').

49 *a calvary or a crib*: representations of the end and the beginning of Jesus's life (Christ was crucified at Golgotha, also known as Calvary, and born in a manger). A calvary is a public monument to the Crucifixion, common in northern France.

myriads of protozoa: protozoa are microscopic single-cell organisms.

antimacassars: pieces of cloth placed over the back of chairs to protect the upholstery from dirt or staining, taking their name from Macassar oil, a popular men's hair oil in the nineteenth century.

50 *chausson*: literally a 'slipper', a *chausson* is a turnover made with flaky puff pastry and, typically, a sweet filling such as cooked apples.

51 *pepsin and Vespers*: pepsin is an enzyme responsible for the breakdown of protein in the stomach, an animal-derived supplement which was taken to aid digestion (like the Vichy-Célestins brand mineral water mentioned here, thought to soothe gastric trouble). From the Latin meaning 'evening', Vespers is the evening prayer service, one of the seven fixed 'canonical hours' for prayer, now typically observed only by the clergy and those in religious orders.

Persian prince: in the Old Testament book of Esther (the story of a Hebrew woman who becomes queen of Persia), when unable to sleep the king calls for the book of chronicles, the record of his reign, and demands that they be read to him (Esther 6:1). A female reader is a mainstay of the *Thousand and One Nights*, wherein Scheherazade staves off her execution by the bloodthirsty king by reading him stories for a thousand nights, leaving each one unfinished at dawn, to be picked up the following night.

52 *respect of a Greek tragedian for the invisible bonds . . . in a family*: ancient Greek tragedy, associated with such authors as Aeschylus, Sophocles, and Euripides, frequently explores and exploits the dramatic tensions of blood relations and inspired many later writers well known to Proust such as Jean Racine (1639–99) and Pierre Corneille.

53 *to use that clever term*: X-rays were discovered in 1895 by the German physicist Wilhelm Röntgen.

54 *the Elevation*: the ritual raising-up of the consecrated bread and wine during the Catholic Mass.

Monsieur le Curé: the parish priest.

55 *get two sous' worth of salt*: in suggesting this errand Madame Octave is contriving a reason to send Françoise to find out the identity of the 'little girl' with Madame Goupil.

56 *'Very good, very good indeed'*: the stories mentioned here continue the prominence of the *Thousand and One Nights* as an important source of wonder and interest for the youthful protagonist.

58 *flowered Gothic capital*: the capital or 'chapiteau' is the architectural term for the topmost part of a column.

King Charles VI: Charles VI of France (1368–1422) was known as 'the Beloved', and later as 'the Mad', on account of his mental illness. He found distraction in tarot cards devised for him.

59 *the age of Saint Louis's successors*: Louis IX (1214–70), known as St Louis, son of Louis VIII and Blanche de Castille, was a crusader and king of France from 1226 to 1270. His successors lived and held court in various territories across Europe in the thirteenth and early fourteenth centuries.

the coronation of Esther: as described in the Old Testament, Esther 2:17. Ahasuerus was a Persian king said to have married the Jewish Esther for her beauty. Racine takes the subject of his play *Esther* (1689) from this story.

lady of Guermantes: the first mention of the fictional aristocratic family whose ancestral lands are said to lie adjacent to Combray. The family's history, entwined with that of France itself, is a key narrative thread of Proust's novel.

Saint Éloi . . . Dagobert, the tomb . . . made of porphyry and enamelled copper: St Éloi or St Eligius (588–660) is the patron saint of goldsmiths and was chief counsellor to Dagobert I (603–39), one of the last Merovingian kings. Louis 'the Germanic' (*c*.804–76) was Charlemagne's grandson. Louis had three sons who are buried at different sites in Germany: their interment at Combray is Proust's invention.

60 *the tomb of Sigebert's little daughter*: Sigebert (535–75) was another Merovingian king. The accumulation of these historical references woven

into Proust's narrative seeks to provide Combray's fictional church with a powerful and evocative historical underpinning.

'by a crystal lamp . . . had given way beneath it': this episode is recounted in *Récits des temps mérovingiens* ('Tales of Merovingian Times') by Augustin Thierry (1795–1856), a writer whose works Proust knew well. The tales, originally published serially, first appeared in volume form in 1840.

Chartres or Rheims: two of France's most ancient and celebrated Gothic cathedrals. The cathedral at Chartres, about 80 kilometres south-west of Paris, was built between 1194 and 1230; the cathedral at Rheims between 1211 and 1275. Both stand on the site of ancient churches dating back to the Merovingian period.

64 *Piranesi*: Giovanni Battista Piranesi (1720–78) was an artist and architect known for his etchings, the *Vedute* or views of Rome.

65 *Lavallière cravats*: a type of cravat similar to a bow-tie (referred to in the twentieth century as a 'pussy bow'), associated with Louise, Duchesse de La Vallière (1644–1710), mistress of Louis XIV.

the sin for which there is no forgiveness: in various passages in the New Testament blasphemy against the Holy Spirit (not snobbery) is referred to as an unforgivable sin.

66 *Gilbert the Bad*: a fictional character, distantly related to the Guermantes family.

67 *an impatiens flower*: also known as busy Lizzies, impatiens are bright-flowering perennials.

68 *quatrefoils*: decorative elements, literally meaning 'four leaves', commonly employed in Gothic architecture.

70 *Second Empire*: the reign of Emperor Napoleon III (1852–70).

71 *Morris column*: still visible in French cities today, Morris columns are cylindrical structures topped with an ornamental dome, used to display advertising posters and named after the printer who held the original concession in the 1860s.

mysterious satin of Le Domino Noir: the narrator here refers to two 'strange works' staged at the Comédie-Française, the most revered of highbrow theatre venues in Paris: *Le Testament de César Girodot* by Belot and Villetard (first performed at the Comédie-Française in 1873); and Jules Lacroix's translation of Sophocles' *Œdipe-Roi* (first performed at the Comédie-Française in 1858). The works he is more used to are popular comic operas, with music by Daniel Auber (1782–1871), libretti by Eugène Scribe (1791–1861): *Les Diamants de la Couronne* was first performed in 1841 and *Le Domino Noir* in 1837.

rice pudding à l'Impératrice: a rich, elaborate dessert made from rice pudding set in a mould, then decorated with alcohol-macerated candied fruits. It is named after Eugénie de Montijo, wife of Napoleon III during the Second Empire.

71 *my first question was always whether he'd been to the theatre . . . an invigorating sense of flexibility*: the five actors mentioned here, Edmond Got (1822–1901), Louis-Arsène Delaunay (1826–1903), Alexandre-Frédéric Febvre (1835–1916), Joseph Thiron (1830–91), and Benoît-Constant Coquelin (1841–1909) were mainstays of the Comédie-Française in the latter part of the nineteenth century. Coquelin was the best known, particularly for his roles in works by Molière.

72 *Maubant*: see note to p. 26.

brougham: a light, four-wheeled, horse-drawn carriage named after the statesman Lord Brougham (1778–1868) who first had such a carriage built in the 1830s.

the most illustrious . . . I was interested in them all: here the narrator lists the best-known actresses of the nineteenth century: Sarah Bernhardt (1844–1923, known as 'la divine Sarah') was the greatest star of all, acting at the Comédie-Française until 1880 before establishing her own theatre, whilst Madame Bartet (the stage name of Julia Regnault, 1854–1941), Madeleine Brohan (1833–1900), and Jeanne Samary (1857–1890) all acted at the Comédie-Française in the 1870s and 1880s. La Berma, also named here, is Proust's fictional creation: some of her accomplishments (such as her triumph in Racine's *Phèdre*) map closely on to those of Bernhardt.

75 *gentleman . . . a cup of tea . . . a "blue" in the morning*: postcards, printed on grey-blue stock, that were sent around a network of underground pipes, in small cylinders propelled by compressed air. London had such a system in 1853, Berlin in 1865, and Paris in 1866. Odette's speech here reveals her mania for English, highly fashionable at the time: 'gentleman' and 'cup of tea' are in English in Proust's text.

Vaulabelle: the narrator's uncle here offers somewhat contrasting examples of what he considers as the figure of 'the writer'. Victor Hugo (1802–85), poet, playwright, and novelist, author of *The Hunchback of Notre-Dame* (1831) and *Les Misérables* (1862), is one of the nineteenth century's most prolific and celebrated literary figures. Achille Tenaille de Vaulabelle (1799–1879) was a journalist, historian, and politician and author of several multi-volume historical studies.

77 *Giotto's allegorical figures . . . photographs*: in the Arena (or Scrovegni) Chapel in Padua, Giotto di Bondone (*c.*1266–1337) painted frescoes of the story of the Virgin and of Christ, below which he created a series of fourteen allegorical figures representing the seven Vices and seven Virtues, including Envy (*invidias*) and Charity (*caritas*). They are reproduced and discussed variously by Ruskin in works familiar to Proust, including *The Stones of Venice* (1851–3) and *Fors Clavigera* (1871).

79 *physiognomic*: physiognomy is the practice of assessing an individual's qualities or character via their outward appearance, especially the face. Aristotle (384–322 BC) wrote a short treatise on the subject.

84 *cuirassiers*: cavalry wearing a 'cuirass', a piece of armour that protects the torso and back.

I saw them in '70: the Franco-Prussian War of 1870–1, also known as the War of 1870, ended in the defeat of the French army at Sedan.

85 *Bergotte*: like the actress La Berma, mentioned above, the writer Bergotte is a fictional creation.

86 *La Nuit d'Octobre . . . Master de Musset*: Alphonse de Musset (see note to p. 40) was a writer of plays, poetry, and fiction: *La Nuit d'Octobre* (1837) is a collection of lyric poetry prompted by the break-up of Musset's relationship with George Sand (see note to p. 40).

"La blanche Oloossone et la blanche Camyre" . . . "La fille de Minos et de Pasiphaé": the first line quoted here comes from another of Musset's verse collections, *La Nuit de mai* (1835); the second from Racine's *Phèdre* (1677). They are examples of the French alexandrine (twelve-syllable) line and, given the prominence of two potentially obscure and exotic nouns in each (Oloosson was a town in ancient Thessaly, Camire one of the tribes of Rhodes; Minos and Pasiphaë are the parents of Phaedra), they demonstrate how in poetry Bloch privileges sound and rhythm over sense.

Leconte: Charles-Marie Leconte, known as Leconte de Lisle (1818–94), revered by Bloch, was the leading poet of the 'Parnassian School', who sought formal beauty and impersonality in poetry rather than Romantic, lyric effusion, instruction, or any moral message.

the Delphic Oracle: in ancient Greece the High Priestess at the Temple of Apollo at Delphi, known as the Oracle, was the highest religious authority and her ('oracular') pronouncements were taken to be prophecies.

the ambrosial joys of Olympus: though he has not yet read Bergotte's work, Bloch, with characteristic bombast, suggests it will be comparable to the food and drink of the gods ('the ambrosial joys of Olympus'), on the grounds that it comes recommended by Leconte de Lisle, referred to here in circumlocutory terms as the author of 'Bhagavat' and 'Le Lévrier de Magnus', which are two of his celebrated poems.

he seldom failed to hum . . . the words: 'O God of our fathers' is the opening aria from the popular opera *La Juive* (*The Jewess*, 1835) by Fromental Halévy (1799–1862) with a libretto by Eugène Scribe. 'Israel, break thy chain' is a line sung by Samson and reprised by the Hebrew chorus in the opera *Samson et Dalila* (1877), by Camille Saint-Saëns (1835–1921), with a libretto by Ferdinand Lemaire (1832–79). While shocking to modern sensibilities, the casual anti-Semitism of the grandfather (a long-time close friend of the Jewish Swann family) represents a relatively common-place attitude in *fin-de-siècle* France.

87 *Archers, faites bonne garde! / Veillez sans trêve et sans bruit*: 'Archers, be on your guard! | Watch without rest, without sound.' The source of these lines is unknown.

De ce timide Israélite / Quoi, vous guidez ici les pas!: 'What! You guide this way | the steps of this timid Israelite?' The source of these lines is unknown.

87 *Champs paternels, Hébron, douce vallée*: 'Paternal fields, Hebron, sweet valley.' This line is taken from an aria sung by the titular character in *Joseph* also performed as *Joseph en Égypte* or *Joseph et ses frères*, an opera by Étienne-Nicolas Méhul (1763–1817), with a libretto by Alexandre-Vincent Pineux-Duval (1767–1842) and first staged in 1807 and reprised, with revisions, in the 1860s and 1880s.

Oui je suis de la race élue: 'Yes I am of the chosen race.' The source of this line is unknown.

88 *the Malay kris*: or 'keris' in Indonesian; a type of dagger, used for defence as well as ritual and ceremonial purposes, often with a wavy rather than a straight blade.

89 *'vanities of life' . . . 'moving effigies . . . our cathedrals'*: the material 'quoted' from Bergotte here has been variously identified, by scholars and Proust's French editors, as an amalgam of echoes and borrowings from Anatole France and Leconte de Lisle.

90 *Athalie or Phèdre*: *Phèdre* is Racine's best-known play. *Athalie* (1691) was his last tragedy, also considered a masterpiece.

92 *more dolce perhaps, more lento than he'd intended*: in musical terminology, *dolce* indicates that the music is to be performed sweetly or gently; *lento* indicates that the music is to be performed slowly.

Bellini: Gentile Bellini (1429–1507) was a Venetian painter who was commissioned to paint a portrait of the Ottoman sultan Mehmed II (1430–81). The painting, completed in 1480, is in the collection of the National Gallery in London. Proust encountered it in the Venice volume (1902) of the 'Villes d'art célèbres' (Famous Cities of Art) series published by Laurens.

Le Cid: tragicomedy (1636) by Pierre Corneille.

93 *the Queens of Chartres*: a reference to the statuary on the western portal of Chartres Cathedral, where figures represent Old Testament kings and queens, considered the royal lineage of Christ and precursors of the kings and queens of France.

96 *the Benediction's over!*: the Benediction (of the Blessed Sacrament) is an afternoon service consisting of hymns sung before the sacrament, which is presented before the congregation in a monstrance on the altar.

97 *A week before the Rogations!*: in the Christian calendar, the Rogation days are days of fasting and prayer on the Monday to Wednesday immediately preceding Ascension Thursday, typically asking (rogation derives from Latin *rogare*, to ask) for a good harvest and protection from turmoil.

98 *in Sens*: the cathedral in Sens, Burgundy, has a renowned collection of late fifteenth-century tapestries, one of which depicts Esther's coronation.

the old Comtes de Brabant: the priest's speech here underscores the ancient origins of the fictional Guermantes family (said to be related to the historically attested counts of Brabant).

99 *Saint Ylie*: Proust's father's family home was in Illiers, about 25 kilometres south-west of Chartres. In 1971, on the centenary of Proust's birth, the town's name was officially changed to Illiers-Combray in honour of Proust's fictional creation.

Charles the Stammerer . . . Pépin the Mad: these two names are fictional, but echo the names of real French kings, such as Louis II, known as Louis le Bègue ('the Stammerer', 846–79) and Charles VI, known as Charles 'the Mad' (see note to p. 58).

Théodebert: there were two sixth-century kings of this name. In providing these background details the priest is presented as the chronicler of Combray's past, just as Léonie, from her window, is the chronicler of its present.

William the Conqueror: William I (1027–87), Duke of Normandy, became king of England and known as 'the Conqueror' upon his defeat of King Harold II at the Battle of Hastings in 1066.

100 *the famous cathedral in Milan*: the Duomo in Milan is one of the world's largest cathedrals. Construction began in 1386 and final elements were still being completed in the first half of the twentieth century. There are in fact over 900 steps in the spiral stone staircase that leads to the top of the dome.

102 *like those in Ecclesiastes*: one of the so-called 'Wisdom' books of the Old Testament.

Le Bonheur des méchants comme un torrent s'écoule: 'The happiness of the wicked flows like a torrent', from Racine, *Athalie*, Act II, scene vii.

105 *'barbarian' (our name . . . Saturdays)*: a possible echo of Michel de Montaigne (1533–92), who, in his *Essais* (see 'Des cannibales', 'Of Cannibals'), makes the much-repeated observation that we describe as 'barbarian' whatever is unfamiliar to us or different from our own customs.

'Month of Mary': the Catholic tradition of dedicating the month of May to the celebration of the Virgin Mary.

108 *the linden trees*: the flowers of the linden or lime tree (*tilleul* in French) are used to make an infusion (also known as *tilleul* in French, lime-blossom tea), which is the drink into which the protagonist dips his madeleine at the close of 'Combray I'.

110 *'theatre in bed'*: likely allusion to Alfred de Musset's notion of *Un spectacle dans un fauteuil* (*A Spectacle in an Armchair*), which played with the idea of theatrical writing conceived to be *read* rather than performed. Musset published three volumes of writings using this title, between 1832 and 1834.

111 *a calash*: an open carriage with a folding hood to cover the passengers' heads.

the Sun King: the name adopted by Louis XIV to reflect how the kingdom of France revolved around him, as the planets revolve around the sun.

112 *the 'machinery' of life at Versailles*: Saint-Simon uses this phrase ('la mécanique de la vie') in a number of places in his multi-volume *Mémoires*.

113 *Les bois sont déjà noirs, le ciel est encor bleu*: Paul Desjardins (1859–1940) was a writer and thinker who established the 'Union for Moral Action' to encourage and promote public debate and discussion of matters political and philosophical. The line here 'The woods are already dark, the sky is still blue' is taken from his pamphlet on the French poet and statesman Alphonse de Lamartine (1790–1869), entitled *Celui qu'on oublie* ('The One We Forget', 1883).

the giants in fairy tales who hire themselves out as cooks: giants (namely Pantagruel and Gargantua) and the themes of cooking and eating are central to the writings of François Rabelais (b. 1483 or 1494, d. 1553), but if Proust has a specific tale in mind here, we have been unable to identify it.

114 *ciborium*: the receptacle for the consecrated host. Since the narrator here is referring to a liquid, he ought to have used the term 'chalice', which is the goblet-like receptacle for the blood of Christ. A 'chasuble', mentioned in the same sentence, is the outer vestment worn by clergy when celebrating Mass, often embroidered with golden thread.

116 *Qui du cul d'un chien s'amourose, / Il lui paraît une rose*: 'Whoever falls in love with a dog's behind, | will believe it to be a rose.' Françoise's somewhat crude, homespun wisdom (and her pronouncements throughout the text) add to the rich sociolinguistic fabric of Proust's novel.

Fabre: Jean-Henri Fabre (1823–1915) was a prolific writer and entomologist who popularized and rendered widely accessible the study of insects.

118 *the Saint-Honoré cake*: a celebration cake formed of a sweet pastry base, topped with a round of choux pastry on to which are placed cream-filled profiteroles (individual choux pastry balls) dipped in caramel.

the stonecrop . . . in Balzac's flora: two novels by Honoré de Balzac (1799–1850), *Le Lys dans la vallée* (*The Lily of the Valley*, 1835) and *Illusions perdues* (*Lost Illusions*, 1837–43), contain scenes involving symbolic bouquets including sedum or 'stonecrop'.

worthy of Solomon himself: see Matthew 6:28–9, 'Consider the lilies of the field, how they grow: they neither toil nor spin; and yet I say to you that even Solomon in all his glory was not arrayed like one of these.'

Jerusalem rose: *sic*. Proust first drafted 'Jericho rose' but changed this to 'Jerusalem' on the typescript of the novel. Jericho roses are desert plants (and therefore unlikely to be found in Combray); the 'Jerusalem rose', however, seems to be Proust's invention (perhaps in keeping with the Easter theme of these pages).

119 *shadow and silence*: the words here are very close to Balzac's epigraph to his novel *Le Médecin de campagne* (*The Country Doctor*, 1833), which reads 'Aux cœurs blessés l'ombre et le silence' (Shadow and silence to those who have wounded hearts).

120 *I'm a Jacobin in the way I see the world*: the Jacobins were an influential, and violent, left-wing group active between 1789 and 1794 during the French

Revolution, in the ascendant, in particular, during the 'Reign of Terror' of 1793–4.

121 *like a Saint Sebastian of snobbery*: Sebastian (256–88) was an early Christian saint and martyr: persecuted for his faith, he was tied to a post and shot through with arrows.

122 *Andromedas*: in Greek mythology, Andromeda was the daughter of King Cepheus and his wife Cassiopeia: they chained Andromeda to a rock as a sacrificial offering to a sea monster, Cetus, but she was saved by Perseus, who then married her.

123 *Odyssey*: the land of the Cimmerians features in Book 11 of Homer's *Odyssey* (*c.*eighth century BC), characterized as a place deprived of sunlight. Anatole France, in *Pierre Nozière* (see note to p. 44), compares Brittany to the 'land of the Cimmerians'.

124 *with Machiavellian subtlety*: Niccolò Machiavelli (1469–1527) was an Italian diplomat and philosopher who wrote, most famously, an early work of political philosophy entitled *The Prince* (published 1532), which advocates that 'the end justifies the means'. His name has come to be associated with manipulation, cynicism, unscrupulousness, and deceit.

   the fabrication of false palimpsests: most likely an allusion to the prolific forger Denis Vrain-Lucas (1818–82), who created and sold falsified manuscripts and documents (a palimpsest is a document that has been written, erased, and then rewritten, retaining evidence of the earlier text).

127 *young houris*: in the Islamic faith, houris are beautiful, eternally youthful, virginal women, held to be the companions of the faithful during the afterlife. Proust's reference to the 'Nymphs of Spring' here is seasonally appropriate and recalls at once the figures of Greek myth who were personifications of aspects of nature; the *Rite of Spring*, a ballet by Igor Stravinsky (1882–1971) that premiered in 1913; as well as the *Prélude à l'après-midi d'un faune* (1894) by Claude Debussy (1862–1918).

   Persian miniatures: small, highly detailed paintings on paper using bright pigments developed as an art form in ancient Persia from the thirteenth century, peaking in popularity and reach in the fifteenth and sixteenth centuries.

129 *Maelstrom*: a violent and dangerous whirlpool.

   the rood screen or the mullions of the window: in church architecture the rood screen is an ornate partition between the chancel (the area around the altar) and the nave (the main body of the church); mullions are the vertical beams of a window.

131 *rococo in style*: highly ornate decorative style in architecture and fine art of the early eighteenth century.

137 *Saintine*: Joseph Xavier Boniface (1798–1865), known as Saintine, was a French novelist and dramatist, known for sentimental, romantic narratives.

   Gleyre: Charles Gleyre (1806–74) was a Swiss-born artist known for Romantic landscapes and mythological studies.

141 *The sculptor . . . less 'righteous'*: as well as depicting religious and historical
figures the sculptor makes allusions to the ancient philosopher Aristotle
(384–322 BC) and the classical poet Virgil (*c*.70–19 BC).

142 *monstrance*: a monstrance or 'ostensorium' is the vessel in which the consecrated host is carried and displayed, often of ornate design in the form
of a flaming sun.

143 *Chanson de Roland*: in the great medieval epic, the *Song of Roland*
(composed 1040–1115), mourning features prominently in raw emotional
terms: the protagonist laments the loss of his army as well as that of his
friend Olivier, and in turn Charlemagne, Roland's uncle, later laments
Roland's death.

144 *scenes*: in the French, Françoise here mistakenly says 'parenthèse' (paren-
thesis) when she means 'parenté' (kinship, relation)—akin to using
'geology' for 'genealogy'. Her errors and idiosyncrasies of expression are
a source of fascination for the narrator throughout the novel.

151 *sophistries*: sophistry is the use of false arguments with the intention to
deceive.

152 *boulevard theatre*: those located on the *grands boulevards* and associated
with popular comedy and melodrama, as opposed to highbrow offerings of
the Comédie-Française or the Opéra.

154 *Viollet-le-Duc*: Eugène-Emmanuel Viollet-le-Duc (1814–79) was an architect and writer, best known for his restoration projects, which included
Notre-Dame de Paris and the medieval walls of Carcassonne. His critics
view his restorations as frequently insensitive to, even destructive of, the
original features of the buildings in question.

155 *the portico of Saint Mark's*: da Vinci's 'masterpiece' is his *Last Supper* (see
note to p. 41). Gentile Bellini's *Procession in Saint Mark's Square* (1496) is
remarkable as visual evidence of how the façade of St Mark's basilica
looked in the fifteenth century.

   de Montmorency: once more Proust combines real and fictional figures.
Louise d'Orléans (1627–93), Duchesse de Montpensier, and Marie-Félice
Orsini (1600–66), Duchesse de Montmorency through her marriage to
Duc Henri II, were seventeenth-century noblewomen, placed here in the
company of the Duchesse de Guermantes, a distant ancestor of the
Guermantes with whom Proust's protagonist is so fascinated.

157 *neurasthenics*: neurasthenia was the name given to a condition diagnosed
frequently among the upper classes in the late nineteenth and early twentieth century in the US and in Europe, characterized by weakness, nervous
tension, lethargy and fatigue, dyspepsia, and neuralgia often experienced
in combination. Proust's father co-authored a book on the subject,
L'Hygiène du neurasthénique (*Treatment for Neurasthenia*) in 1897. Proust
himself suffered from many if not all of these symptoms, as well as from
severe asthma, with which neurasthenia was often associated.

Virgil . . . to catch up: the narrator alludes here to canto 29 of Dante's *Inferno*, where Virgil urges Dante to continue their journey, rather than be waylaid by the sights and sounds of the damned.

158 *the Japanese style*: the narrator here interweaves a number of elements associated with Claude Monet. His widely celebrated water lily paintings were made in the Japanese water garden he created at his home in Giverny.

fête galante: this term was created by the French Académie royale de peinture et de sculpture in 1717 to describe the paintings of Watteau (see note to p. 224), which depict figures in fancy dress or masquerade, enjoying themselves in idyllic pastoral or parkland settings.

159 *département*: created in 1790 as an administrative division of France, the *département* serves a local function below that of the region.

the Underworld: different authors and different traditions have placed 'Hellmouths' in various locations in the real world. In Virgil's *Aeneid*, Aeneas enters via a cave on the shores of Lake Avernus, near Naples; Orpheus goes in search of Eurydice (see note to p. 216) via a cave at Cape Tenaron in the southern Peloponnese.

161 *baccalauréat*: the school-leaving certificate at the end of secondary education in France.

162 *fancy dress ball given by Princesse de Léon*: on 29 May 1891 Herminie de la Brousse de Verteillac (1853–1926), Princesse de Léon, later Duchesse de Rohan, held an extravagant costume ball that has gone down in history, in part thanks to photographs that have survived by Paul Nadar (1856–1939).

166 *Lohengrin*: a Romantic opera in three acts by Richard Wagner, first performed in 1850.

Carpaccio: Vittore Carpaccio (*c*.1465–1525/6) was a Venetian painter, especially of richly detailed series of paintings such as his St Ursula cycle for the Scuola di Sant'Orsola in Venice.

'delicious': Proust was an avid reader and admirer of the great nineteenth-century poet Charles Baudelaire (1821–67), who often uses synaesthesia (the transposition of sensory experiences) in his poetry. In 'L'Imprévu' ('The Unforeseen'), from *Les Épaves* (*Scraps*, 1866), we encounter the line 'Le son de la trompette est si délicieux' (The sound of the trumpet is so delicious).

171 *Delos*: in Greek myth, Delos (the smallest of the Cyclades island grouping in the Aegean Sea) was a floating island, tethered to the sea-floor by Zeus so that Leto could safely give birth to Apollo and Artemis there.

SWANN IN LOVE

177 *play Wagner as well as that . . . Potain*: the music of the German composer Richard Wagner became particularly popular in France in the late 1870s. Francis Planté (1839–1934) was a French pianist and composer whose concerts drew significant audiences in the 1870s; Anton Grigorievitch

Rubinstein (1825–94) was one of the finest pianists of the nineteenth century and founded the conservatories of St Petersburg and Moscow. Pierre-Charles-Édouard Potain (1825–1901) was a celebrated cardiologist elected to the Académie nationale de médicine (see note to p. 201) in 1882 and to the Institut de France in 1893. That Madame Verdurin should hold that her 'young pianist' and Doctor Cottard are 'streets ahead' of these luminary figures in their respective fields is an early indication of the somewhat blinkered overconfidence of the hostess in her coterie.

177 *Madame de Crécy*: Odette, as the narrator learns much later, in *The Captive*, goes at this time by the name of Madame de Crécy as the result of an earlier marriage to Pierre de Verjus, Comte de Crécy, a man whose wealth, according to the narrator's source, Odette drained to the last centime before separating from him.

cocotte: an antiquated colloquial term meaning 'tart' or woman of loose morals.

178 *'Ride of the Valkyries' . . . Prelude to Tristan*: the 'Ride of the Valkyries' is one of Wagner's best-known compositions: it opens the third act of *Die Walküre* (*The Valkyrie*), the second opera in Wagner's four-part epic cycle *Der Ring des Nibelungen* (*The Ring of the Nibelung*, first performed as a cycle in 1876). *Tristan* refers to Wagner's earlier, hugely influential opera, *Tristan and Isolde*, first performed in 1865.

179 *fishing for compliments*: Odette is in the habit of dropping English words and phrases into conversation, an affectation which she believes brings an allure of culture and mystique.

180 *naturalization papers*: the mention here of official documents confirming Swann's status as a naturalized French citizen is a reminder of his complex identity as Jewish, French, and as an individual who, unusually, moves back and forth between quite distinct social milieux.

182 *when I began to take an interest in his character*: this is the first of a small number of intrusions of the first-person pronoun of the narrator of *In Search of Lost Time* into 'Swann in Love', which is otherwise focalized exclusively on Charles Swann. Since its events predate the birth of the narrator of Proust's longer novel, 'Swann in Love' is effectively a flashback, which fills in the back story of Charles Swann, who is an influential figure for Proust's narrator.

183 *Quel est donc ce mystère? / Je n'y puis rien comprendre*: 'What then is this mystery? | I can't make head nor tail of it.' The grandfather here is quoting lines from the end of the first act of *La Dame blanche* (1825), a comic opera by François-Adrien Boieldieu (1775–1834), with a libretto by Eugène Scribe based on scenes from a variety of works by Sir Walter Scott (1771–1832).

Vision fugitive . . .: 'Fugitive vision'. Allusion to an aria sung by Herod in the opera *Hérodiade* (1881) by Jules Massenet (1842–1912).

Dans ces affaires / Le mieux est de ne rien voir: 'In these matters | it is best not to see anything'. A quotation from the closing lines of André Grétry's comic opera *Amphitryon* (1786), which itself echoes Molière's comedy of the same title. By humming snatches of music from works that deal with complex amorous relations involving mystery, betrayal, and deception, the narrator's grandfather is gently mocking Swann's way of conducting his own affairs.

184 *smart*: this word appears (twice) in English in this sentence in Proust's text (see note to p. 179).

186 *Vermeer of Delft*: Johannes (or Jan) Vermeer (1632–75) is recognized as one of the finest painters of the Dutch Golden Age. Little known in his life-time and with only thirty-four works attributed to his name, Vermeer was rediscovered by scholars in the nineteenth century. Proust saw the *View of Delft* (1660–1) during a trip to Holland in 1902 and again towards the end of his life at an exhibition in Paris in 1921. Later, in *The Captive*, in a characteristic moment of one art form illuminating another, the fictional writer Bergotte experiences a blissful aesthetic revelation of how he should have written his novels whilst contemplating the *View of Delft*, shortly before expiring in front of the bewitching canvas.

Areopagus: a large outcrop of rock north-west of the Acropolis in Athens, Greece which, prior to the fifth century BC, served as the site of the council of elders of the city. It later became the site of criminal trials. Odette's reference to a frog here is unclear: a number of the *Fables* (1668–94) of Jean de La Fontaine (1621–95) include frogs, such as 'Les Grenouilles qui demandent un roi' ('The Frogs Who Desired a King'), which is a rewriting of one of Aesop's Fables, but none features the Areopagus.

189 *"the Golden Voice"*: 'la voix d'or' is the name reportedly given to the actress by Victor Hugo after her rousing performance in the role of the Queen in his play *Ruy Blas* in 1872.

190 *smart*: again, this word appears in English in Proust's text (see note to p. 179).

194 *Reichstag*: from its opening in 1894 until 1933 the Reichstag was the site of the lower house of the German parliament.

the Ninth . . . the Meistersingers: just as she holds her pianist to be better than the most lauded practitioners of the time, as we learn on the opening page of 'Swann in Love', here, by mentioning the finale of Beethoven's Ninth Symphony (1824, the last he completed in his lifetime) and the overture (correctly the Prelude) to Wagner's *Die Meistersinger von Nürnburg* (*The Mastersingers of Nuremburg*, first performed 1868), Madame Verdurin is placing the sonata she has 'discovered' in the company of the very best-known parts of some of the most influential and celebrated musical compositions of her century.

195 *Beauvais*: the name of the town in Picardy, in northern France, is used attributively to describe tapestries, and furniture (often upholstered with

tapestry), manufactured there since the seventeenth century. The director of the Beauvais tapestry works produced a series of designs drawing on La Fontaine's *Fables* in the 1730s, though none of these includes Madame Verdurin's 'Bear and the Grapes'. She (or Proust) may be misremembering La Fontaine's 'L'Ours et l'Amateur des jardins' ('The Bear and the Gardener') or 'Le Renard et les Raisins' ('The Fox and the Grapes').

196 *sine materia*: (Lat.) without substance. The phrase encapsulates the immaterial, evanescent nature of the pleasure imparted by the experience of listening to a piece of music.

200 *di primo cartello*: Italian term relating to performers of the very highest quality, who take 'top billing'.

201 *Academy*: the Académie nationale de médécine was established in 1820. Proust's father was elected to the academy in 1879 and served as its secretary from 1883 to 1888.

202 *Gambetta's funeral*: the state funeral of Léon Gambetta (1838–82), lawyer and political leader, prime minister of France 1881–2, took place on 6 January 1883.

Les Danicheff: a play first performed in 1876, this was a collaboration between Pierre de Corvin-Koukowsky and Alexandre Dumas *fils*.

where Monsieur Grévy lives: Jules Grévy (1807–91), as president of France from 1879 to 1887, would have lived at the official residence, the Élysée Palace.

204 *the little phrase by Vinteuil that had become . . . the national anthem of their love*: a great deal has been written about which composers or pieces of music Proust had in mind in creating Vinteuil's fictional sonata. Models are thought to include Franck, Fauré, and Saint-Saëns.

Pieter de Hooch: (1629–84), a contemporary of Vermeer and a major figure in seventeenth-century Dutch painting.

207 *niello*: a black metallic alloy, formed of sulphur and either copper, silver, or lead, and used as an inlay for engraving or decorative design on other metals.

Notre-Dame de Laghet: Laghet is a place of Christian pilgrimage in the Alpes-Maritimes, near Nice where Odette used to live; the church and monastery were founded in the seventeenth century.

208 *Zipporah, Jethro's daughter*: Zipporah, daughter of Jethro and wife of Moses, appears in a fresco series by Botticelli in the Sistine Chapel, depicting *Scenes from the Life of Moses*.

209 *Antonio Rizzo*: the Correr Museum in Venice holds a bronze bust of Andrea Loredan (who was not in fact a doge) by the Paduan sculptor Andrea Briosco (1470–1532), who was known as 'il Riccio' or 'il Rizzo'.

Ghirlandaio: (1449–94), a Florentine Renaissance painter of the same generation as Botticelli. Michelangelo (1475–1564) was for a time an apprentice in Ghirlandaio's workshop.

Tintoretto: (1518–94), a Venetian Renaissance painter whose self-portrait, with prominent nose, heavily bearded face, and 'piercing gaze' hung in the Louvre in Proust's time.

211 *La Maison Dorée*: an elegant restaurant established in 1840 (which Proust sometimes renders La Maison d'Or). This and the other establishments mentioned subsequently (Prévost's, Tortoni's, and the Café Anglais) were all popular, respectable Parisian establishments.

the Paris–Murcia fête: a fundraising event held in Paris on 18 December 1879 following serious flooding in the province of Murcia in south-east Spain in October that year.

216 *as if, among the shades of the dead, . . . he were searching for Eurydice*: in Greek mythology, Eurydice, wife of Orpheus, was killed by a snakebite on her wedding day. Orpheus, via the power of his singing, persuaded the gods to allow him to bring Eurydice back from Hades, but they imposed the condition that he should not take a backward glance towards her as they climbed up from the Underworld. Unable to resist the compulsion to turn back towards his beloved, Orpheus lost Eurydice a second time, this time for ever.

219 *victoria*: a four-wheeled, horse-drawn open carriage.

221 *Valse des Roses . . . Tagliafico*: 'Les Roses' ('The Roses'), a waltz for voice and piano, is the best-known composition of Olivier Métra (1830–89), who was notably the conductor at the Folies-Bergères in the 1870s. The 'Pauvre fou' (actually titled 'Pauvres fous', 'The Poor Lunatics'), is a song written by the French-Italian opera singer Joseph Dieudonné Tagliafico (1821–1900), who performed at the Théâtre des Italiens in Paris from the 1840s. That these pieces of music should be Odette's 'favourites' gives a snapshot of what, to Swann and the elevated circles in which he habitually moves, are her undiscerning aesthetic tastes.

224 *Watteau*: Jean-Antoine Watteau (1684–1721) was a major French painter of the eighteenth century (see also note to p. 158); in an essay on the painter Proust described his work as 'the apotheosis of love and pleasure'.

225 *Rembrandt*: considered as one of the most accomplished artists of all time, Rembrandt van Rijn (1606–69) was a Dutch painter, printmaker, and draughtsman, famous for his self-portraits, in some of which he wears a broad soft hat, often turned up at one side.

in the style of the Vicomte de Borelli, but even more touching: Vicomte Raymond de Borrelli (1827–1906)—Proust misspells his name—was a society poet and, like the waltz 'Les Roses', is here representative of Odette's unrefined taste.

227 *Hippodrome*: a horse-racing arena in the Bois de Vincennes in Paris, established in 1863 and rebuilt in 1879 after significant damage during the Franco-Prussian War.

229 *La Reine Topaze*: comic opera by Victor Massé (1822–84), first performed in 1856.

230 *gentleman*: this word is in English in Proust's text.

Serge Panine: novel published in 1881 by George Ohnet (1848–1918), which was adapted for the stage the following year: it was enjoyed by the public but not by critics.

Olivier Métra: conductor, composer of the waltz 'Les Roses' (see note to p. 221).

232 *École du Louvre*: establishment founded in 1881 for the training of museum conservators.

235 *Blanche de Castille*: (1188–1252), daughter of Alphonso VIII of Castile and Eleanor of England. She was queen of France as wife of Louis VIII and regent during the reign of their son, Louis IX (1214–70), who was canonized St Louis in 1297.

Suger and other Saint Bernards: the *Chronicle of Saint-Denis* (the popular title for the *Grandes Chroniques de France*), a history of the kings of France, was begun by Abbé Suger (1081–1151) in the twelfth century. Brichot is somewhat confused with his 'impeccably reliable source' here, since both Suger and Bernard de Clairvaux (1091–1153, canonized in 1174) died more than thirty years before Blanche de Castille was born.

237 *even better than Rembrandt or Hals*: the painter here compares the contemporary canvases he has seen at the exhibition with long-established masterpieces whose accomplishment resists analysis: *The Night Watch* (1642) by Rembrandt and *The Regentesses of the Old Men's Almshouse, Haarlem* (?1664) by Franz Hals (1580–1666).

238 *the Ninth and the Winged Victory*: to Beethoven's Ninth Symphony, mentioned above as the archetypal musical masterpiece, is added *The Winged Victory of Samothrace*, a sculpture of the Greek goddess Nike, discovered in 1863 on the island of Samothrace and exhibited in the Louvre since 1884.

239 *Francillon*: a recurring topic of conversation in the Verdurin circle is contemporary art, though, as is quite clear, the guests' engagement is frequently superficial. Madame Cottard is keen to show that she is up-to-date here, by mentioning *Francillon* (first performed in 1887) by Alexandre Dumas *fils*, a play she has not yet seen. The play contains a scene where a 'Japanese salad' is prepared: it is a salad of cooked potatoes and mussels, dressed with olive oil, vinegar, a glass of Château d'Yquem, and finely sliced truffles. The name simply reflects the prevailing *japonisme* of the period, the fascination with all things Japanese.

240 *Le Maître de Forges*: (*The Owner of the Iron Works*), sentimental novel of 1882 by Georges Ohnet, whose *Serge Panine* is mentioned here and a little earlier in the text.

241 *Palais de l'Industrie*: (Palace of Industry), built for the World Fair in Paris in 1855. It was where the annual Salons (exhibitions) of painting and sculpture were held until it was demolished in 1897 to make way for the Grand Palais and the Petit Palais, built for the World's Fair of 1900 and still standing today.

the La Trémoïlles and the Laumes: two families are mentioned here: one real and one fictional. La Trémoïlle was one of France's oldest aristocratic families, with a history traceable to the eleventh century. The des Laumes are Proust's invention and similarly formidable in their history: they are a branch of the Guermantes family that lends its name to the third volume of Proust's novel, *Le Côté de Guermantes* (*The Guermantes Way*). The Prince and Princesse des Laumes, already encountered in 'Combray', through inherited title become in turn the Duc and Duchesse de Guermantes.

243 *that gentle anarchist Fénelon*: François de Salignac de la Mothe-Fénelon (1651–1715), theologian and tutor to Louis XIV's grandson, the Duc de Bourgogne (1682–1712). Fénelon is described here playfully as a 'gentle anarchist' since some of his writings, including his book *Les Aventures de Télémaque* (*The Adventures of Telemachus*, 1699), intended for the instruction and education of the young duke, contained criticisms of the reign of Louis XIV.

Those de la Trémouailles: Brichot inadvertently shows his ignorance here by misconstruing the origins of the ancient La Trémoïlle family, as well as corrupting and mispronouncing their name.

244 *Se non è vero*: truncated version of the Italian 'se non è vero è ben trovato' (even if it's not true, it's a good story).

246 *it's not serpent à sonates, it's serpent à sonnettes*: there is a play on words in the French here that alludes to an acquaintance of Proust's. Marquise Diane de Saint-Paul was a gifted pianist with a reputation as an uncompromising gossip, known therefore as the 'serpent à sonates' or 'sonata snake', playing on the term for rattlesnake, 'serpent à sonnettes'.

249 *Gustave Moreau*: Gustave Moreau (1826–98), best known as a Symbolist painter whose canvases lavishly depict mythological and biblical themes and motifs such as *Oedipus and the Sphinx* (1864) or *Salomé* (1876).

252 *Île des Cygnes*: 'Island of the Swans', an island in the larger of the two lakes in the Bois de Boulogne.

261 *the painter of the Primavera*: the reference is once again to Botticelli. The *Primavera* (?1482) is one of his most celebrated works; also known in English as the *Allegory of Spring*, it can be seen in the Uffizi Gallery in Florence.

watch Moses pour water into a trough: another allusion to Botticelli, this time to his *Madonna of the Pomegranate* (?1487), also in the Uffizi, and to the *Scenes from the Life of Moses* frescoes in the Sistine Chapel.

264 *"Moonlight" Sonata*: Beethoven's op. 27 no. 2, the Piano Sonata no. 14 in C sharp minor (composed in 1801) has, since the mid-nineteenth century, been popularly referred to as the 'Moonlight' Sonata, after a critic likened the effect of the sonata's first movement to moonlight on Lake Lucerne.

266 *a play by Labiche*: Eugène Labiche (1815–88), dramatic author of vaudeville and farce, whose plays poked fun at the bourgeoisie.

267 *Plato and Bossuet, and the old system of education in France*: Plato famously
condemns artists on moral grounds in Book 10 of *Republic*, which Bossuet
(1627–1704), a theologian, moralist, and orator, cites in his *Maximes et
réflexions sur la comédie* (1694). French school education underwent major
changes in the 1880s as a result of reforms and innovations implemented
by Jules Ferry (1832–93), then minister of education.

the last circle of Dante: in Dante's *Divine Comedy* (1320), the last (ninth)
circle of Hell is reserved for those sinners guilty of treachery, the misdeed
Swann is railing at here.

Noli me tangere: (Lat.) 'Don't touch me'. Reported in John 20:17 as the
words of Christ, spoken to Mary Magdalene after the Resurrection.

269 *Une nuit de Cléopâtre*: opera (first performed in 1885) by Victor Massé,
whose other works include *La Reine Topaze* (see note to p. 229).

274 *the Carte du Tendre*: 'the Map of Love' in *Clélie*, written between 1654 and
1660 by Madame de Scudéry (1607–1701), incorporated an allegorical
map of the different paths that can be taken to arrive at true love.

275 *grappling with the reality of the external world or the immortality of the soul*:
Swann's state here is likened to that of people who have 'worn themselves
out' with philosophical reflection. Precisely such reflections fill the pages
of Descartes (1596–1650), Pascal (1623–62), and Kant (1724–1804),
thinkers with whose work Proust was familiar; these preoccupations are
also those we encounter as we are plunged into the thoughts of Proust's
restless narrator on the very first page of *In Search of Lost Time*.

initials . . . intertwined everywhere with her own: the church at Brou, in
Bourg-en-Bresse, was built on the order of Marguerite of Austria (1480–1530)
to commemorate her husband, Philibert 'le Beau' (1480–1504), Duc de
Savoie, who was killed in a hunting accident.

276 *'Bal des Incohérents'*: the 'Ball of the Incoherents' was a public event first
held in Paris in 1885. The 'Incoherents' were artists who mocked the official Salon exhibitions and staged very successful exhibitions of their own,
the opening of which was marked by a costumed ball.

277 *my love*: this endearment appears in English in Proust's text.

279 *landau*: a four-wheeled, horse-drawn, convertible carriage.

go to Bayreuth for the season: by the 1880s the annual Bayreuther
Festspiele (Bayreuth Festival), dedicated to performances of Wagner's
works in a specially designed concert-house inaugurated in 1876, was
a fashionable destination for cultural tourists from Europe and further
afield.

280 *the difference between Bach and Clapisson*: Johann Sebastian Bach (1685–1750)
was an immensely influential German Baroque composer; Antonin-Louis
Clapisson (1808–66) was a minor French composer of comic operas.

287 *Lully's shrewd avarice and lavish lifestyle*: the Duc de Saint-Simon wrote
at great length and in remarkable detail about life in Louis XIV's court

at Versailles. One section of his *Mémoires* (which span the period 1691–1723) is dedicated to the dinners held by Madame de Maintenon (1635–1719). Jean-Baptiste Lully (1632–87) was an important composer of the period.

288 *Crapote . . . Jauret . . . Chevet . . . the 'right addresses'*: Crapotte (Proust misspells this) and Jauret were Parisian fruiterers popular with the elegant hostesses of the period; Chevet was a *traiteur* or upmarket grocery/caterer.

291 *the early years of the Septennate*: the French presidential term was historically seven years. The 'septennate' referred to here is most likely that of Edmé Patrice, Comte de Mac-Mahon, which began in 1873, though did not run its full course: Mac-Mahon resigned from office in 1879.

Botticelli's Primavera, his fair Vanna, or his Venus: Primavera, the goddess of spring, appears in the painting of that name (see note to p. 261); the 'fair Vanna' refers to *Giovanna Tornabuoni and the Three Graces* (?1480), which Proust could have seen in the Louvre; and 'his Venus' is a reference to the famous *Birth of Venus* (1484–6).

292 *second part of this story*: a projection forward to the latter part of *Swann's Way*, 'Place Names: The Name', in which Swann and Odette are married.

293 *Mémé old chap*: a familiar, diminutive form of 'Palamède', the Baron de Charlus's given name, used only by those who are close to him.

300 *Balzac's 'tigers'*: in the early to middle years of the nineteenth century, explored in the fictions of Honoré de Balzac, a *tigre* (or 'tiger': the term was used in English), was an elegant gentleman's groom (a young male servant or attendant).

301 *the purely decorative warrior . . . paintings by Mantegna . . . San Zeno . . . Eremitani*: Andrea Mantegna (?1430–1506), Italian painter and engraver who was part of the team of artists who decorated the church of the Eremitani at Padua between 1449 and 1456: here, in the Ovetari Chapel, Proust could have seen *Scenes from the Lives of St James and St Christopher*. In the *Martyrdom of Saint James*, a warrior is depicted deep in thought, leaning on his shield as Proust describes here. Mantegna also painted the altarpiece of San Zeno in Verona, between 1456 and 1459.

one of Albrecht Dürer's Saxons: Albrecht Dürer (1471–1528), German painter and artist, a key figure in the Northern Renaissance, who was influenced by Mantegna and made copies of his engravings.

the Doges' Palace—'The Giants' Staircase': the staircase in the central courtyard of the Doges' Palace in Venice (see note to p. 360) takes its name from the huge statues of Mars and Neptune that flank it.

302 *like one of Goya's sextons*: Proust was familiar with the work of the Spanish painter Francisco de Goya (1746–1828), though it is not clear which work he has in mind when evoking a representation of sextons.

like some priceless statue of a watchman by Benvenuto Cellini: Cellini (1500–71) was a sculptor and goldsmith from Florence. As with the preceding reference to Goya, it is not certain to which work Proust is alluding here.

302 *Aubusson tapestries*: tapestries and carpets have been manufactured at Aubusson in the Creuse department in central France since the fourteenth century.

303 *Jockey Club*: see note to p. 18.

an aria from Orfeo: the reference here is to the opera *Orpheus and Eurydice* (1762) by Gluck (1714–87).

304 *Liszt's Saint Francis Preaching to the Birds*: the Hungarian Franz Liszt (1811–86) composed two pieces of music for solo piano in 1863 described as 'legends': *Saint Francis of Assisi Preaching to the Birds* and *Saint Francis of Paola Walking on the Waves*.

305 *her ultra-Legitimist family would never have forgiven her*: Madame de Gallardon here worries that meeting Princess Mathilde (1820–1904), the niece of Emperor Napoleon I, would horrify her family who, as 'ultra-Legitimists', would want nothing to do with those associated with the usurping of Ancien Régime aristocracy.

307 *Chopin*: Fryderyk Franciszek (or Frédéric François) Chopin (1810–49), born to a French émigré father and a Polish mother, was a composer and pianist of genius, known above all for his preludes, waltzes, and nocturnes.

309 *a clarinet quintet by Mozart*: Mozart in fact wrote only one clarinet quintet: K581, and it is one of his most popular chamber works.

310 *Mérimée . . . plays of Meilhac and Halévy*: the Guermantes' wit is a recurring theme in Proust's novel as a whole and here we are provided with a literary frame of reference for it. Prosper Mérimée (1803–70) was a dramatist and writer of short fiction, notably the novella *Carmen* (1845) which was the basis for Bizet's opera (1875). The libretto for this latter was written by Henri Meilhac (1831–97) and Ludovic Halévy (1834–1908), father of Proust's schoolfriend Daniel Halévy (1872–1962). Meilhac and Halévy's collaborations are characterized by their lively and often satirical nature.

312 *the Belloir agency*: Belloir was a company that rented chairs and sundries for receptions and parties.

313 *the Iénas . . . the name of a victory before it was a bridge*: Napoleon I's forces defeated the Prussian army at the Battle of Jena in October 1806. To commemorate the victory, Napoleon ordered the construction of the bridge (the Pont d'Iéna), which was formally opened in 1814.

314 *famous mosaic table . . . Treaty of . . .*: Proust is most likely referring here to the table variously referred to as the 'Breteuil Table', the 'Teschen Table', and the 'Table of Peace', presented to the Baron de Breteuil (1730–1807) to mark the role he played in negotiating the Teschen Treaty of 1779, which established principles of collective security in Europe that ultimately formed the basis of the Covenant of the League of Nations and the Charter of the United Nations. The table can be seen in the Louvre in Paris, which acquired it via a crowdfunding initiative in January 2015.

Spartacus: Spartacus (*c*.111–71 BC) was a Thracian gladiator who led the slave revolt against the Romans in the Third Servile War.

315 *Vercingetorix*: (?82–46 BC) fearsome warrior king who commanded the combined Gallic tribes against Julius Caesar.

316 *The double abbreviation . . .*: Swann and the Princesse des Laumes are having fun with the sound of the name 'Cambremer', which 'ends just in time' in that it doesn't quite spell *merde* (shit). 'It doesn't begin any better', notes Swann, since the first part of the name is shared with that of a general in Napoleon's army, Pierre Cambronne, who, it is said, cried 'Merde!' when his surrender was demanded at Waterloo. To speak of 'le mot de Cambronne' (Cambronne's word) was a genteel, euphemistic way of saying 'shit'.

317 *that old Bérénice*: 'that awful Rampillon woman' has been 'dropped by her prince', which leads the Princess des Laumes to make an allusion to Racine's play *Bérénice* (1670), whose title character is to be married to Emperor Titus, but is jilted because the Roman public cannot tolerate a foreign queen.

318 *La Pérouse*: Jean-François de Galaup, Comte de la Pérouse (1741–?88) was a naval officer appointed by Louis XVI to lead a round-the-world expedition. He set off in August 1785, reaching Chile, Hawaii, Alaska, California, Macau, Korea, Japan, Russia, and Australia before he and his crew disappeared without trace; their last correspondence dates from February 1788.

324 *as he would that of La Princesse de Clèves or of René*: Swann's points of reference speak volumes about his tortured state of mind. He associates the sonata with 'a conception of love and happiness' as distinctive as that found in two literary classics: *La Princesse de Clèves* (1678), a novel by Madame de La Fayette (1634–93), which tells of the frustrated love of a married woman for another man, and the short novel *René* (1805), by Chateaubriand (1768–1848), whose plot concerns the romantic hero René and his sister Amélie's incestuous love for him.

Tristan: Wagner's *Tristan and Isolde* (first performed in 1865), in a similar vein to the literary allusions indicated in the previous note, tells the story of a forbidden love affair that ends in tragedy.

325 *as inspired, perhaps, as Lavoisier or Ampère*: Proust's comparisons often straddle disciplinary boundaries and bring together that which might conventionally be thought of as quite distinct. Here the creative powers of the artist are compared to two of the eighteenth and nineteenth centuries' greatest scientists: Antoine-Laurent de Lavoisier (1743–94), considered to be the founder of modern chemistry, and André Marie Ampère (1775–1836), a mathematician and physicist who formulated the theory of electromagnetism.

327 *Nicolas Maes . . . Vermeer*: at the sale Proust alludes to (which took place in 1876), the painting mentioned was indeed sold to the Mauritshuis Museum in the Hague and was believed at the time to be the work of

Nicolas Maes (?1634–93); an 1891 catalogue for the Mauritshuis indicates that the painting by that time had been reattributed to Vermeer.

328 *You're never as unhappy as you think*: likely allusion to La Rochefoucauld's maxim 'On n'est jamais si heureux ni si malheureux qu'on s'imagine' (You are never as happy nor as unhappy as you imagine). The Duc de La Rochefoucauld (1613–80) was a moralist and author of the widely read *Maximes* (1665).

329 *Mohammed II, whose portrait by Bellini he liked so much*: in 'Combray II', Swann likens the narrator's friend Bloch to this portrait.

Whitsun: Whitsun, or Pentecost, is celebrated on the seventh Sunday after Easter in the Christian calendar.

334 *Les Filles de Marbre by Théodore Barrière*: first performed in 1853, this successful play (adapted into English as *The Marble Heart*) by Théodore Barrière (1823–77), treats the life of courtesans, who are characterized as heartless and cold.

Dieppe, Cabourg, and Beuzeval: towns on the north coast of France. Between 1907 and 1914, Proust holidayed every year at Cabourg, which lends many traits to the fictional resort town of Balbec in his novel.

340 *Alfred de Vigny's Journal d'un poète . . . one's future happiness depends on the answers*: the lines mentioned here are an accurate quotation from the posthumously published notes of the French Romantic poet, novelist, and dramatist Alfred de Vigny (1797–1863), titled *Journal d'un poète* (*A Poet's Diary*, 1867).

344 *the Desolation of Nineveh*: Proust alludes here (somewhat obliquely) to a biblical story via John Ruskin's *The Bible of Amiens* (1884), which he translated in 1904. In his description of the façade of the cathedral Ruskin points out statues of minor prophets standing above carved allusions to their respective prophecies: the animals left inhabiting the desolated, godforsaken city of Nineveh figure among the prophecies of Zephaniah. The motif of desolation serves to communicate Swann's frame of mind.

346 *the Mirlitons to see the portrait by Machard*: the Mirlitons was an annual art exhibition organized by the Cercle de l'Union artistique (Circle of the Artistic Union). Jules-Louis Machard (1839–1900) was a portrait painter of great renown who first exhibited at the Mirlitons in 1863.

347 *Leloir*: Jean-Baptiste-Auguste Leloir (1809–92) was primarily a painter of historical and religious subjects, though he did produce a number of portraits.

PLACE NAMES: THE NAME

357 *'modern style'*: the English term for *art nouveau*, popular between the 1880s and the First World War (the phrase appears in English in Proust's text).

358 *the illuminated fountains at the Exposition*: illuminated fountains were a feature on the Champ de Mars, installed for the Exposition universelle

(World's Fair) of 1889, which had as its centrepiece the Eiffel Tower, constructed for this purpose.

Finistère: the most westerly region of Britanny, jutting into the Atlantic Ocean.

360 *a dazzling golden background like those in the paintings of Fra Angelico*: born Guido di Petro (*c*.1395–1455), Fra Angelico ('Angelic Friar') was an early Renaissance painter, famous in particular for his frescoes in the San Marco friary in Florence.

the Doges' Palace . . . Santa Maria del Fiore: built in 1340, the Gothic palace that housed the doge (leader of the Republic of Venice), overlooking the lagoon and St Mark's Square. Ruskin dedicates a significant section of his study of Venetian architecture, *The Stones of Venice* (1851–3), to the Doges' Palace. Santa Maria del Fiore is the name of the cathedral in Florence, which is topped by the *duomo* or dome designed by Filippo Brunelleschi (1377–1446).

361 *La Chartreuse de Parme*: *The Charterhouse of Parma* (1839) is a much-celebrated realist novel by Stendhal (born Henri Beyle, 1783–1842), which recounts the life of a fictional nobleman, Fabrice del Dongo.

362 *fabliau*: a medieval genre of usually comic or satirical verse, composed in France in the twelfth and thirteenth centuries. Some of these were reworked by later storytellers in the Italian and English traditions, including Boccaccio and Chaucer.

tower of butter: one of the towers of the cathedral at Rouen (not Coutances, as the narrator has it here) is known as 'la tour de Beurre' (the tower of butter).

of the coach pursued by the fly: the narrator's comment here is an allusion to the phrase 'la mouche du coche', deriving from a La Fontaine fable about a horse-drawn coach that just makes it up an incline in a country road, only for a fly—who had pursued it and bitten its passengers—to take credit for the achievement. The narrator's comments here—lyrical, subjective associations relating to beauty, landscape, and the unchanging elements that make up French rural culture—combine to enrich his imagined journey on the otherwise prosaic 1.22 train.

363 *the Primitives*: the 'Italian primitives', in art historical terms, were the pre-Renaissance painters of the twelfth and thirteenth centuries, the transition towards what we recognize now as 'modern' painting. Proust visited a major exhibition 'Les Primitifs flamands' (The Flemish Primitives) in Bruges in 1902.

364 *medieval domestic architecture*: Proust's narrative here draws liberally once more on John Ruskin, particularly his *Stones of Venice* and *Modern Painters*, where he writes of the Venetian painter Giorgione (*c*.1477–1510).

366 *'majestic and terrible as the sea . . . their blood-red cloaks'*: further approximate quotation from *The Stones of Venice*.

'rocks of amethyst, like a reef in the Indian Ocean': approximate quotation from Ruskin's *Stones of Venice* once more.

367 *Poussin*: Nicolas Poussin (1594–1655) is the best-known painter of the classical French Baroque style. His *Four Seasons* cycle of paintings, which Proust could have seen in the Louvre, all feature clouds above their main subjects.

368 *prisoner's base*: a children's game of two teams, where each side tries to tag and capture members of the other side when they venture out of their designated territory.

370 *Pont de la Concorde*: the bridge spanning the Seine between the Place de la Concorde and the Quai d'Orsay, just a few minutes' walk from the Champs-Élysées.

371 *Field of the Cloth of Gold*: allusion to the location of the famed meeting that took place in 1520 between Henry VIII and François I, in the Pas-de-Calais region of northern France. The name derives from the show of splendour and wealth laid on by the French king, including tents woven in silk and golden thread. This reference is a long-distance connection to the opening page of 'Combray' where it is a question of the rivalry of François I and Charles V, to which the Field of the Cloth of Gold meeting is related (the French king sought to win Henry's support against Charles via his lavish display of wealth).

374 *pain d'épice*: a bread, still widely available, made with rye flour, honey, and spices.

ethnic eczema and the constipation of the Prophets: in Deuteronomy 28:27, the 'cursing, vexation, and rebuke' that God directs at the Jews includes such afflictions as those attributed to Swann here.

376 *'En revenant de la revue'*: a song first performed in 1886 by the café-concert singer Paulus (1845–1908) which then became popular amongst the conservative Boulangistes—supporters of General Boulanger—who wanted to overthrow the government of the time.

377 *the Ambassadeurs*: a café-concert venue that became a restaurant and theatre, the Ambassadeurs was situated in the gardens of the Champs-Élysées on the site where Louis XV received visiting ambassadors.

379 *Philippe VII*: the title by which Orléanists called Philippe d'Orléans, Comte de Paris, since it would have been his regnal name. He is a close friend of Charles Swann.

380 *King Theodosius*: a fictional king, most likely based on Tsar Nicholas II who made a state visit to France in 1896 and laid the first stone of the 'Pont Alexandre III', the bridge over the Seine dedicated to his father.

Michel Strogoff: a novel by Jules Verne (1828–1905), published in 1876 and adapted for the stage as a play first performed, and critically acclaimed, in 1880. The eponymous hero is a courier for Tsar Alexander II of Russia and the tale tells of his adventures and travails in this role.

384 *aphasics*: aphasia is a disorder that affects individuals' capacity to speak, process, and recognize language.

385 *the Trois Quartiers*: Aux Trois Quartiers is a major department store, established in the 1st *arrondissement* in 1827.

387 *her medals*: religious medals, typically depicting patron saints or the Virgin, are worn by the faithful as a symbol and reminder of their religious duties and their faith.

     middlenight: 'ménuit' in the original, an example of Françoise's idiosyncratic French (the correct word for midnight is *minuit*).

     the Madeleine: the church of the Madeleine was designed in the form of a Roman pantheon as a Temple to the Glory of [Napoleon's] Great Army, begun in 1807, before being finally consecrated as a church in 1842.

388 *Allée de la Reine-Marguerite*: the route mentioned here was very popular, amongst Parisian society, for promenading, seeing, and being seen.

     Aeneid: the myrtle grove in Virgil's *Aeneid* (6.440–5) is said to be the site between the river Styx and Hades where the souls of those killed in love and war bemoan their loss.

389 *polonaise*: a 'robe à la polonaise' or 'polonaise' for short (dress in the Polish style) is a woman's dress dating originally from the late eighteenth century and revived in the late nineteenth, consisting of a tight bodice and a skirt usually cut away and draped to reveal a decorative underskirt or petticoat.

     the Porte Dauphine: the entrance to the Bois de Boulogne from the Avenue du Bois de Boulogne.

     Constantin Guys: Guys (1802–92) was a painter and illustrator, much revered by Charles Baudelaire as the 'painter of modern life', and visual chronicler of social life during the Second Empire.

     the 'tiger' of 'the late Baudenord': the tiger or groom, mentioned above, is a staple of Balzac's *Comédie humaine*. Godefroi de Beaudenord (Proust's spelling differs from Balzac's own) appears in *La Maison Nucingen* (1838) and *Les Secrets de la Princesse de Cadignan* (1839).

390 *Coquelin*: see note to p. 71.

391 *the day MacMahon resigned*: Marshal MacMahon (see note to p. 22) resigned as president of France on 30 January 1879.

     Trianon: within the grounds of the Palace of Versailles, between 1687 and 1768 Louis XIV and Louis XV each successively had secondary residences built on the Trianon estate, known as Grand Trianon and Petit Trianon respectively.

393 *Armenonville, the Pré Catelan, Madrid, the race course, and the shores of the lake*: the narrator here alludes to key features of the landscape of the Bois de Boulogne, sites where restaurants provided sustenance (and points of observation) for the elegant denizens of Paris.

394 *Michelangelo's Creation*: the narrator refers here to the frescoes on the ceiling of the Sistine Chapel.

     the cruel steeds of Diomedes: in Greek myth, Diomedes, a Thracian warrior-king of fearsome renown, kept a herd of man-eating horses.

394 *Saint George*: George of Lydda (d. 303) is typically depicted as a youthful man slaying a dragon. 'Childlike' here may indicate a measure of poetic licence.

395 *Graeco-Saxon tunics with Tanagra folds*: in the latter decades of the nineteenth century terracotta statuettes, dating to the fourth century BC, with highly delicate detailing of drapery and dress were discovered in significant quantities around the Greek city of Tanagra.

in the style of the Directoire: the Directoire (Directory) was the name of the small governing committee that ruled in France between 1795 and 1799 after the Reign of Terror and fall of Robespierre. This was a time of economic crisis. In fashion, 'directoire style' was, perhaps fittingly, unostentatious and classical, rather than decorative or indulgent, as can be observed in portraits of the time by Jacques-Louis David (1748–1825).

Liberty chiffons: in 1875 Arthur Lasenby Liberty (1843–1917) established 'Liberty & Co.' in Regent Street in London, a shop specializing in goods, including fabrics, from the Far East. Gradually the company's own designs and prints became popular and widely recognized.

397 *a Dodonean majesty*: Dodona, in north-western Greece, was the site of an oracle of Zeus. There, the rustling leaves of a grove of oak trees, sacred to Zeus, were interpreted as the basis of proposing paths of action.

HENRY ADAMS	**The Education of Henry Adams**
LOUISA MAY ALCOTT	**Little Women**
SHERWOOD ANDERSON	**Winesburg, Ohio**
EDWARD BELLAMY	**Looking Backward 2000–1887**
CHARLES BROCKDEN BROWN	**Wieland; or The Transformation and Memoirs of Carwin, The Biloquist**
WILLA CATHER	**My Ántonia** **O Pioneers!**
KATE CHOPIN	**The Awakening and Other Stories**
JAMES FENIMORE COOPER	**The Last of the Mohicans**
STEPHEN CRANE	**The Red Badge of Courage**
J. HECTOR ST. JEAN DE CRÈVECŒUR	**Letters from an American Farmer**
FREDERICK DOUGLASS	**Narrative of the Life of Frederick Douglass, an American Slave**
THEODORE DREISER	**Sister Carrie**
F. SCOTT FITZGERALD	**The Great Gatsby** **The Beautiful and Damned** **Tales of the Jazz Age** **This Side of Paradise**
BENJAMIN FRANKLIN	**Autobiography and Other Writings**
CHARLOTTE PERKINS GILMAN	**The Yellow Wall-Paper and Other Stories**
ZANE GREY	**Riders of the Purple Sage**
NATHANIEL HAWTHORNE	**The Blithedale Romance** **The House of the Seven Gables** **The Marble Faun** **The Scarlet Letter** **Young Goodman Brown and Other Tales**

TROLLOPE IN OXFORD WORLD'S CLASSICS

ANTHONY TROLLOPE

The American Senator
An Autobiography
Barchester Towers
Can You Forgive Her?
Cousin Henry
Doctor Thorne
The Duke's Children
The Eustace Diamonds
Framley Parsonage
He Knew He Was Right
Lady Anna
The Last Chronicle of Barset
Orley Farm
Phineas Finn
Phineas Redux
The Prime Minister
Rachel Ray
The Small House at Allington
The Warden
The Way We Live Now

Classical Literary Criticism

The First Philosophers: The Presocratics
   and the Sophists

Greek Lyric Poetry

Myths from Mesopotamia

APOLLODORUS	The Library of Greek Mythology
APOLLONIUS OF RHODES	Jason and the Golden Fleece
APULEIUS	The Golden Ass
ARISTOPHANES	Birds and Other Plays
ARISTOTLE	The Nicomachean Ethics
	Politics
ARRIAN	Alexander the Great
BOETHIUS	The Consolation of Philosophy
CAESAR	The Civil War
	The Gallic War
CATULLUS	The Poems of Catullus
CICERO	Defence Speeches
	The Nature of the Gods
	On Obligations
	Political Speeches
	The Republic and The Laws
EURIPIDES	Bacchae and Other Plays
	Heracles and Other Plays
	Medea and Other Plays
	Orestes and Other Plays
	The Trojan Women and Other Plays
HERODOTUS	The Histories
HOMER	The Iliad
	The Odyssey